# WAKE me up

## OBSIDIAN CORVUS

# CONTENT WARNING

Not intended for those under 18 years old. This book contains content and themes that may not be suitable for all readers, including: violence, suicidal thoughts and ideations, sexual assault/ rape, forced pregnancy, and addiction.

Reader discretion is advised.

# PROLOGUE

Voices play in slow motion, but I cannot hear what they are saying.

Their words are woven by separate people in conversations, stitched together like a marred CD. I can feel the pull of my brain glitching in memory, like static that rips through a radio station just out of reach from my signal, my head swelling with the pain of time lost and swarming with an emptiness that nests in the stomach of my soul as fear.

There is a veil in this place. One that stands between what is known and the shallow, unlit corridors of my demise. It is white, wispy and soft as fine fabric, but impregnable by the physical form. The shadow of my thoughts reaches out to it as many bony fingers that curl when its darkness can brush this barrier with even the tip of its form.

*Too eager*, it flutters.

Teasing.

*What is your name?* It calls back from beyond. *Do you* even *know?*

I am writhing in my subconscious, seduced by the promise of

dark magic that engulfs my heart in black fire ignited by knowledge that I am not yet acquainted with.

But I would be.

*Will* be.

Sinking into the dim, snug warmth of all that is ignorant and uncertain, I know the worst is yet to come.

# CHAPTER ONE
## ADABELLE

I T WOULDN'T BE A BALLET IF IT DIDN'T END IN TRAGEDY.
All the good ones do, anyway.

The famous ones.

The ones that we still practiced when, in the midst of war and anarchy, time forgot the classic arts altogether. The ones we learned real lessons from. Suffered with. Felt in the physical sense as all hairs stand on end, and our skin rises in little buds to the sound of music and raw pain.

I told my students this, back when we rehearsed for upcoming recitals that only few would attend—usually not of our own species. They could take what they wished from it. Because life is a dance. A tragedy. The fluid movement of every step we take, posing a not too subtle reminder to all minds alike that the world loves to look in on disaster to help stabilize our own existences.

How we hate to know that we do. For when tragedy finds our own, it transitions from entertainment to torture.

Teaching is one of my only memories since the unconscious

discovery of the white veil. With the same clarity I have staring at the momentous trees before me, I can see rows of little people standing in first position span along a tall barre attached to the wall of a rundown, two-story, grey brick studio, this opposing a full-size mirror reflecting scrawny shapes descending into demi-pliés.

Stout legs still bend quite stiffly. Skinny arms flash a sea of carefully spread fingers and float graceful arcs to the ceiling, drifting back down at my command.

I would like to believe that they enjoy what they are doing, and that I do as well, in this dystopian memory where we still use elaborate light fixtures in every room instead of scentless candles settling in white puddles on a metal plate. A soft pull at the corners of my lips suggests that this might be the case, but a lingering uncertainty robs me of this hope as the reality of what is becoming my life collapses in upon me. My memory lapses, removing the face of any individual present, and leaving their scrawny, underfed figures to interpret the music playing delicate instrumentals in a much too warped background. It becomes a carousel of taut skin stretched over human canvas until the white veil drops, much as a velvet stage curtain might, and leaves me stranded on the other side.

So I can't even know if they are real, or if my brain didn't just invent fictional filler so that I would not feel as lonely opening my eyes beyond the veil in a shriveled, dripping stone room in an unfamiliar land to discover I had no other substantial memories at all.

It has been a single day since the mandatory quarantine that every new arrival in this strange place first opens their sheltered eyes in, like a newborn being birthed into a vivid nightmare. Sunlight unlike any limpid warmth I have ever seen filters in through a permeable lavender Dome that stretches the length of the sky beyond the tall, dark fence that separates myself from whatever rests beyond this holding pen of quiet, subtle deceit. Incredible ferns with yellow-tipped foliage sprout from the one exit of this courtyard, so tall that they cast shadows higher than my head—though I am admittedly not very tall—yet they quiver in the presence of all that grows even further behind it. Beastly knotted trees with ashen trunks weep slender crimson whips that guard the entrance to the forest beyond like vipers, cautioning all who dare approach, yet entrancing those who might. Flowers, blacker than coal, litter the ground and climb what they may in furtive, robust tendrils, coated with a wet sheen visible to the naked eye with just the right amount of sunlight. All of which would naturally draw out the innate curiosity that resides within each of us, having never even remembered seeing a plant outside of books, much less ones of such intrigue.

Only, there is an admission price to not just observe, but to relish in such beauty so close in the flesh, and it is nonrefundable...because once it is taken, it will be spent in the same second. Though from whispers alone, I cannot say why this is so, but I entertain no desire to see my life ripped away so soon, even if that is where the staff of this makeshift hospital center want me to be after just one encounter in dim light. It is all that could be heard from this vantage point, outside where I can no longer be scrutinized, but just close enough to the window that their passing voices mingled with the fresh open air.

*Leave her beyond The Dome*, they snarl to an unknown party for hours before the next grace of silence.

*She doesn't belong here.*

But why?

"Here is the information we could gather."

A shuffling of papers echo to the trees from inside the hospital center. Against the tantalizing edge of The Purple Dome and the stone structure that will decide my fate, a light breeze brings reprieve from the crippling heat that is hard at work, baking my delicate pale skin. My face welcomes the senses of nature. Beads of sweat that had begun to accumulate on the bridge of my nose cool for a moment before rolling off.

"And this is...Adabelle?" an invisible young woman asks in turn.

An involuntary wince curls my toes at the name spoken with such casualty. The one that belongs, without question, to myself, yet one I cannot recall with the same conviction as those who deal fates like playing cards in a sidewalk magic show. It seems more foreign than factual, as if somehow I have been born forthwith into existence and granted a name.

"Yes, ma'am. Adabelle Shay Green. Five feet, two inches tall. The weight taken, according to the state identification we found on her upon arrival, is one hundred thirty-two pounds precisely. She is twenty-one years of age and appeared to be intact at our prior review."

It isn't wrong, I suppose. Even if I can't remember, it sounds right. The statistics on this imaginary chart being read off in a report I have never seen, by people I still cannot quite convince myself actually exist, match the reflection that stared back at me the first day I woke up. Although, nightmares are more often believable than not when trapped in the throes of the action. Whether I had seen a decrepit troll with rotting teeth that curled into her upper lip from a disconnected lower jaw, or a goddess with silky white curls that rolled in sea foam waves down to the barren floor on that day, I was bound to believe it because that would be the only evidence of personal reality that I could maintain.

After all, with no memories, how can I know anything else? Whether I am good or bad? Loud or quiet? Early or late? It is impossible to say in the bare moments of mere existence. How can I even claim that what I do remember is accurate when my own name passes through me with a fearful ambiguity? Is my age really twenty-one? There is no one alive here to verify how long I have slumbered away before being found. I can't tell these people where I was when located, or even as of current.

The one sanity left to claim is that, even if it's felt so, I have not been alone at any specific point so far. Voices of the medical staff and other inhabitants, while mocking and alarming at times, drift into every crevice of space on the property. Even in my nightmares, they are present. Tangible. Like the trees and the grass. The dirt and the sky. In my mind, I hardly remember any of these things at all, yet in an unfamiliar world full of creation the likes of which I never could have conjured in the deepest recesses of my imagination, somehow just hearing anyone at all is grounding enough.

I reach into the dirt beneath my knees where the shade from the overhanging canopy of the forest keeps any green from sprouting, sifting it through the spaces between my bony fingers until I have a few good-sized rocks in my fist. With each sparing moment I have, until my uncomfortable reign of silence ends, I toss them through The Purple Dome.

One by one.

Absent in body but present in thought, as though the air itself could blow right through me and I would be none the wiser, except in unspoken processes. My eyes look far out into the trees, searching for answers that are only provided by at least one hundred other sets that stare back.

I can't see them, of course. Whoever they belong to. Not really. But I can feel them. Hungry...each set starving for something I cannot provide. A disappointment that will never be satisfied.

"Adabelle Green?"

All at once, the watchful stares vanish. A full, swelling discomfort at the front of my skull pulls me back to reality, responding with displeasure at the same high-pitched voice that saw me out of the quarantine unit and into this yard, much to the chagrin of her coworkers. It is softer than the face it pairs with. Misleading and laced with hidden motive.

"My name is Celestyn Smith. Do you remember me?" She pauses for effect. I can tell. "I am here for your discharge."

*Remember YOU? It isn't my short-term memory that I lack,* I think to myself.

A few queer whispers echo in response from somewhere inside, voices drifting distrust through the breeze that carries it back to my ears in muffled phrases I don't understand. I am one of two discharges that I know of today. The other that kept me distant company left early this morning without conflict. It's late evening now, though, the sky a tender dusting of orange blending against a pastel blue with just enough grey clouds to insinuate unexpected rain in the forecast. Much too late to be sending someone with no memory out for the first time with no resources to guide her.

I brush a tangled mop of violet fringe from my eyes, using the same sweaty hands to dust the backside of my knee-length, pale green skirt and once-upon-a-time white leggings that have officially darkened to more of a beige. Clouds of loose dirt fluff into silence, settling as an evaporating mist around my worn red sneakers. It is a struggle to not pump tingling legs toward this girl I don't know so that I can discover the next glimpse of what the future with no memory might look like without strangers glowering down to me everywhere my eyes can see, and stalling so that I will not be forced just yet to step out alone into the unknown. Celestyn returns a peculiar gaze from the open stone columns that lead inside the building, her eyebrows knitting against the space between her eyes, and her mouth twitching back and forth between an undeserved grimace and garish smile.

"Come with me." She settles somewhere in the middle, seething dispassion hiding beneath soft lips that stretch to reveal the best teeth I have bore witness to since my arrival.

"Ok-kay," I choke on my own words. My mouth seems years ahead of my thoughts, yet trying to cling to them all the same, as if the void they'd fill is toxic once released. Celestyn must feel the same way, having turned her back toward me, leaving nothing more than her silhouette casting a bleak shadow on the grass before the word has even completely parted ways with my tongue.

Darkness casts fragmented quiet in the slender hallways that swallow her, bending away in unlit angles until I can no longer hear the padding of her tightly laced ankle-high boots through the open spaces between the stone pillars. It doesn't appear to matter whether I follow her or not. The building is gargantuan, with multiple levels that reach nearly as skyward as the fence and rounding at the distant front in a firm glass-paned ceiling. But, before such luxury, the stone expands for what seems like miles in many directions. Tangles of corridors and units branch in outstretched digits that could house a small city. At the pace in which she left, I would be lucky enough to find her after taking the first right turn away from the quarantine hall that I had been released from not so long prior.

What sliver of bright light remains of the evening is stolen by clouds rolling across the dim burning sun, guiding me near what safety the center brings. Shelter continues to be prime, even if I cannot navigate myself through its depths. Being long out of sight in the time it takes me to register that she has gone without waiting, just as the nurse before her had for my temporary courtyard companion, the path Celestyn carves through the corridors after the first right turn is left to the imagination and dwindling sounds of civilization.

*Maybe if I combine the two, I can actually be as startling as they make me out to be,* I tick nervously in my thoughts, pacing from the courtyard until I can only see folds of it between stone, flipping away like a picture book.

The last section of the scenery that I have become acclimated to closes away between one more mast of round colossal stone and a thickly built wall that extends just a few good feet to a narrow impasse of solid steel. Candelabras burn orange and red at either side of my immediate roadblock, illuminating dark stains that carpet the unforgiving tile floor in dry, crusty browns. My legs maneuver about them, twisting through what I can see, and making educated deductions on where they spread to comply with my anxiety and avoid tainting my sneakers with an unknown substance while still healthy enough to be discharged.

It is archaic for what my gut instinctively feels an institution of its sort should be—unclean and vague, with deep ravines carved into the impasse as if a dozen animals have attempted to channel their way inside. Flashes of white walls, blinding fluorescent overhead lights, and cold sterilized trays of peculiar instruments plague the heart of my intuition when the word *hospital* comes to mind. Tall blue and beige curtains, the smell of alcohol burning the insides of each nostril up to the eyeballs, invasive tubing that snakes without consent into organs reluctant to give way but yet shriveling under the demands of failure until pain bursts in colors like forming galaxies at the front of the skull...and when dry, crusted eyes flutter open once again, it is a steel impasse.

Cold. Dark. Reeling with a heavy wet smell and coated with the prints of many different persons.

What exists in the depression of my false memory fades away into fiction, all intricacies lost in a slow blink that grounds me back in reality.

A delicate clap of a solid pointed heel and the muffled thud of cumbersome work boots tangle from either corner of the jam. Silver metal glitters in the flamelight, held by two opposite gendered persons at the mouths of deep shrouded hallways built into the rock I had not seen seconds ago from the back of the niche. My gaze shifts between the two of them, awe and bewilderment at their sudden appearances bubbling to the base of my throat but producing no sound. The woman is tall, with legs like feeble sticks that balance on nicked stilettos. Her arms reach for miles, with a torch toward the limitless ceiling in one and a blunted spear garnishing the other. With nothing to say, she steps to the side and motions to me with a nod into the sudden void I now see produced her stern, but scrawny form.

The man generates just as little reaction. Shorter than the woman but broad, with gnarled shoulders leading down to swollen knuckles covered in wiry black hair. His own spear rests against the frame of entry that he guards, unmoving and detached from my presence, the hand that should be holding it with the same gusto as his female companion, shriveled at the pocket of his sheered tan slacks. Even at his disfigurement, I am not eager to attempt a test of luck to gander through his entry if they happen to notice me in their statuesque practices.

Both sets of dark brown eyes stare into the void around us, settling into the quiet as if it were a rhythm intended to play at this very hour. Their robotic fronts leave me with my first sense of genuine relief, the lack of the same basic judgment their peers clutch to with taut fists sprouting through the wall of unease I have placed between myself and all that lacks humble familiarity. It feels as though I am both watched and unseen in this moment. I can do everything, or perhaps nothing at all. No further eye contact is being made to signal I should do anything other than what the woman motions, but something about hallways being guarded by simple people with dangerous weapons makes just walking through without repercussions seem delusive.

Curling my lips into my teeth where I can gnaw away at the dead skin—caused by deliberate dehydration—until it bleeds, I tuck a heap of electric blue and green highlights behind my ear. With careful eyes, peeking just far enough below my lashes that I can see in front of me, I shuffle against the floor to the corridor with the woman aside it. I hold my arms deep into the plush of my belly, a brief heat rushing to my face at the frame and filling my ears to the beat of my heart that races against the feeble skin of my chest. Irrationality throttles me faster into the darkness, fear consuming my mind in images of one misstep where the force of the weapon held rips through me, so I am left to die. Trailing this eerie fantasy, a rumble of steel on steel screeches until the final whiff of fresh air is shut away, leaving only distant light to guide me onward.

Doors are sardined in uneven spaces on either side of the thin aisle I walk into, leaving barely enough room to open one without whacking the other side, and none at all to have two in the vicinity ajar at the same time. Not a sound erupts from any containment, the space beneath each door just enough to take in the humid air to whoever might be roasting within the closet-like space. I extend a hand to each wall, using the feel to keep myself grounded in the most lonesome place I have been since quarantine, until a dull glow at the cusp of a subtle twist in the everlasting straight shot propels me to what is unmistakably a waiting room.

A dull orange twinkle casts down between clouds and strikes my face. My forearm raises reflexively to shield what is left of my sight against the onslaught. It is a cruel reminder that quarantine has no windows to filter in sunshine and the courtyard has so many overhanging plants, that the best of it is shut away except in glimpses. This will be my first time seeing it with lucidity, even in what my mind has invented, and it is nearly gone—shutting away behind the horizon, so that the moon will have its time to breathe chilled air down to the earth.

I amble forward in search of the nurse who left me in her dust without providing the courtesy of where she might be going. A way out of this wretched place without seeing her again at all is preferable, if feasible, and I imagine it can be—if I'm careful, anyway.

At the distance of the courtyard, all I could see of my path to freedom was the rounded glass ceiling soaking in beams of white light, peeking up over the top of the building as an invisible circle of grandeur that I could only dream about. In person, this glass ceiling transforms into many glass windows that round to a light wood floor with the same ornate black bars from above closely caging the outside like a frame, but more like a prison. What light of the day remains bounces from each wall of glass to the next, reflecting faint rainbows that dance on the shadows of every item inside. Lumbering brown doors built with clustered logs and rusted bronze rings for handles guard my way out, with little to no one coming or going at this hour.

"Where were you?" her voice creeps from the side. "I've been waiting."

Out of my peripheral vision, I see Celestyn just as she strides away to a blistered rounded desk at the front of the room. Something sinks quickly inside me from my face to my feet, and I follow her this time without hesitating, taking in everything. If I were to make standards in aesthetical beauty, she is the most perfect person in the room. Or the world, even. She is thin and long, with clear ebony skin and glistening black hair that is neatly wound into a tight, curly ponytail. Her face is delicate and angular, with fiery black eyes that scream *I dare you to try* when my gaze falters back to the doors.

If an Amazonian warrior princess undertook deep medical studies and found herself with a doctorate in a locked-down quarantine hospital, I am looking at her in this second.

"It's busy here," I whisper at last, holding my arms against my chest and sandwiching my hands inside my armpits.

A cursory glance around the empty room is all it takes for her to decide that I am either challenged or telling a joke. She doesn't let on to which she believes, instead responding with a single word.

"Observant."

The chill her voice and physique retain could out frost the arctic itself. Her elegant arms ice the chipped surface of the front desk, as rigid hands scribble on crumbling yellow paper with a voluptuous quill in her dominant left hand, while she cranes her long swan-like neck to set eyes on makeshift files she has yet to reach for.

"Follow me, please." Celestyn sweeps all the other files, now amassed in stacks along the blemished desktop, into one elbow while mumbling the faux kindness to no one in particular as though I didn't stand just in arms reach.

Of all the things that have struck me as peculiar over the past day, it seems to me a strange occurrence, not that she has yet to make a move in any direction available after such a request, but more so that she is mumbling. Indecisive tendencies stray far from the countenance she had displayed in peacock proportions when first entering my quarantine room amidst the violent commotion I have since tried to forget, caused by several of her colleagues. Her eyes, as focused as they were in those first seconds, squint at the large print still left at the desk, long after her hand has dropped the quill. And even as a distracted woman, not once in a single meeting we have ever had—as few as they've been—did she strike me as one who mumbles for any occasion.

Brief hesitation ensues from the words she barely speaks in careful poise. Procrastinating. Waiting for anything that might sweep in from atop our glass sky to save her from this more official introduction, and then buckling under the weight of fate when not even an insect crawls beneath the door to capture her immediate attention. She gives me one glance in still air, body facing the hallway, stretching out at the rear of the front desk. I step forward in involuntary response. Whether it's out of instinct from being left behind prior, or blatant fear I will turn to stone if I do not, is unclear. An exasperated rock of her hips begins our short trek two doors down the slim hotel of rooms, orchestrated by faint groaning and choking.

*These people need help,* my thoughts plead when the sound invades my senses, pursuing my conscience, and yet being ignored all the same. Some will to survive, despite the obtuse lack of danger, fills the spaces consumed by misery with white noise and false reasoning.

Hospitals are often uncomfortable and cold, right?

Only, my head gravitates to the door across the way, bruised fingers flexing in the space below it for fresh air.

"Do you *want* to live?" Celestyn's sigh echoes above the shudder that rattles the door belonging to the fingers.

It is a question I'm unaccustomed to being asked without hints of sarcasm and a playful grin or a chuckle to alleviate the severity of the words. In the most coincidental way, the sound of her effort feels as if she is sending forth a forewarned reply to my unintentional fight or flight call. All I can feel instead is the definite raise of her eyebrows behind the ajar door, beckoning me inside before the little patience that remains within the confines of her day wears through. All morals in question, and the fingers slipping away from my vision, I am able to nudge the door open to find a seat for myself in another miniature hell.

Inside, I discover that the space provided for exit examinations and apparent patient stay is no larger than the basic quarantine lockers, essentials not far off in variation. It is empty in the character department, the room itself baring stark stone walls that close into a square, barely bigger than the average walk-in closet space. A couple bales of hay with a ripped, off-white cloth tied around them sit against the far wall as a mattress for the "patient" in question to be reviewed upon. Gnarled candelabras barely hold to the structure, a cascade of rust tinting the dripping white candle wax frozen in motion at the bottom of the iron.

*More like a dungeon than a patient care room,* I think, and leave the door far open as I take my seat with obedience on the sheet. The light of my one known path to freedom is a comfort, if it can stay—a sign that I will not be locked away in here by people I do not know for reasons they cannot say. *Will not* say.

I tuck my knees to my meager, almost flat chest, resting my chin on their ugly round prominences. Just as I had upon waking that first day, alone in a pitch darkness that preyed on my fear and desolation, and just as I had in the courtyard when my only company would not so much as share the same half of limited field, edging on some imaginary line that had been drawn as he left without so much as a goodbye to the single other person available to share the burden of this experience. My only parting sentiment to carry into this new world that I have been taking in is aggressive stares and righteousness that leave me further paralyzed, inundated in what is this person I am still unfamiliar with...and yet the one person I can seek asylum with, even if I don't know her as I should.

After these first twenty-four hours, it is almost instinctual now to cover my vulnerabilities when I can feel the anxiety creeping in for a visit from those around me like wild pack animals, waiting for the wounded victim that has been separated from a herd she isn't sure exists to stumble. I need to conceal the only deviance I can think of that will make outsiders believe me to be vile and pray I can absorb it back into whatever memory it belongs to, as if it is possible to change what has already been done.

"I will be conducting your discharge examination."

A crippled wooden pedestal echoes tired cries across the floor's bleak surface as she speaks, settling with a painful victory in front of the open door where Celestyn folds her slender legs together and steadies yellowing parchment against her lower extremities. She doesn't bother affording me the luxury of a faux kindness when she meets my gaze this time. There are no possible witnesses to my mistreatment here. No one to advocate for my fair processing, other than this body my mind inhabits. I return the venomous demeanor with a small, curt smile, anyway. I need someone on my side here.

"So late?" I mean to say *thank you*. Those are the words that jostle behind a bitter discontentment that wears me through every second longer I strive to be here. They are polite, humble. Something I intend to make myself appear to be, whether or not I am.

The other words, the ones I said instead, happen to slip through, slick as they are and far more honest than I care to be in person. It seems my own mind is the first to betray me here, followed closely by my dumb mouth.

Isn't that how it goes though? It's always the people we think we can trust that drop the ax.

A pause follows, the void it creates filling with heavy heat generated by disgust. My knees push deeper into the underside of my chin in wait, jamming against the gentle pink splotching on my neck.

"Yes," she rejoins.

There is little sympathy in the way she speaks, and even less love for a profession that she chose and the people that she didn't. I did not ask to be here with her just the same, or with anyone else that wants me dead in the forest that they speak in soft voices over. Not to my recollection, anyway.

At her feet, the files amassed from the desk sit in a lopsided array of mystique. Celestyn swipes slender fingers across the top, plucking the thickest makeshift folder and dropping it on to the parchment already in her lap. The papers inside crash, bounce, and creep just barely out the side to reveal pages that are uneven in size. A scrap no bigger than a sticky note floats with skinny black letters scribbled along the middle to the floor, landing just in front of the pedestal. The room is too dim to attempt reading it even with the much brighter light from the hallway to aid, but it doesn't appear important. Celestyn is in no rush to retrieve it as her eyes follow its path, straying back to the other contents immediate to her attentions. She clears her throat.

"It appears that you have passed all of your initial stability tests and physicals to be released into the village without issue," she says. "How do you feel?"

It is a courtesy. Strange, albeit refreshing. She does not actually care how I am feeling. The question is routine. But it feels good to be asked, finally, even if it means nothing at all.

"A little behind," I admit. "Confused. I'm just...I'm not quite sure where I am. Or why I'm here? I'm not even particularly sure who I am for that matter, let alone everyone else."

She bobs her head, holding the point of her chin in the palm of her hand and chewing absently on the knuckle of her first finger.

*Mhm.*

It is like background noise. Is that sound even from her?

I can still hear other patients from down the hall vocalizing a fair number of alarming noises. It could have been any number of them. It was such a soft response, after all, and she did not appear to be the kind to administer gentle sounds, no matter how fair.

"Great. Great," she mumbles, ticking her head in either direction, and begins dragging the quill across the first page of the file in rapid successions.

I have never seen a quill being used before. Perhaps I've never even seen a feather outside of books or in museums, hidden behind dusty glass casings and velvet backdrops. Where did she get that?

*Wait, what?*

"I...I'm sorry." I try to laugh it away. "I—"

"I will need your signature on a few of these release forms stating that The Healing Center will henceforth no longer be of aid or service as housing to you, unless it so happens you fall ill, injured, or in the case of an emergency in where no other shelter can be taken," she interrupts, and slides the handwritten form across the floor with the quill that glistens in pitch hued ink from the sharpened tip laying atop.

My mouth unhinges. I ogle the pitiful joke at my feet with caution and disbelief, reluctant to move.

"Am I going to be injured?" I ask. "Or ill?"

The answer is a lax shrug of the shoulders. "If you're stupid, maybe."

"Can I just…"

"If you don't sign the release, I'll have to stuff you away in quarantine until you do." Celestyn glances over her shoulder again while she speaks, her voice almost a whisper. "Trust me. I am doing you an invaluable favor."

Rejection is invaluable in this place, I'm supposing. Or hate. What did they call it? The Healing Center. As if healing happens in the tunnels of this structure. Has anything ever been rejuvenated inside these walls? It serves better to tear a person apart mind, body, and soul than it does to build them up. They need better staff. More staff. I have seen a scarce number of persons, outside of fingers on the undersides of doors. I think there is a population crisis at hand though. It sounds right. Has it gotten worse since my memory loss?

I reach to the floor and steady the release, skimming along the scribbles with aching eyes, and stroking the white plume of the quill with hidden wonder. I want to touch my face with it, sleep on a thousand of them and never wake. It tickles the belly of my chin as I lean forward, scratching at each parchment with uneven strokes and lapses in pressure. The incredible fancy of it is almost enough to forget. But…

"I'm sorry," I say again, and slide the forms opposite me. "But if you could just give me a few answers. I was listening earlier… through the window…and I just…"

Celestyn stuffs the papers into the back of the file, skims through the stack, and pulls out another. "Have you felt ill at all in the past twenty-four, almost forty-eight hours?"

"No. Well, ill at ease, but—"

"Great." Clockwork. Her voice has taken on a robotic tune. "Everything moves properly still, since your last examination? No pains? No irritations?"

"Just you," I promise.

My jaw clenches, teeth grinding into one another through

labored breathing, and another betrayal of my tongue. Not speaking at all proves to be more useful if I'm craving allies rather than trying to provide answers, let alone find them.

My snap remarks do little to affect her demeanor, however, and it washes away any guilt that remains for being unable to practice basic self-control. I am an object here with a paycheck tied to the end of my stay. I am sure my feeble body warrants quite a collection of bills and coins, given consideration to the problem my stay has presented alone. It is easy to pretend I'm not human to these people when part of the job requirement doesn't include loving the career itself. There is little value placed on a means to end, because there is always another out there if one goes looking.

"I'm going to check your eyes one more time, as well as your reflexes." Celestyn rises from her seat, approaching me with a willing reservation. "I'm under the assumption my colleagues failed to do some of it during the end of your quarantine. My findings will go in your file, and thereafter, turned over to the proper authorities."

She's taller than me, I realize, as I stare into the flat of her stomach before she kneels to maintain eye contact. Nearly everyone is, of course. I'm but five foot two and the boots she dons have thick heels that elevate her already nearly perfect adult woman height to a much more quintessential status.

*Of course* she is taller than me. She always has been.

It's just that defining features are so much more apparent when a person has closed the distance between the two of them.

Quarantine is the closest anyone has been to me up to this point, and it lasted only a short-lived period of time before it all ended in an abrupt gasp and clamoring atop one another to get out of the room as efficiently as possible. There were several girls that entered the room at the time to see me out: one that appeared to be in charge, and two or three others that held linens and dressings. I think my quarantine nurse's name was Rosie.

Roseanne?

She was a young thing when so close to my person. Maybe

seventeen? A baby face with lots of freckles for sure. She was splattered in them, as if someone had tossed her a brown paint tin and she missed the catch. It was cute though, in its own special way, and she seemed kind enough until the examination began.

Comforting.

Bright light the color of searing agony is like needles digging into the whites of my eyeballs in strobe effects as a subtle click graces the room with a blissful darkness once more. A miniature flashlight is smacked into the wall and a rattle juices the batteries of what little life still remains while rocky crumbles rain to the floor in the aggressive aftermath. Defiant flickers, each dimmer than the one before it, bear little use to the action needing to be performed and Celestyn eventually sighs, dropping the instrument to the floor in sheer agitation. It rolls to the bottom edge of my hay bale bed, unable to be revived without new batteries.

"Why the feathers, old paper, and candlelit rooms, but you all still use flashlights?" It feels good to speak an entire sentence.

So I add to it. I can't resist. "And where am I? Who am I? Why am I here?"

It is blurted out into the open air so fast that I provide no respite between questions, leaving an empty and short satisfaction in their wake as Celestyn takes each of them in with tentative agitation. What will I do next if she refuses to answer my questions? How do I even thrive being discharged in a home I don't remember if she won't? Do I have a home?

I could be homeless.

I feel my face fall, and yet I try to keep it together, stuffing the panic deep below the surface to be adult about this.

"Are you done?" she asks.

I nod, squeezing my lips together in an attempt to wet them with the saliva that remains on my dry tongue after a day without water.

"I think so, yes."

She nods in turn, letting out a slow exhale.

"Okay. That's good. That's great."

Another glance beyond her shoulder as if I won't notice, a mindless shuffle of the papers in her lap, and she clears her throat. "There are just a few more pages I would like to go over with you, and I..."

My blood boils, warms and swells the space behind my eyes in an attempt to spill the contents out on to my face and collar. Nothing will satisfy these people more than that. To watch water ribbon down my cheeks and pool in the cup that my collar bone makes. To submerse it with grief.

"*Who am I?*" I scream. My fists are clenched, and I'm standing now. Trembling. My voice falls after the outburst, helpless as I am. "What am I doing here?"

Our eyes meet, and she is tucked away on the stool. Her legs still folded, poise still collected...but her demeanor has changed. Loose papers are scattered on the floor, the files she held tipped into collapsed tents on top. Her shoulders are hunched forward, further shutting me out, though with a rather firm tolerance that is frozen on her face.

When at last she blinks, it is slow and decisive. The dark irises that almost match her pupils dance with a searing, unearned animosity while a faint smile plays the edges of her lips. It isn't as deceptive as once before when she attempted a more customer service façade, leaving little to the imagination in this second as to the position she is taking in the situation of my fate.

"I don't know *who* you are," she asserts. "Beyond words on a paper, I don't know who I am, or why any of us are here for that matter."

"W-what..."

My disappointment is evident, my bewilderment even more so. This has to be a joke. Or a nightmare. I want to go home, wherever home is. I want my mother or sister or brother or someone that knows me, that cares about me enough to tell the truth or give me a hug in this crisis.

"The village here is named Limbo," Celestyn continues. "Sort of a holding pen for the lost, hence the name. A strange place, I guess, if you learn how to survive here long enough to know it.

Most people do not. Most of us don't even endure long enough to have memories of whatever came before this, let alone make memories with what we have now."

"How long have you been here?"

"Too long."

Expressionless, she gathers her files, haphazardly cramming papers into each one and glancing toward the door with each stack complete. The sun's light has almost completely faded, leaving only the flicker of dim fire to warm the hallway in blackened shades of orange and yellow. Most of the stifled groans have hushed now to listless murmurs, and the rattling of bodies shifting against wooden chairs or side tables.

How can they tell it is so close to bedtime in perpetual darkness? Is it because the building empties just before this time? Is it the silence that grows everywhere about them as the staff and remaining patients clear the building? What kind of quarantine unit or "healing center" isn't open twenty-four hours a day?

Something pelts one of the windows outside in the waiting room where it is the most silent of all, ringing against several panes just hard enough to make a sound through the bars without causing a fracture. Breaking into a locked-down quarantine hospital seems counterproductive and will prove fruitless for whomever requires such questionable services, as the staff make a break for home before sundown. But somehow this doesn't appear to be the goal of the sporadic actions. Celestyn swallows, rising from her seat and peering around the side of the door.

I take a breath, opening my mouth, only to be silenced by a wag of her finger. She slips around the corner, feet padding the short length of hall to the front desk in a slow, reserved tip toe. There is a brief scuffling and a heavy *thunk* at the front doors as she returns.

In tow, she carries a long and heavy khaki backpack adorned in bright, multicolored patches that have been sewed on where the hem has not quite held tight, and glittering pins of innumerable advertisements and characters jingling against one another. It is filled to the top flap with supplies of some kind, almost too gargantuan for Celestyn to heave with a single arm, though she had. I take a frayed strap between my fingers as she strolls back across the room for something else, caressing the familiar, and yet all too foreign, edges of this parting gift.

"What is this?" I ask.

Celestyn returns with a dulled stick, motioning for me to let my legs drape over the side of the makeshift bed. Bits of hay needle in through the silky mesh, catching skin and flimsy dressings that had been wound about my knee to mid-thigh. I have felt the laceration there since the minute I opened my eyes, a resilient ache without relief. In the sun, the blood plastered below was felt melting into the dressing meant for protection from outside contaminants. But all that had crossed my mind since then was the lingering curiosity of who removed my pants to stitch and tend my cut.

Was it her?

What had she seen?

Surely everything.

*Damn it.*

I let out a slow breath, choking on the same air I lose when she gives my knee a less than tender whack.

Gentle is not her strong suit.

"We live in the dark ages here," she says. "We have no running water, no power for electricity, no advanced weaponry to protect us from the creatures in the woods, other than what we can make ourselves. Everything we have in this place is owed to what each individual person was found with, the things people leave behind when they are taken too soon, and resources we are able to collect in the small time frame that we are granted. These are the resources you were found with."

My other knee is struck with the same vigor as the first. "The things in this bag...they're mine? From before?"

"Yes." Her voice is that of a mother who has told her toddler the same thing for the last ten minutes. "I don't think a person has ever been found with so many personal belongings. More often than not, people are found with nothing more than the clothes on their backs. There are some cases where even that is not the circumstance."

I linger at the flap that hides away my entire world and what I can know of it in this second. "Why was this not delivered to me sooner? I've been here for a hot minute."

"Protocol." Celestyn eyes the area of my laceration, dancing on the balls of her feet and nibbling on her lip before moving along.

*Not today.*

Not while I'm awake and sentient.

It's too dangerous.

"Prison protocol?" I snap.

She takes each arm, bending and testing their durability. "I am charged with keeping an entire population safe, to an extent. I will not arm a potential psychopath and send them to live amongst people just trying to survive long enough to maybe see their families again one day."

I pull my arms away, crossing them and tucking my hands into my armpits. "There are no families here?"

An audible hum is the only response I receive, followed by another rattle against the windows, only much louder this time. I'm certain I hear the crinkle of glass in the throw, spider webs creasing and splintering the poor craftsmanship into pieces of a puzzle that cannot be reassembled ever again. I jump at the noise, remembering the vague conversations of discarding me in the woods to die, and what might be in there to kill me.

What kind of animals lurk come nightfall? I don't think that I have ever seen live animals, spare a few show dogs on television. Celestyn is visibly unaffected, though her brow furrows and eyes narrow.

At her pedestal, she dips her quill in a small pot of ink and makes a sparing note in the files. She loops enormous letters on several documents, glancing at a separate one each time she does. It doesn't look like her signature from this vantage point, considering how I imagine her name might be spelled. But what do I know? If she is forging my own hand, I hope she's good at it.

Better at it than me.

"You'll need this."

From the inside of her pocketed beige vest, as she scribbles away and turns papers face down so that I will not see, Celestyn produces a small blade roughly the length of my hand from palm to fingertip. It is hard to make out further details from a distance, but when she approaches, I can see my own setup for failure.

"It is mandatory that we arm you for official release, and it is all I could find on such short notice," she offers.

It is thin, speckled with rust that has already begun to flake away from the intact metal and stained a dark brown along the dull edge that should be well sharpened. I take the worn, leather wrapped handle in a shaky hand, feeling no weight to power such a useless tool through bare flesh, let alone a healthy sternum if I find myself in trouble with a living, rabid critter.

"It won't do me very well," I say, wishing my mouth would quit moving. "Not unless you intend to have me as a professional bread butterer."

"I wouldn't touch butter with that if I were you." She picks up each file with care, surveying the hallway without wavering. "But I believe the words you are looking for would be *thank you*. Again. Especially when that so-called butter knife will probably save your ass more than once out there if you use it right."

"Will it though?" A sigh rips through me, my own demise sinking in faster than I care. "Is there a right way to use this?"

Our discharge conversation—if it can be called a conversation —is interrupted by the faint, yet ever resounding, cry of a woman outside the front doors. It is so faded behind the strength of my exit that I could pass it for a trick of the wind through the trees, if not for the frantic banging that follows. A high-pitched whine fills the silence created amongst ourselves in this moment, permeating my senses in the form of gooseflesh that raises each of the tiny hairs on my arms in painful attention, sending chills crawling down the back of my neck, and forcing my body to quiver. My heart races the longer I still hear it and the more Celestyn appears indifferent to the distant and erratic whimpers for assistance. I want to ask her to open the doors, to help the poor thing, but it appears to be the one subject my mouth can remain closed for until the tension is all that fills the space left between the two of us.

Celestyn peers out the door when she is sure the event has reached its end.

"You need to go now," she responds. "Welcome home, Miss Green. Please, don't stay long."

The words sound rehearsed as though she has done this a few thousand times with the same khaki backpack, rusty dagger, and lack of basic care or instruction. Just a cold welcome and a detached goodbye in big, meatless fuck you sandwich.

*Do you need extra salt with those questions?*

"I still have questions," I say, rising to my feet while she shifts around the corner of the door with care.

"I'm sorry," she calls out. "So sorry. We're...um, we're closed, and you have to leave. You can't stay here. You signed the paper."

The backpack given to me swings around each shoulder when I don it. It buckles twice in the front across my rib cage and belly, nudging the curve of my spine and the top of my thighs below my bottom. It is deceptively lighter than the sound impressed upon me by it hitting the ground, and the pads of the straps press on my skin through the fabric of my shirt without leaving burning indentations to tarnish. Still, it is just enough to bend me forward for a few seconds as I lurch against my new center of gravity, finding my footing but looking like a hunchbacked troll.

Poking my head around the corner of the door frame and scanning each end of the hall, I see no further signs of life, nor hear them. Fingers have retreated, shuffling has ceased. I cannot hear breathing, let alone the feverish moans when I first passed by. It was as if I had become the only person to exist at all until I caught sight of Celestyn beyond the front desk. Pacing. Biting her thumb nail and meeting my gaze. She throws her hands out to either side and gestures to the door.

"Please." Her voice is stern. "Leave."

My insides recoil, my gut shriveling in fear.

"I still have questions," I repeat, inching my way around the desk.

"No. No, I won't answer them. You. Have. To. Leave." Her eyes are the size of dinner plates, but her voice remains bold and steady. A flicker of her irises and tilt of her head gesture, once again, to the two oversized wooden doors that both seal my fate to chance living for at least the night and put me in inexplicable danger, according to the complimentary weapon now stashed away inside my pack.

"If you survive the night, Headquarters will assign you work in the morning if you ask right away. Otherwise, you will have to wait for assignments the day after."

I am swimming in a pool of defeat as I grip the bronze ringed handles. This misadventure is similar to thrashing wildly in a pit of hot tar. I am still moving as I have been since I woke but never in any particular direction until eventually, I sink, inhaling the chemical glue so that I cannot breathe. But yet I do.

When I do, it is hot and uneven. Poisonous. My exhales are toxic bubbles that float to a surface I have never seen. Light does not even shine in this place where I drown. I am alone. No hands reach to save me, and I can't move just the same. Yet still I am. Contradiction and alienation are the rocks tied to my feet by those who were set to help.

Celestyn whisks an arm around me, throwing a heavy wooden bar lodged across the way to the side that I had not seen in my daze to unlatch the entry. She gives each entry door a forceful shove, swinging them open just enough to walk through with both shoulders chafing against the unpolished edges, leaving white scuffs against my easily burnt and now much more visibly pink tinted skin in a stream of moonlight that cascades in silver beams from the very open sky. The doors are shut again before I can try to protest my inquiries any further.

It is impossible to feel claustrophobic in this place, though it is a bit more of a disappointment to take in. Not in any of the few glimpses of memory that I have managed to catch in between blinks of my eyes do I remember a place like this anywhere in the world, with the abundant space to walk on a carpet of rich, green grasses and loose, black soils. Smaller trees litter the outskirts of this little town becoming denser, as well as taller, the closer to the forest's edge it reaches. Open sky tinted slightly from The Dome above, stretches in clear view within the gaps among the trees until I find myself closer to the housing where it opens up entirely as a black canvas, populated by glittering white spots of light as a tiny entourage for the moon.

I don't think I have ever seen stars. Not through the thick overcast of smog and smoke, anyway.

"This is it?" I talk to myself, traipsing along diminutive, subpar shacks that are clustered together amongst the land, made out of what appeared to be any bit of scrap that could be rounded together in a structurally sound haste.

It is perplexing in its own right, to see so many outdated and dilapidated structures construct an entire miniature city. I have to be in some kind of off-the-map, unheard-of slum region of the remaining livable Earth.

But how would I get here? And why?

It seems barely habitable at best.

Streaks of rust and sketchy blacks are the only paints applied to besotted, nonuniform metals that make do for protective sidings and doors. Splintering logs are held together with bent nails and yards of thick twine coated in hardened gloss for support beams. Lumps of thatched hay will hardly protect its residents from the elements as durable roofing on the poorest homes, let alone wild animals if they are particularly hungry.

Aside from what appears to be the normal, there aren't many homes that veer off this image. A few with glass windows and some with stairs fashioned out of heaping piles of rocks or bricks, but nothing particularly striking. Nothing beautiful. No sculptures or fake shrubbery to decorate the front yards in a place advantageous to it. Most backyards are just more houses. It is simple to tell which homes are possessed by folks handy with tools, and those who struggle to simply shield themselves from mother nature, as far as to what sets these apart to the naked eye.

*Will I have to build my own residence?* I wonder. These structures were made by someone, after all, and it is very obviously not a band of merry carpenters. Maybe—or I can hope—there is at least one empty lot available so that I can avoid the prospect of building. I can hardly do my own hair outside of giving it a quick brush or putting it in a bun. How would I put together a worthy home that wouldn't crush me while I slept?

*There's something newsworthy*, I think. *Headline: Local Heathen Dies in Abrupt Collapse of Homemade Home.*

If I make headlines, that is.

Or if they have newspapers.

Do newspapers exist? Or did I imagine all the events that transpired at The Center? Am I dreaming now? How do I stop?

*"Watch out."*

A cool breeze jostles a set of shutters wasting on broken hinges. I startle at the clatter more than the astringent voice that gifted me the benefit of caution, skipping deep into the mass lodging, my pack swinging just as loud at my backside until I slow to a jog. I cannot see what it is I should be watching for when every which direction my legs take me appears as similar as the next, leaving me stranded in a sea of self-doubt and with the knowledge that while there are in fact real people that inhabit this new home, they will go out of their way to stay away from what this path has laid out before me.

I duck around a thin sheet of tin protruding from the edge of one building, underestimating my dip and feeling a sharp snag to my cheek. My head nods in either direction, bobbing over either shoulder in an attempt to locate the voice from earlier with the concept that I have long fled it in such a rash fear. The buzz of insects singing to the hushing rustle of millions of leaves in the nighttime air confirms this loneliness in its everlasting hymn of silence. It almost seems funny that moments of silence are never truly quiet. For even when there is nothing at all, the voice inside is invasive, filling an otherwise void environment with incessant chatter to hold the sanity intact.

From high in the sky outside the curious Dome, dark clouds rumble. White and lavender streaks of light break apart the sky in delicate, secondary curves before falling back behind the night once more. The moon isn't yet shut away by the stretched, blackened cotton clouds above, floating in from the distant woods, but it winks down to me now between glimpses it can grasp from behind the wall of rain that has been working its way in all day. I like the smell, the taste this imminent weather brings to my tongue. It's nothing like what my senses remember, but oh so comforting. I could dwell in it, if I wanted to. And I do want to.

But not tonight.

An inhuman groan catches my attention, followed by a pounding of nearby dirt. I turn to the lodging beside me in a brief connection of the sound and location. In every sense, it is different from the other living spaces in the area, mostly made from heavy, uneven sections of log, puzzled together in such a way that its residents could be viewed through a window in between the spaces unintentionally created in the poor design. I brush the unpolished trunks of wood with my fingertips, pressing my face to the abrasive material to get a peek inside only to be met by a huff of hot air that wets the fringe of hair above my ear and another, much louder, groan.

I yank away, breathing so deep my lungs all but combust with the heavy oxygen here. Peering back into the gap, I catch a pair of large brown eyes staring into mine and tufts of hay hanging from wide, white lips, tinged the slightest shade of pink.

I am certain it is an animal.

A cow, probably.

I have never seen one up close. Not even on television. Only in books about the history of nutrition.

Yes.

I love to read, I believe.

I edge closer and extend a hand to the animal's face, touching the coarse hair with limbs that no longer feel like part of me.

Another huff, and I try not to laugh.

It isn't very tall yet, or wide, for the creature I read about. They're supposed to be bigger than this. So perhaps it is a baby.

I wonder if it has a name, and in my thoughts, I have already given it one so that we can be familiar with one another until I can learn more information.

*Gabby.*

I hope the job I am assigned is in this place where she is. We can be friends, for a time.

An eruption of screaming flattens me against Gabby's snout, nudging her backward into the other side of the barn that contains her. I can't tell where I think the sounds originate from, but another set confirms that it doesn't matter. They are from all throughout the neighboring area, shrill and followed by pain-staking pleas for something that does not appear to be granted.

*No. NO! Please. NO. Please.*

*Don't hurt him.*

I clutch the sides of my bag, humming with unease. All around me are the echoes of similar cries, some followed by the sound of steel zippers opening doors to lockers full of pennies that hit the ground in abrupt drops to the rich soil that drinks in their wealth. Stealing it.

*Fuck.*

There is a deep-seated terror keeping me from looking to find my opponent to allow me to understand what I am up against. I haven't made it quite that far yet in my mind, still processing a number of other important things such as how so many screams can call out to a nameless god and not receive a shimmer of hope. Or why there does not seem to be help at all, canceling hope faster than the premiere of a bad sitcom. Or, even more importantly, how the hell I am going to survive whatever is happening here when my eyes are shut.

My lids respond to this notion, lifting, but eyes averting to the ground. Somewhere I don't have to face the music.

Do I have time to search for the dagger before I am also

begging for some unattainable wish? I don't find myself wanting to test that theory much. But I need protection.

Gabby howls with the same apprehension I have on the inside, dancing with four heavy weapons on her feet behind the wall.

"Shh, shh, shh," I attempt to hush her, waving my hands at a downward volume in spite of her lack of understanding.

I glance between her and the shadows thrusting and lurching not so far off. Gabby objects to me as I do, making me put a finger to my mouth in panic.

"Gabby, I thought we were friends," I scold, whipping my head in either direction and toeing the length of the building.

I need cover. I didn't see anyone outside until the screams started, and now everyone is in trouble. This is as close as I can get to shelter in the case of an emergency.

Another shrill cry pierces the forefront of my conscious, filling my ears and making every hair stand on edge. Gabby yells in return, stampeding around her hay strewn barn as I attempt to shush her, poking my head past the corner of the crap architecture to assure my coast is clear.

I don't wait to dive for the barn doors in the middle of the structure's front face when I see darkness fill the empty yard. Jumping the white fence that scantily contains sheep and goats, I trek through almost grassless terrain for my survival, in spite of how my bandaged thigh now throbs with a pulse its very own. My heart skips, touching the unlocked doors that tower to accommodate the beasts inside. I swing them open with a gentle grace, hoping the dying would drown out the agonized creak the hinges make.

I breathe a sigh of momentary relief, another cry calling from a home outside my haven as I turn to face a still frantic Gabby...who is actually a Gabe. His sweet mother, who is now Gabby, stands at the back corner chewing with annoyed vigilance for her calf, stepping in all the right places to run my ass dead. I maneuver with care around both, afraid to start a mother's love for her child if I veer too close to Gabe from anywhere other than the wall outside.

The chaos from outside drives me to the empty back stall opposite of New Gabby, pushing hay up against the open spaces of the wall and covering what I can of my own body so that I can still simultaneously breathe throughout the night. I cross my fingers that Gabe and New Gabby don't find me delicious at any point in our foreseeable future together, letting me sleep in this scratchy plant used for cows, and housing, apparently.

It is the feel of the less humid, fresh night air against exposed skin, making my flesh twitch with relief, that also sends chills across the base of my neck. The feeling that I am not as safe as I thought here is one that I can hear outside all too well.

*He-elp.*

The word resounds in these walls. Lingering. I can't escape it. I have nowhere to go. And I freeze, attempting not to wince at the broken inflections of angst.

I'm not breathing.

New Gabby appears indifferent to this danger, lifting her head in a lazy acknowledgment at the aura of the new presence in the room. But I already feel dead.

Shot.

*Pa-pow.*

Heavy, haggard boots fluff the dirt on the barn room floor in steps that make no sound, similar to a ghost drifting across the arena to meet his challenger. Simply taking his time. Observing all that he could see and listening for what he couldn't.

My eyes trace the form of this creature—not quite human, but not without a hint of mankind spoiling inside him thus making him physically unlike the monster he must have been. His long, slim shape clears seven feet, wiry arms bent so that strong hands hold to the hilt of a sword that could surpass half my own weight in etched gold, stones engraved to it glittering in several shades of green and black. His head ticks to the cows, stilled in the very presence of his being as if in a trance. Through the hay, I can make out his dark brown hair swept into a low ponytail, twisted with hearty braids and silver jewelry grazing the end of his spine. It is in this moment that I notice the shape of his ears. Slender and pointed, they extend nearly to the end of his skull and are adorned in further hanging jewelry that makes me feel more like a heap of trash waiting to be taken to the curb.

New Gabby snorts to him, dipping her head back to the floor and nosing through the food left in abundance. The creature pats her side, serene and soft until the sound of a scream, not but right behind me, stiffens him to attention. The weight of a body slams against the other side of the wall, disturbing my quivering figure inside the hay. A small exhale escapes me, retrieving the same air in the exact moment it left.

Our noses are almost touching.

It takes no time at all for him to cross the room. To locate me in this mess. It is unworldly. Unfair. Unreal.

The heat from his body lights a fire of adrenaline in mine with nowhere to run now, for the eyes of a true titan befalls me in this second, and my whole body trembles in response. Though these eyes that attempt to look directly into my soul are not quite...standard.

They are more similar to illustrious green orbs, like a snake's or even a cat's. Nothing more than a emerald shimmering, like two jewels with a sly black slit for a pupil. Nothing more, and yet everything beyond. It is not human.

No.

It is something far superior.

I inch backward, bringing a single arm up to my face as a shield. His eyes trace this action in quiet thought, eluding the off color that decorates my pale skin in fragile divots and textures from the neck down. Eager fingers tap the hilt of his weapon at this same moment, weighing a vicious choice as I try to make myself small. Invisible.

And then he stands, leaving me be, coupled with a nod and the rumble of thunder that shakes the ground in its might.

Outside, I can still hear the desperate tears of others, and a conversation that I do not understand between two men. I am afraid to sneak around the stall to pry, and New Gabby whips her tail in agitation of my presence without the monster here to moderate. I hunker back, deeper into the straw as a response, resting my head against the wood and squeezing my eyes shut.

I have been set up to die here.

It is the only thing I am sure of.

# CHAPTER TWO
## ADABELLE

MEMORY IS A FICKLE GAME OF THE MIND, IN hindsight. An intangible victor with wrought iron fists pumping skyward, that glides through the rules of basic essence, rumbling around in the back of our thoughts with the perfect recipe for chaos slipping through his clever hands, and each ingredient dealt like unlucky numbers at a cheap, back alley casino.

I know my fate is sealed before I even take a seat at the table, but the odds whispered at the cusp of my ear are just too good to pass up.

What is that phrase? You can't be disappointed if you expect the worst? I don't think that's true. It only allows one to setup with disappointment and leave with even more.

One time won't hurt. That phrase alone has started so many addictions, memory being but just a small portion of them. For I understand in these dreams that I possess now that we crave the things that have become a part of who we are. As humans, we feed off of the brilliant nectar of what has made our hearts sing. We despair and linger even more so on what has made our hearts stop. Weep. It plays right into the game, of course, especially with amnesia.

It has been proven through countless studies that, even if it is possible for a memory to recall the course of events that takes place in a visually clear play-by-play scenario, it is, nonetheless, rather flawed, as are we. Memory changes with us. Within seconds of a sequence, facts blur and cross the lines into fiction. Smaller details blend into the environment, replaced entirely by an immortal fuzz, something that audibly reminds me of the noise my ears make when they ring.

Attempts to sort these details are impractical at best, thousands of distorted images and unmatched words blending through a mental sieve, until I'm left with countless pieces of various puzzles and no corner bits to give me a point of inception. There are uneven slices of dancers accompanied by coarse, strangled instruments. White leggings stretching with hyperextended limbs to capacity. A vast cream-colored house with shattered glass windows in the third story and a rocky driveway two miles from the nearest street. Hospitals and silver skins in sterile plastic baggies. Empty stairwells. Voices. My stomach turns in both conscious and unconscious states of mind. There is heat melting away the blackened edges of the game I try to play.

But it was fun while it lasted, right?

A fractured bleating and the tender nuzzle of a heavy snout returns me to this nightmare of beautifully blinding sun and the pounding heartbeat inside my oven-baked skull. The sound does not belong to New Gabby or baby Gabe, but just the same, hay sticks up from my blood-stained thigh where the laceration must have bled through in my careless stupor to maintain a beating heart just hours ago.

A puff of air fills my cheeks, releasing in a steady stream of pain that I do not dare scream out loud.

*You can fix it,* I tell myself. *It's just a little blood. A scratch. Nothing some water and a bit of rest won't subdue.*

My eardrum shatters at the obnoxious *baa* that feeds saturated air into my thoughts, leaving a sharp, pulsating buzz that blinds me in this daylight haze I'm brought to. A stark reminder of where I have been since last night, and the lies my head wishes to lead me on about it. It feels better to blink away the visions of violence that dance omens behind my half-shut eyelids, letting the barn sink back into my senses with newly blurred swirls of serene color I could not have foreseen in the pitch darkness I cowered within.

It would be convincing enough to be a dream—this section of the world that appears frozen in a long forgotten era, full of vibrant foliage and utensils that are far past their expirations—if I didn't already appreciate what these nocturnal fantasies looked like. Understanding this reality, knowing I'm still here when these picture book images fade and feeling pain where there very well should be agony bursting at the seams of my flesh—barely held together by weak, potentially unclean, threads—is realizing I had lost the battle before the war had begun. There is nothing new to purpose me through this. Nothing useful. *No one* useful.

I shake the pale straw from my upper body, my blotched, aching shoulders exposed to the remaining audience left to entertain—two ewes and a lamb—who are now rummaging in my prior bed setup and hideaway. They flounce in their mighty wool jackets, grazing their paths across the floor as if I don't exist at all when all accounts thus far speak otherwise. Each creature takes turns flicking soft ears to the clamor I make in shifting the hay so that I can sit completely upright and see the gross damage inflicted in last night's terroristic escapades.

It's a blur of recent retention, what happened. Less vague than the collection of histories I stow away in the catacombs of my brain, but just as distant. Repressed even, so that I'm protected for as long of a stretch that ignorance permits, before it becomes an imminent danger. Yet I find it disrespectful that I allow myself to forget the force that incites pleading screams so desperate that they carve trenches through the streets. The violence that makes the hollow pops of breaking bones against the side of the barn echo behind me. The sounds are accompanied by a distinct smell I cannot rid my reminiscent constraints of. What it is that blindsided me with fatality, my body pushes under the sieve, crumbling it away with everything else and leaving me doubly frustrated.

A cheerful bluster mocks my disorientation, invading my cognizance with agitated steam so I can't think coherently beyond. A plan would be incomplete with this nonsensical disquiet, even if I crave the company of anything living.

"I hear that some people eat lamb," I mumble to the ostentatious mothers, feeling a twinge of guilt follow the last bitter syllable to hit my tongue.

They pay me little mind.

In a bashful continuation of my imprudence, I roll my skirt up to my hip, tugging the elastic waist of my leggings an ample length down the naked ridges of my thigh to inspect the bandaging in need of attention. From a brief glance alone, it is intelligible that my fluids have had more than just a few undisturbed hours to ooze through the expertly wound wrap, leaking out the bottom of the suffocating band to dry midway down my knee in a rich, blackening channel. Wavy grooves of it break in the uneven surfaces of my skin, crumbling in a reddish dust at the ginger movements of my leg, and dropping into the mesh leggings like grains of sand.

I touch the pin that has crusted over in the front of the bandage, holding it on with faint uncertainty of how crude the break in the partially healed injury might be. A vigilance leaves my hand fretfully unstable in pulling it free, letting the cloth fall apart so that only the little section of scab remaining beneath the stitching from the cut holds it to my form.

*Not today. Please, not today. Haven't I been through enough?*

The little herd chews without pity, eyes unwavering from the entertainment of my struggle, therein a handful of snaps in clear line on the end of a once finished product, leaving a cruel oval of striated meat winking back at me behind a drizzle of watery blood.

It drips past my fingers in a faded orange tickle, racing toward my pelvis and thinning as it goes. The calculating faces of my set-up stare at the rear of my imagination in this second of faint gore, measuring my response in a vivid flash of inhuman influence that is pushed deeper into my subconscious.

"She's right here," high pitched voices chant at the doors. "Come see, come see! She's right there!"

My heart flutters from my chest to the top of my throat, creating a knot that I swallow alongside a painfully dry gulp of air. Adept fingers fly to my bare leg, securing the fabric back around the gash, and ramming the pin through with such force it almost makes a nest in the warmth of my flesh. I manage to shimmy my bottoms back into place right before at least a dozen small faces peer around the stall with the company of a young adult man clad in a ripped plaid vest and no undershirt. Blue jeans, shorn and mildewed, are ripped from the hem to his knee at the left side, and there are no shoes to conceal gnarled feet blanketed in a chimp's worth of thick curly hair.

I want to swallow again at the sight of him, fear bubbling up from the base of my throat as I stare into a face that's contorted in a deep-set frown that flares his nostrils and stiffens his squared jaw until the blue veins at the sweaty temple of his forehead pop through the surface—but my whole mouth is much too sapped, my body pulling every ounce of fluid left in my system to keep me upright. All I can produce instead is a puny cough, holding my hand cupped over cracked, bleeding lips and extending the other to protect me.

*Stop. Let me explain.*

It is all I want to say, but my tongue is tied like the cherry stems attractive women seeking a sexy thrill practiced to entice more attractive men on cheaply produced television romances.

"What're you doin' here?" the man asks, his speech a slur.

His green eyes are bulging and burdened with purple pillows of exhaustion, the red vessels that have not already flowered into crimson clouds snaking in branches all the way to his irises.

"Well? You think you're homeless, girl? Huh?" His words bite.

I shrivel as the sound exits his mouth, tucking my skirt over my knees and idling within the soulless preconceptions that have already impregnated his very understanding of what is and what is not, planting seeds of misplaced hostility in those below him who flout at my abashment—seemingly undeterred by the majority being less than half my age. The smallest of the bunch could not have been more than just a tot, with enough blonde locks in messy ringlets to create a dirty mop on the top of her head, and still somehow I can see the confidence she exudes in her dinner plate-sized blue eyes far superior to my own sense of self-worth at this point.

"You deaf?" The man raises his voice at me, raking nails chewed bloody to the bed through hair the color of peppered carrots. "You mute?"

"N...no," I rasp.

My voice sounds as though I've been smoking since infancy. Desperation for water smashes through the dam of adrenaline that has kept me alive through cutting dehydration, dragging me to the bottom of an internal dry abyss that rakes broiling talons across my stomach.

"No. I'm...so sorry." I attempt to hold in my urgency to cough at every word, throat sinking into itself. "I was just released last night. I had nowhere else to go. I don't even know where I am."

"Girl," he snaps. His jaw glistens like that of a scraggly wolf, his pack no more than pups teetering on mangled, shoeless paws. "I'm not your damned GPS, and this barn ain't no home for your kind. Get on outta here."

"S...sure. Yeah," I reply, sniffing away the shame melting across my face like a sundae on a hot sidewalk.

Below my waistline, my legs simultaneously work against me, struggling to find their ambition to send me bolting outside with the speed of a life flight helicopter—which, quite frankly, I could use at this moment. A resilient ache blisters my joints, snapping my knees to gelatin with every jolt to stiffen back to my feet.

I wobble and exhale, touching either hand to a wall within the stall so that my scrawny arms can bear the weight of my cumbersome body, only for my fingers to drag on the wood in a splintering slide beneath my nails until I resolve to let myself drop flat to my ass in defeat. Black stars twinkle across my line of sight as my backside hits the floor, making my head feel heavy and numb. My chin touches the start of my chest without conscious movement, and there is a stirring across the room in light of my now shallow breathing. I roll my head to both sides, eyes weighted shut—nevertheless, everything is frighteningly white. My forearm trembles to swipe the heat from my face, but blankets it with much more.

*The show must go on*, the voice inside my head commands. It sounds like me, but it's not me.

My ribs expand against my shirt with two healthy inhales and I rock to my knees, teetering with agonizing care to my feet. Pins and needles rush to each of my extremities at this change, filling them with static waves of torment and renewing what circulation I had lost with my pack at my shoulders all night. I've only straightened from a decrepit hunch when an unyielding thud connecting with my forehead sends me spinning into the lamb at the back wall, frantic blusters rising alongside the beat of tangled hooves.

Another *thunk,* like the sound of bone on bone impact, sends cold pain dripping down the side my face and dribbling beneath my jaw. I do not hear myself shriek, but I can feel my neck tighten and burn with ear splitting sound, my arms rising to protect my head against an onslaught of sharp stones from the fenced enclosures outside.

"Get on out." The man is adamant. "Or they'll keep on throwin. We don't take to your kind here."

My kind? *Female?*

The next few stones clatter at my calves, each folded flaccid below me but filling with sparks of ardor like orange embers erupting from flint and steel that launch me upright. My elbow takes the next bruising for the sake of my face, and I careen blindly through the barrier my miniature army of enemies have created at my only point of exit.

I can hear their bodies roll and shift, feet padding against the dirt outside in air that smells both light and dirty, grass that smells both sweet and tart. My heart races as it did last night but in a different way, whacking against my sternum every handful of seconds in frantic attempts to power a dying flame only strong enough to slide me back over the white fence, leaving a faded red silhouette dripping in slick crimson lines to the bottom of the uneven slats.

I close my eyes to a triple vision of sights that my lucidity is not ready to take in—except for in trepidation that if I did not at least try to relocate, my skull would be split like a coconut in a much too comparable sound. Drawing to temporary focus at this concept, I pick myself off the ground and allow my lids to lift in a gradual sweep so that there is time to adjust to the transition brought by the ball of radiance in the sky alone—something dulled by a foul, toxic shadow in memory of what has been.

The sheer contrast of the village in the two instances I have witnessed it is quite actually night and day in viewing, for now it is lit up in a full spectrum of color and volume, leaving me drunk on fascination like I have been pushed through The Healing Center's front doors all over again, but without the paranoia of being dumped in a ghost town. Instead, a pull between my physicality and soul leaves me feeling improperly drugged while I absorb the panorama of life spilling from rickety wooden stairs into every bare crevice of the jagged dirt pathways made by the weight of so many feet pounding in a hurry to their destinations.

The ages of this conflux are as varied as I might expect in any structured society. Each accumulated clique carries a false sense of normalcy in an otherwise ethereal environment that places no value on rules or human decency. It does strike me in a second take that there might be more men than women standing about in soiled, patched outfits, and far more adults than children. Even then, there is by no stretch abundant, willing manpower to supervise the smallest of them who dart disoriented zigzags about the setup as if it had not been traumatized by unseen forces of the night just hours ago. In turn, I am visibly cringing at the one-year-old wobbling on rounded feet, holding up the caboose of a youthful locomotive weaving among indifferent adults with his neck arched for any brand of attention. His pudgy cheeks are swollen and red amid the rampant humidity that wets his untrimmed bangs to his forehead.

He needs water too, and I promise myself to find him before the end of the night, if not this afternoon if I am able.

The homes feel far less drab than the people in daylight, however, any puddles left from the rain the night prior having been soaked into the dark, rocky soil. This allows the sun to zap sweltering heat onto the shelters, reflecting its light from their metallic portions and casting glittering beams throughout the unoccupied spaces. It is exhilarating in its own right to experience so much natural light fueling a landscape into existence. The warmth it generates screams inside hollow guts that this is what home should look like while my brain continues to fight against the walls of this place.

Of what it is.

I duck into a sea of bodies that hum with the hospitality of a hornet's nest, lowering cold, dry eyes to my shuffling, scuffed sneakers in an attempt not to look any one particular person in the face. A few fits of laughter heighten this anxious frenzy. Whatever conversation that follows immediately fades into the background of fifty other voices while I glide through busy days and private circumstances in makeshift backyards that smell of pungent piss and rot. Overhead, I still see the Purple Dome that encases our minuscule section of what is always a very big world extending beyond infinity like a lavender tinted cake cover.

It is just a shade lighter than it seemed yesterday, painting the sky and all it comes into explicit contact with a voltaic pastel, leaving all inside its more definitive borders as it should be on the color wheel of life. Like looking through a thin film of plastic, I can still see what lies beyond without crossing, such as the cloudless baby blue in the great above, or the flowers on some of the outer edged trees that blow their red speckled petals wayward until they settle on the walkways of Limbo.

That is what Celestyn called it, I remember.

Limbo.

So, it's coming back.

Was there ever really such a sacred place like this on the remnants of Earth prior to my memory being cut short? One so backwards and secluded from the toxins that plagued our very reality, that it thrived beyond reason? And where did the questionable Miss Adabelle Green fit into either of these pictures?

Nothing thrives where I lived. Nothing frail slips through the cracks and blossoms amongst adversity. A good ninety percent doesn't exist as it did once upon a time, except for in history books, most fossils lost to war and waste before museums could recover them. There was a tragedy of sorts, muddied inside this timeline that attempts to retreat from my possession. Or, perhaps, a great many man-made calamities, superseding the next, until all was but lost to the poison we designed, overrun at our weakest summit by something strange.

Unfamiliar.

I don't quite recall. Everything is filtered through my conscience so fast. A diary of dirty laundry that my hundreds of internal hands cannot sort in the daunting presence of so many questions, and an inside-out headache to match.

Upon my forced exit, Celestyn had made mention of a place designated "Headquarters" where I could be assigned work in the morning. If I am lucky, I can weasel the answers from those in charge of work placement where I could not at the center. But the morning for most of these villagers has started—from the appearance, much before sunrise—so trying tomorrow feels far more ideal. It will be much simpler to locate the building today and go in tomorrow anyway, given doubt that I am unlikely to receive directions from a good Samaritan just lingering in wait.

At this rate, who would hire such an outcast anomaly of

society, even if I made an appearance? Especially a late one, with more questions than answers. Whatever mystery occurred within the confines of quarantine has already spread to the community after all, infecting the minds of anyone that I have yet to come into contact with and skewing what little facts remain about what I know of my own person. If I wish to stand a remote chance of survival among them, it must start with what I am positive I can manage on my own.

Tending my substantial injuries somewhere contained and serene would be a positive start, if I can find the space. Preferably away from the incessant buzz of fatal rumors or what hospital of nightmares I have escaped from by the skin of my own teeth. Following which, I will need to search for or provide my own shelter, and set up a fortress against the horrors of this nature that won't crush me while I dream before I get to the section of the game plan where I am graciously dispensed answers faster than fifty-cent condoms at a sketchy, backwoods gas station. But more than any of that, if I wish to elude not being able to walk at all, I will have to find food and water to coat the shriveling edges of my stomach, which feels as if it's pulling outside itself like linty blue jean pockets. I want to drool from the caustic nausea it manifests but am left with the dehydration giving my mouth little to spare. My legs wobble, feeling stunted under my body as if I need the confirmation that I can die soon.

I plod forward, powered by nothing but fumes and desire— only two of the intangible items a living body requires to survive. The other two being the will to live and a purpose. The homes are beginning to disperse the further I go, and I smell something savory just to my right if I just follow the breeze it rides in on. Heavy on the nose and slathered in so much fat I can already feel the acne, I'm enticed by what can only be the hotspot markets of the city calling to me in false reassurances.

*I could go for fat right now,* my stomach cries out to me in a gurgling rage. *We certainly can't maintain these hips without a bit of grease,* it reasons.

But even if I found this food, how would I have the means to pay for it? I'm sure they don't have any card readers if they don't have light bulbs. If I have a wallet to be dug for in this monster backpack of mine, my money will probably be obsolete. I can't imagine that hunters, butchers, and cooks run off of the sugary promises of a paid in full tab as soon as I find work, either.

They wouldn't make a lot of money that way, and I'm not to be trusted with animals in a barn, let alone alongside real people. If I happen to be recognized—which wouldn't be hard after the arguments that brought me here—it could mean trouble. Trouble I'm little prepared for in my current state of affairs.

*She's tainted.*

I can still hear the clamor of the nurses in my head—metal trays with new dressings and boiled needles crashing to the grungy floor while each hurried acquaintance trips over the next in a dash to reach the door before the other. Their words seeped inside my pores in that moment, the same as this one. The echo of the door hitting the wall after being sprung carelessly ajar makes me wonder what would have been had I left at that moment.

It was the first time I could see light since the veil, only this was hot and inviting. It had spirit. I could have run to it in their folly, and not a single person in that hallway would have felt plucky enough to challenge me. But I wanted to bathe in it, this non-mechanical heat. To just roast in it until my skin mutated to a fire engine red, and then sleep in the open air where I was free of all constraints.

Only I wasn't free then.

And I'm still not, in a strange way.

*Get rid of her beyond The Dome, Celestyn. She'll get us killed,* they had argued.

It was my good fortune at the time that there were at least a few who did not see it this way. But the whispers carried much quicker than I imagined when I heard my name slip through tight lips and clenched teeth throughout that day. Much to their delight, they inadvertently devised a new way to kill me where other plans fell short, because everyone else had become privy to information that I am not.

Like a game of telephone where I am the last child at the end of the crisscross applesauce circle who receives the final half-giggled phrase, I peek through timid lashes to the originator and ask, *is that right*, and the whole class riots around me, instead of providing the fact so I'm left beside myself with no tools to clean up the involuntary disaster.

I manage a willful turn from the scent, stumbling to the outskirts of town where houses scatter to a halt down a steep slope, and I can put a steady distance between myself and the things I cannot attain. My brain requires reprieve from the sinful temptation to rob an entire market of its products based exclusively on the motives of my stomach, even if my life depends on having it.

A field of tall yellow grasses and thorns wave in the breeze a few yards ahead, opening in an expanse of listless space occupied by the hearkened remains of things long past. It rattles in a blissful sway as I stretch against my backpack, all strength released in a mass exodus of icy chills running up my spine and out the tips of every extremity known on the surface of my body. It's peaceful enough to tend my wounds here, if I can find the supplies.

There's no one to disturb me, unless the ghosts of empty brick squares with shattered windows want to take a shot through caved-in roofs overgrown in crunchy bramble. I bet they would have a better vantage point from the looming black tower set against the remote tree line, though. It's taller than anything in the dead village as well as the living one.

In a naïve sense, it reminds me of a pillar that belongs to a castle, with rectangular dark-grey stones snugly layered beneath a pointy shingled hat to keep out the elements. A brick chimney juts off to the side, probably burnt black with soot on the inside, even though it hasn't been used in years judging by the curtainless black window placements at the front of the tower, spaced just so pleasing to the eye that a sliver of me wonders if the architect was obsessive-compulsive. The door can barely be seen from the ditch that cradles my body, except for the thick sturdy frame right below the window on the second floor.

*It's probably an old factory*, my thoughts ring, imagining what use each circular floor must have served, if it was feasible at all. *Or a haunted house. Kids like those, right?*

I could live there, if it's as empty as it seems. It is isolated from this chaos that consumes my inhabitance at the hilltop, abandoned for the shambles that still remain uninhabited, despite being far more structurally sound. I won't have to see anyone at all if I learn how to hunt and protect myself, and their unmerited fears can be at a distance farther than arm's length.

I can become a myth, or a witch.

*A hag.*

I smile absently, my face aching with the motion and my forehead feeling like it's been cleaved in two beneath the sunlight no longer hiding behind a canopy of trees. Where the blood has begun to dry is stiff, crusting to my skin and smelling like a jar of sweaty pennies. I inhale through my nose anyway, tasting it at the back of my tongue before it is gone.

*"Thirsty?"* The voice comes from my legs, and I curl at its intensity.

Who speaks that loud right next to someone's body?

My head rolls toward the sound, studying the person attached to it with half-open eyes. My conscious is slipping in and out, but I can speak.

"Is this a trick?" I murmur, attempting not to gag through the pain in my throat and chest.

It's another young girl, fifteen or sixteen on the lower end, but possibly older based on deceivingly youthful facial structures, as well as the tallest person I have seen. Her frizzy, dirty blonde hair is pulled back into two low lying ponytails that sit on meatless slumped shoulders, framing her mousy freckled face, spotted in clusters of cystic acne. Her neck dips in at her chest, where split ends fester like baby spider legs, accentuating a collar bone so visible it can be gripped like a handlebar beneath a stretch of stressed, sun-kissed flesh. However, her most striking feature lies below this.

Something the likes of which I know I have not been witness to, as it's nearly more so extinct than plants or animals. A belly. Rounded in the shape of a soccer ball, it sits just at the top of her hips under a flowery yellow blouse stained with black streaks across the ratted lace.

"Are you fucking dumb?" she scoffs. "Doesn't it look like I have better things to do than pretend like I'm going to water the weirdo?" Bony fingers slosh about a leather canteen, hanging by a string of white yarn, twisting in a limp dangle. "Just take the damn thing before I change my mind."

The canteen hits my lap at the bandage, rocketing me into an upright position so that there isn't any that spills across the fabric. My jaw quivers and my hands are flimsy as I look this girl in her big doe eyes the color of mud.

I want to distrust her, to have the willpower to, but my hands won't give me the time. The opening is already plunged throat deep into my mouth, filling it with razor blades of cold water racing down my lips and the sides of my face, pooling within my shirt in translucent streams. My eyes leak, the growing pang making it harder to swallow urging me to sputter it across the ground, but my body unwilling to relinquish the resource just yet. I wretch at the last drop, holding my stomach in a mix of relief and violent discomfort.

"Thank you," I gasp when I'm finished, still holding the empty container against me. "W...what's your name? I need...I need to..."

I can't catch my breath.

The girl lowers herself next to me, balancing with outstretched arms until she settles on to the grass below. What survival has left of her thighs spreads to touch between the blue legs of her shorts, and she lets out a shaky exhale upon expanding across them from above, letting the tension of moving release until her full girth is present.

I can't help but zero in on the lump of a stomach that takes up her entire lap as she goes, the way it moves and thins in the most alien way, outlining the vague shape of the baby inside when she leans in just the right avenue. A hasty piece of myself wonders how she doesn't bust beneath all the internal pressure brought to the surface, but I manage to keep this locked away for now.

Pregnancy is taboo enough to warrant a question or two, but she did make sure I didn't slip away too soon in this present—I think—so it will do me well to keep my toes behind the white line.

Resounding pains snake from the pit of my guts to my chest, sending diluted bile shooting out my mouth to the ground between my acquaintance and I. There isn't time to squeeze oxygen back into my lungs before it is ejected from my insides in a violent second round that assaults the back of my hand in a thickened, gelatinous sheen. I suppose in the grand scheme of it, I should be grateful there isn't anything in my system to add a delightful variety of chunky colors, but most of me is disappointed to already lose half of my gifted resource to acid washing the grass. It doesn't really need it as much as I do.

The girl wears a disgusted, possibly offended, face when I glance back to see her nose scrunched and flared, though I cannot smell anything—perhaps due to the foul mix leaking out my nose as well. Her brow furrows, pinching the area between her eyes, and lips curling in toward her teeth without saying a word in response to my question. I wipe my hand on my shirt, studying her face for purpose, and returning the emptied canteen to the ground beside her.

I clear my throat. "My name is Adabelle, I guess."

"I know who you fucking are," the girl barks. "Everyone does."

The delusions that have been a silent but existent passenger to the neighborhood voice inside my head fans blue fires to the tune performed by the theoretical devil on my shoulder, making him dance to the beat of the visible waves of its madness. My mind tangos around a few questions presented by both, flirting with the proper way to go about them in a manner that will win me reasonable answers. This girl is the first person to give me the chance to let out an entire sentence, after all. I want to keep a clean slate with her if I can manipulate my position in any way.

"No one will tell me anything at all." It comes off as a whine and I hesitate to complete the idea, grounding myself back to center. "They all act as if I'm so strange, but they don't even know who I am beyond a name and a rumor probably distributed by some flowery nurse who decided she saw something that she didn't like. What she saw, I have no idea—"

It comes out so fast I have to catch my breath. A slow burn singing across my cheeks and ears, blowing steam through my eyeballs as it has nowhere else to go when I waste air on words. My eyes flutter, gating in tears that threaten to overflow and break what dignity I have to spare. Fear is a gas that inflates the space beneath my skin in swells so large that I am suffocating, a balloon of guts that runs out of space to hold anything else inside.

All it will take is one prick to spill everything uncontrollably into the universe.

"What was it that she saw?" I ask, unable to hold back the question, and disassembling my build. "Do you know? I need help here to piece together this mess. I don't even know who I am, but it appears everyone else does."

I wonder if she is paying attention. If she isn't, then why is she here, watering this weirdo, and letting the dark green grass tickle the underside of her legs while only a puddle of watery vomit sets all the distance between us? If I am a dangerous stranger, setting life off its proper axis, should she not flee?

But her eyes are void of reality, fixated on the same tower I had been earlier with a hard-lined grimace, as though this population has sucked her dry of imagination. Or hope.

I try again. "I don't feel like I know this place. It's too clean for everything I remember. Or think I remember. Too...backwards. No cars. Or phones. Restaurants."

The wind whistles through the cracks in the ramshackle housing beyond us. Birds call to one another from different trees, orchestrating an eerie lullaby that puts everything in its vicinity into a blissful slumber, except for the bugs that chirp in a compliant applause, as if compelled by the hypnotic aura of false security like a baby in the house of a serial killer. They scurry through the weeds and bury hard-shelled bodies with prickly legs into the dirt so that they are not found, but sorrow endures that they should call at all to the very thing that takes their lives.

My possibly teenage rescuer places a hand at the top of her belly, folding a forearm over the arch below her ribcage and taking a deep breath, inhibited by the lack of lung space seized from the imperious occupant on board. A subtle twitch responds to this touch below her knobby fingers, sliding along each one, and hesitating as a less-than-palm-sized bump at the side above her hip, until vanishing inside its water world of warm dark dreams. I can feel the twist of an invisible knife upon this sight, not quite painful like the water, but heavy on the mind.

Where is a future tied to a parasite so helpless for so very long? Perhaps she cannot see one anyway, considering her placement, obligations piling, and stakes soaring over her head.

Is it hard to do alone? To wonder what we no longer know about pregnancy and childbirth in the throes of this timeline, where the technology we have left for actual human labor is no longer here at all? Let alone that most fathers only stick around long enough to discover the accident had been made, she is a girl setup to lose it all.

"My name is Zoey Mince," she says. "That's what they told me when I had my 'awakening'." She accompanies the word with finger quotes and a deep voice followed by an aggressive eyeroll, as if she were actually still dreaming instead of having this conversation with me. "I was sixteen when I got here, but it's been a fucking minute since then. A birthday or two or three might have passed between now and that time."

"You...don't want to know more?" I pry, letting my own dilemma wash back into a sea of temporary ignorance. My grip on identity is falling between closed fists, hands bruised from the futile attempts to rein it in when it cannot be touched. Not yet.

"Don't you *dare* fucking judge me, you little twat!" She points a daring finger, scooting across the grass halfway up the hill. "I'm plenty smart enough to figure this shit out on my own. I just thought...well, I was just hoping this would be more of a temporary fucking thing, I guess."

*Is it* ever *temporary? If it happens, it doesn't unhappen,* right?

I can feel a slick smirk hiding under red lipstick staining the base of my skull in a smarting burst of warmth. My hand flies to touch it, finding nothing but a fringe of soft hair too short to make it into my bun.

I try to nod with a degree of empathy, the tremors in my hands bringing them back to the ground, my eyes deepening the concern written across my forehead. But it feels forced when the accompanying words come out to her. I don't know what I'm saying, but I do. It has always been there, nestled in the sarcasm lobe of my broken bicycle brain.

"No. No, yeah. Sure." I sigh through my nose. "Who needs a higher power when we have our all-knowing youth to answer our questions?"

"Don't patronize me."

I roll my shoulders forward, hiking my backpack closer to where the warmth had been. A mental bullet ricochets through the missing persons ads of my psyche, marking actress off the list of people the nefarious Adabelle Green might have been in the fantasy dripping to me.

Does that mean I can also mark criminal off the list?

I wouldn't be a very good liar, even if it couldn't be a terrible skill to expand upon if my life carries some value to me.

Out of my peripheral vision, Zoey uses the balls of her feet and shaking arms to scoot herself back in the spot next to me. I can feel a distrust in her purpose here but, glancing around, I cannot find an ambush waiting to happen. I am close enough to the forest that there would be an impracticality about choosing to toy with me here and while my stomach still rolls with discomfort, I do not feel like I've been poisoned.

"Not everything can be explained with a fucking I.D. badge in the front pocket of a wallet," she fumes, settling beside the sputum. "What we are found with means absolutely fucking nothing."

My shoulders grow heavy with the materials that anchor it, my conscience seizing me in place while my mind slips away. I can feel Zoey's hopelessness scanning the shape of the bag I was claimed to have been found with, a seething bitterness reaching deep within its unseen contents despite her disregard, for I am lucky. Or so they say, in comparison to my many shoeless neighbors.

"Do you mean to tell me that my name might not be Adabelle Green?" I pretend to ignore her less than subtle interest.

She cackles, giving me a start.

"Well, maybe if you're a fucking liar. How should I know?"

Rocking to either side, I catch my feet underneath me and wobble upright. There isn't a lot of energy left, but the water has given me enough zest to get to the tower if I work efficiently. Given I'm still feeling sprite by then, a little venture past the tree line might find me a few new swigs of water and a river to take a cold bath in. But at least if I were to die, I could do it on my terms and not at the mercy of some crude, teenage brat.

The long grasses catch my skirt starting in from the hillside ditch. They pull without mercy at the cotton threads so that little loops are freed from the article until they are loose strings, opening pits to reveal negligible spots of mucky, off white leggings, slick feathers tickling my cheeks in forewarning of the briers not far in front of them. I can't see over the glossy tops of the weeds, disappearing in this ocean of overgrown neglect with the trust that I am walking in the right direction. It's the first thing I can trust— that I know how to walk a straight line in the absence of a manual guide—and I slash my flattening path with all one hundred thirty-two pounds of my resignation.

Who needs answers, right?

They have just as many as I have, their hitch being admitting it to someone they do not trust. But I'll be damned if I wait around to be their scapegoat for this horror flick. I won't be an artless object at their disposal. I'll lay low and ask questions later, when the waves have settled, my name lost on their tongues.

I can be forgotten. Eclipsed inside this timeline. Sequestered to the boundless world while I struggle to remember and, therefore, discover the purpose of our existences here. Because I will do something they apparently refuse to.

I will go home. Where I am welcome. And cold. And free of this stigma which has shapeshifted into my current identity. I am not this monster they have made me into, and I am finished with this version of reality.

I don't want it. Even if that means the air is no longer light on my lungs. That the sound of cars honking keeps me up at night with a white noise machine blasting old distant sounds over a romantic comedy playing on loop atop my nightstand, and where black out curtains are all that fills the empty space between myself and so much light pollution it still feels like early morning.

I'll gladly forget the beautiful trees that tower over me and the way the grass feels brushing against my calves. The animals and their gentle dispositions. Even the children. Laughing. Screaming. Living.

I would sacrifice it all for a shred of myself. To belong somewhere kind and acquire answers. Solutions. Ones that if I had at this exact minute, I could explain away the problem that has been foreseen in my nature causing all the cruelty that has followed.

There has to be record of me being born somewhere beyond this.

No one is *just* an adult.

A strong gust of wind blasts down from above, the jagged points of taller trees swaying sideways at its destructive force, and grass in the vicinity bowing in a hurricane of whispers. Breaking across the sky, a cacophonous growl fractures the different sounds of wildlife into catastrophic silence. Fissures of light, highlighting screens of dust, fleet along my scope of vision until the field bleeds black shadows that bar out the sun, followed by another sudden typhoon of air that knocks me flat against the earth. My face crushes into the dirt as I roll to my side, bracing for another barrage of invisible assaults.

Instead, I feel as though my heart has begun to beat on the outside of my body, vibrating against my sternum so hard that the rest of me feels numb. Asleep on pins and needles.

I can't seem to wake up either, cemented in perfect viewing to the leathery stretch of red wings now consuming the sky. A serrated serpentine tail with thoroughly fatal black spines lined like rows of obsidian swords chases a sleek reptilian body at the top of The Purple Dome, delivering a thunderous whack of agitation as it goes. Crystalline sparks burst from this aggression, showering first in a shrieking tidal wave of bright light around the beast, and then diminishing to individual embers along the lavender contours of The Dome, vanishing just before it kisses the grass where I attempt to make myself small.

The beast is sent carrying on without a second glance or desire to fight The Dome. Its flight is smooth, defying its sheer size, and slicing through the emptiness above like butter. I can just catch a glimpse of its muscled back legs folded snug to an impenetrable underside, four toes on each leg curled into a clawed fist.

Another powerful screech is all that resounds from this creature as it clears the horizon, leaving me to scramble against the sharp terrain, desperate to find cover should more find their way down this venue. Sharp rocks grind into my elbows, flowering red splotches to the surface like blooms of roses. The first set of thorns catch me off guard, unzipping slim lines over my round cheeks in this frenzy until I have the wits about me to reach into my pack, yanking free the dagger from the side pocket. I pull my arm back with abrupt force, swinging down through the vines in messy strikes, pushing at what I do not slice with open palms that explode with the heat the plant causes when it penetrates my skin.

"What the *fuck* are you doing?" I hear Zoey scold in a half-whispered screech.

Cold hands take me by the shoulders, throttling me in the direction I came. I catch myself before the wilting weeds and housing rubble does, ears shutting out all but an incessant ring from the beast that masters the skies in a way fowl only dream of. The dagger jangles to the earthen floor in the same instant, my own clumsy paws trembling too much now for gripping its scraggled handle. My fingers, jellied blobs without feeling, climb up the length of my arms until I am holding myself in a constricted vice. Dry sobs break through the repression, filling the quiet the animal has left behind.

I am smothered.

"I want to go home," I gasp. "Where am I? Tell me. NOW!"

Zoey jogs for my dagger, belly jostling with each heavy stride and face bobbing either direction to our flanks. It is wiped along her pants and turned back to me, handle split but manageable. "Right now? We are in the remains of the *old* village, and both of us are risking much more than death by standing out here in The Dome's second layer like A. BUNCH. OF. ASSHOLES."

It is the first time I really stop to look at where I am standing. What I am doing. How far I got without being stopped.

The old houses are within arm's reach, scattered in uneven rows and old walkways. I'm standing on broken glass as we speak, up to my neck in weeds and bug bites, The Dome above us lighter than the one covering Limbo.

"I don't want to go back," I hiss, covering my face with suffocating intent. Tears begin to fall in gushing streams, thorns still jutting deep from within my palms registering a coarse sting when pressure is applied. "They hate me. I haven't done anything, and they *hate* me."

"Oh, boo," Zoey clicks. "I guess you'll die then."

"They want me dead!" I shriek, unable to compose myself.

I am so far from here. Unmanageable. Lurking beneath the surface of my own pain.

"Then I guess you'll show them by giving them exactly what they fucking want, now won't you?" she snaps back, tossing the canteen she wore over a slumped shoulder to scabbed, bare feet. "Some strength you have! Ha! The way you are spoken of, I'd expect more than a grown child!"

I glower, though she could be right. More than right.

I just need glue to hold together every fracture of this person I know I am, something sticky so that I don't lose a piece while finding another. Impossibility is no longer fleeting, but a permanent state of affairs, a statuesque dictator with a golden scepter that fries anyone who dare believe otherwise. But emptiness is beginning to replace what was repressed pain, and I welcome its newfound attendance, for at least if I cannot feel a thing, there is a neutrality instead of whatever this is.

Uncertainty?

Terror?

I don't like it.

Sniffing, I wipe each wet cheek on a dirty forearm, letting this nothingness consume all that it must in order to restore balance. So that I can feel bare. Exposed. Deadened.

Zoey is closing the distance that remains in the middle of our bodies, taking a dirty hand at my mid-back and nudging me with vigor toward the village of Limbo. Her teeth are grinding in a wide-eyed despondence, something about her urgency reminding me of my own, but wiser. Something that is screaming of bone crunching *thunks* in dead black nights. Of inhuman green orbs with thin black slits for pupils gazing back into mine, filling me with a much-deserved inferiority, our breathing stilled in a life altering measure.

The grass is swishing closer to the forest like hundreds of snakes gliding about its depths, birds twittering again in a harmonious belt. I plant my feet so that I cannot be pushed any further, listening instead, gut guiding me to remain placed.

"I don't want to go," I say. "I don't know you."

She stops pushing in futility, hands falling in defeat, but legs never ceasing to dance in anticipation.

"I know," she replies.

"I will stay in the tower," I conclude. "It's the best I can do for right now."

Zoey is inching further away, biting her lip and holding her hand steady. Our eyes meet. She doesn't want to be here either. What is keeping her?

*What is it you fear?*

But I don't ask. I don't know that I actually wish to be made aware.

"You can't fucking live there," Zoey hurries. "It's not for you."

"No one lives there."

"That's not true," she almost yells, but the world around her is able to suppress this. She raises antsy fingers just below her nose, pinching the space with uneven nails. "You can't fucking live there."

"I can't stay..."

The village looms as a grey silhouette in the afternoon sun at the hilltop. Waves of heat so strong I can see its pulse are swallowed by what feels like fresher air down here. Why would they want to make a foundation closer to the sweltering fireball in the sky? I'm pretty sure I already hate it long-term.

"But I need time. I need you to buy me time."

Her free hand is outstretched toward me, fingers flexing, throat bobbing with the massive amount of thick pride she swallows in a voice a shade above sorrow.

"I don't know you," I insist. Careful. Piqued.

"You will," Zoey promises, nodding. "Because the truth of the matter is, *you need me too.*"

# CHAPTER THREE
## AIDAN

I CAN REMEMBER THE WAY GASOLINE SMELLS. HOW IT burns by just the hint of the first gush, acrid from the top of my nose to the back of my throat on rainy August afternoons when the water should have washed it clean. But the fuel just continues to break across the pavement anyway, burning rugged trenches down streets littered with cars sitting bumper to bumper in motionless traffic.

I should have died that day.

Traffic stilled for hours, honking wildly as though it were possible to remove ourselves from these hollow shells cemented to the warm crunchy seats set ablaze—flames snapping closer and closer to bare skin in the form of long red fingers stretching to consume all that it can reach. The gasoline pours piss down the tank of my imagination, heavy at the base of my neck while my small chest flails diagonally, bathed in cumbersome warmth so I don't move despite the soft voice that crawls its way beneath my nails like little ticks, nesting inside the soft tissue where it spits toxic shifts of insomnia so that I am cognizant.

*Aidan, honey.*

A handful of phones stretch out half-cracked windows, zooming in at just the right angle from the safety of cold leather seats. White flashes, like glimpses of lightning crashing against my conscience, plead to me in the same voice to stay alive.

*But I'm not, am I?*

Alive, that is.

I want to live within a memory so I can sleep forever. To drink whatever poison can be entertained in such an unusual scape of land, and never wake, so that at last I can relive the lush of what had once been my own design for the unforeseeable end ahead.

I crave escape in the only respite left available when the life granted only totes terror cloaked in death every time the stars blister pings of silver light into the night sky, with The Dome that keeps all magical entities at arm's length receding alongside the sunset. In distant melodies of lullabies strung upon a harp in a forest green room of stuffed bears and plastic train tracks, there are white pillows on a pale wooden bed bursting with feathers that I am flung against in a fit of laughter. Free. Whereas now, I'm a broken puppet that clatters on thinning strings and a scheduled stage, my set list branded into the grooves of my shriveling brain.

Wake up. Smell blood.

Shake it off. Button shirt.

Play guitar. Move the bodies.

Go to work. Come home.

Rinse and repeat.

The life inside these moments are husks of existence. Fleeting joy, relative to a captive's when the cellar door is cracked before the onslaught of torture—catching a peek of golden sunlight as it vanishes, and the actuality of what is happening smashes home in the form of a hurricane that everyone ignored until it breaches the shoreline. At which time, it's too late to evade the waves that sweep one below, catapulting entire populations out to the mercy of nature's brute strength, with no prepared lifeboat to spare.

I am not living with *that* in mind.

Surviving?

The best I can.

But it is all cellar door light when I am just as much at the mercy of the Ravagers that live beyond the borders of our community—watching the hurricane that others attempt to disguise as a thunderstorm move in, and knowing that there is nothing I can do to will it away. If I'm right, that feeling is actually referred to as hope, and if I am wrong it is fantasy. So I indulge in neither, buttoning my black flannel shirt as I have every morning prior, and rolling the sleeves in neat sections to my elbows.

It is too big for me, and stained in browned blood from the previous owner who took a bone shattering impalement through the chest, the brutes unhinging his rib cage like the macabre wings of a butterfly. But the shirt I came with two years ago was totaled before I had my first in depth recollection—some kind of hot pink V-neck with the word *donate* scrawled on the back and a list of several organizational phone numbers below it. This was only a more recent addition to an expansive stockpile that had been pulled from bodies that no longer needed them, and it was a fat chance I would ever find something particularly form fitting, considering my rather efficient metabolism and chronic fits of cardio leave little for rippling biceps or glistening pecs the size of my girlfriend's head.

Tough cotton for brier protection. A fold down collar to catch the sweat off my jaw when the sun peaks sometime in the afternoon. Sleeves to ward off the blood sucking insects. Or better, no insects at all and enough beer to put me in a permanent coma —whoops, there's that cellar door again. All these things are factors brought to my attention through trial and error in the line of work thrust upon me since the day of my release, but only rarely granted when the right person kicks the bucket too soon. The markets in the center of Limbo, adjacent my living quarters, almost exclusively boomed off the poor fortune of others after all, and thus the people as well, for the dead do not need as the living do.

## OBSIDIAN CORVUS

I skip the music today, my fingers itching with movement in this morning light, where the sky is still pastel indigo through the brief cleft in my window cover. I stuff my marred guitar inside its black canvas case, rolling both in several sets of blankets that I cover with homemade pillows in a heap at the corner of my shack before heading out the door.

It takes most of my might to open, hugging the thickened steel edge with just enough room for me to wedge my thigh outside, but worth the peace of mind and many sacrificed hours of spare time to accomplish. I had walled in the windows in a similar fashion from the inside out four months back, reinforcing my shelter fragile wall by wall until it felt more like a semi-soundproof fortress of ignorance than a last line of defense.

My head scrapes against the cold, solid frame, popping out the other side, though my shoulders catch and heave, paving extra crimson striations along my already much too raw collar. Outside, the smell of rot is festering in oncoming waves of heat carried on the final welcoming chilly breezes of morning before the sun toasts us alive.

Meanwhile, just a neighbor away down an open dirt path at the foot of the marketplace, a mob of survivors from another night of violent assaults tug at the remnants of assets left on a teenage boy's corpse. Baggage, such as his wristwatch and facial jewelry, hold little value until they're melted down—if they can be. Nonetheless, in mere minutes he will be bare—his body tossed into a wagon and dumped in a mass grave by myself or comrades among the search crews, depending on who draws what straw in the coming hours.

When at first it seemed like an inhuman design to act upon, the smell of bloat and gas building where I refused to assist cornered me into accepting that a great number of behaviors are horrendous until they are chased with copious amounts of repetition. After all, when routine is but a log on the fire, anything can become as mundane as a stroll down a quiet sidewalk on a Monday evening—except, I suppose, those are the extraordinary behaviors in this place.

Fires smoke with seasoned grease less than half a mile from my brick paved porch. Shouting men and women bark orders through crackling stone ovens, leaving me unsure as to who is running the kitchens today while I fight my door shut. I have little time to care, saving the hope that I don't get food poisoning for after I finish business, and ducking my head to the ground while I walk so I can hum a tune of escape without the disturbance of mortality.

*It is more for an instrument of keys than strings,* I distract in thought, brain blinding my eyes so that I see roses in a field of thorns. But it is missing a few lines that beguile me into starting over after every two minutes of struggling to place the notes.

My black sneakers spray dust, stumbling along a bloody pile of rocks and swaying around them without having to make handprints should I fall. A mass of fat buzzing flies swarm to the sky in a tornado of black bodies, most landing before I have reached the other side of their abomination. I despise things with wings just about the same as things that bleed.

The first time I saw both in the same place, I shriveled into a piddling juvenile, ruining my shoes by throwing up the dinner given to get me through the night after quarantine. I was shoeless for three days, my feet swollen and lacerated so that I could scarcely walk when I sat alone in my dark and empty new home, resolving in this time that I might fancy bodily fluids with my clothes after all. It had never been more prevalent than in those seconds, staring at naked walls caressed in the waning silver of moonlight, that I did not want to be known as a boy among men —a useless insect feeding on the leftovers of society.

But the struggle therein lies that I also do not wish to be the leftovers of society.

*Don't be a hero,* they say. *It's not worth the outcome.*

I wonder if the guy who wore this shirt had tried to be a hero. Maybe he loved a woman, or another man. It had been worth the risk until it wasn't. To do what is my job by law—though most of my coworkers don't do the work required—is a death sentence in full, but they call it 'helping others' because 'someone has to do it'. Why that someone has to be me, when my hands before had not known what it meant to kill a living being, is haunting, but we're not permitted to question the decision of work placement without written consent. It is all dusting shit with sparkles at the end of the day and calling it a unicorn. Because it's spray-painted white with glitter sprinkled over the top, the people that don't clean the mess take it at face value.

But it still smells like shit.

I catch a glimpse of the clear glass ceiling of The Healing Center glistening with a sheen of residual rain behind indelible black bars bobbing over the rooftops of the outskirt shacks closest to its outermost borders. Heavy dark stones that construct virtually indestructible walls interlace with the most dusky outlining of The Purple Dome, both welcoming immediate danger to our most vulnerable members of society and allotting a reverse psychology to be the fine line that we tight rope on in our best attempt to lure the Ravagers exactly where we want them to be: away from the weak and confused.

The apparent disaster that erupted in the confines of the old village claims this to be an effective method, in part, or at least our best shot. The survivors that built this village skimped death's hefty toll in a similar fashion, though their biggest building was much less ambitious, and the second layer to The Dome catastrophically less effective at keeping out magical entities than the one we reside in now. But I still find myself ill at ease to this concept of decoy in any event.

It failed once, right?

That aside, I've had many hours to watch *their* shadows prowl unlit streets through the cracks left in my windows, listening to the voices that echo unfamiliar vibrations as they stroll. Never quite in a hurry. Weapons sheathed. More like they're waiting on something in particular rather than seeking out violent confrontations when they arrive, lacking a degree of simple sense.

A good mile ahead of me, trees too thick to ax down without

more clearance than we possess, disperse into short trampled grasses leading to reveal the looming wood doors where the sick are treated and the injured die. Alongside the hearty frame I lumber toward, a prepubescent girl sits covered from her chin to blackened toenails in streaks of grime, dried blood having soaked into her sunburnt cheeks like lotion, anguish buried deep within her pores. I try to avoid looking at her as I approach so as to keep her from feeling uncomfortable, acknowledging the notion that at her age, in this place, it can cause her to bolt faster than I can apologize.

Not everyone is cut out for this environment. Most younger bodies and certain search crew members maintain the morning duties. It isn't entirely uncommon for kids lingering beneath adulthood to creep away somewhere quiet when a brief respite presents itself in a larger crew. Piling severed limbs and heavy stiff bodies on to corpse carts pulled by donkeys is something I cannot imagine doing at a similar age. I sympathize with the need to break free of it, especially when the ones lying in the street are those potentially recognized as a friend.

But she will eventually discover that an honest attempt at going missing isn't necessary if she wants to disappear for a time. No one will fault her, or even care, if she doesn't do her part. I once went six days without working during my starting month, and not a single man I called my new brother noticed my absence. It's one less person to pay, and more resources for those that are working.

Frantic murmuring flows from the jarred mouth of The Healing Center, allowing focus to rein me into the present. I nudge my way inside, giving generous distance from the minor as I do. Common community members are not permitted here during prep hours. It isn't like an emergency room that is operated in consistent, round-the-clock conventions. It is closer to an urgent care that opens after the last corpse cart has drawn away and closes at the first twinkle of night in the sky.

It commands appreciation, the profession being the single occupation here that requires taught skill and impromptu genius to perform at peak. It is a highly sought-after position to work in The Healing Center at all, and it comes with prodigious privileges that leave others sick with envy. But the hard truth, and glaring pitfall, is the lack of convenient hours and constant staff—resulting in preventable deaths more frequently than not, leaving it only the second highest paid work in Limbo.

"Celestyn," I call, rubbing my dry eyes behind thick glasses up the length of my forehead when the candlelight assaults my still adjusting vision. Having eyewear only aids my incredible nearsightedness after all, and not the vampiric terror of glaring lights after living like a mole for ten-and-a-half hours.

When Celestyn doesn't immediately answer, I speak up, this time with a bit more agitation and a lot less patience.

"A little communication goes a long way, Celestyn," I fume, waiting. "Mhm?"

It's hard to stay mad at her. So often when I hear the sound of her echo reverberating from every wall in the room, carpeting my chest to stomach like thick velvet, I feel more as if I could float instead of walk. Like a balloon, I'm filled with hot air in her presence. Dumbfounded. Awed and speechless.

Except...for when she makes that sound.

*Mhm,* as if she has little to no clue what I am alluding to but agrees with the premise of some grand idea that my inferior mind has concocted in her absence, when we both know that isn't the case. She is, less than humbly, perhaps the smartest person gifted to our medical devices under Master Amadeus' protections. She is agility in unforeseen emergencies. She is steel in the presence of grief. Her incomprehensible capacities constructed around maintaining information filters out the impertinent and keeps what matters in private mental storages that can be accessed upon whim. Her aggressive retentions alone laid out the foundations for her special protection orders and living quarters, this so that she can continue research for the survival of humanity in solitude while the rest of us attempt not to wilt away in the meantime.

This is also how I happen to know there is, in no possible

reality or alternate reality, a circumstance where she can bat her long, black eyelashes at me in some kind of basic bitch oblivion to what she has done on countless instances in our history together. She knows why I'm here. The only premise she actually "agrees on", is the one in which she is right, and that means, somehow, I am simultaneously wrong.

I release a burdened sigh, the scuffed cream heels of my tennis shoes scraping against the floor as I pace my way to the front desk where she is reviewing overnighted patient notes and histories with two other resident professionals, both female of minimum eighteen years, or just a bit older, since Celestyn should be going on twenty next month if our timelines are accurate. There is not a soul available that has her memorable experience as an actual medical professional in the time predating this, so all understudies given placement here are not done so by the higher powers as per usual, but by Celestyn herself. All of which provides her a well-earned superiority complex and a not-so-dazzling God complex.

"Are we really going to do this?" I ask, placing my sullied hands on top of her files so that she has no choice but to look me in the face, confronting the subject.

It is the least she can do. And I'm not letting it slide into the background of our foundation this time so that history can repeat itself on the next turn of her axis.

Each resident glowers at her side, eyes bouncing back and forth between our not-so-subtle skirmish, though appearing to avoid taking a definitive stance. There is an earned silence in this place, a frequency that somehow bellows above the noise of wet hacking and moaning, something stiff that sits atop the air it feeds, like humidity so dense I can drink the moisture right out of it.

I have a feeling they are not receiving orders well today, based off the tension in the room alone, or perhaps she denied them time off after clustered late shifts for a whole week straight. It isn't unusual, and as a boss, Celestyn can be a bit impersonal with those she employs. People are a collection of facts and histories for her, open books and torn pages to be studied, and then discarded when they lose their purpose.

Celestyn's full, dark lips tilt in a statuesque grimace, sharp eyes shooting laser beams back into my own as a dare to continue standing between her and her work.

"I have less than two hours to finish setup before the morning rush." She leans away from me. "Are *you* really going to do *this*?"

My shoulders slump forward, shrugging and throwing my open palmed hands out, followed by an aggressively distinguished nod that inch my glasses toward the tip of my nose. It's a wonder they don't fly off my face in my dramatic frustration, and I refuse to adjust them right away as a spiteful determination to maintain eye contact, no matter how much of an asshat it makes me appear. Celestyn is no loser though, flashing a devilish smirk—which, as a man, I have learned is not always a green light—and dismissing her residents to prepare empty units, followed by rounds with pre-existing patients. She then slips the remaining paperwork from her desk in a brisk tug, taking measured steps toward the west wing.

Hesitant. Deliberate.

I follow, though a bit reluctant. A part of me doesn't want this confrontation to be one controlled by her, set on her turf. Another part is uncomfortable with the west wing in general. The inhabitants. The sour memories.

Walking side by side, I can see her frowning at the smudged ink in the shape of my fingerprints at the title of the first page, perturbed at the flaw in her very perfection. But I pretend not to notice, despite a lingering guilt that it causes her undue stress when she already has the fate of our entire village riding her ass. She spends every free second of this unnatural life making important decisions, holding powerful discussions with significant figures, and wasting hours of time reading old books laden with centuries of dust. All time in which she could choose to spend fraternizing with friends—if she actually had any—or holding acquaintances close while they take their final breath, or even catching up on a good night's sleep since she has the protections to enjoy it, given Amadeus' tower is untouchable.

The truth is, I shouldn't mess with her perfectionism at all. I know my hands are less than clean most days due to my line of work, and that her pages are more than often immaculate. But damnit...

"We aren't exclusive, Aidan," she surmises at last, pulling a keyring from her outer vest pocket at the first door of the quarantine units after passing the thick steel entry. "I'm sorry your partner died on the job, but you don't get to take it out on me when you *know* what this is."

Do I know what this is?

I bite my lip, whipping my head down either section of the corridor we parted with to reach this destination, and leaning my arm overhead on the rough gritty wall. Celestyn is shorter than me by a good five inches or so, and it's evident with her shit show of a personality, being much closer to hell giving her the relatability of a demon that wants to "just be friends" in public, but connect intimately behind closed doors as though we are more.

"Okay." I pinch the bridge of my nose, eyes shut, and trying not to chuckle at her attempt of being absentminded. "Not being exclusive doesn't mean that you get to only show up to scheduled dates fifty percent of the time."

She shrugs this away, sort of like she does people, bad memories, and deep sentiments.

"It also means I am not obligated to show up any percent of the time." She jams the first key into the lock with little success, thumbing through a couple more and growling when it doesn't turn. "Quit...ugh...quit being so entitled. I don't have time for it, no matter how many times you call me your girlfriend, or dream that it will happen. This" —she points between us— "means nothing."

Always going for the kill.

My chest hurts a little with that one.

But I wave it off.

She can smell pain like a cadaver dog.

"Okay, how about this," I acquiesce. "It doesn't mean you get to cut out common courtesy. I deserve to know when you aren't showing up. I waited five hours for you after I got home."

"Five hours?" she scoffs in amusement. "That's stupid. You should have stopped after one."

The door clicks with this key, and the hinges shriek into the empty bathroom-sized chasm that Limbo dared call a patient room, lit by nothing more than two candles burnt to the last leg of their wick. I watch her stride inside with little shame to our dilemma, collecting misshapen white wax sticks from a swollen drawer in the boxy side table and trading them out one by one.

I cringe when she waves me in, my stomach unsettled about being here, but still afraid to disappoint her. I swallow, pushing the door open until it touches the wall without creaking back shut. Celestyn crams linens by the armful into my chest when I cross the threshold, pointing to an empty handmade basket beside the bed, while she fluffs the new, semi-white dressing over the square hay mattress so that it appears more shapely than what it is. I can see the stains festered in tragic blooms in the ball of used fabric in my arms, and I'm thankful the color is less brutal in such dim lighting as I wad them deep into the basket.

When I turn to speak with her again, she is on her hands and knees, scrubbing the floor with sweat already splitting across her face in the building humidity. By now, she should be organizing files on remaining populous and what new persons have survived quarantine across town with Ace to be sent to Master Amadeus, so that she can then rush here in time to get a whole day's worth of information set up for the next. It's part of why I chose to speak with her now instead of later, since my work *usually* convenes at Headquarters anyway. She can't just escape the conversation like she can at the day's end.

But this aside, something must have blown her clear off track. Enough to want to do menial tasks rather than the meticulous extras.

Her forehead is scrunched against her nose in heated meditation, brows cross and lip chewed raw corner to corner. Naturally curly hair falls loose of her ponytail in tight waves of midnight, hopping sprightly against her puffed cheeks while she works.

I've always liked it better down, a glorious mane of volume and spirit that encompasses the personality she tries to withhold from everyone around her. But she likes to keep it just about as tucked away as the rest of her true self, safe and neat so that no one can get too personal.

The wire brush she forces over the cold floor could have scraped away the stone in the measure she applies it, while I drift into the clouds of my thought, attempting to decide what to say next. Where to go from here. It's part of the difference between a dreamer and a realist, that I can somehow let reality skip a beat into a never present future in real hope that things can change, whereas she can't loosen her grip on the right now, in fear of what she doesn't yet understand.

Celestyn takes a moment longer in contemplation, dropping the scrubber in defeat. I kneel, picking it up for her to carry on in her place, and letting her rock backwards onto her bottom, watching her press her bony knees together out of the corner of my eye. I think we're trying to get a blood stain to come up by the shape of the spot. Or texture. It's either blood or shit, and a lot of it, dried in an uneven splatter.

"Is it true you were ambushed?" Her voice seems to come out of nowhere after all this uncomfortable quiet. Her chin rests on a closed fist, eyes staring through the files that she brought. Void. Incomplete for this conversation.

"Yes."

The wire brush makes an angry swooshing as I grind it harder to the floor.

"And that is how he died?"

*Swoosh. Swoosh. Swoosh.*

Here it is.

"Don't turn this around on me, Celestyn."

More silence. More swooshing.

"I'm just saying, if you almost died," she counters without the emotion to back it up. "I deserved at least a letter. Or a visit, better yet."

I don't want to think about it. I haven't for two weeks now, not allowing myself to lose a piece of my sanity to the twist of events that ended the life of someone I saw every morning to evening for one-and-a-half years.

It's not that I didn't make an attachment to him—my partner on the search teams. They tell new recruits in Limbo never to make attachments to another person, and it is still unavoidable. Because we crave people that add meaning to our lives, no one ever walks away without pain from this nightmare. But lingering on the "what ifs" and "whys" only draws focus away from survival, so repression and narcissism pay off, even when it doesn't feel right.

Still, when I close my eyes, sometimes I'll see him there against every will not to. On the ground, surrounded by the Ravagers, his legs thrashing in the shallow riverbanks and his cherried hand extending out to my fading form as they gutted him alive in the most unmerciful way that normal healthy individuals wouldn't a deer.

On those mornings, I remain alone for a much longer time, avoiding the meet up of the search teams until they make break, then venturing out for my shift solo, letting nature swallow my mindlessness until it is time to go home. As Second-in-Command, it shouldn't have been my partner to bite the dust when my record since promotion had been spotless.

I should have been more responsible.

"Any new kids on the block?" I look up from the brush, demanding the subject change in everything except the actual words. But she diverts her gaze just as fast.

"No, yeah," her voice changes pitch with each word. "Two. Some girl and an older gentleman. Early twenties and late fifties."

My eyes hit the back of my skull. I toss the scrubber back to the tin bucket hidden in the darker edge next to the door. It doesn't budge Celestyn, all but appearing to expect both the question and reaction, having inched aside sooner than the words left her mouth.

She pushes herself off the floor, bending to scoop the files off the freshly made bed and dropping them into my arms. I scramble to keep all the pages inside, shuffling out of the room ahead of her and watching her lock up. It's clear neither of us are going to get what we wanted in there.

"It's my luck," I insist, my voice an echo offering to return the paperwork she bestowed upon me.

"I wouldn't call it luck," she snickers, dodging my re-gifting and slinking down the narrow hallway past the steel guard.

I call to her, the stack sliding and slipping around with each jostled bounce in my step, "Fifties? Late fifties! It's the kind of luck I'm cursed with!"

The residents are lounging in the lobby when we emerge from the corridor, whispers a decibel above stagnant air thickening the tension over the sound of villagers lining up outside to be checked in as soon as the cracked doors swing wide open. Celestyn squeezes between the two women, clearing her throat in a dive for the front desk that she fabricates to seem much more reposed than what it is.

"You're right, Aidan." She breathes, flipping away more hair that had fought free of its constraints. "You've hit the *fucking lottery. I've hit the fucking lottery.* Now, can you do me a favor and deliver those papers to Ace on your way to work? I don't have the time. Thanks."

I can feel the snide grins hiding under cupped fingers and sets of fluttery black lashes, and I am struck with white rage, settled fast by a singular look at her face beyond the people she hired for help. Softened cheeks, eyes crazed, and face fallen in trapped defeat as they flip through scattered notes loitering the wooden desk that is perhaps celebrating its birthday on the same day as her.

It can't be simple to have the world sit on her shoulders.

But it sure as hell could be a lot harder, when safety is guaranteed in such specificity.

I'm not going to get what I came here for like this, my fists clenching around the crap she enlists me. Unclenching.

"Fine," I growl, turning my back and cramming falling mismatched papers to the top of the folder.

I am touching the semi-cool handle of the door when I hear

her voice shout out to me one more time.

"Date tomorrow, one hour before sunset?"

In my mind, I romanticize the offer. My heart throbs and cheeks burn just a little less than they did the day we met in my own quarantine. But a kind of cool washes over my immediate rash behavior. The idea of spending time with her toying about the strings to every limb on my body like she were the puppeteer and myself her brainless instrument of entertainment whenever called upon causes my hands to shake, slathering them in slick sweat like grease. Her files are going to get wet if I don't get them to their destination soon, and I edge forward without a word.

The sunlight strikes my eyes just outside the break in the two doors, and I wedge between them, shimmying my way out to where I belong inside a mob of hacking and groaning commoners. To where Celestyn remains a steady distance from my vicinity, not because I am so angry with her, but because of who we are—to one another, and ambiguous at best.

I just...need a break.

# CHAPTER FOUR
## ADABELLE

Z OEY HAD FRIENDS, ONCE.

The walls of her shack, just off the fertile divide that leads to The Healing Center, is an undeniable tribute that, at one point, she was a very prominent girl with a world of options at her feet. Like the sides of a shared high school locker that is made of bloated splintering wood instead of dull rusted steel painted over in a somber beige, wallet-sized photographs from her billfold are displayed along a scale of parchment, sporting hand drawn decorations, small feathers, and patches of multicolored fabric.

It is the first time I *really* smile, that evening she brings me home, pacing between the front door and the closet to the left of the back room that serves as a bathroom with a tin bucket for a toilet. I touch the plastic images with inquisitive fingers, tracing each figure of two brunette girls grinning in dorky Halloween costume makeup. Their arms are outstretched, laced around one another's shoulders in a cheek touching hug, naked bellies bare to the chilly midnight air and faint glow of the crowded city sidewalks.

*Tessa and Christine*, they are marked.

I think I would have liked Tessa, but for no particular reason other than the genuine way her smile radiates a light fun to Christine's much darker, tragic aura. It is a beautiful balance to behold—light and dark. What a wonder it must have been to have friends at all, I think.

Along the living area, there are other pictures as well, some torn or bled with water damage from the leaky roof so skin bleeds into sky, similar to my fantasies of what past contains me. Others are more pristine, aside from nails piercing through the top center to keep them hanging. Images that depict a glowing, captivating life begin in a clear shot of a rosy faced cherub in purple-ribboned pigtails sitting on the blue jeaned knee of her clean shaven father, and transform into a lanky preteen kicked back with several friends on a circular canopy bed, their eyes rolled back and mouths agape with words frozen in time.

I can imagine what they might be saying at that age, too cool for anything that isn't self-taken.

*Momma, stop! This is so embarrassing.*

Girls on the precipice of womanhood are rife with drama and maternal abhorrence. They want to be left alone and to feel mature. Like they have this all figured out and the rest of their lives planned, so there is no room for the person that brought them there.

But I bet she is grateful now. She probably even misses her mother.

I miss mine, though somehow, she still eludes me.

The final picture Zoey owns is frayed around the edges, but it is the only one she has that looks even close to what she does now. In it, her worn, but more well-fed modelesque figure, stares into the dense yellow warmth of a lone streetlamp. A pastel pantsuit tucks away a glittery, embellished binder at her side, in a world unlike the one occupied by Tessa and Christine. Because this one is empty. Deadened and stripped of humanity. The sidewalk stretching behind her is bare and dark. Lonesome.

She actually remembers most of it, she tells me after getting settled in our first night together. I will remember most of it too, at some point. It will come to me in pieces, day by day, like jet lag of the mind. Things will be foggy for a while, and then they won't be so terrible. Or they'll be worse, if I start feeling homesick. Not that it matters when there is nowhere else to go.

There's not a lot of going home to be done when no one else knows where we are or why we are here to begin with. Theories are Limbo's only namesake, and there are more than enough of them. It's a government experiment to build a thriving civilization on secret untouched islands that have not yet sunk below sea level, they say. Or perhaps, we are the ill-behaved pets of extraterrestrial lifeforms in a far off galaxy that continues to give us more friends in an attempt to make us happy, only the locals aren't incredibly fond of our newfound presence so the aliens are left continually trying to replenish our populous to be bred for other alien owners.

Maybe we are just in hell.

Or heaven?

I can't bring myself to buy into any theory at the moment, but the options dwindle in lieu of seconds that pass like hours, leaving me burning with the passion to believe *something*.

We pull apart my backpack before retreating to the cellar she has dug out, hidden beneath a stockpile of blankets just below the living area. Zoey has designed the safe scape to keep her out of sight and mind to the locals of the region that the villagers refer to as "Ravagers". A crude title, though they live up to it in most respects from what I've been told, raiding the little space we have as our own a couple nights every week to take what they will—and kill what they won't. From livestock to crops, women to children, up to a third of the population and resources go missing on a bad night. On the worst nights, people turn up dead. These people being anyone with a penis over the age of twelve, though that border has been crossed in severe situations.

The hope this night is that anything useful in such a fight against nature can be found in my backpack big enough for a camping trip. But disappointment follows the endeavor not long after we dig in, Zoey getting a better thrill out of its contents than myself, who all but begs memories to be drawn forth by these items to no avail.

A couple changes of clothes and a leotard are folded over the top layer of my prized possessions, cushioning the area around the more breakable products. Frazzled black pointe shoes with laces for days loop about a travel-sized pepper spray and a half-empty bottle of cheap perfume. A pistol with no ammo provides Zoey just enough hope to dream, but quickly vaporizes any illusions I might be a profitable investment in three seconds flat. A Polaroid camera and a thin photo album piled with hazy images protected by slick sheets of transparent sleeves showcase small shapeless girls in similar leotards gripping tight to an oak barre. Their toothy grins confirm one of my few early onset memories, giving faces to the people I'm not quite able to fill yet. Under this, I have a wallet bulging so thick with grocery receipts that it cannot button shut, a thin band silver ring with the smallest emerald engraved on its front rolling in its pouches. Following is a bottle of shea butter lotion, a double-walled purple water bottle, replaceable studs to several pieces of jewelry in my ears and face, a hairbrush, elastics for my hair, six quarters, and a handful of pennies.

Zoey's disdain eats away at the rest of our first night as roommates.

"No ammo for the gun you fucking carry," she moans as if she were being exorcised. "But, hey, at least you have *a half-gallon of shea butter lotion*! Not only will our skin be *glowing* when we are kidnapped, but thanks to your shit camera, we can capture it in real time. Say cheese, bitch!"

She's serious, but it's hard to take her that way, stuffing the contents back inside the linty void with much less organization. I'm quiet, listening to her feet stomp in anxious paces around the living area, weaving in and out of the backroom. She re-enters the living area only to insult me again.

"Jesus, you twat," she grumbles. "Who carries a gun with no ammo?"

Me, apparently.

Or who I was.

I wonder if she knows that I will sooner die than let myself suffer the cruel, abstruse fate that a vast majority of female arrivals and almost all children—the others passing from "natural causes"—meet.

Instead of answering, I shrug, not wanting to start arguments with the one person willing to grant me living quarters, though she is still reluctant to answer any of my remaining questions about the situation in which I find myself. She would rather insist, with unconvincing repetition, that I need her more than she does me. As all others have bestowed upon me, she claims to also be in the business of granting me invaluable favors that I will humbly repay by buying her time. As for what I'm stealing extra time for, I am not told.

It's a relief for the night, to shut the world away under the cellar door in unlit eternities that are soundproof to the potential terroristic swells of inhuman yelling that I have suffered prior. This leaves me nothing at all but to dream of a woman who laughs something both hot and cold, like ice on a summer day. She occupies a strange allure that doesn't quite make sense, presence swelling and dominating entire rooms. The people she surrounds herself with do not know whether to chuckle in apprehensive unison or wait out the storm to the words she speaks, ones I can't quite hear, muffled as if there were a wall between us. Her pouty ruby lips are dipped in the middle like butterfly wings, elegant and symmetrical, and matching a slim dress that hugs her hips.

*Click, click.*

A stuttered noise reverberates over everything else, spilling urine out the leg of one man's knee-length jean shorts, his hands raising in submission.

This woman is not me.

She isn't like me, if I can dare say that.

But, somehow, I understand who she is. This concept bringing an unsettled heat to my unsuspecting conscience, as callous laughter builds and fades into the snug black tunnel I'm crammed inside next to Zoey's encumbering stomach that takes up so much space, I actively attempt to not bother it with the accidental elbow or knee. I'm still half-asleep in this state, taking back the stage of my slumber and grasping at the seams of its curtains until I'm forced to perform a dance most frantic in the new half dream. In a blur of reality and fantasy, my heels kick to the screeching and wailing of a very strangled, indescribable, high-pitched inst-rumental. The sky above me cracks in white breaks of crooked lines that bellow deeply, causing me to stretch my legs in an ambitious leap over a roaring thunderous quake below the ground as I hit the surface once more to toe along the fractures it creates.

And then I fall.

My eyes pop open. At once, my arms flail apart to catch what is not actually my catapulting through breaks in the earth, but the unparalleled feeling of weightlessness. I choke on it, an empty tickling at the back of my throat. My heart gallops straight out of my slack jawed mouth, and my neck throbs to the beat of my pulse, aching from using the bony nubs of my fish belly legs as pillows in this tunnel Zoey dared call a cellar. It is expressly big enough to sit completely straight up in, but not wide enough to fit more than one person in a single place. I had been forced to sleep in an awkward, upright fetal position that kept my breathing shallow and paced most of the night to accommodate us both.

I cup the base of my skull, feeling the sweat that soaks the underlining of my bra wetting the subtle rolls of my stomach, and every crevice in between. It cools the fire of static nerves sending fight or flight pumps of adrenaline swooshing through my extremities, allowing me to ground my wild imagination back to the real world, only to hear an elongated moan followed fast by a whimper above me.

My head lolls to the side, Zoey absent from her place, and the hatch thrown open, letting a faint trickle of dark light filter into the underground. It singes my eyes in this sensory deprivation bunker. Like a bat in the brightest part of hell, I am blind as I stretch my legs in the space she left. There is a temptation to fall back asleep now, wave after wave of endless needles racing down the height of my major limbs, spasming, until the blood flow is well restored. But another sharp, audible inhale turns me over, crawling to the exit and inching my way out of the hatch looking like an ill-rested goblin.

Zoey is catty-corner from my right in the living area, a mottled blanket wrapped about her entire body like an oversized shawl on a one-hundred-sixty-year-old grandmother, smashing her forehead against the wall aside our closet bathroom. Her hands overlap on the soccer ball cameoing as her stomach, a trail of slick red juice stealing little pools of remaining moonlight from the partly sealed window at the kitchen counter. It starts at the trapdoor in smaller droplets that have already been swallowed by the thirsty wood floor, leading to my roommate in a trail that becomes a puddle at her feet, the hem of her blanket shawl attempting to drink it up and making it suddenly seem more like a warrior's battle cloak.

I blink—hard. My hands steady weight borne on shaking arms without a ladder to hop up on, and I hoist this weary body out onto the floor less than quietly to let her know I'm here. I am anxious, tilting my gaze over the room in a brief sweep, hoping that since Zoey is out as well, the locals have long left the village, if we were paid a visit at all. It is easy to forget the little information I've retained since our walk home, to plunge potentially traumatic events deep into a suppressed shelf at the back corner of a dusty unkempt storage shed in my head so that I can focus on the problems that directly affect me in the moment. But it all lingers anyway in dreaded spite of me, because if fear fuels a populous without a realistic plan of action to combat it, it only makes its at risk citizens even more so.

That being myself.

That being Zoey.

And from what she elaborated upon last night, every man, woman, and child who is just trying to exist with no explanation as to why they are here. Because Celestyn didn't lie to me, in technicality. She only did not tell me all that I needed to know at the time.

We're all at risk. And we all suffer a different expedition after our "awakening".

Zoey doubles over and vomits, dribble glopping from the ends of her hair and smacking to the floor, followed by a mix of snot and tears. She is gasping in shrill intakes, mumbling through bubbling lips, and howling as quiet as she can manage.

My brows knit together, gaze swiveling around the room, praying someone else can take my place. Fuck.

"A-are you okay?"

It's a dumb question. Why can't I come up with something more reassuring? Something like, *Hey, want me to call a cab? Hey, an ambulance is on its way. Just take it easy.* Or even, *Hey, you want some of my expired painkillers that I keep in the drawer of my nightstand?*

Do I really keep expired drugs?

I am on my feet, reluctant to meet her at close range, but feeling a direct obligation to assure her that she is going to survive this. Stumbling in this morning haze, my hand extends, grazing her slumped shoulders with the tips of my fingers, and then hesitating. Trembling. She stiffens, waiting in my presence for something more, and so I follow up with an awkward pat between her obtuse shoulder blades that remind me of the plucked wings of a baby bird.

*There, there, little bird.*

For a single moment, she slumps in relaxation, sniffling and dabbing away the wet sheen on her face with her gross blanket. But the tragedy of the situation doesn't wait to tense her back into mania, fist slamming against the wall, and causing me to jerk toward the hatch in alarm.

"P-please," she whispers. "Help me, please."

I hold my arm to my side. Her words take a minute to absorb. "Oh..." My teeth clench. "OH, I don't...uh...I mean, I just—I don't think I know anything about this. I'm sorry."

Another horrible cry ascends the meager confines of our

home, and my hands wave instinctively down in a volume gesture that goes unappreciated. Her desperate pleas are moaned into dark air, chanted like a spell she can cast to make the pain slow and lose its power, a fruitless undertaking that is empty of her desired effect. I watch in helpless abandon the way her cheeks puff red and hold air, fists berating the wall when she has to free it until her knuckles split at the bone like stage curtains, ribboning a watery ooze around her wrist like a bracelet. I pucker my lips, phasing out the disturbed intermittent sounds, while I attempt to withdraw a solution.

Can she walk to The Healing Center like this?

It isn't that far away, but I'm not strong, or tall, enough to carry her if she can't.

What I need is a cab.

Or a sled, a hill, and some snow.

Is it still assault to push a pregnant woman downhill if I'm also trying to get her medical care?

What am I doing right now? I can't think straight over this noise. It creates a dense mind fog that blankets my common sense in the way a corpse bag does a body at a crime scene.

I'm brain dead right now. I have amnesia, and I'm stupid. This is my life.

Who has a baby in a place like this anyway? Or sex?

*Who has sex here?*

Fuck. I need coffee.

Zoey's words are a panicked mumble of *wait, don't leave me* as I pivot on my heels in galloping strides to the mess of blankets and quilts that are usually slopped over the cellar door. I gather as many I can into my collective arms, one by one, giving them a firm shake for spiders as I heap them into the corner next to the bathroom under another boarded window, all amid the uncertain supplication of my young companion.

"I'll be *nice*," she bargains under heavy gagging, breathing uneven shakes.

It would be easier to believe her if an exasperated *fuck you* hadn't followed the pleas, making me wonder whether she is talking to myself, the baby, or the pain as its own entity. Zoey doesn't seem capable of unmotivated kindnesses, and she has a hard time looking me in the eyes when speaking more than a couple words, so I can find no genuine agenda or hideous deceptions lurking at the outermost article of her person.

She's just here...holding the boulder attached to the front of her body that shivers in pain, eyes nailed shut and sweat slicking down the stray hairs from her widow's peak to her brow.

I approach her with care, taking her clammy palm in my own cold hands, fighting to lace my fingers through her own. It enrages her to start, distrust foaming over like a pot of boiled water. Her face deepens red with veins that pop at her temple, and her scraggled nails drill at the slope of my knuckles. As I drag her to the nest of less than luxurious comfort I have designed, I can hear a faint guttural hum of agitation. A feral growl.

I try to explain this away to myself as the weight of her body resists mine.

It's so easy to want help in moments when we are afraid, after all. When we are terrified, it might be just as simple to ask for it. Beg for it.

But it can't be easy to accept the help once it is offered. Not from a stranger anyway. She hardly knows me. It's weird for both of us.

I feel the bones pop at the back of my hand during our short excursion, digits bulging purple in less than a full minute, and pulsating with trapped blood. Yet no fear wins me over, taking each step by step in growing confidence.

I *have* done this part. At least once.

Not this exact procedure, of course, but something similar.

The sensation of knuckles cracking, the captured swelling of my tiny limbs filled with blood as if they might pop right off when squeezed any tighter. The pain rocketing from the point of inception to my forearm. The things that give me a tight lipped, upward tilt of the mouth and offer reassurance, though I am now in pain too.

*Squeeze,* my past echoes inside, *as hard as you like. You can't hurt me.*

The scuffling of plastic bags and rattle of metal instruments on an icy, sterile tray are so close to ear, I can all but touch them.

*I promise. I'm* right *here.*

Comforting. I have comforted people, perhaps? But haven't we all? That doesn't seem accurate.

*There is screaming.*

I shake the sound of my own voice from priority and use my free arm to remove the bloodied cover from this girl I don't know. Her inner thighs are browned, painted in something that can be smelled more than seen, and I try not to linger on her indignity any longer than I have to, a brief respite presenting that there doesn't appear to be anything new gushing forth since at least my waking.

"Sit, please." It's more of a command than it is a suggestion.

My eyes bounce along the boards nailed to the window, seeing the faintest trickle of dark orange light creep inside. Will I be late for work placement today too? I can't afford to be, but I can't just leave Zoey like this either.

Her arms are bonier than mine, a tragic tangle of malnourishment snaking through the space between my underarms and toned biceps, weight more of a breeze than my initial inclinations suggested, and the baby a surprising fraction of her wispy form. Zoey groans, hitting the floor and leaning gingerly so that she can rest her head against the blankets I stacked.

I do a quick scan of the unit when she is in place for any health-related items that can hold her over until we can get her somewhere...better. But the bare bones of this home haunts each step I take in mocking, pitted echoes of defeat. Every room, from the makeshift living room to the kitchen and closet bathroom, is worked through inside and out, barking failure in each step.

The living room is mostly empty, other than my backpack and a single wooden chair that I wouldn't trust a gnat to sit on. The bucket in the closet is contaminated, and nothing else resides in there other than rough paper for wiping that will only tear against dry blood if wet. However, there is a slightly swollen counterspace with two tin cups and a wooden plate atop it, her canteen we refilled on water rations from the barn on the way here last night propped against the back room with my water bottle that we filled prior to bed.

I snatch both containers, pulling away the dingy fabric nailed over the cabinets in place of doors to see if there is anything useful below deck, but all I see is one carrot with a singular bite taken from the side, half a dry—and potentially fossilized—potato, and four beetles that scatter in the dim light.

*Cool. I am definitely okay with this.*

I move on next to the door, ripping apart my pack in a semi-successful endeavor to find a change of clothes she can wear, pulling a pair of spandex shorts and an oversized grey T-shirt from the unfolded mix, as well as red laced underwear and black socks. My hips are considerably larger than hers, breasts considerably smaller, and height much more dwarven than modelesque. But clean is clean, and I kneel in front of her with my bowled arms, juggling what can be found on her behalf. Zoey eyes each item with bugging whites, breathing slowed to a calm panting, but also deepening.

"What are you doing?" she spits, mouth still soured by bile.

*It's fine,* I remind myself. *This floor probably isn't that clean anyway. There is a pile of vomit and blood at the other end of the room, and neither of us have even given it a second thought.*

"I'm not doing anything," I reply. "It's what you are going to do while I get ready to find Headquarters for job placement."

There is an animalistic panic to her face, like a dog that has been cornered. "You can't fucking leave me yet. Not like this. Please. Hey?"

"Take your canteen when you're ready—drink all of it." My voice is steady. I need her to relax. "When you are done, take my water bottle and use one of the blankets to clean yourself up with. My clothes will be a bit big on you, I hope. But seeing that I couldn't find any others that might belong to you, they're at least clean. So we will start with that. Okay?"

She hesitates, but consents. I assure that I can see her throat jounce up and down with timid swallows before I am satisfied enough to grant her the privacy she will need at the room's other end, and I drop back again to my pack in the living space to pull out a change of clothes for myself. There isn't much I see that I can both wear and be comfortable in, despite my "good fortune", making me a bit curious as to why I even own such apparel in the first place. My need for clothing practically demands long thick articles everywhere I can place them to save my humility. But I settle on a high-necked handkerchiefed tank top, jean shorts with black leggings underneath, clean white ankle socks, and fresh panties.

It will cover the worst of me.

I section myself off in the closet bathroom with the door cracked, letting in minimal light to change and check on my leg wound. I feel like a flaky snake in old skin, peeling off the soiled crusty clothes I woke up in, and exchanging them for new. I already feel cleaner as I stand naked in the bathroom closet, looking over my injury and prodding it gently as I wiggle into my fresh shirt.

It looks great. Too great.

It is soft and smoother. A light pink and riddled with faint bruising.

If I'm being honest, it almost doesn't hurt anymore. Like a bad scratch, but no longer an oozing laceration. The remaining stitches will have to come out tonight or tomorrow if I don't want a different set of problems, but I can probably do that on my own to avoid seeing The Healing Center staff. I definitely cannot explain this expedited healing away, no matter how I try.

Uncomfortable but feeling fresh when I emerge, I stuff the dirty set beside the backpack and brush my hair, twisting it into a messy bun on the top of my head, hoping that it makes me at least half an inch taller so people can see me in a crowd. I scuttle to Zoey who has quieted since earlier, almost finished cleaning what she can see, and breathing slowed to match her decreasing amounts of distress. I wet my hands with what is left in the water bottle to dampen my bangs so they don't look as frizzy.

Zoey rises like a sloth on sleep medicine, waddling to the bathroom with the change I gifted and calling out through the crack in the door.

"How's your damn leg? It looked fucking nasty through your pants yesterday."

I had not felt it all morning, forgetting as much as the weight of the bandage around my thigh until I had looked at it just a few moments ago. And now it is almost completely better. How do I explain this away in a spontaneous second and answer her question?

I bite my lip. "I looked at it just a few minutes ago while you were cleaning up. It's definitely fine. I'll recheck it after work to be sure. Are you okay?"

Grunting, but no horrified death screams. "Peachy. Fucking incredible. Give me a goddamn second, and I'll run you to Headquarters."

I want to protest this offer after seeing her struggle this morning. But I don't know the way alone, and after sitting for a couple minutes with a gut full of fresh water, Zoey does seem more herself. Or at least the version of it that she has exposed to me. She isn't using her fist as a wood ax anymore, at least, and I need her vague wisdom more than I care to admit to her face.

"Fine. But only if you go straight to The Healing Center afterward to get your little problem checked."

There is no aggression in her reply. Not even a sigh. We're both aware—even without having formal knowledge on pregnancy or childbirth—the kind of pain she experienced, doubled with heavy bleeding, can't be normal unless something major has changed. She needs professional help, or the best Limbo has to offer in that department, not performed by an outdated dance teacher. It isn't until we've made it outside, though, that I can see the true frailty that has overwhelmed her in the past night.

It could have been there all along, I suppose, and I could be overthinking in the painful hysteria clinging to her situation, but she seems paler. More sick than hungry. Off.

I should make her turn back, if I'm a good person and a friend that has her best interest at heart. But I don't, hoping she will come to the decision on her own in absence of my unwarranted hovering. I'm merely a stranger who claims no business telling this girl how to execute her personal care, or that of her unborn. The shirt I gave her is ample help, however, covering her whole belly without any skin showing, unlike the other one, and the shorts are a bit loose but manageable if she can keep a proper posture.

She can't.

There is a quiver in her legs, a lag that my mind questions as to whether she can make a double trip without permitting strength as her arms brush me in faltering steps. She doesn't have shoes to go over the socks she now wears with pride. The sharp rocks crunching beneath my sneakers dig ruthlessly into the bottom of her feet until we hit a patch of shaded green grass where she releases the painful tension. She lets her toes fan out, writhing against the fabric. I hear her sniff at the sensation, but the glimmer in her eyes refuses to give way to tears. There are only pitted lines of concern that stretch across the contours of her face—a frown so heavy, she cannot pick it up from where it fell.

My eyes draw to my own shoes in selfish discomfort at her distress.

Leagues of people are swarming from their houses the further into town we get, with streaks of black gritting the dirt into clumps on eroded tan roads and covered carts pulled by mules trotting in the opposite direction that most of the population flocks toward. Many do not see us, letting us blend into the audience of foul body odor and unbearable heat, shoulder to shoulder with regular people who see me as little a threat as a child. But the tension still wells at the side of my head in a striking pressure when I recognize the features that enclose New Gabby in absence of Baby Gabe outside, bellowing a quite lonely salutation to those who pass her by in an elongated *moo*. It's too early for the farmer and his bite-sized mobsters in training to be out yet, and I allow a twitching curl of my fingers when I meet her sullen brown eyes, our spirits one in the same.

Heavy. Detached. Spotted.

We break past the final inhabitable shack heading north, away from where I departed this asylum to meet Zoey for the first time. An expanse of somewhat clear field grazed down by livestock opens to reveal a saturated market not much farther ahead. A smaller, fatter tower looms over it at the end before the next outline of dense forestry and wildlife collects at the border of the town.

An unusual weightlessness builds in my chest and stomach at the first finish line of many in this new life, letting the grass give under the girth of my foot as I am halted by a bruised elbow jutting into Zoey's side by one of two women swerving around her into the open and trekking over the remaining weeds with hard-won steps in ragged gladiator sandals.

I wait to hear the train of expletives that will surely follow, but Zoey has paused where she was shoved, with her eyes on the ground and gears turning as if playing out the action in a daydream at the back of her mind. Her eyes break back to the socks instead though, a faint smile at the wiggling toes forming in the dimples on each end of her lips.

I wonder if she had been one of them. Well liked. Thin but supple, skin aglow and still covering a meaty distance between her bones. Probably even accompanied by friends. A social elite, rather than defensive brat, losing it all to one round in the sheets. Now what?

Another shoulder plows around her, this time the assailant making eye contact and spinning to spit at her. Something she appears to both expect and skip, so it only wets her exposed ankle in a warm gelatinous blob.

"Get lost," he says.

"You get lost." My nose scrunches and the words fire just as quick. "What kind of person shoves a pregnant woman? Or spits on her?" Our eyes connect, and he slinks in with the crowd in a hurry. But I raise my voice. I'll make damn sure I'm heard. "Are you afraid of a girl? Or repopulating? Are you afraid of babies, you bastard? Huh?"

*Have nothing to say to this real-life monster?* My inner thoughts taunt his cowardice long after the blond fuzz on his head fades into the dispersing cloud of villagers. Zoey clears her throat, joy forlorn and fading from her being as though it never existed, if even for a second.

"The markets will take you roughly five fucking minutes to cross if you can avoid getting into trouble," she says. "Three if you run. Looks like you're able, as long as you're not lying about your stupid leg. But Headquarters is on the other side. Ace will give you your damn job placement when you get there."

My hands gesture to the vanishing crowd, mouth agape. "You chewed my ass for dying, but you'll let them douse your fire?"

Zoey takes a step away from my wave of the arms, sheepish as she shrugs her shoulders. Her eyes flutter up and down, evading my desperate attempts to meet her defeated gaze.

"I need to go to The Healing Center and get checked out. I'll fucking see you whenever I get home, okay?"

I look to the markets, and then back to her, my toes curling inside my shoes with a rising anxiety. "Don't you work?"

The question catches her off guard, her arms crossing over her chest and her eyes darting along the ground. She shakes her head in a decisive "no", still looking...pained.

"Not since the pregnancy was discovered," she admits. "Ace claims it would be too much of a liability. Whatever the hell that means."

The image of her bare cabinets settles into the back door of my mind, along with the empty home and the way she appears at this second, standing in the wide open with her hair reaching in the wind for something unseen. I want to question it all, to be angry for her youth, and bring her up to Headquarters with me.

I want her there. To demand a change or face a lawsuit. This has to be some kind of discrimination. Who wouldn't employ a pregnant woman? How else will she maintain a healthy pregnancy? This has to be why she needs me. To have the fearsome freak make a stand for her? How hard would it be to have her make bread? Or feed cows? Something?

I open my mouth to speak, but she only shakes her head, throwing up an open palmed hand and turning away from me.

"Go, Adabelle." It is exasperated. Quieted with shame and abuse.

Her body is cold and rigid in every syllable. She lowers her arm and rubs the other as though she can feel the frost of her own breath blending into the humidity. How it is tornadic, not just outside where it can be seen but also inside, shaking up the foundation of who she is and swaying it to and fro, like a violent cradle. I nod as if she can see it, stepping into the firm weeds that populate the field.

But a lingering question won't release me to let her go like this: alone, to endure some sort of walk of humiliation to get attention for what ails her. Not yet.

"Zoey?" I call, setting a proper distance.

"Yes?"

She has not moved.

I cringe when the words leave my mouth, unable to stop their flow. "How did you get pregnant, exactly?"

It sounds terrible when I hear it. There is a sniff, followed by a cynical chuckle that warns of danger. "Jesus, Adabelle. How old are you? Haven't you ever missed a period?"

It is alien. The words coming from my mouth are not mine, but they are. They have been, since the beginning, the words inside my head. I can't keep them silent, or cased where they belong, if I tried.

"No." My brow furrows. "No. I've...never had a period."

Zoey turns around, eyes glittering wide and her mouth contorted into a subtle sneer.

"No?"

"No," I repeat, knowing this is true, hand extending over my empty pelvis and strolling toward the smell of sweet grease and bread.

Something about that isn't right.

Her answer, that is.

# CHAPTER FIVE
## AIDAN

I N AN ALMOST EMPTY WHITE ROOM THAT SMELLS OF FRESH paint, I can see the heat come off the walls in waves that are like notes from the sun being hand drawn to life for the pleasure of the naked eye. Kind of akin to today, outside of this recollection, where the packed grey stone that paves the steady entry from the Markets to Headquarters feels equal to that of coals broiling the rubber bottoms of my black sneakers to murky shoe glue, and I know for certain I am in actual hell. But the memory is a better kind of torture than this current reality.

Because I can't stay in it.

I feel indulgent at the fork of my thought, where I nurse my theoretical wounds after such a bitter morning engagement, followed directly by the best bakery getting a late start with their goods. I'm left hungrily irritable to say the best. I won't yet speak about the worst when the amnesia is worn so thin that I can touch the open glass door of my dreams decorated in tiny fingerprints and letting in muggy brown air so dingy and polluted that it is thicker on the lungs than one thousand cigarettes being smoked in the same room at one time.

I inhale here inside my recollections and try not to cough, stilling the tremble in my chest. Checking my phone for the seventh time in one minute. Thinking the same thing at every peek.

*This can't be* right.

But it is. So, so right.

I want this. This *feeling.*

I crave it.

The wood floor is polished in my fantasy room, albeit old. Pale and divoted in places the finish has worn thin. I pace around a tired grey piano, lackluster flakes peeling from it in uneven paths. Waiting. Staring for hours. First out the metal framed glass door, then up a claustrophobic stairwell donned in brown shag carpet steps and flyers for lost children plastered on either paneled wall.

Concerned isn't the right word for what I feel in this safe hollow of history, but I'm not at rest either. Sitting on the rustic red-cushioned bench placed at the breast of the instrument that does little to set my mind at ease, I am in the company of so many yearning, misplaced eyes.

Nonetheless, I'm not unhappy.

I would kill to be "not unhappy" now, in the apprehensive way I flex my fingers in these delusions over yellowing keys, and bounce over a handful in a labyrinth of melody that impends the best kind of news. I hope. I cannot think of another reason I would perform in such delightful vigor in absence of a proper audience, other than something so futuristically forward that it radiates positivity. Unlike many in my retired line of work, I played better in joy than pain, stress putting a damper on the natural flow of creativity I had held.

Not that things don't change.

I can remember playing the piano in expert measure for the extent of my youth—or what is left of it that isn't ruined by fresh air and trees. I played a little violin too and, per my mother's request, a bit of cello as well. For a time, I even dabbled in the ukulele as preparation for a trip to one of the few remaining islands in the United States not yet consumed by rising sea levels. My oldest brother had taught me how to play beginner's exercises on the saxophone when we got home that month, but that was more of an unintentional mistake that bore the consequence of tempered screeching for the next year until I laid that aspiration to rest in its rightful grave alongside him.

Looking back on it as an adult well past my brother's expiration forced to relive all the scattered ashes of every second we coexisted as if it were the first time, I immerse in solemn abandon when I'm left behind again. I'm left with nothing more than the flash of his floral adorned casket being lowered out of view in an empty yard of battered headstones. Nothing more than confusing and vivid, yet so vague, memories.

And for all that, I can safely assess in absence of guilt, that my good brother was wrong at least once in his short life—the saxophone will not draw in hordes of women, nor will it make them feel any kind of longing if played with "just the right amount of heat".

It might actually repulse them—or I might have repulsed them playing it.

It is one of two instruments I never found skill for, the other being the clarinet, which led me to believe for a time that reed instruments were the death of all good things, and only a special breed of sorcerer could play them. I never did pick them back up after Oliver's death to test this theory out either though, his personal saxophone being buried beneath crossed powdered fingers to hide the bruises and deformations involved in his passing, that I allow to be shut away in eternal suppression. The starter sax, that belonged to the house for everyone's practice, was auctioned off against my will less than a full day later, as it was the one item unique to our family.

*Someone will pay solid cash for it,* I had been told when I fought. *You can't play it anyway, kid.*

I wince at the bogus consolations playing like antiquated

records on loop, the devaluing of familial objects as if they mean nothing but dollar signs when someone's time comes full circle. When they cease to exist in this macrocosm of convoluted space. Or at least the version of it that I actually remember. The one I yearn for at the end of every night, imagining tall buildings that sit above the general cloud of smog, swarmed with a host of bars and auditoriums. All of these places are littered in vast night life, with people wearing elaborate colored beads and no clothing, and sporting glow in the dark lipsticks and shimmering liners that made the eyes pop like neon when the rooms grew dark. I can smell the throat scalding sour of liquor in these desires, the blast of air conditioning against the heat of shameless masses smothering the chill of my skin, making me grow clammy.

I had three older brothers that performed in these places exclusively, a mother and father to add. All competitive mentors when I was still smaller than the mics and too young to make sense of the words flowing in stilled vibratos. But somehow, we were the less-than-average family of the twenty-sixth century living the dream, being just a little bigger and more put together.

A tad stranger. Funnier.

It didn't ever seem to bother me when people stared back then. Not like it does now. They were supposed to look, my father so often explained. We were an entire family of musicians. Our own circus. Each set the precedent higher for the next, appearing on stage younger and younger, beneath the label my parents worked so hard to create in their divine success. If people were not at least taking a bashful gander behind restaurant menus when we left the house for dinner, we weren't doing the business justice.

Or the world.

I relished the idea of *different* as a child.

I wanted to have magic powers. Super strength. Speed like a cheetah.

What boy doesn't want to be a hero?

Every kid wants to be special to the world, to know that they are the only one of their kind out there, and irreproachably celebrated. It is the only time we get to excite in being bright and lustrous, discovering ourselves for this brief period of collective innocence that melts away into what we become: dull. Sleepless.

As an adult, it is dangerous to so much as glisten without status. These strangers are ostracized like lepers. A complete circle from everything we were brought up to know.

I'm nothing but a grown sack of meat here. Blood and bones with a dumb smile, and overgrown hair that gets in the way of my glasses, much too large for my own half-blind eyes, matching the edges of my jaw, sprinkled in just enough cacti tipped fuzz to almost shave...if I were a post-menopausal grandmother battling a hormonal imbalance.

And what a crash it is to be so ordinary when the circumstance that consumes general society is everything but. Until two years ago, I didn't understand what it meant to breathe air so concentrated in oxygen that it's both light and heavy at the same time. To see a tree that was not already a weathered lamppost sway with leaves the color of extravagant paintings, or animals wild enough to gnaw fingers to the bone—if only the hand was extended within reach. To hold mourning strangers in arms doused to the elbow in blood, while they plead to a god that was not there to bring back the only family they had ever known since waking up. To bury a body with ice blue eyes glazing over, shrouded in crimson maggots and guts stretched along my very steps like endless spools of bloated sausage.

*This is my ordinary.*

Even when I can't suffer it, leaving me helpless beyond routine. For I am a powerless adult, swept in the world's current like rotted autumn leaves in an everlasting storm. I float above water with each thrashing wave, but just barely.

Breathing.

Surviving.

But not the same.

Loud boisterous laughter catches my attention not far ahead of these sentiments, and I follow it like a dog seeking out its purpose. It is impossible to discern amongst others like it in the open lawn, expanding out the other side of the frenzied streets snaking through the markets, but I don't require extensive focus to find the search teams today. Not when we have been in need of a new qualifying member since my partner kicked rocks. It is beyond doubt that they have been antagonizing Ace the last two weeks without slack, the concept that one team member is without a partner a practical crisis in the event of another ambush with the Ravagers—like so many we have experienced already.

I duck under swathes of colored fabrics decorating the last few carts set out in front of rat infested shops like twisted hammocks pressed against the sky, flapping in the smallest caress of breezes, so that the shade it provides swings back and forth from sun spot to sun spot. The file Celestyn forced upon me grows heavy in the hollow of my sweaty underarm as I shoulder between collections of people shifting through the motions of their routines. Murmuring abrades my senses like white noise on blast when I cross the wood and stone threshold that erects a steady wall around the property sectioned out by Headquarters.

It is better protected than The Healing Center, I believe, although many others would claim that the indiscretion of the Center makes it a forgotten target in the raids. The grass is more than figuratively greener here by all accounts, and rich pink flowers blossom on fruit bearing vines around the darkened entry of the timber-framed, multilevel building that is left open during daylight and litters secrets across miles of land that the gate withholds from the public come nightfall.

Not that these creatures are much after our secrets. They have enough of their own to keep them busy.

There isn't enough packed dirt for the lot of people awaiting payment and new job placement to stand on, with grass growing in each patch that is cleared without fail and providing relief for the masses that have no shoes. Not that I mind either way, but a weight writhing its way free through my pores and dissipating at the iron creak of the gateway shutting out the markets to conduct business in absence of interruption, leaves me with a temporary guilt-ridden security. The noise sways at the change, hushing and rising in the same instance, congregating closer to Headquarters but also keeping the proper distance to allow Ace to exit. It reacts as a body—a mob—but with each member reading the mind of the next.

I scurry into its heart, the file's contents slopping forward and nearly flopping to the ground under the restless feet of people no longer paying attention. My hand flies to the edges like lightning, ripping through the air so fast, I brush the scrawny leg of a woman standing on the tips of her toes to see over the people in front of her. I mutter a brief apology at this, slinking onward before I realize she didn't even see me, nor did I really see her.

At the leading edge of this congestion, I spot my group of eight other team members lined in a semi-circle. Our First-in-Command, Ethan Cline, takes a long drag off the cigarette he bought from the markets early this morning, the same as he does every other. His bald head is like a beacon, sunlight glinting in sweat trails rolling down the back of his thick neck and sleeveless white T-shirt that has started to yellow around the collar. He's lost a bit of weight since we last talked, his arms having slimmed so that the skin appears looser around the firm biceps he had when brand-new to Limbo, a sloppy notch carved in his belt to keep his jeans up on his waist.

Out of the corner of his dark brown eyes, he catches a glimpse of my face and waves me over with an upturn of his chin.

"Over here!" he calls.

I've never been one to refuse him, glancing to Headquarters to assure Ace has not yet made his exit and pushing my glasses up the bridge of my nose as I jog to meet them. The others begin to snicker at my approach. I try to pretend like I don't see it, the way they lean forward with insults at the ready, despite my being Second-in-Command. It is one of several ways they attempt to feel superior in spite of me, most of them being built with better bulk than myself, who has remained quite a bit leaner in my time here, earning me the title "boy" on my first day.

"Morning," I say, forcing my voice to exude confidence. "Sorry I'm late."

A chortle erupts before my words are completely out, as Dennis flicks his own cigarette into the grass and grinds his boot against the stub.

"Did ya sing Celestyn a pretty song, boy?" he croons. "Ya don't have to strum a guitar to get 'er into bed with you, ya know. She purrs just fine fer anyone, if ya ask 'er real nice."

There is a heat in my face blowing steam in waves from anywhere it can escape, and a tilt to my lips as they curl in toward my teeth. In a less professional environment, I might have tried my hand at clocking him square in his crooked, milky-white nose so hard I could practically hear the satisfying crunch. Or I could shoot him with my bow, an action accompanied by a riveting *thunk* through flesh, if I could con him back to my home where I keep it. It wouldn't be hard. He isn't that smart. No one would miss sharing air with his waste of space, and if I timed it at right about sundown, I could blame the Ravagers without facing trial for the crime.

But...

Ethan studies me for the appropriate reaction over our charges —what makes or breaks me in moments when reprisal is coveted —and I need to assert my own authority whether or not I am "boy". Dennis is my inferior, his abilities lacking in comparison to myself who has dedicated every second of on duty time to perfecting such skills.

And shouldn't he be concerned to speak to his Second-in-Command as such? Unless he thought my position was up for grabs after the most recent incident.

I meet Ethan's stare for a second and look back to Dennis, sweeping dark brown hair away from the lenses that zero in my misleadingly calm eyes to his unwavering smirk.

"I don't know what you're doing with the local cats, Dennis, or why you're naming them after Celestyn," I respond, striding in line next to Ethan. "But it's illegal."

It doesn't make me feel any better, but the explosion of sound coming in swells through my shortened team leaves Dennis with a frail, bruised ego that allows me to get through a week without his crass commentary. Enough time to adjust to a new, older team member that will inevitably slow me down where it counts. I would watch them die off within the month just for this scene to play on repeat for the next decade. Although, I guess if I wanted, I could have any partner I preferred from the already existing team. If I live that long.

I hope I don't, though unfortunately I'm rather good at it.

Ethan grins through clenched teeth. The cherry at the end of his cancer stick glows like a violent sickness at another heavy inhale, ash falling in skinny tubes to his weathered boots. He bobs his head to my underarm.

"What's that?" he mumbles, lips crimping a protective bite around the yellowed paper.

I remove the file from its place, holding it out for us both to examine in the pale sunlight. The pages wave in succession like a deck of cards being shuffled. It looks like every other file Celestyn has ever handled in my presence—plain on the outside to allow an extent of privacy to the new patient and filled with sets of parchment, cut in uneven segments, scrawled in her illegible smeared ink.

Boring and without purpose.

There are only three sets of eyes that will ever grace the surface of each page and understand its worth. Celestyn, the one who fills the form to completion, is the first. She has never explained the value of each set to me, why she makes personal copies before allowing the primary to slip on to Ace, or why Ace even requires them when most of these people will be lost before the end of the year. I do know that Ace stores them inside the walls of Headquarters when they are complete, in secret cubbies carved to look like the rest of the building, holding the information of hundreds, if not thousands, of people that are eventually transferred out to the one referred to as Master Amadeus. A person rumored never to have been seen by living eyes outside the chosen few. One fabled to hold a key to escape this place, if only one was bold enough to ask.

"I dunno." I sigh. "It goes to Ace though. Don't you go see him today?"

He chuckles, head shaking and hand wiping away the sweat from the back of his neck. "We all do today, boy."

That isn't what I meant. He knows that, but I let it slide anyway, my attention turning to the entry of Headquarters where the shadow of a man proceeds him, allowing his figure to fall into view for the split second allotted by these jackals until they notice him, jolting forward in joint anarchy.

Phrases like *late payment* and *job opportunities* are screamed from front to back like children fighting for candy from a busted piñata, hands waving as if they won't get their turn, while actual tots cower in set distance at the closed gates. Ace's voice can be heard little above this, asking for their silence before continuance. He will wait all evening if he has to, something of which I have witnessed in the past, the man's patience and stern demeanor outlasting the test of time itself.

If I'm being honest, I've never been particularly fond of him in the way most others are, more oft than not women. The man is peculiar, taller than anyone I have ever seen, with uneven pitch-black hair tucked away in a blue beanie too big for his own head. Not that I have ever witnessed him take it off to discern for sure. He is informal that way down to his clothes—jeans that drag to the tops of his off-white sneakers contrasting his piercing green eyes that melt into a soulless black when his mind is made up, which is usually right away and without further question.

Residents are nameless in his understanding but remembered on sight, like stray dogs that show up at his doorstep to be fed and then later butchered by legions of natives—all without any recognizable attachments. Compassion. Because he is suggestively absent of everything that makes this place bearable since I have met him and possibly long before. Yet this has camouflaged him to become the model citizen of Limbo, and something like a mayor of impossible delegations. An honor no one asks for, but one that holds its value in every circumstance, whether physical, emotional, or mental.

It only begs to question the obvious that people don't want to see though. There is a glaring problem with someone that has the ability to flip an emotional switch at the bat of an eye like a humanoid bi-polar robot, being more relative to a bomb hidden in plain sight. We can keep telling ourselves he is actually a clock, and that our lives are dependent on his operations, revolving like the small hands around every snap of his fingers. But time is ticking at either end, and whatever is on the other side can either be harmless or fatal.

Take your pick.

The swarm of villagers grows quiet at the sound of a group who take it upon themselves to produce unified hushing. Ace is like a giant, encircled by throngs of children leeching to his every breath as if he were their messiah, handfuls of papers and small sacks of coin poking out the bottom of worn brown bags snapped tight at his feet far below wiry arms clothed in tight grey sleeves that button at the wrist. His voice is like thunder when spoken into the silence, the lack of wind in the moment allowing it to carry much further than normal so that the people in the back do not miss a beat.

"Welcome back."

In spite of its commanding force, his tone is soft and neutral.

Harsh, but kind.

Cold, but warm.

It has always been this way, careful and programmed to avoid the slightest misstep. Enunciated. Matter of fact enough to eliminate grey areas in comfortable amounts of small talk and refusing all intimate contact with others—including prolonged eye contact. The closest he comes to physical touch is a less than committed wave to the people who come to eavesdrop on the latest news every morning, hand rising from waist level and fingers not quite uncurling to his subjects.

*No one is welcome here*, I retort in the sanctity of my mind. *The public is dangerous for you. Heartbeats are like the flu.*

But my hand waves in a polite rebuttal against this, an unsure smile playing my face while regret I left the house at all lingers behind every visible tooth.

To my side, Ethan keeps his arms crossed, his hawk eyes darting around the expansive crowd for the new face to become our charge. I imagine he is already aware of who the man is, an inevitable occurrence if he arrived as early as he tends to so that he can speak with Ace alone, hoping to have some gravity with the decision if he is unsatisfied. Not that he ever had a final say, but there is consideration at stake for those who know their brand.

*There isn't a person here who knows better than Ace.*

It isn't my voice this time, resounding off the inside of my skull, but Celestyn's. The smug upturn of her lips following the words in the vibrant visual of my imagination is coy and dismissive. An acrid, rotted part of me wants to shut my eyes to this, to rock the image from my mind, thinking once again of this morning. How she acted. The same as any other day—but different.

Avoidant.

Frightened?

That doesn't seem accurate. Not Celestyn.

A plume of cigarette smoke rolls to the grass, a grey miasma of defeat, at the sound of Ace's voice saturating Headquarters' lawn. Ethan's eyes deepen in dark lines that stress trenches along his reflective mirror of a forehead. The new trainee will more than likely do rounds with everyone, at least one time, to get a feel for the position until he's assigned an official partner, experiencing a relative amount of hazing the first week of the job to harden him to the misery of irreversible calamity. To force a grasp on the inescapable helplessness, knowing he cannot save someone while he hears distant screams just within reach.

Admittedly, I'm a softer instructor of agendas that involve

mass fatalities and the crumpled faces of people who will never see their friends again. I don't force trainees to perform under pressure when they have perhaps never experienced it in this life still, and I try to not be cruel while I recall what it is to be new here. My voice remains ever patient and I try to smile alongside simple mistakes. To reassure. It isn't always the end of the world to fumble. So someone should do at least that, right?

"It has come to my attention that there are both old and new issues in need of address this morning."

It is melodic at the end.

Stark.

But hypnotic.

I shake my head, raking my nails against the sides of my scalp in discomfort. It is easy to zone out when sleep is so elusive these days. I need to change my routine. Shake it up to stay awake to the events creeping inside the edges of our lives.

"We will start with old," Ace continues over the obnoxious reply that is the need for immediate satisfaction, "ergo the replacement of the fallen comrade of the search teams and the need for another guard at The Healing Center. After this, I will read off a list of names due for late payment, and you may report to my colleague, Melody, inside for these matters."

I can hear teeth grinding to white powder at the border of my reach, but I can't tell who is doing it in a trickle of conversation forming at the heat of the villagers. Dennis and his assigned search partner, Sammy, fall back toward the sound in intense whispers not for my ears, while Ace bends to pull a stack of parchment from his largest bag. It takes just a second of brief shuffling, his lips moving in words I can't read beneath his breath, then he is straightened once more, all voices ceasing to hear our man's name.

"To The Healing Center, I would like to welcome Mr. James Albright to the night guard of our local quarantine," he reads at a steady pace, scanning over the document and skimming the information from the surface he requires.

There is an abrupt gentle applause at the sacrifice of an official guardsman, a silence creeping over it to wilt the pride he should feel from it, and Ace allowing rare seconds to it. In most ways, night guards make more sacrifices than the search teams to keep our frail society functional—often the first line of defense to ignorant newcomers and one of the few high risk jobs allowed to women, due to the end risk being somewhat the same in all scenarios. Yet, it ranks fifth under the best paying jobs one could possess. The guards get to go home at the end of the night, nine times out of ten.

"Yes, yes. Congratulations to you, sir."

It doesn't sound real. Almost sarcastic. Or I'm almost paranoid.

Both are just as likely.

The gate audibly creaks ajar to allow exit upon this announcement for whoso requires it. A parade of feet marches in the rhythm of gossip to its high-pitched whine, either having killed all the time they can manage before having no choice but to work or needing nothing more from Ace than seconds of news.

"Report at once to The Healing Center for further instruction, and the best of luck in all your endeavors," he calls to James.

Sammy prods at the space between my shoulders, grinning dimples ear to ear. He looks boyish this way in manners he usually does not, fifteen years old and round in the face, brown eyes bugging bright with foul humor. "How long you bet he lasts, boy, huh?"

It's all I can do not to roll my eyes, but I manage, holding in mind that the boy only retains what the others have taught him to survive. A mime of much older men and a slave to their mannerisms without a proper role model to leech from. Not that they are terrible men in their own lights, most a hair younger than me and self-sacrificing when it counts. But fear brings out the ugliest part of people and it pays rare exceptions, none of which are here.

I open my mouth to speak, stunted by the next page Ace retains being shuffled to the front of the stack.

"The search teams have waited and mourned their fallen brother for a proper time." He and Ethan are deadlocked in a silent disagreement, invisible fists flying and berating one another. It is enough to make the audience as a whole violently ill, seeping with discomfort. "And so, for the first time since I have been here, I am giving them a female comrade to work alongside. Welcome Miss Adabelle Green, if you will."

My jaw is slack, trembling though I can't feel it. Or my hands.

Are my hands shaking?

I glance down, fingers curled to fists and pale to the knuckle. Ethan flicks the last of his cigarette into the dirt next to my feet and pivots to the rest of the team for discussion. But I'm frozen. Dumbfounded. This can't be right, can it? I shuffle, stiff inside the circle of men as the outraged voices of the town climb like ladders of panic, crashing over and over in waves that Ace could not speak louder than. Like drowning, but worse.

How do you speak while drowning? Or breathe?

"He can't do this, can he?" My tongue finally finds the words I want to say over others, but I'm not comprehending them. "I...I mean, I don't know. Ethan? If we are ambushed on patrols with a woman in tow—"

"We?" Dennis interrupts, incredulous. "We? Ooh, nah, boy. Hell nah. The bitch ain't gonna be my damned sidekick. No way."

Sammy panics. I can see it in his face, the idea that he might have to patrol with a less knowledgeable teammate and tasked with protecting her life in the event of an ambush early on setting in before Ethan has the chance to deny it will happen.

"*No*, no," he almost shouts. "I won't do it. Make Ace change his mind, Ethan. Can't she trade jobs with that James guy?"

Ethan sighs, pinching the space between his eyes and squeezing them shut in a moment of weakness. I feel it, the way he attempts to contain the worst blossoming inside a belly of despair—the risk of a woman on the team immeasurable. What it means in standard is even more frightening.

"Don't ya think I've tried, kids? Ace won't budge with me."

"And he couldn't make the whore a baker or something?" Brandon shouts behind Dennis, words like a slush of diarrhea running into the conversation. "Ace can't force us to work alongside her."

I want to say that is true, but it doesn't sound that easy. If it was, Ethan would have already explained otherwise.

"Yes." Ethan shakes his head. "Yes, he can. Because he won't pay us if we don't."

It is a blur of reality I can't keep up with. The conversation builds in the same way shattered bricks would make a castle, words soaring from one person to the next without structure until it collapses in on itself. Expletives are roared in defiance, the insult *bitch* feeling kind, the pinker faces flushed in blind rage. I purse my lips, wishing Ethan had slowed on his cigarette enough to save me a drag, knowing this was coming. Although, maybe he needed it more. PR was never his strong suit, his voice too gravelly to tame the masses and his demeanor too commandeering.

"Bitch better be a big ole fuckin brute," Dennis yells to the others who try to make light of it in their panic.

It is better than the yelling, of course, and I want to join the hum of bitter nervous chuckling that follows it.

Desperately.

Because if it were true, it could be managed.

Only...

She isn't.

# CHAPTER SIX
## ADABELLE

I CAN'T PLACE MY FINGER ON THE EXACT WORD THAT rings red like swells of fire consuming the raw, faded paper of a stark, unlit hallway.

But it's there.

Hanging on the edge of Zoey's tone are notes that sing passionate tales of unspoken pains, like things lost and yet not forgotten, haunting my every step like a parasitic phantom I can't shake, screaming life into the possibilities of her situation—of what it encompassed since the time she awoke this morning, to perhaps long predating our so far short-lived companionship.

It is fear.

No—terror.

Love?

That can't be right. It's more sinister than that. I can't ask her either, can I?

Not now that she's gone, and not whenever it is that I'll see her again back at the home we share. My memory is swept clean, but my manners aren't so rusty I don't understand it would be rude to so much as even implicate anything other than what she decides to tell me on her own. It isn't any of my business, after all, to pry as if I've known her any longer than a day. My careful silence in her wake camouflages me as the brusque stranger she invited without question into her home on condition—a stranger she knows nothing but rumors of, no less. It is similar to a grim fairytale brought to life from a bookshelf for her, the situation telling its own story akin to the pictures she treasures like cautious secrets that could expunge all the wrong for every whimsical glance she thought I didn't see when digging through the contents of my own life, picking apart facts as if they are fiction.

It is easier this way though, isn't it?

To pretend like I'm not real?

And that she's not ripe with the feeling of a girl who has not yet grown in her own right while she bears the true burdens of womanhood in each place she wobbles to, like a horrid sideshow she cannot detach from?

It must be a nightmare in which she never wakes, cruel stares from countless eyes, condemning the prints she leaves in the dirt until there is nothing left for the sake of comfort aside the stripped cellar walls that box her in each night, winking within glimpses of impossible, shapeless shadows to keep her company.

Then she finds me.

In the grass. Bleeding.

Melting into flexible bones that are growing soft inside a dry flesh casing that appears, somehow, as her only attainable hope for help. Some kind of help.

And for what? This?

To become an untouchable? Sanctioned from formal society like a diseased animal to be put down at their earliest convenience?

When does this treatment become acceptable?

No. When *did* it become acceptable?

The crude folds of my withering brain ache with the stretch to retain any further material, new or old, as the aggressive roars of Limbo's citizens gathered on Headquarters' gated lawn build in intensity all at once when my name is dropped to the wind like hot garbage on a sidewalk. It leaves me a kit among ravenous hounds, avoiding the cries of slack jaws and panicked howls that pound the grass in thunderous herds, a pit of disaster shifting forward and sweeping me into their torrential vortex of anarchy.

My hands shake to the sides of my head at the pulse of the intolerable sound, pressing loose hair in tight bands over the cold steel of my heavily pierced ears to drown out the flamboyant protests from infantile adults eager to get their way till they break in agitated clusters of defeat to the day's work. Or to spread more toxic news of the day. But relenting, nonetheless.

It is one of few moments already that I wish Zoey had not needed medical attention.

Because I need her right now, in my own selfish ways.

I'm lost in understanding the fit involved with my placement, or if it has anything to do with the riotous reactions at quarantine. Am I just this much a horror to behold when I feel so average in my own body? It is crippling in a way that leaves me sucked inside myself, leeching to what I know, and rejecting what I don't.

What is a search team?

What are we looking for?

I shouldn't be here. People are talking. I'm not deaf.

I need to find these teammates that are like "brothers" to one another. The ones who so hastily push away a woman from their exclusive leagues in connection with the entire population of Limbo. Such lewd discriminations would never have been tolerated in the history I recollect, women making up the better half of the population and sixty percent of the work force.

Was that a real statistic? My thoughts agonize over what is real, begging for confirmation I cannot have.

Another tandem of men brush past me, leaving the man known as Ace exposed in full, clear view from where I stand in what remains of the middle audience. Our eyes catch briefly in this second, his stone features from up high lapsing as if he had recognized me on sight, knowing what he had done to my already blemished reputation. My hands slide from my ears to my chin in an absent caress, lips parting to speak and his the same. I take a step ahead, watching his arms tense from his biceps to the tips of his fingers. Unsettled.

But...

My head whips in the direction of a gathering of voices that echo off the paved walkway that leads inside the building, hard and flouting. They shout amongst one another, arms waving in wide gestures and hands holding sullen faces, ranging in what appears to be mid-teens to early thirties, riddled in despair.

They don't see me in turn. I'm still protected by several legions of bodies passing intermittently to and fro, but I pivot on my heels in their direction, the sound of *bitch* poisoning the atmosphere.

I skirt the perimeter of their semi-circle, listening to their insults and complaints that fill the divide between us, though nothing makes me cringe quite the same as The Healing Center. This, in itself, is more crass than hurtful. It is indirect and it lacks the substance to cause pain, simply pointing fingers at a victim of their law, rather than pounding out a solution.

*Victim.*

My guts churn at the attachment this term makes to me, like one of the tattooed numbers resting in delicate black ink on each of my fingers, but more flagrant. It's a bigger advertisement than that, written on my round baby face in neon paint, complemented by industrial black lights for everyone to exploit at its highest degree.

Is that what Zoey intends to do? What I intend to let her do?

She has the same brand. A matching logo.

*Victim.*

Everyone is a victim, if they think about it hard enough.

I toe onward, peering at a distance between two men—the loudest one pasty like glue and thin like a stick. Or a snake. Without the muscle tone to stand straight, his spine flashes in solid knots through the pastel blue V-neck shirt he wears, his jeans sagging at the waist, and boots stepping on the tattered legs every time he leans forward.

The other man is much darker, like coal, and with a head admittedly smoother than my knife-shaved legs. His voice is like power itself, strong and deep, much like his prominent muscle tone that flexes in stiff distress at every firm snap to the group. It is something that commands respect, the confidence in which he presents himself, and they do—respect him.

*Hell*, I want to.

Respect him, that is.

If he respects me in turn.

But there isn't much to see, leading on the meager space created along the outlines of their hairy arms. Flashes of clothing, mostly. Some less than attractive legs. The tops of heads belonging to members knelt in the grass, and yellowed cigarette paper being flicked aside in streams of pestilent grey.

I purse my lips, biting the bottom, and inching around a taller blonde woman blocking my view for a moment. I teeter on my next move while I eavesdrop.

*Bitch better be a big ole fucking brute*, Glue Man shouts as I creep forward, leading the group in a loud, but nervous chorus.

Except *him*.

Pasty White and Dark Reflections of a Bald Head fall away in the knee-splitting jest at my expense, bending sideways and elbowing their "brothers" in the ribs who join without air, reflecting sounds like seals with bronchitis more than real people. This allows me to view the majority of the faces on the other side. Turning and writhing. Clapping and losing their wits in an attempt to relax back into a safe place. Normalcy. To clear their damaged egos and forget I'm here.

Or would be here.

My arms cross over one another, gripping my elbows in self embrace at the second I know I cannot be unseen lurking about. It is reflexive, shuffling away at the catch of his face among the shouting, and protecting as much of me from his sight as I can manage.

My spectator's eyes are strangely blue for the olive skin they dwell in. Pale, like precarious ice behind thick black glasses sliding down the slope of his nose slick with sweat. But dull, as if they had been muddied by centuries of trauma. Though he can't be older than twenty-five at an initial glance, one of the older men in the group of condescending jackals I've been misplaced to, and the others appearing to lack certain wisdoms acquired by their elders.

Still, my mind wanders looking at him. I wonder if his glasses were a necessary accessory to his face, or if he wore them as a fashion statement to keep others from noticing how tired he appeared when there was nothing but a blank canvas to showcase. The rectangular frames he wears do little to conceal the pillows of exhaustion camping out in fluffed sacks at the fringes of his cheek bones, bouncing just a touch when our gazes lock.

Right before he nearly joins his brethren in hateful laughter, catching himself just then.

His mouth pauses in a careful, open turn that drops for a split instant, so the sun catches a silver flash of stainless-steel caps concealing his bottom canines and one on the top. It takes him this time to gather himself, to take in who I am, and then he shoulders past two of his group members so that they produce tumbles of disoriented yells. This so he can greet me before they have the chance to say anything else incriminating, probably.

*Human resources*, I assume.

My inner voice is snide and bitter. Searing.

"Aidan Powell," he announces, thrusting forth a calloused hand and interrupting the remarks that build an inner wall against my once not-so-rigid exterior.

My fingers twitch in response, hand floating just off my arm and elbow extending in a mere stretch, changing my mind at the beat of my inner warning drum. I use the hand to clutch back to my skin instead, nails pooling pink and white below the surface of my skin. Aidan's lips only retract at this response, his own digits curling with hesitation into his palm.

"I see."

It is all I can manage that is appropriate, connecting cold glimpses at each member he protects like some vigilant knight, his black sneakers planting a firm barrier between us.

His hand drops to his worn jeans, sliding over to the folder he holds in the other at his side, and chin dipping in a subtle nod of concession.

"You...erm...you must be Adabelle," he confirms. "Right?"

If I lie, can I get a new job?

It is a passing temptation, one I weigh with heavy consideration. All of it could end right here. A single yes or no, and all I have to do is drop the hammer.

*Say no.*

It would be better for everyone, wouldn't it? And there is a better possibility I'm not lying at all, because I don't know for sure.

Aidan interrupts these inner thoughts again, mouth twisting in a coy grin.

"Can I call you Addie for short?" He leans closer to my absent eyes, trying to assess whether or not I'm still present, while simultaneously bringing physical emphasis to the word *short*. "You know, nickname sort of thing? We all have one."

It wants to be reassuring, the design in which he leaves himself open again. His arms spread in a gesture to the team, and his eyes light with impending humor I don't translate. But I find my body instantly firm by this, deep pink creeping along my face in a painful trickle that I can't hide, my fallopian tubes sucking down my ovaries into my uterus that crumples like a wad of chewing gum.

Is it possible to dislike someone this much?

My temple, where I was struck a day prior, pulses so violently my head pounds to its beat in a way that feels as if it should be audible, but isn't, forcing me to squeeze my eyes shut to keep them from watering.

"Please," I say, my voice exasperated. More so than even I anticipated. "Please, never do that."

The others chuckle, erupting into unified *oohs*. But I find it much less amusing, spinning away on my heel and contemplating whether or not moderate to severe starvation is a viable option. My stomach growls in protest to this idea though, still running on mostly empty thanks to Zoey's personal rations being less than scarce to share with even herself, let alone me.

I sigh, attempting to tune out the clamor behind me. I would have been better trying my luck in the forest, I think.

"Aidan," Dark Reflections calls, hushing the group to a murmur. "You need to see Ace today, don't ya?"

A pause, awaiting a response that doesn't come. I look over my shoulder when it doesn't, Dark Reflections carrying on as if it had.

"Take our new friend with ya," he insists. "I want Ace to get her...comfortable, please."

There is something dissatisfying about this that lingers on Aidan's face, however brief. The folder he carries crumples at a gentle squeeze of his fingers, packed tight with scripts and notes slipping out of the borders. A notion the man in charge gestures toward at every given opportunity so not to let him forget.

As if he could.

Aidan relents to a half-smile, swinging back to me halfway so he can see us both at once.

"Ah, yeah. No problem, Ethan." He bobs his head. "I'll get little Miss Addie set up with Ace in time for break. He's a swell guy. I'm sure it will be no problem."

There's a hint of sarcasm mingling in the mix of this, but I can't decide at which word it sits. He masks it well with an undeserved faux courtesy that keeps the others satiated as they buzz to each other.

"Adabelle," I correct him. "Just...normal-sized Adabelle."

"Aidan is our Second-in-Command here," Ethan's voice softens unnecessarily. Like he pities me. "He'll take good care of ya, and Ace will get ya sorted out."

Sorted out?

I can feel my face scrunch inward, as if I were smelling

something awful rather than staring it straight in the ugly face. I rub at my head wound, breathing deep and trying to sort myself out. It feels more similar to a deep bruise than a gash now, the edges closed and scabbed well.

Strange.

"I can take care of myself," I grumble at last. "Thanks anyway."

The air is more abrasive as I stride the opposite direction, the facetious droll bursting like fireworks at my rear keeping my stilled lungs from inhaling their insidious natures within to rot me where it counts. Instead, the abhorrent behavior weathers the barrier I have been working to build on the outside. Warm, forgiving gusts of wind that gave me relief at one point, now seem stagnant, life becoming unmoving at this juncture.

Sharp tides of dead heat rips across my skin like rusty barbs on a fence burning down the trunk of my neck to the subtle curve of my chest that heaves into the pain the faster I walk, letting it strip away the barrier I've made, as well as the flesh, and leaving me raw to their careless insults where I wish to be indifferent.

*Tiny bitch, ain't she?*

*No tits for being so stout.*

*She has a fat little baby face, though. Like a fucking bowling ball, that one.*

*More like fat ass! Am I right? Have you even looked, dude?*

Laughter. At my expense.

I can almost feel them pointing, and my hands twitch to shield my backside. But my inner woman pleads that this would only fuel the obnoxious flames of their disgusting manhoods.

*Flames.*

Everything is on fire outside of my body, burning up what I'm caging in by biting my tongue, letting my much stronger self run this bitch. Tree bark sandpapering my face to frayed bloody tissue would feel like silk in comparison to this slow verbal torture I can't seem to escape fast enough, the etches of white sunlight heating my already scorching cheeks to a rolling boil, and blood pooling underneath the surface of my ears spilling forth a battle cry of furious swooshing that drowns out the softer noises produced by my new "coworkers".

In the preservation of my own dignity, I find it is in my best interest to see Ace alone, rather than tote around the messenger boy of the "search teams" that they dare call their Second-in-Command to do all the dirty work, simply because I am the one person who does not know what is happening. But I haven't been granted a sliver of pride to cling to in this new life, my balance disrupted by the weight of his arm connecting along the length of my shoulders, providing it a quick squeeze, so that his feet find pace with mine.

"*Nonsense,*" Aidan beams, letting the arm retreat in a fast drop to his plaid shirt pocket when he knows I won't try to outrun him. As if I could outrun him. "We are a team, Addie, and that means we take care of each other. It's part of the job."

*Oh, yay.*

I run bony fingers through my bangs, letting out a sigh that shakes my abdomen against the marbled scarring of my forearms.

"Adabelle," I correct. Again.

It doesn't seem I will be part of the job any longer after this confrontation, and I'm okay with that. I would request the change without their help, if they weren't trying so hard to both pretend and not pretend that they are inclusive. The bigger truth of the situation is that I don't want to become the community project of a group of strangers who despise me as I am, when I am still trying to figure out who that is. They don't want the sideshow, and I don't want the trouble. Because having a set of breasts, small or large, is only convenient for some men when they aren't required to work side by side with them, and if they are, it is family to aggravated assault.

Heaven forbid my practically nonexistent sacks of chest fat keep them from doing their job. Like a straitjacket made of such sparse cleavage, you could row a canoe down my sternum. My nipples could be pistols aimed right for their dumb heads, and they still wouldn't be able to spot them if I took my A cup bra off and pulled my tank top up over my neck.

Not that I would. I'm a bit more timid than that. Not quite like other women of the day and age, and not that I would be a prude if I didn't have to be.

And I DO have to be.

Like it matters either way.

Why do I even care?

Being ugly isn't why they don't want me here.

The very concept of being a woman is the likely culprit for why they have sent Second-in-Command: Please Don't Kill the Messenger, Aidan Powell, with me to seek out Ace. Right?

I will get myself sorted out in person without the excuse in just a few minutes, pending Ace was not also intimidated by small women, boobs, or vaginas. Although, opportunities for approaching the almighty job dealer solo are growing distant, leaving me out to reclaim what is left of my own voice.

If I have one at all.

Our shoes click in unison on the stone footpath coming up off the somewhat overgrown grass, every stride taken in tempo with the next, as if we are both in the same hurry at each individual second of time that ticks away on the invisible clock set when we wake. The pace is what pacifies me, satisfying a mild OCD rattling the scrambled wires of my brain, and allowing my natural color to return in patches of sweaty white, bulging veins receding below the shallow surface in passive throbs.

It is a solace, almost, when I look down in this flurry and haze to discover that we match on any level. A comparison, sort of, that I can identify with and lay an adulting foundation upon if nothing else at all.

It is mutual ground.

Our footwear, that is.

Other than color and size, it would seem the same company had designed the skinny, absent arched apparel that laces just above the ankle into dingy double knots. His, being black, are visibly smeared in dirt with fabric tearing from the white rubber sole, while mine are cleaner and far more dainty, blazing redder than my current mood and abloom with sketches of white flowers. A strange thing to have in common, despite our typhoon of animosity, dusty diamond tracks from the bottom of our shoes brushing a dirt trail residual from the markets in our gait.

But I attempt to allow myself room to fall into it—a bare bones chance for objectivity so I don't appear too disgruntled at our coming request.

I could try to sympathize with Aidan's cause until our conversation with Ace is complete and I could move on. Because that's what adults do. Right?

Working with people they would rather not?

I want to be that person when others cannot, I think.

I think it much more as the distance between ourselves and the party of asshats ripens, and my soul floats back into my meat sack of existential crisis. I'm able to relax my stiff arms so they swing at my side when the soft slope uphill makes my heart rate climb with it. The reminder that I am starved is abrupt with this. I am missing fuel for minor pursuits, and I need an actual meal.

*Did I really* ever *dance? Moving doesn't seem to be my thing?*

*Nothing is my* thing, I remind myself. *I don't know who I am. This person does not have a* thing.

Headquarters sits within reach at the end of the pathway, looming damp and cold in spite of streams of sunlight blasting it in absence of clouds. It is a monstrous piece of determined architecture in person—more like an erect cave, built in tower formation, than a man-made structure. It is practically windowless, save for a few that are carved with poor shape and barred over in black iron at the top floor, singing empty songs in shrill whistles at every breeze.

I let Aidan take the lead as we reach the resolute wooden doors that have been left open so that the chatter from inside the chasmal entrance filters out to us in ripples of foul breath and natural body odor. The textured stone walls exhale dirt and metallic scents that I can taste in thin films over my teeth and at the rear of my tongue...something that appears to bother Aidan a lot more, judging by the way his tongue glides over each row of teeth, attempting not to cringe while his hand raises in a noncommittal wave to those that spin about to meet his entrance. He is recognized on sight here, favored by many, according to the sea of smiles flashing in just as pleasing emphasis echoing his name.

*Hi, Aidan.* My thoughts mock this cordial display, sneering, forsaking yet more questions in its wake.

Can she really sneer, this inner voice, for instance? Am I sneering? Right now?

My nose is scrunched, eyebrows pressed together when his head cocks to me, checking that I haven't yet lost my way as we are shoulder to shoulder amongst average-sized people demanding late payments to pocket, so they can eat by noon. The smile he puts on display is contrived when our eyes meet, lasting less than ten seconds, then dipping to a thin stressed line that none of the arms swinging out to slap him on the back pay attention to.

Like a magnet of fraudulent friendship, people are drawn to him, shouting familiarities, begging attention that I must duck under in order to keep up. I am watching as he feeds their desire for companionship and getting nothing in return. After a time, I begin to feel more as if I am a lurking, uninvited guest than the second member of this venture.

*A stalker*, using tiny elbows to knock unintended space invaders in their place.

But he is efficient. With brief tilts of his mouth and head. *Hi's* or *hey's.*

*It's been awhile. How are you?*

"Not dead yet, huh?" someone calls over the crowd, a few laughing in response as though the joke were aimed at them.

Aidan chuckles. "Not yet, Melody. Check back tomorrow."

At the left wall is a smaller lobby interrupted by a spiral staircase laden in a broad coat of fluffy grey dust along its rickety exterior. The iron rails it employs to keep patrons from leering off the dry, rotted steps before reaching the next floor is perched on by a group of teenage boys and girls chatting one another up while they wait for the chaotic line leading both out the door and down two different corridors to shift forward. An extended counterspace runs along the farthest wall to this, where the head of the line fans out in rampant discord, smothering the physical sight of this woman named Melody except in temporary glimpses of slender tattooed arms stretching around warm huddles to drop ringing change into open palms.

She is undeniably swamped in this sea of shit, tufts of black hair slipping over her scrawny shoulders and curled fingers hesitant to deliver the next payment when several yell her name at once for it.

*Melody! Here! Here!*

*C'mon, woman! Hurry up! I don't have all day.*

I wish I could see her face in place of the way her elbows retract, misshapen metal rolling in between white knuckles that beg retaliation for the impatient clamor pounding on the squalid barrier that protects her from being mobbed. Her forearm tenses at *woman*, vigilant in my imagination, as I picture her tossing the coins straight into the crowd that would squabble for them like fish in an overcrowded tank that scramble after pinches of crusty flakes floating on top of the filtered water.

But the money clinks into an angry hand that snatches it away, the response attached to the flow of her tongue making me believe against all odds she is a genuinely beautiful woman when compared to those I have already met.

*Yeah, yeah.*

Simple enough.

The curt attitudes are excused in a single breath in a way I cannot seem to resolve, as if she can understand it without enjoying the aura and leaving me intrigued at the quality of its inflection. Both soft like velvet and commanding well earned respect.

Like she owns the building and everyone in it—we're just cattle for her prod.

*Why can't she be Ace?*

I would bet my whole life she wouldn't let a pregnant girl starve to death.

Dozens of people lurch forward at this thought, Aidan shuffling against the unpolished grate railing the boundaries of the staircase and ignoring the kids who call out to him this time, pulling the folder closer to his core. The papers are beginning to slip out now through the object's loose confines, bold letters at the edge of many parchments legible, but not enough to make out exact words.

I drift closer to him, slinking out the other side of the crowd on his haunches and into a different lobby that takes up the better half of Headquarters' ground floor. Both of us appear to relax at the relative vacancy regarding this section, an unlit brick fireplace riddled with soot and logs of scorched wood lined on either side of the farthest wall by expansive bookcases. Shelves bow under the immense weight of this literature as dusty spines face out to us in greeting.

A rhythmic tick swelling inside my skull wishes to make a beeline for it. My legs are more and more indulgent to the subtleties of my brain's desires, my body sagging in that direction giving little warning to my hesitant feet that slip across the dipped and darkened floor to keep up. My fingers catch the back support of a crusty white chair to keep my balance, the seat unoccupied, along with three mismatched others that center around a splintering box for means of a table, each glazed in flaking paint for a homey effect. I stumble forward, letting my nails run the length of what they could reach, taking in the reality so to keep in mind that I'm not dreaming, and stopping short of the left bookcase. Skimming the titles.

*Autobiography of Kayla Lilianna.*
*Autobiography of Cassy Isaacs.*
*Autobiography of River Lee.*
Aidan's mouth drops free at my actions, his sneakers skipping ahead with the hint of a groan at the base of his throat, then deciding against it, whipping on his heels toward the tremendous

counterspace enclosing a host of stacked crates from ceiling to floor. I'm able to free myself from the magic of the book arsenal for this, stunned into awe at the innumerable scrolls rolled inside each one, white wooden boxes of others stacked higher than I am tall throughout each walkway.

Ace stands in the middle of this secretarial hell, shifting warped and snaggled boxes from one side to the next in a single scrawny arm, while holding his dark blue beanie in place with the other so that it loosely covers his ears. Breaking little more than a sweat, he's claustrophobic to watch in such refined space. His body is a magnificent stretch of skin over bone, like a taffy person, who bows at distressing angles to collect the next batch of items in wispy limbs corded with just enough muscle to make me believe he could lift anything over thirty pounds at the cost of his elbows disconnecting from the rest of his body.

I follow Aidan in this direction, cringing when the folder flaps against the counter in a reverberant echo that climbs the walls like the black vines around the staircase calling from the invisible top floor. Booming. As would thunder.

There is a distinct pause before Ace noticeably reacts to this sound.

Still, everyone in the whole building must have heard it at the same time in lack of being nearly as close, a few heads instinctively popping over slumped shoulders to investigate as lines draw ever forward and vanish.

But Ace only stiffens at the pop, dark eyes wide, yet narrowed, as if attempting to concentrate on something else across the room shrouded by endless work that blinds him bored. Though I could swear that he recoils slightly at our approach, a sideways glance from his peripheral vision shooting lasers clean through us, followed by a huff that rattles his chest, his biceps flexing under the burden boxed away in his arms.

But I could have just imagined it.

The preemptive acknowledgment.

A box snaps to the floor in a haphazard clatter, the scrolls inside bouncing sideways as he shakes his bruising hands and straightens like a cell tower to allow us a full view of his seven plus feet of sheer enormity. He is a true giant on Earth, and I am inconsequential in his shadow that lumbers toward us in the awkward grace of someone who is used to hitting their forehead on everything that even Aidan would not, at what had to be at least, if not bordering, six feet tall.

Ace does little to resolve these perceptions, dead eyes retracting none of the hostility emanating from the rigid posture he presents. The absence of a healthy smile takes away from the concept that if his brows weren't knit together in such stringent disinterest, he might actually appear normal. Bashful even, the way his cheeks redden just a faint pink over his nose.

"Celestyn asked that I deliver this to you." Aidan clears his throat, tapping the folder with his first finger. "Today. Before scouts."

There is a blatant discomfort scripted along every line in his face. Grooves stressed in dips around his mouth attempt to brand the same smile he delivered me into the heart and soul of the job dealer, reassuring that his visit wasn't tainted with ill intent. The charisma isn't lost on Ace, however, gaze shifting back and forth between Aidan and myself, and trying to decide whether or not he wishes to buy what this boy is selling. The huff he eventually releases from his nose and mouth is somewhat alight in amusement to this, but dead of joy.

"She asked you?" he responds, flipping amongst the pages and laying it closed again. "How very unlike her."

Aidan laughs, but it's forced through the clenched teeth of his jaw wrenched shut, the pitch unnaturally high. His tongue glides athwart the metallic covers within his mouth, and he bobs his head once more, allowing himself to take in the insult while I absorb the information they permit to be said out loud at the mention of Celestyn's name.

It wasn't much.

Just enough cordial small talk for me to lose interest, and for my eyes to wander along the endless space collecting mites and rot behind Ace. It isn't anything that I couldn't get better of in either of the lobbies lined in untouched leisure text, but more unusual than anything.

Eerie.

Hundreds of boxes and crates bulging with even more scrolls and loose parchment stack far beyond basic candlelight into a sea of pitch, seeming to serve no purpose other than to be organized and reorganized. Cobwebs and broken slats for other boxes fill empty spaces, reflections of broken glass and several daggers poking out the tops to be seen with still no purpose. Sparse tables are laced between the piles to balance heaps of folders similar to the one Aidan laid down, many slopping out faded content that would have to be placed back into individual files, the one closest to Ace dawning a dirty lace cover.

His canteen is strung beside two open folders that have lines struck through the first four sentences, along with a hunk of bread and its shower of crumbs covering a majority of the rest of the text.

I lick my lips. "What do you do here, exactly?"

Both men silence, and Aidan mouths words that don't come forth.

I have an intuition telling me it wouldn't be anything kind if they managed to blossom into an actual sentence.

"I keep records," Ace explains, icy as ever.

"Of what?" I lean forward, hoisting myself up so the counter digs into my belly and I can get a better view of *everything*, feet dangling off the floor.

Ace takes a firm step away from the counterspace, as if I carry the plague.

Mindful, but permitting.

"People," he replies. "Of everyone in Limbo. Their lives, and the end of their lives. Their well-being, or what they do."

"Each scroll..."

"Each box" —he bobs his head to the ever-accumulating collection— "represents a life."

Aidan clears his throat again, drawing the room to focus and demanding attention.

"I actually came to speak with you today," he presents. "About...life. Specifically, of matters concerning the safety and *well-being* of...well, *life*, I suppose."

I had almost forgotten our task in polite investigations, swinging backward so my feet touch the floor in a delicate thud of my heels. It's foreign to do, as if I had charge of the room for a moment, and I'm reluctant to yield it while I slide in place next to Aidan, allowing him to take the lead in spite of my earlier enthusiasm to do it myself.

"I see," he muses, monotone and robotic, watching me teeter in constant anxious motion from heel to toe. "So you believe I made a mistake in Miss Green's placement, Mr. Powell?"

There is no time wasted hitting the underlying problem, like an overt bullseye was painted in vibrant color all over each of us. The abrupt drop of the search team's do-good façade catches us both off guard, Aidan avoiding my desperate glares but his face glowing red with unbridled abashment. He shakes his head in well-meaning deceit, his hand waving frantically.

"N-no. No," he affirms. "It's...I am sure you are careful. And I am sure Addie is...great, but the consequences for all of us are dire with her on the team. That is, considering we do our job at capacity and appropriately."

Another flush of red prickles the surface of my skin, individual spines of hair rising to a higher call of pitted rage. Not that I should expect otherwise, but it strikes me as an open-handed insult the way it rolls from his tongue.

*Great.*

The '*t*' on the end could go on forever in the stretched hollow his mouth makes, saturated in sarcasm and antagonism. Like I was the small girl that begged the club leader to come on an all-boys outing, and the Great Elder Ace couldn't help but relent despite the tangible sighing the little fellows in his wake produced.

*Ah, c'mon, sir. She might have cooties. It's daa-ngerous.*

The lobes of my brain swell against bone, reaching for the danger they speak of that can only be amplified by my presence.

Mosquitoes don't discriminate when blood is blood. I'm pretty sure man-eating beasts don't either when guts all taste the same.

Ace's lips hint at a coy smile. The first genuine twist upon his face I have seen. He takes a swig of water from his canteen to wipe it clean.

"There are no consequences," he claims. "*If* the men on your team are performing their jobs appropriately."

Tense white knuckles crack against the countertop, and my feet shuffle involuntarily in the opposite direction. Aidan leans forward in direct follow up, heat glazing over the shadows bounding across his face.

"She's a *girl*," he growls just as fast.

"A woman," Ace corrects in nonchalance, lowering the canteen to where it belongs on the table.

His skin has split like steep canyons where it hit the wood, warm trickles spinning down a veiny forearm he thrusts outward in dismay, glasses falling tight against his face while he tries to contain a series of aggravated chuckles.

"You *know* what this entails for *her*, Ace. This isn't just the pre-existing team here."

Ace shrugs, shoulders broad and rolling. "That is not what I am told. Ethan appears to disagree."

"People could die." I watch him word this with care to my presence, delivery precise and quieter. "She could die. Or worse. We know what is worse now. And you can't make good people sacrifice their lives for the sake of being inclusive."

My chest drops, innards wilting into pink slush that festers in sweltering heat down to my toes. I open my mouth to speak, but Ace dilutes this squeak with the power of his own inflection.

"People die anyway, Mr. Powell." He nods toward the towers of history at his rear. "Or worse. But they do. I am not the one who decided this time that Miss Green would be an asset to your team."

"Master Amadeus cannot delegate jobs!"

The same fist slams down on the counter once more, the weak

fibers of wood giving way to a crack that divots the space next to the folder, and causes a handful of papers to slide outward, skittering scraps to the floor at Ace's feet.

"Don't try to put this on him when you know it won't be resolved." I can feel him giving in, caving like the tenuous bottom of a plastic bag under the weight of over-packed groceries. "You can't lie your way out of what you've done."

I swallow. Hard. Pivoting on feet numbing to the inner surface of my shoes, my mind sprints leagues ahead of what I am able to construct with the twisted vocal cords boring tunnels into my throat. My other motives are lost to a barrage of questions battering the walls of my sanity and I cradle my head in dirty palms, letting them settle to ash while I debate my next step. Whatever it may be when the outcome could be death in any direction I go.

Or worse.

*God*, what is worse?

The bickering is still climbing when I face them anew, the term *coward* slung more than once at my recently introduced coworker, who has grown splotches of crimson painting down the trunk of his neck from his ears and face. His bottom lip curls at the newest tongue-lashing, letting the reverberation of the emptying tower give it to him twice so to be certain he doesn't forget.

I creep forward, quivering in newfound ignorance and unable to get a word in edgewise through Ace who never raises his voice enough to yell, but wields authority in each word as if he were the only real adult in the room. A commander of finality and an egregious disciplinarian who accepts nothing less than total compliance at worst.

But he isn't the face of this attraction, is he? He answers to someone else. A Master Amadeus, is it?

The folder in the middle of their quarrel waits to be put with the others in a disarray of familiar eloquent scrawls, a pleading distraction for my mind. The letters at the top of the foremost parchment are traced bold and underlined, capitalized so they will be noticed before anything else when examined. Which I do—notice them—slipping further by Aidan to behold its secrets as the text arches over the distant ledge, ready to flutter down and out of sight.

The men shift in a blur of words from the object, intensifying the recognition I draw when I reach the wooden barrier separating us from Ace. I don't think anyone else sees what I am coming witness to, or they don't care. But I do, stretching a thoughtful hand over the folder's frame at the epiphany of what it is. What it's about.

There is a friction when the item slides forward—a minute hushing beckoning immediate scrutiny, like a home security alarm when the front door is cracked just a wedge during an attempted burglary. A fresh crack follows this warning of my attempted thievery at less than a drop of a hat as the painful swooping of Ace's considerable-sized palm plummets down upon my knuckles, freezing the subtle maneuver as my eyes reflexively well up.

I attempt not to whimper, gasping instead at the sudden pain that stops Aidan mid protest, his last word stuttered to severe silence. Stringent purples and blues flex across individual fingers, fabricating nauseous swells beneath the skin that bloats through the weight of his palm folding over them, firm and unmoving, his eyes bulging in apparent panic at the deed done. His fingers ease to the pull of mine, struggling to breathe life back into inanimate logs that lock flat in hyperextension. When they twitch, I exhale in a sputtered shriek, pain tingling in full force up the length of my elbow and resonating inside my bones which feel inexplicably hollow.

Our eyes connect at this noise, low and pitiful as my mouth hangs agape, and he bends to meet me halfway in our confrontation.

There is a change in his demeanor that is quite patronizing, though it dominates the building, rolling off of him in a tsunami of strict control and robbing him of all previously attentive qualities. I'm shaking when my voice finally comes, quieted from the torment burning holes into my hand. I'm not sure either of them can hear me speak above the bare whisper I attempt.

"Let. Go."

I manage the sounds, but I don't feel the utterance leave. Just my lips moving and my tongue writhing to form syllables smothered against the wall of my teeth ground closed. Ace flashes a quick smile, mindful not to display too many teeth and be mistaken for friendly.

"You. First."

I swallow.

My head bobs fast in generous, agreeable nods. The floodgates to accumulating tears welling within my sockets refuse to break, while I wonder if it were possible that a slap on the hand could break bones if it was done by a giant. Pain is a remarkable motivator for obedience in me. I don't tolerate the feeling of agony well, even if I have experienced it in the past.

Here I am, a lab rat, and I learn from it. In my mind. Sort of.

I want to learn from it.

But as it trends, my words betray me anyway.

"No. I...it's mine." I tremble. "At the top. It has my name on it."

The disobedience solidifies my form like gelatin, but only if it were dried out on the outside, rigid and inflexible. A sweet burning smelts rivers of molten fire beneath the surface of my hand, receding at the same second to an ache cooled by sweat slick in the crevice made by our layered hands, and I ease the tension of my jaw in defeat. Sighing.

"Y-you should change my job." My heart throttles furious kicks against the plate of bone protecting it, but I just can't help myself. If I were more daring, I would bring up Zoey while I dominate his floor. These concepts are lost, though. "If it's dangerous. You should. I don't want to die."

A muffled tapping interrupts the steady eye contact we maintain at the other side of the lobby, cleared of nearly everyone but the woman approaching us in sleek black heels and a bright red beanie, styled similar to Ace's, pushing down her mop of straight black hair.

"I like it!" Melody claps, her laugh startlingly loud, but voice recognizable in the still air. "Down with the man, or whatever they say now. But Ace, hitting a girl? You weren't raised to strike girls."

She clicks her tongue, almost curveless hips bouncing to the side on legs almost as long as his, leaving me able to pull my hand home with dignity intact. Ace retracts his own digits with the folder sliding between them. He sways from the rest of us, back bared so his shoulder blades protrude like the bony stumps of demon wings. His voice softens to the course of blows he still intends to deal now, slapping the host of papers on the nearest table I couldn't reach, and gripping his own hand as if it had been wounded in place of mine.

"Will that be all?"

More tapping. The smug grin pulling at plum stained lips sours to pity for his invisible injury, and Melody hoists herself up over the counter to meet him on the other side in less than any hesitation. Her fingers stretch over the shrug of his shoulders, her face peering around into his for a quiet word.

But I am *not* done.

"No!" I shout. "No, I didn't come here just to—"

"Yes," Aidan speaks over me, forcing another famous smile, though this one far less committed. "Thank you, sir."

"No. I'm not—"

"Yes, you are. Come on, Addie."

I am pressed to listen, resilient but willing to settle for anything as the rush of adrenaline fades to weakness in my tissue. Our march back is set first to the beat of Melody's gentle insistences cooing frantic messages at the ear of her coworker, swirling about to look him in the face, and then to the shrill song of nature consuming the path back to the team.

*Our team*, I try to reassure myself.

Ethan gaits with a lazy swing of his legs ahead of the others when we arrive, Glue Man a small pup at his heels ready to piddle in ecstasy. Both carry cigarettes in hand, lit and half-smoked, with ash tipping off the end.

The smell is both nauseating and desirable when it wafts our way. Like I had craved this once.

Possibly even now.

But not like this.

I don't want this.

"Why's she still here, boy, huh?" Glue Man throws his hands out toward me, as if there were another *she* waiting to be inducted into this joke, pinching the cancer tube in tight lips.

"You knew it wouldn't be that easy if he had already said no to Ethan," Aidan responds, his voice even and collected. "Ethan has twice the pull I do. Sending Addie with me to see Ace, like some kind of abandoned dog we are trying to surrender at the nearest shelter, was a pretty weak attempt at a last second save. Don't you think?"

Ethan's eyes roll back at the next inhale, blowing dark grey clouds to the sky, then following the shape of The Dome down around the tree line as he tilts his head in position to view us once more.

"Ya can't expect these men to take her out there." He won't look at me when he spews this garbage.

"I don't," Aidan replies. "I never did."

"Ace can't expect it either, damnit! They've been through 'nough without the added threat of a woman on the team. Those creatures would skin us alive for half of her."

I wince, my mind's eye snapping to the barn where monstrous eyes roll over the length of my huddled mass, measuring my reaction. Then leaving.

He left.

*"Uh uh, boy!"* Glue Man shouts. "Won't die fer her, boy. Won't do it. I've made my sacrifices and she ain't one."

Several cries from the rest of the team edging closer shout expletives to lend him support, each one combining into an out of tune chorus that derails the next verse. Swarms of eyes sneak spiteful glances my direction, finding me even when I fall closer to Aidan's backside, using him as a human shield the more uncomfortable I become.

"None of you will die for her," Aidan speaks above the others when he's sure they've had their turn to voice their complaints.

"Because I will. If I need to."

"That's absurd," Ethan growls.

"No," Aidan responds with a nod. "You are. All of you are. I was. *This* is absurd. It's crazy."

There is a grim silence. Reluctance to fight him, their Second-in-Command. But Ethan speaks up again with all his power and authority.

"She is not allowed near this party," he declares. "Not for rounds. Not for updates. She'll get those from you."

Aidan rubs his temple, scoffing. "No, yeah. Fine. I guess if her presence is that threatening within the safety of the goddamn purple igloo in the sky, you should probably slip on your purity ring and chastity belt too. I'll buy you each a skirt and heels, and you can take turns standing on my feet at the next daddy-daughter dance night."

Whatever else Ethan has to say is drowned out by an influx of people entering the gates from the markets. Aidan snatches my elbow and drags me their direction before I'm able to halt our progress. Ripping free of his grip at the stone archway leading into the busiest part of Limbo, I look up at him. His cheeks flush pink at this, frustration building to color his ears, and he pauses to see me. Really see me, for the first time.

"W-what is this job like?" I ask, breaking the tension. "Am I going to die here?"

It's indescribable, the grimace that breaks across his face and how he pales to it, shaking his head but, at the same time, not giving an answer to either question.

"We will talk tomorrow, Addie. I promise. I'll show you everything. But today is not that day."

"No," I breathe. "NO. I...I don't have any money. I'll go hungry. My roommate. She doesn't have a job and she's...she... she'll go hungry. And she needs me, and—"

Aidan puts his hands up in protest and steps clear of me. Not that I blame him much. My objections run awry and make little sense.

"Look, I'm sorry. I can't today. I thought I could, but I need a minute. Meet me tomorrow, right here. I will explain everything. We will get this sorted out. Okay?"

Aidan speeds away from me, rushing into the markets with his head tucked to his chest, watching the ground move beneath his feet. I can feel myself groan at this, spiking rocks up from the grass with the tip of my shoe at the sound of the rest of the search teams closing in. Mocking.

*Ooh, Aidan come* back.

*I need help. Please.*

*I'll go hungry, Aidan.*

I break past them, knocking into Ethan with the brunt of my shoulder, and traversing to Headquarters one more time. At least then, perhaps, I can get "sorted out", and find my answers all at once.

# CHAPTER SEVEN
## AIDAN

THE BEAST.

That's what clusters of blathering stooges dressing the condensed walkway of the markets call her as I brush along them. Addie's panicked call builds quarter at the back of my conscience, like pressure inside a water balloon ready to burst. It's tormenting me, antagonizing and belittling the promise I had boldly made to lay down my life for hers out beyond the first layer of The Dome where we most often work.

It was a stupid call to pass, I realize now, the buzz of rumors on the street ringing above the voice she left inside of me, knowing this could all end in one day. The first day. People are practically chanting in a cult mentality that I have effectively committed suicide in more sense than one.

But I don't see it.

The reason for the title placed upon her, or why so many people hate her after only having existed for less than a week in our village—I just can't see it. Not when her dainty hand prickled a mottled indigo at the brutal swing of Ace's palm down onto her. Not when, just like anyone else taking a slap that resounding, her knuckles took on a dark crimson hue. Not when her temple blossomed with green bruising, swelling beneath the half-healed gash already present. Or when her whole body quivered from the starvation she claimed as she watched me leave her in a pool of defeat and mockery filling the emptiness around her. I can't see it.

It isn't that she has to be invincible to fill the role of *beast*, or that she wouldn't grow accustomed to the jabs of a society so corrupted by fear it has made itself sick in hate. But for a girl, she appeared average at best, potentially even a little naïve to her new environment and the events surrounding her. Brave, for sure. Brazen, if I could go as far to say.

But she wasn't cold. Or callous.

She didn't seem any stronger than the average man or woman, and she certainly didn't overpower Ace to retrieve her file, no matter how bad she wanted it. There is nothing clear and overt in the core definition of who she is that terrifies me at all, and if I were being honest with myself, I think she is spunky as hell. If moxie makes a person a horrendous sight to behold, this whole village might be asleep. A scary thought in its own right, like a nightmare that grinds to climax every time I saw her mismatched eyes staring back to me today.

They were mystifying, those eyes that had locked with mine in a very instant. The left is a vibrant, unnatural green that fires bullets with each bat of her long black lashes, taking in every ounce of conversation I couldn't stop. But the right, it is a dark blue, almost grey. It is more relaxed in color, though just as fierce beneath the surface.

Raging.

Swirling with determination and spirit.

And I was breathless.

Looking at her in that first moment, I couldn't breathe.

Like a panic attack, there was something about her initial presence that was stifling, fitting me into a small box where my chest could not broaden with the breadth of my lungs. Unable to process the why's and how's that brought me there. Suffocating on this enigma that enraptures such a small person. My mouth hung open while the others had made their jokes, while I was merely trying to find my own words. And air. And sanity.

What was this?

Who was she to prowl the perimeters of a full group exclusive to men without the same shred of regret or hesitation held by wiser villagers? As if she were already keen to our protocol. Or knew who we were without having to be introduced. And yet she is no less green herself, in truth, a small woman with a round, youthful face that bore holes through me, ready to take my long-lost soul to hell as retribution for crimes committed by my peers. For probably what she thought I was doing when my jaw slacked in stupor.

Not that it wasn't a fair assumption.

I think she expected answers upon approach. It was to be anticipated she would have questions regarding the occupations and the teams, the drama that withholds its answers. If she were a man, no one would have had a problem delivering any reasonable solution begged into existence and more. It would have felt natural. Clean. Effortless.

But for her, I didn't have anything. I scarcely have the ideas to keep me alive come tomorrow, should I live that long. How could I tell her that every trip will be an extraordinarily calculated risk for us both?

Maybe she already knows. I couldn't say yes or no, now. I just left her there, pleading with me to return, because I couldn't face her in this siege of panic, this wall of recognition that I could be facing the last day of my life for what? Pride? Anger? Why did I do this?

I will have to take her out for scouts tomorrow. Show her how to mark corpses for retrieval and collect food. Explain how to use her dagger and where the dangers lie. Help her to understand the rules, the limitations, and where she might walk straight into peril if she were not paying attention. I would have to burden her with the darkest concepts of our short careers, bleed the very secret that our teams hold so dear to give others hope where there is none at all against her porcelain ears and pray she understands.

Because she must.

The soul crushing fact that has grown to be acknowledged by every member of the search teams is the very acceptance that the living are not worth chasing. The essence of our job front is a falsehood, and we have not brought home a living person from the raids since before I started my work as a member.

That entire night passes in sleepless unease, my fingers pressing quiet remarks on the worn strings of my guitar so it blends gentle sound over the screaming outside. The melody blasts against the thoughtful confines of my ears, just loud enough to hear over the bloodshed, until I'm able to all but phase out the gurgling thud of a wet body crashing against my front door, which I am propped up against. Mumbling lyrics to this song I make. Unable to open up even a wedge to let this still living person inside, never blinking as I let the sobbing fade to somber silence.

The body has been moved before I'm able to find my feet come morning, most of the corpse carts chugging fast beyond my home at the first hint of orange light striking celestial cracks through the window covers so that I can now see shadows of the personal I.D. I had been found with, rolling my thumb over its plastic surface. Back and forth. Like a windshield wiper made of dry, calloused flesh.

I never liked cars.

And it showed.

My identification never registered me to drive. Most of the details next to the grinning photograph of a man I no longer know designate the most obvious facts of my person that could be seen just by looking. My height. Weight. What color my eyes are, and my hair. I'm near sighted, and I was born December 23rd of the year 2547. The back of newer age identifications allots even more information to keep the agendas of each person in check at all times for those that invaded our home planet.

*Letviations?*

Something like that. Strange creatures, though not entirely hostile once Earth was secured. They aren't here with us as of current, but I would prefer if they were. This ID is the best clue I've had to understanding what happened, and it's what I cling to in times of crisis. A sure identity. Even if it isn't who I am anymore.

I pocket the laminated piece of shit, listening to roosters crow at the butchery not a mile down the street, so loud that I can't fall asleep while I'm safe. I groan, reminding myself they wouldn't be squawking for much longer, and pulling on a better attitude than yesterday coupled with a yellow flannel. Today is my opportunity to turn over a new stone, to teach someone who is being failed by the world's superstition and icy demeanor.

*I will do better*, I promise myself, again and again, summoning the willpower to stand in the form of a self-pep talk. *Better than panic. Better than them. I will do it. I am Second-in-Command and I can do better.*

My guitar rolls off my absent lap in a sharp shriek of strings, making me cringe as I scramble to my knees to pick it up, my glasses rolling down my nose. I can't afford to be careless today. Or tired. Or as burnt out as I am. I need to pretend that I'm not toasted, inside and out. I can be chipper and sprite. Pushing my glasses into place and stowing my guitar in its case—shoving it under the usual sea of blankets and pillows—I rush out the door.

I take less than a straight shot through the markets, making my first stop by the local bakery to observe their selection and pay for the few rations that survived the overnight raids. The ovens are still being fired up when I catch Brett and Penelope fixing their makeshift awning, a couple fledgling villagers inside learning the foundation of making dough, and three others stimulating the brick oven fire to life. They have gardeners out back that grow most of their ingredients and a fellow that comes by once a day to help clean up. It was a breezy job, compared to mine, and I like the people. But I don't stay to talk this time, bidding them a good day and moving on to the butcher for salted beef that could last Addie and her supposedly starving roommate until they build up enough funds to buy their own food.

Being paid daily, this shouldn't be much of an issue.

The biggest problem comes when I finally return to the place I had left her, as long gone as I had imagined she would be when I thought over my poor reactions across the span of the last twenty-four hours. Her absence outlasts the morning rush, from the markets into Headquarters where people are demanding payment, and it drones past new job recruit placements until Ace is long inside, the expanse of yard emptying out. I remain through all of it, waiting, as Ethan approaches alongside the remainder of our crew, slamming a rough hand down on my shoulder.

"Relax, yeah?" He grins. "Maybe ya lucked out and the little bitch went on and sat on her knees for Ace long 'nough he reconsidered? She went runnin' off that way after ya split on her."

I tuck the food into my elbow, my cheeks growing hot. It's too early for this. I am not prepared for *this*.

"You didn't see what happened in there yesterday," I grumble, shrugging his hand from me. "If she got on her knees, it would only be so she could be at the right angle to disembowel him."

"Ah, don't ya be a big ole puss now." Dennis laughs, ripping into some dried meat he must have bought before I was around. "It's all good fun."

I hope he gets food poisoning.

Ethan chuckles, reaching into his jean pocket and producing a loosely wrapped cigarette to light.

"Regroup at sundown for report." He smiles, gripping my shoulder tight once more before strolling through the gate into the markets to branch off in the forest.

I shake my head, spinning toward Headquarters with a sigh. It takes a piece of my ego to traipse back to see if she might still be there, or if she survived the night at all. It takes a bigger part to wonder if the strength she demonstrated in defiance of Ace—the strength I have taken a personal stand for—was just a farce. Was Ethan right? What would I walk in on coming here? Is this the kind of person I want to be on a team with? One that only barters to hold her own?

Did Ace accept those kinds of bribes?

I have never seen him come so close to another person in our history of knowing one another. He's never touched anyone, willingly, let alone deliver them a crack to the hand so loud it shattered my own blood vessels by default. But he was so focused in that moment—on her. It was like he missed something, if only for a second, unrelenting to her release as they spoke.

What did he miss?

Inside Headquarters, it is quiet, except for Melody's heels clicking behind her individual counter, setting stacks of remaining coin behind pockets in the wall for safe keeping. It was guarded overnight when she was not present, but I had never been clear on who they trusted enough to guard the glorious cash safe of Limbo, or if they had ever been required to replace that person.

I look away when she doesn't see me, glancing over to Ace's side of the court where Addie sits in rundown chairs, slumped over on to the table like a small, broken doll. Her face is smothered in the pages of several books, the shelves she took them from in disarray, after having not been touched in at least a year.

Ace carries on at his station in great disinterest of her presence, filing what he must, though his eyes roll to meet me as I edge closer.

"She's been here all night," he confirms, not looking back up to see me stare after.

"You let her?" It is a daring question, but one padded with curiosity. This is not typical.

"Her friend was not home." He stops. "She is confused. And hungry. She would not have lasted the night. But I gave her my lunch from yesterday. She appeared to enjoy it."

Guilt creeps in deeper, latching tight. I stride across the lobby, bread still relaxed in her closed fingers when I give her a gentle shake that rockets her upright. She blushes a rich pink over ashen skin when she realizes what has happened, mumbling a quick apology for oversleeping and lowering her mismatched eyes to the books she passed out upon. At her feet sits an enormous khaki backpack fit for a camping trip, littered in glistening pins, that she opens up to put her leftovers inside. She jerks backward when I step toward her, caution glinting in her eyes as I am abruptly reminded of the dark pigments shadowed at her temple from yesterday, though a few shades lighter.

I need to approach this in a different way.

"I...I brought food," I offer, holding the goods out in a peace treaty and attempting a hopeful smile.

She wants to accept it, her eyes glimmering at the protein and lips pulling inward to keep from drooling. But her pride denies her this, and she pulls the backpack closer to her core, head tilting toward Ace.

"Hey, can I keep these?" she calls to him. "Just for a while, if that's okay?"

*He didn't run on her*, my thoughts antagonize as Ace, the ever-dutiful librarian, nods.

"If you wish."

He saunters among the stacks of crates, disappearing into darkness as she smiles. Behind her lifeless lips are secrets shared between the two of them. Scenarios that I am afraid to know and conversations I've been left out of. But it's genuine, and it makes me smile too.

Addie has a friend. Perhaps her only friend so far, considering most of Limbo doesn't seem to be incredibly welcoming to her presence. However misguided it is to assume Ace could be a friend to anyone, she feels safe somewhere, and that's what counts.

The smile dissipates from both of us when she twists back to me. I'm unable to hold the friendly façade with my arms full of crap she won't take, and my brain winded by Ethan's words swimming inside of it.

Addie is very small compared to Ace. Child size, if I could side by side them for proof. She might be over five-foot-tall, and he is for sure leagues over six. Her round innocent face and violet mop of hair folded up into a very messy bun didn't match the image he presented to the world or his personality, at all. As in, she had plenty of spark to spare, and he had none.

She shoulders the backpack on as I shake these insipid thoughts from my mind, buckling the accessory twice in the front, and looking to me with a degree of impatience. Waiting. She grips the straps for extra support to its girth after a moment, her hands spotted in mottled grey scarring up the length of her arms, shoulders, and visible neck.

*What happened to you? Before this place?*

I had wondered the same thing yesterday when I had noticed it, but I had hoped not to have to think about it again. See it again. Deal with it. Again.

Did she remember where it came from?

It's not subtle. I'm sure it hurt.

She follows me outside into the heat of the city without a word. Whatever questions about the job she had at one point have evaporated, vanished, and ceased to exist. It's possible Ace could have explained the functions of it to her, I suppose. No one else would. Even I failed her on that front. But she could also be deterred from asking now that she has a feel for who she thinks each of us are—what we stand for.

We continue to shoulder through the markets in considerable hostile reserve. Her gaze wanders from stand to stand, studying the surroundings still so new to her as sets of eyes leer back, coming out of the inner safety of rustic shops and peering around display carts. There is a fear burning holes through her like fire on parchment, a hope conveyed in fleeting whispers that she will be lost to the trees.

It's almost a relief when we arrive at the clearing between the markets and farmlands, next to the outskirts of housing where I live just a few feet within. I walk her across the weeds chewed down by cattle in the afternoon, cutting diagonally to the edge of the forest where monstrous trees twist proud appendages toward the sky and the first layer of The Purple Dome ceases. It is the beginning of beauty right here, the one step into an arena exploding in color and life. A breath of fresh air. A cool drink of water.

It is the one step into imminent danger, and Addie has stopped.

Her eyes trace the length of each tree and the distance between them. The reluctance she presents is rooted in blatant distrust, her brow furrowing and body hunching over while she rubs her own arms for comfort. Like this could be some kind of joke played at her expense. A prank. A body disposal, or worse.

It must be the first in a series of many ideas she creates by how her mouth falls open, and her stare narrows onto me, her little feet shuffling backward. I throw my hands out to stop her, the food jostling in the crook of my arm. Slow. Gentle.

"It's okay," I promise at the same time, although it means so much less to a stranger. "I know what this probably looks like. And I'm sure yesterday was strange, maybe even a little harsh. But I won't let anything happen to you. We are safe."

"Safe?" she scoffs, repeating the word with abhorrent sus-picion.

She clings tighter to herself and her backpack straps. Indecision chips away at her like a chisel to a marble statue. Shaping her. Creating her. I can see it, the way each extra piece falls off to leave what is left as the person that will stand next to me when the horrors of the day are through. Addie is afraid right now, but she won't always be. It's not in her nature. I can tell.

I glance up to The Dome above us, stretching for miles beyond into the woods. I don't tell her that it seems a bit lighter today than it had been. People have laid claim that it's been getting lighter for years without it ever letting up a shade. It was yesterday that I finally noticed it for myself, and I'm still unsure today. It could just be fearful paranoia and that isn't what I want to instill in her at this time.

"Do you see that?" I point, and nod to The Dome. "Did they ever explain it to you?"

Addie purses her lips, her feet digging into the ground. She avoids eye contact, but her interest is piqued. She is listening.

"No," she mumbles.

I smile to be reassuring.

"I had a feeling," I reply. "Listen, The Dome is like...hmm... magic? But real. During the day, nothing gets in the first two layers —usually. Not the native Ravagers, anyway." I wave her forward, but she remains, so I keep talking to appease her insecurity. "It has three layers, you know. It's hard to tell from this angle, but when you walk, it's more evident. The first layer ends right past these trees and each layer gets just a bit weaker until it's completely gone. But we won't pass the second layer if you're not comfortable today."

The distrust again. I catch it when she thinks I'm not looking, turning back to see home and wondering if she's making the right call.

She's not, but food comes at a price. For everyone.

"I'm getting special treatment?" She continues to look around her. Searching.

I shake my head. "You're in training. I just want to take it one step at a time. None of the Ravagers are much of a problem until the night when The Dome gets weak, anyway."

"I don't know." She gives the indecision a voice, letting it resonate with me.

But I'm patient, I can wait. We have time to kill when the people we look for aren't alive. A lot of team members spend at least a couple days a week fucking off by the river, and the people who worship them for their hard work are none the wiser.

"It's okay." I reiterate my promise. "Hey, I've done this. A lot. It's our job, and I'm right here."

She has no reason to trust anyone. It's probable she does not so much as trust herself, not knowing yet who that is or how she's gotten here. I've been there. We've *all* been there.

I continue to smile for her, attempting to be sympathetic against all odds. Friendly.

"What do we do when we leave?" she asks, shifting closer to the border. Her skinny fingers trace the low-lying fronds of a fern growing between the closest trees, grasping its reality. She is still tense, as if she suspects I might leave her out there when we get far enough.

"We look," I whisper. I don't want to tell her the whole truth yet. Partial truths seem okay, for now. She would have to be trying to get herself into trouble on her first day.

"For?"

"For people that were taken," I tread. "Or dragged. We help them if they're alive. If they're dead, we mark their corpses for pickup. We collect their things, items that can be reused or sold. Anything we find, we report to Ethan who reports back to Ace so he can finish their files...I assume."

This takes less time for Addie to process. Whatever holds her back, leaves in an instant. She launches herself into the tree line, bramble crunching below her feet as I follow close behind, catching up so I can lead the known safe trails while her eyes reach to the treetops, studying all above her in awe. It's always a wonder to see it in person, a land thriving in intricate creation the likes of which Earth as we knew no longer contained.

Squirrels leap in leaf shuffling hurdles from branch to branch. So many birds nest on twiggy limbs, twittering to one another. Deer graze out in open space, if I can keep her quiet enough to see. I've noticed some elk too. And dragons, though most are small, no bigger than the average house cat—which there are probably also plenty of. I've seen a few younger felines prowling the shops in town to catch the rats that inevitably raided our stores when the Ravagers failed to. I'm sure there were older cats and much bigger dragons too, but I haven't seen the latter and most beasts any larger only passed overhead to faraway places, paying us no mind at all.

Like we were invisible.

Addie thinks she is invisible.

She walks, touching everything she sees. Initially petrified, she is growing comfortable in this solitude provided by nature. More so than I have seen her in the village, as if she had belonged here the whole time and we had stolen her from it. Though there were never any trees on the Earth we knew. Or animals.

But her eyes skitter with the patter of feet, singing with the chirping and chittering. She likes it, the sound of nothing. The joy of everything. It's better than the silence of quarantine, more innocent than the drawl of the village spinning spools of hate like spiderwebs that can't be seen straight into her soul to catch her off guard. Nature is harmless, compared to everything else.

I liked it too, for a while.

Until all it became was what coupled with it.

The Ravagers...they ruin all things good.

We are skirting the outlines of a clearing of trees leading to more forest and the smell of water not far off, given an hour's time. Weeds grow waist high here, some tipped in white petaled flowers and others in wheat like fuzz. I've taken this path before, and most bugs are repelled by the smell of these flowers. Last week, I gathered some to rub on my clothes and skin for scouts, but I ran out early on. If we had time, I could grab more for tomorrow.

"How long has Limbo been around?" Addie calls, pacing herself.

Dragging like a toddler in the summer heat, her head and shoulders bob above the grass, studying the squirrels that tumble overhead, chasing one another to endless skies.

"I don't know."

On the other side of the clearing, I take a sharp turn against the trees. The hillside it stands upon veers to an abrupt and unexpected end. Without the experience of understanding the land, we would be plummeting down a marbled, rocky slope to a flatter bank of land that would eventually lead to the river where we could fill our canteens if we weren't dead. It's fortunate I know the routes to get us there in one piece.

"It could have been here awhile, I guess," I speak to her again. "Ace has been here longer than anyone I know, and he isn't sure either, if that says anything."

"It doesn't." She tries not to smirk. "Have these creatures attacked since the beginning?"

She stumbles on thorny briers at the edge of the ravine, still distracted, and catching herself on a tree. Her hands shake at the bite the pale bark makes in her palm, fraying it a touch raw.

*She'll pay attention now, I bet. That would have been a steep drop.*

"Attacked is putting it lightly." I chuckle at her expense, feeling the glare reach me without having to look. "But I think so. They're pretty aggressive. At least, with the men. I don't think I've ever seen them damage a woman or small child...physically...well...in a way that would kill them. Ah, what do I know?"

We stop.

She is staring straight at me, or through me. I can't tell. It's cryptic and alarming, as if she is trying to process what I'm saying. I don't know if she does, letting her slip around me to take the lead for just a few minutes. It gives me a chance to distract in the delight of open space, watching smaller saplings reach for scarce light between thick overgrowths of canopy above.

"Do they kidnap them?" Addie asks.

The grass at her next step swishes as a small lizard whips away underneath a cluster of rocks. I am quiet for a moment, but she is insistent. Demanding.

"Well?" She stops. "Is that it?"

"Yes." I want to deny it but protecting her from that information would do neither of us any favors.

We walk further, this time Addie slowing to meet my pace.

"Why?"

"Why else?"

The sound of the river draws closer. The smell too. It's one of my favorite smells—damp and metallic. Cold. When I glance next to me, she appears confused still. Frustrated at my reply, as if it weren't enough information for her to draw her own conclusions. I don't want to elaborate on this if I don't have to.

"I'm sorry," I say, and I mean it. "It's just...being a woman is what makes it dangerous for both of us while you are employed with the search teams. Those monsters would kill any of us if it meant getting their hands on something female."

She draws closer to the remaining trees, holding to her backpack straps again. Squeezing them until her knuckles flash whiter than her normal skin hue.

"I can't change that I'm here." Her tone is defensive, but it loses the build it makes just as fast as it started. "I tried, I mean. But I can't."

"It doesn't matter," I reply.

It doesn't.

She's here.

I can't change that.

Everyone tried and no one could.

Our eyes meet for a second, hers a glittering offset of color trying to grasp an understanding of who she is working alongside. In this shade, the right eye is so dark, it reminds me of an abyss. Almost black, but not quite. There is still some life in there that hasn't been beat from her. It is more like a *navy blue*. Like a warrior.

I force one more smile.

The sound of rushing water catches our attention. Addie pauses, her heels crunching pebbled dirt and sprinting through the brush. I chase her, bounding through trees and plant life growing down a permissible piece of the hillside to the shoreline that extends a good half-mile to the most tremendous freshwater river I have known in either existence. Greater than oceans, it stretches without end in this part of The Dome, amiss in clear blue waves that roll in a gentle pull when the weather is forgiving, much like today. Its tides often bring it up over the cleft we just ran down from, delivering with it small fish that are scavenged by early morning. The remaining schools are left to swim in shallow waters, or dips in the bank that trap tiny ponds of inescapable death for all forsaken there.

I had never seen anything so pure until two years ago when I started. The river I had once lived next to, a few miles down the driveway, was a black sludge of human waste and garbage. Grey moss and crushed beer cans rocked in stagnant slime on real stormy days, creating toxic ripples that nothing survived below. The snow fell black when it could in winter, the ice it made like shit stained ink, so it carried no gothic aesthetic.

But this was beauty. The river. I adored every inch of it each time I came for refills in my canteen.

Addie stumbles down the hillside to the uneven banks, stones clattering against each other and flipping at the front of her shoes. I try not to laugh, recollections of my initial time seeing it rolling in the back of my head. The clumsy boy I had been, scraping bruised knees to plunge his face deep into the water for a better look at the mysteries swimming out of reach. I didn't realize then how much this would sting my eyes, but it had been worth it.

Addie wades knee deep in gentle sways of water that still manage to knock her backward at their height, soaking her clothes completely through. Not that she cares. She is more stunned than anything. It probably provided a touch of relief in the open sun with all the layers she dons. She timidly dunks her head below— just as I once did—to complete the look and sensation, careful not to tread where her feet could not reach.

I stroll closer, pulling my canteen from inside my flannel to fill it twice after taking hearty drinks each time. Addie spits at another pull of water crashing against her face further out, gasping but alive.

"It's not...I mean, it's fresh water," she breathes, inching toward me so she's not pulled beyond her means.

It wasn't uncommon that people didn't know how to swim. I did, but only because my parents were endowed enough to afford lessons in a purified private pool. Most were not so lucky, and many would drown in the sludge if they slipped.

I could teach her eventually, if she let me, or if she lasted. It is a proper lesson to learn in a place like this one. There are many lessons she will have to be taught, of course, but most of them wouldn't be as difficult considering, so far, she sinks into the environment as though she owns it. The others would dread learning her simplicity in comparison to their own hard starts.

We dredge around the banks for some time after this, hours upon hours of Addie sloshing in the water like a child in rain boots wading through a kiddie pool, marveling at the life swirling at her feet. I try to explain to her along the way what we look for when it comes to bodies, and the details of what we do. It isn't as easy as just telling someone up front. The search teams are a bit of a hands-on job. Most of the Ravagers travel along the riverside after raids—which is all they ever do when The Dome weakens come nightfall, so the vast majority of our job can be done here as well.

In the village, these beasts take our livestock, break our shops, and rob us blind of our abilities to protect ourselves. Once, our forges were down for a whole month in repairs, and they took all the blades still being finished. Newcomers had to use broken glass to defend themselves if their homes were invaded, not that it did any good.

They take everything. They leave us empty and vulnerable.

And at the end of the day, we are the people that clean up the mess they leave.

Admittedly, they are very unusual creatures in spite of their criminal behavioral dilemmas—like things we could open a storybook to find, but far more terrifying. They are taller than the average person, towering over most men and women by at least a solid foot or two. Extraordinarily beautiful, yet harsh, they are savage warriors with long slender ears and teeth like polished knives. They are able to gut human men with bare, clawed fists whilst carrying glistening swords in sheathes as a mocking show. They take children from the streets, wrapped in long blankets tied like straitjackets if they put up a fight, though the smaller ones are a bit more compliant. I heard once that some women go with ease as well, but generally there is force applied.

I've seen them tied. Shackled. Carried.

Originally, our task was to find these people—the women and children—to bring them justice and freedom. The older search teams would follow the trail of misery for days alongside the riverbank where old bandaging and lost possessions could be found, like a much too obvious paper trail leading to the culprit. The hotter team members got on the trail, the more they would follow sounds instead of items. Pleas for help. Idle chatter and sobbing.

The Ravagers allowed for it, granting our teams the opportunity to scope the perimeters while we were none the wiser that our presence had been discovered at all. But death always followed.

Sometimes, they would temporarily release their captives for a jog, to lure search members closer. Who refuses the cries of a desperate woman running for her life? However, those who found her were killed on sight by the ever-clever Ravager, camouflaged close behind. Quiet. Careful.

It is rare they slip up.

It wasn't until the six months prior to my wakening, we stopped traveling beyond our means to find victims. As of current, we search for only what's left behind, as victims often still drop personal belongings in their last hopes someone will look anyway. But the position is altered to protect lives.

We are professional collectors now. Corpse Counters.

Not that I tell Addie any of these details specifically.

Just the important bits.

It's good to start the job with hope for something better, and she looks like she's been through hell and back in every aspect of her life. I want to paint her a proper picture of her new life here, but not too much so. Outline safety concerns but keep a little naivete for as long as it can be managed. Chances are, she meets a terrible fate in the near future. Why not keep her innocent for just awhile?

Addie removes herself from the water after another hour, tiny ponds sloshing out of her sneakers, and the black leggings she wears underneath her shorts that cling to her calves, are practically steaming in this humidity. She sits down to rest, enough past noon it is going on evening and nothing to show for it. Her fingers rake through the gravel in this frustration, finding part of a shoelace and a shard of grey shell under the first layer.

I sit next to her, offering a piece of the bread that had made the journey with us. To my surprise, she takes it, squinting with relative caution, yet too hungry to actually care. She's ravenous, stuffing the whole piece in her mouth and laying her hand out for another. Her shirt is still damp from her aquatic adventure, the water that had drenched her body outlining the vague dip between her ribs and belly.

Despite having lost a bit of water weight overnight, leaving her face a bit wan and sunken, the girl was heavy waisted. Not overweight by any extent, but not scrawny like Celestyn. Addie's thighs are larger, thick and lacking the space for breadcrumbs to fall through, instead piling in her lap like a human dustpan. She also has love handles, just big enough to notice, her belly rolled over ever slightly while she sits, balanced back on delicate scrawny arms...much like her chest.

Not that I was looking...

But she isn't one extreme or the next. Just...healthy. She is healthy, for now.

I hand her the rest of the bread after taking a small piece for myself, and I push the meat into her arms as well.

"It *is* for you." I nod. "And your roommate. I-I shouldn't have run off on you like that yesterday."

It isn't an accepted apology, but it's a start. She puts the meat into her backpack, and chugs water from the container she brought—one that wasn't made here. I nibble in silence for the second it takes her to feel satisfied.

"Do you make a habit of running?" she asks in between one gulp and the next. "Or...did you?"

I straighten. "Um, no. Not necessarily. No."

"So just me then?" She shoots back just as fast.

I scoot backwards, shifting against the discomfort of the bank and averting my eyes to watch the waves roll.

"That's not a fair accusation," I snap. "You don't know—"

"No, I suppose I don't," she answers without giving me a chance to finish my sentence.

In any event, she would have been right.

"All we do is run here," I admit when the sounds of nature become overwhelming. "We run here. Run there. The village was uprooted twice before we realized that it didn't matter. The *actual* first village was turned to dust much longer ago than the one you still see, and I don't know how anyone made it out alive to rebuild...but you can still find pieces of it if you look. We're flightless birds here, Addie."

A grimace.

"Sitting ducks then?" It sounds like a joke, but she's already spent too much time with Ace.

"Broken ducks." I laugh anyway.

She smirks. Relaxing. Brushing away crumbs and crossing her legs.

"What do we know of this place where broken ducks quack and no one listens?"

She looks out beyond the branches overhanging in the shallow waters to the sky, The Dome still in the second layer, but almost the third, and more a faded pink than lavender. Translucent.

"Not much," I reiterate to her less-than-subtle probing. "Ace would know more than anyone. He's been here the longest. But I don't think he knows anything either. Other than that, we are simply here."

Addie gives this some thought. "Does he ever talk about home then? There must be something he remembers."

"He's not that person," I counter. "Ace never speaks about himself."

She looks as if she wants to argue this, but she lets it slide instead, following it up with another question.

"What about you then? Are you also secretive?"

A bird yells shrill screams further in the woods and a different one calls back. From the brush at our left, the glinting yellow eyes of kitten-sized dragons creep forward, inquisitive gazes drifting to the numbers tattooed on Addie's knuckles. Purring. Growling.

It's not often I see so many grouped together in the second layer of The Dome, but it is their breeding season and they seem harmless. I clear my throat, my fingers clutching to my dagger's handle.

"Ask me anything."

She scoffs but obliges. "Do you remember home?"

I'm ashamed to tell her I don't remember as much as I feel I should after all this time.

I shouldn't be. But I am.

Two years have passed, and there is so little that I have retained. Understood. It feels like small portions of my brain were removed between here and where I came from. Sort of like a more personalized lobotomy, where instead of cleaving off a whole fraction of the brain, smaller wrinkled segments are removed and blown full of cotton.

"Kind of," I say. "It isn't as simple as remembering. There are pieces still missing."

"Okay." She shrugs, stuffing more food in her mouth. She closes her eyes to the taste, savors it, and carries on. "But what is still there? Humor me, Aidan Powell."

I screen through my memories, collecting them one by one. There are many singular images in this place I try not to visit. Phrases. Houses and streets, I would walk from or to. Faces and lack thereof. Smiles and sounds ricocheting off invisible walls return to my ears in real time. There is pain resounding in each of these moments, heavy on my chest like a bus grinding bumpers straight into my skin, cracking the bone.

*Don't look at me, okay? Just close your eyes...*

I don't want to hear that voice. I shake all the voices from my head. Addie is watching the water move, the way the current rushes the shores and retreats. Her eating has slowed, and she looks at the bread now as if she feels horribly guilty for what she has done, setting the rest in a side pocket of her backpack to take home with her.

"I...um..." I laugh. I didn't mean to, but the sound caught her attention. "Um...home. Home was...I mean, it was something... um...ah..." Another laugh. "It was just never home, I guess. I'm not sure I had a real home. You know?"

She looks cautious of this. Perceptive. "Home is always home."

"Do you feel at home here?"

Quiet.

"But you weren't here before, were you? You were somewhere else."

I look away. "I play music, you know."

"That's not home." She glares.

"It is if you don't have another." My voice is soft, not low enough to be a whisper, but gentle. And she accepts it.

"What kind?" she asks.

"Any kind I want," I remark. "I did best in guitar and piano, though. Wrote my own lyrics when I needed them. But what about you? Do you remember anything?"

There is no response. She side-eyes me as if I've interrogated her in a full courtroom without a lawyer present. We remain silent like this for a time, enough of it for me to decide we should start heading back so we make it home while there's still some light out. My legs and bottom ache from the ground, shifting as my weight moves until I freeze at a sound growing loud in the distance catching Addie's attention right away.

It is shrill. Ear-splitting. Gut-wrenching. Unexpected.

And it takes a moment more for me to register than for her.

Her backpack lurches when she stands, the top hitting the back of her head that spins in every direction to try and find the source of the noise. I turn my head from the river, leaning back on my hands and tensing. Several dragons have skittered at the sound, leaving fluffs of magenta feathers that Addie steps on moving toward the drop off.

"Addie, wait," I shout. "We need to talk about this."

It is everything but watching her hyperventilate when an actual scream cuts through the dead air.

*Help me.*

She wants to. I see it.

I raise a hand at the sound of another scream and Addie looks back to me. Gears are rolling in her head faster than I can convey alarm, and the cry comes again.

And again.

"We have to," she tells me, just a hair above the sound of water.

I am trying to gather my wits.

"Addie, no." I beckon her forward. "We need to—"

Her face contorts into one of disgust, and she shakes her head to me, lips forming to mouth *no* before she hurdles ahead across the bank, scaling the drop-off to exit the forest. I can feel the word *fuck* leave my mouth at least a hundred times, flipping to my feet to venture on her trail, the trees a blur of thick pale bark and many different colored leaves like an oil painting swimming by. Her backpack slows her down, yet not enough for me to catch up with the head start she had, and she weaves through the forest as the sound grows closer.

We are entering parts of the environment I have not yet traveled in the third section of The Dome where the magic is weak and fading.

I gasp for air while low-lying branches covered in rich red leaves catch my shoulder and toss me sideways, tearing at my shirt and leaving me confounded for just a few seconds. My teeth grind and my glasses drop into my fumbling hands as I race to shove them back on, my legs pushing harder. Faster. I catch glimpses of the sky in some places, where the trees are starting to recede in number, inciting panic while I try to keep sight of her.

My shoes slide at the next elevation in the ground, still holding water from a prior rain. But I'm closer. So much closer.

I grab for Addie's heel and miss. The distant voice pleads again, this time with a frantic *hurry* at the end, and Addie yells back to her, frantic and devastated.

"I'm trying!" she shrieks.

I yell, hand swinging out again. "Addie, stop!"

She glances over her shoulder but ignores me anyway. There is something in her body that freezes in between, as if she wished she could stay, but it doesn't last.

"Don't!" I call over and over, but she disappears over the hillside.

I climb after, panting. One more sprint and I loop through the trees from a different angle, completing the edge of a circle and tackling her from the side. We spin together, my grip firm around her shoulders and locking in the front, rolling us inches from the last wall of barrier that separates everything we know from what we don't. Hitting the ground, rocks and thorns and grass smelt through the side of my face, taking my breath out when she falls on top of me.

Addie shrieks, holding her upper thigh for a minute, and struggling back to her feet. The screaming is growing distant, and my eyes roll around us, trying to locate the danger nearby. My lungs fill with air as I wretch, trying to find the oxygen she crushed from them. We are both shaking, and Addie is wobbling—weak in the knees.

I sit upright, panting, hand on my chest when she lurches forward. Diving, I catch her forearm and pull. She attempts to yank it away as the echoes fade further into the forest, but I squeeze tighter, groaning as her fist—somehow clear of its prior bruises from yesterday with Ace—berates my knuckles until we are both a brilliant red.

I squeeze even tighter, feeling nerves and veins crunch and pop beneath my thumbs until she lets out a defiant screech, dropping her ineffective fists of fury in defeat, though not quite giving up.

"It's our job!" she shrieks without looking at me. "It's our job and we are losing her! It is important. What are you doing?"

The truth. She needs the truth this time.

"It is our job to save those who need us!" I yell in return. "Not to die with those who don't."

"Did you not *hear* her?!" she squeaks. "She *does* need us. It is *our* job. That is what you said."

My eyes veer away, looking out beyond a steep valley rife with snakes from the river bleeding down the middle, and into ample parts of the world I had never seen until now at this vantage point. I have a choice to make, right here and now. One that I didn't want to make because of who she is.

I could keep lying to her, withhold more information that would lead to further mistakes and problems down the road, even fatality under the right circumstance. I could do it all over and train the easy way, because she is a girl. I could keep her innocent, because I want her to enjoy what little time is probable to her here.

Or I could tell the ugly truth.

I wipe rotted leaves and small pebbles from my hair, knowing some would stay there as grit until I could get a moment to wash myself in the river—not that I would have this opportunity today. The sun is getting a bit low for my taste and we have a long way home. I need to make sure we arrive in time for report, and for my next "date" with Celestyn, if she shows. We will have to run part of the way, no doubt.

"Have you seen these demons in person yet?" I ask, trying to keep my voice level. She opens her mouth, but I stop her. "No, definitely not, or you wouldn't be here right now. They don't leave women behind when they come across them. I'm sure you've never went into combat against them either. So don't ever, for one second *at all*, Addie, tell me what this job is about. Because I am the only one on these teams who knows for sure. And we don't cross The Dome. Ever. Not on my watch."

There is an immediate deflation in the willful attitude that she strives to keep.

"We have to help," she insists one more time. "You said we helped people."

I let her arm go, the red from where I'd squeezed her staining to what I imagined would blossom into dark bruising. Or not. She doesn't seem to keep injury at all, something that disturbs the blackest, most hateful hollowness building inside of me.

"That's the glamour of it, isn't it?" I reply. "But it's just a show. If you cross that part of The Dome, Addie, you are not coming back alive. Or maybe you would, but you would never be the same. You wouldn't last in Limbo as it is now."

"Then what's the point?" her voice quivers.

*The point is what they leave behind,* my thoughts answer. *We need their clothes and their weapons and their personal effects because we can't make them fast enough on our own. We're dying here and people are dying there.*

I don't answer out loud. Not right away. I get off the ground and offer a hand to get her stable. She spits blood pooling behind her teeth from the fall at the ground, having bitten part of her tongue, and stealing one more gaze over the valley. There is a fear seeping in, seeding its way into her mind and corrupting it.

Just like mine.

*Good.*

I turn my back on her, knowing she will follow and hearing the shuffling of grass to confirm it. The return home after the explanation of the truth is more silent than a morning of corpses, trees bleeding occasional breezes through their leaves to assure I don't hallucinate from the madness of it. Hardly any animals cross our path this late that we can see, bugs chirping the song of impending nightfall and birds settling in for the evening. When I am finally gutsy enough to look behind, I can see her loping at a distance, holding the arm blackened with dirt above red blooms where I held her so tight, I could make out my fingerprints.

*Though, it's better than what could have happened,* I remind myself, the guilt not seeping inside this time when I remember the way my body almost skimmed the final color of The Dome at the edge of the world as I know it.

As the adrenaline wears down, I can feel pain sneaking into my bones that feels like rusty piping ready to break apart in time for us to emerge into the village. The sunset looks like a proper masterpiece at this angle, highlighting the teams toward the mouth of the market across the divide, which is emptying out to shut up shop for the night.

Addie peeks up at me when they notice us, seething in warm striations of orange beaming through our lavender shield from the horizon, and looking flushed. I pass a look back to her as I leave her there, going to speak with the group as demanded, though it feels wrong.

They each expect our expeditions to go fatally awry, for her to fail, and me with her. Dennis wants to unseat me from my position. It must have felt like a betrayal to them, to choose her. But I didn't have much of a choice. Not when getting paid was contingent on keeping her on our side, and the others would have left her to die.

So I tell them nothing happened.

With grass in my hair and dirt on my face, bruises spotting along visible flesh.

We found nothing. We saw nothing.

*I tripped* down *the drop-off.*

How clumsy.

And then I leave, to bid Addie goodnight, who stares away from our circus back into the trees.

Does she miss it already? Or does she wish she would never have to leave and behold its horrors?

She pulls her hair from the wrecked bun that binds the remaining knot that hadn't escaped during our tumble, shaking it free so it blends in an array of color halfway down her back. She shakes it, fluffs it out into the mess it truly is.

*She* truly is.

I edge closer and she pivots to meet me, dropping the ponytail holder in a panic, her eyes stretched wide and mouth agape.

"I'm sorry," I say. "I didn't mean to startle you. It's been a long day."

"It's fine," she mumbles, but I can tell it's not. "I'm fine."

"That's good to hear," I lie.

She nods, rubbing the scars on her arms.

"Do...do you remember anything at all?" she asks again. "About home? Please."

My mouth falls. She needs this for some reason. Her question smashes into the wall of my conscience, making me strictly uncomfortable. It forces bubbling cataclysms of voices and faces out beneath the lid of a pot that boils over, making me warm from my head to my feet as I cross my arms together in the way I so often see her do.

"Clouds." My bottom lip quivers, but I let loose an unintentional chuckle.

"Clouds?" she repeats, peering up to the ones left in the sky.

"Not those." I shake my head. "But, yes, kind of like them."

It's strange to say out loud. To admit it. But it appears to satiate both her curiosity and the overwhelming terror written across her face.

"I miss home," she says. "The one I don't know. Whatever it had been, other than familiar...I don't think I can stay here."

"Of course," I sympathize. "None of us can."

Her hands cup her face, sliding down to cover her mouth.

"I had a home too," she reassures. "And now...I have a void where my life used to be. It's just an empty space being replaced with trauma after trauma. Fear and insanity. Like a never-ending nightmare where there is no one I can turn to when I need someone to tell me it's okay."

The trees rattle with the start of night life making their salutations to the universe. I inhale as deep as I had when chasing her through the forest, taking in the purity of the air, trying to feel real in a place that, to this day, seemed only a figment of my imagination. Addie seemed to be taking in the gravity of it too.

It is when my brain resets.

"Dinner," I murmur. "Fuck, I have..." I stop. "Would you, um, would you like to have dinner with my girlfriend and I? It's a...better void you *can* fill."

Her voice is dead of emotion.

"No."

And she walks away, leaving me in day and night's haunting in between.

# CHAPTER EIGHT
## ADABELLE

HELPLESSNESS.

That's the right word.

A bleak term, but proper.

It is a broad feeling that encompasses several categories of emotion and situations, I find.

It is a burden of understanding, a multi-faceted design that comes in various fashions. The concept is like cosmic beams of color filtering through the same prism to paint reflections of despair atop a snug, one size fits all jacket every person has worn at some time or another. One that the residents of Limbo all squeeze inside in absence of choice, wondering when the eternal winter of their unnatural lives will finally let up and allow a mild spring to replace it.

*We* are helpless.

*I* am helpless.

Here, where I am, being helpless is a confusion. Waking in an outdated quarantine unit with no memories to keep me warm and no family for comfort. It is alienation and division from potential peers without logical cause—a witch hunt that casts its fear like bleak shadows in a forest, waiting to prey upon the weak members of the pack at large.

Helplessness is knowing every place I set foot is a guilty verdict in absence of fair trial.

It is convalescence.

It is an innate knowledge that trust cannot be earned in a career pre-chosen for me, because someone has made their own fiction a fact.

Because I am different somehow, and being scared is another form this emotion wears.

Being helpless is inevitable when my gender is the subject of violent attacks every week, with the village being no match for the enemy. It takes the form of being forced to hide in lieu of fighting, because the knowledge of danger fuels this rich abandon. It becomes an understanding that home, and going home, could be all but an improbability.

Or a matter of wills.

Last night, helplessness crossed paths with its longtime soulmate, hopelessness. It was gifted a voice of its own, a scream in the forest I could not answer. A cry for help that haunted my conscience. The pair took center stage behind my eyes while I had been toeing through the dirt pathways of Limbo in late evening. It peeled my throbbing heart apart down the middle, wider than ever, bearing witness to bulky mismatched families cooking meager dinners on self-made spits. Starving, their eyes had murdered my spirit with furious passion until I made it home. And then it took form of coming full circle to another night alone and being unable to find sleep until it was too late to do so.

The walls of this place are closing in on me as I am, and I am unable to move the air in my chest. Guilt is a stagnant pool of piss settling dark orange inside my lungs. Bloody. Toxic. Like this way the villagers call life. It invades the space between my mind and heart, similar to ants that spoil a picnic, spilling black shifts as permanent stains that can't be scrubbed off the surface of my blood so it has no choice but to circulate within every inch of my being until I am numb to this unordinary poison they call normal.

The new normal.

*My* new normal.

It comprises of letting others suffer an ill fate so I can survive to do my new job that actually has nothing to do with helping anyone, a moral crime that rots me from the inside out.

A lie to make society feel like their overseers are doing the best they can when, really, we are nothing but thieves.

Liars.

We lie, and that is our line of work. To steal and to lie.

And for what?

This?

I don't know if I want to survive in a place where it's every man or woman for themselves. Of course, selflessness is an ideal concept at the end of the day in any societal construct, but I can't make people be something they're not. They have to want it on their own.

Unison.

It is a powerful approach to tragedy like this.

But they don't have the vision for it, not yet. Not when they have their own self to look after, and there is not one guiding figure to corral them together. I have nothing to work from to make this place worthwhile until I can find a vantage point for the future.

Ideals without motivation always crumble—of which I have neither right at this moment.

No, especially at this moment.

It is early morning before scouts to my exhausted, and yet restless, dismay. The horrors of another night dragged until I couldn't summon the strength to sit still any longer and departed home for Headquarters where Ace watches me read from behind the counter in his section of the lobby, skimming through files I can never touch, with cursory flutters of his eyes popping back up to glower at me. As if I shouldn't be here. As if I might get up and run away before Aidan meets me to go on our next adventure.

Admittedly, I don't want to go. Not after how yesterday went, and not after learning what I now know about the search teams. But Ace couldn't possibly know anything about my discomfort. Not unless he had spoken with Aidan this morning prior to me getting here right as he was unlocking the flower embellished gates —which was impossible.

Most of the shops in the markets weren't even trying to open when I trekked through. It was a ghost town, chilly with dew and pastel blue light. I think I had startled him just by showing up, my head leaning against the bars in patient despair, trying not to study the wasteland of my surroundings. I could ignore the corpses if I tried to, something about death ingrained in my psyche and uncomprehending at the same time.

*I'm not here.*

But I am.

I was the first person *here* this morning, other than Ace and Melody. So Aidan couldn't have talked to Ace at all about yesterday, could he?

I mean, why would he? It won't change anything, and they don't exactly seem chummy with one another.

Although, Ace doesn't seem like an intimate person with gaggles of friends at all, so I shouldn't be so embarrassed that he might know about my "screw up". It isn't like the information could go any further than what it has. He just documents individual lives, and it was probably in yesterday's report anyway, to go down in a file that no one would ever look at. I just don't like feeling like a prisoner...or a zoo animal.

I attempt to feign a smile to him from the crusty chair I'm settled in, my thick legs crossed and impatient foot bouncing up and down. Somehow, I think we are resolved since our first meet, though I am still quite bitter about my hand—which happens to feel much better now—and he is more cautious than humanly possible about leaving me to my own devices when no one else is present to bear witness to my shenanigans.

But I'm comfortable in his presence.

Shamefully safe.

He is the only person in Limbo that *really* treated me like they would any other person right out of the gate—stern and unforgiving in his laws to all who try him. So, I myself am able to absolve him of panicked, unintended assault on my good hand, as long as he acquits me for being a bit ambitious. Not that I can promise it wouldn't happen again.

Our eyes meet for a split second and his cheeks flush, breaking contact in a scramble for more work at the other end of the counter and giving in to a grimace while I smirk, my eyes dropping to the page I left off on.

I definitely like reading, as I had initially thought, and the diaries are interesting without a doubt. Haunting. They're mostly written by previous residents of the older villages, but several are from when this one was still a dirt foundation being constructed upon, each compiled into warped parchment laced together by cheap string. I've found six that are crumbling into the same dust that coats them, words grey and fading so each sentence is almost illegible, talking about the first introductions to the region's natives or "Ravagers", as the current villagers call them.

Not that I can deny they have vicious after dark activities, but I think most of the population would be surprised to learn from the context of these words that it didn't start out this way.

The oldest diary I have read this far, claims they came from the forest one night in overwhelming numbers after two years of lone human dwelling. In legions of men upon the ground, they marched without sound through the breaks in the trees, filling the empty streets where children had played before dinner in emotionless vigor. Standing as tall blank slates, witnesses from around the same period had written the creatures appeared devoid of emotion, each inhumanly beautiful face wearing a plain expression absent of a smile or frown, with sharp eyes that focused on an unforeseen target, like thoroughly trained hounds on a blood trail.

They were just...everywhere.

Armed. Dangerous. But not...hostile.

According to an eighteen-year-old girl named Ginger Little, there were a lot of hungry children in the old village. Possibly more than what we have here, if I am reading correctly. A lot of our youth slept on the streets, instead of in housing out there, or died out close to the woods looking for food or parentage. Love.

These natives hyper focused on *them*, and the maintenance of their well-being by feeding them and bringing them water or treats that the rest of the population at the time had not seen before then. Specifically, *fruit*, and dried fruit. But other things too—strange beautiful clothing and hair clips to wear, medicine for their wounds, and handmade toys.

It was almost like a get out of jail free card for that generation of villagers. Children haven't held value to society for a good two hundred years, and no one has ever enjoyed raising them. I'm pretty sure if manufacturers could design a pesticide in the form of a child repellent—without murdering a few by accident—the industry would have boomed. Hell, parents might have been able to ditch their kids more efficiently and womankind would be considered officially liberated from the constraints of our most natural design—the womb.

Letting these children become someone else's problem was a godsend for the old village. But...that is where the problem started, too. In more ways than one.

No one ever cares about what comes next. Not the sentence. Not the paragraph. Not the page or event. Not the *generation*. Society has built itself up to fail, focusing on the right here and now. What we want today, not what we need tomorrow. These villagers didn't pay attention to motive until it was too late. A motive that is still unclear, thanks to weathering pages and potential untimely demise.

Women and children started to disappear in the months to

come, and they have continued to ever since. Except it has grown more violent in our current stage of living—however long it's been since these diaries were officially logged. The natives are out for death to satiate whatever the kidnappings do not, but I haven't found a conclusive point to causation of either event.

"Good morning, Addie." Aidan's voice is tired, shooting to me from across the lobby.

I slap the current diary shut, sneezing at the puff of dirt liberated from its pages by the force, and turning my head to see him shuffling through the empty floor space. Melody waves him in at first sight, a coy grin playing on her lips from her half of the bottom floor. She had sat with me for part of the morning when I was still deciding which diaries to delve into. I enjoyed the company without Zoey to fill the silence when I came home in distress, and she had no problem talking my ear off, though Ace appeared conflicted with it at the time. He treats her like she is one of the stray cats that sneak in through the open door. Specifically, a stray cat that won't leave him alone, even when he asked for her to be here.

*He's the stray cat more than anyone. A straggler.*

Their relationship is a strange one, no doubt, but for a moment this morning, Headquarters almost felt...homey. Like I could relax and dissolve. Dissipate. Melt, like butter on hot bread. Something I wish to do more than ever.

I push the book I have deep into my backpack, rearranging a few clothing items to help it fit. I haven't had the opportunity to change yet, still wearing the same dirt smudged clothes from yesterday, and cheeks clinging to streaks of black soil. But I have every plan to return to the river today. I can wash the few extras I own, and commence searching for the crying woman—whether Aidan wants to or not.

"Morning," I mumble back finally when I close it all up.

As I stand, he takes longer strides, meeting my attempt to swing this beast of luggage over my shoulders with gentle hands ready to help while I bend with its weight like a rubber woman.

His fingers only get to brush the strap before I jerk backward, slinging it on for myself as I learn how to manage this new, but old body, realizing one thing in the process.

I don't want to be touched. Or helped, more than I have to be.

My spinning head catches Ace in this recognition, tensed and frozen as if he were trying to make an impossible decision about an invisible subject. Aidan must have caught the abrupt start as well, his brow furrowing, but hands flying up in defense as he attempts to smooth over the informality with small talk.

He pulls out a piece of bread to chew while he talks. "Did you and your roommate eat well last night? I hope you remembered to get paid after leaving so fast."

I didn't, but Melody took care of that this morning when I came in.

"No," I start, treading with care. "Well, I mean, I did, yes. But my roommate, she didn't come home last night. She's been at The Healing Center since I started work."

There is a pitiful look on his face, one that is difficult to read, but full of sympathy that I don't want. His reply is steady and soft. Sickeningly kind. I would be happier if he told me to fuck off.

"I'm sure she's okay then," he offers with a shake of his head. "Celestyn and her charges are great at keeping the residents well cared for. The Center has only ever been broken into here and there, and the raids are never anything major."

I don't mean to glare, but I do at the mention of *her* name.

Celestyn.

The reigning *mistress* of Satan himself, because she's too evil to be his wife. She'd overthrow him in a position of power and look glorious doing it.

I should be grateful that she didn't leave me beyond The Dome to die like her charges suggested. There are a number of creatures within each layer of the explored Dome so far that could kill me without effort, and no one really knows what lays outside of it because no one has ever returned from the deepest explorations, to my knowledge. But knowing who I am right at this very second, I think it's easy to say that I would have died if I had been pushed that far out.

So, by theory, I should adore her for saving me the misery brought on by the dangers of nature.

But she condoned the spread of whatever false information entrapped my entire being, and she dampened the vital facts granted to me at release from The Center, which could have gotten me killed right away. Or I could have been kidnapped, had I not lucked out that first night—given the current nature of the natives.

It was enough by my standards to hold a grudge, even if the end result was that I'm still alive to see another day out.

"They're never *not* major," I reply with venom after taking a second to wind down, walking to Ace who retracts himself from the counter's edge as I do. "Can I come back later?"

He hasn't removed his eyes from the situation, the current file wadding in his closing fist. I can't help feeling like if I got any closer to him, he'd have to shower in bleach just to feel clean again. Still, he nods. Slow. I nod too, tapping my fingers against the countertop and turning around to find Melody monitoring the situation across the room, much closer than she was but not intrusive. She flickers a nervous smile to us all when I wave in acknowledgment, worry dancing behind stretched lips that are twitchy and stiff.

*How long have they been here?* I wonder.

I feel rude for not already asking, but Melody is the one person Ace is truly comfortable around, so it feels like a valid question. At first, I thought maybe in another life, they could have been in love. The longer I'm around them, I understand it just doesn't fit their image. Their dynamic is more than that, I think. It is rooted in unspoken trust and trial, annoyance and failure.

*Failure* and defeat.

I brush any remaining crumbs from my early breakfast off my clothes, and give a small wave to the entire lobby, following Aidan out the doors and into the bright light that isn't done justice by the grim, almost windowless building. It is refreshing, burning comfortably against my skin for the walk across the grass to the markets, where it becomes insufferable. Ducking under the twists of cloth used to shade the local hot spot helps this to an extent, but the river is ever the more inviting the longer we move. It's all I can think about when we breach the walls of foliage guarding the entry to the rest of the world.

That and Zoey. But she would have to wait.

I veer away from Aidan almost right away, slipping through the first several trees and a patch of dense brush to march back toward the riverside where we sat yesterday. Or at least where I felt it might be, based off our point of entry the day prior. At my side, Aidan shakes his head in immediate astonishment, his agitation clear as he spins ahead on weary heels. He stops short of me, pulling me by the same arm he had already brutalized when I attempt to walk around him, and swinging me to face him.

He gives way to a slight involuntary chuckle.

"What are you *doing*?" he growls with a smile. "I thought we talked about this. Yesterday? Do you remember? You don't know what you're doing here. Your job is to follow me. Listen to me. Do what I teach you. Stay in the lines that I *will* draw."

My eyes narrow. I pry my arm free in a fast, hard shove as the pain of what bruising is still present from our last incident prickles up to my elbow like the bone itself were being struck with a mallet over and over. Aidan shuffles with arms spread to keep his balance, shifting and glaring behind his black glasses.

"People are missing," I hiss, checking over the area he touched. It's a string of luck my injuries never stay long. "They deserve to be looked for. That is what the books on Ace's shelves said the original search teams did. That is *why* we are *paid* so damn much."

He reaches for me again, and I sidestep toward a set of trees.

I could do this all day if I had to, but I won't. I'll leave his infant ass here if he won't commit.

"You're tough." Aidan crosses his arms. "I admire that. I *like* that. But here's a question: did those books also tell you how many people died in those outdated efforts? Did it mention how quickly we burned through search teams back then? *Entire* teams, no less? Using antiquated strategies with the knowledge we have now, won't help the people that need saving and going to the same place twice over one woman is moronic. At. Best."

I step further from him and he stays still. Watching. Breathing deepening.

"I'll go alone," I warn, instead of hearing out his logic. "If you're scared, I'll just go by myself. I don't have anything to lose helping someone else."

I can't stop myself from wanting this. Wanting to do this. Every action I have taken since waking, every word spoken, is a calling from the most carnal parts of myself that I can't deny, and my brain heeds each command without hesitation like it has no choice.

Aidan sighs at this, head shaking and eyes trailing to the sky in thought.

"Fine," he muses. "We will take a *different* path, but we will go deep into the second layer of The Dome today, staying next to the river where these creatures often walk. That is my compromise."

I don't want to compromise. Compromise means neither of us get our way and no one is happy, but we pretend like there was a fair trade off somewhere in the deal that should make everyone smile. It's just...he knows these forests better than me. He knows the trails missing persons are generally led down, and where to avoid so we aren't gored by wild animals.

If I'm being honest with myself, now that I've had a moment to think through my own actions, I am terrified. Out of my mind. Not because I don't feel what I said, but because having nothing to lose scares me more than if I did. If something bad happens, I don't know what I'm leaving behind, or if I'll miss it. I'm in a permanent state of ignorance.

But I have to know for my own sanity that I made every effort to find the screaming woman. Not just for her, but for my selfish desire to have a clean conscience. Because I can't get the sound out of my brain, nor the weeping that followed it. The pleading. The panic.

I can't unhear it long enough to shut my eyes.

And if it wasn't the sound of her voice, it would have been another. It would have been the ones that are more tangible just beyond the front door, coupled with the smell of blood spilling at the peak of night when I should be asleep in a bed somewhere far from here. It would have been the children in the diaries that never came home, or the innocence robbed when the natives pulled human men out of bed in the dead of winter to gut them in the snow. It would have been sorrow, a shrill cry for humanity somewhere in the midst of people who lost it in a scurry to survive this madness.

It would have been me, because if I don't take some kind of action against it, it will be.

So, I acquiesce.

"Okay."

Even if it's a bitter agreement, it's something, and supposedly that's better than nothing.

Notably, Aidan is content with the decision. He must feel like he has made the proper call, straightening and uncrossing his arms, leading the way toward the river in a different path that felt like more of the same, despite it having the same result on my psyche. A positive one.

I don't feel so caged out in the open, away from the village and its variety of clowns. The plant life and smell of clean water barreling in waves toward a rocky shore cleanse my brain of bitter discontent and building rage, erasing my feelings to a blanker state. A more focused state where I realize that all around us grows the sound of birds and bugs and small chirping dragons. Somewhere overhead in the treetops, I am sure I also hear the mewl of a cat that had spotted us first, calling from where it hunts squirrels and fowl.

Melody helped me chase down a feral cat in Headquarters this morning while we ate, the pitch-black feline roaming Ace's countertop and looking for mice undoubtedly hiding within the stacks of paper he hordes. The delicate combination of pace and race to get within arm's reach of the slinky ball of sleek fur was incredible, adrenaline inducing and fun loving—a wad of emotion

I wasn't sure could go together since waking up. I had a desire in that moment, to touch something new, to brush its fur with the tips of my fingers and know what it was like when the animal was still warm instead of cold taxidermy in a museum.

I wanted to understand everything. To know what cats eat and where their favorite spots to be touched are. Do they like hugs? Or are they as aloof as they like to appear? Will they bite? Or is the hiss all talk?

Being away from the constant reminder that I can die any second without knowing who I am gives me hope one day I'll have my answers.

The sound of the river's elegant tides breaks my thought process, and I stumble around Aidan, slipping down a small embankment in a hurry to have a drink, my water bottle having been empty for several hours now. My partner follows at an even pace, careful and wading alongside me in the ankle-deep shallows. He doesn't ever seem as amused by the ebb and flow as I am, going straight to the business of filling his canteen and stepping out to sit ashore. Meanwhile, I retreat to set my bag out of reach from the wave-happy water, a complex system that is breathing in and out with every push of clear blue. I take a handful of clothes I brought for the adventure and sit where I know it is safe for me, scrubbing them the best I can with my hands given the time I am gifted.

When I finish, I wring them tight and lay them over a blanket I use overnight to guard the less waterproof items in my backpack. Aidan leads us back up the embankment, and we follow the edge of the river out, as he suggested, until we are well through the second layer of The Dome, the boundaries of its containment looking a bit lighter than they did yesterday. Pinkish.

Out this direction, there are no signs of men or women alike anywhere. No children either, though we find other trinkets. Wallets and watches. A unicorn sneaker and a plush bear missing his button nose. I find an earring dangling a turquoise gem, almost busted free of its silver base. Aidan finds a dagger a bit further ahead buried in a pile of large grey rocks, and the long sleeve of a purple shirt, shorn off without any signs of the rest of the garment.

But no actual people.

Never any living, breathing bodies.

I watch hours pass in disappointment, the top of the embankment we walk along becoming denser with foliage, pushing us further from the riverbank and up into the forestry. Waves crash against the grassy ledge we climb, moving uphill in unfamiliar spaces. Half a mile more, we are forced closer to the trees where Aidan warns me to watch for snakes, as being bitten by one is described as a "not fun" journey to The Healing Center where life and limb are not guaranteed.

He makes me walk in front of him at this time, so he can be a better help in case I fall off the ledge to the greedy fists of river waves below—though, as a dancer, I probably have far more grace than he ever will. I've been rediscovering these gnarled toes as crooked windows to my past, learning my practically nonexistent limitations and balances. So I can't pretend like he's doing me a favor this way, but I won't fault him for his mother-henning either. Something tells me his share of experience is in the art of fragile women.

Not that there is anything wrong with a woman who *isn't* a fighter.

But that's not me. It's not who I am in this day.

Another fourth of a mile grows more space for us to walk amongst, the river growing too loud to hear over, but Aidan's interest in conversation heightening. He's restless, calling to me in a voice that screams of anxiety, despite every attempt to keep it steady.

"So, where...uh...I saw you've been reading those dusty old books. Where is your research leading you?" His arm curls around a tree so he can scoot between two others without risking a dangerous plummet. "Anything good in there? Or useful?"

I do my best to indulge, to get along.

"No. Erm...not really." My hips almost block me from squeezing through two smaller ashen trunks. I make it, but it will smart come morning, scabbed at least. "It's just a bunch of diaries, I guess? Autobiographies? I don't know, but it *is* interesting."

We can walk side by side again when he pulls forward and wipes the sweat from his forehead with a half-rolled sleeve.

"Well, thank god it's not boring," he remarks, shaking his hands.

I roll my eyes.

"Laugh all you want," I reply. "You asked."

He does laugh, unaffected by my bitter tones. Carefree, but still somehow guarded.

"I never have time for reading, and I was never great at it either. I was what they call...hmm...dyslexic? Well, I mean, I guess I still am. It makes writing music a real bitch. But I've always wanted to know what the old fuckers before us had to say about living here."

I shrug. "Not much. It was hard and it sucked."

"That's not interesting."

He's persistent.

"A couple of the really old diaries are firsthand accounts of the initial appearances of the locals," I admit, gauging his reaction as I go. "The people then just weren't as afraid, and by all witness statements, they had no reason to be. The locals didn't start out aggressive and most people didn't really think about them for a while."

"They're the *locals* now?" Aidan chuckles, his feet crunching grass and stone beside me, head turning each direction.

He's surveying the area.

Should I too? He hasn't mentioned it.

I smirk. "Well, yes, sort of. The way I see it, this might be their land we have taken up residency on. It's not like the thought hadn't occurred to the older residents as well, when the attacks picked up. Surely, you guys aren't so naïve that you believe otherwise. They're more well-dressed than us and they have better weapons. It seems pretty obvious they were here first."

The ledge thins once more but the drop off is steeper. Falling would be like hitting concrete from this height.

"It's not that obvious." His breathing quickens, grunting as I stumble. He catches my arm, so I don't have the chance to slide, shimmying me back to stable dirt. "Maybe we have all lived on the same land this whole time and just never knew about one another, and they just advanced faster."

"That wouldn't make them any more aggressive by default," I point out. "Plus, they don't primarily speak any of our languages, but a lot of the journals make claims they can speak about any other that they come into contact with at least once, so they can communicate major problems. Their brains are comparable to super computers. Hardly deserving of the term *Ravager*."

We stop.

"That's impossible." Aidan sighs.

He glances up toward the sun through the break in the canopy. It is scalding, and searing white in visible squiggles of heat bouncing off the exposed ground. His skin is well-adjusted to the fiery death ray that heats this world, but mine would look like a cooked lobster by the end of this.

"Not necessarily, if you take into account that we wake up with no memory, under a Purple Dome, and that none of this is really possible."

He grimaces. "If they could, it would mean they understand exactly what they're doing when people plead for their lives or beg to stay. It wouldn't be something as simple as turf confusion."

I think about this.

"I suppose you have me there. But I feel like we are missing information. They're intelligent, and by all firsthand accounts, kind, to start out. That doesn't just change for no reason."

He's been holding back, I can tell. But something about this protective wall snaps, and crumbles like a paper house.

"They rape women, you know. *After* they kidnap them. Sometimes they do it before though. But the end result is always the same. You can't paint a pretty picture on that."

There is a brief silence. I'm stunned into quiet, trying to find the words I want to speak.

"I don't want to paint a pretty picture," I heave. "Just an honest one."

"I can respect that." He half smiles.

We trek on from here in awkward speechlessness until the ledge steeps down into another lofty bank where we find a small mountain of rough grey rocks jutting from the ground to sit upon, overlooking the late afternoon tides. The water still looks really deep further out, like it didn't have any shallows at this edge, but more of a drop off into a bottomless abyss. How does one river have so many depths in so many places?

My mind begins to wander, and I cross my legs.

Is it lunch time or are we just resting?

I never thought I would miss routine until now. Lunch was always between noon and two, and anyone could go find a safe place, like a coffee shop or a bookstore, to eat in peace. What happened to that? Where are the places I'm recalling in such detail that I can smell them? My memory is coming full circle, just like Zoey said it would, but I'm no closer to home given each one I collect.

My fingers search through the dirt and grass and rocks from our perch of stone. Did anyone lose anything else I could find? I don't want to remember anything more right now. There's so much to take in, and I still need to check in on Zoey eventually. I promised I'd help her to an extent in exchange for crashing in her cellar. And I can't do that if she's stuck at The Healing Center...

Not to mention, we need to have a serious talk in light of recent information.

"The Healing Center is the safest place to be during attacks." His earlier sentiments ring at the back of my thoughts when I speak, absent. I don't want to be here. "But no one is allowed to stay there unless they are sick or injured. It's meant to protect the vulnerable and weak, but isn't that kind of the whole population? Why has no one thought of that?"

Aidan pauses. His arms tense, and he doesn't look at me. He can't seem to take his eyes off the shoreline.

"When security measures in The Center were looser, and Celestyn was still sort of new, there was a freshly quarantined resident that escaped during an exam." He shakes his head as though reliving the disdain. "I mean, not that anyone could blame her for snapping. It's not like staying at a five-star hotel or anything, and the girl was both young and terrified. Practically a baby, but still an adult, if you catch my drift."

I raise an eyebrow. "Ah, the boundary of an undefeatable liver and chronic back pain."

"You've got it." He nods. "She was eighteen? Nineteen? Well, she was young, and she just...freaked out. The door opened for the first discharge exam and Celestyn looked inside. She was surprised not to see anyone right away, but she said the girl just came out of nowhere. Took Celestyn by the back of the head and slammed her face into the door so hard it broke her nose. And then she just...ran."

"No one caught up with her?"

"The guards tried when they figured out what happened. Screamed for her. *Hey, it's not safe out there.* But she went into these woods and she never came out."

"Never to be seen again." I apply ghost fingers for effect, but only to conceal how uncomfortable the tale has made me. I can't cope with it right now. It resonates inside the best parts of me, despite my will to push it away, souring.

Aidan smiles like he always does. He's weirdly happy for a guy stuck in these parts. Or he's possibly psychotic.

"My point is, the people in quarantine—the sick, the injured—they're all far more vulnerable and frightened and unsure than we are. They require more superior protections than informed individuals, Addie. If we put everyone in the same place, it would just lead them to the jackpot of our population."

"Is that why a massive part of quarantine and holding is separated from the rest of The Healing Center by a big steel wall?" I counter. "To keep them safe?"

I look to the clear sky. It will be getting late soon. From the corner of my eye, I peer back to Aidan, awaiting his reply, though this seems to startle him to an extent. His body jerks and his brow furrows as he shifts from me with subtle care, monitoring the ground between us, as if he could not continue to look me in the face for this conversation.

"They keep potentially infectious or dangerous people separated from The Center by a steel wall, yes," he replies. "It is left open to the forest but guarded from the village. If these people are kidnapped or killed while hazardous, we still win. And if they aren't..."

"Who wins?!" I snap. "Who? The people don't win. It isn't their fault. Why do they get to be the sacrificial lamb?"

He bites his lip. I'm an electric fence with a warning sign, and he knows it. He knows *something*.

"I'm sorry you were separated. I am. But you made it out..."

"Great!" I zap right back at him. "And you know who didn't? People. Just. Like. Me."

"That's not true!" Aidan shouts over me. "It's not. The Center hasn't suffered a direct attack in almost a year. It's like the Ravagers have forgotten about it altogether while they focus on the village. Our plan works."

There is a crippling silence, and I pull my legs toward my chest, the heat radiating blasts of fire through my black leggings and baking my jean shorts.

"You're underestimating your enemy." My voice is tart. Hard. "They can interpret and learn any language just by hearing it once with little flaw, and you're telling me that they just...forgot? Forgot about every single one of your sick and injured and confused? I would say that's fucking precious, but it's actually just stupid. The Center needs assigned guards throughout the night. The search teams have enough people to rotate that duty."

He waves his hands, sitting straighter than before. "And who's going to risk their neck for that, huh? You tell me. It's a fast way to lose your own life as you know it, that's for sure. What we have right now is enough because it has to be. The system was broken prior to us getting here, and it can't be fixed with a little clear tape. If you follow the rules as they stand, you'll last longer."

He has continued to inch further and further from me as our conversation ensues. Part of me wanted to believe I was imagining it at first, but now he is on the edge of our rocky pile, and he is trying his best not to look at me. Instead, he is watching smaller waves crash against the cleft of warped stony shore further out.

I stand to meet him where he begins to rise, looking down as several shapes emerge just out of sight from my previous angle. When I see it in focus, I have to double take to assure that my eyes have seen it correctly and I understand, at once, why he couldn't concentrate on our conversation.

From the crashing water crawls half-naked humanesque forms with thick scaled tails, varying in sleek patterns, flipping back and forth like pendulums to beach them. At this height, I can see both genders are extraordinarily long, the men alone having been at least as tall as Ace or longer. Their glistening skin is tinted individual colors from pitch to grey, occasionally green, and scaled in patches on their cheeks, forehead, and jawline. Wet, tangled hair is long and uncut, laced with webs of moss and pale shells, a few of the women donning cages of bone to surround their skulls like morbid crowns strung with rotting guts. Those who do not wear these elaborate headdresses sit nearby them in servility, singing haunting melodies to the wind.

I creep forward, watching the spot on their heads in place of ears, opening magnificent frills to the gentle breeze, folding to the sides of their face when nothing responds to their tune. Thin gills part as ridges along their cheek bones, reacting to the oxygen, yet not suffocating. Only...adjusting.

"Are those..."

Aidan lunges so that I cannot finish my sentence, covering my mouth, and stepping us backward. Small rocks clatter downhill when we move, drawing attention to where we stand and causing the lesser women to lift their heads. Bloodshot, coppery eyes glint with feral intent as they open wide mouths to expose a sharp toothed hiss that shrieks murder through the trees.

Several of the crowned women fling themselves into the water, but the lessors remain with the men who whip around on yellow nailed fingers, raking their way our direction with heaves of their powerful fish ends.

Without looking back, Aidan yanks me from the rocky hillside, pulling me higher up on the ledge we descended from and across the upper cliff sides. I allow him to drag me along in a stumbling stupor until their high-pitched hissing is little more than a memory that only the insides of my skull can remember, worse than nails on a chalkboard.

I am shaken. Paler. Wiser.

My whole body quivers while I try to find a single word amongst the millions waiting to spill off the tip of my tongue. Aidan holds his face while I panic, pulling on his olive skin as though it were a fake mask he wore, and he was ready to reveal his true identity. Instead, he finds the words I have lost.

"Those were mermaids," he confirms, letting out a heavy breath and catching it again. "Not quite what you'd expect, I'm sure. They weren't what I envisioned, anyway."

He's trying to regather himself, but I'm afraid to stop moving now. I shuffle around him, wandering further from the riverside now that we have emerged back on the other part of the cliff we came in on.

"They're beautiful," I only half-lie, listening to him move in behind me.

"They're fish," Aidan replies, "and vicious. They'll eat anything if they're hungry enough, including each other. This time I think they were only trying to scare us, so they must be well fed by *something*. But if they wanted to, they could have caught us pretty fast. I've seen it happen."

I frown, catching glimpses of the water through the trees as we pass by, thinking of all the time he had let me spend out in the shallows with the knowledge that these creatures dwelled below the surface. Was he also trying to get me killed?

"We should go home now," I whisper.

Through the trees, I can see small rings ebb out on the river's surface just beyond the shore. Aidan must see it too, nodding.

"I agree."

As we start to diverge further from the riverside we came in on, I look behind us one more time to see tens of heads emerge further out where my feet would just barely touch. Each set of eyes glitter with desire and curiosity, yearning to ask questions unheard, and yet knowing none would be answered.

I duck closer to Aidan, fingers reaching for his plaid shirt but not quite grasping. I wonder how fast these creatures could crawl like spurned nightmares over rocks and bramble before they exhaust themselves. No amount of distance makes me feel safe enough, and again, deep in my ears, I can hear their fetid, dusky lullaby. Reaching for me. With an invisible finger, their scramble of words lock around my very willpower so that leaving is hard. Harder than it should be.

It is a relief when we arrive back in the village, the group waiting for us just off to the right and already amid discussion of their finds, throwing blurs of items into burlap sacks to distribute at the markets. Ethan looks up at the sound we make coming through the tree line and first Dome layer, waving Aidan over—though he doesn't break eye contact with me.

"Ace is on out in the village, boy!" Glue Man delights as my partner breaks from my side, flashing me a brief apologetic smile. "Now, ya damn well know what that means."

I don't, but the rest of them seem to. It can't be good, as Aidan leaves our end of the report vague and to the point. He drops all of his personal finds into the bag, and hurries into the village housing, nodding to the rest of the team in a half-assed goodbye and claiming to them that he had to find Celestyn.

They wave him off, and I feel their many sets of eyes settle on me, daring me to approach. I rub my thumb along my upper arm in dismay, debating it since I have junk to turn in as well. That and the human contact, although negative, is to die for in some drastic change since this morning.

Loneliness is beginning to swallow me whole, eating me alive and digesting this guard I have set up. I slump off their scrutiny in a blush, deciding against approach and making a break for home, opening the door to find once again, Zoey is absent.

The home is empty.

The blood-stained sheets from our morning together is only slightly askew from where she left them when we made our way to get me a job, and the cellar door is just barely ajar.

I'm afraid to go to The Center to look for her, remembering all the ill faces of people who wanted me more than gone—of people who wanted me dead. But I can't help wondering if she needs me right this second. If I am failing my very purpose to her.

Am I failing her, waiting for her to come home on her own?

I scuttle to the corner where her blankets rest, pulling my photo album out of my backpack from beneath the wet clothes and blanket, and some cheese off the counter that I left this morning. I flip through each page of four until I can't make out the images in the darkness, every colored print-out a gateway to my life and my studio. My world.

There are a few pictures of myself with my students as a class, smiling. Laughing. Beaming.

There is another of me dancing on a brilliant stage, just a little thinner, though not by much. Stretched from head to pointed toe, fingers spread like feathers ready to help me fly.

One more of myself staring out an open window to a smoggy sky high above the ground, overseeing other rooftops.

My personal favorite is one where I stood on the base of a stone statue of an elephant, posing in front of one of the last zoos in the world, though I have no memory of going in.

I can't help but wonder who took all of these pictures, if not me. Or if my camera had a timer.

It looked like a lonely life I led, but I didn't appear unhappy at all. It shouldn't be this hard to feel happy, ever. And if no one else, I will make sure that there is not a woman more that should suffer the pain of this life. There will not be a woman out in the woods I will refuse to save. There is not a disappearance I won't try to solve. Not a soul will I forget.

A heavy burden to carry but fitting for this new person I am creating within myself, as I shimmy down my shorts and wrap

Zoey's blood dried blankets around my shoulders for warmth against the nighttime breeze.

These stitches are coming out now, and I will pull each one free of this damaged flesh with care to this healed body. This *very quickly* healed body.

Because this is my unraveling.

The protective paper that hides the person beneath is falling away to reveal the gift Limbo doesn't know it needs.

Compassion. Empathy. Understanding.

*Me.*

# CHAPTER NINE
## SAHANNA

A SLINKY GREY CAT WEAVES THROUGH THE GLITTERING lavender sawteeth of the battlements, roaring in delight as it slips along each smooth edge. It stretches, its rubber body stumbling as it lets the uneven grooves of pale amethyst caress the slim density of its glassy fur. Carved and polished, the perfect defensive shapes sitting atop the packed, pearl white curtain wall veined with black press in all the right places for the ultimate stone massage this morning, before the guard takes needless shift in the sanctity of the Fae.

Less than casually, I creep at a distance from my latest victim— the current target for my unbridled affections. I call her Mouser, although considering where we are so close to the sky, perhaps I should call her dove. Or bird.

*Bove? Dird?*

I don't care. It doesn't matter.

It's quiet high upon the world where I like it best. Far away from the primary castle sights and sounds and duties consuming my existence, I am free to pursue the true ambitions anchored to the person I consider my real self, rather than the blissful front I pose to fly under the radar.

Trauma doesn't exist here in my safe space. I've convinced myself it can't reach me, the same as the cat has convinced itself I can't catch it. Being left alone in these water-locked lands, I can breathe every time we visit like it is the first I've done it for each second I spend roaming the height of the wall walks.

Which I do, roam. Whenever I get the chance. Not that I often would if I didn't take matters into my own hands.

It is warm at this hour, the pink and blood orange sun just getting around to rising over the checkered white and magenta treetops reflects generous beams of light off the surface of the water surrounding the castle of the Fae. This all separates its king from the actual island cities, as well as the intricate land bridges, drawbridge, and whatever swims beneath the endless depths of surging currents belonging to the ocean-sized river which pools around the islands and set of mountains wherein the Fae reside, forming a thunderous waterfall at the castle's rear entrance.

A complete natural beauty of this world, if one is lucky enough to be a Fae.

I am not.

Mouser skips ahead on tiny pink toe pads, peeking back at me, who follows from a careful distance. Dainty. Curious. Grinning. I like to pretend that this isn't a game we have played all morning, as if I have not been behind every cautionary glare I've been given.

*Not me, no.*

I look away into the wide-open world, subtle for this short duration while I side eye the clever fluff trotting onward.

*You're so paranoid, little one. I'm not following you at all. I was already going this way. I definitely, one thousand percent, did not stalk you from the courtyard.*

Once the distance is set, I carry on, running my fingers across the stone. It feels foreign in places, other-worldly and smooth on the amethyst. It has an earthy smell only rocks have, mingling alongside pungent, bitter tangles of dark green ivy bearing sweet blooms of night blue and purple flowers, climbing away from the violent rush of river water and rooting itself between deep seated creases in the white walls that outline each individual block of rock used to make this structure.

I pick at the greenery I can reach, my heart pounding and breath quickening the faster I move and the more anxious I become. Walking for several hours is a lot of work when most of life as I know it consists of bed rest and studies to catch up on the culture I've been enslaved into. But escaping my decorated prison cell to avoid these mandatory activities is far more taxing than I imagined. My body makes sure to remind me of this when my stomach pangs less than quietly with sharp regret that I didn't take the breakfast sent to my room prior to climbing out on the balcony with nothing but my bony hands and footholds to guide me to the gloriously expansive courtyard, where I made an early break for the open gates while my "husband" attended his king brother in yet another meeting.

It is something I know will cause me severe penalties if he were to find out—though he rarely does. Not when duty calls at all hours of the night, and the hours in between beg for what minutes of sleep he can rake in. Not to mention, he would be a fool not to understand, after the seasons we have spent with one another, that containing me is a laughable endeavor. I'm a restless soul, and the manner of which the wheel this society turns is not one I'm well suited for. Not that I think any woman is befitted to adhere without question to the demands of men, but there are those who adjust faster than others.

I suppose though, if I really think about it, I have it lucky when compared to most women chained to this purpose.

What am I lacking other than personal choice?

I have chronic access to The King's personal serving staff since I am wed to his closest brother. I can eat whatever I ask for—locally sourced and fresh grown foods lacking modern chemicals or mutations, learning in this process that I possess quite the affinity for peaches. I am sheltered and warm in the brutal winters, protected at all costs due to being imprinted upon by a member of the royal family. My clothing is stitched without flaw and my wardrobe is bigger than the three outfits I laundered on repeat when I lived at my real home on Earth.

Hell, I don't even have to do my own wash now.

I have a relative freedom others do not have, in my last life and this one combined, even if it's a forced freedom.

Or so I like to tell myself.

It gets me through the day to pretend as if I have some kind of privilege others do not, like it would be selfish to complain that the reality of my liberty couldn't be further and further from the truth. Because the truth is, like most women, I live in basic bondage to this universe of sick, hormonal creatures. A life without the choices that matter.

I am stuck in servitude.

*Yes.*

*Of course.*

*As you wish.*

Disgusting.

All of the rules my husband has made are clear and defined. One of them states I shouldn't be out here at all without him, so high on the curtain wall in this...condition. It's dangerous. And I can fall if I lean in just the right avenue. My balance is already a bit askew anymore, being five—nearly six—months pregnant. I had slipped a week ago following cats in the stairwells to the kitchens. The tumble down the last few steps sent the help into a frenzy against my pleas to pretend it didn't happen, all of them dropping their duties to seek out the man who placed this burden upon me.

*The dumb hens.*

I don't mean that...I think.

I'm only bitter.

Really, the Fae is built on kind, peaceful people. Nothing like the race who kidnaps and brutalizes women. The Fae king is extraordinary and powerful, older than time and space itself, with a young face and a few children of his own who are just as exceptional. Trusting. The four-year-old makes me look like a regular useless piece of shit.

But even so, I actually like it here—or, at least, I like it better than our usual residence where I sit alone in a dark castle, stripped of any feeling. When I'm here, there is more. Overlooking the expanse of a whole city and knowing there are people out there that I can talk to is a breath of fresh air after spending much of my life thus far in what feels like a coffin. When I'm home, it is the memories of what I had, prior to this mess, that keep a light in my fire.

Mouser hesitates at the stairs, beginning the descent from the battlements, bobbing at the first flight as if she might launch off into the space below. So much braver than me. I pause too, holding my sad stomach and wondering if it will hinder my ability to run if I can't see my feet. Will I really be upset if I tumble hard and fast to an imminent, neck-breaking agony?

*Too bad I can't pull the whole unit to the side,* I remiss, traipsing slower toward my prey of love.

Our eyes meet, again, and the sweet baby's ears fold flat against her head. She growls, releasing a cool hiss as she leaps in a daring dart for freedom that I find myself racing after in absence of thought. I bound for the place where she stood, slapping onto the wall in a solid miss, and my body flinging through the space between the merlons. The force of it grinding into my stomach makes me gasp, my hands frantic to find the stone and throttling me backward when they meet their mark.

I growl at this failure, all in good fun...for now.

My hair catches the stone when I move along the wall, attempting to keep my balance closer to solid structure. I rush down the stairs after Mouser, still in my sights, though just barely. My fingers flex with each curve we hug, each stumble we make righted on our descent into madness, my hands yearning to touch her. Just once. Whether or not it hurt.

At the last step of this chase, she speeds into the courtyard like the fastest creature known to man, burrowing under an open wagon filled with buckets of produce and grain. I'm panting, starting forward then stopping at the sight of armed guards advancing in my direction, gold armor sleek against their skin. Lightweight, as it always is in the Fae. The image of them is enough to remind me that I shouldn't be here, though it does bring a sense of normalcy in comparison to my usual travels.

The Fae have much shorter ears than their dark elven counterparts, though still pointed, it feels more human. I had noticed it when we first visited their lands after my marriage was privately...consummated. They were much shorter people than I had expected since witnessing the average of my husband's father race—so much closer to the size of regular people, instead of lumbering giants—that I had been thrown off. I had actually believed, for just a second, that I had been taken home.

Thin. Large. Muscular. Wan.

It is almost...normal, and it is always less intimidating being around them in general when I am supposed to be. Though at this minute, I am not.

"Is that..." one of the guards start, and my legs pump faster than with the cat.

"Wait!" I hear them shout.

But I am the cat now—far gone, though they don't chase long.

It puts too much risk on the baby, I think. Pregnancies don't end well with me, but this is the fourth, and it is the closest I've come to the big finish. The *live* finish.

My husband has become hopeful, I believe.

Too hopeful, but it is fair.

The King is a renowned medic. More so than anyone in the land, and he's chosen to remain rather close to us throughout this particular pregnancy at my husband's request. It is his family too, after all, and family is an important piece of their culture.

But it doesn't matter. It never does, if I can help it. Because I don't want this.

I never did, despite following this insanity.

The dark elven customs are cruel to women. Oppressive in the name of protection and rampant population crisis. Wives are entirely submissive to their husbands with so few rights in comparison to what I recall having in times prior, it makes my head spin. All I am required to do is present my husband with heirs, to whatever shit storm this is now, that we will raise together, and in turn I have his undivided protection and everlasting life.

The kicker being that he cannot live without me. Literally. If I die, it will kill him too. But I would give anything to live without him, including die—when I am brave enough.

When I was a little girl, I had a shelf of books in my bedroom that I shared with my older sister in our first home. Like most girls my age, I had many pink books painted with princesses in beautiful dresses and tiaras. They donned fragile heeled shoes and big smiles with perfect lipstick. Prince Charming was a savior from a terrible life and not a gateway to a horrible existence. Everything was perfect then, though I didn't know it.

I would beg my mother on those nights, every night, to read me one specific book about a princess in a blue dress. It was easiest to fall into that fantasy as a little girl who knew no better, dreaming of being hunted down by a special person willing to take away all the nightmares I thought I had then.

I would give anything for that book. To read it again. Just once more.

Because I need the fantasy.

And I need my mother.

*I have the dress, Mom,* the voice inside my head is much less confident than the one on the outside.

I let out a slow stream of steady air, flattened against pale gargantuan arcading. Several maids pass me by without a glance, laughing amongst themselves and dressed in white silk flowing past their ankles. On Earth, I would have been envious, of course, but real poverty is almost nonexistent in all regions here. Everyone has something to work with, somehow. It's a strange mix of heaven and hell.

I duck my chin toward my chest and pace fast along the empty corridors where I know no one resides. Not a soul is allowed in these sectors, other than an occasional guard when The King holds his meetings. He's furtive this way, always several moves ahead of those who dare fight him, though I don't know who would. I wouldn't.

The archways stream sunshine inside that bounces off the stone floor, shimmering in flecks of dazzling light. I follow them, wondering if I can remember where my room is at without scaling the castle walls. When I was a normal teenage girl rather than a strange, miserable adult, my whole family fit in a one-bedroom trailer. My parents slept on the living room floor while my siblings and I all shared a room...until I moved out, anyway.

The castle, though, is enormous. All castles are, I am finding, and most of the villagers' homes. There are entire towers here dedicated to servants' quarters, halls dedicated to dining, and rooms dedicated to drinking. My last home barely had a kitchen and we didn't have a table, let alone benches where hundreds feasted in celebrations, or courtyards big enough to fit an entire city. We had a lot of weeds in our old yard though, enough to get lost in a couple times when my father started yelling.

Voices catch me off guard as I pass the massive double entry to the throne room where two kings and my husband sit, addressing the concerns that brought us here to the restricted lands of the Fae to begin with.

I teeter on my heels, glancing over my shoulder to see no one there, and imagining it means the guard is changing as of current to relieve the last. Or the current guard had to relieve himself. Either way, it grants me some leeway and I shuffle toward the entry, just slightly ajar so I can hear.

The Fae king, Kai, is the first voice I hear, collected as he is and serene in comparison to my husband and his brother.

Unlikely to start a war with people weaker than him out of resentment.

"I am afraid to ask of the human village to our south," he claims, pacing. I'm late to the conversation, I realize, but I'm good at catching up when I eavesdrop. "Of the business conducted in that region and what becomes of it when it returns to ash."

There is a clatter of something hard across the floor, and a silence that follows. I'm afraid to peek around the door's edge, their eyesight quite keen when compared to humanity.

"It is almost endearing," my husband starts, avoiding the question, "that they've come to name it as their own. Their disregard for their situation, as well as their fight, is admirable at points. Limbo? I've heard it called. Interesting."

"They are stuck." King Kai seeks information in a curious dig for gold. He's desperate but trying to keep composure. "Lost. I would have the rest of them in the Fae to avoid their slaughter, if you allow, of course."

Another silence.

The King, my husband's brother, speaks in turn. "Pity would continue to perpetuate the very parasitic complication that has brought them here. They will die after the completed evacuations are filled."

"They are but trying to survive." King Kai's voice is softer, with more reason. I don't pity his job, trying to persuade what cannot be. But I enjoy him. If I have to be in this place, I would rather it be under his command than the one I have. "The only creations of both..."

A pause.

"I see." He submits to the authority of The King, for he is only the Fae superior. "Very well."

"Many of our primary troops require a soft recovery," my husband tells them. "Quite a few were critically injured in the last wave, as the humans have developed a few items of self-defense. Others would like to spend a month with their newer offspring, perhaps less. If their king approves or denies it."

"If it is so they are injured by human steel," The King scoffs, "perhaps they should be called to training in place of recovery."

I can hear my husband scrawl something on paper. "Mer-folk have moved closer to the villages as of late, taking advantage of those unfamiliar to the region. A few of ours were gored in the last wave by a school that emerged from the river attempting to take human children. The children are intact, though one did lose an arm to the elbow."

"Have him brought to the Fae if he is not placed," Kai commands, though he has little place to do so in presence of the true king. "He could quarter within the castle walls, and many of ours learn to fight with only a single hand, our weaponry much lighter and versatile."

"It is a girl," my husband comments, and they fall silent.

My heart is decimated for her.

"Absolutely not," The King replies. "As for the troops, two weeks with family will have to suffice while battles have yet to be fought. When the eyesore of a village is razed to the ground, we will see to it they spend a proper year with their families and in training before the next phase of operations begin."

"Does that mean you will be making your departure soon?" Kai clicks closer to the door and I skitter away, looking either direction down the hall only to catch the new guard closing in on me, his eyes growing at the knowledge of who I am, and mine at who he is.

Icarus, the son of the great Fae king, who has often trained in the guards and sat in wait for his father's position for millions of years. He still looks like a boy, in most senses, young and sprightly. He carries a spear haphazardly with no real threat having been apparent in the Fae since The King of this universe took over, and his hair looks every bit a similar mess to his father's—bright red to almost orange, and unkempt. I would bet money on his skill though, his intense green eyes narrowing.

"I—" My voice starts before I recall the exceptional hearing of the elves.

Icarus levels his hands in a hushing motion, shaking his head, and looking the other direction, as if I am not here at all, eyes attempting not to stray to the scars painting my wrists in slender, parallel lines to the crook of my elbow.

He pities me.

I pull my sleeves down further in abashment, nodding and creeping toward the door.

"It is pertinent we see Bastian in the weeks to come, and bring him full circle on our plans," The King echoes. I've missed something. "I trust he is well enough to accept visitors?"

Silence. "He would have no choice but to welcome his king into the city—well or not," my husband replies. "But as far as intermittent sickness and reckless abandon, Bastian is fit to receive us. I will write his staff at once to forewarn our impending arrival."

"Then we are finished for the afternoon," The King replies. "I will return in four to six months to inspect the capabilities of your soldiers, Kai, so assure they are acquiring proper training. I will call your people to aid if it is demanded."

"Of course." Kai is gracious, accepting. "Although...if you wouldn't mind, I understand you have maintained visits to the other world in preparation for your endeavors and I thought, perhaps—"

"There were complications," The King rings, severe and dark. I hear them moving toward the doors. "Leave it as such."

I stumble backward, and Icarus faces forward, somewhat ashen as he attempts to think of proper excuses in light of my presence. My husband is the first to exit—tall as he ever is and towering over me, golden eyes veering to my crumpled form without hesitation, like he knew I were here the whole time. His hair is silver, nearly white, almost as long as mine and laced with strong braids at the sides. A beautiful monster, as they all are, making humans look like bridge trolls.

I am his bridge troll. Or his personal human incubator. *Wife*. Whatever he calls it.

The King walks out in pace with Kai and they turn to see me as well, Kai gracing all with a slight bow and nodding to his son to excuse themselves from the situation.

*I wish I could duck out that easily*, I contemplate trying.

"You are supposed to be resting." My husband is firm,

thwarting me with reality. He never dances around a point much.

I duck close to the corner of an arcade, eyes dropping to the floor in their looming shadows.

"It is lonely in bed all day." I force a smile to draw him in, though it feels sick. "There are no friends there. I am a social woman."

"It is not a choice you are to make," he replies. I feel the heat of his glare and I blush, realizing his twin brother is still present to witness my humiliation. "These decisions are made for your safety and for our unborn."

"I am safe. I just—"

He cuts me off. "I've been told you spent much of the morning on the battlements. And the guards at the doors never saw you leave."

I am full of panic, unable to breathe. Trembling. The words I want to say are stuck in my throat, and I can't bring them out.

"Take her to bed," The King intrudes upon our conversation, and turns from us, killing the argument before it begins. "She has not eaten today, and there is no point stressing her further. I will send for her next meal and assign guards to the inside of the room, so you need not worry of it. Meet me in the gardens when all is well, brother."

I shrink from him, quivering and reluctant. The sound of his voice in person is enough to ward me off, but I remain in wait for a proper dismissal. My husband bobs his head to his twin brother, and I inch closer to him, shaking my own in a fearful agreement. He places a hand at the small of my back to guide me where I should be, but I hesitate, still paralyzed in my apprehension.

The King shifts, pivoting from us and departing, though I swear I see the cocky bastard smirk.

*I'm on to you*, it says.

I hope he isn't.

The stairwell at the next corner taunts my imprisonment, and I stop with force, looking to my husband and batting my eyes. He peers down to me in return, but with little sympathy for the pity party I host.

"It's lonely, Silas," I repeat, garnering hope on hope he will listen. Sometimes, if I'm lucky, he will.

His hand cups the side of my face, sliding under my chin, his long body bending to meet me on my turf lower to the ground.

"It will not be lonely forever," he claims, and I wince when he kisses my nose.

It would be easier to die and it's all I can hope for now.

# CHAPTER TEN
## CELESTYN

THE WALK FROM THE TOWER OF MASTER AMADEUS TO The Healing Center in the morning after just waking up is cold, freckling my dark skin in dewy chills under the quilt I've wrapped about my shoulders in absence of long sleeves. It is icy enough to wake a girl from a dead sleep for certain, my lack of slumber over the past week wearing thin on me while I spend my spare hours rummaging through old books for solutions to the mess of Limbo, avoiding the Master where I can, though I can feel his presence looming at the top of his spiral staircase.

Watching. Waiting.

Not that I mind the pressure. I wouldn't make a very good substitute doctor if I crumpled like autumn leaves under work boots every time someone made me uncomfortable, but sometimes I wonder if the way I nose around disconcerts him. Makes him weary—the way his eyes gleam and shimmer a barbaric red from unfathomable darknesses that candlelight cannot illuminate to call the rest of him from hiding.

I *do* hope he's unsettled, in the most vindictive way. I hope he knows I'm onto him, or whatever *this* is.

I want him to tremble when he discovers that I'm learning, understanding that every day I am peeling books off his limitless shelves and deciphering their strange texts that will lead to answers. Freedom. We won't continue to need him and what he provides—that I cannot privy the public to much longer—if I can just keep going. If I can just keep chugging along in rich knowledge and thriving under his care for the time.

Because, later, I want to see him in person. And I want to see him squirm, just like I am now—as well as every other resident of Limbo out this early feeling the cool air, waiting for the space heater in the sky to do a few warm-up stretches so that it can make the day comfortable. Of course, this temporary perfection only lasts about an hour before it becomes unbearably hot, just to make me wish it was freezing again.

At least when my skin is pimpled in cool weather I can use a blanket as a wrap. Or maybe this year I can find a jacket instead. Although I miss my proper jackets, like the ones my dad used to buy me. Those were expensive. Soft. Lavish and warm. He would bring them home in threes to try on when he had the time to visit his only legitimate child succeeding long work hours. If I close my eyes real tight, I'm able to recall how the silky lining brushed against my skin. Simply heavy material was the only love I'd ever known that hadn't abruptly bitten me like a snake among tall grass...until Aidan, that is. But I can't force myself to lay down investment in other people, no matter their commitments to me, and at night when I lay the books on the table aside the sofa I sleep upon, I rock myself somewhere beyond this horror to the dream of what I may have when I am released of its grasp.

I miss dreaming the right way, though.

All my nighttime sentiments now are different than they were back when I still *felt* like a real person. Nightmares really felt like they could end back then. I knew when I was falling that I could wake up and it would all be over. The family maid, Jackelyn, could brew me the blackest coffee known to man, a blend that stopped just short of making my heart burst at the seams at the first real big gulp. And I could ponder. I had the luxury of wondering at that silly time what the meaning of the ill-gotten fantasies of my own subconscious designs actually were until I crashed from the caffeine, shutting my eyes for another brief time.

It's only...when I open my eyes again, I'm here instead of my bedroom or the living room. In this place rather than home. I'm at my desk or in the tower. Dead on my feet but marching on.

I shiver, nudging open The Healing Center's front doors and unlocking the secret safety doors that close over each wing at night, creaking them wide open so they blend in with the wall and fresh air filters in once more. I wonder as I do, how many patients I will find dead this morning, or close to it. My curiosity agonizes over which rooms will fill with new injuries and illness, and which will remain desolate. Dusty.

Some nights I sleep here just to stay close to humanity, to feel like less of a robot and more like a person in light of circumstance. I tell myself it's for the people though, for the riskier sufferers, so they stood a better chance when the rest of the staff jumped ship at sundown, sharp. Master Amadeus has cautioned against it explicitly in the times we have spoken, considering how I am the sole person alive in Limbo to know a fraction of his written secrets and bear his protections—things not even privy to his slave boy, Ace.

But I know the truth when I take the risk. That I do this to make myself feel anything at all, even if I don't like the bitter taste it leaves behind.

I am invaluable to society. To its higher ups.

I have proven my worth.

But nothing lasts. Not here. And I won't last when the Master has lost his amusement with me.

I know this. It doesn't have to be said, and I fear it. But sometimes, I think I want to see the end. To know what it looks like and visualize it for one time, good or bad. I want the end of... *something.*

Anything at all.

Nothing is ever so easy, however, and that goes for today as well, my heeled boots clicking to the anthem of unyielding pain, legs bare to the sharp sting of the fresh breeze. I never wore shorts in a professional environment until this Center was officially set up, where it became mandatory on the hottest summer days if I wanted to breathe properly, coupled with avoiding yeast infections all in the same go.

I'm not sure I knew girls could sweat down below like piss through panties, until I spent a full day in snug skinny jeans in a non-air-conditioned building that just seemed to collect heat the way greenhouses did back when we had them. By the end of those shifts, I looked like I had jumped straight into the river, only I smelled like the sewer.

Today, I smell fine though.

I'm only sleepy and a bit cold. My shoes are a touch noisy and my bag booms when I swing it on to the front desk. From it, I pull endless files to be sorted, most of which will be given to Ace after I grant them a cursory glance. I don't really do that much with them like he does, but I like to learn what I can from each case, if I can. Specifically, if the files had a case of fatality in them.

It isn't likely I trip up when I can help it, if I trip up. But if I do, I don't do it again.

Most people in Limbo come to me half-dead, and I have learned to shut off remorse in their passing, even if I pretend to the face of their friends that I hold their feelings at heart. It is a lesson hard learned that I focus more on patients clinging to life when they arrive than those already at a loss.

I cling to the hope of those here when I can, having little of my own.

The front lobby doors creak ajar as my favorite charge, Ebony, weasels her way inside with a similar satchel in arm. Her hair is braided in small sections over the surface of her head, rattling with beautiful beads that she has had since I met her a year ago. She was eighteen then, still a young sprout at nineteen years old a month ago, and plenty of naïveté in tense situations to prove it.

But damn, when she is good, she is *very* good. Almost like myself at that age.

A stroke of genius and talent.

I wave to her, dismissive, as I feel her roll her eyes. It's expected that she is still displeased with the last major decision I had made. But she knows better than to speak up. Not to me.

Instead, she shoves her bag in the open space filled with supply boxes below the front desk and digs out yesterday's paperwork from a box in the same area. There is more than enough to catch up on so we can release charges today.

I clear my throat. "Are Chantille and Rosaline coming in today?"

Both girls have been here longer than her, Chantille doing my good work before I had even made move to set up this abandoned shithole as a hospital. She and Rosaline were inseparable during their shifts, perhaps a couple behind closed doors and always coming in together—not that it needed to be a secret.

But the ladies were a private sort, uninvolved in basic drama. Uninvolved in almost anyone they didn't have to be. I hardly knew them, other than that they worked below me, and Rosaline held to Chantille's metaphorical skirts like a prison bitch.

"Rosaline's dead." Ebony's voice sounds as cold as Rosaline's corpse should be about now.

I let go of my files to face her, hand on my hip, and my eyebrow raised. "Excuse me?"

"You heard." Ebony pouts her lips, dipping a feather into the ink pot and refusing to face me. "Rosaline went and got herself killed."

It doesn't make sense. I can't focus.

"Not funny," I reply, my voice stern.

"You think I'm having fun?" Her full lips part in a sneer. "You think I found somethin' I enjoyed seein'? That girl was like a sister. Worked with her everyday."

I turn back to my work.

"The Ravagers don't kill women in the city limits," I counter. "Or. At. All. The penalty for death in Limbo is—"

"You think I'm here cause I'm stupid?" Ebony snaps. "Chantille is gone and Rosaline's dead. Had a stab wound straight through the heart with a dagger handle still poking out like a fucking daisy in May."

Silence. Unbearable, agonizing silence. And then adrenaline.

This would be a busy day.

"I will tell Ace we need more help this afternoon."

Ebony slams down another stack of papers. "You go on and fucking do that. While you're at it, go on and turn yourself in for criminal negligence."

I feel myself glare, my brows pinch together, though I try to remain calm. Professional. Those inferior to me could become quite the nuisance.

"I've done nothing to warrant such an action," I respond smoothly. She scoffs.

"Nah? Cause the way I see it, things have been getting worse and worse since you let that little demon bitch walk out those doors."

There it is. Of course, it's that. It had to be, though I have been admittedly startled myself. Witch hunts and mob mentalities accomplish nothing productive and inhibit intellectual growth. What is wrong with that girl could be explained, if I'm given a little time. I am close to cracking this case.

So, I roll my eyes this time, listening to the influx of people beginning to fill the streets.

"She hasn't committed a single crime." I am firm but as understanding as I can be. "Adabelle Green is flimsy and soft. She will die or go missing before she causes a single problem for the village. In fact, she is probably gone already. I make no mistakes, Ebony."

"The attacks have been more violent since the day her body was discovered, and The Dome has been growing lighter every minute since she was set free. The first layer is now the color the second layer used to be. Don't bullshit me, lady."

I throw another stack of files on the desk in a thunderous boom, and I whip toward her in aggravation.

"Go do rounds, Ebony," I hiss, pointing down the wing leading to the quarantine hall. "Or I'll have you arrested for abandonment."

Her eyes grow wide, her nostrils flared. I've never made such a threat until now, but she can tell how good it feels for me in the moment, the surge of power and adrenaline cocktailed through my veins, exhaling my stress in a single breath. Ebony tosses the rest of her work back under her desk and turns away, starting down the direction I pointed her to, where our most vulnerable laid. It was doubtful she would get it all finished without our regular help, but an early start couldn't hurt. It means I can attend to the more at-risk residents in between.

I hold my head in my hands for a moment, the first bustle of patients climbing through the cracked doors and making me regret not taking advantage of an even earlier start than the one I had. I smile anyway though, glancing up and nodding to a few men who help a sobbing buddy stay standing, breathing through clenched teeth as the lower half of his leg drags behind the rest of his body by bloody strings.

The swords of the Ravagers could chop a limb off in a single blow, but this is still hanging on. Which means the one who did this to him must have not been trying hard, more or less toying with him like a cat would a mouse.

God knows I don't have the skill to reattach this mess.

So...a cripple he will be.

I lurch forward to meet them, shoes slick in the new blood the wound dripped from not being handled well. I cradle the bit with bare palms to stabilize it and keep it from swinging, nodding at his friends to assist me in lifting him down the hall to a bed where I can see him to a proper end of care.

Undoubtedly, I will hear this story...and journal it.

Cursing and pleading rings empty in my suddenly ruthless ears. I feel nothing at all for his pain but emptiness. Hollow and clinical, I am going through the motions in my head on where I'll bury the leg out back later if I had the time, or if I will have to feed it to the wild animals for a more efficient clean up.

There is a body dump somewhere around here where we take our corpses, but I won't dare go that far out even with the search teams to help. Not if my life depended on it.

And it always does, as a woman.

Down the middle hall to the left, we find a suitable room. The man has nearly lost consciousness from agony, and I release him to the soiled mattress used by many in much worse condition prior. His friends beg to keep his company while I request leave to grab some supplies, and I allow them, promising to be back in a moment with the material to fix him right up.

Leaving the room is almost a relief, but not for long. The lobby is growing loud and distressing, leaving me a bit regretful for sending Ebony away so fast. My ears ring, stumbling out of the hallway and emerging into the light, feeling even more exhausted than what I thought I could be when I realized I had only a few hours' sleep.

I duck under my desk for the supplies. We are running lower and lower on absorbent dressing for injuries, fingers gripping a small roll of bandaging that would scarcely cover the aftermath of what I am about to do.

Another topic for Ace, I suppose.

When I straighten, I am stilted into shock. Frozen.

At the doors, standing like a dwarf in jean shorts and black leggings, is the very being I had set free to die. Her vibrant mop of hair is an unfixed pile of torment spilling from a slept-on bun down to her speckled shoulders. Our eyes lock, as if I had vocally acknowledged both the subtle attempt to spare and end her life, and she can no longer decide whether she is furious...or accepting.

My hands drop to my side when she approaches, clenching the material tight while I maintain composure.

"Are you hurt?" I ask, my nose scrunching and eyes scanning the lobby for a way out of this conversation.

She shakes her head. "No."

"Please take a seat." I nod to the few chairs available. "I'll be with you when I'm able."

"I'm looking for someone," she raises her voice when I turn away, tone commanding that I listen.

I am compelled by it, for one reason or another. If not for the fact she is so grim and stern, maybe it is the strange guilt making a home deep in the hollow of my vacant soul as I make every attempt to smother it, burying it where I can.

Another scream echoes from the open door down the hall, and I sidestep behind my desk to disappear down the hallway. But she swerves around the wooden barrier that protects me from regular people, racing after me so I'm unable to refuse her.

She isn't going to be denied for a single second, a spirit I both admire and despise.

Besides, help is the least I owe her, considering her disadvantage, isn't it?

"Wait," she calls.

No.

I hesitate.

*No.*

She owes me.

More than she knows.

# CHAPTER ELEVEN
## ADABELLE

I T ISN'T A FAR WALK.

She was going the direction I was in need of anyway, and I'm sure getting rid of me so that my presence didn't disrupt the lobby of frail asshats was a primary bullet point on Celestyn's long daily agenda.

But I'm known to be wrong.

Turns out, it is a way cooler power move to make me wait a whole hour in spite of this, demanding I sit in a sea of condemning faces while I wish over and over that I hadn't made the decision to visit The Center at all.

It takes a slew of foul whispers and chairs meeting the wall's firmest edges in ear bleeding scuffs across the floor, trying to escape my unmoving body crumpled next to the doors, before I'm called back by the devil's new boss, her hands drenched from her fingers to her elbows in blood. More than eager to avoid the topic of the conspicuous hushed rumors surrounding my existence, I all but fly off my ass to meet her while she both balances and stains another set of supplies in the crook of her arms.

Our trek down the center wing is the same I followed her upon when I first tried to retrieve her quick attentions, stopping at almost the same door we stood outside when she requested I find a seat before she asked security to remove me. It could have been a simple nod of her head to land me right here so that I could have managed breakfast by now, but I can't hold my train of thought long enough to bear grudge as the heavy gateway to my roommate's containment screeches open, filling the cell with light for the first time all night.

Celestyn bobs her head to me in an absent motion to allow me inside uninhibited, departing in a swift whoosh to lend us some silence and vague comfort. Privacy, or close to it, though I decide I will sacrifice a bit of secrecy to keep the door open.

Fresh air could do nothing but benefit Zoey. And I seem to remember a very similar room in quarantine full of oppressive grey breaths, candlelight, and dim hope for the future burning out faster than the wicks. The room could use a little happy to combat all the dreariness that will take place when my conversation has reached its end.

Around the brief corner of wall built in the place of a shabby plastic curtain to protect a patient's identity, Zoey quivers in a ball, at the far end of the room, upon a mattress stained dark brown. She waits, paying mind to who the footsteps are attached to, her eyes pleading for comfort to settle the visible shaking of a young girl with a life gone wrong in a place no one knows of, without the knowledge or skill sets to fix her problem.

Or care for it.

Although, there are factors that complicate caring for this case. Little ticks on a list I must know so that we can carry on. It just... will not be easy to confront.

I hike my backpack further up on my shoulders, studying how her shallow breathing quickens as clean air fills the room in waves. Her canteen is empty next to her—once again—bare feet. The cap for the container is gone somewhere in the shadows of the room, and the socks I gifted her are missing in action, along with the weak thrill I had last seen on her face at the soft texture cradling her toes. Here, it is transformed into a vacant stare targeting the alien stomach she has spent time growing, fresh pants spotted in old blood and the bed...

I can't even tell what is hers, or what belongs to someone else on the mattress. Though it is a positive all of the stains are dry. It implies she stopped bleeding at some point.

But when?

Have they even checked on her at all since placing her here? Or are they too afraid?

Zoey doesn't look up as I toe in her direction, not so much as flinching when I slide in next to her, as if I were some sort of ghost rather than a useless, living sack of crap. I purse my lips, my hand shaking as I reach out and rake my fingers through her hair in the best form of comfort I know how to offer. Over and over. Until she registers that someone is touching her, and she stiffens under my fingers, taking in a sharp inhale.

"What kind of sissy ass shit is this?" She swats at my hand, but the power isn't there, nor the commitment. "Are we going to fuck each other too?"

I attempt not to let it get under my skin.

"You haven't been home," I reply. "I was worried."

Her hands scratch through the places I had touched her, as if trying to scrub herself clean of any evidence I had placed a hand on her. In the light of so many candles, I can see her cheeks glisten pink in warm tears, dampening the fringe of blonde that hangs low in her face without braids to contain it.

"Gee, sorry," she huffs. "I didn't realize we were fucking married. I'll make sure to get in touch with your needy ass next time."

I don't wince this time at the anger ringing in her voice. It isn't directed at me as much as she thinks it is and, if I am being true to myself, I have almost missed it. Her company and the sound of her belligerence, though I hadn't been around it long enough to really miss it—but I did.

I've longed for her fiery nature in the most selfish ways. A series of verbal assaults that weren't quite hate but rang just as true as pure hate does from the mouth of someone who feels it.

She is someone I can trust, even when her feelings of betrayal and sadness and fear are misplaced, shot at me like bullets at the slightest touch of her nerves. The first night with her was the safest I had felt.

But there are boundaries that also need minding and questions I need answers to. I'm her roommate, and whatever else she has asked for me to be in exchange for shelter, not her punching bag.

She chose me.

Not the other way around.

So I need just a little compliance.

"It couldn't hurt to communicate with me a little," I insist, handing her my water bottle.

"Fuck you." She sniffs the rim as though it were laced with poison, some sort of trust lost during her short stay here.

"I was worried about you."

"You don't know me."

It is a snap, the feeling of something inside her breaking. She throws the open container at my lap, the water sloshing out onto my pants as I scramble to clean it up and cap it, so the resource isn't entirely wasted.

There is a heat building behind my ears in this process, my face flushing crimson. But I don't leave yet. I have that much restraint...for now. Despite the fact that I want to yell at her, that I want to ask her why she hasn't left if it has worsened her condition, both physically and emotionally, sitting in this locker. I want to know what's holding her back, though the answer is clear if I take time to think about the fact no one ever just walks out of here when they feel like it.

A scream rises in the hallway, shrill and making the little hairs on my arm stand at attention. Zoey pulls her knees to her face at the same time, burying against them so only her eyes peek out from over their tops. She shakes more violently than before, with so much force her feet bounce as the sound dies down to muffles and a steady gurgling, like the sound a baby makes when it is out of air from crying so hard.

Something about this turns my stomach.

*It's familiar.*

But I shut it out, reaching for Zoey's hand and dusting her bony fingers with my own. Just enough that she feels my presence this time, but not overbearing.

I don't want to startle her with my touch or smother her with my comfort if it scares her. I just want her to know she isn't alone as the next scream builds, begging for the perpetrator to stop.

*Just please, stop. No more. No more.*

I try to imagine what it must be like for her to sit in here with no windows and no shoes, wearing dirty clothes with only candles that light the room being the primary décor, trying to get comfortable while she saturates in her own blood—of which she doesn't know when it will stop, or what it even means.

She knows nothing about being a mother, having no one to guide her, and she has no partner by her side to tell her it will be okay. Meanwhile, rooms all over the building fill with the screams of people needing stitches or having rotting limbs severed.

When we met, Zoey told me her last known age was sixteen... but she had been here for a few years. Younger than me, in any event, but still a teenager whether sixteen, seventeen, eighteen, or nineteen.

She is a teenager with no job, no food, and barely a home. A home that she has now invited a stranger to live inside with her and her baby to be. Life is a garbage fire for her, and I need to be patient.

I fight the urge to close the door, allowing the fresh air to stay and fill our lungs. A soft weeping replaces the echoes of the screaming we had been privy to, and when I'm sure that there will be no further disturbances, I glance back to Zoey who is digging into her own skin with fingers chewed raw.

I need to present every word from here on out with care.

"So...you, I mean...the baby..."

This is smooth. I'm winning at life today.

"The damn bastard is still fucking shit up from the inside out," she growls. "Yeah. Don't act like I don't know what you're getting at. Just spit it out."

I don't know anything about babies, other than their exit route. The thought makes my legs twist and lock together like a helix. There was never a lot of focus on childbirth and reproduction in my memories of Earth as it was. No one needed the information because there were hardly any individuals having babies.

There was a population *drop-off*. And a war. Why is this important?

A lot of information had been lost on the subject during recovery, and in the matrix of my still muddied thoughts. Schools had downsized so much, they began using only a fourth of the old buildings to fill classes. The younger kids were less than a good fraction of school aged populous.

I still don't recall ever seeing an actual newborn baby in my entire life. I'm actually almost positive I haven't, which is unsettling.

"Are you close?" I ask, shifting against the wall, feeling more confident.

"Close to fucking death?" Zoey groans. "Absolutely. I'm way past due for it."

I frown, hoping for a more specific answer.

"I want to take you home, Zoey," I propose. "I have a job, and it will be easier if I can count on you to do your part too. But I need to know what is going on here, what I've unknowingly walked myself into. I can't help you if I'm blind to the problem."

I can see her tense, her eyes going cold and dropping to the floor. She removes her fingers from mine.

"What job did you get?" she evades my inquiry. "Is it a good one?"

We are both on edge. One of us has to give, and it will always be me. I need her on my side, more than anyone, because I have no one else.

I try not to sigh, but one escapes my lips.

"I'm on the search teams," I reply. "It is great money. I've been there a few days, and I already have enough money to buy us meals for the next two weeks if we spend *wisely*."

"The FUCKING *what now*?" Her voice is rising above mine before I have the second half completely out, interrupting me as I carry on. "They NEVER let women on the fucking search teams. Do you understand the amount of danger you're in? The kind of fucking danger THEY'RE IN? And Ace is fucking ALLOWING this? THIS?! That goddamn piece of *shit*. It's like he's trying to get me *killed*..."

She's still ranting in a shrill yell when I start talking again. I'm finding it is becoming easier to ignore her.

"It doesn't matter, Zoey," I reply slowly. "It's good pay. We can eat and have fresh water every day. Maybe we can have proper baths more often, if I can find the safest routes to the river."

She stops talking at the sound of *proper baths*, winding down to a mumble that trails into silence. Which is a good thing. I've enticed her enough to listen, and I need the quiet to think straight for the rest of our conversation. I've had enough happen in the past several days to last me another few lifetimes, and I don't need this riot too.

"I want to go home." Zoey blinks, staring at the floor. "Celestyn is afraid to let me go until I have the baby, but I want to go."

"I want to take you home." I nod. "But I can't be your residential stranger. I need to be familiar with you and your situation. I need you to be honest with me."

This incites a reaction. I jerk sideways as Zoey slams her fist into the wall, spinning to lean her head on her closed hand and shutting her eyes tight, as if the concept of truth pained her in every degree. But this time there is a tiny sob when she talks, though she attempts to restrain it, to control it—just as she does all other situations.

"I can't do that, Adabelle. I can't."

"Then I can't help you." It slips out fast. Faster than I wanted, on a whim. But I'm already on my feet, tucking my mostly empty water bottle back inside my pack.

"What do you want?" Zoey yells, frantic and moving toward me against all desire not to. "I don't have anything to give you. The information I have is fucking useless to you."

"You know."

My voice comes out harsh, and she cringes. I don't like this part of me when I hear it. Unable to keep the innermost pieces of me in check and falling backward against the wall in defeat to it, though my backpack cushions the blow, so it just resounds as a crunching mess. The sounds of women speaking clamor past the door frame as I hear a metal tray crash to the floor just a few steps after.

"It's all...fucking complicated," Zoey murmurs when she's sure they're gone.

"Try me."

There are obvious markers of distress in the lines written across her face that tell me she doesn't want to. She is practically dying to keep it inside, while simultaneously letting it kill her by allowing herself to carry the burden of her secrets, and the rumors of mine, to our graves.

But this is precisely what I am trying to avoid.

Our funerals.

I need to know what I'm dealing with.

Zoey takes a deep breath, practicing her words in voiceless whispers so she can speak them out loud with the same vigor as usual.

"I..." she starts, "I need some damn time."

I throw my hands up, almost laughing.

"We don't have it. In fact, we have negative minutes, Zoey. Time has been up for a while now. This has been drilled into my head since I opened my eyes. And since working the search teams, I've figured out, hey, there are things out there. Killing us. Kidnapping us. *Whatever.* I need you to give me anything to work with here so that I can help you. Help *us.*"

She sniffs. "I didn't fucking ask to be here, you know."

"Do you think I did?" I scoff. "I don't have a clue who I am yet. At least you have some solid memories making a home up in your brain, instead of my dropped gelatinous massacre of a head. I mean, I have zero memories that mean anything at all, a whole city that acts like I grew horns and a tail that I can't even see, a job that could get me...*whatevered,* a partner that's so fake that I can't tell if he is a real person or a mannequin, and a roommate that can't tell me a single damn thing about what is going on without falling apart. Do you think this is some sort of wish package I drew up on the drop of a dime? Who WANTS to be here, Zoey?"

My yelling diminishes into guilt but, to my surprise, Zoey is unfazed. She's not wounded or hurt by my frustrations. For a second, she smiles—a small smile, short and untrusting. But it wants for something. It hopes.

"Worst. Vacation. Ever," she attempts to joke.

My exterior melts away, and I laugh without meaning to. A frantic, crazed, noise that holds a simple degree of joy. I take a deep inhale in between bursts, another round coming in waves. Like I am going mad, but I can't stop it.

This makes her laugh too, snorting and covering her mouth with both her hands. When the joke clears, I'm back on the floor next to her, my legs stretched and crossed as I stare at my shoes side by side with her feet.

"Just one thing," I pry one more time after a moment. "One thing, and I will check you out of this hell so fast, we'll spin Celestyn on her ass walking out the door."

She smirks, though it is reluctant. "She's good, you know—Celestyn? She means well, but she's swamped. We just need a better game plan than me living in The Center."

I don't answer this right away. The woman was as unhappy to see me as anyone else. Maybe even more. She practically set me up to die in the dead of night when these locals were prevalent, and without giving me an inkling that they even existed or that the attacks would happen.

"I'm not used to having fucking help, okay?" Zoey admits. "I asked for it...but...I didn't fucking think you'd say yes. It almost seemed unfair."

"Unfair?"

She swallows. "Every damn person and their sister talked about your release before it happened like you were the biggest, meanest, mother fucker around. A beast. A brute, with tree trunks for fucking arms, and fangs. They called you *hideous*. So, imagine my surprise when I find your five-foot punk ass in the weeds, bleeding from the head like a little bitch because you wouldn't knock a few kids through the barn wall. The beast was my last real hope, but it wasn't you. I was going to just leave...but I couldn't fucking do it."

*Okay, ouch. Hideous? Tree trunks?*

I extend my arms out in front of me, toned but soft, like the green twigs that belonged on the trunks I was foretold to have. There aren't much to them at all. Just shriveled, mottled skin and bone. Scars and indentations where I'm lacking some of my muscle tone.

Pain...and numbness.

"You could have gone." I grimace.

"I couldn't." She shrugs. "It's kind of fucking selfish, but you sort of became my redemption here. What I did for you, or what I was going to do, it was for me either way."

What could she have possibly done to need redemption for? I'm afraid to ask.

As if she can read my thoughts, she speaks again, carrying on without looking at me in the face for her confession.

"I haven't done the best fucking things since I started living here. I...I wasn't always so damn dirty, and I need to do better before I'm not fucking here at all. You just seemed like you had the potential to be fucking better than the losers that run this place, so I hoped that I could teach you to learn from my mistakes. That way you'll survive...and remember me? Maybe you'll even get out of here one day."

Get out.

I haven't thought much about that yet. So much of my focus has been enraptured by finding out where I am, I hadn't dreamed of leaving beyond a few passing thoughts.

But it's true. I can't envision a life here. At least not a happy one...or a long one. I won't let myself live long enough to become a victim if it comes down to it. So leaving seems to be my only real option in the grand scheme of things.

Still...

"Zoey," I say, "I'm not saying I need to know who the father of this baby is or anything, but I have questions. I need you to cooperate."

Her face drops and her knees fold close to her body—as close as her belly will allow, anyway.

"It's none of your damn business."

A soft sobbing in the halls diverts her attention from me, so I move on my knees to block her view. Stern.

"You told me when we first met that you needed me to buy you time," I say. "How can I buy you time if you're making me walk in blindfolded?"

She still won't look at me, shuffling closer to the wall.

"Do you listen? I just fucking told you that you can't. You're not the damn beast. You're just a tiny woman with a stupid fucking target on her back."

I bite my lip and lunge forward, gripping her by the shoulders and giving her a squeeze. "I can be the beast, if you tell me what I'm dealing with."

Zoey jerks from me, shoving me away and waving her hands.

"Stop giving me the sweet talk and fucking bedroom eyes, you stupid twat, or we really are going to fuck each other."

I roll my eyes, standing up and curling my lips in, ready to leave. But I can't seem to stop trying. It's not in me.

"Don't threaten me with a good time, Zoey." I sigh, holding tight to my backpack straps. "We both know you're not sixteen anymore, no matter what age you identify with. Although, I'm afraid I wouldn't be a very pleasing partner, considering my quite celibate history."

She doesn't want to laugh, but her body gives in to this subtle admission of age. I'm finally on her level, and she relaxes, shoulders slumping forward and hand finding her belly to rest upon.

"Has anyone told you why the Ravagers raid this fucking village?" she murmurs.

I think about this. "I...have a few ideas of my own. They seem to kill their fair share of people on the way through. The old journals Ace keeps make it pretty clear the murder is reserved for adult men...and teenage boys, but that doesn't give a cut and dry answer to a purpose."

"They don't kill women," Zoey replies quickly. "Or children. Or, well, damn I don't know. Maybe...but it's always some thirteen-year-old boy or something. We didn't really fucking know what was happening with any of the disappearances during my first year here. It was just...One minute someone was here, and the next they were gone. It's what happened to my roommate before you."

I lean in, mindful of her space this time.

"She was taken?" I interrupt as she finishes her statement.

It takes a minute for her to catch up with my eager attitude to understand, and I try to steady myself to avoid frightening her away in my quest for answers.

"Yes," she replies with unusual care. "Our home was...fucking breached, eleven or so months ago. There were quite a few of the fuckers standing around, throwing shit off the shelves, and prowling the house like we weren't right fucking there, clinging to each other for dear life."

It is when she is finished with the sentence, I realize that the care is to keep herself from crying. She's chewing her fingers, sniffling as her face grows scarlet, her body shivering with anguish.

While she takes her time, my thoughts flash in reverse to my night in the barn again. The way I was looked over, the measurement and disdain. I recall it all through the repression, wondering what was said in the strange language outside when he left. It sends chills down my spine.

"There were four...no, five. At least fucking five," Zoey carries on after she composes herself. "Maybe more. It's...hard to recall exact facts. It's all a blur. But there was one that guarded the door so we couldn't leave if we fucking tried. There was another saying something in their weird fucking language to the guard, and I know that they laughed. The others destroyed shit for no reason, just tearing the house apart to make sure we weren't hiding anyone else...and those two fuckers *laughed*."

I cross my short legs as buds of gooseflesh prickle every inch beneath my leggings.

"When they stopped searching," she pauses and sniffles. "One of them rounded the corner from the counter and stood in front of us. I was shaking, trying not to breathe even though they were right there. The one in front of us smiled like he was fucking friendly, Adabelle. Fucking. *Smiled*. And he offered his hand to my roommate, June. He said his name was Azariah...and it was almost charming. They were beautiful, up close. But June didn't fucking touch him, okay? She didn't. She didn't fucking ask for any of it? She didn't want to let me go..."

She's looking at me, waiting for me to make it clear I believe her story, so I nod.

"Okay."

But my heart hurts at this, only to shred when Zoey's voice raises an octave to continue her story.

"She held on so damn tight. I...I remember...her nails, they were digging into my arms, and I secretly just wanted her to let me go so that it didn't hurt so much anymore. But, when she didn't fucking take his hand, he just sorta...shrugged. He pried her from me, kicking and fucking screaming. I begged him to let her fucking stay. Begged. Take me instead. Just leave her here."

The crying in the hall intensifies, as if in tune with her story, and I move to shut the door just enough to drown it out so we can talk unhindered. When I look back, Zoey's face is beginning to wet with her own tears.

"Did he?" My voice quivers.

"They don't operate that way," she whispers. "The...um...the damn guard, he...well, he motioned them all out when my roommate was taken. And he..." she pauses and holds her breath, letting it out steady. "He closed the fucking door."

I wince. Knowing what comes next. What my gut has insisted this whole time.

"He introduced himself. Kasismis, he said, is what his fucking name was. He was...nice, I guess...tall as they all fucking are. Fucking brown hair, long as hell. Longer than mine. Armor, and a sword. He had enough to be damn well scary, but he didn't try to scare me..."

I purse my lips. "The earliest journals I've read, they stated that the creatures...they were kind. When people started disappearing, it was assumed that they left willingly until the villagers found out otherwise."

Zoey bobs her head and clears her throat. "He told me that I couldn't fucking stay here. That I would be leaving with them. Very, very fucking calm. Like he'd done it before. And when I refused, he put his arm around my back and waited, ready to carry me out...except he fucking stopped at the touch...and..."

I put my hand up. I want her to stop. I can't take hearing it, and I don't know if she can take saying it. Knowing that kind of fate is the likely outcome for those still here makes me tense, red, and filled with upset.

But I am filled with more than just rage.

I am uncomfortable. Afraid.

Zoey's lip trembles, tears spilling over her jaw.

"How did you..." I take a deep breath. "How..."

She takes the reins. "When he was done, we sat there for maybe an hour...I...I'm not sure. Time seemed to last forever and stop all at once. Just dead quiet. Then he said it was time to get out. I would have said hell no, but everything he did took very little fucking effort, Adabelle...I just wanted to cooperate and have it done with. He didn't have to drag me. It was all so fluid, and I felt like such a little bitch. Weak and disgusting, like him.”

“You were raped,” I counter, shaking my head as a fight to her self-loathing.

“It doesn't fucking matter.” She meets my horrified gaze. “I...I'm fine. It's just...We were almost fucking gone, and I was going to be with June. I was so sure. It was my only fucking consolation, because at least I would still have my best damn friend in the whole world to cry on...but we were stopped.”

“And it...upset you?” I ask, but Zoey is quick to deny this.

“N-no. I'm grateful, almost.” She's crying so hard that it's becoming hard to understand her. “Some fucker loaded Kasismis up with arrows and he couldn't fucking keep a grip on me through all the pain and blood. I got away...sort of. But I became a pariah when everyone found out I was pregnant and being this far overdue doesn't help it much. People are so damn afraid to be around me because 'he might come back'. It's not like anyone ever recovered a body...but the dumb fuck is probably dead.”

I unburden myself from my backpack for a moment, scooting across the room, hesitant. But my arms do the work for me, wrapping tight around her shoulders and squeezing her face against my collar bone, laying my head on top of her hair. There is a willfulness to my act of love, a part of her that wants to reject it and hide, but she sinks into it for a minute, crying harder against my neck until there is a river soaked into the chest of my shirt. When she's done, she is so still, I'm not sure she's still breathing until she talks again.

“Where are your fucking boobs?” She tries to shift focus, to humor me while she suffers.

My ass got what my chest needed, but it makes sitting on hard surfaces less cumbersome, so I take what I can get. But I don't answer this aloud. I don't want to let her make this about me when she has been alone for so long.

“Do you miss her?” I ask instead. “June, I mean.”

Zoey shudders in my arms, limp.

“All the fucking time,” she replies. “You are fucking nothing in the space she left behind."

I take the blow. I'm hardened to it, and I understand.

Pain. It is *my* armor.

I am okay.

I will be everything for her, to protect her. Whatever she needs me to be, I can be. It will be the purpose I grant myself.

I pat her on the back and release her, though she doesn't seem quite ready, leaning into me as I do. I rise, shoes clicking against the floor and stepping toward the door, peering back to her.

"Are you ready to go home now?"

She flashes a quick smile.

# CHAPTER TWELVE
## ADABELLE

THERE IS A PUZZLE TO LIMBO THAT I HAVEN'T QUITE figured out how to piece together yet. But I'm trying.

For me, it starts with Zoey, by removing her from this prison ward and getting her home where we can begin a proper care regimen—a piece of *her* puzzle that starts with food and ends with a more comfortable sleep, stretched out below deck while I guard the cellar hatch.

Considering this circumstance, I don't bother notifying the staff that I am checking her out of this joint. I don't want to give them the time to tell us I'm not permitted when her contractions have slowed and she is drastically overdue. Given the level of dehydration that the pebbled corners of her mouth reveal and the starvation she has endured prior, it is fair to say she has lacked the medical attention she deserves in this hell based off immediate need. So, *if* she has the baby any time soon, I'd rather deliver it myself than let her spend a minute more in this hospital room.

When I get her settled in at home after her bad vacation away from it, I show her the upgrades my work has been able to allot us. There are jars of fruit and vegetables that sit on top of the meager counter surfaces, a hard loaf of bread next to it just waiting to be scarfed down, and bars of soap with lemon peel stirred inside to exfoliate that are wrapped in cloth at the other end of the space next to a bucket of water I gathered earlier this morning. I was able to purchase actual quilts at the markets, so we didn't have to reuse the ones smothered in her blood—and a little of mine from pulling the stitches with my dagger—and a metal pot to boil stew in.

I want to let her imagine what it will be like when I work more consistently, so she can feel comfortable. Maybe I can find her a pair of shoes if I look hard enough. And hire someone to sew clothes for her baby? The possibilities are endless, and we will arrive at these destinations as we go. For the time being, keeping her off her feet and hydrated is the focal point of our fresh start.

Creating a sense of normalcy in this difficult pregnancy is next on my agenda, though getting her regular medical attention without making her sit in a room for eons will be tough. The reality of our situation is that The Center is too overrun with patients to give round-the-clock care to a high-risk pregnant woman in a labor that comes and goes. Ten to eleven months of pregnancy can't be normal, and Limbo lacks the tools to cut her open to remove the creature within—let alone the skill. But maybe I can set something up where she can be checked just once daily, if I talk to the staff woman to woman.

I take a week off work to make sure I can get our affairs in order. It isn't like I can be at her beck and call all the time, but getting into a routine could benefit both of us. And I want her in prime condition to deliver this baby when the day comes. Celestyn is agreeable to this concept, though I feel she would agree to anything if it meant keeping me out of her safe place of work.

The time off I use is beneficial for me as well, after the most important things are cared for. I am taking time to rediscover my love of dancing in the morning, most of my wounds healed in miraculous time frames that I attempt not to over think for the sake of my own sanity. This is easiest to do at the twinkling moments predating sunrise, where I creep around the hatch that conceals Zoey's huddled body below ground, and I dig into my backpack, pulling free my pointe shoes for a test run.

I am stunned to learn my arms recall the series of graceful flutters and bows, fingers stretching above my head to reach for an unattainable dream that comes and goes like the days of my absence from the search teams. I am limber and sprite this way. Much like water, I am fluid and weightless. Soft, and powerful.

The more my muscles are conditioned, the less contained I feel. The less *helpless* I am. And with all our ducks in a row, discreet and proper, I am comfortable today with the idea of going back to face the crew of obnoxious asshats I work alongside. I can even run without regret now, better than ever—not that I'm hoping I'll need to. But I will if I have to, assuring each muscle is stretched for the event, should it happen, and taking ten minutes after to have a little fun.

To dance.

Rising on to the tip of my toes and down, I pull my weight from my feet and lift a leg parallel to my body in a joint defying movement. Over and over. Up and back down, switching legs after one set.

At my last leg lift, the hatch rattles. I lose concentration right away at the noise, my foot catching the floor but the other trying to compensate, sending me stumbling into the corner of the counter, snagging my elbow so I yelp. My funny bone feels infinitely less hilarious, reverberating into the darkest parts of my meat and making me clench my teeth.

Still, I'm able to manage a smile when Zoey trudges out from underground, lifting the latch with hooded eyes that scream *get this baby the fuck out of my body.* Below her breath, I hear her call me stupid, and I can't help but agree while rubbing my arm, watching her reach for her canteen. I grab my water bottle next to it and, together, we swallow heavy swigs of water that I will have to replace when I go down by the river today with Aidan.

But Zoey seems...satisfied. More so than usual.

She isn't as sickly as she was when we met, and she hasn't called me a bitch or a twat in two days. So, dare I say she is a touch more patient? Less abrasive?

Zoey gasps when she's finished with her water, taking a big inhale before reaching for our pot of piss poor stew that we managed to conjure up yesterday evening. I had purposely left its contents for her when I realized our finances have dwindled faster than I imagined they would when I took absence from work. I'd been confident we would have the money to see us through a solid week, and I had spoken with Aidan about the time off in the bare amount of advance I could give—something that seemed to be a sort of relief for him.

It isn't like it's a secret that no one wants me there. Aidan never wanted me as a partner, and it was plain to see from the day I started. But since our last adventure wrapped up at the riverside, he has been far more avoidant than before. Cringing and flinching, he tries his best as a gentleman not to be too obvious, but it has been impossible not to notice.

Strange, too. Something that makes me wonder for a minute if he has caught wind of these beastly rumors at last. Not that it matters. He can believe what he wishes, and I'll let him think it.

We are supposed to meet at The Center for our next task this morning. A fortunate thing since Celestyn—against my better judgment since I won't be present—needs to check in on Zoey's condition.

I yank on my backpack, assuring Zoey chows down the last bite of food and drinks the murky meat water, while I lace on my regular sneakers. It isn't until I have pulled my hair into a sloppy bun that she second guesses this decision to eat, her mousy face glowing with shame.

"Did you..." She clears her throat. "You had some of this shit too, right? This morning?"

I lie. "Yeah, yeah. Good stuff. Are you ready to go? I'm already running late."

Zoey shakes her head, shedding the blanket she brought out with her that had been wrapped around her shoulders, and baring sun-kissed skin to the chill morning air.

We travel through the parts of town where less people roam, off the main roads of housing and closer to what is left of the old village where people won't bother her, the lump of child she carries protruding outward. Here, it is queer to see the tower that I noticed the day we met again, isolated and quiet behind the remains of old housing.

I don't ever see candlelight in the dim morning hours, or at night when I'm preparing to turn in. The door has never opened. But Zoey said someone lived there.

"It's fucking gorgeous against the sky like that." She nods its direction, as if reading my mind. "Until you look at the rest of it, anyway. Then it's just a damn shame."

I stop, admiring the damn shame. "Who lives there? You said once someone lives there."

Zoey grabs my arm, dragging me forward in a not-so-subtle reminder that we are still late, and I am going to make us even later. My feet tangle with one another to keep up, catching myself and straightening to find Zoey glancing at it once more, this time with spite.

"Master Amadeus lives there," she seethes. "He is...You know like how some fucking cities have a mayor or some shit? Well, he's like...the president of our little toilet of a town. He oversees our higher ups, like Ace and Celestyn, and dumb shit like that."

"Does he ever leave?" I pace next to her.

She is so much taller than me, and her strides are longer, but the waddling of the baby sleeping low in her pelvis slows her to my pace.

"No," she replies. "No one has ever really fucking seen him and come back to tell the tale. Except Ace...and Celestyn...and maybe Melody."

"Why?" I don't mean to sound so incredulous, but it hangs dense in the air.

The Center is just in sight now, looming less than a mile ahead and making me wish I had just gone back to bed.

"I don't fucking know." Zoey sighs. "I've heard rumors and shit, but nothing substantial. I heard once that he's one of the Ravagers and that The Dome is his design to protect us from his own people. But it's all just muddied together. I don't know what's real and what isn't."

I frown.

The rest of our walk is spent in silence, and the sun has nearly peaked the horizon when we arrive at The Center. Aidan is waiting at the doors with agitation spread across his face like cream cheese on a bagel. But this changes when he sees Zoey.

His whole demeanor changes.

His hands drop from a cross at his chest, his face growing dark and sullen. Behind his glasses, his eyes drift to the ground so he doesn't have to look at her long, flickering up one time to meet her gaze out of courtesy. Zoey shuffles toward me in response to this quiet greeting, her cheeks growing darker and her arms crossing behind her backside. She seems so...timid all of a sudden, tucking a strand of hair loose from her braids behind her ears and giving him a brief wiggle of her fingers.

"Hello, Aidan," she murmurs, the faintest of smiles playing at her lips.

"It's good to see you," he replies, stepping aside so she can rush inside without so much as a goodbye.

He means it, and I wonder if they dated in the past. If they were now?

No...Zoey doesn't date. People are too afraid of her.

But maybe they were in love at some time? Aidan had his... charming moments. It wouldn't be hard for him to snag any girl he wanted.

Something about this thought doesn't sit well in my stomach, which flips and coils. My fists clench and unclench, then I hold my arm to ground myself back in reality. The ugliness of my outer core envelopes me and tugs me here to what I know.

There is a life altering silence in Zoey's disappearance into The

Center, both of us trying to find our ground to stand on.

Do I ask him about this? Do I just let it go?

He doesn't have on his plaid over shirt like usual, I notice, peeking up to him from the ground I stared holes into. Instead, it's just a plain black T-shirt stretched over his body, a hair baggy for his shape, and covering the belt loop on his jeans.

It isn't as if he were abnormally muscular or anything of the sort, but it's weird to see his arms for the first time—more like seeing a fluffy cat without fur. Scrawny. Spindly. He has *some* tone to his tattooed biceps, a bit of muscle from all the heavy work we do together. But he isn't the biggest man in town, and without his usual shirt, he feels almost...naked.

I feel myself retract somewhat, bending so that I'm not as upright as I was and looking more hunched over, staring at the ground again. My face hurts and my ears are burning like someone had poured melted wax all over them. I don't like it.

"What are we doing today?" My voice stutters in pitch.

There is a pause, and I tilt my head to make sure he heard me. But he is staring through the doors where Zoey had been, his eyes somewhere beyond where we are now. He shakes his head after a second, brushing his dark hair from his glasses and stepping around me while he talks.

"You were gone for a week." He states the obvious straight away.

Carts are beginning to line the streets we intend to approach, the whining of a few horses cutting through death weighing down the air in heavy scents of manure.

"Zoey needed the help," I reply tartly, shielding my sensitive nose.

"I needed your help."

"Are you having a baby too?" I snap. "Or are you just being one? Because I can't say I'd make a good mother."

A dark chuckle, though it isn't because he enjoys my humor. His arms are tense, veins popping as if he is taking the time to imagine strangling me.

"Ah." He laughs. "So funny. Well, I suppose we will have

*plenty* of time to laugh together about your lack of competency while we are on civic duty today."

We turn down a row of houses a ways into town, a damp and heavy odor saturating the air as we come upon three bodies that lay like plush dolls, their limbs twisted in listless contortions that immortalize the way they had crashed to the dirt upon their deaths —one missing an arm altogether, ripped from the socket like paper from a perforated journal.

I wince, afraid to look at their faces and see the final terrors captured in their open eyes—to know what they felt past the screams I have learned to repress so I can sleep come nightfall. Though Aidan is less shy, bending down to a corpse while I turn away fast, diverting my focus to The Dome above...even lighter than yesterday.

"What is civic duty?" I ask, hoping he doesn't hear me.

I'm more concerned to know, but I think I already do.

"I'm glad you asked." He takes me by the elbow, spinning my resistant feet to face the problem full force.

We walk far, against my personal will, toward different homes, stopping short of taller grasses at their sides where he releases me like a disease and saunters into the weeds. Aidan rummages in these weeds for a couple minutes, giving a gruff *aha* when he pulls forth the missing severed arm, giving it a quick wiggle.

I cringe in pure disgust, retracting into myself as he comes forward, shoving the piece of body already crawling with reddish brown maggots at my unsuspecting arms. I can see sanity flee from him in emotionless slithers, like it was a stage prop and not part of a corpse. He doesn't care. He's rigid and unbothered.

"I'm not touching that." I look between the arm and my partner.

He rolls his eyes. "Yes, you are, because you are the reason we're doing this."

"I didn't ask for it," I scoff.

"No one asks for it," he elaborates. "However, at the beginning of each week, the worst performing team on our search crews get put on what is called civic duty. This week, due to your absence, that is us, Miss Maddie Addie. It means we get to spend the day committing ourselves to the better good of the community. So, to start our morning, we help by picking up cadavers in the street, stripping them of their valuables, then carting them outside the first layer of Dome to dump before noon where nature can run its course."

"Who determines who did the worst?" I reply, putting my hands up to refuse the limb that he edges closer and closer to my arms. "That doesn't sound fair, considering the whole team hates me."

Aidan fumbles the limb into my grip with force and skips back so I can't return it.

I'm breathless holding it. It's much heavier than it looks for such a small part of who someone once was. I jerk at the sensation of its weight against me, taking a sharp inhale at the maggots dropping down onto my shoes.

"Lucky for you—and for me—it isn't up to them." Aidan watches my reaction with intrigue. "Oh no. That would be your good pal, Ace."

The way he says it makes me roll my eyes, not that he notices. He turns around in search of more dead bodies, motioning for me to follow him, which I manage in shaky strides at his heels while anger builds and topples over in a tower of words.

"You mean to tell me, that even with every girl practically throwing their cat at you, you can't screw your way into getting at least one of them to bribe our way out of this with Ace?"

This makes him turn around fast, eyes narrowed, but the rest of him relaxing.

"I don't know what you're implying." He laughs a little. "But I'm quite good at what I do when I'm not a committed man."

"Okay." I shrug. "So it's just the sex with your *girlfriend* that sucks then."

Aidan stops at one of the carts that had been set out, placing his hand on top of a worn sack resting at the handles where they would attach an animal to help haul it.

"Don't be so bitter." He smirks, picking it up and tossing the burlap piece of crap to me. "And make sure you get the rings off those fingers *before* you throw the arm in the cart. We need to be done by noon so we can eat lunch, and then go to The Center to babysit the discharges until sundown. We are on Celestyn's clock today, mind you, and she runs a smooth operation. We won't go home tonight until she tells us to."

*Oh perfect. That's what I need.*

But there's no point fighting it. I can't fight it. Not when Zoey and I need it so badly. Though I realize right away, it's hard to rob the dead.

I mean, I am certain the glassy eyed man with flies flitting in and out of his mouth could care less since he is not alive to enjoy the aesthetics of his jewelry, but I find my mind creating sentiments for each item I have to take.

I wonder if the rings had any importance in his life prior to this.

Was he married? Did they belong to his father? Brother? Maybe a grandfather?

The one on his middle finger looked chipped and dented, showcasing rubies at the center and diamonds on either side. That seemed like a grandfather thing, right?

I drop it in the bag all the same, just like I was told to, but questioning my ability to keep this job or ever missing another day of work if this were a potential consequence. Requesting a new job is far out of the realm of possibilities, too, so it is a caging feeling to endure.

I help Aidan carry the bodies to the corpse cart, pretending deep inside my imagination that these people are just big meaty dolls. That we are just cleaning the bedroom of a giant's child who has left her toys out.

*We take off the accessories first and put them in their sorting bags.*

I see Aidan pocket the money from the jeans of a corpse and pretend I don't see it.

*The clothes are next. The giant child needs a clean slate for the next play date.*

It is fair to say by my reaction to stripping men to their

birthday suits, I never came into contact with a penis on the regular. This confirms at least a few basic facts I was already sure of before this—one being that I am an incredibly celibate woman with no drive to change course any time soon.

Just...god, no.

Another fact becomes evident that, while I am safely attracted to men, their genitals are one hundred percent the least attractive thing about them.

The last fact?

When today is over, I never want to see another corpse or dick again. Does womankind really need man to move civilization forward?

*Together on the count of three, we lift the doll into the cart to be put away.*

*One, two, three.*

Crash.

The cart sways and groans.

There are other people assisting now, moving this task along and loading up bodies. Piling them like timber. Just pieces of wood to burn.

My arms ache at the last of them, Aidan taking the brunt of the weight in complete pity of my exhaustion which quivers down to my toes, my stomach feeling sick in waves.

People from the markets pass through in groups of two as we finish collecting valuables off the wagons that weren't bummed by the more dishonest thieves stripping the bodies. It takes several minutes until they are gone, and when this happens, the children under the care of the farmers walk with donkeys and horses to attach to the carts.

Aidan pulls out a small cloth from his pocket with the coins he collected inside while we wait, removing half and dropping them into my palm with a momentary smile.

A peace offering, perhaps? Or maybe I earned it?

I feel disgusting.

I put it out of sight in the pocket of my backpack, focusing my thoughts on the hope they'd let me pet one of the animals on the way out to the dump site. Aidan takes the lead of our assigned cart when we are set up, grasping the reins of our donkey and leading him forward. In his pockets, I notice him dig every now and then for treats of encouragement. I catch up to their pace following the first treat, unable to help myself from running my hands through the animal's coarse fur in absolute amazement.

Fast pets. Slow pets.

I am overwhelmed with the desire to hug the fellow, giddy and not abashed in the slightest when Aidan chuckles at my excitement. Through the escape of animal introductions, we join the little caravan heading out on a cleared path to our dump site through the forest.

I keep my hand on the donkey throughout the journey there the whole time, hoping he doesn't try to bite me in return for my enthusiastic love. I decide along the way I want to call him Terry, since he doesn't appear to otherwise have a name. Terry felt like a proper name for an ass, and it rhymed with another name making home at the back of my thoughts that I can't quite focus on enough to recall. So I keep my full focus on Terry, showering him with compliments and affections to keep my mind off of the fact we are being lead to a mass grave.

I can smell when we get closer to the dump site, gagging on the perfume of rot, and pulling my shirt up over my nose. Aidan grimaces at our lead, the other carts ahead of us slowing to a stop as we, one by one, toss our given bodies and pieces down a steep ravine flooded in carnage.

I steel myself to the guts and bones, the flighted scavengers ripping loose meat from unrecognizable faces while I attempt to stonewall my sentiments. But I am the only person to say a speedy, compulsive goodbye to each person we set free, wishing it were possible to give them all a proper burial. Or something better than this.

Terry brays at the duo waiting behind us and we finish up, walking home to Limbo in a solemn silence. I let Aidan take him to the barn in an agreeable fear that I might try to kidnap him if I did it, coupled with the secret I have withheld that I'm still anxious of the keepers there. When he returns, the cart has been hauled away by a set of people employed to do so, and he grants me another half-smile, stretching his arms that are probably more sore than mine.

Or maybe not. He's had practice.

"I told them to give Terry a carrot," Aidan says. "They said it was a strange request, but they wouldn't say no."

I smile to him, just a little. "He deserves a carrot."

"And we deserve lunch." He points to the markets. "On me, Addie. We can go grab some food and chow down before The Center. I know a place that started up a few weeks ago that usually sells some real good cooked pork. They salt it and everything. I bet you'd love it."

My stomach flips.

"No meat." I shake my head. "I think today has made me consider the wonderful world of veganism."

He pats me on the shoulder, like he would one of the guys on the team. Except, it's more awkward. Kind of like he both meant to and didn't mean to at all.

I scrunch my nose, making a face I can't quite describe as good or bad. But he ignores it, walking on ahead in the knowledge that I would follow, though I fall a bit behind as we enter the marketplaces, and whispers start to fly.

I am the beast, after all. If they choose to believe that crock.

Does he believe that?

I refuse to think he hasn't caught wind of it by now.

We stop at a fruit stand. The prices of sweet produce are astoundingly expensive compared to the more easily grown vegetables. Aidan uses our corpse cash to buy two bruised pears and a cloth tied shut with dark berries. We travel a few vendors down and buy fresh bread that I accommodate with cheese to make myself feel as if I am contributing something. We opt to take our goodies back to The Center with us and eat there, so we can sit longer, our legs powering through exhaustive miles as we reach the doors.

Sweat is dripping down my forehead when we enter the lobby. Celestyn is at her desk with one of her charges that I know, and another that is new and fresh enough that she must have arrived this past week. Pale and meek. Shaking. Young.

She's between eleven and twelve by initial appearance. Just a child—a fact that makes me uncomfortable.

The mistress of all that is evil glances up when we click through the doors, zeroing in on Aidan and finding me at his side. Short and homely, I'm like a troll, or a garden gnome.

Aidan waves to her in a simple flash of his hand and a nod, about to move toward the quarantine hall when she dismisses her charges, slipping out from behind the desk like a lioness, and creeping over in predatory grace. She steps between us as I teeter out of her way, her fingers wringing to his shirt, and pulling him in for a deep kiss. One that lacks the passion it displays, full of tongue and lust, but empty. Robotic and greedy.

He breaks the seal their lips make, abrupt and cold. His face is twisted with disdain, to which she appears both offended and furious over. Her mouth begins to form words to speak, her hands coming up to the side of his face as he jerks away, waving me on as the uncomfortable third wheel to this party.

"C'mon, Addie," he shouts, sweeping from Celestyn's touch toward the quarantine halls. "She'll let us know when it's time to leave."

I'm sheepish, peeking up at Celestyn, who appears stunned at best with her jaw slack and eyes falling down to me from above. I excuse myself so I don't have to confront her rage head-on, ducking around her elegant form and chasing my partner down the familiar hallway, past the steel impasse and out into the courtyard.

There are four discharges out there this time, three women and a man. Aidan sits at the entry to the building on the hard ground and stares around these people. Beyond them. Listless.

I sit next to him, pulling out our food so we can dig in, and thankful for the break it gives my legs. I find that the berries are the best part of eating this afternoon. I hadn't eaten real ones in my time predating this, but I could get fat off them, the dark purple juices staining my fingers that fight Aidan who tries to steal at least a few. But he gives up with another ornery grin, plucking a pear from our lunch instead and taking a bite.

"I thought you might like those," he admits against the pale skin of the fruit. "Celestyn loves them. Says it's the only good part of being here. Especially since these berries never existed back home."

I don't appreciate the comparison, but I keep eating anyway. I can't stop. I'm a glutton.

"Not much of a fair trade-off, if you ask me." I roll a smaller berry between my fingers. "All of your sanity and life's memories for exotic berries? No thanks."

A quiet laugh. "You still don't remember that much, huh? You've been here...what? Two weeks. Less? More?"

"About two," I reply. "I...remember basic things now. My name for sure, where I worked, and that I lived alone. Just not... major things."

Two of the girls start to yell at one another close to the trees. They have to be close to my age, maybe a bit older. Both brunette beauties and fair skinned. I don't catch what caused the predicament, but the first reaches for the second's layered bob haircut, Aidan yelling above their clamor and having little of it.

*Hey!*

And he points at both of them.

"Knock it the fuck off," he follows up, taking another bite of the fruit.

It is hard to tell from this distance, but considering how they curl away trying to hide their faces, I could swear they each blush.

*Gross.*

How can someone with glasses like his be considered this attractive? Is it just the status of who he is? Women love status.

Is he really a magnet for estrogen?

I don't look at him, but he starts talking again anyway.

"Jobs are pretty major. It's your livelihood," he carries on. "What did you do?"

One of the brunettes is called out from behind us by one of Celestyn's charges to be released. I jump at the unexpected shout, and the girl steps unnecessarily between us, almost stepping on my fingers and her bare leg brushing against Aidan's upper arm.

She apologizes to him instead of me with a shy smile, hesitating and waiting for his generous reply, but nothing comes vocally. He simply smiles and waves to her, making eye contact with me in wait for my response to his question.

"I was a dancer," I say when she is gone. "I had my own studio and everything."

"You look like a dancer," he says with a mouth full of food. "I can picture it. You're short and pale, but you have really muscled legs. Like those porcelain ballerinas that old women collect and put on their knick-knack shelves."

I try not to snort or smile. "Please, don't picture me as anything, ever."

Another girl is called forward, and this time, I scoot aside so she doesn't have to try as hard to be rejected. Though she doesn't put forth the same effort despite my good nature—more focused on proper survival than the last. Meanwhile, the gap I've made fills with animosity and I pull my knees up to my chest, nibbling on some of the cheese now.

"What did you do before this?" I ask him again to fill the awkward quiet.

He folds cloth back over our food now that we are getting full and slowing down as the afternoon rolls by in a blur, bugs taking notice of our feast and trying to find their own meal.

"I was a musician," he reminisces. "Well, sort of. I didn't get paid much. But my parents were also musicians. They made bank, so I had time to pursue my ambitions, I guess."

"They were together?"

It's unusual. Relationships are more often casual than not. Co-parenting, if there were children at all, is a reality for almost everyone.

"Oh, yeah." He grins wide. "Super in love and all that junk."

"Adorable." I smirk.

"Sure, sure." He hands me the wrapped food to put in my backpack. "What about your parents? Who were the lucky makers of Miss Addie Green?"

The last girl is called forth, leaving the man by himself, sitting as close to the borders as I had with the sun casting rays behind the trees. It must be a decent time past noon now, closer to evening or sundown. Every day passes faster than the last here. The silences are all that feel as though they last forever.

"Well, the unlucky makers of Miss *Adabelle* Green are still quite the enigma," I say. "But it's safe to say her father wasn't an active role in her life. She...just had a mother."

Aidan's smile falls, his lips turning sour. "Ah, the traditional family."

The next several hours pass in another steep, steady quiet. The sky is dusting blue when the last man is called, and Aidan rises at the same moment. But the charge puts her hand up, swallowing hard.

"Celestyn says you have to stay," she whispers. "She needs an escort home and it will be a late night. She'll come get you when she's ready. The Center guards have been sent home for the night, so you will each fill the temporary role until she is ready."

The words make Aidan very unhappy in an obvious way, his brow dipping together, but giving in to whim by default. We would have to collect our late pay for the day in the morning, and hope we made it home in time tonight to avoid a slaughter.

He doesn't sit down next to me again when the charge and patient leave together, standing and staring with paranoid caution out to the open forest. The focus grows harder and harder the darker it gets, and we are more silent than death himself, listening to the sway of the grass and hush of the tree leaves until the moon is bright above us, casting dull swathes of light to keep it just bright enough to see in aid of the candlelight still going on the candelabras.

I am nodding off in place, mind racing with paranoia about whether or not Zoey made it home on time when I feel Aidan shift against me. One of his hands claps down on my shoulder while the other reaches for his dagger, waking me completely. My heart pumps loud and sure in a split second. I writhe free of his grip in a befuddled mess, clamoring for the dagger in the side pocket of my backpack.

While I pull it free, he turns around to rip free one of the candle sticks from its holder, inching forward to get a better clearance of our area.

He whispers, just loud enough to hear. "Go. Ask Celestyn when she will be ready to leave."

I don't hear or see anything, but he seems serious.

I squint into the light cast by the candle, seeing nothing but dark shades of colored plants and rocks. The trees.

I am rising to my feet when it becomes clear. A high-pitched whine, but...no. No.

It is a scream. Crying.

I glance to Aidan and then to the trees, hearing it draw closer as he steps away from it. His free hand holds tight to his dagger, but our history resounds like furious echoes in his reflexes, and he drops the weapon to catch my arm to stop me from rushing forward.

*Hello? HELLO?*

It comes from the forest, howling and sobbing. I purse my lips, jerking forward as he tugs me close. Stern.

"Go inside," he commands.

"Someone needs help," I whisper in return.

"Everyone needs help at this time of night. Lay low. Go. Inside."

Crying.

It is getting closer, and I pull against Aidan's grip. It makes him squeeze tighter, so I yelp when my wrist feels crushed within his fingers. I rear back at the sensation, swinging and punching him in the shoulder with my free fist so he yells back. This flexes his grip, but doesn't free it as he growls obscenities that would make Zoey blush under his breath.

When I swing again, he swings back with the candle in hand, whipping the fire at my face and trying to fend me off with the threat of fear, keeping his grip all at once. He stops when the light hits my face though, freezing at the illumination and hand releasing me so that I tumble against the weight of my bag.

I skitter into the dirt as another sob and scream for help reaches through the trees. Aidan's mouth hangs open, his whole body frozen until the next plea comes, and then he lurches forward. But I am on my feet again, racing toward the trees, and returning the calls.

"I'm here. Where are you?"

*Don't! Stop, Addie!*

I can hear Aidan shouting somewhere behind the tree line, but I have a better lead. His voice is a second thought. Insignificant and growing distant.

My legs pump harder to keep our distance, praying he doesn't follow and, at the same time, wanting to believe he will. For my sake.

The voice answers back.

"I don't know. I-I barely escaped. Please, help."

More crying. To my right, I think.

I'm breathless, having jumped the forest edge in a row of thorn bushes and plants, my arms searing from the blind movements against the bark as my eyes take their sweet time adjusting.

*It's too bad I don't have night vision.*

There is a break of sticks behind me and I hear the grass move. I stumble to my right, trying not to pant too loudly and focusing on the shapes that come into view better when the canopy parts to let in delicate beams of moonlight.

"Hello?" I call as I go. "Hello?"

My voice begs to be weak, but I don't allow it. She said she barely escaped. That almost all but affirms tonight there will be an attack. I don't want to be caught in the middle of it. I don't want her to have to go back to whatever is still coming.

"Hello?" I call again.

Hands grip to the backs of my shoulders, pulling me inward so

I careen into a warm body, and a steady orange glow. I yell, but Aidan throws his hand over my mouth, pressing it between my teeth so I gag on the sweaty dirt taste of his hand.

"Shut the fuck up," he growls. "You're so fucking reckless, you know that?"

I punch him in the stomach, and he groans, letting go of me and trying to suck in his missed air as I turn around to a pair of blue eyes staring back at us. Terrified.

I gasp, scuttling back at her unexpected presence and knocking Aidan over in the process. He holds up the candelabra when he recovers so that we can all see, still coughing but otherwise okay.

The girl that stands before us is about his age, perhaps a touch older, with hot pink glasses cracked at the bottom of the left frame. Tendrils of lime green curls fall over each of her shoulders and a messy bun littered in leaves and debris sits at the back of her head.

She is wearing a tan cardigan, something that is baggy and was probably once a comfort outfit, but is now ripped at the side. At her upper thigh, where her jean shorts do not protect, is a growing red stain blooming and racing down her leg, but she doesn't seem to notice.

"A-are you okay?" I breathe, inching toward her.

Aidan waves the candles all around like a mad man, holding the air in his lungs.

"We need to go."

The girl sniffs, whimpering and nodding.

"I-I fell," she sobs. "I don't know where I am...but there are these things. And they...they...and then I escaped...but they're not far behind. And I fell."

"You're very brave." I offer a hand, but Aidan grabs the free one by the wrist to retract it. "I couldn't say I would do the same."

"Leave. Her," he demands. "It could be a trap."

"You leave, if you're scared." I shake free. "But I'm here to help. So I will."

The girl limps toward my gift of freedom and stumbles, Aidan shoving the light in my open hand and catching her underneath the arm as she goes down. She cries louder at the near impact and he shushes her with soothing sounds, motioning for me to work as a crutch for her other side. She follows our lead without question, mumbling in joyous remarks again and again that we are human as though she hasn't seen one since arrival.

When we get back to The Center, the village is still quiet. Deadened. We take the girl inside and down the quarantine hall, where Aidan rattles each of the doors until he finds one that is empty.

Once we're in a room, we help her down on to the makeshift mattress, Aidan moving across the small space to search amongst the items left in the corner for new admits.

I give the girl my water bottle and uncap it, giving a brief nod and a smile, then jogging to his side.

"Have you ever done this?" I'm nearly frantic. "Isn't Celestyn still here? Maybe we should go find her?"

"Celestyn has special protections with Master Amadeus and would be one thousand percent out of here by now," Aidan replies hotly. "She's angry I spurned her, and left us here as a bad joke. She probably thought I'd be smart enough to leave anyway."

"That's fucking perfect." I throw my hands up. "Great girlfriend, Aidan. The best ones are the ones that will get you *killed* for fun."

We whip to the girl who is downing the rest of my water in between gurgles of sobbing. The blood from her leg is thick between her toes now, slick and making prints on the cold hard floor. I swallow, approaching with familiar care and placing each hand at her knee. Aidan is behind me, carrying silk thread and a needle, attempting to figure out how to set it up.

But it's okay. I know this. I've *known* this.

I meet her gaze.

"What is your name?" I ask, soft, reaching a hand back to Aidan.

Her lip curls. "C-Celia," she answers. "Celia Rodgers. I-I'm...I mean, I was...a biologist. I was at work...Where am I? Who are you? Who were they?"

"Shh," I hush, rolling the blue leg of her shorts further up to reveal the meaty gash pumping out lines of blood. There is dirt inside too, but I don't have much to irrigate with.

That can come later when Celestyn sees her, and maybe reopens her. Right now, I just need to stop what's started.

"My name is Adabelle Green." I talk to her, motioning for Aidan's canteen, and dumping it in back and forth streams down her wound, dabbing at it to dry as she flinches and cries. "My partner here is Aidan Powell. You are in the village of Limbo now."

She sucks in a breath at the last dab, but I wait until she relaxes to begin stitching—a procedure she covers her own mouth for to stifle yelling.

When I'm finished with the stitching, the rims of her eyes are nearly as red as her pants from crying. Raw and tired. The same as my arms, battered by the unforgiving growth in the forest and a full day of constant work.

*I better get paid so much overtime*, my thoughts scream. *Ace and I are having a HELL of a conversation about this shit.*

"What are those creatures?" Celia asks again as I wrap over the stitching for the night with a bandage that looks as though it has been used a time or two before.

"I don't know," I reply. "The natives to this region, I guess. They're aggressive, but at least here, we can equip you with weapons to give you a fighting chance."

"Don't let me go back," she pleads. "Please. Please. Please."

I glance to Aidan, clipping the bandage. Aidan rubs the back of his neck and glances out the open door.

"You will stay in here for the night." He nods. "The Center has pretty much never been *seriously* broken into, so you'll be safe for now. Our doctor will see you in the morning. Okay? Just try to get some rest."

Celia grips my arm with a painful passion, shaking. I grunt, placing my hand on hers, and giving it a soft pat.

"It's scary." I smile. "But it will be okay. Nothing will happen to you here. The worst part is over."

I don't know what I'm talking about. But I need to go home too, so I lie through the weight of my conscience. It nags, wondering if complete and total isolation is more of a punishment than sanctuary after being assaulted. Aidan glances back to the door one more time and nudges me aside, sitting next to Celia and taking a deep breath.

"Go home, Addie." He nods. "Make sure Zoey got there safe. I'll sit with the new girl until she falls asleep."

I'm relieved, though the guilt stays.

I thank Aidan and I close the door all but a crack behind me, in case it has some kind of automatic lock.

The Center is still lit up in the lobby when I emerge, though Celestyn is little in sight. Down one of the other halls, I see a door open wide, but I hear no noise coming from it, and pay it no mind. I turn to the lobby doors instead, bursting free of them into the chilling night air.

I want to get home fast with a nearly guaranteed attack on the brain and locals searching for Celia. It would take at least ten to fifteen minutes from where I am at right now, and that's if I run, which I start to every time the wind blows, trying to lay low like it matters if these creatures are as superhuman as they've been described. If anything, I probably look like a moron. Weaving through shacks and huts, I'm spinning in every which way, attempting not to get lost and make sure I'm alone.

But I am stopped quite suddenly, running into hard bone and muscle. Clothes that smell like dirt and earth.

Uncomfortably shifting, I look up right as Ace stumbles away, holding to his treasured beanie with one hand down over his ears and flinching for a moment, as if he is pained by the mere sight of me.

"We have to talk." My voice is full of frustration, but I find myself glancing around again. Calming down and letting the feeling replace itself with fear. I frown. Neither of us have time to be out here, to talk. "What are you doing out here, Ace?"

"I was in a meeting with our Master, and Celestyn had not returned home for her dinner. I was asked to check in on her...and you."

My heart stops. "Me?"

Ace digs in his pockets, pulling forth folded parchment and placing it in my hands, nodding.

"We will talk tomorrow." He bobs his head, and moves around me, disappearing between further homes.

I look down at the paper I am given, sitting in my shaking hands. On the front is written only two words in delicate scrawl.

MASTER AMADEUS

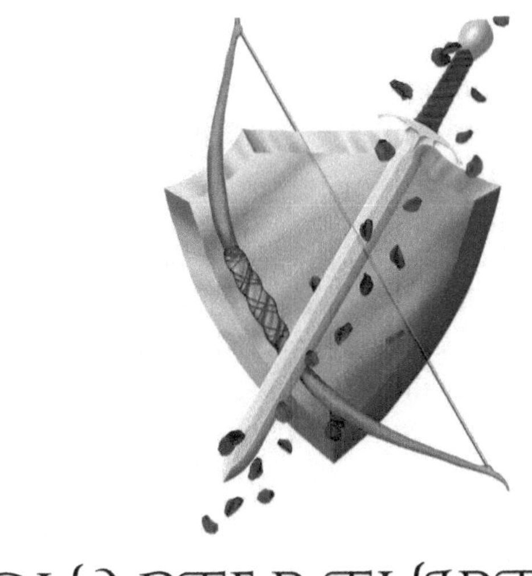

# CHAPTER THIRTEEN
## AIDAN

IT TAKES SOME TIME FOR CELIA TO DRIFT INTO A comfortable sleep. Not that I blame her for it.

She's watchful of me in the hours that pass when the door is shut, more so than Addie, the champion for freedom and basic humanity, who she fell right into with ease. I think she's trying to convince herself that I'm not here to assault her already traumatized body, a stranger with no motive to help her, not to mention a person who shied away from helping her to start with.

I can't take her survival instincts to heart, all things considering. It's inappropriate. If I were in her position—a recent victim of violent assault on the run with little memory to guide—I probably wouldn't particularly care for the company of the gender that perpetrated the attack either. And I'm only here to complete the task I embarked upon with my partner, so feelings of offense have little duty in this place.

I'm here to keep her safe until she falls asleep, not to be her friend.

I don't need friends in Limbo. No one needs emotional

attachments if they want to live.

For this girl's sake, I hope she wants to live. She'll need more fight than what she's shown if she wants to survive the fallout to come from being a high-paced rescue. And for more than just being ostracized by regular society.

Rescues usually don't last more than a week before recapture. She would have been luckier if Addie had left her like I asked, to serve out whatever fate comes next, so she's spared of the bitter taste accompanying despair after lost hope. Not that there's anything we can do about it now, except hope for the best.

I am hoping...for her.

And when I'm certain that she's drooling on my shoulder instead of crying after scooting closer to me at the sound of an owl flapping outside the door, I shuffle free of her dead weight. My hands cradle her head until it touches the lumpy mattress of straw and thin sheets, and I conceal her body with a cheap blanket, making sure to cover her shoulders so she wouldn't wake up alone feeling exposed in any way. Like the most primitive form of comfort I can recall when I was a boy, I want her to feel swaddled in warm blankets tucked below her blotchy chin. I want her to wake up thinking of a time when this nightmare wasn't real, and she could duck her nose below the covers for an extra five minutes of sleep past her morning alarm, even though she'd have to skip coffee on the way to work.

I want her to recall ignorance and innocence. Just to be young for a minute longer, even if it is just for a fleeting second. Everyone deserves that, especially when it will end soon.

On my way out, I look back to her once more, just to be sure. When I am, I shut the door. It won't lock without a key, of which Celestyn has right now, but I have my doubts she'll leave any time in the near future. The room is strong and safe, not to mention her body will want to recuperate all the energy lost since she started running, which I can't imagine was any small feat, considering the stamina of the creatures she was escaping from.

She'd be exhausted at best, and I am too.

Today was longer than I expected it to be—not that I foresaw an entirely smooth operation. But Addie and I are...incompatible as partners, piling on top that there are some rather concerning aspects about her I can't force out of my mind, no matter how hard I try. No matter how hard I try to convince myself she's a normal girl being subjected to a real-life witch hunt.

She's just...strange.

It isn't a secret that I have been listening since the day she was assigned to the teams. It isn't easy to miss what people say about her. Stories have begun to emerge about the details of her appearance now, depicting how an unnamed person found her just at the edge of the third layer of The Dome. How she was curled into the fetal position with her backpack strapped to her shoulders, her chest rising and falling in gasping inhales, as though she hadn't yet woken up for the first time.

There was nothing outwardly wrong with her then—at least nothing that could be seen. At least a small fraction of the people in Limbo appear on the wrong side of The Dome and make their way here to seek refuge. I don't care about any of that.

My problems lie in the stories of what occurred after she woke up. The details of those particular stories call into question why Celestyn passed Addie through quarantine at all, and why she wasn't sent back to where she came from. Or, at worst, killed on sight.

Not that I want her dead.

I don't want her dead. I just...

I run dirty fingers through my dark, messy hair, letting loose a sigh that I have repressed since this morning. I wish I had thought to bring my bow from home. It's not like I use the thing very often anymore. I'm trying to save arrows for emergencies, and without a proper quiver to hold them outside of the house, it becomes a bit of a hassle to tote around.

But tonight is ripe with friction.

I can smell death in the air, and I feel its presence lingering close. Lurking. Smothering.

The hallways are quiet, save for the sound of my footsteps and the occasional groan of the few patients taking their last breaths. Addie's words resound within the walls of my skull as the echo of each step feeds back to me. All of them rattling about in waves of chaos, trying to make sense of one another. Paranoia rises at the same time in veiled threats to greet me, in noises I'm not sure are real, forcing me to debate taking a room for shelter overnight rather than walking out.

I am growing more and more pissed at Celestyn with each passing second as these feelings overwhelm me. Taking advantage of her position over the masses like a toddler with a knife could very well get *me* knifed, and I decide against my better judgment that I will definitely check to see if any patient rooms were available to bed.

As I approach the lobby, I pull my dagger free from its sheath out of habit. I had picked it up on the way into quarantine from the yard. It's flecked in dirt, but otherwise okay.

*What an unusual habit in a hospital.*

My thoughts ring a painful truth.

At the final curve of the hallway, I hear a gentle shuffling and the clap of shoes on the lobby floor that all but confirm my worst fantasies about how tonight could go. My heart gallops in my chest, the whooshing of every beat is a drum in my ears as I freeze, edging forward on my toes so I can get a glimpse around the corner. When I look, squeezing the handle of my dagger so intensely my fingers burn with anticipation, the rush fades out in an instant.

The life drains right out of me through pores zapped in pins and needles at the sight of Celestyn sorting through papers on her desk, her forehead dented in thought. I slip my dagger back into its sheath with shaking hands, pivoting on aching heels out into the open, where her eyes flicker up just long enough to acknowledge my presence without an ounce of shame for what she did.

"Why are you still here?" I approach, leaning against the desk and trying to get a good look at what has stressed her into foregoing her safety.

Her delicate scrawny arms pile two different stacks into one as fast as she can, and she turns away, flipping through each one in an even bigger hurry.

"Where's your little girlfriend, Aidan?" she mocks, avoiding my question.

I roll my eyes. "My partner, you mean? I sent her home, since you obviously weren't going to release either of us, which I shouldn't have to mention was awfully fucking careless, you know. We could have died. We could still die."

"Don't be such a child," Celestyn remarks, turning to face me with a small grin settled on her full lips. "I wouldn't have let you die. Her, maybe—but not you. I have too much fun with you."

She winks, and I attempt not to react to it.

It's better to keep my mouth shut on the matter. Or at least attempt to, for now. Instead, I adjust my glasses, shaking my head at her, and gripping the desk to relieve the pressure on my tired legs.

"What the fuck is with you, anyway?" I all but shout, rattling her from her work to here. "You want to shut me out? Fine. You don't want to be exclusive? I'm okay with that. It's your call. But you can't have it both ways and expect me to read your crazy mind, Celestyn."

She shrinks back, her shoulders slumped over and her back hunched, seeming almost smaller for a second before her eyes find mine. Wounded. I'd call bullshit, but bullshit makes itself known in a stage presence when she speaks.

"I'm not jealous, you know," she declares without my asking. "Adabelle Green is a rag doll, at best. Ugly as hell, with all those scars making her skin look like she's the human version of a patchwork quilt." She shrugs when she explains this visual, as if it drove her point home. "It's just...I'm concerned. For your safety."

"My safety?" I guffaw. "*My safety*? Be concerned for your own! I mean, what the fuck. Why are you still here at night? You do realize it is night, right? If you knew what I've been doing for the past hour or two, you'd have beelined it out those doors at sundown. It isn't safe here."

She doesn't take it seriously; Master Amadeus has made her cocky. She opens a black bag she had sewn herself out of old shirts to dump the papers inside. In the entire swift movement, she refuses to look me in the face. There is a frosty chill radiating from this that reeks of the murder undoubtedly on her mind.

"I have no reason to be afraid," she replies, her voice biting like winter. "The Center is basically never attacked. And I have special protections from Master Amadeus, so I'm untouchable. This isn't the first time I've overnighted here either. I sometimes have patients that need round the clock care, and I can't just abandon them, Aidan. That would just be selfish."

"You've never been anything but in your personal life, and you're telling me that kind of behavior doesn't just transfer over?" I hold my forehead, squeezing my eyes shut and regretting the words as soon as they leave my mouth.

I don't really mean it, probably, but she's grinding my nerves, hard. She takes these protections gifted to her—by someone who's able to provide them for one reason or another—for granted, while the rest of us suffer in her wake. Not that I'm upset that she's safe, but at times I wonder if she really is that safe in one event or the next. The Master offered her help very quickly into her stay here and, to my understanding, she never questioned his motives or what it is he would be getting out of the deal.

There must be a good reason the Ravagers don't attack him too, after all.

Nonetheless, my words don't appear to poison her as I'd worried, much rather they make the walls she's built around herself that much stronger. Fortified. Reinforced. She shuts me out harder, but this time with a smirk and a laugh. The ultimate female way of saying *fuck you*.

"Run home, Aidan," she cackles. "My life is more valuable here than Ace himself. I don't need your pity escort."

She waves me away with a flick of her wrist as though I am a pest. But I can't leave. I'm unwilling to leave her like this, with this knowledge and curiosity building of how many overnights she's truly stayed without me knowing. Ten? Twenty? Is this how she gets everything done?

She glances up from the remaining junk littering her workspace in the time it takes for a few minutes to pass, raising her eyebrows, and throwing her hands up. It's a gesture that screams the question of why I am still here, staring at her like a dillweed.

I wonder the same myself, in part.

I don't *want* to be here. Not right now. Not with her.

The day I met her was on my discharge from quarantine and, on that day, amid my confusion and massive head pain, I would have killed to spend a few more seconds with her, though I admit she was borderline a bit young. Eighteen. I've been persistent since sometime after then, groveling at her feet like most men here do when she passes them by. I have no doubts she's slept with most of them, or at least half—back then included. And I don't mind her experience in physical intimacy, except that she wants an on and off commitment to the people she includes in it at her own design.

Starstruck faded fast when I realized I had been used as a tool and discarded when her fun was over. It wasn't what I was about at all, and it infuriated me...at first, until I got to know her better. Somehow, through all of our ups and downs, she has been my security blanket at every blink of an eye. Something soft and cold I hold on to when things get to their worst, and the pieces of my life string into alignment to become painfully clear.

When odds stack against me, she grounds me in reality.

When the days are dark, she reminds me that night is not everlasting.

But, damn, I just can't tolerate her methods in between.

"Do you know what I did today?" I ask her, my voice quiet and drowned out by the sounds of muffled groans down the hall.

Still, she heard me.

"I don't really care." She shrugs, dipping a feather into a pot of ink to write along empty parchment.

She really doesn't, but I'll tell her anyway.

"Addie and I rescued a girl out in the forest, just a few hours ago," I continue. "We put her in quarantine, despite being wounded, and Addie sewed her up."

Celestyn laughs, again. "Addie? That's precious."

"Are you paying attention?! Where were you if you were here the *whole* time? The girl was screaming and crying. You must have heard it at some point."

Her shoulders bounce up and down. "You guys seemed to have it locked down okay. I wasn't worried."

"What if we didn't?" I yell, inching closer to her face. "What if Addie didn't know how to stitch like she'd been making quilts with her ninety-seven-year-old grandmother her whole goddamn life? Huh?"

Celestyn pauses, her dark eyes void and feather pen stilled. She taps the fingers of her free hand restlessly, pursing her lips that curve downward into a frown. An expression that is genuine, for the first time all night.

"She's fine," she mumbles at last, staring at the windows. "But, she's obviously why you've stayed here this long. I can tell. So, go ahead. Ask."

I glance to where her eyes had laid, but the only thing looking back at me in the glass windows surrounding us is my own reflection. Still, I put a hand on the handle of my dagger just in case, turning slowly to her.

"Why did you pass Addie through quarantine?"

Her rock-solid exterior attempts a full return, but it has weakened.

"She wasn't ill. I saw no reason to keep her."

"They're *afraid* of her," I counter around her bullshit.

"Who?" She doesn't look at me.

*She knows damn well who.*

"EVERYONE!" I roar. "For fuck's sake, Celestyn. Don't play stupid when it doesn't fit your image!"

Her hip pops to the side and she crosses her arms. "Define everyone, dear."

"Every single person alive in Limbo, and some of the dead ones!" I shout. "And *me! Me!* I'm fucking terrified of her. She's fucking feral. She hit me at least twice today, and I'm thirty percent sure she tried to bite me earlier. And have you seen her *fucking eyes*? C'mon here. It's not normal."

"That's not a very high percentage, Aidan," she taunts, her voice level. "Are you sure it wasn't a love nibble? You looked awfully cozy out there with her, watching the new charges."

I laugh to try to keep myself from lunging across the desk and screaming some sense into her. It wouldn't do me any good.

"Celestyn. Have. You. Seen. Her. *Eyes*?"

"Yes, Aidan," she says with a sigh, as though it was a routine question she's been asked every day and she is tired of hearing it. "Adabelle...*Addie*, has full heterochromia. Blue and green. Very beguiling, but I assure you it's not dangerous or spooky, nor does it mean that she's a witch."

Oh, the mocking.

"It is more than that," I growl. "Can you fucking stop this bullshit?"

She hesitates, our stare down going much deeper this time. "Stop," she commands.

I know I have her cornered. She knows it, too.

"You. Know," I press. "And I deserve to know too. I fucking work with her."

She rolls her eyes, but I can see the wall break right in front of me, as if it were falling apart brick by brick.

"Her pupils dilate into the same slits worn by our favorite locals in reaction to light. Fine. You got me. But what do you want me to say? It isn't like it makes her dangerous. It just makes her... strange. What's wrong with strange?"

It isn't necessarily a lie, but it isn't the entire truth either. Another moan echoes down the hall from behind her, and Celestyn's head whips to it, her eyes breaking into an emotion I don't often see on her face.

*Sadness. Genuine pain.*

I relax, taking my hand off the desk and looking at the doors. I'm unable to ward off the paranoia filling my glass to the brim tonight.

"Things have been weird since she showed up, I hear," I remark.

There's guilt there, but she covers it well. People that don't know her as well wouldn't know it as such.

"Coincidental. Things are bound to get weirder here. That doesn't make it Adabelle's fault."

"The attacks have been more frequent and more violent—it's indisputable," I reply. "Do you think that she...well, I guess, do you think she might be one of them? Or that they are looking for her? She wasn't really found inside our own boundaries, Celestyn. Maybe, whoever found her, picked someone up that didn't belong to our community."

A pause.

"I...I don't know."

It's quiet, and I sink against the wall between the two hallways behind the desk, looking up at the sky through the bars above the glass ceiling. I've always loved the view in daylight hours, but sometimes I wish I could camp out in this lobby. Just to get a glimpse of something other than pitch darkness and fear.

Following what I've learned tonight, I wonder if Celestyn actually stays for the same reasons and view. She probably has better opportunities to see it, living with Master Amadeus, but this is independent of him. A place he never went where she could be free.

And she needs to be free.

Celestyn is pulling on a jacket I've never seen from her makeshift bag, closing it back up when an earsplitting screech sends shattered glass spilling to the floor in glittering fragments. A rock zooms past her head and several others ring against the bars that protect the outside of the building.

My eyes shoot toward the doors, closed but unlocked as I take a hesitant step forward. Celestyn's face is contorted in a similar horror, holding her breath and taking a step in the opposite direction toward the center hall. I shake my head at her, holding my hands out and inching forward a little more when another rock blasts through a perfect pane of glass. It finds its mark against the desk, hard enough to splinter the wood, the doors edging ajar in a simple creaking crack.

Out of the corner of my eye, I see her bend low to run down the hall, but I haul ass to her before she can. In a split moment, I take her by the arm and sweep her onto the floor. I inch her under the lobby desk, following at her heels and cramming us each tight against the medical supplies, then shifting the boxes in front of us with the hopes we won't be seen right as a thunderous crash shakes the whole floor.

I know what it must be, although it doesn't all register at the same time.

The whining creak, the door brushing open, and no one coming through. The resulting crash that snaps the floorboards and rocks the desk closer to the hall as our attempt to stay under it is followed by another boom sending dust and flecks of wood down upon us, thankfully not quite breaking the item in half.

It is just the doors coming unhinged and slamming down into The Center, but it feels like the beginning of an earthquake—violent and unsteady, erupting clouds of dust into the air that speckles our vision behind the boxes. Celestyn is trying not to inhale it, her tiny body convulsing while she pleads to me with wide open eyes to do anything at all. But there is nothing I can do, maintaining our place as I brace her close to the wall of the desk furthest from the boxes.

I lean at the sound of footsteps building in number through the lobby of The Center, unable to see much through the barricade of boxes. The candlelight emanating from the start of the main care hall has blown to a gentle glow, flickering in paced shadows that pass us by.

I hear the first doors creak open nearby within seconds. No time wasted, despite the noise being slow and ominous. I reach my hand out to hold hers when I hear the mumbling. The begging.

And then...

Screaming.

The sound of weapons shriek and crunch against bodily resistance. Wet gurgling and coughing accompany the smell of blood spilling out into the air. The thick essence of crimson can be felt seeping into the cracks of the floor, watering the foundation below in sticky drips of goo.

A set of steps click beside the desk we have sheltered beneath, stopping short of the boxes so that I can see the fabric fibers on the trousers of this Ravager. Coarse and dark green. Like the forest, and yet unlike the forest, not made for comfort. More for skirting the terrain on the regular without being hurt by wiry brush or blending into the surrounding area when time grows a little darker.

I don't move away in fear I will be heard, but I pivot my head to see Celestyn who squeezes the meat straight out of my hands, more silent than the ghosts of those who have already died here.

*No. No, no, no. Wait...I just...wait...*

I hear the familiar voice in frantic sobs from the quarantine hall, and my chest sinks faster than a car to the bottom of the ocean. I recall Celia's terror just trying to fall asleep next to me, the person who kept her safe for a mere couple of hours, her pulse throbbing so hard I could feel it through her skin. Sniffling and breathing so light, I was sure she was dead at one point in time.

It takes all of me to remain still. To not move while listening to her cry and call for help.

For me.

For Addie.

Hobbling and grabbing anything her hands can grip, until I can't hear her footsteps any longer.

*Sometimes they will pick up resistant women*, I remind myself at the start of panic. *And Celia is wounded. She can't walk well, so it would make sense.*

These creatures speak to one another in their own language, not vocalizing to the women they take at all, contrary to the stories. Celia's voice is a memory out the door, among many other

English speakers being taken tonight, each a lost cause and something I hope Addie won't bring up when she finds out what I had predicted came to pass. For a moment, this also leaves me paranoid that she might actually be a spy for the Ravagers, here to infiltrate our lifestyle.

Celestyn flinches at the Ravager standing in front of our hiding place when he nudges one of the boxes with his foot, the scuffle of her body concealed by screaming down the hall from a man drawing his final gasp of air, yet fighting for more. I cup a hand over her mouth before she can cry out at the next nudge of our barrier, studying the figure that stills.

The sound of his sword pulling free of its sheath makes me uncertain of what motion to make next, other than to play as if we're not here at all.

If I burst free, I'm dead and she is caught. If I move, I'm dead...and she is caught. We can't be here if we want to make it out.

Another woman stumbles down the hall, barefoot and tired, though she is much braver than the others around her. It reminds me of Addie and her pride, giving a quick sniff and nothing else as she stomps by with her head held upright.

The Ravager at our front yells something in their language, booming down the hall so that he is heard quite clearly, and bringing all who are still present to respond in unison. A word that rolls off their tongues with fluidity, then everything is suddenly blocked out by the point of a thin blade through the opening I have been using to keep watch.

I lean to the side, careful not to knock over a stack of gauze at the back of my head. Celestyn follows suit, her hair grinding against the backboard. Footsteps file out in an ordered fashion, sounds fading and voices diminishing. Celestyn's tears are now visible by the reflection of candlelight off the purest metal I have seen in my life, and I'm praying she can repress the panic long enough for us to go unnoticed.

The blade lowers to the wielder's leg, stopping, and then ripping through the boxes at the edge of my face with lightning speed, grazing my cheek without resistance from my skin at all and missing Celestyn entirely. I press my hand harder to her mouth in the motion, so much so I'm not sure she's breathing or if I'm smothering her. I bite my tongue when the blade slithers back, taking its time on the second go, until it is returned to its sheath.

From here, the user's footsteps turn and exit the building, though we stay in place for hours. We convulse beside one another in this time, until Celestyn has no more energy to burn.

Her eyes are the size of dinner plates, bloodshot and dead to the world around us.

I'm relieved that we made it out alive, my body melting against the support of the desk and holding my head until I can see natural light filtering inside the building, indicating the arrival of morning. It is only then that I push the boxes over, letting the supplies tumble to the floor and stretching my legs that feel as if they had atrophied overnight.

Celestyn follows me, ducking under the caved-in place where the door hit the desk when it crashed off its hinges, and surveying the damage done to her life's work. I want to tell her I'm sorry— not that words could fix what had been done to this haven.

All the windows have been smashed behind the protective bars —now bent like straws—allowing a cool breeze that the sunrise hasn't killed yet, to float inside. The double doors are knocked flat, breaking much of the flooring where they had bounced and tearing out some of the wall with it. Down the previously semi-sterile hallways, blood swirls in trails, with handprints like finger paints smeared across the stone where attempted survivors gripped for traction and crimson footprints of the women who walked through the demise leading out into the village.

Every door is open down every hall. Celestyn's hard and never-ending reams of paperwork are blowing a little throughout each one, smashed candles glued atop some of the scattered sheets.

I pick them up, still looking around each corner for survivors while Celestyn remains frozen. Stunned.

I won't get any help from her right now. It's been awhile since she has been witness to these atrocities, considering she's been housed by Amadeus for most of her existence in Limbo, and it would take time to process. Because she doesn't remember. She doesn't know what *worse* means in relation to attacks, except for what she sees on her way to work every morning.

But it's different than experiencing the events of every other person's reality in the heat of it.

Our nightmare.

I look at her, pity overwhelming my previous fit of rage. She stares in shock at the blood on the floor, her arms beginning to tremble all over again, though it's nothing she hasn't seen in the past.

I walk across the room to meet her, opening my arms to pull her in, and pausing as she skitters away, breathing heavy.

"No." Tears drop off her chin, dripping down her cheeks in waterfalls out of her control. "NO. NO."

My hands drop to my side, my head swiveling to the pink sunrise outside.

"It will be okay," I try to reassure, as I have others.

She shakes her head.

"No," she repeats like a dogged child. "No, it won't. No."

"It was bound to happe—"

"NO!" she screams. "No, it wasn't, Aidan. It was safe here. I made it safe here, and you brought *her* here. It ruined *everything*. *She* ruins everything she touches. Like a cursed...fucking cursed *bitch*. No!"

I am still staring out the broken windows, now wondering if Addie made it home safe.

"You're scared. You said yourself that these attacks are a—"

"It's not," Celestyn's voice quivers. "Don't try to tell me it was. It wasn't. You don't know what she is, okay?"

"Celestyn..."

"Don't talk to me," she shrieks. "Don't. I need...I need to quit. I just need to quit. I'll hide in Amadeus' tower for the rest of my life. It's fine. I'll just quit. I'll leave."

I grab her by the shoulders, steadying her so she has to look at me. Focus on me.

"You don't have his protections unless you work. This isn't about Addie, and you need to calm down."

She breaks. Snapping like the bones of the people lying dead in their rooms right this second.

"All of my patients are gone. They trusted me, and I failed them. They're all gone."

I give her a squeeze and pull her in, letting her head rest against my chest under my chin, wetting my shirt with liquid despair.

Has she ever cried like this until now? Truly cried?

It was alien in the moment until she pushed away, drying her face with a sleeve and racing back to her desk to gather her bag.

"Celestyn," I call. "We need to look for survivors. I've seen people live through attacks like this. It's not impossible. We lived."

"Mhm," she hums, tuning me out. "I...I need a personal day. I need a vacation. I'm going on vacation. A big break! I need something *good* today."

"What about everyone else who needs a personal day?" I raise my voice a little. "Everyone else that needs something good that only you know how to provide?"

Celestyn chuckles darkly, shaking her head. "I'm not the only one."

"You are."

"No. Nope. You, uh...you want to know about your little demon bitch partner so bad? Your little Addie? Well, I'll throw you a bone. A little extra information, since she hasn't had the decency to tell you herself yet. But you know her personal ID we found her with? Well, it said that she was a medical student."

I pause.

All medical students that have come through Limbo are assigned to The Center. So why wasn't she?

I open my mouth to speak, but Celestyn stops me.

"It wasn't my doing." She catches the accusation. "If I could have kept her contained to where I could control what I set free, I would have. Our *oh so great* Master assigned her before I could though. He wanted her out there in the forest with you guys for some *sick* reason. But today...he doesn't get a choice. I'm assigning her here to clean up the mess that she is responsible for."

"She didn't do anything wrong," I snap without thinking.

"She's here," Celestyn retorts. "That's wrong enough."

"I'm here. You're here."

She steps on top of the broken doors, rolling her shoulders, and wiping away more tears.

"Maybe we shouldn't be."

"Celestyn..."

She puts her hands up in a stopping motion, treading distance between us.

"No," she affirms one more time. "I'm done. I can't take it anymore. Sweet little Addie? She's your problem now."

I raise my hand, but she has raced out of the space where the doors used to stand.

And then I am alone.

Alone in a pile of rubble and a house of corpses.

# CHAPTER FOURTEEN
## ADABELLE

*Adabelle Shay Green, and current resident of Limbo, I hope this letter has found you well, or at least alive. It would be preferable you not perish so soon when we have so much to discuss. You see, I have had quite a few conversations with certain associates of my own, about you and your very existence in our little town. And what can I say?*

*Legend of your enchanting nature, and tales of your brutish appearances have sung songs to my ears that can only be fulfilled with my eyes. We will meet tomorrow night at sundown, should Ace deliver this on time. My schedule is open for the time being.*

*Be present and I will see you then.*

Master Amadeus

I FEEL SICK.

I reread the letter over and over while Zoey sleeps and, by the time she has woken up, I have stuffed it away into the depths of my backpack in an honest attempt to pretend I had not received it at all. It was that easy, wasn't it? It could be.

Most people wouldn't know I was still here if I didn't have a job that required me to be seen in public or leave the house. Maybe if I laid low for long enough, the Master would think I was dead, as long as payroll isn't reported back to him and I don't see Ace ever again. Who would keep a written payroll in a place where everyone dies, anyway? It isn't logical.

I'm frowning when Zoey finishes her breakfast of bread and fruit from my lunch with Aidan yesterday. She's filling out a little better, but I think I'm losing weight. My shorts have been sliding when I walk these last two days, and I'm pretty sure my ass is the only thing keeping them from dropping straight down my thighs all together.

Maybe it was more the dancing than the lack of food though. I've been doing a lot of it, burning extra calories, and trying to keep myself distracted to avoid the thought of tragedy playing out around me. I have the energy to do it, even considering most of my job requires being on my feet, and it's sort of like a warm-up in wait for the big game.

"Are you ready to blow this shithole?" Zoey creeps alongside me, peering down into my dead face.

I try to smile. I don't want her to worry about me or get skittish about my lack of sleep during the attacks.

"Yeah. Let's get you to your check-up, so I can go to work."

I want to commission someone to make baby clothes from things no one uses any longer. It's a subject that has been on my mind a lot lately, and I have high hopes for a girl to complete our household in the coming days. Just a tiny little female, someone that we had a better chance to lead by example to and teach what it means to be a person. A task that would be exponentially easier than what I imagined teaching a boy about manhood would be.

But I'll have to see what happens between now and then. Knowing what I know, and having what I have, we both need to be prepared for anything. Which also means I need to speak with Ace at least one more time before I go off the grid—if that is even possible.

Maybe Aidan will give me a few seconds or something.

I shoulder my backpack on and I step out ahead of Zoey, helping her down with what little bit of waddled grace she can muster. I don't take in our surroundings until I whip back around, catching Zoey's *whoa* as I do.

It is a blood bath, painted on the sides of each shack in crimson that bakes to a rich brown as it ages in the dewy sunlight. Two bodies are strung out in pieces around neighboring homes, and four more litter beyond that, their torsos marred in stab wounds and deep slices. Slash marks ooze puddles that soak into the nutrient rich soil, feeding it the sour taste of evil that it drinks with indifference.

I swallow, trying to shut my mind to it the way I see everyone else do, and hurrying through the maze of houses to the grass that leads to the old village. Zoey waddles at my tail, her breathing labored by the unborn baby jutting angry feet up into her lungs like a straw meant to suck the air out of her. She grabs my elbow as I rush ahead, pulling me in reverse until I can find my footing, then glancing in the direction of the village.

Why isn't she panicking too?

"It's...more violent than usual." I breathe, swallowing the lump of frenzy that comes with each syllable.

"O-only in theory," she replies, voice shaken. "This s-shit has happened before. A-a-and we recovered from it just fine. They have periods of aggression and such, but it always goes away. It's that small dick energy shit coming out and so on."

Her voice rises and falls in pitch. I don't know who she is trying to convince now that she has opened her mouth, but I decide that I'll need to do some light research between talking to Ace and Aidan this morning. I've fallen behind since having Zoey home, and this situation screams for help like none predating it.

Together, we hurry in synced steps to The Center to drop her off, the bodies of men all around growing sparse the closer we get to this side of the village, but also bringing in another newer thought no one has asked yet.

Why are there never corpses from the Ravagers? These men don't just lay down and die, and not every fight can be escaped unscathed when the opponent is not in complete control of their victim.

So where are their bodies? Have we ever looked into it? Or them?

We reach The Center in record time, stopping short of the broken door frame and crumbling wall letting in beams of sunlight and warm morning air. My stomach hurts.

I hate being right, and my innards turn to slush while I catch my breath from not only racing all the way here, but the view in and of itself.

The windows are shattered across the lobby, fractals stained in smears of dried blood and the bars protecting the glass bent like plastic toys—snapped in half all together in certain places. Where doors had stood at one time to protect the masses are now hinges that hang in haunting squeaks by nails freed of their frame, ready to drop down to the pieces they once held, buried into the wood floor that has fractured into aggressive splinters.

Upon entry, I can see millions of microscopic flakes of dust floating against the light, drifting midair as if it had nowhere else to go. In the tattered hallways, silence screams back to the wall of mortality presented here, stripping the building and its people bare so there's not so much as a tear to grieve with.

Zoey's fingers tangle along the back of my shirt while we move inside, step by step. The girth of the right side door creaks beneath the weight of us, the eyes of people who had arrived as soon as moonlight became sunlight seething against our degenerate persons. Still, rare others can't seem to take their eyes off of this decrepit, *untouchable* museum of bodies that have been haphazardly yanked from rooms along the middle hall behind the desk. None of which look alive.

At the desk, caved slightly in the middle so it looks like the kind of *v* birds that art teachers show children to draw, is Aidan. He turns to see me at the start of murmurs, the bags under his eyes heavier than ever and the dry whites bloodshot.

The limp sound of more bodies being dragged further down the hall in rotting shadows can be heard through the animosity filling the room, begging questions between us.

So many questions.

I pat Zoey's hand, asking her to take a seat next to another woman crisscrossed on the floor with two children under the age of ten, dark crimson smeared across their faces with no visible wounds to cause it. When she puts her hands up to Zoey in a refusal to let her sit, I notice the gashes across each palm, wounds dripping little rivers down her arms through the cloth she partially tied over them.

I can see the initial pain of rejection cross Zoey's face at this, her inner defenses flaring as she tells the lady to *fuck off* in search for another seat. But she still does as she's asked, for now, and so I approach my partner. Careful.

"Where's Celestyn?" I whisper to him, glancing around the lobby again.

She should be here.

It is getting fuller by the second, and it doesn't seem like anyone has escaped this attack without injury. The optimist, somewhere deep down, wants to point out that not everyone was killed for a reason. They can only cover so much surface area in our town within the confines of a single night. Which means the numbers the locals send out are *limited*.

They can't afford to lose anyone if we fight back. Most of the time, until now, it seems like they send groups to focus on particular areas, since not every home or collection of houses has been attacked every night. They are methodical and cautious, if we can take some time to pay attention. Maybe we would be more successful if we conjured a game plan from our studies and fought back as a unit, instead of this "every man, woman, and child for themselves" bullshit.

*We need an army.*

Aidan looks out the glass ceiling. There is a subtle tinge of grey in the isolated clouds that insinuate rain might be in our forecast later today, collecting the strength to move in from somewhere over the horizon, slow and smooth. Currently, it is more like the distant growl of a furious beast in the expansive sky than a sure predator ready to attack. There will still be time to go out and search for a bit this morning if we leave soon after what will be an imminent clean up, and I can talk to Ace later if I am fast.

Aidan rubs his face, breathing deep into his hands. "She is... ah...she's taking a break."

I cringe. "A break? Has she seen this place? She can't take a break. People are..."

My voice runs away without me. Aidan is staring at me between his fingers as though they are part of a prison cell that I put him in that divides us straight down the middle. When I fall quiet, his hands drop to his side and he motions with a tick of his head to follow him through the halls of death. I don't want to go. The memories of our little corpse removal street team gave me nightmares throughout the night that I could not escape with each flutter of my lids. The final vulnerable expressions, frozen on the faces of people begging to live and trying to recover from illness or injury, could push me over the edge when I don't quite know where that's at right now. But I find myself moving with him, nonetheless, refusing to let my fear set the boundaries for what I can and can't do.

The lobby becomes a distant buzz while we shuffle around corpses laid out like dolls from a gory toy box. Papers thrown from the desk and candles ripped from their holders are smashed into this disarray, bleeding into the mess of other broken doors and frames snapped clean.

The pain goes on forever at times, like a parade I'm being taken down on purpose, though I can't figure out why. And when the hallway does end, it stops at a singular door with a brass handle and dead silence.

Aidan lays his hand across the handle, flexing his fingers along the metal in thought. He glances at me out of the corner of his eye when I don't mention how off putting it is, waiting for his order.

"You said you were a dancer." His voice is thick, dark. Accusatory.

I step away from him with a slight laugh.

"I was? I mean, I am. I could show you just about any dance you could—"

"Where did you learn to stitch people up?"

The calm in his voice is eerie and militant for his tone. He waits out my resulting silence, pulling a key ring from his pocket and thumbing through them.

"I don't know."

"You don't know?" he scoffs.

"I don't," I repeat, my head swiveling up and down the hall in disbelief. This has to be a joke.

"Really? You don't remember at all?"

I cross my arms. "I'm sorry, did you hit your head last night after I left, or something? You're acting...stupid."

*Smooth.*

I couldn't get any smoother with an eloquent word choice like *stupid*. Here I am, the high and mighty genius of Limbo, using childlike words to describe my sleep-deprived partner's actions.

Although, it isn't really wrong? Is it?

"Why didn't you tell me that you were a medical student, Addie?" he roars, spinning around to face me so close I can feel the warm air he breathes. "That is *really* important information in this place."

*What?*

"I...I didn't know," I admit. "I—"

"*You didn't KNOW?* How do you not *know*? It's on the damn identification card they used to figure out who the hell you were when you got here!"

I stumble backward, rich reds creeping up my neck and ears to my cheeks.

I am on fire.

"I...haven't looked at the ID much, yet," I mumble. "I was afraid to know...you know, I was afraid to know what kind of person I was. Especially when the memories so far have been so positive. I just kind of thought I had the time to take it slow."

He spins back to the door in a flash, cramming a key inside, and flinging the metal beast open in an earsplitting shriek that allows what natural light is still present through the oncoming clouds to sprinkle inside, along with a terribly familiar odor. The reality hits us both at the same time, and his shoulders slump forward, his head hanging.

"You didn't know." Aidan nods, talking more to himself than me. "Okay."

He holds on to the door a little longer. Void. Hitting his temple against the sharp edge a few times. For a moment, it looks like he falls asleep in this position, growing still and lax where the outside heat scalds him in a blanket of sweaty warmth. It doesn't look like he's breathing in these minutes, until voices commence at the end of the hall we came from.

My eyes pop up from my partner's despair to see Ethan and Glue Man strolling in our direction at a slow, uneven pace. Aidan lifts his head in response to their presence, straightening upright and stalking forward until I can feel him behind me. He leans closer so I can feel the heat radiating off his body, rigid and preparing for the onslaught of verbal attacks they will have at the ready.

A proper mentor here to defend his student, though I shiver at the contact—reluctant to leave, but anxious to stay. He smells nice...like soap.

Ethan gives him a hard look at this, clenching his usual cigarette in lightly yellowed teeth that roll it back and forth with care, in thought. Glue Man is like a dog at his side, balancing against the stone wall, and his bitterness about my attendance at work more than evident. It's amazing he keeps his mouth shut for the cleanup today, with his hands shoved deep in his pockets and his body bent in an unusual contortion in the poor lighting.

"Good morning."

Aidan is better at the pleasantries than any of us standing here.

"What happened?" Ethan nods around us, leaping straight over the bullshit like a mountain goat.

Aidan's arm brushes my shoulder when he reaches up, adjusting his glasses and sighing. "Exactly what it looks like, I'm afraid. But now that you guys are here, we could really use the help. There have been three...err, *survivors* found so far, by the only two volunteers I've had this morning, who are also injured persons. So this hall is the only one that has been touched."

"Unnerstood," Glue Man grumbles.

Aidan also seems put off by his compliance. Suspicious. But at second glance, I notice his posture more and how he holds himself, the uneven tilt of his body and the weight he shifts to the left side. At the end of Aidan's explanation, he rocks upright, a hand coming to Ethan's shoulder and fumbling closer to The First-in-Command. It is then I notice his right shoe is missing as well as the stump of where his foot had been, wrapped in dozens of discolored shirts and tied off with a belt.

My inhale must have been steep, attracting the attention of all three men, Aidan of which is now leaning over my shoulder. He sees it too, how much more pasty Glue Man is, and the copious amounts of sweat pouring from every micro inch of his skin. He can't work with that kind of injury.

"I-I'm so sorry," I scramble for words. "He just...um...he really needs help, and I..."

"He's gonna be fine." Ethan is resolute. "We'll be well off 'til Celestyn comes back to post."

I part my lips to protest, but Ethan is already helping Glue Man to the lobby to give orders to the rest of the team. I look to Aidan, my mouth quivering to find words in the overwhelming disappointment I had that he didn't say anything for his friend's sake.

He is eying me too, something cruel lingering at the forefront of his thoughts and shining through his blue irises like a mirror into hell.

But it's not just cruel. I recognize this look.

*This,* I know.

He hates me.

Hates. Me.

There is so much of it. So much misguided blame and detest consuming him from the inside.

"I didn't do..."

"We should have never rescued Celia," Aidan interrupts. "I told you it was a bad idea, and it was."

"It was our job," I hiss. "She needed help."

"She was *their* problem," he yells so loud that the trees could hear. "Not mine! Not yours! They caught her. She belonged to them."

I push him into the door so hard his head rings against the metal. "She's not a fucking fish, Aidan. You can't *catch* a woman. They *kidnapped* her and she *escaped*. By the skin of her teeth she did, but by *God* she was brave enough to do it at all. And we helped *rescue* her because. That. Is. Our. Job. Whether you fucking shits are brave enough to do it or not, it is. Celia never, *ever*, belonged to anyone."

Aidan rubs the back of his head, visible anger blossoming in the way he clenches his fists. "She's gone, and innocent people are dead. They came *looking* for her, *Adabelle*. I was here when it happened. I had to listen to her trauma happen *all over again*."

For some reason, his use of my actual name bites. I don't like that it's ugly.

"You heard her grief." I grit my teeth. "Not her trauma."

"It's. No. Different."

"It is everything," I insist. "And the fact that none of you can tell the difference, only tells me that you shouldn't be working in this field."

"Neither. Should. You." He sucks in air, trying to hold back. "You're impulsive. You are unable to work as a team. You're... naïve. You can't figure out how to weigh the needs of the many against the needs of the few. You just see...*need*, and that's a problem."

"The many will become the few if you don't start helping them before then."

He shakes, his whole body convulsing with the energy to summon the amount of restraint it takes to keep his bottle-capped temper in check.

"It's your fault," he says. "It's your fault, and I'm going home. I'm taking a nap, and you're cleaning up the mess you made here. The bodies go out this door here. The paperwork is...everywhere. Ebony will be along soon to help admit new patients, a-and it looks like the rest of the team will help clean the rooms and drop bodies for nature's cleanup. Good luck. Get your shit sorted out."

He brushes past me, but I yell after him. "This is your fucking cop out, isn't it? This is how you guys get rid of me from the teams? Having me work at The Center gives you what you wanted all along, and Ace won't bypass it because your piece of shit girlfriend can't be found."

This stops him dead in his tracks, his gaze narrowed in fury upon me. "You don't know her."

"Neither do you," I reply.

We are stilled in this moment until he breaks it, stepping over bodies like they weren't human at one point, and leaving me to sort out the mess that has been made in our wake.

There are even more people in the lobby when I emerge again. Most of them men, with a couple women and some children mixed in. They stand all along the doors and walls, many trying to sneak peeks down the other halls or catch glimpses of the number of bodies being pulled out by the half a dozen or so members of the search teams, minus Aidan, myself, and Glue Man. I wonder if maybe these people are looking for someone they know.

Ethan resurfaces from the left most hall without Glue Man, trotting to my side and looking at our mass gathering of villagers.

"The orders are comin' from you today," he says. "This once, 'til Celestyn comes back."

I have no experience on how to keep this place operational. I don't know anything about how it operated in the first place, other than that ends barely met.

But I try my best.

"Send half the team to empty out rooms and dispose of bodies." I swallow. "Make sure they get names if they can find any identification...just in case anyone asks. Send the others to quarantine. I doubt there is anyone left, but if there is, take them out here for a room closer to civilization. They at least deserve that. And if you see Ebony...tell her to start taking patients."

There is a part of him that wants to argue, but he doesn't. This is for more than just me, and there is an understanding of this. He turns away, shoving his hand into his pocket, and strolling to a hall where there are more than a few members handling bodies. I can hear him bark my orders as if they were his own, and the team responding without delay. I would more than happily give him the credit for the demands if it meant everyone acted like a cohesive unit.

The rest of the lobby draws me back in, however, the crowd large enough to stomp me clean into the floor alongside the doors if I tell them all at once to find their own room. But I'm not sure what else to do. I'm not sure what Celestyn does.

The doorframe is clustered with people leading out in a line. Bleeding and gored. Some sneezing. Two children to the left of the lobby chase one another back and forth, one with a large bruise swelling over her eye so she can no longer open it.

I suck in air.

"He—" The swarm of people grow louder. I raise my voice a hair. "Hello? Hello, everyone. I am...um..."

"Shut the fuck up and listen, you goddamn pieces of shit!" Zoey yells over the crowd all at once, right next to my ear, giving me a solid thumbs up.

She is going to be the disciplinarian between us in a household with a child.

I smirk at her nearly bragging grin, letting the crowd simmer into muffled retorts and coughing. For a dancer, I've never much liked a ton of eyes on me.

"I am..." I hesitate, trying to find my confidence. "I am taking over for Celestyn today."

I can hear murmurs right away, and a group of four exit on the spot. Not that I take it personally. It is four less people that I care to deal with.

Zoey claps at my side, slow and sarcastic. "Givin' the woman a break. Fucking get the bread, girl."

It is hard not to smile when she talks. Is this friendship? Or what friendship is like?

"My name is Adabelle Green," I carry on with the announcement. "Just in case you would like to call me something other than *beast*, and I mean no harm. We are going to work through Celestyn's break the best we can, with what resources we have available."

"Fucking right!" Zoey yells. "So, in case you cracks didn't fucking hear, if you have a problem with my girl here, running the show today, find the mother fucking door!"

I'm certain she's trying to be supportive, but I don't think her words are going to win me any love.

I laugh, body so on fire with nerves that I can't feel my fingers.

"I...I didn't say that. But I don't know when Celestyn is returning. So, for now, if your problem is a sickness, please step to your left. And if your problem is an injury, step to your right. Major injuries that are immediately life-threatening should be up front where I can see you better, and more minor to the back. If you're here in a group, I will try to keep you in said group for comfort."

People storm around in a stampede of trouble, pushing and shoving to arrive at their designated side of the room. The doors groan beneath so many sets of feet, wood splitting in loud cracks here and there, until the room starts to look a little more organized.

Ebony comes forth during this mess, reporting to me, and introducing herself with words that feel like acid melting through my flesh. I offer to let her take the reins of the sicker patients in hopes she will finish with them quick and meet up with me for the rest—a job she doesn't seem to mind, either.

In the meantime, I attempt to assign my massive group of injured individuals to empty rooms right away. We are still stepping over bodies in the hallways for the first half of the afternoon in this process, but by the next, almost all of our dead are out the back door where animals can have their way with their corpses, and most patients are stabilized enough I can take a quick breather while Ebony works through it.

Quick enough to be yelled at, anyway.

I wince, listening to screaming a few doors down the hall, in demands for a nurse to attend their problem so they could get back to work. The words make me cover my face with my palms, trying to decide whether it's physically possible to spontaneously combust, or if I actually have to go see what these people want when I have yet to eat breakfast or lunch.

I can't imagine I willingly took on a medical career if the abuse of providers was the cornucopia of the profession. But it would fit...with the nostalgic smells and the sounds reverberating at the back of my skull.

*Chronic beeping. Groaning. Screaming.*

The misery is familiar to my heart. I am hardened to it, but open to it at the same time.

I wander the few doors over it takes to meet the entrance the yelling emits from, entering a room with a man and three children. The paper written up on them at the foot of their door had their names, ages, and problems listed out accordingly by search team staff to quicken their care with me.

*Oscar Hudson: 30 years old. Injured arm and deep gash at temple of head in need of examination/cleaning. Claims he was protecting children from kidnapping. Saved three out of six by hiding them under pile of blankets at back room compartment before attack. Was assumed dead in attack after head busted. Back room was never checked.*

*Genevieve Dixon: 7 years old. Mild contusions to face and arms unrelated to attack. Possibly work related. Check for concussion.*

*Ryan Miller: 13 years old. Stab wounds to chest, stomach, and arms. Suspected miss of some but not all vital organs. Child pale and lethargic. Coughing up blood. Check first in group. Parental guardian claims the child removed himself from blankets to draw attention away from two other female children.*

*Brookie Williams: 10 years old. Moderate contusions to arms around infected cuts from untreated rooster attacks. Clean, and refer stay until Celestyn returns for monitoring and self-made disinfectant cream.*

My heart jolts, looking at the group of them huddled on a single mattress. Little hands compress crimson pools on the crumpled body of the one who could only be Ryan, and I'm choking on my air.

No one had said anything. I was never told about the urgency of this situation while I handled others of less severity. Stitching wounds, sawing away limbs, calling death at the hour it struck. And yet not a single person warned me of the urgency attached to the writing of this case.

Why? Is this another way to throw me under the bus as some uncaring monster?

I sweep inside the room, around the corner of protective wall, dropping to my knees for a better view in the candlelight. The hands belonging to the children aren't doing anywhere close to an adequate job of plugging the injuries while I attempt to figure out what I can do to preserve his life. The boy's eyelids are fluttering under the pressure of each bacterial prod into his gaping wounds, the whites flashing back to me when I move a set of candles closer to better my view.

I don't have the equipment to transfuse blood or start an IV to replenish the fluids he has lost. I'm not super sure how he has stayed alive this long, pumping out blood as fast as he had to of with these injuries, other than maybe Oscar had helped keep the new vacuum in his chest steady right before calling for my assistance.

But I notice the children around him more now, how their sticky hands grow stiff and slick, wobbling as they try to keep him here. Each one has wounds of their own to concern over, and they're growing weaker. Too much so to keep up this endeavor.

Ryan is leaving us.

I can't prolong him in this place. I know I can't.

I'm not the person who can do this.

I can feel myself start to shake at this thought, sucking in a deep inhale and moving a single hand over one of theirs, experiencing the flail of his chest and quivers of agony. My fingers press into the cold of his little body under all this heat, counting the frantic beats of his brave heart as they become further apart.

I could wash him up now and stitch the wounds shut. I don't want to blame myself for this, but I feel the guilt burying itself inside me, making home in my guts. Like cancer, it eats away at healthy tissue while my brain fights to rationalize this.

Whether or not I was alerted to the urgency of this problem on time, it consoles, there are perhaps so many sources of internal bleeding, I would have never been able to save him. It would have been too late when I woke up, and it was definitely too late when they got here.

So much has gone wrong here. So much *is* wrong here.

Why kill a thirteen-year-old boy? What did it accomplish?

At the side of the bed is a bowl of water that has gone cold, and a washcloth that I wring until it is damp. I press it around the assumed sources of blood for a cleaner view, but he's no longer reacting much to the pain of it. He's not writhing beneath the pressure of my touch to his gaping wounds.

He hardly even gasps. No groaning.

It isn't until the tears start dripping over my stupid round cheeks, that I realize I haven't been successful for a single second in stopping the helplessness that overwhelms me in Limbo. I can't avoid the frustration. I'm crumbling, seven-year-old Genevieve a more hardened warrior than I, as her hands slide out of the wounds when Ryan's struggle begins its end.

I can't shut out the negative thoughts now. The ones that antagonize me and tell me Ryan would have lived if I had just organized this building better.

I shouldn't be in charge here and it's all a big mistake. Why did they put me in charge here?

Each of our hands collapse from Ryan as he deteriorates, Oscar pushing Brookie out of the way to plug the wounds he can, hanging on with a face that grows redder with pain by the minute. I blink away another bout of sorrow, licking my lips and staring into the abyss of a room marked with the murder of an innocent little boy.

"I can...um...I'll go get some wrap," I whisper. "The wounds. Maybe we can..."

"No." Oscar's voice is dangerous, and I find myself rigid to a tone I know all too well, alarm bells ringing like a declaration of war. "You've already proven to be worthless. If Celestyn were here, he would have lived. She has talent."

I acquiesce.

It's true. I'm a piece of shit.

"O-okay. But...if you would let me see the other children, I can still..."

"NO!" he shouts.

The other children curl away at the sound, and Oscar reaches his bloody hands to the back of my head, wrapping blistered knuckles into my hair before I can run, and ramming my face against Ryan's chest...like a dog being poorly disciplined.

I squeak, just enough to be heard, then I'm winded by the force he floors me with.

"Do you see this?!" he screams again. "This! This would have never happened if they let you die. You worthless piece of fucking shit. Ever since they let you in, the attacks have only been more violent. Now, because Celestyn is so kind, children get to die in higher volumes just because they're boys. He. Was. A. Boy."

"I...I'm sorry." I inhale the scent of blood, my nose pressed so hard to his flesh, one nostril is sealed shut. "I'm so sorry."

"Y-y-you're s-sorry?" Oscar is crying now. "That is all you have to say for yourself? Is that you're fucking sorry?"

His free hand connects with the side of my face, and I feel warm blooms pool copper to the surface of my mouth, staining my teeth and leaving the skin hot and tingling with fire. I'm dazed through it, my eyes wide and body frozen as he keeps his grip on my hair so tight that I can feel strands free up from my scalp. I open my mouth to speak and crimson free flows, my words just an endless pitch when he hits me once more at the corner of my eye in a thud that lands me on the floor beside Ryan's now lifeless body.

I reach for the wooden bowl full of soapy water, my fingers brushing the rim as Oscar raises his interlocked hands in a hammer above my spinning head, ready to come down with all his might. But a voice interrupts us.

"That's enough."

The words make him hesitate, allowing Ebony to stride into the room and clutch his arm with a warm compassion I don't usually see in girls her age. His face breaks into grief laced in denial as I spit the gushes of blood bubbling between my bit tongue and split lips, dribbling down my chin while his sobbing bounces off every wall in the room.

"It's all her fault," he weeps. "He was a *boy*. He didn't deserve that, and she...she..."

"She didn't go on and wield the sword," Ebony protests in my favor. "That baby boy was gone as soon as it happened, and he knew what sacrifice he was making when he did it."

I slink upright, climbing to my wobbly feet, and granting Ebony a quick nod as I exit, hearing Oscar scream out behind me.

*Don't you dare come back. I'll wring your neck myself, you* bitch. *Make the sacrifice. Do what's right.*

I am running faster through the halls now, faster than I have in my life, adrenaline coursing wildly inside my veins. At the back door Aidan and I had stood in earlier, I force myself outside in its somewhat ajar crease, despite the insistences of voices at my back, whirling around stacks of bodies, and breaking into the forest past the first layer of the Dome.

I stumble along overgrown roots and sticks, wiping my face with the crook of my elbow so smears of blood paint my forearm. The air is thick with humidity that has intensified since this morning causing the rotting of the bodies, somewhere I can't see, to smell more horrendous than I thought possible. In fleeting darkness overhead, thunder erupts in bright savage flashes of burning white, like the blinding click of a camera times a million, and I find myself startled, darting from this sound I cannot escape.

Dizzy.

I can't think.

Everything is just...blurred together.

I'm not sure what to do next, collapsing against the abrasive bark of a tree to catch my breath. Fear pulses like a sickness here, padding me in a sea of cotton so I am suffocating. My own blood turns to sludge, fighting with me to circulate through a body contaminated by this poison. This sickness.

I hold my head, humming to the pain that blinds me in another flash of lightning. The resulting thunder gets me moving again, past the second layer of The Dome, like I was told, and into the third layer. The thinnest one.

It crosses my mind, when I reach this place, not to leave like they want me to. Frightened and grieving people do horrible things to cope, and I should try to understand them. Reason with them, like I had intended to in the first place.

But out here, I could pave my own path if I wasn't caught. I could be somewhere I'm not a sitting duck waiting to be plucked from the flock. I could thrive somewhere my flock doesn't hate me, or reject me without a word as to why. I could do all of it without ever having to face Master Amadeus and unknown consequences, because people go missing all the time.

No one would ever know the difference.

It doesn't have to be a hard choice, and my feet do most of the work for my brain, toeing through these parts of the third layer

Aidan had left unexplored with me so far. I notice it takes longer to get through, moving around trees and shrubbery, but not hearing the water for hours. I can't tell if the time passes this way because I am walking slower, or if it is actually bigger than the other layers.

My head throbs the more ground I cover, and all smells point toward sweaty pocket change. Rain has started to drop in inquisitive plops upon my skin, chilling the swells of heat smarting in throbbing pain where I was struck. Up ahead, I can see the outline of a large wooden shed with two glassless windows.

I have enough time to make it to the door before the downpour if I hurry, which I do, realizing it doesn't have so much as a lock to keep its contents safe. It pushes open, unlatched and lacking resistance at the touch of my fingers, right as the rain washes to the ground in sheets that splash inside to the floors.

I scuttle inside, taking in the view when I break the threshold to realize it isn't so much a shed as it is a small house...but not quite that, either. There are small trunks lining each wall of the inhabitable area, stacked in some places to the ceiling, and in shorter clusters the closer they come to the terse hallway. I sweep my fingers along the ones at the back wall, made of white wood with intricate silver inlay and golden latches clicked tight.

More thunder roars outside as I do this, and my head whips back to the window, fear creeping in that I am not alone out here. The aura in this place is tense with a presence, strong with unfamiliar sweet scents, and the overwhelming sensation that I am being watched.

How could I be so stupid to go this far out of Limbo without someone alongside me? I don't want to meet Zoey's fate. I don't want to lose the fight before it's begun.

Aidan had told me, at one point, that these locals occasionally penetrate the third layer in daylight, and I didn't listen. I couldn't help myself when the anguish settled into my bones.

I never can.

I have a habit of just...acting. Just speaking.

It's an uncontrollable urgency to will myself into existence, a tendency I can sometimes catch, but more often than not...it is this. This chaos. This mess that I am.

My fear takes a back seat and shuts off when my senses are overloaded, and my common sense dies with it. I just can't fight it. I can't...

I shield my face with cupped hands at the next strike of lightning, jumping at the sound of intangible white ripping apart the sky. In my dreams so far, it's never stormed like this. Not with the winds and the ferocious lightning and booming thunder. The rain didn't lay siege on buildings or bend plants sideways, and nature did not gust haunting moans through the open windows.

But a part of me recognizes the sounds. The sensations and the cleansing odors.

*It's only thunder, girl*, a harsh reminiscent voice snickers in the back of my thoughts. *Go on now, get up. On them feet.*

I drop my hands to my side, sucking in a steep breath. I'm still dizzy and a bit unbalanced, but I let it all go, shutting the weight of this place out. My feet become charged with my comfort, my arms like wings, spreading with grace to help me fly.

Delicate.

So much more than a porcelain doll on a shelf, and so much stronger.

I am strong, spinning circles with my eyes shut, so my heavy throbbing head can't keep up. I let my leg pivot, commanding the other to keep me firm on the wood floor so I can finish this one endeavor of self-love.

Because dancing is like breathing for me. Necessary to my being, a natural function for my body, and effortless to my soul. I could do it forever, right here, and it could be my happily ever after.

Every girl gets one, right?

I pivot again, but my shoes hit the rainwater and I stumble, crashing into the open window space and careening into a stack of trunks that smash to the floor, latches from the top containers splitting open to spill contents along the wood surface. I collect myself, head pulsing while I sit on my ass and take in the view of items littered around me. My jaw unhinges at what I see.

The closest trunk is a heap of leather-bound books and papers, decorated in illegible scrawl and detailed pictures of...people. I scoot closer, scooping up its contents in armfuls, studying the unusual letters and symbols bleeding across the page like book script, realizing that artwork accompanied the insides of certain books from the torn edges.

Around me, other trunks are elements of intrigue and survival. A fractured lid on one reveals stacks of skinny white candles awaiting use and medical supplies beside it, another spilling over with peculiar purple flowers with sharp, wilted petals tied and dried in clusters. The trunk below this stores more daggers and rapiers wrapped in clean, pale cloth than I could have imagined— each one gleaming perfection down to their leather hilts and jeweled pommels. The last trunk I touch makes me sick, and I'm reluctant to dig further inside as I discover nothing more than...

*Shackles.*

I drop the weighted restraints in a hurry, looking around me as if I would be locked in place any second.

What is this place? Is it ours?

It can't be ours.

Who knows about it?

I take a swathe of soft bandage from the candle trunk, wrapping a cluster of books, flowers, daggers, needles and rough thread so that they are unrecognizable in the little package—other than that the material is cleaner than our own. Softer, like silk.

It has to be silk.

I press my face into the plush of it, like a brick pillowcase with everything I've stuffed inside, placing it beside me. I'm sure to follow this up by returning what I can to the other designated trunks and restacking them like they were, though I'm hesitant at the shackles.

What if this place was the housing of stored consequence for meeting the Master? What if it belonged to the locals and we were dumb to it this whole time?

No one has ever mentioned it, at least, and I can't meet Master Amadeus like this.

I need to go.

The rain has begun to recede outside, regressing to touches of water tapping at the inside of the building through the windows. I flip hair away from my face that had fallen apart when my bun had been manhandled, damp but drying as I take the shackles as fast I can, pushing them inside the trunks until I can find the courage to burn them at a later date.

Though after this I am wrought with the burning indecision of what happens next—to go home or leave forever.

What lies beyond this, anyway?

I wouldn't be such a target with more ground to cover. I couldn't be a monster with real ones lurking about.

What do I have to lose?

If I leave, I need my backpack first. I left it under the desk at The Center, and it carries all the history I can't bear to part with.

I clutch the items I'll take back with me to my chest, ready to leave when I hear something other than the sound of rain drenching everything in its path. Just barely, but it's there, though I can't quite make out what it is.

My better judgment should tell me to run. But I turn around instead, slipping between two sets of trunks that guard the hall and inching along the tall, skinny walkway. I peer my head inside two tiny rooms as I wander, only to see more boxes packing each crevice.

From the last two doorways, I'm positive of the sound—a gentle crying. I tilt my head to the right doorway, guarded by stacks of trunks that give way to a hidden walkway upon approach. I maneuver amongst them, peering around the shelf they create to find a familiar face sitting at the center of a circle created by tiny articles of clothing.

"Zoey?" I'm breathless, but relieved. I set my wrap of supplies on a stack of trunks, then move to the floor with her. "What are you doing here?"

She jumps out of her skin, unaware of my presence at all in her trance until my voice came at her. And then the emotion hits her all at once, her bottom lip trembling, her eyes swollen pink and red.

*Does she know why she's here?*

I pick up the infant clothes around her, examining each piece as I do. All of which are so sweetly small, delicate, and sewn together with experience and love.

Dresses. Trousers. Little long-sleeved shirts up to child sizes. Soft slippers and blankets.

But the design is...off.

Intricate. Beautiful. Powerful.

But not of our own.

"What is this?" I ask her, and she sniffs again, tears pouring down her cheeks.

She tries to wipe them away, so I don't see, but it's too late. I am just in time to see her snap, sobbing too loud for comfort this deep in the forest.

I can't help whipping around, catching another glassless window toward the other end of the room as the sound of tree leaves hush a song of consolation. On the broad sill is her canteen, and I rush to pick it up, nearly fumbling it out the other side. She takes the item from my hands like it would be her last drink in this world, nearly gagging on the water in her hurry.

I grimace. "When did you escape The Center?"

She gasps when the water hits her core, wiping her mouth, and holding back another whimper.

"You fucking suck at running The Center," she mumbles. "People were literally walking out all over while your dumb ass was at the desk. It wasn't hard."

"I...I'm sorry..."

"I want Celestyn back," she seethes. "We need to get her back soon, before I have this damn baby...and judging from your stupid face, you need her, too. It's not like that'll be the first time someone beats the fucking snot out of you, otherwise."

It isn't easy to forget. The pain hasn't left since it happened.

The swollen bruise at my temple throbs with its own pulse, and the place where I had bitten my own tongue at the first hit is sore. I won't be able to eat right for weeks, sure enough. I reach my fingers to touch the bruise with care, cringing.

Zoey is starting to whine louder than my pain, pooling lakes of saltwater in her collarbone. My attention returns to her and I drop the baby clothes in her lap, looking in the open boxes for more. Whether or not they're ours, they could be handy.

"Are..." I don't know how to pose my question. I'm so bad at this. "Does it hurt? The labor pain?"

"Are you fucking stupid?" Zoey snaps fast. "Is that just it? You're fucking dumb?"

"Yes."

I blush, digging through heaps of clothes in open trunks.

The tiny dresses are soft and lacy. Softer than my own clothes, and floral. Gorgeous.

*This baby better be a fucking girl.*

I grab a few and lay them over my forearm.

"No." Zoey sighs, rubbing her eyes in an attempt to calm herself. "You're not...it's just...it does *really* fucking hurt. A lot. And...I'm just super scared."

I stop. Her braids are partially undone from this morning, and she's looking out the window. A similar debate to my own plays in her eyes.

"They're fucking looking for me, you know," she tells me. "All the damn time. They always return for anyone they lose, and I'm the longest any damn victim has ever managed to stay. They just can't find me underground, and..."

"And they won't," I finish her sentence.

"They fucking will," she resists. "Or they'll kill more fucking people trying. It's just a matter of time."

"They might not. We don't know."

"Adabelle, could you just fucking listen?" I'm upsetting her by fighting this point, but I can't let her hope die. "They don't just pass people up. And they definitely don't fucking lose captives. It doesn't work like that."

*That first night.*

I remember a little more each day, the way that creature looked at me then. Like I was...pitiful.

Unworthy.

*Vile.*

"It can," I suggest.

"It doesn't," she combats. "Adabelle, they're fucking methodical creatures. They almost never fucking attack The Center, okay? But now they did. And all I can fucking think is, what if it's my fault? What if it's my fault that more women who should have been safe, who probably didn't even know what the fuck was going on, now have to suffer?"

"Is that why you're here? Because you feel guilty?"

"The longer I sat in that room waiting on you, the more it just...made sense. I started walking, and I was going to walk until I hit a border. I was going to wait for them to come take me back, to make it fucking easier on everyone. But it looked like it was going to storm. I just got scared, and I saw this place. I took shelter maybe an hour ago or so..."

I crawl back to my knees, shifting toward her. "You aren't to blame for the actions of other creatures in this world."

"They're coming for me. I am responsible for how I choose to deal with that shit."

"You are also more than a prisoner of your circumstance."

"I used to be more than a prisoner," she replies just as fast. "The old Zoey was going to school to be a fucking counselor. She was going to learn to save lives and then she was going to learn to cut hair. Because what girl doesn't want a good haircut when they're fucking depressed, right? Perfect business plan. But this Zoey...she's a prisoner. I'm not who I was, Adabelle."

"You're exactly who you choose to be," I insist.

She looks at me again.

"I didn't fucking choose this."

"But you choose what happens next." I grip her shoulders. "And if you choose to thrive, I promise, as your friend, I won't let anything happen to you or your baby."

She wants to trust me, but her inner defenses are built too strong. It takes more than words to make her believe now. But I feel her shoulders fall and relax beneath my fingers. The promise is enough to make her consider coming home, and she diverts her focus to something less complex.

The clothes.

She holds them against her round belly in sets, starting with the dresses and moving on to the shirts and trousers. The surface of her enormity is so large, she can balance a tiny pair of the slippers upon it, imagining her baby in them for a few freeing seconds right as we hear another noise at the door frame pulling us into an adrenaline surge.

I dart for my wrap of perfect weaponry, reaching them in time for a figure to round the corner, putting their cautious hands up, and shaking their head.

"Slow down!" Aidan leaps, moving his hand in a motion that directs us to also lower our voices. "Slow down, it's just me."

Zoey's whole face falls, suspending in the moment, and yet unable to take her eyes off of him. When he catches sight of her, it is the exact same.

A trip into unexplained despair. Familiarity. Pain.

The room is whirling in fragile silence, eating away at the people within it.

Aidan turns his head about the room, taking it in inch by inch, and reaching for his pocket.

"We need to leave," he directs. "Now."

# CHAPTER FIFTEEN
## AIDAN

I NEVER MAKE IT HOME TO SLEEP.

My feet don't want to carry me that far and I can't face the general emptiness of my personal life yet. I'm not ready. It hasn't completely eluded me that I am unable to face my problems, the coward I am, and I know it should be a sanctuary where I sleep—a steel fortress with covered windows and silence. But all it has become is a vacancy.

Here. There.

Everywhere I am is an all-consuming shell I retreat inside of when days grow dark.

Not safe and not shelter, home is more like a fleeting shield about to split in two at the tired wound upon it that the world continues to reopen time and time again.

*Home is where the scar is.*

At least that is honest. At least I am being honest right now.

Someone should be honest, damnit, and it should be her.

Celestyn. Or Addie. Or anyone!

I hide within the red sea of blood and rage after leaving Addie, listening to her try to wrangle the people that despise her and failing long enough for Zoey to take over. The pair complement one another better as friends—or partners—than we do, and when I'm certain she has a solid grip on our problem community, I beeline for the west wing where I know Ebony will be working. Where I won't be seen, and where I can grab a few hours rest before the work ahead of me.

It's just...I slept longer than I intended.

There are days I find my dreams of what has come and gone a relentless riptide of secrets that eat me alive from the darkest, squirmiest parts of my rotten entrails. Images will consume me when I can't resist them, boiling over in savage, hair raising, screams of a history long gone. Voices will scatter in my mind, swelling my thoughts like the pus beneath an infection, stretching my skull paper thin while it aches to break free.

All I have to do is say yes.

I could say yes, to the better pieces of my history in these dreams of running through the grocery store with a shopping cart full of junk food and a smile. I could say yes to this grin, glasses tipping forward, and cookie boxes crinkling against the cold metal edges of the basket, spinning through aisles. If nothing else, I permit the sounds of laughter from someone buried in the sea of snacks, shrieking out of careless delight.

I don't understand these sounds like I used to, but this particular one is familiar to my heart. I feed off the pitch, like it was the best high in this world, and it nurses the parts of me I can't find a way to fix. The memory is foggy like so many others, but still I can catch wisps of straight, fiery locks of hair, fanning across grave porcelain skin in ginger tangles. It burns warm colors back into my black and white psyche and eats away at the drab circumstance and pessimism I can't outrun.

It is all I need.

And then I am awake again. Long past noon and groggy, my

eyes pop open and reality confirms what my subconscious already knew—I've overslept.

I poke my head out the open door and down the wall, creeping on tender toes out to the quiet lobby where Ebony is reading over files in the comfortable stability of a hustle well done. But it is when she sees me that the problems arise. The look on her face, and the tour of the room showcasing the blood Addie spilled from her mouth during the assault wherein after she fled out of fear, brings guilt back full steam ahead.

In fact, it boils over the edge of its containments. Steams and stews.

It is common knowledge to any fool she isn't readily accepted by the public, but this lesson should have been a learning one for either side. Not a fear-inducing project. She doesn't deserve an attack, and her service to the community should have gravitated them closer to her protections. And then there was the consequence to be understood about Celia's rescue, not that she would grasp any of it now.

Looking for her was easier than I anticipated, however. She didn't bother to clean up on her way out. Ample blood spats remain from where she had spit, bramble broken where she had trampled on her expedition far away from civilization. Signs of life became a little more discouraging the further I tread in the rain though, and I sent myself in circles, twice, losing clues to the wash of cruel sky water.

I didn't expect to find the small structure cloaked in trees after I discovered my way once more. It's compact like a shed, only a bit bigger, with the door left open just a crack. But I have also never particularly ventured this way, nor have many of the search team members, considering the attacks never stem this direction. We travel in these parts where we have to, and that usually means where the Ravagers clock in and check out.

Creeping inside with the mere prayer that it is my partner who decided to shelter in this place, I'm careful not to let the door groan on its hinges to alert my presence. The trunks inside are alarming right away, swarming my thoughts with stern red bells, pleading for me to step the fuck out. I don't think these belong to The Center, or Celestyn wouldn't be reporting back to Ace that we are so low on supplies. But if they didn't belong to The Center, there wasn't another race of beings that had made themselves known, outside the Ravagers, that could claim its ownership... which is another problem.

I need to get out of here, fast.

Inching down the narrow walkway, I can hear voices that make my heart breathe a deep sigh of relief. They're female, and I pinpoint Addie's right away. What surprises me when I round the corner, holding on to the creaky door frame so I may slip through unencumbered by the clutter, is Zoey. Our eyes lock before Addie realizes it is me coming to their rescue, guilt and pain and frustration bubbling to the surface like a dormant volcano impending eruption. She swallows when we see one another, unable to find the right words to say to me after all this time. She glances to Addie, who has more than enough conversation for everyone at all the wrong times—though she is surprisingly quiet now.

Everyone is quiet.

It isn't until I'm sure Addie won't break my skull with her brick of extraordinarily clean gauze that the eerily dizzying aura of the room crawls back up under my skin. I can't quite put my finger on it, or maybe I just won't, but this place isn't...*right*.

To start, it is better built than most of our structures outside of The Center, despite the glassless windows, and I can't much count The Center, since I can't prove we were the ones that built it. This place is sturdy though, and smells like proper, well-constructed wood. Each room flows with the next too, the trunks of supplies stacked in each one making it a fortress of hoarded treasure as soon as the front door is breached. But even the foreign gauze Addie has snaked about a collection of items unseen doesn't look like our own.

It's too sterile. There are no stains from a previous owner. And it looks...soft. Like it wouldn't simply abrade the room. The wrap looks as if it would feel more like getting bludgeoned with a brick pillow when she hit me with it, rather than an actual weapon.

But that doesn't conclude all my finds here.

In Zoey's lap are clothes much too small for adults, and even too little for children. They look to be much more suitable for *infants* or smaller, followed by equally miniature quilts that would hardly cover a lap. The recurring idea that first made home in my thoughts gives me chills, causing me to look at them with as much calm as I can manage so that neither of them panic. I need to remain logical here.

"We need to leave," I say quietly. "Now."

Neither my partner or Zoey protest, nodding in agreement and following my watchful lead out the door. Our walk home feels faster, the group holding a slow jog that jostles Zoey's full-term belly, the darkening sky casting insidious shadows below our feet. We make it to The Center in the late evening, rain clouds making their thundering exit and nightfall painting the world above in the faintest pastel blues—the growing dark making me uncertain as to where I should command Addie to be.

If I am being honest, she deserves to be home, but The Center and its staff are operationally dependent upon her and Ebony today. I don't know what the right call in this situation would be, but she fixes this for me, excusing herself in a humble squeak to the caved front desk where paperwork is being filed in uneven heaps at the somewhat stable edges.

Zoey is abandoned with me, her eyes traveling the length of the still broken and empty halls in quivering discomfort. She doesn't want to be here, especially after last night. I can tell. This is her part-time home since the pregnancy complicated itself, and she gradually grew more and more overdue. Except now, this partial home is no longer a sanctuary, just like her regular home.

I don't know what else to do, other than attempt to smile in her presence, nearly eye level with her extraordinary height, aside from maybe an inch or two I have on her. It's been a long time since regular people showed a friendly smile her direction, myself included.

"Do you need an escort home?" I ask.

Zoey shakes her head, stumbling over her words. "N-no...I...I still need to be seen."

She won't look me in the face. It's been a minute since we have had this much...contact. I'm not sure she knows how to accept kindness like she used to.

"I'll take you to your room." I look away from her in hopes it might make her more comfortable, or at least less pressured.

She doesn't speak for a moment.

"Okay."

I let her lead me down the hall where she is accustomed to residing, a proper escort, allowing her to set the pace we move by until we reach the room that is hers. Based on instinct, I walk in ahead of her to assure it is truly clear. She follows me in, setting her armful of clothes and blankets on the stained mattress, and sitting down before I have a chance to be thorough. Exhausted from so much walking, she pulls apart the rest of her braids, the tight waves of her hair spilling over each shoulder and down her back while she spreads out to keep the baby's feet from launching into her ribs.

Seeing her this way makes me give way to a real smile this time, gripping the door frame and tipping backward to leave when her voice finds me.

"T-thank you," she calls. "For everything. I...well, it was really great for you to go fucking finding us and stuff. I'm just sorry you had to. I'm also super fucking sorry, for everything, Aidan. I really am."

*Everything.*

My lips continue to curve a little, but they lose their auth-enticity. My face falls against it and my chest drops to my knees in memory.

"Don't ever be sorry," I assure her. "If I ever made a mistake worth the fallout I received, it didn't start with you. Saving you that night was never a mistake. It had purpose. Now...rest here or go home with Addie. I'll bring Celestyn by tomorrow. I promise."

This is the reassurance she needs, her hand on her rolling stomach.

On multiple levels, I had never thought to lay our past to rest with the promise that loading Kasismis up with arrows wasn't a problem. Thinking about it at this time in my life, Addie and I weren't so different when I was a touch greener to the new world. Despite the pleas of others, I also wanted to save everyone I could see in need, suffering a huge blow in status on the search teams when Zoey was discovered to be pregnant and solidifying Ethan as our First-in-Command.

It was reckless, but I don't regret it. To this day, it is the one good service I know I have performed right.

I turn away, ready to leave, but Zoey's voice yips at me again.

"Wait!" she snaps, and I spin on my heels to greet her, attempting to maintain my patience.

"Yes?"

She's looking at me unafraid this time, but her voice still betrays a lack of confidence.

"Adabelle isn't a shit person," she shoots out of left field. "I see the way everyone looks at her, and I'm sure you've heard the fucking rumors. I was sorta relieved when I fucking found out she'd be your partner, but...she's just...I don't fucking know. She's different, and you have to learn her quirks. She acts fast...but I've watched her work. She doesn't *mean* to."

I frown at this, but my head bobs as if I understand how someone could not mean to act without a basic thought process. Part of me believes Addie's bigger problem is that she doesn't know how to stop and listen to reason, but it really couldn't matter less.

Zoey is through with me and I leave her room, walking around the front desk where Addie is drowning in responsibility. Only this time, she embraces it.

She doesn't really seem to know what to do with it, reading with tight stress lines raining havoc down across her forehead, and tapping her foot like an angry rabbit. But something has caught her interest over the situation that she intends to take advantage of. I wonder if it has to do with the unfiled paperwork Celestyn has forsaken. She was enamored with her own.

I pat the desk, and she looks up to me, eyes not filled with willfulness this time, but with something that hits me square in the gut. I just can't place a finger on it, other than the defined pain creased along the edges of her mouth where dried blood remains in a dark brown stain.

"I'm out for the day," I tell her. "We'll meet back here tomorrow?"

"Sure," she replies, rigid.

We don't sneak another peek at each other. Something about it is too much. I step on the doors that are still weighted into the floor, leaving and racing to the border right next to The Center to do a shorter, riskier round of patrols.

I normally wouldn't. Not at this hour. But the building in the woods behind The Center on the borders has me curious, and also concerned that we should embark more in the areas we don't often attempt to go.

Though at initial appearances, nothing about these regions feel any different than others I have explored. Most of the trees are the same shade of ashen white here, as far as I can tell in the greedy darkness. The plants are just as large and the mosquitoes still bite. The relative few species of birds that haven't settled down to sleep, still make their shrill shrieks across the endless expanse of forest like they are laughing back and forth about my bewilderment, and crickets chirp in response.

We never go alone like this. Not so late or as brazen either. A lot could go wrong. But I think I need the reflection time, somewhere away from the chaos. Away from her.

I can't think clearly around Addie. She moves so fast and she makes me question my own judgment calls, when I have time to make them. She's almost obnoxious when we work together, except that she's not—and I detest to think I might be a bit attached to her style. She's just...difficult.

I stop less than a mile in the forest, still a bit tired and not seeing any signs of things I could gather or more sketchy sheds sitting around. But I will send word to mention it to Ace come morning. He would send more people out to investigate if the shed isn't ours. From there, we will decide what to do next.

I lean against a tree, and then jolt forward again just as fast at a light sting on the back of my arm. On the bark where I had touched is a small dragon no bigger than a lizard staring back at me. Its glistening white teeth that had not quite punctured my skin are bared, and it hisses in my direction, miniature wings folded up to present a beautiful world of colors mirrored on the other like that of a butterfly.

"Little bastard," I mumble, rubbing the place he nipped.

Another few crawl out from the opposite side of the trunk, chittering back and forth, flapping their paper wings in aggression. I yank further back, counting teeth as they make their way down the tree to the ground, screeching and lunging. I snatch a handful of rocks off the ground, tossing each one into the middle of their tiny mob in hopes to separate them.

Instead, I watch them scatter and come back in greater numbers, legions of tiny bastards hissing around their vicious ringleader. Certain breeds are more active at night, and thrive easier when The Dome weakens, so this was bound to happen. I'm usually more well prepared.

I toss my last rock and veer in a wide turn around them toward the village, but the painful little shits aren't finished. The ringleader is quick, zipping through the grass and fluttering wings that buzz like a dragonfly's launching him airborne. He sinks black claws into the leg of my jeans, writhing up in violent zigzags. I bat him off in a lucky strike, stumbling toward the village in a hasty escape.

Tiny feet patter along the ground as we run, chittering battle cries and laughing in pitchy chirps at my heels, until I break the tree line halfway back to Limbo where their territory must have ended as they cease pursuit. While I catch my breath, I listen to their series of hisses and growls, yowling at my backside to return for fatal playtime. But I make no mistake. A group of these small beasts could end my life.

I've never much liked reptiles anyway, but there is no dismissing that dragons are intelligent creatures. Wise and fickle, they always have been a grade above our own depths. They are conniving and strong, some poisonous and venomous. Dragons are the current foundation that my hate for reptiles stands upon.

The first time I ever witnessed one with my own eyes, it was much bigger than the group I faced today. I was out on patrols, and it had come from the water in a hurry, long and serpentine, like an oversized snake with stout little legs and ice blue scales shimmering against the midday heat. I had almost lost my foot for a dip in the river that day, and I discovered with horror that it had the common sense to follow me when I evaded the attack within the perimeters of its territory.

I have noticed since then that they are highly capable of complex thought, understanding the search for weaknesses or meek attention spans. They stalk prey for miles or concentrate in areas where the food is easy. Ace had once told me that very few of them could speak as well but, to this day, I have been privileged more toward the screeching and hissing.

By the time I officially hit Limbo again, the sun is fully set, and it is late enough to call it yet another day, if I can make it home in time to live. I pass The Center up instead of checking on Addie, hoping she is smart enough to find warmth in the comfort of her home, and going straight for the despair of mine so I can chance playing some music before sound is forbidden.

The night is still young when I arrive at a soft run, the door echoing agitated groans when I open it, crying out with a thud when I heave it shut. I'm stunned by the distinct shimmer of candlelight I didn't spark when the darkness should have consumed me. I whirl around, staring into the momentarily startled eyes of Celestyn seated at the other end of the room, wrapped like an expertly bound burrito in a thick, well woven, quilt. Scattered about her are at least two dozen books, written in peculiar figures and letters, that are translated into English below each line in her own delicate scrawl.

Her face is deadened when I approach, void of all sass and feeling, as if she had left the building and not returned just yet. I close several of her archaic texts, slipping others off my guitar case and stacking them against the wall. These details procure information about her secret life I have been unaware of, and the insight is troubling. It is not that I am necessarily bothered that she reads, but more so that she translates. *A lot.*

"What is all this shit, Celestyn?" I open my case and pull out the instrument, sitting on the only chair I have at the corner by the door.

I should be more perturbed she is here. Or that she came in without my permission...not that she isn't always welcome, but still.

She smirks, dropping her inked feather on the floor and flexing her aching fingers. "Medical journals...from Master Amadeus' library. They're written in a different language, of course, but I've been taught enough to translate some of it. It's easy enough to fill in the gaps of what I can't."

I play familiar chords to get started, warming up my all too eager fingers. It can be easy to get ahead of myself when I have been out of practice all day.

"I see," I reply, watching my own fingers, yet not seeing them at all. "Why aren't you safe at your own home then? Does Master Amadeus know you have taken his exotic library for a walk around the neighborhood?"

It comes out harsh. I mean for it to, this time. My love and adoration for her is like acid in the moment, eating away at the good left in me most days, and taking hostage what is remnant when I am empty. Our relationship is a dependent toxicity that I can't seem to rid myself of, bouncing back to it every time either of us fall so deep into hell that we can't find reality.

But even so, she has never stayed within my home until now. It was always beneath her, and the longest she stuck around was for the time it took us to have sex. A few hours of fun was all she ever required of me, and then she would turn tail. I wouldn't see her until I sought her out myself, where the cycle would continue. Never has Celestyn once brought personal material with her when she's come here either. And I'm not sure I want her to.

As always, though, she refuses to answer my questions. She

won't grant me so much as eye contact. Her gaze follows the path back to her books instead, a guilty expression warming her cheeks as she attempts to decide what exactly she is going to tell me.

I carry on the tune playing in my thoughts—both awake and asleep—like fevered madness all week, listening to the way it comes out, and providing tweaks at each restart. I just can't seem to get it right.

"Ace is looking for you." Celestyn changes the subject when she can't make up her mind. Of course, it has to become about me.

I glance at my secured window, then at the door, continuing to play. There's one reason Ace ever personally seeks me out. He can forget that mess.

"He can keep looking," I tell her.

"He'll find you one of these times." She frowns.

It is genuine. I'm hard pressed to resist her legitimate feelings, taking notice of the stress lines creasing her small forehead, and the hard swallow she takes in wait for my response.

"He can try," I tell her calmly.

I play louder in an attempt to keep her from speaking again while I sort this out. But I stop as soon as I start. Spite won't fix this, and we need to talk anyway. I set my guitar up at the corner of the wall and fold my hands under my chin, resting my elbows on my knees.

"Addie is wrecking your hospital." I'm upfront, like she would have been to me if the roles were reversed. Celestyn needs someone to be curt and honest with her.

"I'll go back tomorrow," she defers.

But I can see it in her face. She doesn't want to.

"And?"

"Why does there have to be an and?" she snaps, pulling the closest book nearer to her chest.

"Because there is always an and." I remain calm in her storm.

So, she relents.

"I want to live with you," she mumbles.

"What? Why? Do you have any idea what you'd be giving up?"

She won't repeat herself, but she meets my concern with more than enough of her own. There is a look of desperation settling in her expression. A deep-rooted fear. An anxiety I had not known of her until yesterday, and more than that.

There is insecurity. Instability. Vulnerability.

In all of this, there is a spark of hope. Not for us, but for her as a person. How can I deny her growth?

"Okay," I relent. "Okay. Just...make it home every night before sunset."

She nods. "Of course. Your home, your rules."

It's a vow I'm unsure she will keep, but it's for her own good.

"*Every* night," I drive the point home, raising an eyebrow.

And she bobs her head again, this time faster in confirmation.

The room feels more settled as she closes her book and sets it aside. I lean back in the chair, wondering if this would make it easier for Ace to pinpoint me. I'll have to be extra careful how often I'm home if I want to avoid the Suicide Missions.

"I...I don't trust him." Celestyn's voice pulls me back from my thoughts. "Amadeus."

"He protects you," I mumble, shutting my eyes and listening to the unusual quiet outside.

"You don't know him," Celestyn fires in return. "It's not what you think. He's not what you think."

I've heard rumors. Limbo is full of them. People claim Amadeus is a Ravager who pities us, and that his magic sustains The Dome for the bursts of daylight hours, taking the night to recover.

It isn't like there's a lot of proof to confirm this as fact, making the whole story a bit silly and hard to put stock in. But Master Amadeus has also never gone out of his way to talk to anyone or make himself known to the people he protects. The people he issues consultations to have to trek to meet him on his turf in the tower out in the old village.

Most people don't come back from it. But Celestyn always does.

"Are you saying the rumor mill has actually produced a fact?" I pry.

Celestyn doesn't answer right away, mulling a secretive response over in her mind.

"It isn't like that," she finds her words. "He...he doesn't protect me. Master Amadeus doesn't protect people. He protects values."

"You're still valuable," I counter. "Addie can stitch like hell, but your work is beyond her capabilities."

"I'm making mistakes." Her admission makes the unusual silent calm feel like the humid suffocating moments before a tornado. "Severe. Mistakes. I can't elaborate right now, but leaving was definitely one of them. I just...I don't feel safe there anymore, Aidan. I've seen people go into his office and never come out. I'd lie awake for hours, just waiting, but..."

I have never considered the long-term problems her protections could incur, or that it might be a risk in and of itself. Nothing ever comes without a price, but the tradeoff for her services haven't been clear. They still aren't. I didn't think she cared.

"Has he ever hurt you?" I'm quick to ask.

"No." This is assured just as fast. "I've...well, we only talk through a curtain, when we do. It is how he taught me to translate these books, though he had never been clear as to how he knew the language. But it doesn't change the fact that our visits are limited. So, it wouldn't be possible for me to accumulate damage. I saw a glimpse of him one time, when the wind blew too hard, but...there was someone else in the room with him. I left before I could see any features that I remember. It's a bit of a blur."

I look at all the books in the room, realizing at this time that they were probably not borrowed from the library as much as they were stolen. How do we turn back from that?

"It's not safer out here, you know," I point out.

"I know, but..." She fidgets. "I have you out here?"

My heart catapults straight out of my chest and my throat goes dry.

"Yeah. Yeah, you do. But you know what happened with me and Zoey. If Kasismis returns for her, I might not be the safest person to bunk with."

She shakes her head in dismay. "If I were a smarter woman, I'd leave Zoey out in the woods and let nature take its course with her. But I can't bring myself to let another woman be injured or taken, if I can help it."

It makes me smirk, just a little. "You and Addie both, then. She refuses to leave anyone behind."

"It's different." Her tone grows dark. "Adabelle Green would not be here if I had the backbone to eliminate residents based off the threat they might pose to the rest of us. I shouldn't have let her stay. She shouldn't be anything at all."

I wince at this, but I don't reply. The memory of her pupils flashing away into serpentine slits, startles me both into agreement and far from it. The truth of the matter is that Addie is an eerie person. Haunting and mellow, but bright and fast to act. She doesn't belong in Limbo, but she also fits right in. A walking contradiction, she wants to help, even at her own expense, and that sets her aside.

"She was knocked senseless today," I comment. "Whenever I found her, there was dried blood all around her mouth. She had a bruise next to her eye that could have its own zip code, and she was in pain. But when we got back into town, she was ready to help again. I mean, she's weird, Celestyn. But I don't think she's threatening."

Celestyn laughs, but it isn't a funny laugh. It is scornful and mocking.

"Just threatening? Oh no, Aidan. She. Is. A. Monster. With the eyes of a devil. She is evil."

"She's never done anything to prove that," I snap. "In fact, everything she has done speaks strictly otherwise."

She lets it go, for now. In fact, she drops everything altogether.

The quilt she has wrapped around her slender body slides to the floor in a fluttering thump, revealing her supple bare legs and black panties under one of my plaid shirts hanging loose over her body. It must have been her back up plan if I denied her quarter in my house, but now it's a tool to shut me up about Addie as she paces across the room. Each button of the shirt is twisted free the closer she gets, the feathery weight of her heat brushing over my lap, where she places her mouth over mine in a deep kiss that I can't bring myself to refuse.

My hand cradles the back of her head, lacing through her endless curls while my tongue finds hers as an eager, violent force of lost passion, playing her self-hating tune so it matches my own. But this time, I'm not the fool.

I'm not the monkey. I'm not the boy.

I know what this is today, and I know what it will be tomorrow when she is in someone else's home, grinding into the tented lap of some other loser. I'm okay with that, because I have to be, and it's a stupid choice not to be.

We aren't exclusive, after all.

We never have been.

And when we are through with this wanton routine that we always play out to the vile, bitter end, she returns to her corner of the room. She immerses herself in quilts, wrapped tight with her eyes closed, and face resting on her books. Meanwhile I am as alone as I often have been. The relief of release is gone when our fun has met its end, and my wallet is out, the ID I was found with rolling between the calloused fingers that Celestyn claims to love.

At the tip of my bruised and absent nail, the word *Engaged* stares holes through me under the category of marital status. There's a vicious guilt at play just looking at it. A sickening pit in my stomach, though the unknown woman who was to be Mrs. Powell is nothing to me now. No more than a wisp of orangish-red hair and pale, milky skin. Chewed lips and a weak smile. A laugh. An addictive dream and a far-off memory. A shell of a person that once existed.

She must have been everything to me when I didn't know Limbo. But now that I do, she is almost nothing. I can't even remember her name and I wonder if she can remember mine. I want to know who she is and where she might be. Or if she has missed me. Or missed the thought of me.

Does she know I suffer?

I've attached myself to Celestyn like a child, craving the

emptiness left in my life and trying to move on all in the same go. But it's for naught when I can't release the past.

I've come to know Celestyn is more than empty as well. Running on fumes, she's detached from her feelings to cope with the loss of everything she thought she knew. Today, I am her tool. Tomorrow, it will be someone else. And the cycle goes on because we let it.

But it is not love.

It is not affection.

It is survival. It is coping.

And it is not enough.

# CHAPTER SIXTEEN
## ADABELLE

S OMETIMES, ON THE NIGHTS I'M PERMITTED MORE THAN A few hours of uninterrupted sleep and I'm able to visualize the vivid nightmares of the life I have left behind, I would run— fast.

Next to my mama or behind her. As a child, my stubby legs would pump against the sharp wall of cold air, like they were preparing to take flight on a runway. She would drag me without mercy by my sunken, fragile wrists below a ratty red cardigan that smelled like urine, while I hit my max speeds that felt so fast at the time. Like a superhero. Or a super villain.

Lights, white and red, flash bright off the bare surface of my bald head, blinding the field of my tender eyes, but evading us in most versions of the dream. It never quite catches up on our ground pursuits, as we dart below metal bridges spilling over with rancid shadows and pass scraggly men with jagged yellow stubs for teeth that smile as we go.

I'm often grateful they never approach us at the end of these visions, as if they know better than to cross Mama. As if it were no secret what she carries at the intimate places below her skirt, cold and dark. Clicking with aggression. Can they smell the coppery heat of their own demise?

I cry out to her at the end of this specific version of what my brain is willing to reveal, Mama yanking me forward with a force that brings forth a familiar ache in my shoulder, ringing torturous pains across my back until my eyes flit open and I am alone again in the house where I reside, static and sweating.

The fear of the past lingers while I hold my breath, having no one to tell but the conscience inside my head since Zoey stayed at The Center overnight after a series of late contractions made us both too uncomfortable to pull her away from steady medical gear. I was also informed by Ebony prior to leaving that there is a fresh water well out the side of The Center I haven't yet traveled. So that fact solidified our choice, as I had only imagined having a baby would require more water for cleanup than just what our canteens could carry. Letting her stay in a quiet, well-stocked building in spite of the risk it might carry felt like the right call at the end of the evening—even if I regret it currently out of emotional need.

Outside the window, right above the back of my head, I can hear birds twittering to welcome the morning. I hadn't slept in the underground hatch last night out of hyper-focused remorse that I planned to skip the meeting with Master Amadeus. The repercussions could be severe if he decided to retaliate for my disobedience, but they could possibly equate out to what I'd face if I went anyway, considering people don't often return from their ventures there—or so I've heard.

It doesn't much matter in any event. Now that I've done it, I can't undo it. The stress of it has caused me to oversleep, strong beams of yellow light having already shifted from the early morning's dull blue and faint orange, burning my face and leaving my mouth feeling sandy. Dry and painful, like my chapped lips that I have chewed to a raw and bloody agony, out of habit.

The boards of the floor groan when I stand, ready to give if I jumped too hard. I pray they last a few more good years as I reach for the door frame that grants entrance to the backroom where a bolder blast of sunlight scorches my eyes in spiteful flashes. My hand reflexively cups my brow, lids squeezing shut as the foundation of a headache commences preparation to launch a full-scale migraine so intense, I almost don't catch the chuckle erupting from the living room.

I allow my eyes to open a little, squinting to find Aidan seated on the floor beside our thoroughly unhinged door and three bolts. He gives me a small wave, and I return a brief, uncertain wiggle of my fingers to him, wondering at the same moment how long he has known Zoey, since I never provided him directions to our home. I want to ask, but instead I go for my water bottle, guzzling what is left of my well water with my bed head and neckache.

"You drool in your sleep," Aidan comments from the other side of the room to kick start our morning. "Like an infant."

I almost spit the water back in the bottle, being delicate as I wipe my mouth, and capping the container to be put away in my backpack.

"Don't watch me sleep," I choke, digging for a ponytail holder, and twisting my hair into a sloppy bun.

"If you were on time for work, I wouldn't have." He shrugs. "But you were late, and I'm responsible for knowing whether you're alive or dead. Zoey and I have a bit of history, so I thought you might be here, and it felt rude to wake you when you were sleeping like that. Real heavy. Didn't flinch an inch when the door came undone."

My head throbs more where I was hit yesterday the longer I'm in sunlight. The adrenaline from that day has most definitely worn off, and a strange metallic scent keeps hitting the rear of my nose so my eyes water. It makes me want to spit, but it sounds like I've already slobbered enough in front of him, so I swallow it on second thought. I cough again at the sensation, turning away and digging around for remnants of breakfast foods Zoey might have left behind. Aidan doesn't leave.

"What are you still doing here?" I grumble, finding old bread below the counter and whacking it on the wood with a sigh.

He shrugs, his feet finding the ground so he is tall and sprite. "What else? We have work today. I convinced Celestyn to return to post after she realized what a disaster you made of it, and I needed my partner."

I try not to smile, but it feels sort of good to be needed just a little. My cheeks redden to the beat of the words, replaying them in my head until the corners of my mouth burn and I turn my face out of his view, letting out a steady breath while I figure out how to compose myself.

"Okay," I relent, my voice pitchy. "Fine. But I need to see Zoey first. Just to make sure she's okay and that she doesn't need help getting home."

There is a short shuffling, and the weight of my backpack is thrust over my shoulders by his eager hands, setting me off balance. He gives it a swift pat, lifting me upright under the arms, and providing a gentle push toward the door. I am a robot, dazed in the fresh air while he moves the broken exit in the frame, so it won't fall, but covers the entry.

*He better fix that.*

"No time." He interrupts my thoughts. "We're already late thanks to you, and we have work to catch up on."

Aidan doesn't give me time to argue. He knows better, and swoops around me, leading us to the markets where he uses his gentleman's intuition to buy me a small, late breakfast of bread, cheese, and berries to sit in my stomach. In the process, he separates a cloth of food that we put in my backpack to serve as our lunch of more bread, cheese, and dried meat. I ask for butter, but he denies this, claiming it would melt and ruin the contents of my bag. In his explanation, it's different than the chemically compounded junk we used to know. It won't stay an oily solid, and I will have to wait another time.

When this business is finished, we stop at the clearing between the markets and housing to meet with the rest of the search teams in advance to our departure. I stand at my usual distance, unable to approach, but noting Glue Man's absence in the huddle.

I don't much like him, nor do I miss his sizable mouth, but I can't say I wish ill on him either. I actually hope he's okay in my own secret way. A bad personality shouldn't equate to the death penalty, especially when the circumstances are so extenuating. If nothing else, it is opportunity to grow.

I eat until they are through speaking, awaiting Aidan's grim return. When he approaches me from the split, he's frowning, but the effort to smile is never gone.

"We scored our usual route." He is concise, treading grass ahead of me without any further elaborations.

This part seems like more of a relief to him than usual, as though for the first time since we met, he's content to explore our regular path and not veer from it. It is eerie, the way my feet light fires inside my sneakers, stepping into the tree line like I should have been here all along. I dance closer on his heels, weaving on either side of him, and speaking whenever I notice disturbances.

I'm becoming more comfortable with the environment, touching the trees and discovering sap, labeling body parts for later disposal, and identifying potential blood patterns on rocks, which I pick up to investigate. To my surprise, they're not all dusty and brown. Some rocks are jagged and dull, others smooth or shiny. A few glitter in the sparse sunlight below the foliage, and Aidan shows me how to skip the flatter ones across the river's edge as we walk—though my attempts sink right away, plopping to the bottom of vast disappointment and effort.

We snake along the water's edge for miles, burning hours of daylight and occasionally nibbling on the food we packed as we go. I find a cheap wristwatch partly submerged in the water a mile into our ventures, and a plastic doll with no hair a bit further along that we leave as a memorial to the lost child. But the investigation of missing people and their missing possessions is at a crawl today, and it's discouraging enough to wonder whether or not we should call it quits.

OBSIDIAN CORVUS

At the final layer of The Dome—almost not visible any longer by how much it has lightened since my first day here—we stop. Together, we look through the final barrier like prison bars out to an open field littered with hundreds of trees beyond it. It's a maze of alien vibrancy I could never dream of conquering, something that leaves me wondering how the Ravagers maneuver through its sometimes lightless, twisted depths. A couple guesses come to mind when I put work into it, but nothing substantial I can prove without leaving Limbo's boundaries.

My best bet is that they have markers that lead them from one place to the next, or that they have primeval tribes set up nearby where they take prisoners after capture, locking them away for unspeakable uses. Uncivilized as these creatures have proven to be, my imagination only runs away with me from this logical foothold, creating scenarios of hate fueled rituals and child sacrifice.

*It must be why they took the children from the village*, my brain fabricates, *so they don't have to use their own.*

Paranoia is an incredible beast. I find myself unable to stop lingering on the possibilities of what lives across the endless horizon of land not belonging to The Dome protecting Limbo. Aidan stares into this same unknown with more disdain than myself, spinning from it while he massages his temples. He freezes. Bending down, he picks up a small white scrap of plastic off the ground. I race closer to take a look, finding that it's not a laminated note or name tag, but a small, wallet-sized picture.

I snatch it from his hands, absorbing the visual of a young girl, no more than eighteen, with long brown hair rolling down her shoulders in thick plumes. She is grinning from ear to ear, freckle faced and beautiful, with a pronounced strawberry birthmark stretched across her upper nose and eyes like a raccoon mask. Her hands are poised, folded over the top of a very small boy seated in her crossed legs—perhaps her younger brother, based off a similar birthmark he wore down his cheek and across his nose.

The loss takes the wind out of me, studying their similarities and thoughts racing to create a backstory for the two, something I can sympathize with to motivate me through my fears. Whichever one of them were here had to be lost, looking for the other. It could have been days since this image was dropped, but still...lost does not mean forsaken.

I inch forward to the last wall of safety we have out here, but Aidan grabs my arm. He swings me backward so hard I lose my footing, stumbling into a tree.

"Whoa, whoa!" he shouts. "Where are you going? Are you insane or just stupid?"

I open my mouth, recalling The Center and its damaged contents vividly. The pit of my heart feels the tragedy the locals brought down upon it, and the calamity I brought by saving one woman. Does that mean I should let others suffer for the sake of the population? Does that right the wrong?

"I have to go look for them." My mouth is the first to answer the questions my heart presents. "Someone needs to advocate for *everyone.*"

Aidan's free fingers thrash through his hair, eyes closing and head shaking. "Do you listen to me at all? I've made it quite clear—it doesn't work like that. You won't come back if you go out there."

"Well, then I guess it takes care of a couple problems." I writhe free, shaking him away with a snap of my arm.

He groans in response, tearing the picture free of my grip so hard it perforates at the bent corner. In a flash of motion, he tosses it through the final layer of Dome, glaring back to me in defiance.

"Don't be such a child," he huffs. "Do you think anyone gets away without being hated here? These people are scared, and they live for blame. I've made these same mistakes, and I'm trying to teach you, but you need to *listen.* The goal in Limbo is to LIVE!"

I'm searching through the side pocket of my backpack for the dagger I keep without luck. Aidan reaches for the busy arm to halt the action while we speak, but I slide away, flailing my clenched fist to punch him in the gut if he tries a second time.

"Your goal is to live," I make clear, my words stark and

unforgiving. "Mine is different."

Quiet. Unmistakable, unabashed silence. Aidan's gaze diverts to the ground, his eyes wandering the surrounding area and keeping low. He is taking in what I have made known, and yet it's like he hasn't quite heard me at all.

It's a partial lie, what I have said. The truth is, I want to live. I want to live long enough to set myself free of these restrictive societal constraints. I want to live long enough to free the true victims that have endured the horrors of this mystery for much longer and send them home where they can recover. I want to live long enough to discover who each and every one of us is, and why we are here to begin with.

I want my happy ending.

But I understand that this daydream might be a loose grip on the gravity of our situation. More than anything, I am growing to understand the magnitude of what might be forever, even if I don't understand the reason why it has to be.

"We don't know how long ago this picture was left." Aidan's words bite back at last, but they aren't fighting words. They are kind and gentle words of reason. "This is a section of our usual trail we haven't walked yet, and a bit further from the riverside. Acting on uncertainty won't help them."

I whirl away from The Dome to face him, approaching with as much respect I can garner. It shouldn't be so hard to reach each other in a mature, adult manner.

"It was sitting on top of leaves and grass when you picked it up," I point out. "It wasn't dirty or smudged. The area around the picture didn't look like it had been walked on, or disturbed by animals, and it also didn't appear damaged by rainwater."

This simmers in his thoughts. I can see the gears turning in the back of his head while he entertains my whims, rubbing the back of his neck in the sweltering heat. The motivation is there, to do the right thing after all this time. We are both just a yes away from changing the world.

"What if it's too recent?" He crosses his arms, an edge creeping into his voice. "They could be baiting us right now. And then what? Some of the stronger Ravagers are able to cross the third barrier for short spans of time, and it isn't unheard of for people to materialize within this layer. She could have been caught as soon as she showed up."

"All the more reason to look for her right this second," I reply quickly. "The people from this picture wouldn't know where they're at. Add kidnapping as a whole new suffering on that list. It's a fresh, confusing hell. If we catch up, maybe we could take advantage of the disorganization involved with new people. I mean, we could learn a thing or two about *why* this is happening, and what we can do to stop it. It would be a victory."

Aidan's laugh is grim and cynical. "It is a fantasy, Addie. If we're caught, then I'm dead for sure. If I'm dead, I can't protect you from them, and then you're gone. Helping no one. Who takes care of Zoey when that occurs?"

My hand is searching once more. My shoulder extends and aches, my hand digging deeper until my fingers graze the handle of the dagger in my side pocket, ready to go.

"I won't get caught." I shrug. "It's that easy."

"No." Birds call over him to one another in the stocky branches of foliage we can't reach from the ground, flitting from one tree to the next. It is hard to focus beyond their songs. "It's not. I don't think you understand what these Ravagers are like, at all."

"I don't think you understand what I am like, at all. I don't give up on people, Aidan."

A look spreads across his face that is almost murderous. His eyes are narrowed and twitching in rage, as if he's imagining twisting my head right off my body. It would be a joyous trip home, one met without question as to my disappearance and, better yet, a viable promotion.

The fingers on his right hand tap in succession upon his bicep, indecisive. He curls his lip, sighing.

"No." He is adamant. "No, Addie. No. *Absolutely not*. I'm putting my foot down. No."

"Fuck you." I look him up and down, channeling my inner Zoey. "Just go home then. I'll look by myself and check in later."

"Do you *hear* me?" He throws his hands out, blocking my path. "Can you hear? I said *no!*"

I step around him, closer to the edge of The Dome. My heart is beating out of my chest, thumping like a log against my ribcage.

"I don't have to listen to you." I try to breathe over the suffocating sensation of my heart overtaking my upper body. "Subservience is a choice, and this is still the modern age as far as I'm concerned. This job is just like any other, and I can quit."

"You won't get reassigned," Aidan warns. "The person who assigned you won't just give a reassignment because your stomach growls."

"Then just agree to split up!" I groan. "You're too scared to cross, and I have nothing to lose. It won't hurt either of us."

"You have everything to lose!" He grabs me by the shoulders, squeezing so hard I squeak in pain. "Have you lost your mind here? HAVE YOU?"

I stiffen under this grasp, swallowing down the urge to yell back. Tears threaten to emerge from my sockets, boiling in my eyes, but the release is interrupted by a whirring screech through the air. Aidan yelps in pain as the thud of an arrow finds it's mark in his lower back, two others raining down, grazing his abdomen while he attempts to face the onslaught.

My mouth drops wide at the tear of his shirt, blood oozing from clean rips in unrelenting gushes down his jeans. His hands drop to each injury in shock, gingerly touching the feathery end of the weapon embedded in his body. I'm fast to put an arm under his, reining in a portion of his weight and bobbing us toward the edge of The Dome. My eyes whirl in every direction, looking for the assailant.

*It came from inside*, my thoughts chide.

Aidan's voice is soft at the cusp of my ear. "Addie...Addie, I need to sit. I-I need..."

The force of his weight pulls down on my short stature. My legs quiver, my back straining to keep him upright and my lungs struggling to still my breathing. He slumps to the side, away from me while I jerk him closer, shouldering as much as I can bear.

"No, no, no," I grunt. "No. You're okay, Aidan. It's okay. This is fine. It's just a little poke. Okay? We all get stabbed sometimes, right? Just stay on your feet. We have to get out of here. Remember? We were going to go home? Just like you said?"

The leg on his injured side stumbles, snapping like a rotted stick as another arrow slides in the side beside the bone. He almost drags us both to the ground, crying out as nine figures emerge from around the trees guarding the path back to Limbo. These warriors are not familiar, but what they are sinks in without pity.

Tall and lithe, each male warrior, other than the two at the left, has long hair braided and decorated in macabre bone jewelry. Slender, intricately pointed ears move, just a touch, to zero in on the sound of my partner's suffering, while the three archers they brought each load another sleek arrow to be fired. The others carry swords though, and spears long enough to split me down the middle like a roasted pig.

At the well-guarded center of their fortified octagon is a smaller shadow of a person, just a few inches taller than me, and female. The girl from the picture.

She trembles in slivers of sight behind the group of locals, shaking like a small dog in the arms of extravagant women in late night films back home. I can hear her cry so hard it is hoarse, her whole face bright red to match the mask she was born with, her eyes rimmed raw with pain. Her lips move, mouthing a silent *sorry*. But at initial appearances, she is also outwardly unharmed, and I am not sorry for that. In fact, she is heavily guarded, the creatures forming a ring around her as if she were precious cargo.

"Addie..." Aidan's voice comes again, softer this time.

*Shh.*

I am hushing him. It's all I can think to do. My heart is throbbing inside my ears, burning rubber against my chest, going a million miles a minute. Adrenaline builds at the core of my thighs, tickling like dozens of tiny feathers caressing the muscles, granting me speed.

One of the archers at the side of the ring aims his bow, eying the swordsman up front for command. The swordsman is motionless—so rigid the air around him tastes like steel to match his silvery eyes focused with contempt upon me. I get the feeling Aidan has become an afterthought when he speaks, the language beguiling and commanding as though I should know exactly what it is he intends to say. But I shake my head, gripping Aidan's weight as he grows slicker in my hands.

"I don't..." I gasp, pulling and pleading. "I don't understand you. I don't know what you're saying."

The string of coarse language is ceased, and the swordsman peers back to his comrades in curious delight. They all let loose riotous laughter, the girl at their middle darting fearful puzzled stares between them. I wonder if she has ever witnessed such a sight in her life. Laughing. Belittlement.

I feel much smaller than I am, hunched beneath Aidan's arm, feeling the heavy crimson stains soak into my clothes so it wets my skin in turn. He leans sideways, panting as his hand grips the arrow at his leg while we are stilled.

The swordsman speaks to me afresh, still at a distance, this time in English.

"Strange," he croons with caution. "I did not think they let your kind travel this far in life. Certainly your presence is known."

Aidan grunts in a high-pitched whine as he tugs the sleek weapon, swallowing another deep breath. I squeeze him tight, keeping my focus on the enemy and attempting to create a subtly growing distance between our groups.

"M-my kind?" I stutter. "I-I'm a *woman.* Not a breed. I'm allowed to go wherever I want."

This response brings more laughter, and Aidan screams in a gory, squelching shriek. At the same moment, he tosses the arrow from his leg to the ground, holding his hand on the overflowing wound as I scrunch my nose. Between the sweet smell of warm crimson consuming the air in dread and wondering how being a woman could be funny at all, I am unsettled. Flighty.

"Indeed," the swordsman agrees.

His head ticks to each of the archers who draw their loaded bowstrings with different arrows this time, their glittering tips hooked and aiming for Aidan's head.

*He's losing arrows and is in need of a refill.*

The girl in their circle can be heard whispering a series of *no's*, begging the situation come to a halt despite its slow continuance.

The swordsman gives a booming foreign command and, this time, the warriors with spears raise their weapons in unison. Again, each silvery tip has target on Aidan, little concerned with my kind.

Panic rises in my partner's body language, not quite as composed and sagging off of his hurt leg. The pain has made him sweaty and cool to the touch, paling, and breathing staggered. He speaks my name into stagnant air, just loud enough I can hear, but I shake my head in resistance to it. I shake him, and his dead weight.

The time to leave is now. It has to be now.

Another foreign command and each soldier stiffens. Their swords are drawn, arrows pulled taut, spears leveled, all locked and properly aimed on Aidan's imminent demise. My left foot extends through the last piece of The Dome, careful not to make any move too abrupt. At this moment, I can feel Aidan straighten without removing his arm from my shoulders, lifting some of his weight off of me as the leg of his jeans stains warm and sticky.

The girl we had found is a mess of nerves, sobbing, and I find it strange in this instant that my heart could tear for someone else, while understanding that there is nothing I can do better than what I have. Not today, or maybe ever. We are heavily under armed in comparison, not to mention one man down.

I jump, Aidan's slippery fingers wrapping around my elbow and his head drifting closer to mine, in an attempt to adjust their aim. Ruin it. But it follows, ready to pierce both of our skulls, as killing me does not appear to be an issue. It sends every hair on his arm standing straight.

One last command sends spears and arrows firing our direction. Aidan darts through The Dome, yanking me with such vigor, he nearly pulls my arm out of socket. I follow when I regain my equilibrium, our legs pumping as fast as our feet will take us, tripping over inconsistencies in the earth and scrambling for life.

We cross the field in a trail of cherry red that Aidan secretes, dipping down into a short plane of tall pale grass that blends into another patch of densely packed trees. I haven't checked back to see if we are being followed, terrified to turn my head too soon. But I can hear the way the grass sways, sharpening my paranoia as it whips my cheeks throttling through its maze. It will lead them right to us, if I can't get Aidan's massacre somewhere with a little less clarity.

We bend into the cover of more trees, condensed and winding so that it abrades my arms on the way through. I choke, out of air, and bursting forward as Aidan tugs my hand sideways to keep me from smacking headlong through a bush. I can hear him panting up ahead, his free hand that's not being used for balance gliding between his injuries for protection against the threat of low-hanging brush.

In the distance, I can hear voices, and my legs shake from exhaustion. Aidan's stamina is wearing thin, and his breathing has crawled to a more labored rasp. He grips a nearby tree for support at the sound of trickling water, in no condition to fight should we require it, as we reach a smaller branch of the river.

At his side, I huff, my hands on my knees looking him over. Outside of the arrow poking out of his lower back like a tail, his shoes are much darker than their usual black, velvety and wet where the blood has dribbled down, sides where he was grazed mucked with crimson. His whole body shivers, his face sunken and wan as he resists every urge to give in, though I don't know his body could endure much more mileage if he tried.

I duck back under his arm on the most damaged side, hoisting half his weight until we hit the shoreline of the smaller water branch. It is so clear, I can see the bottom no matter where I step, and it is perhaps not so deceptively deep if we trudge the right places. I can't swim, so I have to pray I'm right, and that we reach the other side unscathed. Especially when it could be our one ticket to lose the enemy.

I parade Aidan's tired noodle of a body like a lavish fur coat down the slope of grassy bank. He puts pressure on the injuries he can hold to reduce a further blood trail until we reach the cold, rushing water that is ankle deep at the most shallow edge. Deceptive, as I hoped it wouldn't be, its current is strong enough to shove us sideways until I can plant my feet against bigger stones, Aidan gasping as the wall of force swirls against his open wounds.

My head spins back and forth, seeing no one at the tree line still, to my relief, and pushing onward. The water is chest deep if I stand on my toes at the middle, splashing up against my chin and pouring into my mouth when I try to catch a breath. Aidan tugs further and further behind in spite of my dragging, both arms now wrapped around my neck for balance as I slosh toward the sharp upward bank at the other side. I reach for low lying tree branches when we are close enough, my grip slick but my willowy limbs flexible and durable. Aidan slumps away at this motion, his grip weakening as I yank him with every ounce of my remaining strength to land.

Eyes closed, he is reduced to pitiful groans.

"I know, I know, but not yet." I push him onto his ass, arms screaming to give out while I help hoist him to his feet. "You're tired, and you're hurt. I promise we will rest soon, but not just yet. Okay? We need to go just a little further."

I can't tell if anyone is home when I look into his eyes. I haven't been able to check how deep the wounds are that he has sustained, nor have I been able to staunch them at all. But he has lost a lot of blood and he looks dazed right now, as if he's no longer sure what is happening. It's miraculous he listens at all, staggering ahead with the silent promise that he isn't all gone.

Just...glassy.

We inch deeper into the forest, meeting places Limbo has not dare known or touched. I don't know what has touched this forsaken place, zigzagging between moss-covered trees and clusters of vibrant mushrooms blooming in steady patches from the rich ground floor. Thorns from briers of berries and flowers tug at our clothing, splintering off in our skin as we force our way through.

I let us relax only when I'm sure I can't hear anything or anyone else, sitting down with Aidan at the top of a bowl-like indentation of trees. When he has settled, I swing my backpack next to him, pulling out and unwrapping the white dressing I stole like a string of endless handkerchiefs. He touches the arrow at his back while I do this, thankfully not so close to his spine it would be problematic but definitely requiring my attention.

I shuffle closer on my knees, tearing the fabric of his shirt around the arrow and lifting it for a better view. Apologizing in advance, I take the shaft and wiggle it a touch. The range of motion gives me an understanding that it is not impacted by bone at all, though he yells, reaching for me to stop. Instead, I purse my lips and give a hearty, thorough yank that rips the arrow out with a wet sucking from his shallow muscle tissue.

It wasn't as deep as some of the other wounds, thank goodness, but it's a bleeder in spite of the weapon not being a hooked one. I take a pair of black underwear from my backpack and fold it thick, pressing it onto the wound and wrapping it so tight with a bandage it could suffocate him. I have to hope all of his vital organs were missed, moving on to where he was grazed, one injury in particular running a bit deeper than I had anticipated as it bulges with dense meat while the skin around it swells in patchy discolorations. It is drenched in blood, still oozing so I can't get a proper look at it but slowing.

*Christ, I hope it's slowing.*

He bends his neck to meet my gaze, and I swallow. There is an apology at the tip of my tongue, though I can't seem to say it. I don't want this to be my fault. So I dive back into my bag of goodies, unzipping all of the inner pouches as I search for extra supplies and items to pack wounds with. I have a needle and strange threading hiding somewhere in the mess. Coupled with the gauze, I could probably suture him up if only I could think straight.

I reach further, digging blindly as cold wet fingers wrap around my own, giving a brief squeeze. I jerk, peeking up at him, my cheeks on fire beneath a layer of sweat glazing my skin as I realize that he is not looking me in the face, but rather concentrating upon the tattoos inked black across my fingers. He tries to speak, choking and gulping down words he can't manage to find. I yank my hand away before he finds new ones, my heart pounding faster than it did when we were running.

"I...water," he croaks. "Please."

He clears his throat, but I put my hand up to stop him.

I get it. I pull my water bottle free, popping off the lid and making sure his hands are placed on it firmly, like a child. The water spills down his face, soaking the collar of his shirt while I thread more clothes from the bag to the grass. I decide to pad the wounds and wrap them until we get home where Celestyn could look at them. She has more experience here, and medicines that could help that I don't possess. I'm terrified to make the wrong move with so much of my memory not intact.

Stretching the remaining gauze between my hands, I use individual wads of clothing that I have left to apply pressure to his injuries, wrapping them tight in an attempt to staunch the bleeding. He sputters out what he has in his mouth when I roll up his pant leg to address the small hole left there. I finish it fast to avoid further discomfort, tying it off with a big sigh, and pulling my backpack into my lap to find easy food he could chow on to build his strength.

We have to head back tonight without a doubt. Preferably soon, considering his grave state. But he needs more strength than what he has at this second from all the blood loss he has suffered. I can only help him so much in this way, and I'm fearful that he won't have a fraction of the panic-fueled strength he purchased off time itself to get this far.

I make the choice to risk going back to the river branch for more water to hydrate him while he chows on cheese and dried meat. I can only cross my fingers and hope that nothing serious was punctured, causing him to vomit or aspirate in between getting here and there.

I wish I were a better medic...or a tactician. Controlling my impulses thus far is proving to be a real sore point in my life, and they're getting us into a lot of trouble. He might be better off if I sent him home alone for that reason by itself, while I learn to do my best out here like the village suggests.

I'm proving to be a rather awful person.

A terrified, awful person that doesn't want to die.

I don't want to move, let alone make the trip to the river branch by myself. Not without Aidan there to reason with me. But I take my mostly empty water bottle and his canteen in hand anyway, promising to return.

It takes some time to get there, trying to remember through the haze of running the way we came in, and hesitating behind the trees lining the shore to make sure they weren't there. A few minutes pass this way, and I inch further into sight, awaiting the same arrow that crashed through Aidan's flesh like the nail of a cat through a mouse in play. But life goes on in the way it most often does, signs that a single living soul tread here at all gone—including us.

Birds sing hollow tunes into the fresh air, played back by the buzzing of insects. Fish swim in schools of thrashing tails, helpless to the flow of water that carries them downstream. A bright yellow snake slithers in tugging grace to the water, all of which ignore me as if I'm not real. As if I am not standing right here.

I march forward, making a show of the motions, my head spinning while I fill our containers.

*Come and get me, assholes.*

They don't. No one does.

I come and go, angry. I am spent, slinking through the overgrowth where Aidan was left, hope dwindling on sight that we will be leaving tonight. He hasn't moved an inch from when I departed, some color blending against his olive complexion again, but clammy as hell to the touch. Limp.

I press my fingers into his wrist, checking for pulse. He's sleeping, and I let him do so for maybe an hour while I make plans. I *need* a plan, troubled and understanding that we may not be safe crossing the same way we came in. It would be the most obvious path for traps. Or death.

Nothing concrete comes to mind by the time Aidan wakes up. He is more than aching now, consumed by violent thralls of pain that I can do nothing for, except be a poor excuse for a friend and a pat on the shoulder.

"We have to get going," I tell him. "If we want to make it home by nightfall."

*If we can make it home by nightfall,* I mean to say.

He isn't a great conversationalist this way. Most of his responses are quiet grunts or groans, flailing bobs of his head in compliance, crossing the bowl-like dip we sit on top of and making a wide circle of evidence we might leave behind. We will cross through the river branch at a later section, if we can, preferably one a touch shallower.

I give him another drink, then I help hoist him on the worst side to his feet. It is harder this time, his weight more resistant to help and his legs unwilling to bear the girth of his body. We manage to trudge downhill though, slipping through long tangles of bright, wiry trees and velvety flower petals blossoming from the branches. At the bottom of the impression upon the ground, a hollow snap resonates beneath my feet, and fractals of pale bone scatter around my shoes.

I let Aidan stop to recharge for what feels like every fourth mile, counting the minutes in how long it takes him to stop holding his breath while we walk. It's going to take forever this way, but we aren't left with much choice. No one will come looking for us, and I can't help him out here.

We are about to commence our death march when a soft swish of movement nearby startles us into a panic. Aidan shuffles for balance against a tree, patting himself down for his dagger while I draw mine with ease from my backpack. I survey the area, ducking under Aidan's arm for support to keep him close and safe. We inch toward the slope ahead leading out the other side of this earthy bowl, but another bout of shuffling makes me stop.

No, it's not just a shuffling.

There is a sniffling.

I guide Aidan to another tree to keep his balance, listening while I scope the area to where the sound takes me. I am brought short of an older rotted tree, twisted and gnarled, black in its decay and baring no growth. I shift around it, my fingers touching a break in the trunk that splits into a damp crevice for an opening.

Rushing forward, I drop to my knees to peer inside. I can hear Aidan panting to catch up with me, nervous that I've strayed too far, even in his deteriorating state. I yelp at what I see, scurrying backwards in shock as two small brown eyes blink back at me.

Aidan gallops on a limp, extending his hand to jerk me up off the ground so we can run, but I refuse him. I crawl to the tree, breathing deepened and heart on fire.

I am not a failure here. I haven't failed everyone yet.

"He-hello?" I call into the tree. "Are you okay in there?"

A high-pitched voice whimpers. Streaks of remaining sunlight touch ebony skin in blinks through the canopy, and I can see the wet sheen of where tears have stained the small sunken cheeks of a little girl.

"W-w-where's daddy?" she sobs.

*Daddy?*

# CHAPTER SEVENTEEN
## SAHANNA

I HAVE ALWAYS LIKED DUTCH BRAIDS. THEY'RE USEFUL. Taming.

My hair is a mop of tight natural curls with no agenda, other than to run roughshod over my face and head, so it looks like a mess on a normal day. Or a not normal day. Both of which I have plenty of. But it's the kind of rat's nest I won't touch with a brush unless I have to look presentable. That is where the braids come into play.

Wetting my hair and weaving it in strands so tight my scalp burns with tension gives me the only kind of control over my autonomy that I can outwardly manage. It makes me look pleasant...on the outside. Voluminous and neat, instead of five-foot-nine and homeless from ruining yet another dress scaling castle walls against my husband's wishes. Not that the latter was a problem right now.

I have more than enough time to perfect my art of wily hair when my ability to stare off the balcony too long is inhibited by guards The King has stationed outside the doors to check in on me every half-hour. He was also *so kind* as to send in a "friend" when Silas made it aware I was feeling isolated in our quarters—an elven maid named Dee who assists our travels from home and keeps me company when not attending to her own children.

She is much better at the craft of braiding than I am, not that I wasn't made aware the first time I came into contact with The King's personal staff. He mostly hires families with children to support his castle staff, housing them within the castle walls or on the grounds out back with the livestock where they can keep close watch on the animals. But elven mothers, specifically, have a longstanding tradition of teaching both sons and daughters how to braid their generally long, soft hair. They are raised as young girls to understand that this is one of the many duties they carry into motherhood and become very skilled at creating elaborate designs.

Everywhere I look in the elven villages, there are these creatures donning swathes of long hair mixed with a few loose braids, or obedient women twirling tails of twisted hair decorated in beads or metal clips. The men will often take bone from their victories in battle, carving pale pieces to wear as jewelry or fixtures to wear as a badge of honor signifying a job well done. I've seen others of the race in a higher social standing lace fine gems and precious stones into the mix, tied in with soft ribbon or pearls conspicuously placed in at just the right angle. All these things that they must spend a lot of time on in the morning before going to work or providing for the household. Feeding children and livestock. Nursing babies.

My baby is fucking screwed.

My braids are not interesting, sophisticated, or time consuming. Sometimes, I just get upset and stop twisting after finishing the first half of my head. Not that I can't immerse myself into the culture and learn how to perform up to par. I have all the resources available to me, being the wife to The King's advisor. All it takes is a single word, and I'm sure Dee and her daughters would spend endless, joyous hours slapping my wrists until I picked up the trade.

But the kind of power that sort of command entails makes me uncomfortable. I loathe it, to an extent, knowing that despite the lack of poverty present in this thriving society, my life still varies from the average woman below. There are things I will always be able to have that someone else will not. Things that I can get away with, that someone else may not, though The King's law on his own household, siblings included, is rather strict. It is still yet a drastic difference in lifestyle, compared to my setup back at my real home.

When Silas first took notice in my interest of braiding, he brought me home a silky blue ribbon made from the carefully shed coat of a live ice dragon. It is not an item easy to acquire, and one most men would die on a quest to have, but he had presented it to me as if it were unproblematic. For my braids, he claimed it was not an issue, and I spent hours just holding it. I gripped the softest fabric I had known in my entire existence, unable to decide what it was I would do with it, until he helped grace my head in its beauty for the only time.

I stuffed it under our mattress at the end of the night, claiming to have lost it when he asked. But the dark truth of the matter is, the power I felt wearing it in the presence of other *human* women populating the villages made me feel disgusting. More like a prize than a person. His very own incubator with a title to match.

My reluctance to accept items has never stopped him from gifting me other things since then, small tokens of appreciation or devotion. His obsession since imprinting upon me knows no bounds. Our quarters in his brother's castle are swarming with vivacious, exotic flowers and strange plants I had not known existed, with walls of ivy draping around our bedding and enough grassy flora to start a proper fire vying for the sunlit balcony at the door—all treasures I force acceptance of with a brief smile, an expression of gratitude because I don't know what else to do. Because I am afraid of him.

I am bound here, and we both know it.

I am helpless to this forced matrimony, and the duty thrust

atop my shoulders.

I'm powerless, as are all women here. And isn't it convenient?

When they're so much bigger than their opposing gender, more aggressive, stronger—why not?

Silas could tear me in half. He could snap an arm off in what would look like the flick of a wrist. In the beginning, when I was a more willful bride, he had taken both my wrists in one of his hands to prove he could subdue me without effort, cripple me without pain in spite that he knew very well how to cause it. It was a big deal when I was even more fearful than I am now, my whole body trembling with the knowledge of what always comes next. Again, and again. Like a point driven home in a car wreck.

*I'm such a good girl now, outwardly*, my mind prods at the still open wounds of my history here.

But it is true. Silas's point was received at the conception of our first baby...and the loss.

A small grin tugs at the corners of my lips at the word.

*Loss.*

Sometimes, I imagine actually having a baby, like the one that lives inside me now. I toy with the idea of what it would be like, and if I could finally have a little someone to keep me company that wasn't out to make me hurt if I didn't abide by these inhumane laws.

The creature would probably be a boy, to my dismay. Almost all of the babies that made it to this world, prior to The King allowing the kidnapping of human populous, were male. It was part of the problem, after all. The elves did not have a sustainable female population, but a surplus of men. The King had done medical studies to prove humanity and elves were so close in makeup that it was considered suitable for men to imprint upon the women and create children—which are *always* elves. Their genetics somehow manage to override our subpar, helpless, piece of shit ones, turning them into the very same killing machine as their parent.

Still, I can't stop myself from the daydream of having a girl.

Just for a tiny while. Just for long enough to know better and pull a genuine smile from it.

I tell myself my daughter would probably have my hair. My mother and sisters had it too—this untamed, wicked bush of curls that no brush could overpower. It's practically a rite of passage to hate hair in my family, although the baby would have *his* silvery color in my mind. She had to get something from him and, really, his hue came from his mother, so it doesn't *have* to be from him specifically. It is admittedly prettier than my muddied blonde, but I still like to think most of his features would get cycled out of a little girl.

No girl wants to look like her dad. She is better off looking like me, or mom, or even Diamond and Candy. My sisters would have actually killed someone if it meant they were allowed to be aunts. My little brother would have done the same to be an uncle.

*Blu.* Uncle Blu.

I like the ring to it, even if it will never happen.

I practically raised Blu and Diamond while my mom ran around with my dad. In a way, I guess I have that experience up on most human women introduced to this civilization. Child rearing. Most of these girls hadn't really even seen babies until they were in the villages or birthing one. It is more like a strange sideshow when Earth no longer managed or sought out pregnancies.

*Ooh look at his bald little head.*

*They're like raisins that were dropped on the floor. See his hair?*

*Something that big is going to exit my...*

Yes, they can bet their ass it does. Dead or alive, the puny life sucker comes out of the lady bits—or in rarer cases, an incision at the lower belly—in a blaze of blood and goo. It is a terrifying experience for a woman ill prepared to the facts. I wish I could say the fear and depression gets better with further pregnancies.

No one ever addresses the depression, aside the father who caused it. Not like a self-proclaimed emotionally advanced society should, anyhow.

But they *should* address it.

Not that it matters.

Nothing matters if a person has a vagina in this world. Things that mattered to me before this have changed in exorbitant shifts. Though I am years inside the madness, I can still count the old matters on one hand. The most important things in my life, when I was truly living it, I could bend a finger for, each number representing a simple freedom I took for granted lost to my "husband".

Drugs would be the first finger. It was an all-consuming void in my life and I never held a job long because of it. I wasn't picky about the high I took, as long as it was a good time and, at the time I was high, it was *always* a good time. My detox occurred in this world, with Silas, however. I've been able to look at life without a glassy filter since then, and somehow, it feels both easier and harder to live.

Casual sex with a stranger would be my second finger. My middle finger. It sort of goes with the first finger. I don't remember an occasion I had sex where I wasn't high, until I was here, and it was no longer consensual. But I miss the choice. I miss going out on a thick groggy night and wondering whose bed I would wake up in. What stories would I have to tell my friends the next morning? Would my mom be angry I came home smashed when I was supposed to be watching Blu?

Mom would be the third finger, as if it isn't obvious. Nothing is the same without her.

I miss her. More than anything I have ever missed. I want to be with her, knowing I can't, and yearning all the same. She is the first person I called for when I opened my eyes to this dank hell, and the last I scream for at the end of each dream I have.

Silas told me once that I talk in my sleep. Sometimes, I wonder if it's her that he hears me crying out for when he is deep in his studies. Is there any piece left of him that pities it?

It wouldn't help if he did, but I am still curious. Not that I can be sure, but I have grown an intuition that there is a deliberate separation of human families in the world The King has brought forth. The fact that I have no one grows this paranoia into truth through each passing day, from every second I am away from home to every minute I must return home. It's a returning paranoia today because we are leaving the Fae in the next couple of hours.

The King's business here has concluded, and thus ours has as well. We are duty bound, and he is satisfied. There are other ventures calling his attention that he needs to attend to, other places that cannot be ignored no matter how badly I want to stay here, where I feel safer than ever. The only negative aspect of remaining on the island of the Fae is the lack of access to my teas, but it is a fair trade for sanity.

Now...

I stare at the trunk I've packed full of clothes and shoes sitting atop our bed. It carries some wrapped food I intend to take from the kitchens at the top, and some basic medical supplies should I need it on our travels. I threw some interesting rocks in the bottom to add to the live plants consuming my room at home, and an arrow with a crystalline tip I found out by the curtain wall in my cat chasing adventures. The Fae king, Kai, gifted me some translated literature to read and paper to write my own should I grow bored in our travels. His medical staff provided special blue leaves that grow on a separate island that are foretold to aid in pregnancy nausea when eaten.

But I won't need any of it if I am brave enough. Smooth enough.

In between my fingers, I clutch a razor stolen from a barber that had left his tray of tools a little too open as he tidied up for the day. The blade is small, but keen, glistening and gleaming, cold like ice. Just the slightest touch to my fingertips prick the skin apart to reveal beads of crimson, sending shivers of pain up my spine as I suck the small dots on my digits dry.

I've thought this through, more than once. My wrists are so small and vascular, bulging with skinny blue snakes ready to spit red venom as fast as I allow myself to give in to temptation. But I take more convincing than I used to that I won't be caught, knowing there are at least two guards posted outside my door that will drop everything at the first whiff of blood from The King's kin. The Fae aren't as skilled in the art of magical healing as the elves are, but they're no rookies either. They'd hold me off long enough for my husband and his brother to receive notice.

Then I would be in real, steep trouble. Regular protections are child's play in comparison to suicide watch.

Not only that, but endangering my own life, coupled with that of an unborn child, would be a grave crime worth punishing. The King would be furious, further agitated by attending to his twin brother's impetuous wife, being forced to take time out of his endless schedule to dole out appropriate punishments that Silas would be helpless to stop.

It isn't just my imagination that believes The King has an eye for torture and devastation. There isn't a person in all his domain that would dare cross him. He would ruin me for the inconvenience alone if Silas refused. Because Silas shows leniency, and he doesn't. Hence why Silas must account for and keep his brother in line as the role of advisor.

So I have to be precise.

I have to find the right spot. The sweet spot. The one that sings death on my wrists or my neck. A quick split of the flesh, that will only take seconds to fulfill, and then I am assuredly gone. I want my heart stopped before they can reach me.

Just one *real* good go.

It's all it will take.

*I won't even feel it,* I assure myself. *It will be like slicing through butter.*

I like butter. Butter is good. It tastes good. *Feels* good.

I *want* butter.

*Damn it*, I deserve butter.

I'm in hell.

I say it out loud for effect.

"I'm in hell. I'm in hell. I'm in hell."

It is a chant. I'm getting amped up for the big finale. My own death. The baby inside beats against my belly as if it is also revved for the experience—obviously a girl. No female should suffer this life, and she would forgive me if she knew what I was sparing her.

She kicks again, stretching as I talk, a wave of little drumbeats.

*I'm in hell. This is hell. We're in hell.*

She writhes. Little bubbles that pop from within, like joy.

I can't remember what joy was like. But maybe she does, right now. For now.

"I'm in...I'm in..." I breathe, shaking.

The razor hovers so close to the edge of my arm it catches pale hairs, pulling them up in painful pinching sensations that make my eyes water. The baby heaves one more violent kick against my insides so that I feel as though I could pee myself in the same instant, and I take a deep inhale, attempting not to cry. I drop the blade into the trunk, placing it beneath all of my clothes for later when I have more courage.

I fidget with my braids in the mirror at the other end of the room while I calm down, leading them around my head in a delicate circle, and plucking soft yellow flowers Silas had brought in the other day from their stems, tucking them around the design to frame it. The dress I change into is newer—baby blue with billowing sleeves—and flows looser over my rounded belly than the ones I brought with me at the start of our journey here. For a moment, a part of me is grateful Silas thought to pay a seamstress to make me one anew, so I can breathe outside of nighttime when I undress. Not that I would need it at all, if he were a decent person with feelings.

I don't want anyone to think I need new clothes. I don't want to pick them out, or have Silas bring me new ones. It feels so... small, this way. It hurts me. I shouldn't need a thing at all. I shouldn't be here. Right now, I should be home, listening to my mom scream while I screw up her perfect mashed potatoes. I should be in *my* clothes, getting ready for work.

Jeans. Or shorts. I liked short-sleeved V-necks on a workday, but between employment, I loved crop tops. I craved something my skin could catch air with on a hot day. We didn't really have actual winters anymore. The lowest it got most Decembers was a crisp eighty degrees, so my wardrobe was all a series of smart choices, really.

But I never felt...delicate.

Back then I felt hard. *Tough.*

I could kick some serious ass. I did kick some serious bitch ass. Unlike now.

Expectations are different and I adapt. To survive. I'm a survivor.

I touch the last yellow flower remaining in the vase at the mirror across from me, squeezing its velvety petals between my fingers when a shrill noise carries from the open balcony doors. It is a sound I recognize without mistake, due to having done quite a bit of it myself in this past time.

Screaming.

Inhuman waves of shrieking and screeching couples with sobbing, the clatter of swords dropping to the earth, and groans. Soldiers are being called to aid the helpless in bold voices, yelling for warriors to guard the gates and more hysteria ensuring.

My head whips toward the doors that lead out to the halls, the shadows beneath the wood frame no longer present at post. I toe for it, inching closer and fingers gripping the cool metal handles. I give it a soft, quick tug so the door squeaks open and a blast of warm air from the hall bites back at me. Men screaming from the distant floors to take cover makes me hesitant on leaving, shuffling away instead, and taking delicate strides to the white balcony overlooking the courtyard.

It is a tragedy for softer people. From this height still, I can see bodies in the hundreds, piled in pooling crimson heaps at the gates. Men, women, and children alike, there is no mercy shown. Stretches of fabric from lovely shimmering dresses mangle over objects, children, and food baskets strewn across the ground. There is a clear path carved in this massacre, from the draw gate that has been blown apart through the middle, down the rich blue and gold flecked lapis stairs leading inside the castle.

My heart gallops inside my chest. I lean further out for a better view, catching a long, thick, trail of chunky red leading toward the main entrance of the castle and stopping short of the stairs, though strangled figures litter each step. Something that either screams incredible danger or unforeseen salvation.

Is this what I have dreamed of since this nightmare began? A rebellion to spare me this life? How would it fare against the oh so mighty Elven King and his twin brother?

The onslaught has murdered hundreds of Fae in the minutes since I have been made aware of its presence. The Fae have no known enemies, but still it wreaks havoc without care. Should I be afraid of what comes next?

A long, strong arm wraps about my shoulders, pulling me backward as I gasp. I shriek, kicking wildly until I am turned to face Silas, calm, though I can see the way his breathing has deepened. His chest pumps up and down, his honey-yellow eyes tracing every inch of the room. As I calm down, I can see his traditionally white attire is soured in blood, his face smattered in wicked droplets.

He steps around me, closing the glass doors to the balcony and sliding yellow curtains over it so sunlight cannot enter the room. I touch my hair with absent fingers, assuring it is still in place and that nothing has fallen free, dipping into a subtle curtsy while I fall from reality.

"I...Is everything alright?" I ask, as polite as I can manage.

Silas does not respond though. He yanks me out of position before I can complete it, guiding me toward the wooden wardrobe where we had kept our clothes, and lifting me up inside.

*This is new. Do we put our wives on hangers now?*

I resist this, just a touch. I am not afraid, but I want him to think I am. I want him to believe I am the slightest bit reluctant so he will feed me information I will understand. As I hoped, he hesitates when I push back, meeting my gaze over my slumped shoulder. I spin around inside the wardrobe, letting him take in the full form of his baby in this dress for this once. His hand holds to the sword sheathed at his side while he does this, swallowing hard and eyes narrowing.

"There is an invader to these lands," he asserts to calm my fictitious concern. "I am not too certain of what sort this creature belongs. Stay silent."

And the door is shut into darkness for a time. How long, I cannot say for sure. I have no good estimation of time in this state.

Five minutes? Ten minutes? An hour?

I can still hear screaming in faint drones, though Silas never leaves the front of the wardrobe. Armed. Waiting. Patient. He has always been patient, ever the tactician. He is a thinker, perhaps another reason his brother hired him, among all their siblings, as his advisor when all others begged him not to.

It is hard to say with wildcards in mind, what purpose is entrusted with any particular reason. Although, to say they are the biggest wildcards in the family would be a grave mistake. Bastian, their second youngest brother, has a hint of their father in everything he does. How they trust such a creature with the charge of the biggest city in this universe, I will never know.

There is a distant shuffling resounding from the halls, making me curious as to whether the doors are open. Or maybe my senses are dulled, and it is from outside this wardrobe. I turn my head, pressing each ear against the wood doors of the container to listen better. But I am knocked backwards at a deep, violent thrashing not from this room that shakes the floor from down below, rattling the contents of the whole room and sending in an aggressive, loud gust of wind through the window.

I push the door of the wardrobe open a smidge after several quiet moments, watching Silas lower his sword to the fury of the world around him as if it were a kind of divine sign. I brush the door open further, and he tilts his head to look back at me in a gentle, not all too stern warning to mind him.

A clicking of boots outside our door catch me off guard in the same moment. The lack of reaction from Silas allows The King to enter the room, uninhibited and slow. I shrink backward, Silas providing a curt nod in lieu of the traditional bow all must do in the presence of their King. Though I am nervous in his presence, I push the door open completely, sighing so that the baby and I can both stretch from this wooden box.

The King gives this a strange look and a queer smirk.

"Such little faith," he remarks, bypassing his brother and holding forth a hand to help me down.

I refuse him. I don't trust the motion. He is searching for something he knows I don't want him to find, like a fucking crack dog. So I keep him at arm's length, like a junky, gripping Silas' arm and stumbling to the floor. Cowering at my husband's backside, I attempt not to look The King in the face this time as I had last. There is a satisfaction in this refuge I take, as if it hints more at an adjustment than a survival reflex.

Silas' hand reaches back at my arm when I press closer, touching my elbow gently.

*I'm here*, it says.

I wish he wasn't.

"Not at all," he responds when sure I am settled. "I could not locate you, however, when the assault began. My priorities set accordingly."

"Did you find a proper view of our invaders?" The King asks.

He is trailing strange colors across our floor from the bottom of his boots, a thick ooze like blood but different in color. *Orange*. Really *orange*. The slick, sludgy texture of the fluid makes my stomach roll, fingers twitching to my mouth and gut.

"I did." Silas nods. "I detained one of the few aggressors in the cells at the start of the attack, though I am afraid by such time, casualty had already incurred. It is noteworthy that each of the creatures placed a separate coordinated attack in the castle walls, after breaching the draw gate. It does not appear to be coincidental or on a whim that they struck the Fae."

The King neither agrees nor disagrees.

"We have handled their species before, though in absence of near the casualty." He frowns. "I have disarmed each of the animals of their advanced equipment. We will burn it come morning. How many of the beasts are there total?"

"Three," Silas answers. "Four, if you count the unborn."

"I do."

"You do," my husband repeats at the same moment. "I do as well."

I squeeze closer to Silas at the sound of The King moving back through the room, treading closer to us from the balcony. He has no reason to sift through my trunk. He wouldn't dare touch my belongings. I have nothing on me...right now...to get me in trouble. Why am I so on edge?

"An unborn child does provide me with a bit of leverage, does it not?" He sits in a comfortable cushioned chair nearby, sinking into the rare luxury of rest.

Silas loses tension as well upon this sight, his shoulders slumping just a bit. It is common, for he is on guard when The King is on guard.

"It could." He smirks. "Under the right circumstances."

"Entering the Fae without explicit permits is a war crime," The King muses. "Killing the Fae in absence of just cause? What is a proper sentencing for such events?"

It's a game I have witnessed them play in the past. It is a gross, twisted indifference to what they perceive beneath them that makes me cringe in silence. A learned cat and mouse ploy, an unfortunate shit show, the brothers could probably make a good game show out of their deplorable natures, if it were regular society.

*Wheel. Of. Tortuuuuure.*

*Who is it suffering today, Silas?*

*Well, today, we have a special on WAR CRIMINALS!*

Cue the sirens and strobe lights for good television effect.

*Is there a woman?*

*Yeah, buddy.*

*What about a baby?*

*In her belly!*

*Woooooo! Do we have leverage?*

*We have leverage, brother!*

My fantasy of their heinous natures is how I cope with the terrible. Laughing is the only way I can stomach this talk.

"We could certainly find out tomorrow as the sun rises," my husband's voice grows wild with amusement.

"Sahanna," The King calls my name, drawing me away from this vivid daydream.

"Y-yes?" I answer in a squeak, still sheltered behind Silas, boring holes into the floor. "Yes...sir? I mean, your highness? I mean..."

"Would you care to stay in the Fae a touch longer while trial proceedings carry forward?" he interrupts my insolence, unconcerned with how I choose to address him. "It will not take long."

This feels like a trap.

Why wouldn't anyone want to stay in the Fae?

It is heaven compared to my current residence, and I would never leave if they offered to let me stay.

Does Silas not want me here? Is he going to send me back alone?

I have never been anywhere without him, as far as travel. But my due date draws closer with every month that passes us by. It would take time to get home without outside sources, and if we traveled by foot, it could be a very close call.

What is the aim here? Do I have a choice? What if I tell him no?

"Y-yes," I reply. "Absolutely. I would love to stay, yes."

He chuckles, satisfied and poised. It makes every hair on my body stand on edge, and I tremble.

"Very well. Be sure to unpack for the night then. I am sure my brother will manage this for you so that you may rest. It has been a *busy* adventure for you here, after all."

My fists clench tight, but I bob my head in understanding. I don't know how he knows, but he knows.

I'm helpless as to how he knows and the best I can do now, to preserve my dignity, is play the fool. I will be caught due to this evil monster of a deity. There is nothing I can do but hold my head high and await consequence.

"Thank you," I speak through clenched teeth.

# CHAPTER EIGHTEEN
## AIDAN

T HE VOICE THAT EMERGES FROM INSIDE THE TREE IS small and gentle, like a lamb.

So young and new, clusters of sounds tremble between indistinguishable words and gasping sobs, mumbling yet more obscure pleas in the panic that binds this little girl to the only shelter from the elements for the miles we have traveled outside Limbo.

My heart drops to my bloodied feet hearing the sound, such a small vocabulary limiting the age range of the child to no more than three or four years of age. Unsteady hands scramble to hold my body parts together over the thick bandaging Addie spun over each puncture wound, feeling the wet ooze of the slow trickle, proving they have either reopened or never stopped gushing while we decide what our next move should be in light of the present dilemma.

It isn't a simple choice for either of us, and there is no time we can afford to stay much longer. It won't be long until dark sheets of color overtake the sky, leaving us with another set of impossible choices, as walking straight into the village during a potential attack would be a play at madness. Not to mention we have probably already overstayed our welcome out in the forest. The creatures were playing with us like a cat does a dead mouse, or they would have caught up to us no problem when we ran like prey. Not to mention if they wanted to actually kill me instead of wound me, they would have. But it won't stop more from finding us to finish the job if they've alerted their friends to human activity beyond The Dome.

The people of Limbo deserve to know The Dome is growing ineffective as it lightens too, or that the Ravagers are getting stronger. I can't remember ever having seen so many in the third layer at one time prior to this afternoon, and we don't have much to spare before things get *really* bad.

But...

I slide into the dirt, grunting as I collapse within the bed of grass and dead leaves. Insects skitter home, weaving up the decrepit tree while I pant in pain. The pressure, the change of movement, it is all but crippling each time I force myself to try, and I'm growing low on energy.

I can see better this way though, past Addie's shoulder into the gaping trunk of this tree where the child inside is balled up at the rear, in a fit of dirt and tears. Her skin is dark but unmarred, a soft complexion that reminds me of Celestyn, despite her cheeks being soiled with mud. It is hard to make out much more, or assess whether she has sustained life threatening injuries, without conning her out a bit further, but I wonder how long she's been this far out. Did one of *them* place her here with the intent of returning?

Is this another trap?

My mind cannot form a coherent string of thoughts. Everything begins to spin and muddle together so it is like a dysfunctional carousel of events with each new occurrence being another seat on the ride running out of control.

I take a drink of water from my canteen that Addie refilled. I'm so damn thirsty. I can't remember being this thirsty in all my life, and I swallow painful gulps as fast I can, knowing full well I will need another refill on our way home. At the next swig, I sputter into hoarse coughing, unable to force more down my throat, yet pining for it.

Addie's soft coaxing hesitates immediately, and her shoes crunch against the broken sticks and rocks to look back at me. She mouths a couple words in my direction that I barely make out in my daze.

*That's enough.*

And then her attention is focused again on the little girl's plight.

I attempt to behave, listening to her ask questions that I worry might be a bit too complex for a child of this girl's age. It needs to stay simple if we aren't going to take the barbarian approach. She is young enough, after all, that we can swing her up around our backs and leave without dispute, other than a little yelling and a fair prick of shock.

But *no.*

It's Addie who happens to be my partner at the conjunction of this shit show, which means we have to gain the little runt's trust first. Trauma is always a top priority to sidestep if it can be helped in Addie's mindset, and she always wants to help more than she hurts. In a regular, sane world, we would need more people like her. Here in this horror flick, she only creates more problems than she resolves. And unfortunate as it is, Addie's most charming beams of sugary words aren't getting this kid to answer questions.

*Do you remember where your daddy went?*

Bitter silence.

*Can you tell us what he looked like?*

Distrustful glares shooting laser beams of death straight through our skulls.

*What was your daddy's name? We can look for him tomorrow if you can come out?*

A whimper.

I can feel Addie losing her patience the further the sun sets. It's abnormal, but it suggests her mind is learning. She tries to maintain her composure in spite of it, sitting on her knees and taking a drink of her own water while she sifts through our dire outlook in the privacy of her thoughts. But it is failing. She offers the little girl a sip from the container in this panicked stupor, sloshing it back and forth to make the fluid within audible. It is a rebuffed gesture, without hesitation.

I scoot drunkenly forward, light as a feather and heavy as lead. My arms are tingling down to each finger pad, my face both hot and cold. This is taking way too long in so many different ways, and my partner has an interesting lack of people skills for someone who wants to help every single one of them. Although, in hindsight, it could also boil down to lack of skills with children. It isn't like there are many where we come from.

"Hey there, hey," I speak soft and quiet. "It's okay. You don't have to talk to us if you're not ready. But we want to help you. Did your daddy tell you not to talk to strangers?"

My breathing is labored amongst words. I can't catch an adequate amount of air to fill my lungs in a satisfactory manner for my brain. I need more water, and I reach for Addie's water bottle, which she jerks from my hands with a look of disgust. Or fear?

Why do I care? I'm sure I've given her the same look at one time or another.

The little girl's dark, earthy brown eyes peek up at me, studying my face and my ruined clothes. When she speaks, to my delight and disappointment, it is directed at Addie instead of myself.

"Daddy say no," she crumbles, sucking in little puffs of air and a plump bottom lip. "I want daddy."

"I bet you do." Addie nods, frowning. Her voice is buttery and babying, digging deep to stay on this child's level. "I bet your daddy kept you real safe. But my friend and I have been all over this place, and we didn't see him. No daddy in sight."

The child breaks into further sobbing, wiping her cheeks against dirty knees and pink scuff marks, where it appears that she might have fallen.

"Daddy say no," she wails. "It...water...and *nooo*. I'm scared!"

It is almost incomprehensible, other than the last part. Fear is understandable and recognizable at any age, but more especially in someone so young. There isn't much of a right answer to address her concerns that is honest, either. It is harder to be truthful in regard to children when the balance of life and death is such a thin thread.

To add, no one has biological family in Limbo that they know of. Not in the history of being here has anyone located family that they didn't make for themselves during the extent of their stay. But this girl is so small, I can see where it might complicate things. If she and another person had taken form far beyond The Dome at close to the same time frame, and the man she calls daddy assumed responsibility of her...she wouldn't remember anything to know otherwise. It could be like a baby duck effect.

In my experience inside the village serving Limbo, children often remember even less than adults do for their entire lives. Celestyn had made note one time that the younger kids never seem to recall anything at all for their entire stay before capture, which can be years depending on the caretaker in their charge. It's as if their whole data card has been lost to amnesia, and they have started on a clean slate of memory. The words are there. The skills come back. But the people are gone.

Still...it would have been hard to survive out here without help. That much is undeniable. This girl is too young to fend for herself, and she smells like stout, pungent urine from inside the tree. Considering her condition, there isn't much of a chance her "daddy" is alive at this point. Who knows how long they have been separated, and the kid isn't answering questions the way we need. Time was up hours ago, prior to setting eyes on her, and we need to get home.

"Listen," I start, wincing at Addie's harsh side eye to soften my tone. "Okay, let's start over. My name is Aidan, kid. And this is my partner, Addie."

"Adabelle," Addie corrects, though I can see her hiding a faint smile. "It's Adabelle."

I pretend to ignore her, but the kid soaks the information in, eyes beginning to sponge Addie in like she was the only person alive out here in a forest plush with heartbeats. Looking at my injuries right now, she might be the only person alive out of each of us, but I try not to focus on my grave state. This is an opportunity to rush in on, and I nudge Addie in the ribs as hard I can, which is rather meek anymore.

She catches on fast, however.

"W-what's your name, sweetie?" She smiles, resting her round cheek against her closed fist.

I like warmer looks on her, sometimes.

"I'm Simone." Our child straggler plays with her own hands, but finds Addie's gaze for longer than a couple seconds. "I'm three. See?"

She holds out several fingers that do not add up to three.

"Well, Simone," Addie uses the name with convincing compassion, "I don't see your daddy out here. But maybe he lost you and found our village. Would you like to sleep with a blankie tonight? We can look for your daddy in the morning, okay?"

At last, a feisty, but definitive nod. Simone creeps forward on her hands and knees from the rotted tree trunk so she comes into full disturbing view. It is a gaunt, chilling realization right away that she is very small for any age she belongs to—scrawny and bleak with an entirely bald head, save for a few patches of black fuzz fighting to come in. She stands up, dusting off a lacy lavender dress that fluffs well past her ankles, embroidered in extravagant beads that remind me of a more expensive princess dress up item parents buy their daughters for Christmas at home. Except this one is more intricate, weighted and better pieced together.

It has no modern twists—billowing sleeves quite modest and laced in gold...gold that looks all too real, drifting well past her ankles so we cannot see her feet.

Addie takes notice of these details as well, snatching Simone into her arms as soon as she is in arm's length, and casually letting the lacework slip through her fingers. Twisting her head I am just fast enough to catch Addie checking the child's ears.

"It's beautiful." She smiles to avoid startling Simone who fights to keep her pouty lip. "It's beautiful on you."

I struggle to stand with the two, clutching my side and my leg. No one has attacked us yet, and I have no doubts if this were an ambush, they would have by the time we came into actual contact with the child. But we need to get on our feet and start moving before we are brutalized.

It takes a few more minutes studying Simone in her peculiar attire to convince Addie to get moving, exiting the other side of the depression in the earth before I need her official help achieving the motions of mobility. The wounds are feeling slicker by the minute, and I can feel the gauze growing damp above the clothing Addie used to stifle the gushing. My breathing is arduous, my lungs trying their best to keep up with my pounding heart while I fear the smell of blood will attract predators from the shadows if we don't pick up the pace.

But Addie isn't adept at holding children in a single arm and shouldering my weight at the same time. Our pace is the one she can continue to balance upon as a small, unsteady crutch. Like a true warrior, she powers through the lower currents of the river without complaint, huffing up a different trail and hoping all paths lead to home. It's a weird minute to realize that, despite sweat and the brute reality of nature swarming around us, she smells nice.

Sweet. Light.

Like perfume. Or soap.

I bet she bought some from the markets earlier in the week. They make really good ones for people that can afford it, loaded with a variety of fruits, plants, and flowers. I have some at home, made with a batch of honey and some gel from the insides of a bitter grass outside The Center.

Addie's definitely smells more appealing to the senses, and I settle into the familiar comfort of her aroma while we trudge home.

It isn't until we get a mile out from Limbo, having pushed our way through the fields and into The Dome where Simone's head is rubber-necked in awe, that I notice Addie is shaking. She is huffing to carry on, her knees threatening to buckle in overtly dangerous staggers.

It is easy to forget how much weight she is burdened with between Simone and I, and I grunt, bucking up enough to release her from my part in it, though she never asks. She shouldn't have to, and I pressure myself to take the last mile like a proper gentleman would, hitting the village borders as the stars come out in silver winks of light.

My whole body shivers when we pass what is usually our safety net. The Dome is more anemic tonight than it has ever been, and concern overthrows me that this could be viewed as yet another game in the Ravagers' fatal arena.

I need to rest, to build energy for tonight's inevitable attack, and hope it doesn't happen on our way through the door. We all do.

"I'll take you home." Addie wipes a sheen of sweat from her face onto her shoulder, hiking Simone up as I realize she has fallen asleep on the other side. "I think I can make it okay after that."

"You can't," I choke, shuffling through the pain. "It's already too late."

"I've made it befo—"

"Just stop." I make sure she is following so that I can go on. "It's no big deal, Addie. You can stay with me tonight and check on Zoey in the morning."

It is an obvious break in her morality. I can see how her expression is torn, the language of her body bouncing from one direction to the next, her face craning out over her shoulder in the direction of home. The kid will slow her down, and she knows it, but leaving Zoey alone another night weighs considerable consequence on her.

It is way too late to make it to The Center to put the kid in a quarantine room so she can make break for home by law's standard, and knowing her, I'm not sure she will be keen on the idea anyway. It is possible Simone has had to overcome more obstacles than most of us have, getting from the forest to The Center in one piece. It seems unfair to leave her all alone in a cold dark room with no personal contact or comfort, more especially on her first night with strangers.

Simone's presence muddies waters that Addie has made clear to start. Zoey has always been the top priority in the trickle of Addie's life this far and keeping her in check has been the first task on her agenda every day. It is the purpose she has designed herself to stay distracted from this...mess.

But it is possible to have more than one. Purpose.

We reach my fortress of desolation and despair, and I groan, climbing the block to the door. I pull it open with Addie's robust help, who feels so much stronger than I remember. Stronger than most women her size or age or...anything. Though perhaps I am just paranoid, and weak.

Celestyn isn't home when we get inside, as I had requested her to be. Her books are in the back corner, partly translated, with rough pillows she took from Amadeus' tower and heaps of quilts fanned out like the padding to a quack house. My guitar is under a different pile of stained fabric I pass off as blankets, closest to the tallest book stack, and I approach it, my hands yearning to play.

But the strength isn't there.

The will isn't either.

I drag my feet to the wall aside the window, collapsing into the harsh siding and fingers flexing over my injuries. Exhaustion is a limitless vacancy in this state, each inch of my skin and bone firing on all cylinders like acid melting me to ash.

I stretch my injured leg down flat to the floor, groaning.

*Damn.*

The door closes, and my eyes flicker open to Addie padding across my floor. Her eyes dart anxiously to every corner in the room as if this was a trap I had set up to have her killed, rather than a haven I offered from the storm ahead. As if I, specifically, intend to hurt her.

Has she been hurt? Aside from the distraught man at The

Center, I haven't much thought of the possibility. Everyone believes she is a monster, and they have taken it upon themselves to carry out their relentless witch hunt, so I can't rule the horribly daunting thought out.

Who wouldn't hurt a monster if they kept faith that it was for the better good? But...I don't see her the same as I had the first time I'd watched her eyes change. Not tonight. There has to be a bigger explanation to it—to her. We are missing something.

Addie shoulders off her pack, laying Simone in Celestyn's heap of quilts and pillows. She sits upright against the wall close by her, watching me from across the room as I return her stare. I can't imagine it's much different than her post at home with Zoey —the lookout.

She'd be good at it. I'll grant her that.

Her devotion is unmatched.

However, exhaustion is a look I know all too well, and it wears on her until her lids droop against her every will, shutting out the terrifying world around her so that I am all that stands between the door and them.

When the Ravagers come, my cold, quivering body is entering a state of stunned shock at the immense, grievous injury in the forest, just to make it full circle to another attack. I am beyond help, beyond pain and the urge to sleep, unable to take my eyes off of Addie who is huddled in the corner with Simone, the girl stirring a few times to move up in her lap. Closer to warmth. Not that Addie has much of the heat to give. Her clothes are still drenched from the river, and she trembles under a thinner blanket from my guitar case so that Simone can have all the quilts she promised.

It isn't until I hear the first true swell of horror from the attacks outside, that I realize the attacks might be heavier than usual, and concern takes hold. Loud, thundering bursts of wood and metal from the neighboring houses splinter and scream from their structures, crashing to the ground in tired moans. The people that had taken residence within fall into a clustered mess of hysteria, feet crunching by my home as they run for their very lives, though the sleek pierce of sword through bone by the window tells me at least one has not made it.

Both girls sleep through this massacre, adjusted to the torture. Or maybe just that deep in collapse.

Addie twitches a single time, enough to make me think there is potential she is paying attention, small hands wrapping about Simone's bald head and subsequently shielding her ears, calling to mind a time my mother had done the same for me in a crowd of angry protesters.

I lean forward, testing the creak of the floorboards to see if it would be safe to nudge the two coherent, when a rattle comes in the form of subtle tests from a powerful sword to the metal siding of my home.

In the past, most attacks have overlooked my reinforced shack, an endeavor of love I embarked upon since I made nest here. It is far more protected than other homes, a lot of my spare time outside of Celestyn having been poured into its perfection so that it would be more of an obstacle to the Ravagers, requiring more time to dismantle it than I assume they have available. It is a pain to upkeep, and it has worked so far, but I'm not dense.

Nothing is invincible.

I lean further into the wall, reaching toward my pocket for my dagger and eying the blankets protecting my guitar case where my bow is concealed behind. There is a tapping of fingers at the covered window aside my head, and I hold my breath. Their senses are keen, long ears listening for anyone that might make a reaction. Or a sound. A stunned gasp.

My eyes flicker to Addie again. I am undecided as to if I should wake her up, to move across the mine field of a floor to warn her. I need to guard the entrance to this structure, but I can't guard them all by myself. And if she wakes up unexpectedly during an attack, it places a different problem on my shoulders as well.

I push up on my knees, rocking forward and sucking in an involuntary gasp of air at the same time. All of my injuries pang with agony at the motion, drying to the bandaging but tender as ever. The arrow puncture at my leg trickles, pushing apart in smarting tears and making me lightheaded.

The room is spinning, and my hand catches balance before I hit the floor, though it's not too late yet. I can no longer tell how far away the floor is, my depth perception drawing in and out of focus like a camera adjusting to a faraway image but never losing the blur.

I touch the leg wound with my free hand, putting a slight pressure on it and then freezing still. A crunch at the door freezes me solid, the glistening, bloodied blade of a sword pulling back through and another coming just above it like it wasn't a solid metal door, but rather air. Two more of the blades plow inside, creating small slits in the primary exit like peepholes, and awaiting response from residents inside.

No one moves, to my relief.

The shadows of our perpetrators make one more toying, sweeping hole in my door while my adrenaline keeps me up a shade longer, as still as a statue. At the corners of my mouth, I can feel myself drooling a sick taste to the floor, though my lips seems dry. Cracked. The words of another language are spoken in the streets outside, sounding satisfied and secure that there is not a living soul in this house.

But I can't be sure.

*I'm still alive*, I remind myself while the outside breeze squeals inside like the high pitched, haunting wheels of a toy train through the holes in my door. *I'm just hurt. So very hurt.*

I let myself sink into the floor face down, growing cold as I shut my eyes for a time. It doesn't feel like sleeping when I do, my ears still collecting the cries of the people suffering outside and the booming of vile creatures ransacking our way of life in an aggressive, crimson twister—but I must have garnered some rest.

The sun is welcomed back to civilization in warm throbbing beats when I am brought around to another forceful shaking at the door. The sound is pain, like sharp fractals of glass being used as ice picks to shovel out the ugly contents of my skull.

Across the room, I catch Addie's eyes opening to the discontenting noise, squinting as my knee-jerk reaction flings me upright. I rip a dagger off the floor that I don't remember taking out, swinging it around as Addie squeaks and Celestyn screams, stopping me just short of splitting open her belly. My breathing is heavy when I freeze, head swarming so full I can't feel my face in this position.

I crumple to the floor, letting the blade drop against the wood in a hollow ring, muttering apology after apology, though I can't be sure she hears it. She must have. She doesn't spend time acknowledging the fact I almost killed her in confusion when she sees my state of affairs. Her knees hit the floor in an instant, shaking the empty room and pulling at my clothes to get a better look at the places I've bled through.

"What happened?" She swallows. "You don't look so great. Hey, Aidan?"

I clutch her hand as it touches my clammy face, smothering my cheek along her skin to absorb all its warmth.

"I'm okay," I rasp. "I'm fine. I ju...it's..."

I can't catch my breath. Celestyn pats my face, trying to pop me back to reality, keeping me from falling into deep sleep.

*I'd love to sleep. Just a few more minutes.*

The floorboards groan, creaking at the fluctuation of her weight as she is standing, ready to cross the room to the corner where her bare minimum supplies pile amongst books, blankets, and two people that kept my company overnight. Celestyn freezes at the sight of them, setting me loose to die when she takes notice of the pair who are still groggy in her space, Addie coming to in a series of yawns and a broad stretch after her scare.

"Why is *she* here?" Celestyn almost shouts, and I wince, curling at the metal bat assault to my already present migraine.

Addie's eyes pop completely open to this, her scrawny, powerful arms squeezing Simone a bit closer so the little girl twists sideways. There is a fragile trust shared in this, something in Addie hitting the ceiling of how much emotional torment she can handle when it comes to the child.

I open my dry, aching mouth to answer, but Celestyn's voice shouts over my pathetic excuse for words.

"Why the fuck is she here, Aidan?!"

"I didn't have time to get home on my own," Addie answers for me, firm to her opponent, and knowing my current state better than anyone. "I don't see the big deal."

Of course, Celestyn ignores her, the lesser person she is deemed to be.

"Did you fuck her?"

My eyes roll hard. I think I saw hell when they hit the back of my skull, and it was more manageable than this. In the corner of the room, I hear Addie's response of *God, gross, what?* leaving me unsure as to whether to be offended or jubilant. I cock my head at the bloody imprints I have dragged around the room since arriving home last night.

"D-does it look...like I have the capability of fucking anyone, Celestyn? Ugh...Look...a-at this blood."

She crosses her arms, pursing her lips.

"It could have come from her."

I drop my head onto the floor twice.

Can I be dead yet?

"Where?!" I shriek with every ounce of energy remaining. "Where, Celestyn? No one bleeds that much during sex, ever, and outside of that...ahh...out...side...of that...she's fucking invincible. Meanwhile, I have...m-multiple, potentially life...threatening injuries."

"THEN WHY IS SHE HERE!"

I can feel my blood pressure going up, pounding drumbeats in tides of swooshing waves breaching the shores of my sanity. Like a bad rocket, I am three seconds from going sky high, to hitting the ground and cracking into a billion pieces.

Addie lays Simone into a nest of the quilts, covering her with a dry blanket she wasn't using. When she has the child settled, she crosses the room, approaching our squabble and crossing her arms.

"I'm not sure what the problem is here." Her hip bounces to the side, lips dipping into a distressed frown. "We are coworkers, and I couldn't carry that little girl home safely. Aidan offered what any decent human being ever has or would. I accepted his offer. End of story."

I feel the feral rage of Celestyn glowering straight into Addie's soul, but my beast of a partner is durable. She doesn't melt like ice on the sun, and she doesn't back down, watching in return as the fury fades from her opponent's expression. The truth seems sturdier coming from Addie's mouth to Celestyn, and I sigh, my fingers coming to rub my face—though I'm starting to wonder if I am hallucinating.

I can't feel much of either body part.

Celestyn throws out her arms in frustration to assure me I am still balanced by the hairs of survival in this reality. "Fine. Whatever. I just don't understand why you both didn't call me right away. These injuries aren't child's play. Aidan could still die."

*Please, yes.*

"Oh yeah," Addie growls in a vicious lull, a wolf in sheep's clothing. "Let me just get right on my cell phone and do that. Wait a minute, I don't have one that functions here. And even if I did, what were you going to do, Celestyn? Were you going to drive over here before the attacks in your armored tank? Maybe you can teleport now? Is that it?"

Celestyn remarks a biting reply, but I can't hear it. Everything is fading to black, shifting and blending and spinning on its side. The whole world rolls to the left, growing into a cosmic void that builds large and bloated with infinite carousels of imagery.

Gasoline dreams, shiny things. Dark plumes of ashy grey smoke. Mom. Dad. Oliver. Nathan. Gregory. Fire stretching flutters of warm, smarting fingers up a seatbelt jammed in place. My fiancée, an orange haired, flaming mess of pale skin and battered lips beaming in a shower of windy, rare sunlight, floating her finger to her face in a mischievous smile.

*Shh.*

I am hushed.

Her mouth parts in a familiar laugh, each giggle a distant song.

I am drunk on the music, the scenery a merry-go-round that can't be stopped.

I can't breathe.

I'm not breathing.

I'm falling and I can't catch myself from hitting rock bottom.

My arms flail, and my eyes pop open again. I am in an exam room at The Center, basted in ointments Celestyn has made to speed healing efforts, and re-bandaged so my wounds are clean. At my side on a rickety chair, Addie is sitting next to me with her hand on my bicep while Celestyn examines Simone from the other side of the room. I'm startled as she smiles at me, but I can't knock it, relaxing for a second.

"Good morning." She removes her hand, burying it between her thighs to keep from fidgeting. "You've been out for a few hours now."

The panic starts to set in at these words.

"No," I murmur, flinging myself upright despite the pain and seizing up at once. "No...no. I can't be here. I can't...no. He'll be looking for me, and I can't..."

Celestyn drops what she is doing with Simone, switching places with Addie who trots to the child that holds her scrawny arms out to be picked up.

Firm hands push me into bed for rest, holding me there, and allowing me to take in the full weight of how hurt I am while I look my newest, never present, roommate in the face.

"The visit is not logged," she tells me with care. "Ace won't know about it, so don't think for a minute I am going to let him sign you up for the Suicide Missions."

I have avoided them since they started, the Suicide Missions. Limbo has not always been able to produce the goods they need as fast as we need them and, on occasion, Ace would lead small outings beyond The Dome to collect materials outside of our procurement so we can keep surviving for a little while longer.

More often than not, most of these missions go unfulfilled. People die, or get lost, or don't come home.

Ace attempts to recruit me for each one he schedules, and I'm always able to avoid him until he is forced to leave without me. But it is getting harder. It would be impossible this time if it weren't for Celestyn, who comforts and reassures me so I can relax.

She turns to face Addie and Simone when she is certain she has set my mind at ease, and that I won't try getting up. The little girl clutches to Addie's shirt with tight fists, face buried below her chin, and legs kicking about as Celestyn strides toward them.

"We have to decide what to do with her," she says out loud while making strict eye contact with my partner.

*I can't believe she said that out loud...to Addie, of all people.*

It won't end well.

Addie makes the exact face of disgust I knew she would. "We assure she receives proper healthcare until we can figure out the depth of her situation. She's not an object, Celestyn. This shouldn't be a difficult concept for someone like you."

"She is dressed...weird, Adabelle," Celestyn argues with her hands. "And she claims to have survived under the supervision of an adult that no one could find. I think I need to do a routine checkup, followed by *at least* a day long containment to make sure she didn't acquire any illnesses that could be fatal to us."

"Take her in that shit space of a quarantine, and I'll make sure you're left for the next ambush," Addie roars, holding Simone tighter.

Celestyn slams paperwork down on the floor, whipping to Addie sharp and fast.

"If you want to continue wasting breath here in this god forsaken village, I suggest you check yourself faster than I can."

I raise both my hands in clean surrender for both of them. "Hey! Hey! Let's just...stop. Okay? Inhale. Exhale."

"She needs care," Celestyn is adamant.

I pause. "That is true. The check is alright. And necessary. But...I think Simone has endured more than enough stress without quarantine as long as she isn't outwardly sick."

"She could have something contagious. Quarantine is protocol."

Addie hops out of place, fingers grasping the pocket on her backpack where she keeps her dagger, and sauntering for Celestyn. She is going to leave with this child one way or another, with or without permission.

"Leave. The kid. Alone."

There is a grave quiet while Celestyn contemplates this. Could she take Addie? Maybe. But she puts her hands up after a full minute in the same surrender I offered. She resigns herself to finishing the check on Simone and allowing for dismissal. Addie doesn't hesitate to carry the child out the door when it is through, whisking her somewhere safer than The Center.

Celestyn returns to me when it is done, empty and dissatisfied. She sits in frustration, face resting on her fist and quivering with such deep upset, it looks as if she were cold.

"You didn't back me up," she growls under her breath when the silence is too much. There is an apparent disappointment lingering in every word.

"You were wrong," I tell her.

She shakes her head. "I don't care. You aren't supposed to side with her. She's not one of us."

"She is one of us."

"She's not. You've seen it. Alright? She's a monster."

"And if the monster is right, I should side with you anyway because at least that way we can be wrong together? Come on, now. This isn't logical."

Celestyn sniffs, repeating herself. "You weren't supposed to side with her. It isn't fair."

"Why do you care?" I groan, sinking deeper into the makeshift bed, tempted to suffocate myself with the sheets.

*"Because,"* she shouts. "We were a team until she stumbled straight out of some fresh hell to ruin our lives here. And now, you're going to let her divide us. It's not right."

"She's not doing anything!"

"You talk to her all the time, more than you talk to me." Celestyn's chest heaves, lip jutting out while she attempts to contain her distress. "You act like she's better than me."

I've never seen her this pitiful, this vulnerable. But I break. The toxic cloud that we have created clears.

I am thinking well when I return her hate.

"Why. Do. You. Care?" I hiss. "Why do you care who I talk to at all. We aren't exclusive. *Remember*?"

# CHAPTER NINETEEN
## ADABELLE

IT WAS NOT MY ORIGINAL INTENTION TO BRING SIMONE home with me.

It isn't part of my long-term plan to care for a child this soon, really. No less a child that can't make their own breakfasts or efficiently wipe their own butt. It is a big commitment to take on, and one I'm not all certain my job will allot for without a little support on the side.

Simone is a sweet, shy girl, a bit too shrunken for her age, and antisocial around strangers so far as I can tell now. I knew right away in the forest, despite the grueling effort it took to pry her from that tree, I wanted to rescue her as I do all those a part of my mission here. I wanted to help set her free of fear and provide her haven from the elements until her situation could be sorted out effectively by *someone else*. But things change, as they so often do in this flippant world of terrors.

How could I say yes to an abhorrent, desolating quarantine when this little girl's fists curl into the chest of my blouse so tight, my scent is the air she breathes?

For the first time since opening my eyes, I have a person looking at me like I am a vital component to their being. To her, I am water or oxygen, a necessity in absence of the man she calls daddy. In his place, I have become the substitute for a healthy existence, and the one person she has decided she can place trust within. An honor, though a temporary title.

I promised her that I would look for the lost father she claimed to have, which brings to mind that I need to be asking around today to see if there have been any newer male residents lurking about. I'm not sure Celestyn will give me that information at this time, taking into account our current state of affairs, but maybe Ace would give up the goods.

I glimpse down to Simone while we leave The Center, attempting to get a peek at her face the further distance I set between her and potential suffering, realizing when I catch the features in my sight, they are unchanged. Bare and deadened. Unaffected, as if she were well-adjusted to the visual and audible experience of adults at war over her future.

It shouldn't surprise me like it does, or sting all that much. A lot of children, dare I say the majority in my century, lack a proper home life. Or joy. There is a raw, bleeding focus on making tiny tots small, exceptional adults before they are old enough to talk, and the proof of breakage from their distress would seep through in my classes in the ways they refuse praise. Feelings. Treats.

This little girl looks hungry. She looks like she has been for a really long time. Would she eat if I provided a meal? Does she feel like she deserves it? What kind of dad leaves a child if they have a choice, anyway?

I trudge us home for the day, to the one I am familiar with. I can imagine Aidan won't be in any condition to work for the next twenty-four hours, and that is the bare minimum amount of time I will need to get my whole agenda in order as far as taking care of a brand-new, potentially toddler aged child.

I wasn't kidding when I told Aidan I wasn't cut out for

motherhood, and it shows. Constantly. I'm not sure what to do with a child this fresh, or how to interact with her.

How do I talk to a girl who approximates about three years old? Do I baby talk her? Do people still baby talk at all? Or is that just something they do in movies? Is the buttery tone too much? Does she already hate me? How did I teach a classroom of young kids to dance if I don't know the basics of communicating with them?

I must have been a different woman then.

The variation of creature I am here is a bit clumsier than the swan that took stage in my memories. I am rash in Limbo, with a brain muddled by amnesia and tragedy so my decisions are fueled more by flip of the switch passions and less by sound logic. The person I am from the thickened outer shell of defenses to the gooey moral insides has metamorphosed into traits I no longer recognize, or maybe I do, but in different ways.

I can't just be a dancer here, for example, and even if I could, it wouldn't be the same as it was. The brave potential I once held to branch out and become a sensually suggestive teacher to adult audiences wanting to find their intimate strengths at my studio is repulsed by my inner self when the thought of what could have been occurs, the person breathing in the same shoes today having all but taken a vow of celibacy.

I'm meant to be a hag in Limbo, set up with everything I need outside a ratty shawl that smells like pee and a herd of several hundred cats. Taking in Simone was a mistake, largely considering sacred virgins don't really dabble in raising children that often. But as with all things since opening my eyes, I couldn't stop myself, and I can't turn back from it.

And she's adorable. So that's a bonus on the everlasting list of cons. Right?

We acquire some strange stares toeing through town at this hour, heading toward shelter instead of work, rocks and dirt crunching beneath tired, aching feet. Simone has shoes that look handmade in comparison to factory-glued, tiny pastel slippers that are sturdy and rough, but soft as well. Cushioned on the inside, they are decorated to appear more feminine and scream delicacy.

I find myself liking them in a funny way, but their durability is questionable, making me fear that letting her walk in them might take us more time getting from one place to the next. Should I get her some different ones to wear during the daytime? I really need to purchase her more practical clothing, considering costume attire won't last long if they labor children her age. But one step at a time.

At home, I open the unhinged door wide for her to see inside first, helping her through the empty frame and stepping in her tracks. I check the hatch, finding Zoey isn't home, again, and mind racing for the ill conclusions, the worst of which that she was kidnapped after being failed by my absence. The second option is she is still at The Center with more pain and bleeding from being so overdue. But she had mentioned to me a couple nights ago that Ace was looking into finding some odd jobs for her to do to help contribute. It could be as easy as that, couldn't it?

I show Simone around our brief, humble living space. I demonstrate our cabinet curtains and explain the cellar door in the simplest terms possible. She doesn't present ample responses to my introductions, bobbing her head up and down or back and forth for "yes" and "no", or pinching her brows together when she disapproves of a particular smell. I give her some berries picked from the forest out of my backpack's side pocket when the grand tour is over, doubling it with cheese for an early lunch. If I had managed some butter, I would have laid it on some bread for her too, but she doesn't eat much, anyway. She simply nibbles, brushing aside half a berry for a new one or pushing away at the cheese all together.

It takes an hour of playing with food bits to meet her completion of a single meal, and I clean up so we can carry on with our day. It doesn't take intense convincing for her to let me piggyback her through town so we can find clothes her size from the markets. It actually appears it is where she is most comfortable, as if this had been ritual for her, as we reach the vendors selling used clothing.

There are some youth sizes from adolescents that passed on a few weeks ago, and it is the smallest sizes that Limbo runs in as of current. This upsets Simone, who is less than eager to relinquish her beautiful, but stained, gown for a long-sleeve plaid shirt that I tie into a sleeveless dress. Though, she is in admitted awe of my creative feat, marveling at the act as if it were magic and making me feel a lot smarter than what I am.

In the end, I pack her costume dress into my backpack and decide to let her keep the shoes as a fair trade off, not that she has any intention of letting me touch the footwear if I wanted to. She doesn't speak a lot at the moment, but I understand the aggressive shrieks of "daddy made it special" loud and clear. I follow up the semi successful clothes shopping with a purchase of enough ingredients to make dinner tonight, and we walk home where I prepare the individual components of the meal to boil in a pot over a fire while Simone explores our tiny yardage.

I get us both cleaned up before eating, spot cleaning Simone first with residual water, soap, and a spare cloth, and leaving myself second so our bodies will truly be ready for bed after dinner— which isn't much. It is mostly boiled carrots and potatoes with a small touch of pork and salt I scored with my last amount cash until I collect my past due payments. I should have skipped the meaty addition in case of an emergency predating tomorrow, but I am addicted to food with flavor and protein, even after all this time without most of either. Plus, food is a good way to start off with any young lady, not to mention a good motivator when it comes to getting obstinate children to do as they're told for their own good.

The promise of an underground camp out is how I manage to convince Simone to head down below with me for the night. We spread out a blanket in our little hole, laying extra food down and my water bottle that we share. I light a candle and we eat in awkward silence, waiting for the other to make a better move until we are both asleep, or close to it, huddled from the horrors of outside in growing darkness as the candle burns out. Though she is light, the weight of her bears pins and needles upon my lap in the stretches of time we remain still, making my legs weak and numb so that come morning, each limb feels like gelatin.

I decide early, amid breakfast, we will visit Zoey first and get introductions out of the way. We can follow up with finding out whether or not Limbo, in all its glory, requires toddlers to pitch in and if there have been any grown men inducted to our society. Hopefully by the time all this is complete, I can meet with the search teams in the clearing to see if Aidan is there, ready to go, or if he needs more recovery time.

Our morning meal of cooked potatoes is scarfed down our gullets faster than our first lunch together. I ask her if she likes it, to which she makes it clear in her own little, non-filtering ways, that it would never compare to her father's glorious cooking expertise. A bitter part of me grinds away, shouting that while the motherfucker outdoes me in every arena, at least I didn't abandon her in the woods. But I frown as soon as the full sound of my own inner voice comes to fruition, allowing the jealous and competitive parts of me to fade over.

There was a better chance this unknown man made a huge sacrifice to get Simone somewhere safe on the off chance just *someone* might find her passing through. I've only been her guardian for a day, and she doesn't know me that well yet. She has no reason to trust me as much as she does. There is no place for these cruel feelings right now.

I let her finish eating in peace, cleaning up and poking my head outside to make sure the streets are largely clear of corpses before zooming her out into the open. To my shock and awe, as we move and fresh air hits my face, it doesn't look like there was an attack at all. The streets are clear, aside from collections of people talking as they get ready for the day's work, some relaxing on their makeshift porches and soaking in the morning sunrise while the breeze still has the slightest bite to it.

Simone is enamored by the sights of the village while we make our way toward The Center, and perhaps a bit disgusted. Her nose wrinkles at the smell of piss wafting through the air as a blond man buttons his jeans at the wall of a neighboring house. His head swivels over his shoulder at the sound of our footsteps, flashing an unabashed grin as I look to the ground, pretending I have no idea what he is doing.

This is apparently not as simple with a small child in tow.

Simone pulls on my hand, slowing down and bottom lip pouting.

"EWWWW!" She shouts as I feel my heart race, my hand jerking her raggedy body along faster. "That's gross!"

It's not like I can tell her it isn't true. Men are disgusting. It's a fact of life.

*Jesus, I could run a nunnery.*

I could also raise one hell of a no shit taking girl if need be, not that I need much help with this one. She has it all taken care of as far as I'm concerned.

I can hear the man scoff, as Simone jabbers on at my back, like an elderly man slighted by a bunch of jackass kids.

*Peeing is for potties.*

*Eww, it's on shoes.*

*Daddy say no!*

*You're GROSS.*

She calms a little when we are out of earshot, falling back into step with me, instead of resisting to yell. I relish our single second of silence until she speaks up again.

"I don't like here," she whines. "I want daddy."

I rub my forehead with my free hand, my backpack feeling a bit heavier than usual for some reason.

"I'm sorry," I sympathize. "I don't like it here either. But it is safer here than it is out in the woods."

"No," she grumbles. "Hmph."

"I'm going to try and find your daddy," I promise. "But it may take time. It might take less time if you can answer some questions for me though. Can you do that?"

She considers this, quickly.

"Yes."

The agreement isn't a happy one, but it is the only one I have to work with.

Up ahead, I can see The Center coming into view between the sparse trees growing in the village limits. It is more of a relief than it's ever been, and I try to think about the best way to compose my inquiries in this excitement.

I pause, presenting the most obvious item on my agenda. "What does your daddy look like?"

She grins for the first time, but it feels uncertain about the criteria of my question. The thought of her daddy is an obvious delight to her, eliciting a response in any event, but I can tell this is going to be difficult and I will have to try to be more specific.

"Daddy's perfect," she beams, her dark eyes glittering.

I try not to giggle at this, covering my mouth to remain serious. "Is he little? Or is he big?"

"Hmm...daddy's big!" she exclaims. "He this big!"

She stretches her hands up toward the sky, fingers fanned out and wiggling.

"Wow." I try to match her enthusiasm, but I'm not feeling it. This response wasn't as helpful as my dumb brain thought it would be as I remember she is a very, very small child. Literally anything could be tall for her. "What else?"

Simone racks her thoughts for answers, the grin never parting her face.

"Daddy's nice." She shows off tiny white teeth with one missing on the bottom.

"Okay," I hum. "But what about his physical appearance? What color are his eyes? Does he have long hair? Short hair?"

The smile fades, and a frown replaces it at the cluster of questions. She is confused, fingers twisting together, and her foot digging against the ground. I stop, making her freeze as well.

"Nevermind." I breathe, calming my voice and placing trust in the one thing only this little girl could know. "He's nice and tall. What else?"

Simone shakes my hand from hers and begins to skip, gaze flashing to a white butterfly passing her by.

"I dunno," she says, slowing down the more she thinks. Maybe I am pushing her too hard, too soon. "He, um...he's, um..."

*I need a professional's help...*

Tears jump to Simone's eyes, and I can hear her sniffling as the skipping ceases. I stop with her short of The Center doors, taking her by the shoulders and flashing a reassuring, quick smile.

"Hey, hey." I brush away the liquid sorrow pouring from her eyes. "It's okay. Alright? Nice and tall and perfect is a great start. You can tell me more about him when you're ready. Okay? Let's take it slow."

"Yeah," she whimpers. "Let's go slow."

"Of course," I affirm. "This is your pace. I'm just here to support you."

She bobs her head, swaying back and forth and holding to the edges of her dress like a small princess would while she follows me inside The Center. Celestyn is at her desk, attempting to catch up on her paperwork as the lobby is hauntingly empty for once. She looks up at me to the sound of my feet knocking against the still caved doors.

I wonder when they plan on fixing that.

"Aidan was released yesterday," she growls.

It is a bitter taste in her voice, and I have a feeling she is still upset that I slept in her boyfriend-but-maybe-not-boyfriend's home. Somewhere inside, it makes me feel a bit guilty. If it were me, I might feel a bit upset, too.

"I-I wasn't looking for him," I manage. "I was hoping to talk to Zoey about our...new addition. And, um, maybe start some kind of paperwork search going for the new addition's lost daddy. I've been told he's...nice and tall?"

"And easy on the eyes too?" One of her newer charges snicker at my description, and I feel my cheeks bloom red.

But Celestyn doesn't join the symphony of laughter. Her face droops in exhaustion, relaxing and softening so the stress lines on her forehead aren't as visible at the sight of Simone.

"All children of any age group up to twelve, bypass assignment with Ace and are given farm work during the day." She slides the fluffy end of her quill along her jawbone, her voice just as gentle. "Simone needs to get to work soon, Adabelle. Try again later."

"I'll be fast," I plead in an instant. "Please. It's important. I don't want to throw any surprises on her at the end of the night, last minute, when she's already under this much duress."

She slaps her current paper onto the desk, exasperate behind heavy eyes. It looks like she has lost a bit of weight recently too, as though she could afford it. But she relents to my desires this time, unable to find it in her to fight me and grabbing the key ring.

"Come on, then." She motions us forward with a tilt of her head.

We follow her into the main hallway, which has acquired suitable repairs since the attack upon it, most of the blood rinsed off the walls and debris taken out back. A few of the doors are fixed or barred off as uninhabitable at this time, and Celestyn stops us at the sixth functional room down, unlocking the door and shoving it open a crack, looking me dead in the face.

"Quick," she warns. "Your friend isn't in good shape, and I don't know much about interrace pregnancies, but by human standards, she's dangerously overdue. She's having... complications, and she doesn't need a lot of stress at this time."

"Okay," I promise, bobbing my head up and down.

Celestyn leaves us to it, shoes clicking in retreat to her desk. I take Simone inside the small, candlelit room, feeling tiny fingers gripping around my leg as we approach Zoey who is propped upright on the mattress. She nibbles on a plate of stale bread bits that I would have happily replaced if I had known it was all she had, and holds one of the journals I took from the library at Headquarters in front of her face. As she finishes the page she is on, she holds back an upturn to her lips, closing the literature and straightening to greet me. Until she notices Simone.

"Who the fuck is that?" Her defenses are made of steel guillotines ready to decapitate anyone who comes close.

Simone weasels behind me, hugging so close she stands on my heels.

It isn't the most welcoming hello, but Zoey is a person that needs to be...acclimated to. We can fix this.

"Hello to you too," I brush it off, slipping off my backpack and unbuckling the top flap. "I brought some leftovers from dinner last night. I thought you might be hungry, and your attitude screams yes."

She laughs, but not in a ha-ha my friend is so funny way. "Adabelle, fucking stop. Who's the pint-sized shit?"

I hesitate, skating the thin ice she's laid. "Calm down. She is actually the reason I came all this way today, aside from visiting you, and I'll get to it. Just let me..."

"You'll get to it right now, or you'll get the fuck outta here, you dumb cunt."

"I'm scared," Simone cries at my backside, whimpering the ends of my shirt wet. "She's mean."

I set a hand at her little shoulders, giving them a gentle squeeze, though I am losing my patience with Zoey.

"This is Simone." I keep my composure. "We found her yesterday beyond The Dome when we were ambushed doing patrols. I'm a...*temporary* guardian until we find her father."

Zoey's head spins between us, eyes zeroing in on Simone. "You don't have a daddy, you little twit."

"Stop it," I bark. "I didn't bring her here to be insulted and attacked by a grown woman."

"I didn't fucking ask you to bring her!" Zoey raises her voice. "This is a damn stupid choice, Adabelle. Have you even read these journals you borrowed? She can't fucking stay with us."

"She has nowhere to go," I counter. "And she's so sweet. She barely makes a sound."

Zoey's face grows splotchy and crimson. I am afraid to stay

much longer for her baby's sake, her eyes steeling away waterfalls of tears begging to break the dam she has created.

"Cats barely make a fucking sound either. You don't see me keeping their furry assholes around."

"She's a child." I throw my hands out. "Not a pet."

"She's another fucking mouth," Zoey shouts. "I don't think you know what you've done, but it's fucking bad."

"I've helped someone."

"You've screwed us!" she snarls. "Just like you fucking screw every goddamn person you come into contact with. Don't you think that being that far out in the fucking woods, she probably belonged to one of the Ravagers? Huh?"

The phrase never ceases to enrage me.

"You can't *belong to someone*!" I shriek. "Why does no one understand this?"

"*We do*," Zoey insists. "But it doesn't matter to them. How many of these stupid journals have you fucking read since you brought them home? Huh? Even a full one since you started working? Tell these monsters they can't own someone. Go on. I'll fucking watch. They'll own your ass faster than you can say wait. It's not the same for them. Women and children are fucking delicate possessions by their viewing standards. A fucking showcase to the world. Taking that little girl back here will have a con-sequence."

"Having you here has consequence, and I didn't abandon you," I point out.

"And that's fucking great," she pants, stomach tensing with agony. "But without my ass, you would have fucking starved to death. We don't need any more risk in our household than what we already have. The fact that you and Aidan were both ambushed before finding her isn't a promising fucking sign. You could have been viewed as a prospect by someone, which would only mean that we are in more danger than just me being pregnant."

"I'll deal with it," I swear. "Just give me time. I'll work more hours so that we can reinforce our home like Aidan's if you can just help watch Simone every now and then."

Zoey shakes her head and raises her hands defensively.

"Huh uh. Oh, fuck no. You took responsibility for the brat. You can do this by yourself. It's not my problem. At. All."

I can feel my skin steam, rolling with waves of heat dampening the air.

"I am supposed to help take care of your daughter when she's born," I snap. My whole chest hurts. "Even at risk to me."

"*Then get the mother fuck out*," Zoey challenges. "Ace has me doing odd jobs here and there now, thanks to your points brought up in his lobby while reading his books. I don't even fucking need you anymore. You're just the village freak."

My lip trembles, and I exhale. My whole face stings, my hands shaking in tight fists.

"Fine," I whisper in defeat.

I guide Simone by the hand, leading her out and shutting Zoey back in the pit of her own misery. I need to maintain what cool demeanor I have left for the fragile, already frightened little girl clinging to me like a baby monkey, but I'm seething.

The lobby passes me by in a blur. I don't recall thrashing through it, or passing Celestyn on the way out, or bursting through the entry where the doors stood, but the sunlight scalds me as soon as my shoes hit the dirt. It is past time I should be meeting the search teams, and I don't have time for it, racing us home where I gather everything inside that is mine, minus a few items of food so I don't leave Zoey and her baby completely dry.

The gears churning in my mind are stuck, grinding as they try to pinpoint where we will live now, but lacking the time yet to think it all the way through. I have to get Simone to the farm, and I have to see if I'm too late for work. The best I can hope for the time being is that one of these homes would show to be empty or abandoned by nightfall.

My consolation for the day is that the farm is quite close to the clearing between the houses and markets where the search crews like to meet. Still, I am more than a bit skittish around the same red haired farmer that approached me with a gang of stone-bearing children my second day here, reluctant to relinquish Simone to him, and studying the grass when I speak to him following a hollow, stuttered greeting.

"This is Simone," I tell him when he does not return the regards. "We...I mean, my partner and I, we found her not too long ago. I was told to bring her here for work. I am sorry she is late."

Every alarm bell in my body rings like the shrillest clock in the world, screaming to take her with me on patrols, rather than leave her with a man that treated me so poorly. But I am the beast, and Simone is a girl that turns this tall ginger nightmare to pudding as he bends to one knee so they can be eye level.

"Well, hiya there, Simone." He holds a meaty, calloused hand out, but she doesn't take it. "My name is Ray. It's good to meet ya."

I can feel Simone's little eyes on me, her arms wrapped around my leg and my promises echoing in every motion. She isn't familiar with anyone else, and she was left once already. This couldn't be easy, and it wasn't going to get easier.

"I'll be back," I tell her, running my fingers through her fuzz. "At sundown, or sooner. We will find somewhere to stay when I come get you. But I do need to work if we want to keep eating. Plus, I'll have a better chance looking for your daddy out there."

It doesn't appear to soothe her. She grips tighter, tears spilling over each cheek. Ray puts his hand down in submission to this, taking a different approach instead.

"Ya know," he muses. "I have a couple oth'r munchkins yer age that could probably use a new friend to feed ducks with. Ya wanna go feed some ducks?"

I can feel her hesitation, but I don't want to encourage it by speaking. My silence leaves the ball in her court, and gives her the strength to nod her head, taking his hand to leave. Ray grants me one last look, bobbing his head in farewell as he takes her to the animals.

I sigh, brushing my fingers through my own hair, and leaving to seek out the search groups, or Aidan, so we can do patrols. Through the field, I see no sign of either, making my way through the markets and hoping they were at the Headquarters lawn instead. I stop at one of the vendors who sell ready to eat foods, digging through the bottom of my backpack until I scrounge up enough loose change I had forgotten I had to buy the smallest, driest portion of cooked meat, and holding my face as soon as I do.

I forgot to leave Simone with food for the day. It is the first week, and I am failing at each aspect of this task at hand. But it is a farm...so maybe she can eat some of the crop?

*Please, kill me.*

As I finish paying the vendor, I turn around to see an all too familiar face.

Ace stands behind me, towering from a healthy distance, clinical as ever. In his full hands is a tied sack of cash, and another stack of files bigger than many others I have seen him with in the past. My name is written across the top one, and without missing a beat, I reach for it. My fingers graze the paper as he steps away, holding himself in a rigid, stony manner. As though I am as vile as everyone claims.

"Why are you such a fucking prick?" I groan in distress, lowering my needy hand.

He ignores the question.

"Have you been doing patrols with Aidan?" he counters. "Both of you have seemingly fallen off the map as of late. Neither of you have collected payments, and I haven't seen much of your pair anywhere near Headquarters. Strange, isn't it?"

I feel uneasy about this question, my subconscious guard rising like a rock wall around my words.

"No," I reply, slowly. "I've...been doing patrols alone. Fuck if I know where Aidan has been. The team doesn't value my life enough to risk theirs if there was an ambush."

His gaze narrows in disbelief, arching an eyebrow at my statement.

"Which...there was? I hear?" he pries. "How is the little girl you brought home?"

He knows more than I'd like him to.

"Fine," I affirm. "She is...fine. I was ambushed at the edge of the third layer of The Dome. Obviously, I was being a bit... careless, but you should know that it was breached. The locals chased me far into the woods, and I waited them out for a while where I found Simone. I narrowly escaped with my own life, so I'd say we are both a little traumatized. But we are both doing *great*."

Suspicion lingers, but he can't prove I'm lying. He is forced to let the subject lie on his schedule, though I could swear he enjoys watching me squirm in his presence, hunkering into myself a little and crossing my arms. I am feeling flighty the longer I am standing here, disconcerted by the way he looks at me, though I can't quite describe it.

His fingers flex at his free hand as if he wants to reach out toward me.

"Is that all?" I swallow, holding myself and eying his hand.

Ace shakes his head, plopping the bag of coins into my hands. "Split it between yourself and Aidan, if you see him. As well as one other thing."

He reaches from within the top file, and pulls out a small, leather-bound book with a letter clipped on top. I hold my breath, studying the crumbling cover and flipping it over.

"Is this..."

"It comes from our Master's personal libraries, fully translated." His voice is strict. "It should aid your...research. But, please do arrive on time to meet him, this time. Our Master is an impatient man with very little time."

*Translated?*

My hands feel cold and clammy on the book, and I touch the letter at the front with disdain. The rumors dance at the front of my mind, swirling about each other. Fuck.

"I...You're telling me I should meet...a Ravager?" I look to him.

Ace's eyes grow to the size of dinner plates, and he bends his incredible height low to meet me at my level, processing this term I have finally used out loud. I'm not sure what to call them anymore, if I am being honest.

"Who told you he was a Ravager?" He grins in a startling way and whisks away before I can answer him.

I look again at the book with the letter attached. My name is written across the envelope in scrawl that could only come from a man...or me.

I turn to go down the road where I am at when he completely vanishes from sight, ready to continue my search somewhere else when I catch a pair of glasses amongst the crowd staring back at me from another shop entrance. Curled over his hip and mouth agape, Aidan's eyebrows knit in concern, legs shuffling him over to me in slow, careful strides. I can hear him take in sharp inhales as he moves, straightening to appear less hurt than what he is when he reaches my side.

"What did he want?" he asks, staring at the book and letter. "And what are those?"

My heart throbs faster than I can breathe, and I tuck the pair of objects into the side pocket of my backpack with my dagger.

"We should go," I murmur.

# CHAPTER TWENTY
## ADABELLE

PARANOIA HAS BECOME A CANCER. I SEE THAT NOW, sweating bullets as we journey deeper inside the environment designed to kill us, questioning the point of the walk like never before.

We are both on edge, though the difference being clear that I am more nervous than my very first time out here, and Aidan is simply prepared for the worst as the perceptive pessimist he is. This being so, in spite of last night proving tame in comparison to its predecessor, I am paranoid in the same way the flu is contagious. It is spreading from my partner to myself in seeds of violence that have bloomed to fruition. Like the worst of carnivores, it eats away at the most vital parts of my being with hungry serrated teeth, feeding off the live fears I didn't know I truly had as Aidan consents to going back into the danger zone this soon.

The danger became more sentient when he agreed. It drops the veil of protection I have surrounded myself with and taints it black, giving strict reminder that I am fragile. I am *human*. And I have made myself blind and ignorant this whole time, even with the best intentions.

Locals or not, it is clear to my inner workings, as it should be to all, that we did not ask to be here, and we don't deserve to be attacked while we try to wiggle our way out. But I can't get close enough to reason without tragedy incurring, and yesterday was my hardest night to date waiting out the unknown.

I am suddenly afraid for my life, and therefore Simone's as well, having clutched her tight to my body overnight while my legs went numb until I was sure we were safe, questioning how it would come to pass I would protect us both if it boiled down to it. The panic each potential scenario played out in my mind incited more anxiety, unmatched by any I experienced protecting Zoey. I'm more confident protecting Zoey than I am Simone. If I die, Zoey can protect herself. But Simone...what would happen to Simone?

Is this what it means to take guardianship over another, more helpless, person? Am I going to wonder what happens to her in the event of disaster every night and arrive at no definitive game plan that works, just to spin myself in the same circle for eternity?

It is clear death will not elude me during daylight hours either. If I die out here, who will take Simone on? She can't just live in a barn forever, and I doubt Ray would let her stay past hours.

To my luck, we can't travel as far today, which plays to the advantage of my fresh, but clear concerns. Aidan had woken up earlier than myself to trudge his painful, aching limbs through town to meet with the rest of the teams while I had been busy competing in a screaming match with Zoey. He claimed he'd stay home if he didn't need the money so badly, but I can't shake that there is more to the story than that, remembering his outburst at The Center. He doesn't want to be here and he's desperate to jump town for the day, despite the worst of his wounds bulging forth, swollen and red below his shirt that raises when he lifts his arms to move low hanging branches out of our way.

I can see it *ooze* while we walk, an injury much too late to stitch, even if we could have without sealing in infection, when Celestyn and I carried him in that morning after he passed out. They have to heal as is since I didn't act with what I had, and each puncture will leave him one hell of a scar, though it appears his vitals were missed, much to our relief. But I try not to imagine what the injuries under his jeans look like at this point, cringing when I remember them looking brand new. At least he's changed out of his bloody clothes into something fresher to help their appearance.

The white shirt Aidan wears is only speckled with dots of dark brown and watery pink where the wound below creeps through the fabric. He attempts to conceal the weakness with yet another piece of his famous plaid shirt collection that keep out ticks and mosquitoes in the danker parts of our crisis playground, but it is white and blue plaid, so it sneaks through this as well.

The layers are a good investment anyway, in hindsight, not that I'd ever tell him when he's using them to be stupid. I've never seen a bug bite on him in town when he's not wearing the sleeves, and my own arms are infested with swollen lumps upon my sensitive skin. I wonder in secret if this is why all locals wear long sleeves as well, though come to think of it, I can't lump them as a race in that concept when I've never seen the women of the race.

Aidan and I spend an hour walking in a straight line once we hit the riverbanks. His discomfort, following the first thirty minutes of sweat dripping in slick lines into at risk wounds, is apparent in the way he leans close to large rocks or nearby trees for balance, hunching over in pain and trying not to breathe too deeply. It is something I can pretend not to notice for the sake of his own dignity, and I keep pace behind him as the reverse, less experienced lookout.

It isn't until the next fifteen minutes pass I notice his respirations have grown labored, and he cradles the wounds he is able, bending in half like his back has gone bad. I have no choice but to demand we stop at the riverside to rest for a moment, impending turning around so we can go home. Not that he fights it hard.

I take long strides ahead, watching out of my peripheral vision as Aidan stumbles down the rocky banks at my heels to get closer to water. He holds his chest still in these motions, reaching for my shoulder to keep his balance in check when it becomes harder to pick up his feet. I lean him up against a cleft of dirt and grass with ashen willowy whips shading the ground he sits on dipping into the water, blowing loose red leaves when the wind blows.

Does this world have seasons? I've never thought to ask.

I set my backpack next to Aidan, rummaging through the contents for my water bottle as I notice him still staring holes into the side pocket where I put away the items given to me by Ace. Instead of assaulting him with words at the yearning to intrude upon my privacy, I flash him a brief smile that is about as fake as any of his have ever been.

"I can fill your canteen with my water bottle if you hand it over," I offer.

He snaps out of his daze, reaching for his canteen at his backside, but hesitant to pull it free, testing his strength to stand up and do it himself. But the effort fails, and he winces, inhaling sharply as he huffs, handing me the container without a word. I sigh at his frustration, curious if all men are like this, and if catering to ill, stubborn behaviors is a permanent part of my life now...on top of stabbings, kidnappings, and travels to places I don't want to be.

What happened to dancing and watching television in my underwear with a large pizza and a tub of cookie dough ice cream? The only distance I had to travel then was wherever my remote could take me in the next three clicks. Who needed allies when I had pepperoni? Cheese never hit me in the face or called me a bitch.

A woman's real best friend is whatever she can fit in her mouth when she's sad.

Still, wishing and wanting won't solve my real-life friendship and homelessness problems, the latter of which is a pretty big problem when I have a small child to care for. Shelter is a greater necessity than ever in the age of endless desolation and despair.

What if it rains? Where are we going to stay to keep dry?

I'm certain that even if she "works" there, they won't let me camp with the cows again—being Simone's guardian or not.

If Zoey weren't so bull-headed, this would all be so much easier.

I've tried understanding her point since we argued, searching for solutions around the single one she gives me. But I can't get past the conclusion that she is blaming a child for her own insecurities about the potential situation at hand.

It isn't that her fears are unfounded either, so much as they are irrational. These creatures have no way of knowing who or what lives where, to my knowledge, making their raids a lot of guess work. If we are found, it wouldn't put us in any more danger just because our household had a higher count by the standards I've seen placed since existence began here.

I stay ankle deep in the shallow water for a few minutes, letting the waves rush up over my knees and cool off the heat my black leggings absorb beneath my jean shorts. Sometimes, I wish I were a bit bolder. I wish I were brave enough to not wear them at all. I could just...show what it is I am so afraid of the whole world seeing and live this second life like I should have the original.

But I can't bring myself to stop caring, holding my arms so the wet bottle and canteens touch my biceps. Not for a second can I allow the worst parts of me into the world when so many people already believe they've seen it.

Aidan groans short and low when he thinks the nearby sound of two small dragons squawking at one another can drown it out, and I tense, trudging back out of the cool relief with both containers filled to the brim.

I don't appreciate the manner in which he accepts the water, but I don't mention it either, noticing his quivering fingers wrapping around the canteen with caution, blue eyes full of danger. Distrust. We don't have to speak for me to know it when I see it, and I have always seen it. Not that I feel much for him either.

I turn my back to him, facing the river as I hear him shift, lifting his shirt to check the wounds he can. I'm not fooled, hearing the sound of his water hitting the dirt around the same time and the threading of the cap popping back on. My brain pleads against my paranoia to understand it might have been him cleaning the injuries, but my emotional turmoil has already sprint free with a different idea in mind.

It isn't like I've done much to earn his trust, other than helping him get home directly after almost being the reason he dies. He hasn't done a lot to earn my trust either, though. In fact, it seems as if we have put each other in more danger than we have helped.

This partnership has been a sham from the start, and we've put our best efforts into it. But the rumors must scare him, whatever they are. I must scare him. And when I think about how I terrify him, I know I can't trust him, as fearful people perform cruel acts.

There are fractions of time where I really believe, for a second, we can be great friends. But I shatter the illusion like a hammer to glass as soon as it starts—a picture so delicate and light, it is unable to survive the brute force of my baggage.

I crumple into the ebb and flow of water beneath the tree a safe distance from Aidan, letting him rest upright while I dig through the grainy piles of tiny rocks, finding delicate white shells and skinny fish. A breeze sways the low hanging branches against the water's surface, making the ripples dance in dripping swells for as long as it takes the calm to return. Aidan is half-napping when I turn to assure he is okay, having crawled further from the shade to the heat of the sunlight as he shivers in pain.

I can feel my face drop. "We should go home."

He pauses, jaw clenching and shoulders tensing. Frowning.

"C'mon, Addie. We have barely been out today."

"You're hurt." I focus on the ground. "Still, hurt. This isn't right. I can finish scoping this section of riverbank by myself, and we can start again together when you're feeling better."

"I'm okay."

His insistence is admirable, but the energy to smile is fading fast. His voice is a low grumble, cracked and whispered. Unconvincing.

"I'm not your girlfriend, okay?" I snap. "I'm not Celestyn. You don't have to act tough around me when you're not, because I don't care."

"Addie, I'm not—"

"You're slowing me down." I say it with a bite. "It's no big deal, but I just really need your crap together, and if it's not, I don't need you at all."

He blinks away the verbal lashing, pursing his lips. "You can't go out here alone every day it takes me to recover. It's too dangerous. And you'll miss out on really good pay waiting on me."

"If you die, I will miss out on a lot more," I reply. "Just go...go home."

The truth is, this isn't just for him. It's for me too.

I'm terrified. And empty inside.

My first real purpose has abandoned me, and it has left me with so much to do, lacking any of the time to do it in. I just...need a few days to figure myself out. To figure this *shit* out. I need to dwell on some positive memories. I need to get to know this kid a little better, and help find her a much better caretaker, or check in with Celestyn to see if her father has been located. I need air to breathe, because it feels like I'm suffocating.

Aidan sucks in a deep inhale, wobbling upright, and shuffling for the less steep part of the hill we came in on. He swats gnats with his free hand away from his wounds, and I grimace, the tiniest part of me wishing to go with him to aid him home. At the same time, as if reading my mind, he whips around faster than he should have, his gaze hardened but exhausted. He eyes my bag one last time, straying slowly to me, and giving in to curiosity.

"What did Ace give you?" It is so firm, it's almost not a question.

I think about this.

"I'll tell you." I sift through the rock water. "If you tell me why he is looking for you, and why I just covered your ass some hours ago."

There is a temptation there, something flashing like police

sirens in the rear of his mind and pleading in his eyes, begging for a yes. But, instead, he shakes his head with a ragged sigh.

"Alright. You win."

It is a bitter defeat, but he takes it in stride, climbing the hillside in staggered paces, lumbering out of sight until I can no longer hear the sound of his feet slipping through the grass and dirt. I can only hope he makes it home okay. It will be awhile until I follow him, as I need the time to heal alone and think, but he has forgotten his canteen in his hurried plight. It will be a dry night if I take too long getting back, and I stuff it in my backpack for safe keeping after another sturdy refill.

In the time that passes, I spend my hollow solitude eating the remnant food I intended to gift Zoey. The waves crashing along the horizon of this river are hypnotic, swooshing over one another and drowning out smaller sounds. It is undeniable that the world outside our poorly built hellhole is beautiful, swimming with life I never believed possible, and some I wished that weren't.

I flip through a journal while I snack, keeping watch on the small collections of dragons skirting the perimeter of my items and hissing at the contents of my backpack. It doesn't feel like I'm missing much, skimming pages among pages of similar tales weaving the same epic stories, cut short by destiny.

*Destiny.*

Is this destiny?

It's impossible to say how long I stay here, flipping through books of people long past and chowing on food, tossing the remains to my nippy, hungry observers. When the sun is glowing a bit lower in the sky, I pack up my mess. The food, the journals, my dagger I laid out to distract the reptilian scoundrels tearing pages from my text and skin from my hands if I didn't swat fast enough, it all goes in the bag.

As promised, I walk along the willowy, shaded shorelines, scanning for evidence of life or items to bring home. There isn't much, outside a single purple sneaker and spindly fish bones. In the water a couple miles from village limits in the dim sunset, I find a curved, rusted dagger that couldn't possibly be one of ours, pommel etched into an emerald dragon with ruby eyes. I say a silent prayer that a vendor would give up their home for emeralds and rubies before I chuck it recklessly into the river as far as I can throw, screaming into my hands where no one can hear me.

But the sound of water lapping in resistance to the surging waves makes me peek up from my palms, keen yellow eyes glinting back to me from a safe distance. I jump out of my skin, almost out of my shoes, shouldering my backpack further up my body and panting in fear. My feet shuffle for higher ground, my hands gripping loose soil from around the tree roots, and rocks from the bank, ready to throw.

But the mermaid is lax. Pleasant, floating amid the current like it wasn't moving at all, but rather stagnant and lifeless.

I step away, reaching for ground to hoist myself up on, and she bats her eyes, flipping rich brown hair off her shoulders to reveal her ample naked chest, armored over the sternum and ribs in the same blue scale that covers her voluptuous tail which flits back and forth. Open gills ridging her cheekbones lead toward facial fins in place of ears that fan out in her delight to see me, her playful smile loaded with pointed canines.

Without effort, she glides through the water to beach herself in the shallow riverbank. Though I am not within arm's reach, she acts as if I could be, rolling to her backside with her neck arched so her eyes never leave this prey. If I were smarter, I would flee as fast I could, but I find myself concerned about making movements too sudden.

Isn't running what cues the predator into chasing the prey? The chase is what they're looking for.

"Hello, human girl," she coos, voice false and sweet. "That is what you like to be called, is it not?"

My lip quivers. I am unsure what to do, or to say, scooting in subtle slides up the bank where the previous hillside turned into tiny cliffs.

"Y-you...s-speak English?" I swallow glancing behind me at the gnarled tree roots poking out from the earth. I only need a firm grip on one to hoist me up.

She has rolled back upright in the time it took me to remove my eyes from her own, angular face glinting with mischief.

"I speak many, many things, strange creature," she replies. "But you...you only speak what you know."

Rocks roll under my panicked, clumsy feet. My backpack seems heavier all of a sudden and I scramble for clearance. Has it always been this heavy? Is my fear this heavy?

"I...I don't..."

"Don't be afraid," she lulls. "We are all creatures of the Great Mother and Father."

"The gre...great what and what?" I pause. "Wh...what...Who is that?"

A snicker, and giggle.

"You do not know?" she teases. "Come closer. Bethesda will tell you."

She motions toward herself when she speaks the name, holding webbed hands outstretched to me.

"No thanks." I swallow. "I'm okay, really. I am."

"Ah, but don't you wish to know your origins, lovely?" Her grin grows wider, revealing teeth that are only sharper and sharper the further back they go. "The origins of all creatures can be explained here."

"Then explain it from there." I shuffle, but something inside my head shatters like dropped china at the same time.

I find myself unable to move at all one way or the next. In the background of my conscious mind, I can hear a soft song being sung like waves of visual notes blasting over me, swallowing me whole in melody. But there is no one else here, and Bethesda's mouth is not moving.

"Secrets must be kept, girl," she insists. "It will only take a single moment of your time to change the course of your life."

"Save it for someone who cares."

I fight the paralysis to grip my backpack straps, as my feet begin sliding back down the incline I have climbed thus far. My mind screams no to the motion, but my body...it has other plans.

The mermaid watches me, bemused by my struggle to stop this zombie march for water. She whips forward with her powerful, muscled tail, beaching herself just a bit more and sitting completely up.

*Why can't I stop?*

"That's it," she croons, extending a hand showcasing black talons at the tip of each finger. "Just a little further. I will tell you everything you have ever wanted to know, lovely girl."

Our hands connect, her flesh cold and wet against the heat of my own, the music from beyond luring me closer until my shoes are inundated. Her tail swishes to and fro, the force scooting her further from the shore until her shoulders are submerged, leaving all that remains of me as a head and neck floating over the surface.

"W-what is going on?" I gasp.

I can't break eye contact with her. I don't know how I did it earlier, though she is no longer paying my words mind. The caress of her soft, webbed fingers slide over my throat and collar bone, sharp nails pinching the skin and stopping between my breasts, inching across my sternum with a childlike, delighted glee.

"Your heart is so full of dark energy," she squeals. "So precious, so terribly strong that it all but bursts inside your fragile chest. They must all be terrified of you. It is lucky that I am not."

I gulp down a deep breath, and I am pulled under water.

# CHAPTER TWENTY-ONE
## SAHANNA

I WOULD HAVE BEEN A FOOL TO BELIEVE SILAS WOULDN'T find the razor unpacking my trunk later that night, but I must be one anyway, or I would have said no to an extended stay in the Fae.

I should have known better than to let my desires speak louder than my common sense, sipping hot tea while my eyes wet with tears, I all too quickly understood his quiet pause, and the look passed between brothers. Knowing.

It was all over, my scarce freedom in that minute.

The King is a malicious bastard in sheep's clothing, and I am little more than a prisoner—a sister to him by forced marriage, carrying his future family in her womb, and not a friend to purchase sanity for.

*He doesn't have friends.*

This is more evident than ever before in my cage of a life, as I have been placed on "suicide watch".

*Fucking yay.*

To my dismay, it is, down to the letter, exactly how it sounds. It is brought to my understanding, following the official introduction of human women into civilization, suicide watch is a common protocol set in place when an individual female in previous question displays a series of red flags in place of acceptable adaptations to her new environment. It prohibits me from roaming the halls unattended until I am shown to adjust.

There is no leaving the bedroom by myself. I'm not to go anywhere. I cannot go to dinner without a guard to escort me. I cannot find a bathroom without a guard or husband to escort me. If I am wearing a clip in my hair, the edges have to be dull enough that I cannot split skin with it, or it is to be locked away in a box that only my husband has access to for the foreseeable future.

To worsen the destitute matters at hand, my one given companion, Dee, has been sent home in advance of our small procession to assure the castle is still in good function for the royal family's arrival home. So, my extended stay in the Fae has morphed into a lonesome, eternal nightmare, leaving me wishing I had carved my wrists like a jack-o-lantern when I had the chance.

Not that I can't throw myself off the balcony if I'm desperate.

I'm still game for it, maybe.

If I had been clever enough, death should have incurred by now one way or another—though maybe it isn't a question of wit as much it is courage. Not that it seems to matter if I am either smart or brave with The King lurking about these halls to save the day for his younger twin brother.

He is an excellent healer.

Skilled.

A rare exception among beings of his own kind.

If one were to ask his subjects, they would make claim he is not an actual being at all, but a creature long ascended above our ranks to become something much, much more—an entity of pure magic.

He does not even bleed, they say. Not that anyone has dare touched him to find out.

I've never seen him bleed.

Of course, I have only tried to kill him one time. It was an attempt that was ill-planned, ending with the blade of a kitchen knife shattering into crystalline bits in the twitch of a closed fist, and a strict reprimand to Silas who was asked to "keep me in line".

*In line.*

As if I am an unruly child in need of discipline, an object out of place on an unreachable shelf, it is not I who receives the brunt of my own actions, but rather Silas who is tasked with keeping charge of me as the role of "husband".

*Keep her in line, brother, lest something horrible befall her.*

I knew he meant it when he spoke it. This…abomination, would hurt me and there would be no one to challenge him other than Silas who cannot live without my existence. I would have deserved the consequence by the standards of his kingdom. The King is adored by his public, considering his quite successful millennia of reign, and I would be thought of as a traitor. No matter how vigorously Silas would attempt to protect me, it would pale when matched against his monarch.

Still, today is a new day. I've been locked in this shithole of a room for too long, and I'm eager for release. I would even take a short walk around the castle halls with the guard, if it was just granted to me.

Who could fault me for wanting some fresh air?

There are plenty of eyes to watch me in the confines of the castle walls, so it isn't an unreasonable request if there isn't a guard available. If anything, it is more dutiful to my current family's restrictions upon my life, as there are no guards to actually be spared for the servile watch over my quarters while the threat of aggressive invasion still haunts the island. Rather, I receive passing visits from Icarus on the hour to assure I am well or not in need— each check timed and considerate so as not to disturb my ever so busy life.

Or naps.

I've thought to scale the castle walls again any time I wish to escape, weighing the possibility that I am as bold as to accept the consequences that follow it should I not return in time for check-ins. There were so many casualties, the families in mourning wouldn't notice me for the sake of tattle, and Silas has been so preoccupied with The King, it would be improbable he would spot me. They have not gone outside since the impending investigation circled them back to the dungeons withholding their prisoners.

Well, criminals.

Oh hell. It doesn't matter. Nothing matters.

I braid my hair achingly close to my scalp this day, lacing in soft pink ribbon and a few white petaled flowers Silas has yet again plucked for me. Weaving the snapped, skinny green stems between bundles of hair, I keep my hands occupied with something other than my own demise, trying to maintain the tricks Dee taught me to perfect the look. But I hate it, this blend of twisted texture my hands create to make it appear I have accepted their culture on the off chance it might score me a touch of freedom.

I hate *me*.

It feels...weak. I feel weak, and sick, fingers working faster than my mind can catch up, so I don't have time to tear it apart in a fit of depression, looking at this ugly pathetic girl in the mirror.

I reach to pick another white flower to finish off the look I have attained when my protruding stomach taps into the vase at the wooden ledge of the vanity, sending it crashing to the floor. I cringe at the shattering of decorated glass, awaiting the frantic padding of footsteps from somewhere down the hall to come check on me, and kneeling to the floor to pick up the sharp slivers when I remain alone.

It is strange no one ever thought of glass as a weapon when the room was seized and locked down for the suicide watch. They take all the obvious things a person could use to end their own life—knives, needles, medicines, or sharp clips. Even writing feathers are subject to confiscation.

But glass vases? Who would break a perfectly good vase to murder themselves with?

Why, it is holding flowers, delicate buds of white and blue and indigo. What anarchist would disrupt the painted coffin for bundles of dying flora? Isn't that, like, a felony or something?

I can't be too harsh. It's not like I realized I could use it either and I hadn't intended for my belly to knock it to the floor when turning at the vanity. In fact, I try not to pay attention to my belly at all as an extension of myself unless I have to, or unless I require items I would not otherwise be able to get without the leverage of being pregnant.

But it is so quiet, picking up this mess by myself...

I splay my fingers over the swell of skin and unborn, tensing at the rise of her little feet into the palm of my hand as the other brushes wet glass and shaven stems into a dainty pile. Broken and bare as I am, I relate to the stems that can never grow since being plucked, the protective thorns bent on keeping the flower safe flayed clean so that there is only vulnerability and a bleeding vibrant green to adore until the plant is dead.

The baby pops against my finger pads, and I gasp at the aggressive nature of the movement, peeking down to her as I pick up the last piece of vase. I rub the shape of her inside me, gentle, and then rough, muttering an apology as I slide the slender shrapnel in one fluid slash across the stretched skin on my wrists and hands.

Crimson pools in thick, rich lakes onto the floor with a steady flow, though it is a weak attempt. Not enough to kill me if I act soon. I don't want to, but the promise of death makes me panic. I toss the shard onto the floor, wobbling upright and rushing over to the nightstand where I tie a handful of cloths I use to clean my face in the morning around the rash injuries.

They would probably need stitching, but for now, it is a proper excuse to leave this room if I am caught wandering. I step over the golden ticket out of here, pushing the doors wide open, and hurrying out into the sunlight streaming through dozens of windows lining the vast, glittering white hall in shimmering crystal arches.

I can see the ocean's worth of river water from this height, so many stories in the sky in the lockdown safety of the Fae king's castle. I find, all at once, that even perceived freedom can be a new containment when surrounded by all this glistening blue. I press my face to the clear glass, meek crimson fingers caressing the tan worthy warmth it radiates, trying to inhale the scent of faraway beaches and picnics in the sand, but only getting stone. Cool, impenetrable, uncompromising stone.

I sigh, taking what I can from the experience and adventuring along the endless hall, moving by door after door over a perfect red rug laid upon rock floor. My soft, silky slippers barely make a sound in the abandoned, quarantined wing where The King's family stays on visits, swinging left at an impasse of intricate murals to a grand spiral staircase that I descend to find exit in the one of several strangely deadened, celebratory halls where public ceremonies are held or name days are celebrated, or where parties are hosted just for the hell of it.

If only for a moment, I let myself be a young girl, spinning across the sapphire floors of this hall to the doors at the other side with my arms held out to balance. I never knew how to dance, despite a lesson or two when I was sixteen taught by a girl not much older, but I don't have to try as hard when I am alone. I twirl and jump and kick my way to the doors in madness, catching the curved handle of my exit at the final spin and creaking it ajar so the fresh air outside blasts my face in refreshing swathes of heat.

Life springs forward in the courtyard, as if no one were allowed in the actual castle and have been called to do a summer camp out in the extravagant gardens of King Kai's palace.

Guards. Cooks. Maids. Scholars. Medics. *Children.* Vendors.

I squeeze past them all with little notice, trying to appear as though I am supposed to be here. Because I am, right?

Silas is just a rank below his brother, next in line to be king by technical standards, so long as his brother acquires no heirs. And I am Silas' wife by their wonky standards. So I can be wherever I want as far as most common people are aware, if they are aware at all.

*Most* common people, more especially in the Fae, don't have infinite knowledge about the royal family. The King prefers his privacy and would rather most events in his coming not be excessive in nature. By default, Silas falls in similar pace, advising his brother from the right side, and keeping in touch where need be. They don't even often use their given names in front of others, referring to one another as "brother" instead, and The King calling me "sister" or "sister by law". The one time my appearance was made public was for the ceremonial vows we placed to one another.

It is close to a wedding by human standards, but a bit more... intimate. A touch bloodier. And there is no specific guest list to attend. Pretty much anyone is invited to these events, as marital celebrations in these cultures are for all to enjoy.

Everyone *loves* to celebrate a marriage in each kingdom clustered to make this universe a reality. It usually means at least three things are sure to come—future children for an ambitious struggling civilization, a lot of free alcohol to share, and an opportunity for current children to run themselves sick. In reality, having an eternal audience of gawking strangers to witness my vulnerable, painful, crimson humiliation less than two months following capture, still brings back nightmares. In my dreams, I can still envision how the kingdom smiled at me as I sat high above them on the platform overlooking the primary ceremonial hall, feeding off my vows of submission with coos and head tilts.

In my reality, I scuttle through seas of shoulders, finding a snug cove between a row of rose bushes to conceal myself out of sight, out of mind for any sets of curious eyes. In this sanctity, the sun is beating down at just the right angle so it hits my face in searing streaks, pulsing atop my already sweaty skin while I taste the water surrounding the island without having to touch it at all.

People come and go in this time, talking as they do or laughing, sometimes weeping of the tragedy that unfolded.

I try not to eavesdrop on their sorrows, focusing on myself, and letting my hands fold over my stomach to get comfortable now that little feet can make home in the lower half of my rib cage. But it is a guilty motion, really, my attempts to evacuate this creature from my body through means of poison having failed through and through. It is becoming more of a person by the day as I grow it, and it is getting harder for me to deny this. Because she is a fighter. Like me.

I would teach her to fight this horror too, if I could only accept the idea of birthing her alive...except that I don't want her. And she shouldn't ever have to fight like this. If I can help it, her struggle will be over with before it is had. But...I want to savor her a bit longer, this bonding of her feet rolling under my fingers, into my lungs.

I laugh just a bit, my lips curving. Breathless.

Words carry effortlessly to my ears as I do, conversations being had by strangers visiting the castle or by serving staff and their families who house here. I am pulled in to avoid further positive interactions with my baby, doing what I do better than anything else—putting my nose where it doesn't belong.

*Nice day for a swim,* they tell one another.

*The work's been heavy since the attack, but they can't work us forever, you know?*

*You're wrong,* I think to myself. They can, and they will. Everyone works up until their death, and it never changes.

But do go on.

*The King has been lovely,* a high-pitched woman joins the chorus of voices. *Extending his stay to seek justice for the slain families of the attack. He's been so busy as it is.*

I can hear the beating of wings, combustible extensions in the Fae that come and go at their own will. Though in this case, it sounds as if someone might be...flapping with infatuation for my criminal family?

Gross, but okay.

*It is an obligation. We are a part of his heritage.*

*But did you see how he took the beasts down?* Another man pipes in. *I've never seen anything like it myself. Fluid. A single raise of his arm is all it took, and the ground tore to pieces out front.*

*Is that why the main entrance hall is blocked off then?* The woman asks. *I wanted to give him...personal thanks, and all that, but I think he might have left down that way.*

The men laugh together. I cringe.

She's going to *what* now? Do Fae give out those kind of favors? Last I heard, they're virgins till they're dead.

Does The King even accept sexual favors? Have I missed something? Am I missing something?

I am almost definitely sure he hates everyone, and lives to hurt those who inconvenience him.

*What are you going to do, Lynn? Do you intend to propose? He'll have none of it, you realize. You can't give him sons.*

*I can give him other things,* Lynn chuckles. *Maybe he doesn't like sex, anyway.*

Another round of riotous laughter. Lynn joins in this time and raises her voice to speak again.

*Alright, alright. But I can still say thank you, can't I? He's very handsome, and his brother is wed, soooo...*

Oh, my god. Take him, please. Have them both, if you want them. Create your own harem, woman. Save me.

My mind screams to plead these sentiments aloud, but I keep my mouth shut. I'm becoming rather dedicated to the art of silence, and I wouldn't want to be caught anyway.

*They'll be gone soon,* the first man replies. *The King in a few days when he sentences the beasts, but the advisor intends to take his wife out on dragon back tonight by talk of the guards.*

My stomach drops through my feet. I feel sick, and my innards roll with the baby, meshing into one lump of despair.

*Poor girl. She does seem to enjoy it here. The elves are so protective of their partners, I can't imagine she has an easy time at home,* Lynn remarks. *Why so soon?*

*It is all the advisor's insistence.*

Of course it is.

*Our borders were strictly guarded. The brutes were able to slaughter three entire units of soldiers on duty that day. The advisor insists the breach of security is a problem for his wife and baby, and The King agrees. He won't risk a baby for certain, not him.*

Fuck. I knew I should have jumped off the balcony. At least if I had, I could have died somewhere semi-pleasant.

*What about our borders though?* Lynn asks frantically. *What will we do when they leave?*

*Nah, don't you worry about none of that,* the other man chimes in. *I asked King Kai myself if they needed soldiers to spare for the borders. He told me The King has it squared off.*

*Our population hasn't even recovered its number since their Nameless Father's Day. We can't not have guards.*

I feel for Lynn's fear. I wonder if she knows this advisor's wife faces fear as well.

The first man speaks once more. *Kai has explained to me that The King will send his brother out with a dragon to a rendezvous point where soldiers are already stationed to pass. His lead commander* —he snaps his fingers, trying to concoct the name in question— *Kasismis! That's it. Kasismis. They will talk to that fellow about sending more troops to guard our borders from further danger.*

Dragons.

I can hear quite a few screeching over the curtain walls if I pay attention. They're everywhere in this hellish world. Mischievous, unpredictable creatures with a lust for anything brilliant and shiny. I've heard of them lighting entire villages on fire if they're ired. Although, they generally leave people alone if they returned the favor, and water dragons are more likely to drown a person just attempting to play.

Sort of like a dolphin.

I don't much care for them however, but my brother-in-law has a way with the beasts. They're like kits or pups around him, purring in his presence, taking commands without hesitation as if in a life-altering trance at each syllable.

There weren't dragons back home.

But there might be soon, if The King and my husband have

their way. Our home was once theirs after all, and we have ruined it.

I am pulled to reality by a sharp pang on the ankles of my crossed legs, and a crashing of bodies to the ground beside me. I retract my limbs closer to my body, flinging myself upright to see a small woman hovering over her even smaller daughter at the ground, gathering fruit in a basket that had spilled over during the fall.

I blush, breath quickening in my chest at the fumble.

"I-I'm so sorry." I try to smile, but I'm afraid, embarrassed. "Let me help you with that."

The older woman glances to me, face dropping and blue eyes doubling wide in terror. At her shoulder blades are delicate yellow wings, like that of a butterfly, that span out and fold over her biceps, shorn and damaged at the edges, but not wholly ruined. It occurs to me she probably does not have the energy to expend to produce more, or drop these nuisances in light of the attack. Her daughter is a spitting image of herself, but marred with bruises and cuts stitched shut over her right eye.

"Oh. No, no, no, no," the mother squeaks in a hurry. "It is we who are sorry. So very, very sorry. We were not watching where we were placing our feet, and we never meant to step on the advisor's pregnant wife. It was a complete accident, I assure. We cannot speak this strongly enough."

"S-so s-sorry," the little girl repeats, tears already welling in her eyes.

I shake my head, waving my hands.

This is one of the worst parts. The fear instilled to damage me, accident or not.

"Oh, no, hey," I soothe, reaching for fruit to help them recover their goods. "Don't cry. It's okay. It was my fault, honest to god. I kind of just sat down, and there is no way you two could have expected someone to be here."

There is a familiarity to this girl, her scrawny stature and messy hair reminding me of my younger sister. I can't stop myself from wrapping my arms about her, patting her back, and pretending. For a moment.

*She smells so good, just like her.*

"It is fine," I reaffirm, for myself and for her. "This is fine. No big deal. I'm not hurt. At all. And the baby is fine too. She's certainly not in my feet."

Did I say that out loud? This is getting too personal.

But the truth is, I don't hate children. Not really. I loved my siblings with every piece of my broken heart, and helping to raise them when my mother was unfit was one of the greatest joys of my life. It's only...I don't want children of my own, and the thought of childbirth disgusts me.

The little girl laughs.

"That would be funny." She smiles a cheeky, dimpled grin.

"It would be *so* funny," I return the favor.

Would it be inappropriate to squeeze her face? I love it so much.

The mother appears relieved at the contact, squatting to finish collecting the remaining items for the basket. I move in beside her, hurrying as best I can with twenty extra pounds weighing me down. This endeavor of mine is visibly appreciated, though I can see the woman is still frazzled.

"Where are you delivering to?" I try not to sound as nosy as I am, but I haven't talked to another woman not associated with The King's staff in so long.

I miss conversation.

The mother's cheeks redden, white teeth flashing in a reluctant smile.

"We don't usually deal food within the castle walls." Her defenses come up at the sharp edge of her words. "I mean, sometimes we do, of course. But we never venture beyond Icarus."

I nod my head in understanding. I don't want to push a subject she's uncomfortable with.

"Sure," I reply. "Alright. Sounds good. I bet these taste great."

She hums for a moment. The daughter moves down beside us to help pick up. It is when I notice the gauze wrapped from her chin to the neckline of her dress. When I look back to the basket, I am face to face with the mother, leaving me unsure as to whether I should apologize or not. It feels rude, but I hadn't meant to look.

Her vicious glares settle at my discomfort.

"My husband passed protecting our borders in the attacks," she whispers, pulling a few flowers from the rose bushes and minding the thorns, to place in the basket.

"That's terrible," I reply. "My condolences."

"Thank you." Her voice quivers with grief. "My daughter is without a father now...but, because of your husband, as well as The King, she is alive to tell the tale. And I am forever grateful. We just...we were hoping, perhaps, we could meet them, and give a proper thank you."

"With fruit?" I am smiling. I can't help it. I *like* the innocence of the gesture, and it feels so...pure, unlike 'please fuck me Lynn' standing over with the gaggle of gossiping guys.

"It is all we have to give." She places a cloth over the basket. "I know it is silly, but..."

"Why don't I take you to them myself?" I offer faster than I think to know better.

Fuck.

"You would do that?" the mother asks in return. "Truly? That would be lovely. Thank you."

"It is not a problem," I swear. "I...I cut my hand earlier, and I am sure one of them should take a look at it anyway."

The daughter reaches for her mother's hand, and my imagination runs with it, thinking of myself and...

*No.* No.

No.

We take off, meandering inside the castle once more, but through a different entrance. I wonder how much trouble I will be in when I show up at their feet, not because I am bringing them villagers, but rather that I have escaped another shit lockdown they have set in place for "my benefit". The villagers would ebb off initial ire, I suppose, and that would help. Silas and The King enjoy speaking with their subjects, not only as a routine part of their work as higher authorities, but as a part of their own natures. It must be grounding to understand the complications of their plights, a regular part of Silas' job when not at The King's side being the collection of information about the struggles of the common people to better their reign. But I am not supposed to have left our quarters, and this cut is at least an hour old by now. If they know I'm missing, and they're not at the dungeons like I figure, I'll probably be toast.

We pass through winding walls of painted arches, rising higher than most skyscrapers and open so that I can see the free blue of the sky above me. Tendrils of cerulean ivy blooming dangerous green flowers climb the structure, reaching for the sunlight to fuel its growth. The insidious blooms are dewy from a brief rain shower overnight and, for a second, I hold a leafy vine between my fingers, letting it pass through when I realize there would be too many witnesses to this version of my death.

As we reach the mouth of the dungeons, I realize it is in worse shape than it had been the first time I crept this far. The little girl reaches for her mother's hand behind me, paying mind to the mass of dusty rubble and broken mounds of stone that used to be laid as floor, thick and elegant pillars smashed to bits. Caverns of darkness that stretch to the left and right to us are roped off, further blockaded by packed tight mounds of earth and disaster that we can't cross through without effort. But the entrance to the dungeon I am most aware of is guarded by two brawny men who follow our every breath as we approach.

"Hello," I whisper, trying to maintain a respectable distance. "Do...do you know where The King and my husband have gone, or if they are down there? I have brought visitors who wish to meet them."

"They're in the dungeons." The guard to the left shrugs, feathered helmet covering most of his chestnut brown hair. "They'll be back in a little. Haven't heard any screaming in the past hour, so I assume it's close to wrap."

I frown.

"Could I just...run down by myself and find them?"

"Sorry, my lady," the one on the right responds. He doesn't sound sorry. "The King has given strict orders than not even Kai himself is permitted to go below. Best just sit tight."

I look back to the mother and daughter. They can't spend all day waiting on these two twits to remove themselves from happy torture time. It will take a second to find them, max.

I dart forward, and their spears come down, but I take a different direction, veering to the side and slipping under a section of unguarded rope. I shrug my shoulders, inching toward the dungeons with the weak smile of a weak victory.

"Best stay put." I wink. "King's orders."

It is a guess that they also aren't allowed to pursue a single soul further than the rope. I'm sure they have protocol to follow if someone presses by, so I won't have a lot of time to get myself into trouble, but this is my way of pushing the boundaries. Of maintaining *some* stupid kind of control and feeling like I have power beyond my husband's name and title.

Besides, what guard charged by The King himself to fend off intruders is going to say he was so off his game that he accidentally failed at keeping a slow, fat pregnant woman out of the dungeons?

If they can play this cool, so can I, and no one has to be punished for disobedience. As far as I am concerned, I can claim to have come in through another entrance. There are at least three other hidden passages into these places.

The stairs descending to the underground caves filled with cells are railed for protection against the slick, slimy stone. I take care when I walk, though my fingers squeeze the cold metal, white in fear of falling to my death, scant torches providing dim lighting and miserable groaning echoing at the ground floor.

It isn't often full up in the cells, and I have seen children playing fictional crime games around here when they're empty, the incidence of misdeed quite low since The King inherited his father's position millions of years ago. Not that criminals will be eliminated entirely based on prosperity, but more that he gives little mercy for egregious activity, seeing fit to punish many criminals himself.

I find most of the cells empty on the ground floor though, walking through a maze of them carved out in the blackened cave walls and not seeing a soul in sight. I feel somewhat duped, peering about sharp corners while shackles clamor at the sound of my footsteps tapping below. Following what feels like twenty minutes and six dead ends, I huff an aggravated sigh, deciding to turn back empty-handed when I remember what way I came in from. I lean along the icy bars of the nearest cell, stretching my stressed spine so my aching bones feel a chill of relief snaking through them.

Everything else happens too fast for me to react.

There is a quick, close rattling of chains, an aggressive shuffling of heavy body weight and a metallic ring on the bars behind me. I am pulled tight to the poles of metal gating the enemy from myself, my head bouncing off the cell, so it swells with waves of pain as I yelp. Two voices race to my pain response, hushing and cooing.

"Shh, shh," a woman's voice excites. "Please, quiet, sweet girl. They'll hear if you fuss."

"HELP!" I writhe, hoping they'll hear if I fuss. "SILA—"

Another hand presses over my mouth, the chains to its wrist shackle broken free of the floor.

"Here now, little human woman," a man's voice responds, incredibly calm. Relaxed, though he's missing a finger, and as of quite recently—according to the meaty, bony, unhealed stump on his hand. "Quiet, now. All is well."

All is never well.

All has never been well.

I open my mouth wider to bite him, but he closes the advantage, pressing sharp into the hinges of my jaw so that I whimper, forcing my limbs to hang loose, and yet unable to stop the shaking all at the same time.

I am going to die here. I can feel it.

And I'm not ready.

*I'm not ready.*

"There," the man's voice soothes, letting his hand fall from my lips to my throat where he holds me firm. "There it is."

"She is frightened, Marcellus," the female voice panics. "This will not work."

"I-I s-shouldn't be here." I tremble as his finger pads press into the soft underbelly of my chin.

I am afraid to tilt my head, to look at them this closely. Their hands are frigid, pointed at the ends without fingernails, and tinted inhuman colors. Strange.

"Neither should we," the one named Marcellus replies. "There is an irony to it, isn't there?"

"I-irony?" I murmur. "I just...I was...I don't belong here."

The hand below has still not released my arm, squeezing tighter than the one at my throat so it rings with pain. I realize I cannot use Silas or The King as leverage here, that it could prove to be dangerous for me under these circumstances.

"No human belongs in these lands," Marcellus insists. "We could amend this, if you let us."

I am quiet for a moment, thinking it over. Shivering in fear.

"Let me go?" I present it as a barter.

There is a hesitation, but it is desperate and naïve. The hands collapse away from my body, and I lean forward as a test to assure they will not pull me back in. And then I dart free, the woman screaming as my legs propel me through the slick, wet floors of the dungeons.

*Come back! Please! Come back! HELP!*

I swing myself through the halls like a frightened rat in a maze, panting through the corridors until my feet find purchase with the stairs, scrambling up where I emerge into fresh air that I swore I'd never see again. I slink through the shadows of rock unseen to be safe, hearing the buzz of voices as I climb. I swerve around the rubble at a separate entrance hall, climbing over the dirt and ducking under the rope into the light, making it appear as if I am emerging from anywhere but the dungeons.

Silas and The King stand at the front of the guards, towering over the woman and her daughter. The guards catch sight of me from the dirt pile, nervous but flooded with apparent relief, the mother turning to see me with a brief smile.

"There she is." She nods, and my heart skips a beat. "She had... went looking for you both in a couple places down the hall. Thank you, Lady Sahanna."

My head bobs, throat panging with the agony of serrated blades when I swallow, The King eying me with a brief, coy grin.

"Did you find what you were looking for, sister?" He is smug, deep voice booming in the hollow around us.

I hesitate, knowing he knows, and eyebrows diving together. My hand reaches up to fix a strand of hair that has fallen from my braid, and I wince, lightly touching a bruise at my cheek and temple. Silas raises an eyebrow, demanding I answer.

How much does *he* know?

"I...erm...yes. I found you both...just now. The vase in my room fell earlier. I cut myself on the glass. I just need..."

It happens before I can stop it. I am crying, sobbing.

I don't mean to, but the adrenaline is leaving me in waves of cool chills, and the fear is catching up. My chest heaves, and I wipe my eyes with a soft sleeve, hugging myself tight.

"Can...can I be excused, please?" I plead.

Silas nods, his features hardened and body rigid. I can't tell if he is on to me or concerned over my mental state. I dip in a hurried curtsy to The King upon departure out of my required due respect common etiquette begs I offer, and I break from them, rushing back from where I came when Silas' voice follows me in a soft raise of his voice.

"Don't go far. We will be leaving shortly."

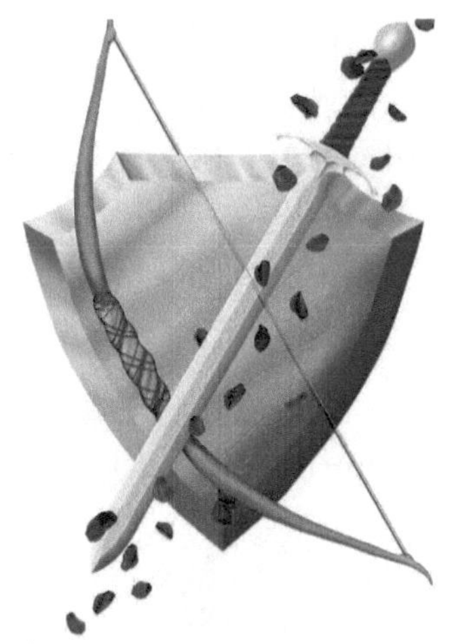

# CHAPTER TWENTY-TWO
## AIDAN

A DDIE WILL BE FINE ON HER OWN.

She is independent, tough as hell, and I have given her all the training she could ever need for a short solo adventure.

It won't kill her to stand on her own two feet, I've realized as of lately. Nothing can kill her, and nothing can stop her.

Who knew invincibility could come in such a small package?

I've never seen any single person heal up faster from agonizing cuts and scrapes like her, as if she can perform slow regenerations upon her skin versus being forced to tend delicate wounds. It makes her a powerhouse of mystique, and more so a source of fear for all those around her paying attention.

I'd like to claim that the other villagers are acclimating to her strange presence in our new world, that they are beginning to come around to the idea that she means well, or at least that she's someone on their side in this calamity. But the notice of my injuries between regular acquaintances over the past day or so has ignited another stream of rumors that she is vicious and filled with malice, a harbinger of death himself.

There is no persuading ignorance laced with actual malice.

I can't tell them that Addie couldn't be a harbinger of hard slaps on the face if it meant someone could be hurt in the process, because no one is ready to listen.

She is their monster, the person that gets to shoulder the brunt of their darkest fears and the outsider looking in. Addie is the untouchable—the epitome of our enemy and the concentrated version of our pain.

Addie is the unknown.

She is the darkness, no matter how desperately she reaches for light, tainting everything black in her path.

No one sees her for what she really is though, and today, more than anything in this world, she was finally right. Because I *am* slowing her down. I am slowing me down.

I am slow. And I need to be home where I can rest off these painful, unhealed wounds just a bit longer. A day or two more should do it fine, if it can be managed without disturbance. I can probably hide out in The Center for some of it to keep Ace off my back. He should be leaving town soon anyway.

But right now? I want to get home. Home is a great start.

In the comfort of my own metal prison box, I can take a nap without the risk of infection lurking about every corner, allowing my mind to drift from the intense agitations weighing down my life. Although, if I were a smarter man, I realize as I remove my hand from my hip to see fresh red painting my palm, I would haul ass to The Center for my rest. It has bled through again and I knew walking this far would do it.

It was a piss poor plan, but I can't escape the consequence of it now that it's done and over. Celestyn will be home in a couple hours—at least, if she wants to continue living with me, she better be—and I don't have the energy to trek two different places, so she can look at it after hours and spread some more of her special ointments on it then.

I pop out the other side of the trees, shifting in a swaying limp through crowds of people where I am carefully concealed amongst them, holding my plaid shirt over the worst of the fresh blood.

When I reach my front door, I all but drop against it in an icy shudder of relief. The air being expelled from my lungs is unsteady, meshing into a grunt as I pull the door open and shuffle inside. I make it to Celestyn's pile of pillows and quilts where my knees buckle, and I yelp.

My whole body seethes with pain, burning and racked with chills at the same time. My teeth chatter together, loud and cracking, my legs folding with care until I am curled like an unborn baby on the hard floor.

The door is only open slightly when I blink away slender streams of white light igniting my flesh, but I don't have the energy to shut it. I simply reach behind me, wrapping myself like a human burrito inside two quilts, shivering against the humidity. I cover my head for good measure with a couple hard pillows, shutting my eyes for what feels like a small section of time.

It is unusual to sleep so heavy this way in summer during the day. I haven't taken a nap of this magnitude in daylight hours for a year or more. Perhaps I haven't shut my eyes since I first opened them, or at least not this comfortably.

But sometimes, different feels good. In this case, it is magical.

I squeeze my eyes tighter than ever, trying to keep myself under the spell of endless sleep as the rest of my body trembles violently, the poison of my apparently infected injuries sending jolts of jagged ice shooting through my veins. My breathing comes out in staggers, teeth chittering drumbeats into my dreams. My lungs feel like they are lifting a million pounds with each respiration. All of which I hardly notice in the deeper parts of my slumber that fades fast as the duration pushes along.

I stiffen at the sounds of children playing, squealing and pattering past my door outside. I knew I should have tried harder to close it, the buzz of people talking and moving about pulling me from infinite comfort to their gossiping and misery.

*I can't believe so and so is gone, they say.*
*What will we do without blank?*

It isn't that I am entirely unsympathetic to it. I have lost people too. I have lost people I care about like family, and I have lost people I don't even feel like I really know anymore. I've lost a whole lifetime of people between the past, and what I have now.

But we all have to adjust or die.

I'm adjusting.

And I am dreaming.

In my vivid memories blending into the subconscious desires of my dreams, my mother sits on the piano bench with me at her side when I am no more than five. Her fingers glide over the keys, delicate and fanciful and long, like the spindly legs of a venomous spider. My stubby little pigs in a blanket follow, a bit clumsy and still learning, but she smiles at me with the reassurance only she can give. It lends me the confidence of an expert at the time, fingers bouncing as if I am one of the greats.

We are the best team in the moment, happy and unaware of what comes next.

My mother sings, and it sounds like everything I have ever missed in this whole world, a song that I have carried with me to the day. Slow and full of love, its tune puts me on the edge of serenity, remembering her this way while my older brother moves in with his saxophone for a solo no one asked for.

But it ends, as it always does, with screeching and blood and fire. It ends.

It ends with undeniable pain and desolation. Betrayal.

It ends with a heavy pounding on my door, forceful and loud. Agitated.

My lids lift from this haze caused by the memory, sweat pouring from every pore in my body. I shift the blankets further over my own head, heart galloping like a herd of horses and head seething in agony. It is all I can do to remain hidden, pretending I'm not here, and hoping for the best outcome as another round of knocking breaks through the house. Again. And again. And again.

Then, there is a pause. I think it is done until a sharp voice yells through the crack I left in the entry.

"Aidan fucking Powell, if you're in there, you better get the fuck up right now before I beat your dumb ass."

Zoey.

Why Zoey?

We hadn't spoken since the day I saved her until Addie entered our lives, and now that she has, it feels as though we can't stop running into one another. Finding one another.

I have always attempted to avoid her, not that she deserves it. She probably craved the company more than ever after her rescue, and I stayed by her side that single night. But I had my own life to think of, too. Staying at her side any further without the certain recovery of Kasismis' corpse was, and is, a risk all its own that I wasn't willing to take.

The Ravagers always come back for people that are rescued and I never want to be a part of that crossfire, no matter how close Addie takes me to that edge. But I often wonder if Zoey blames me for how her life has turned here. For the endless isolation she has endured, the hateful stares and the menacing action taken against her.

No one wants her here now that she is tainted with *their* kin. But maybe that is why she sought Addie out. Or maybe their friendship is a happy accident. It is good, though.

I wrap myself in a couple quilts that haven't been stained with blood, trembling upright and wobbling for the door. However, Zoey flings it open at the sound of my lumbering footsteps creaking across the floor before I can reach it. She looks me up and down, almost the same height as me, if not a little taller now that I am slumped over in a pitiful, sluggish excuse for a person. I feel her resounding pity at my serious state, though not much.

In her hand she has a burlap sack that she hands over to me more than a little fast. My arms don't have time to keep up with what my eyes perceive, leaving less than a second for me to suck in my breath as the item is thrust into my arms.

"What the fuck is this?" I groan, peeking inside briefly and spotting some food under a couple changes of clothes that I definitely cannot fit into.

"It's the rest of Adabelle's bullshit she forgot on her way out," she replies, glancing outside over her shoulder, paranoid.

I can see why. The sun is setting. I don't want her here either, and I must have slept longer than I thought.

"It has some of that pint-sized shit's old crap in there too," she carries on, crossing her arms over her belly. "I don't want any of it sullying my home, now that they're not fucking living there anymore."

I freeze, setting the bag on the floor in a low drop so I don't have to bend. In the forest, I recall Addie seeming a bit more frigid than usual. Distracted and tender.

I am having a bit more trouble reading her lately and it makes me nervous, but these feelings were conveyed loud and clear in her body language. Knowing that she is so strange to start put me on a very guilty edge but, coupled with her silence...I had been so out of focus with my own pain, I hadn't bothered to pry beyond her business with Ace.

"I...Is everything alright?" I probe.

Zoey's demeanor falls apart. Her shoulders slump and the faintest puddle of tears well in her eyes. I'm not great with feelings, but I brace myself for her needs.

But the needs never come.

Zoey wipes away the sadness like a dry erase marker on a white board, bobbing her head.

"Yeah." She clears her throat. "Yeah, I'm fucking great. It's just...I can't chance it, you know? There's too much on the fucking line for me, and I just fucking can't."

I do understand, to a degree. But I can't imagine she was this gentle about it with Addie. Not for her to look like she did.

"Okay," I pause. "Why didn't you just bring it to her then? We both wrapped the day up early. I'm sure you can find her around here somewhere."

Zoey's eyes drift to the floor.

"Well, fucking duh." She frowns. "I'm not fucking dumb, okay? I tried that. But no one ever received report that she fucking came back from the forest, and her little shit was never picked up from the barn. I thought she must be hiding the fuck out here or something."

I try not to smile at the notion. My face hurts, but I laugh a little.

"No." I shake my head, ignoring almost everything she has said. "That's crazy. She was right behind me. There is no way she is still there."

Zoey shrugs. "Sucks to fucking be her, I guess. It's not like anyone else has fucking seen her today. That little girl sure is going to be fucking sad though if Adabelle turns out to be a deadbeat bitch."

*That's not Addie,* my heart thrums, skin building with heat.

Addie is...loyal.

I drop the blankets to the floor, stumbling around Zoey as she talks, her voice like elevator music inside the confines of my mind.

*Hey, are you fucking okay? Where are you going? Aidan? FUCK. Hey!*

But I am gone. I rocket through the village, rippling agony taking a backseat as I plunge into the forest in a race against the setting sun, trying to remember the path we took and where she would travel after I left. The trees seem more eerie this way, casting bleak gnarled shadows on private niches, making the ground a soup of midnight blooms.

I can feel my hip and leg and backside tearing at the crusted reddened seams of where scabs have started to form again, itching as it unlocks from the healthy skin.

But I don't care. I can't care.

I fumble over hidden roots, snaking up from out of the ground, unable to trace our exact path out, but finding my way to the banks where we sat. It's hard to see now, but I charge along the direction leading home, watching the hillside grow from a steep descent to a sharp cliff with willowy branches hanging off gargantuan trees into the water.

I dig in my pockets, my fingers fumbling to find a memento of my past life for assistance.

A lighter.

Tearing a leafy branch from the lower hanging limbs of an ashen tree, I set the bramble alight, waving it around as a torch for visibility. To my dismay, there isn't much to see. Our things are no longer present and, other than deep rivets made by the sliding of shoes on the cliff side where she may have had trouble climbing out with that giant backpack weighing her down, I don't see much to prove that we were ever here to begin with, except...

There's a stale, satin shine on a patch of rocks closer to the shallow water. I edge toward it, flashing the light to reveal smatters of blood thinning from a dip in the mud to clusters of dots zigzagging around the water line. I try to tell myself this could have come from anything. It could have come from me right now, though I don't feel any squirting or gushing.

But my heart drops all the same.

I wade knee deep into the lapping, turbulent, nighttime waters, swinging the light to the crystalline depths where schools of fish swim. Through the roping tree limbs that hang overhead, black coatings of goo paint bundles of the tree whips in desperate slides that have shorn vibrant leaves from place, some foliage still rolling about in shallow waves.

*Fuck.*

# CHAPTER TWENTY-THREE
## ADABELLE

THE GRIP IS LOST ON MY FOOT AS SOON AS I AM UNDER, and I thrash against the force of the water. The currents heave high and spin low, tossing me further out, but bringing me close to where my feet can touch in the same wave. I find purchase with my heels between two large rocks where miniature fish scatter, using the leverage to scramble toward the shore. I can still hear the singing that rendered me immobile earlier, much louder now, but with panic muddying the sense I had to remain paralyzed.

When Bethesda resurfaces in search for me, I refuse to look her in the face, my gaze bending high up at the overhanging treetops and fingers dancing for traction to pull me faster to safety against the brute weight of the water. It is a bad time to be a short girl.

"What is wrong, lovely girl?" she calls, swooping through the resistance with grace. "Don't you wonder what you are? Why you are here? Bethesda can tell you, sweet girl."

The water laps at my face, rushing inside my gaping mouth so that I spit it out with an unsuspecting cough. I can't swim. Aidan has yet to teach me, and I have never been out this far. I push off the ground, my legs throttling me up toward vines of wispy branches to no avail as I am yanked by the ankle once more, my face crashing into the water's surface like concrete.

I am shell-shocked by this, spinning on my backside, my body tingling like television static and limbs flailing as I vie for cold evening air. Bethesda holds me in an iron grip, a hand on my shoulder and the other cupping my neck just tight enough that the attainable air is coming in squeaks.

"Your breed is invasive." Her long brawny tail coils around my legs, dragging me further out, her voice a gravely whisper at the back of my skull. *"Vile. A parasite* is what you are. You, a speck of a creature on the surface of this world, who has stolen the beating heart of another."

I claw at her webbed hands, my feet rearing back to kick her and set distance between us that I can use to escape. She squeezes when I get my broken nails under her skin, hissing like a gargantuan snake. My hand balls into a fist, connecting with the side of her scaly face. I have enough time to shriek—a sound that is cut fatally short as my whole body is submerged, in turn sinking to the vast bottom of the river, despite how I struggle. My backpack is like an anchor this way, pulling me into the abyss like a brick.

Plummeting from existing light, I hurdle to slick vibrant algae. To tall grass and rocks. To multicolored fish and creatures with tiny claws waiting to pinch. I squeeze my burning eyes shut, drifting and swinging my arms and legs. Scrambling for unattainable life and getting nowhere close.

When I pop them back open, I choke on the water I inhale, face to face with dozens of Mer-folk gleaming hungrily back to me, rows of fangs bared in a display of toothy grins. I wave my arms, kicking my feet like an idiot, trying to set down the basic mechanics for swimming, or at least moving through the water. But all it seems to do is create a shroud of bubbles that float toward the surface as the two closest to me lurch forward, cutting through the water like it was absent space.

The lack of oxygen is dizzying as I realize I am running out of time. My cheeks bulge as if they could split apart from holding in air for so long, and I use all the strength in my legs to push away from the two mermaids coming my way. I shove the ground from me again, letting myself float instead of fight as I am circled like prey. It takes me a minute to reach ground I can bob to the surface from, gasping for a gulp of fresh air before I am yanked under again by the wrist.

I can feel the skin tear at this jerk. Like a zipper, it splits apart around my bones to expose inner flesh, blood spiraling out in fresh ribbons to the faint orange glow of the setting sun. Four sets of teeth dart for the source of vitamin-rich red, nostrils flaring and heads knocking in their frenzy, but one finding my palm instead. My gut instinct is to yank back, my free hand swinging through the water to punch the beast in between the eyes for release.

They split to circle once more, and I push far enough backward that my head surfaces on the tips of my toes. Razor sharp nails rake along my calves as I start to wade for shore as fast as I can backwards, attempting to keep my eyes on movement in the water. I reach for the side pocket of my backpack, feeling for the space where I usually keep my dagger—adrenaline pumping through me.

I've gotten lucky to make it this far, but luck doesn't stay.

I can't be dragged back under. If I am, it will be all over.

*Fuck, where is it?*

At my left, Bethesda resurfaces, speeding forward and reaching for my shoulders to rein me in for feeding. I pull away, splashing for shore, and grasping the handle of my dagger as she grips my shoulders, yanking me closer to finish the job, her teeth puncturing the skin at my neck.

But it is shallow when I rocket my weapon up below her rib cage, driving it in deep until I hear a sickening crunch, ripping it free to make another go. She releases me right away, screeching as a lake of blood spills from the lower half of her chest.

It is earsplitting, and I fall, scuttling toward land as streams of blood pump free from my various wounds. I catch the willow limbs the closer I get, using them as an anchor against the water, my ears ringing a hollow noise I can't quite describe. They feel as though they could burst, explode like balloons filled with cherry rain while water spills free of them, slick and warm.

I cover them in defense against this onslaught while balancing myself upright. I writhe toward the edge of the banks where I came in from, limping and scrambling for the ledge of small cliffside that I hoist myself over to freedom. It doesn't take long after this for me to run, weaving between trees and slamming into thickets of overgrown brush when night draws closer. I am so close to the village, I can almost taste it, but my pathetic legs buckle, collapsing under my useless body into a mess of dry sobs and heavy coughing. The water on my lungs feels heavier than any physical item I carry on me, trying to expel from where it doesn't belong.

In the forefront of each memory that slithers to mind in this moment, a woman's laughter jars me deep with unwritten trauma. Fear.

*C'mon, girl. It's just a bit of water.*

I close my eyes to the sound of her laughter, taunting in the creases of my thoughts. I can remember myself a bit younger, rolling through fields of dirt as someone calls for me. Louder and louder the less I listen. Angrier.

But I don't care. I can't care. At this age, in this memory, I am freer than I have ever been. Smiling. Giggling.

Another round of coughing makes me gag, and I vomit where I kneel in the grass, pushing the water from my scalding eyes. I try to prevent myself from inhaling the acrid smell wafting in hot fumes back to my nose, retching as another round makes its way to the open.

It isn't until I am done that I hear the sound of my name being called.

Over and over.

Louder and louder.

Angrier.

More desperately.

Around me, the sunlight shies away from the sky and the trees. I stand up, pain boiling up the length of my leg in sharp aches and stings as I swallow, gathering the energy to race faster than ever toward the call of my name. Toward the sound of everything I could have hoped to hear.

I burst through the trunks of thick trees, stumbling into the field between the markets and housing, glancing in wild turns of my head to find Aidan not too far down the barrier wall. His mouth hangs when he sees me, his clothes painted in blood, same as mine. He draws out a slow labored breath, shoulders slumping forward, then charging my direction. I don't have time to react before he scoops me up in a safe strong squeeze, so tight it draws the air right out of me. His arms are locked in place, pulling me so close my feet dangle off the ground, and my head is draped over his shoulder, nose pressed against his neck.

I'm not sure how to react. What to do. But my arms perform the motion for me, crossing behind his neck and pulling myself in closer as I sob.

Something about it feels good. Like home. Like help. Genuine.

"Addie," he repeats over and over. "Are you okay? I looked for you. I promise, I looked. I just didn't see...I didn't see."

"I'm okay." I cough, weeping and wetting his clothes. "I'm okay. I'm okay."

He squeezes tighter, letting me down to my feet, though neither of us have released one another. I can't release him, because I need this moment. The human contact. The very human contact.

I peek out from the intimacy of our embrace, vision sweeping the area about us in the growing night. My arms drop as I see the barn.

At the other end of the field, at the edge of the pens containing the animals, is the one person I didn't want to see, coupled with the one person I did.

Celestyn stands, mouth agape and eyes narrowed.

Hurt, but rigid, holding Simone's hand.

# CHAPTER TWENTY-FOUR
## ADABELLE

I CAN SEE THE TIGHT COILS OF PAIN CREEPING IN OVER Celestyn's face, whether she wants it to show or not.

Like so many other things, I understand the intricate workings of suffering here, and the brute unstoppable force of it. The very nature of internal agony is insipid—a relentless vice grip putting a suffocating hold on one's very life, haunting everything they do. Everything *she'll* do, if I can't pull myself together.

This is my fault.

No one deserves to suffer for being unpleasant and I don't want to rob her of any form of relief in this place, up to and including Aidan. It isn't fair and I don't want Aidan the way she does.

I just want comfort. Close, needy, selfish human contact. Willing hands on my ugly, stout, disfigured body.

Just for a second.

I am more than a bit guilty when she approaches, my cheeks to my ears flushed a searing hot pink, Aidan's lock around me lingering a second longer than my own before dropping to his side.

It doesn't appear that he expected her any more than I did, adrenaline of our reunion wearing thin as he stifles a series of grunts by holding his breath, quivering in the darkness.

"The bitch has been found."

Celestyn's voice is placid, as if she couldn't care one way or another, though the bite of her words sing a different song. I bite my tongue to withhold my response, more than catty enough for rebuttal, but making me no better than her. I have to remember that pained people say painful things. It cannot be excused, but it can be met with compassion...maybe.

*We'll see how we feel in a few minutes*, my inner woman swings a metal bat like ice through my skull. Waiting.

"What are you doing out?" Aidan's voice stays low, careful not to disrupt his wounds more than he had already. "It's close to dark."

She stops short of us, releasing Simone's frail hand to cross her arms, hunching her shoulders in a defensive curl.

"Zoey mentioned something concerning you being a dumbass over the community project right there." She motions my direction with a flip of her head but refuses to meet my gaze to own it. "The little tot was left all on her own at the barn, so I picked her up on my way to see if you had found her or not. Which you had. Just now. Not that I really care."

I bend down to squeeze Simone, gathering her canvas of thin flesh over bone into my arms. All at once, I am apologizing to her over and over for my failure to retrieve her from the place I abandoned her for cash when I should have been here. I have fallen short of guardianship, losing us a home, and skirting my responsibility to find another in my despondence of rejection, damn near costing me my life.

My arms slide from around her neck to her shoulders, brushing in a tender descent to her tiny malnourished fingers I hold in my own. She winces at the cherry red trail it leaves, frowning but unresponsive to the shock of it, as if it were another piece of the collective universe she had been desensitized to.

"You're bleeding," is all she mumbles, rubbing her eyes with the back of a fist she pulls free.

I smile, tucking wet globs of hair behind my ears. "It's okay. I'm fine. I'm great, and we are going to be okay." It is a promise I intend to keep, somehow.

I rise to my feet from skinned knees, ready to leave Aidan and Celestyn to work out their misgivings and find a place to stay for the night with my assortment of issues. I raise my hand to wave ourselves out, but Celestyn snatches it away from the farewell movement, whipping my shoulder almost out of socket to get a better look.

"Are you stupid?" she growls, reaching into her pullover bag for gauze and cloth to staunch the continued dribble. "You're going to need stitches, if it isn't too late. Not to mention that this needs some serious cleaning and some antibiotic ointment. We have a little time to look at both you and wonder boy over there, but I swear to God, I'm not doing this again. You both are ridiculous."

She prattles on about this for several minutes while securing my wounds, but I can't seem to take my eyes off of her wonder boy, Aidan. He can't seem to remove himself from me either, holding Simone's hand with one of his, and using the other to steady my jerky arm so I can be stabilized.

Is this what teamwork feels like? Does Aidan have my back? Can I count on him?

I don't understand. It is all a dizzying blur of events I can't keep up with. But following another round of tactless insults from Celestyn, I don't have time to find logic in it. I am up on my feet and cringing when she tightens the gauze so that I am sure not to lose more blood than I have to, though that can't be much since the major bleeding stopped as I ran from the riverside.

I am okay, I think.

We walk to The Center anyway, at Celestyn's insistence, where she meanders about the lobby for supplies. Under the desk she retrieves clean needles, flexible strands of suturing string, and supple lavender cream only partly filling two ceramic jars. It is all she appears to want, and we go straight to Aidan's home to do the work when she has placed each item in her bag of medical goodies.

I let Simone have the leftover food in my backpack when we get settled, creaking to the floor below a mostly sealed window while Aidan gets her fixed up in a tower of blankets with a pillow from Celestyn's stash. He offers us an indefinite stay until we get on our feet, his teeth chattering as he fluffs out the bedding so my foster child is in prime comfort for Limbo. There isn't much choice but to accept, for at least tonight, and I try to make myself look stronger than I am as Celestyn unwraps my arm to dab away at my injuries.

She starts with the worst of them on my wrist, using water and reusable rags to clean up the crusty red and working toward the fresh trails until there is a visible field to work upon. Simone criss-crosses her legs without the distraction of my audible pain, tiny fingers snagging journals from multiple piles and popping them open to look at the pictures. I suck in air as she pours cold water into the open wound and pulls out a needle to dig free any fragments of dirt or debris. The outline of my inner arm glistens to her from watery, pale wrinkles of meat.

She doesn't ask how I acquired the injuries. My prime guess is that she doesn't care. Not that I want to discuss it much when everyone else is on a hunt for my head. Bethesda's words are still too clear for my liking, echoing in my sore ears still full of river water.

*You, a speck of a creature on the surface of this world, who has stolen the beating heart of another.*

What does that mean?

Aidan thumps over to see us when he is satisfied that Simone is happy, taking a sloppy drink of water and hovering over his girlfriend-but-not-girlfriend's work on me. His eyebrows pinch together, calloused hand adjusting his glasses so that they don't fall off his face gawking at the damage done in his absence.

*God, he's never going to trust me again,* I agonize inside.

"Back off, Romeo. She's fine." Celestyn waves him away with a flick of her dainty hand. "It's not as deep as it looks, and I have seen worse damage done by mermaid teeth. But it *will* get infected if you don't butt the hell out of my light."

There is a brief blush I can spot rising to his face, but an undeniable weakness races ahead of it. Aidan holds his side, hunkering next to me so that I can smell the infection on his exhale, rotting him from the inside. He tries not to confront Celestyn's comment the best he can, pursing his lips—not that he needs to be flustered. We both know what this is, but he makes it easy to forget in sporadic junctures of our partnership, the tips of his fingers at this one touching the back of my arm in support to the pain.

Firm. Warm.

My head tilts to them, and they retract faster than I can enjoy it. He frowns at this, his hand still floating in air, but withdrawn all the same.

"Sorry," he whispers.

I don't want to embarrass him further, so I turn my attention to the unyielding question my mind begs of Celestyn.

My mouth drops, my voice a stuttered squeak. "How did you..."

Her eyes flicker up to meet mine, lips curving to reveal a sarcastic grin. She tugs my hand up by the thumb to showcase it to the room in light of my ignorance.

"The puncture at the base of your palm and thumb is shaped like a bite wound," she presents. "Unless you have another friend nibbling your crispy skin, mermaids are the likely culprit. Which also makes disinfectant all the more important. Their bites are mildly toxic."

She yanks my arm closer to her lap at the sound of a page turning in the corner with Simone. From her bag, she pulls one of the two jars of lavender cream she had taken from The Center and mixes it with a spoon until it gradually grows to a darker purple verging on black. I lean forward at the sight, spotting gold flecks whirling in the mix and inhaling the sickeningly sweet aroma of fruit and flowers.

"What's that?" I nod at the jar, eying the other in her bag.

Celestyn wets her hands in water the best she is able without wasting too much so they may be clean, sweeping two fingers through the light, yet velvety mixture. She studies the length of my injuries in heavy concentration.

"I don't know the exact translation for it." She shrugs, acting as if the word *translation* or the fact she wasn't one hundred percent sure what she was translating were not alarming at all. "I... haven't learned the whole Ravager language thus far, and now that I don't house with Master Amadeus, my knowledge of their cultures will only be stunted. Or, at least, limited to the medical journals I stole."

"You what?" Aidan's voice rings in the background of our conversation, though not sounding all too surprised.

"Stole," Celestyn reaffirms for him. "I stole them, Aidan. It's not like you couldn't have guessed it."

"Is the cream a part of your studies?" I ignore both of them.

A bit more relaxed in her own arena, she nods. "It is hard to say, but from my understanding it is named something like... purple ice? Whatever. Purple Ice is a strong, battlefield disinfectant made from the gooey innards of galax villosus and azolla flowers native to this region alone. A whole field of both were found a couple dozen or so miles out behind The Center. I add some of the indigo berries the smaller dragons eat to my version since in the journals they are said to promote faster healing."

"You went beyond the first layer of The Dome?" I can't help but sound skeptical.

Celestyn is...not a warrior type of a woman. She is strong, but in a fight?

"No." She laughs lightly. "No. I've offered a few of the search team members favors that they can't refuse."

My nose wrinkles in disgust. But I don't want to assume the worst.

"Money?" I guess instead.

"Adabelle, no. *Favors*."

"Food?"

"Child in the room." Aidan clears his throat, though I can sense his presence growing darker at my side.

"Are you really that stupid?" She presses the cream into the actual wound, slickening the inner edges and meat like it was lube rather than disinfectant. I groan, my lungs seizing up inside my chest. But it chills the broken skin almost as fast as it bites into it, much like ice, budding frosty flowers of numbness until I can no longer suffer the riveting pains of my own stupidity.

"I just don't..." I try to explain, but she cuts me short.

"Sex." She sighs at my lap, bending to mend the wounds. "All men want is sex. All I want is knowledge. We trade. It's like a business deal, and because of that, the fact that I am about to run a needle through your skin will feel like less than a pinch."

She's right. It is more of a nuisance than anything, a prick, a pop of sound, and an urging to zip my wrist back together. Twice, my eyes water in the tedious motions, but it doesn't take long for my wounds to be shut tight. She rubs ointment from the second jar, a lighter shade of violet, over the finished product for a barrier against bacteria. She subsequently moves on to Aidan, who has looked more and more rigid since her conversation with me.

He is silent, refusing to look her in the face, and neither of them speak a word as she lifts his shirt, rubbing each cream on top his first injury. I look away when she cleans the leg wound out, giving them time to work out their stresses with one another to no avail. She finishes attending to each puncture on his body and wraps them tight, turning in for the night when all is complete.

We all follow suit, blowing out candlelight and assuring the door is barring the outside effectively. Celestyn inches close to Simone with the pile of books out, taking one from her game of Name That Picture and reading three pages, so that she can strain her eyes hard enough to fall asleep. Aidan goes straight to guard the door, pulling the dagger from his pocket and laying it at his hip.

Several hours pass in sweet, sacred quiet. Simone has stretched out against Celestyn's lap, propped together in a furtive bundle below the blankets stretching up over their heads. But I am restless. I watch Aidan leave his post long enough to retrieve his guitar from a separate stack of blankets, returning to his position and sitting back. I scoot forward from the window, uncomfortable and homesick and intrigued.

"You still have one?" I smile, extending testing fingers to pluck the strings.

"Yeah," he repeats my randomized melody, adding a few notes to give it substance. "I was found with it. Well, wearing it, thanks to the strap."

"Do you still play often?" I tug a few more, catching the small grin tugging at his mouth.

"Not as much as I wish I could."

"Did you really write your own music? Or did you piggyback off mommy and daddy's success?"

I grin, playful. There is a larger smirk lurking between both of us, hidden behind dustings of moonlight sneaking through the slivers carved into the door.

"I learned from an early age to write my own," he replies.

I lean up onto the wall opposite him, heavy eyed but attentive.

"Would it be too much to ask you to play something?"

There is no answer.

Aidan glances to the shape of his own hands curved over the instrument, studying his own intricate movements creating melodies. Painstaking, sad melodies.

The notes reverberate throughout the room, both like a red flag of someone who lives here, and a white flag...as if the person that dwells within these walls is already gone. As if they have given up. Low notes, high notes. They all weep the same symphony of despair, a tornado of anguish that spins me into haunting dreams of bright lights. Of bedtime tears and muffled roaring. Snapping. Voices and choices.

*What is your name?* Memory calls to me as it had so long ago. *Do you even know?*

I open my mouth. To speak myself into existence.

Opposite of me is a satisfied smirk. A patient waiting.

*Say it.*

I gasp for air waking up the following morning, as if it were my first breath and my last. Around me, the day has already started. Celestyn is standing at her miniature library, tugging on her coat and getting ready for work while Aidan is absent, his guitar propped against the wall. Simone is nibbling on trace amounts of food when my eyes find her—potatoes stewed nights ago from the look.

My heart is still racing, galloping, as I approach her, sitting down and opening my half-dried bag. I should probably let the contents dry out here today, and I very much doubt Aidan would mind if I left some of my things inside. It isn't going to be forever, after all. Without incident, hopefully I can find a new home this evening and we won't have to freeload off of anyone else.

But the question of Simone's parentage hasn't yet left my mind, my promise playing at the rear of my thoughts, and the need for files from Ace boiling into overflow at another failure in the bucket. I don't know where to start anymore, and I hold my head, mussing damp musky hair in need of a wash.

In a quick decision, I lay all of my backpack crap out below the window to dry out, glancing to Celestyn when I'm through, and studying her library of stolen mystique. Each book is a durable, leatherbound item with delicate gold or silver inlaid in an untranslated title—the thickest of the stacks on the bottom to balance and the thinnest at the top holding no more than twenty pages at best.

As I approach, Celestyn lurches forward, sweeping every precious ounce of information to the back corner that she can as a warning to back off. And I get it. She doesn't want me touching them? She doesn't want the help? Fine.

But why wouldn't she want anyone else to learn her trade if it were vital to saving as many people as possible? Keeping these types of secrets seems cruel if she has a couple keys to understanding the race, the language, the medicines, and anything else she wanted.

I suppose it isn't my place to understand, though. Ace gave me my own ill-begotten book to look through, and I don't have time to learn a language on top of it. I just need to wait for it to dry out and hope the pages aren't completely destroyed.

*God, what would he do if the pages were destroyed? I can't return it like that.*

I huff a sigh, holding my hands out to help Simone to her feet, assuring she gets her shoes on right, and fixing her clothes so they don't appear so baggy and sloppy. Unhappy, but as joyous as I'll ever be, I pick up two more potatoes for my hungry baby and usher us toward the door.

"We're out," I call to Celestyn while she works through her own mane of hair.

"Don't care," she sings, waving me off.

I roll my eyes, wondering if she actually doesn't care or if it is all part of some tough girl façade like Zoey. A girl has to do what she needs to in order to survive. Who could blame her if she distances herself entirely?

I can't blame her. That's for sure.

I am just as afraid to make long term attachments myself, though my mind can't seem to help itself. I can't seem to help myself from doing anything at all. I'm mindless. Senseless. *Stupid*.

At the barn, I drop Simone off with the other children. The younger tots welcome her with goofy smiles, tugging on her to go every which direction with them as she tries to chew the potato still packed in her cheeks. I grin, waving to the man in charge of the barn who has all but flipped a switch in his opinion of me, and ducking low to retreat.

"Be on time fer now on!" he calls.

"I will." I sideline the fence to watch Simone draw closer to the animals. "Be careful, Simone. Don't move too quickly!"

Her head swivels to see me when I call her name, but it isn't more than a second and she is out of sight. It is a bittersweet exchange, her hand reaching to return my wave coupled with the most sheepish smile. My heart already aches for her to be home with me.

I move on into the clearing between the markets and village where the search crews have gathered, speaking in the form of yelling, minus Ethan but adding a one-footed Glue Man. I grimace, keeping a distance as I am permitted, and skirting the outline of their formation, trying to catch words being thrown around. It takes less than a minute before Aidan notices me, his eyes strict and full of concern.

Nothing like last night.

The disinfectants and healing promoting creams must be doing well on him, however. Other than a slouch, he isn't quivering or holding his side in lameness. My cuts feel pretty decent too, other than a tender ache and a touch of nausea. For being toxic, I feel almost too good.

"Addie, over here." Aidan bobs his head, throwing me off my game.

The rest of the group grumbles, but I approach as I am told, squeezing in next to Aidan. I face Glue Man from the opposite side, shoulder to shoulder with his pasty allies of hate. I dart my vision to the ground, shuffling closer to my partner as the anxiety sets in.

Is this a joke? A trap?

"What's going on?" I pry, tucking my hands into my armpits.

Glue Man responds faster than Aidan can get a grip on the situation, spitting words like acid.

"Yer lil bitch boy here went on and skimped out on them Suicide Missions," he accuses. "Hid like a big ole pussy 'til Ace had no better choice but to take Ethan and get on outta here on our last horses with two other boys from our crew, and six others from round these parts."

I feel so small here. I don't want to be here, to fight this fight.

"I don't mean to be...thick..." I start.

"Oh, you're thick alright!" one of the other men yell as the others howl and whistle around him.

I cringe.

Aidan's voice belts out harsher than I've ever heard it. "That is enough. I think she has been through plenty without your jabs. It's safe to say she is a hell of a lot tougher than any of you. Be respectful."

He nods at me to continue when he is finished speaking, and I feel as light as air. Protected.

"I don't mean to be *dense*," I try again. "But what are the Suicide Missions?"

For once, Glue Man is helpful.

"We aren't the best at what we do." He shrugs. "Our supply logs go runnin' on empty sometimes, and Ace goes roundin' up some fellas to take 'em on out beyond The Dome to get some. Most 'em don't come back, but ole Ace has been tryna grab ole pussy boy here since the day he woke up. Like some sorta personal ire shit."

I think for a moment.

"I didn't realize the things we need for our supplies are that close," I mull over. "Just outside The Dome a ways? And people aren't coming home? It sounds sketchy enough. I don't see what the problem is with what Aidan has done. I'm sure he isn't the only person on that list who decided he didn't want to die."

Another man speaks up.

"Wouldn't have been a problem if Ace hadn't taken Ethan in his place. Seems awful convenient for your buddy here, doesn't it?"

"Coward!" another member shouts.

Aidan doesn't bother denying the accusation. He frowns, face wrinkling as he is forced to embrace the term, trying to find the proper words to release him from this mess he helped create.

I shrug so high my shoulder bumps into his arm.

"I mean, yeah. I guess it's pretty convenient not to die. Ethan should have hidden himself better. You all sure did. Any smart person wouldn't go after the First-in-Command straight away when they serve the position so well."

"You shouldn't even be here, ya ugly bitch," Glue Man growls.

"Stop," Aidan speaks up. "Until Ethan returns, I've been promoted to First-in-Command. Thanks to her experience and my power to grant it, I have decided to make Addie your Second-in-Command for the time."

My mouth drops.

I have done nothing to deserve this.

If anything, I have done everything to deserve a demotion.

The group knows it. I know it.

The band of men are crying out and yelling it so loud I am sure the people on the Suicide Missions can hear them. I have caused more problems than I've solved just by being alive. I've been nothing but put down since I joined this shit show. They won't let me command them to get a drink of water in a desert with one oasis.

"There ain't no damn way I'll take orders from your pint-sized slut," the man behind Glue Man shouts. "Dennis deserves this more than anyone here."

Aidan shakes his head in response.

"I don't think so," he says. "*Dennis* doesn't take orders well, but he sure enjoys doling them out. He won't listen but expects to be heard. Experience is half the battle, and Addie has proven herself competent under my watch. She's always had my back and she's the most dedicated member of this team. As far as I am concerned, she's at least twice the man any of you are, and more useful than most of you. She could carry the weight of at least ten of you, no problem. Now, I think it is time to get to work. We will reconvene tomorrow with the Second-in-Command present."

I am floored. I don't believe a single word of what he has said, even if I want to. As the group parts in a discord of grumbles and middle fingers, I am still muddled with confusion. I look up to Aidan, wanting to believe there is even an iota of truth to what he told the rest of them.

"T-thank you," I mumble while the last pair of partners disappear. "I appreciate you standing up for me and all."

"Don't..." Aidan replies just as fast, holding a hand up and setting a safe distance between us. "Don't thank me. Don't. We... we aren't friends, okay? I just...can't trust the rest of them to have my back."

I hesitate, all the wonder of his act dissipating like I knew it would.

"Yeah. Yeah...of course. I know."

*I really do.*

Aidan shakes his head, stiff.

"Honestly." He sighs. "You are absolutely terrifying. You are strange, and I understand why everyone around you seems to hate you. I hated you too...when I saw your eyes do that *thing* they do in the light..."

*My eyes? What??*

No sounds free from my vocal chords, but my jaw unhinges while Aidan's speech comes back into focus.

"...but you have been my responsibility since the day they assigned you to me." I'm grateful he hasn't caught on to my lack of attention. "I'll be damned if I hear anyone disrespect you like that *ever again*. So prove them wrong. Prove me wrong. Okay?"

I nod my head. Slow. Dumb.

"Okay," I repeat.

I need a mirror.

# CHAPTER TWENTY-FIVE
## CELESTYN

They think I'm asleep as he begins to play for her, Aidan's guitar strumming notes I'm all too familiar with, having heard them on several occasions as he attempts to perfect one tune in particular for the eternities that he spends here with amnesia. It is a song I have always loved, even on repeat in the evening sun, though glum in its composure compared to who he is on the outside, revealing more of his true nature than most see in person and that I have had witness to in private. Not that I can fault him for his painful, guarded secrets, when we are the exact same in that respect.

I will always understand him in a way that no other woman will, having seen him at his lowest in quarantine, frightened and shut away with earth-shattering memories rushing at his conscious like bus lights that tear apart his life at the seams. Recollections that I am sure he has kept at arm's length from the monster seated opposite him, refusing to allow her to see the ugliest sides of him, and therefore not allowing her to know him twice as well as she thinks she does. Like I already do.

It is one thing I can take away from their interactions that helps me sleep at night, wanting to keep Aidan safe from what I know she is, and yet understanding that this may not be feasible when I see the way he looks at her in the sweet, tender swathes of moonlight escaping through the holes in our fortress. It is impossible to miss, peeking out from this corner and catching his weak warm smile as she plucks away at the strings of his guitar, testing the sound of each one. Though it was even harder to escape earlier when they hugged, his strong arms wrapped tight around her body, clutching in a greedy desperation that I don't think he knew he was capable of until he saw her alive in that moment.

In my head, listening to the two of them talk and gawk at one another in shallow playful whispers, I can concede to the idea that this might be my fault for saving Adabelle in the first place. Everyone begged me to have her dragged to her death out in the woods after the incident with her release from quarantine startled my residents, but upon my examination of her, seeing the same thing in her eyes that they had, I couldn't come to the conclusion that she deserved to die for it. I wanted to make the right choice and to feel like a good person doing it. I questioned the most harm Adabelle Green could do to Limbo, finding the answer inconclusive and in turn, walking the one person I care about in this shit storm straight into the jaws of evil.

The night passes in slow strokes of several chords being played, dutifully pulling the puppet strings of my guilty conscience so that I grow angry rather than sad, regret swelling in my chest and making it hard to breathe. Come morning, my eyes are raw and sandy feeling, more alert than I'd like to be while Aidan gets ready to leave. We don't speak to one another, and he doesn't look at me in the slightest, pulling on a clean shirt with care to his tender wound sites that my inventive creams haven't completely healed up yet. I don't give him the satisfaction of saying bye, knowing he is angry at me and obviously retaliating for my sexual honesty last night.

At my side, Simone flinches at the beams of pastel sunlight

drifting inside through reinforced windows, a bleak reminder that I am not going back to sleep whether I wanted to or not. No matter what way it pains me, I've gone this far to keep Adabelle in good health for Aidan's sake, and I'm not going to turn my head to this so soon. After yesterday, she needs the extra rest, so I allow it, sitting upright and awaiting the start of babysitting.

It takes about an hour for the sleeping bitch to get whatever she needs to power her through the day, the stout dwarf of a woman still groggy while I am putting on my vest and lacing my boots to leave. Simone chews away on breakfast as I watch Adabelle like the venomous widow she is, cringing as she dumps the contents of her sopping wet bag onto the floor and laying each individual item out to dry. I realize at once it is off-putting the way her attention begins to roll across the room in waves, bouncing from one place to the next like it has no important place to center on. I suppose, if my research is doing me any good, I should expect this from her. If I'm right, and the books I stole from Amadeus' library provide the most accurate information, this lack of focus is a focal point of the problems encompassing her person—of who and what she is—though it is a slim possibility at best, and most of the time I wonder if when I hear her metaphorical hooves, I am looking for zebras rather than horses. But I draw the line at my books, giving her a strict look that commands her to buzz off my property, which she does, less than gracefully when I sweep them out of reach.

Her attention moves immediately to Simone while I inhale a quick potato breakfast, wiggling the girl's shoes onto the proper feet, and minding her clothes so that they don't appear as sloppy. In spite of all her faults, it is apparent to me that Adabelle did indeed teach small children to dance before as her state issued ID suggested, making the morning drag fun for the little girl who missed her nonexistent "daddy". She sings to Simone while they prepare, placing her hand to her ear when she has finished a cat scratch on a chalkboard line and awaiting the tiny, incoherent echo to sort of repeat her, both girls laughing and dancing to inaudible music of their own design.

"We're out," Adabelle calls to me, almost forgetting her own ungainly appearance and combing fast through a mop of hair that has begun to show roots.

"Don't care." I wave her away, hoping it will make her leave faster.

I really don't care.

I just don't want to leave until she does, to assure that she doesn't steal anything in my absence. Not when I have so much riding in stolen text and studies, unable to return to Amadeus' tower for more now that I have abandoned his good graces in pursuit of his identity and where we are. Not that I have come much closer to either, outside of what I know as of current. I just knew after the attack on The Center I couldn't risk being that close to someone in his position when I am within sprinting distance of the truth.

When I'm sure Adabelle and Simone have skipped far enough out of sight that they won't be coming home all too soon, I slip my shoulder supply bag on, and step out the door. In my time living in Limbo, I have grown accustomed to the intense heat straight out the gate of every late morning to afternoon, learning to relish slight discomfort over unfathomably sweltering heatstroke weather. But I hope it rains soon, just to get a little wind and chill going for my walk home later on.

Arriving at The Center, I do not receive half the busy day I expect, and it gives me time to see Zoey for light contractions. I note her visit in my personal logs to copy and give to Ace at some point, creating a summary of the pain followed by her lack of dilation or crowning baby. Having nothing else to go through on, I provide her with more water to hydrate, and discharge her to avoid the potential for Adabelle to kidnap her again.

In my life prior to this, I was just a nurse—if anyone can say the phrase *just a nurse*, considering all that we do for the sake of our patients. I never did amputations like I do now, or diagnosed ailments based on the sound of a cough or how high a fever accompanying the symptoms is. Pregnant patients and children were a rare sight to be had, and I'd never seen a baby born alive in the hospital I worked in. Most of Zoey's pregnancy I have winged based on what I know about the laws of health in general, and studies I have read courtesy of Amadeus' library. I do know that most pregnancies go for a span of nine months, and that Zoey's is going on eleven and a half.

But what can I do?

It's not like I have anesthetic. Not to mention, I don't trust myself to do something as delicate and intricate as a C-section without killing the girl, unless it is an emergency, and the baby is still moving. Still weirdly small inside her womb where I can feel it.

Waiting out her body's natural course seems like the best plan of action...but I hate it. It is sketchy. It reeks of anything that can go wrong.

I bury my face in my palms, letting the hours slick by. People come and go, my residents leading them to rooms while I work on file copies to give Ace. My hands ache with burning cramps on the inside of my wrists the longer I use this quill, side of my pinky smudged in dark ink. There is an intermittent buzzing of voices, building and ebbing, never staying like a tidal wave of need I can't allow myself to stay on.

The sun rises further into the sky, officially allowing daylight to take the place of night as I send my first resident on a brief break before lunch in a couple hours. I appreciate the days that don't involve the brutal sawing of bone and flesh more and more the longer I remain working this batshit crazy job, and I flex my fingers in a subtle gasp so I can return to the documents I should, by all logic, have a computer for. But a clamor of footsteps catches me off guard, and I poke my head up to see Farmer Ray walking inside, carrying a tiny body in his arms.

It isn't all too uncommon that he takes a child to The Healing Center every couple of days. Working among animals large and small, there are bound to be run-ins with small children and the hooves or claws of irritable animals that need mending. The worst I had seen was a four-year-old girl who had run too fast unsupervised up behind a horse getting ready to be led out for Suicide Missions. It had startled and clocked her in the head, making the farmer sick as he carried her to our hospital. Though it had been too late when they arrived, as she was already gone.

Ray approaches the desk, and I peek up to see him, avoiding the sight of the child wrapped tight, cradled in his arms. His job is hard enough without feeling the condemnation of being unable to watch thirty small children at the exact same time.

"What is it this time?" I pull out a new piece of tough scratchy paper. "A hoof to the face? A split lip?"

His teeth grind, jaw quivering as he shoves the limp body toward me in distress. "I...I don't know...she just went on and...I mean..."

He isn't making sense. I take the child in my arms, hand stroking the shape of its head, smooth and soft. Small. I stop.

"She just went down," Farmer Ray explains as other children pull at his arms, talking over him. "I don't know..."

When I look down, my heart ceases to beat inside my chest. I am frozen, sick and shaking as I attempt to maintain my cool. In my arms lay the last person I wanted to see here, dark skin sunken against my own, little chest rising in staggered breaths, eye whites fluttering behind shut lids.

"S-Simone? Honey?"

# CHAPTER TWENTY-SIX
## ADABELLE

I HOLD A COMPACT MIRROR IN FRONT OF MY FACE, flashing candlelight close to my eyes and watching my pupils dilate to monstrous slits. Over and over.

Is this real? It doesn't feel real, but it doesn't stop happening either.

It is quiet in The Center where they keep Simone's peaceful resting body, and I had not known she was here at all until I came to pick her up from the barn following an uneventful evening report. The sun was beginning to set in a glow of orange and pink, leaving little daylight to spare, so I had to run for The Center, but Ray mentioned the incident occurred that morning, shortly after I left her for drop off.

He said she just...passed out. Fell down.

The stories changed depending on who I asked. I don't know which one is real, other than that it doesn't matter when every road leads to her laying on a gross mattress in one of the very sinister rooms I had tried so hard to keep her out of.

The first night, I hurried to Aidan's place to gather all of my things while I delivered him a hurried rundown of the situation at play. I resigned all of my duties—effective immediately—until there was a change in her condition, expecting a fight but receiving unexpected grace and understanding. He explained to me that he had more pull than ever now as First-in-Command, so if I handled all the written reports that are left unattended with Ace out of office, I can keep my position and my pay. Moreover, I would be free to be at the side of my foster child.

I borrowed one of Celestyn's quilts that night as I walked out the door, in the same way she borrowed Master Amadeus' books, collecting anything I could that appeared clean enough for Simone to lay on top of that wasn't previously sullied with death. At the time, I had wanted her to feel as comfortable as possible when she woke up from this nightmare or illness or whatever it was.

But she hasn't, yet. Not for very long, anyway, before whatever it is that ails her takes her for another round.

It has been two days.

Celestyn had told me the evening it all started that they had expected her to wake up prior to reaching The Center with her small lifeless body, from the farmer to the nursing staff. It is easier for children to succumb to heat exhaustion or dehydration in a climate that promotes it. Or it could have been that her body wasn't ready for strenuous activities and she needed a job where she could sit down, like providing the animals some love and care —work that I would be envious of. But as several hours passed them by, followed by small seizures, bigger concerns would arise.

It has become...complicated.

Yesterday, Celestyn had come in to wet the corners of Simone's mouth with dabs of water, gently pushing fluids during periods of semi-consciousness, and hoping these periods would lengthen in time. But in the absence of technology, there isn't a definitive answer as to why this is happening, or a solution to make it stop.

We have no x-ray machines. No MRIs. Not even IVs.

Celestyn and I have concluded, together, that we could rule

out anything such as poisonous foods or bad water, since there were so many witnesses to the area where the event occurred. She suggested it is something that might have already been present this whole time.

I am pressed to agree.

She permitted me to read some of the more recent logs she has kept to occupy my time and assist in finding Simone's "daddy". This isn't an isolated incident. People can get sick in Limbo, for no outward or apparent reason. They'll leave quarantine fine and come back days, or even months later, with symptoms concurrent to cancer or really terrible flu bugs. It's documented, but most of these people die despite intervention.

I have allowed Celestyn to attempt new means of treatment in light of that information to preserve what we can of Simone's life. Every two hours, she enters the room to swab new, self-made medicinal mixtures she has drawn up from her books along the inside of Simone's cheeks and around her mouth. Two of these procurements look like dark gooey honey, whirling around the spoon she uses in thin strings and taking time to dissolve. Another one looks like water with lime green food coloring, made with the water from inside the roots of what she said is called a parrottia plant. She claims it is used for internal restorative purposes and can be found anywhere in this universe, at least to her understanding of the text. I tried some for myself and it was gag worthy, making me happy that the coating brushed along the inside of her mouth is done while she is asleep.

But, for the most part, this has been it. It is just Simone and I, occasionally seeing Celestyn when the time calls, but no one more. Aidan does not drop by at all to check in, burdened perhaps by his own responsibilities, and more than that, not caring. Since we aren't friends. Even if I need one now more than ever.

The Center is lonely with nothing but reports and the contents of my backpack to keep me company, if I can admit anything of the sort to myself. If I were stronger, I'd go out for some fresh air. Some sunlight. I'd go do my actual job if I was able to stray that far.

I just can't bring myself to walk away.

I unshoulder my backpack for the afternoon after collecting a handful of files from Celestyn's desk to add to my pile from the search teams. At my side, Simone's tiny, frail body pumps oxygen into her limbs at slow uneven paces, bracing for another brief open of her eyes that doesn't come. I didn't think it were possible for her to drop more weight off the little chicken bones inside her flesh casing, but somehow, it blooms to fruition.

I extend my hand, grasping hers in mine and giving her little fingers a soft squeeze, holding firm as I dig for the book inside my backpack that Ace had given me. I frown, tugging it free from the crap above it, and noticing some of the script on the inside is smudged. But it doesn't stop the text from being mostly readable, the title translated out in familiar handwriting I can't quite place.

*A History and Lore of Race. Written by Grace of the Crows. Finished by Ceridwen Rose.*

*The authors sound like another book title,* I smirk to myself, reading on and rubbing my foster baby's knuckles with the pad of my thumb, hoping against hope she moves in response.

Nope.

I sigh, bending over my lap in despair.

The first page is written in a different language with the same scrawl underneath it entitled *The Master Races*. I flip the page to see two separate humanish diagrams, decorated with varying degrees of height. The first makes my heart stop, leaping into my throat and sticking at the base so I cannot swallow it down. There is a label at the top of the page over a hand-drawn image depicting an oversized creature with pointed ears protruding past the back of its head and eyes like that of a cat...or snake, the black ink naming the race category as *The Dark Elves*.

The discomfort is felt right away, forcing heat to my ears and aching down the sides of my neck. I take a deep breath in the realization that this is a bigger favor than I can ever repay Ace for, begging more questions of this Master Amadeus I refuse to meet.

My eyes bleed over the page of written text, translated below lines of foreign entities as the entries of none other than Grace of the Crows.

*Until my arrival in the cities, I had never seen a dark elf in person, let alone had the opportunity to journal such extraordinarily powerful creatures. In my previous writings, I had taken many accounts of various creatures and plant life I did not understand away from the sprite tribes to bring light to their natures. But due to circumstance, I am afraid these will be lost forever, and that this will be my new start into documentation and research.*

*To begin, of course, the dark elves are one of two Master Races devised at the beginning of our planet's birth. These divine creatures were a gift from The Great Mother to the Father of Civilization, the sprites being his present unto her, and each created in the image of the other so that in death they will live on. So, for reference, we will assume that Our Nameless King is one of the dark elves, and The Great Mother is a sprite.*

*I would like to start off in the department of physical characteristics to help sustain my drawn image, since one reading this later might not be able to imagine the full girth of what it is sketched on the page without context.*

*These creatures are giants among many of us, countered only by the Mer-folk (this only due to the ever-so-long tails they sport). The men are almost always taller than their women, ranging from seven feet on the short end to just over eight at the largest—though most are in between. The women, however, can range six and a half feet to seven and a half feet. But the tallest ever known was a solid eight feet before her abrupt death riverside at the webbed claws of a ravenous mermaid.*

I know that feeling. I stop, looking at Simone and granting her a brief smile and a wink, though she can't see it.

"The mermaid was ravenous," I repeat, jokingly. "Starved, the poor fish. Have you seen them? Beasts."

*Beasts. I am a beast.*

I decide to read aloud at this point. Just so if Simone can hear at all, she knows someone is still here with her.

*Our Great Mother was quite generous with these beasts, you see. She gifted them many things equal to that of The Nameless King so his image could be exacted, perfected. Carried on, if you will, because to her, he is an unsightly thing—his lineage should never carry on through his own seed.*

*The dark elves are his allotted legacy, a magnificent present with many of his abilities and quirks. I have done my own testing to see the truth of this.*

*They're quite brilliant, really. Readers will be enthralled to know that dark elves, like their image, have superior hearing capabilities when focused, surpassing most, if not all, animals on this earth. Like cats, their long, pointed ears can turn ever so slight, zeroing in on sound up to three miles out. We are reminded to be gentle in the presence of such sensitive ears if they are focused and in their element, not that they mind if things get a bit loud otherwise. These creatures are quite friendly and seem to practically pull reasons out of thin air to host a proper celebration.*

*Still, it should be noted that these creatures are omnivorous predators, and their diets are protein based by over half to support their magics, more so for expecting mothers, though the population does seem to suffer in comparison to others due to lack of living female children—but this is another problem we will cover later.*

*As for the danger in their predatory skills, I have found that they have exceptional senses of smell—sniffing out traces of blood for up to five miles if it is untampered, as well as being able to differentiate individual smells. Sort of like hounds, but better.*

*In the sight department, I must admit, I was a bit startled by their vertically slit pupils, but it does not seem to have much an effect on anything other than their night vision and ability to stalk prey. These creatures want little for candlelight, except for in the presence of guests. With exceptional depth perception and clarity, I find that their eyes are better than even my own.*

*They are all around wonderful, beautiful creatures, though flawed in a particular...disturbing, aspect.*

*If I include my worst fears, it is that Our Great Mother did not create this Master Race to survive in her spite. Or, at least, not functionally.*

*It really starts with the imprinting, I suppose.*

*Imprinting is a process performed almost exclusively by the men of this race. As I have seen, it is a very intense physical, chemical, emotional, hormonal, and mental bond to a fated mate. It is through speaking to those who have endured it that I understand these men do not choose this mate on their own. This is a spontaneous incident that many in the natural world refer to as "love at first sight", however it is much more aggressive.*

*It is made clear to me that a small portion of women may also do this, but more often than not are compliant victims to it.*

*The bonding with men has been created to be very instantaneous. Think of it as a grand realization. A great truth they have newly discovered in their lives. An awakening.*

*It begins at sight, but it is initiated by a single touch of sorts that marks the unknowing mate with a hormonal stamp warning other men to stand clear until consummation, when a separate set of hormones secreted through the skin from both parties will darken the mark into more of a brand that their wives will wear for life.*

*Therein lies the problem.*

*Many of the women are compliant, as they have been raised to be, but if this race continues to fail, and permission be granted to look further than within their own lines, the results could be criminally devastating to the eyes of others who do not understand the culture.*

*These men perceive their doings as an act of love. Their first attempts at bringing on a family and welcoming a new age, for they are the primitive Master Race. But...it is unbearable for me to think that, should they never find a way to patch the hole in their race, there will be tears shed for the thirteen months it takes to gestate these Elven children to completion. For these men will pay no mind to the culture of their wives, and—*

I feel sick. Really sick. The kind of sick that one only understands if they have read about the fears of a woman they never knew, describing the potential systematic rape of an entire civilization.

For the sake of love? What kind of bullshit is this? What kind of race is this?

Is this what "Ravagers" are?

It looks like them. The dark elves.

Are they kidnapping women and raping them for companionship? For children? For destiny?

It isn't possible they imprinted on every human woman they came into contact with upon attacking the village if it is left to chance, and they had no problem making it clear they would fire straight through me to slaughter Aidan. Nonetheless, the reported attacks on women are quite low, the attacks on children under a specific age nil. But they kill every man they can find without hesitation, sometimes with unnecessary brutality.

The door shrieks at the opposite end of the room and a voice rings inside the hollow of misery as it does.

"Hey...are you there?"

I stuff the book under my legs, suddenly content with my own thickness as Zoey enters the room. As if she could get any bigger, she seemed as though she had—enormous for being so thin and frail. But, if the journal entries are correct, not overdue at all.

Her braids bounce on her slumped shoulders as she waddles across the floor, trying to make her way as delicately as possible to the one seat across from Simone and myself. Her dark eyes remain at her feet, abashed and afraid. Juvenile.

I almost feel sorry for her, thinking of the fresh detail my brain has absorbed, and wondering if it were just possible that she had been one of the victims of Grace's future. Was she a fated "mate"? Or a victim of circumstance? Was this her destiny? How could someone be destined for rape? For childbirth?

"Why are you here?" I say instead.

Bitter and ice cold.

I shouldn't be. She is terrified and has every right to be. I am terrified, and I have less right to be. But neither of us can help it, and I am still seething with resentment. Hurt. An unashamed piece of me wants her to know this. To hurt with me.

Zoey doesn't take it personally however, rolling her eyes at my attempt at her perfected craft.

"Don't say fucking hi or anything." She attempts to laugh, but it fails.

"I didn't want to fucking say hi, or anything." I force a curt smile. "What do you need? Did I forget something else on my way out?"

She is quiet for a moment, pursing her lips, and bobbing her head.

"Sorta," she mumbles.

"I have all my shit," I bite back. "All of it, plus a little more. So you can leave. Thanks, bye."

"You forgot something," she insists, angrier this time and clenching her fists.

"Leave, Zoey," I huff, combing my fingers through my hair that is fading out to a lavender and showing color at the roots, wishing I could have a hot shower to wash it clean.

Maybe I can bathe in the river, or somewhere close, when Celestyn comes in for rounds. I wouldn't have to walk too far.

"Not until you fucking admit it!" Zoey yells, pulling me out of my hot water fantasy.

"Admit what? You're acting like a freaking lunatic right now and I don't have time for it."

"Admit you forgot something!"

"Absolutely not!" I throw my hands up, feeling a pang of sharp pain ripple across my temple as she pelts me with small rocks from her pocket.

*The bitch came prepared for me to say no.*

I pick one up and throw it back at her, missing and hitting the door.

"Say it!"

"No!"

Simone's hand twitches and I freeze, dropping to her side and squeezing her hand again, hard. I just need her to wake up.

Zoey is quiet for the duration of this, minus a series of sniffles and a rattle of her rock stash hitting the floor. I swivel to see her still standing in place, eyes rimmed red, and body quaking.

"You forgot *me*," she whispers. "You forgot all about me, and the promise you made to help me. You brought in that little brat, and didn't give a second thought about me, or how it would affect me. You abandoned me for her."

I am a volcano. I have made myself a volcano, the absence of who I am and the person I am now being the crashing plates that create my rigid exterior. The suffering I have met at the second of my arrival is now the force pushing thick seething magma to the surface to scald all in its wake.

There is too much pressure down below. In my gut. In my chest. In my head.

I am ready to blow.

"All I have done since arriving is think of you," I ooze. "I haven't had time to think for myself, or of myself, or literally anything about why the fuck I'm here. And then, I happened along Simone, another cast off in this hellhole that needed help too. So I helped her, because it can't always be you, Zoey, and you pushed me away for it."

"I know," she whimpers. "I'm fucking sorry, okay? I'm just... not in my element. I've been reading those damn journals and I'm really fucking scared. Having that little shit running around would have made it all worse. But I also underestimated your dedication to, well, everyone. And that's my fucking fault."

I relent, for a minute.

"She was alone." I bite my lip. "And more than anyone else, you and I know what that's like. I only wanted to give her someone to count on—safety."

Zoey nods, wiping her face with the back of her hand. She sniffs, rubbing her eyes relentlessly.

"I'm sorry," she repeats. "I was just fucking—"

I put my hand up to stop her. I don't need it.

"If we let fear dictate everything we do, we will never leave here alive. Chin up."

"We?" She scoots closer, chair screeching over the surface of the floor.

I don't look at her, instead watching the way I squeeze Simone's fingers, desperate for a reaction of any kind.

Nothing.

"If you are apologizing, I assume it is because you have decided you want the protection of 'the beast', again."

Zoey smirks. "A bit, yes."

My heart is pumping, throbbing fast and furious. I swallow.

"I will oblige on one condition, and I need you to be honest. Open."

"Yes?"

I look her in the eyes.

"Do you have any strange marks on your body?"

# CHAPTER TWENTY-SEVEN
## SAHANNA

I AM GLAD WHEN THE DRAGON FLIGHT HAS MET ITS END, and we are on safe, sturdy ground to walk.

I don't really possess an appreciation for airborne heights where the trees look like a phantasmagoria of color blending into the seams of different regions marked by unending, changing vibrancies. I spend the majority of these day long journeys holding to Silas for dear life and praying for the sweet release of a death that doesn't include becoming a puddle of blood.

There is a preference I hold, better enjoying where my feet can touch the ground and make a break for it at any opportune time in the naivete of my imagination. It equates to the wonder of mischief, an uncontrolled adventure wherever I step, and the distraction of nature all around me.

I haven't laid claim to this much luxury since before I was pregnant, again, and it won't last long considering the beast will return to meet our next location upon retrieving The King to deliver him to his. No one wants me on my feet too often this far in, considering the early failed attempts of the past, and if it means sparing his own means of transport to see this through, I have no doubts my vile brother in law will assure it happens.

Family is important to their race, even if that family is only so by marriage. Seeing his brother achieve fatherhood becomes a priority when the depression of losing children affects his ability to operate at capacity as his right hand. The men of this race crave fatherhood like they're the ones with the biological clock and ovaries, but pregnancy hasn't vibed well with my body in the past due to a little...intervention.

Only now, I don't have my teas.

I haven't been this anxious in a very, very long time, cradling my head while we loop through the maze of a forest, and breathing heavy into the bony cave created in the pockets of my elbows.

I shouldn't be here.

*No human should be here.*

If I knew I could outrun him, I would. In a second, I would take off like the fastest mammal alive, and not look over my shoulder for anything in the world. But I have seen him move faster than cars in less time. I am barely faster than a three-year-old double amputee right now anyway, and that isn't getting better the bigger this baby gets. All that changes is that my waddle deepens.

Below my dress, I can feel this creature stretch in alien ways, waving and writhing until an agitated foot lands a heavy blow to my hip. I grunt, stopping and cradling my face instead, as if I can shut it out as long as I can't see anything. Silas' warm hand on my lower arm keeps this from being a reality, however, his fingers gentle and firm.

Alarmed.

*God, please don't be alarmed.*

"Are you alright?" He asks, moving my hands to the side so he can get a clear view of my face.

It is to see if I am lying.

He isn't as skilled in this technique as his brother when it comes to me, but even through the rosy veil he looks at me through, he can understand several cues. I am sure his mother was an excellent liar of sorts, considering the history and lore surrounding this family. Silas probably watched her tell at least a lie a day.

"I'm...fine." I clear my throat. "I just have a headache, and the baby is not so kind today."

I don't try to smile for his reassurance. He would know that it was a straight out lie this way. I have never been happy to be here, nor have I felt pleasured to carry his rape baby to any degree. Smiles are reserved for when I can actually manage them, and not when I think it will get me out of an actual excuse. I have a list six miles long filled with excuses to give him for any time of day to avoid suspicion.

Silas studies my face a minute longer, analyzing everything I have told him in one little sentence alongside my body language. At our side, the river swooshes in soothing currents, a sound I have fallen asleep to for three days, staying at an inn for one and sleeping at the banks for the others. I preferred the inn, if I were being honest, the comfort of a bed on my aching backside after spending all afternoon lumbering around like a fucking sow, and the cooked food. Light music.

I have always enjoyed music.

I used to sing.

But, despite my depression, the outside has its benefits as well.

For instance, I can go completely crazy out here. If I scream? Who's going to hear me?

No one, that's who.

The trees, maybe.

But what are they going to do? Get up and *leaf*.

Oh Christ, I'm making jokes with myself, again. This can't be good.

"We will take a rest here." Silas tugs me by the hand closer to the water, and directs me to sit on top a couple of larger, smooth stones. "You haven't much to drink today, and I believe you must be feeling the worst of it."

"Sure," I grumble, wincing at the realization of the twinge of sarcasm lingering on the edge my every word.

Silas takes a seat aside me, handing me a leather pouch full of fresh water. I take it with caution, quivering so the fluid sloshes within, and guzzling it faster than I intended to as he folds a hand over my belly for a feel of the baby he helped make.

I am uncomfortable, in part, knowing that he is bonding to something that is inherently part of me. More so than it is him. But it responds to him, and his touches, indiscriminating in the rises and falls. Rolls and thrashes. Like a game they had made without knowing.

*Catch me if you can.*

Oh, he could.

I hold myself together, letting him carry on without choice as to otherwise. I focus on something else instead. The water, the limitless expanse of the river. How big it is, or must be.

I've never heard of a river being so large before. It is more like an ocean, or a sea in comparison to Earth measurements. But the water tastes like the best nothingness I have ever had, rather than the fucking salt swish of usually bigger bodies.

Silas doesn't let me approach the water alone on most cases, or at all, if we can avoid it. They have a certain degree of less advanced plumbing and waste than the completely primal tribes of Earth history, so unless we are traveling, there isn't a point in being in the danger of the river. Because it is "dangerous". It is deeper than it looks, more often than not, and I am still in the kiddie stages of learning to swim. But there are also too many beasts lurking in those depths.

There was a time he told me a story about his younger years, when he was just a boy learning how to grow up and become a monster. His father apparently did not let his mother, or himself, leave home all that often, guarding them fiercely, and accompanying all their trips out. He was a protective man, as they all are.

But his mother was what they called "a bit of a struggle". She took Silas close to the water while their father was conducting business, and a mermaid had attempted to pull him in for an afternoon lunch. Luckily, or not, his mother was one hell of a woman. A powerful, magical creature who defended herself without the help of a man, and who saved her son from an imminent death.

Still, when his father was made known of the situation, they weren't allowed back out of the castle walls for years after in blatant fear she would wander more, guiding them into trouble.

Because whenever the cage bars were open, Ceridwen would wander as fast as she could get along, and as far as time would allow.

There is a level of admiration for that kind of push. If I were a magical entity, I would attempt more escapes as well. It is unfortunate I am human, and more so that I know better. Both of which don't stop me from wanting to approach the water on my own, though. Wishing.

There was so much of it back on Earth that had gone sludgy and rotten, I remember. Sea levels went crazy high at some time prior to me being born, and there were alien invaders that had taken over hundreds of years before that, building structures to sit on top the trashy goo so there were more available places to live. Especially since not every person was lucky enough to live on what little land remained.

Drinking water was a whole other story. It was so murky and stagnant it would have to be processed and filtered at least twice to be safe to drink.

In hindsight, it seems unfair that I get to be so close to the real deal, and I am denied more often than not.

I lean away from Silas, scooting to the edge of the rocks, dipping the tips of my fingers into the cold wash of water under his watchful stares. It makes dozens of little ripples where my fingers dance and drip, blooming like sound waves calling back to me.

I wonder what babies hear in their little room of sound waves. It isn't like I know much about them. They stopped teaching a lot of that garbage because we all ceased having babies for the most part.

I'm still not ready to have one. I don't know how to get rid of it anymore, and I'm running out of time.

I am failing myself, my past, my future, and everyone in it by being so complacent. But I lack a game plan.

The sound of footsteps make me perk my head up, and Silas shifts to his feet as a couple hundred men march into view on the subtle path carved up above the river bank. The lead of this small army hesitates before reaching us, examining both of us with caution until he understands his target and who he is greeting.

"Kasismis." Silas nods in salutation, confirming that this was not just a rest, but also our rendezvous point. I whip around to pay immediate attention, shrinking behind my husband. "I did expect to meet you in Praesidia first, but circumstance does change, doesn't it?"

He is as tall as the rest of them, but maybe a bit smaller than Silas. It is hard to tell from below the hillside. The callous eyes of Kasismis find me, studying the situation and measuring his response, as if he were afraid to speak too much in my presence. But given a second, he carries on as expected when addressed.

"My claimed wife will be laboring any day," he booms. "It is vital I retrieve her soon, so we will march through the night."

*Retrieve her? Disgusting.*

I think I throw up in my mouth a little. Poor soul.

"Regular operations, I assume?" Silas questions, but it is clear he already knows the answer.

He is testing, to assure The King's plan is being carried out the way it is intended without any fuckery.

"Not quite, sir," Kasismis replies. "Bastian made it clear to me upon our departure several weeks ago that our King has sent explicit orders to have the human hospital burnt to ash this visit. The letter he sent in advance of this rendezvous point suggests the Operation of Elimination begins now."

Silas bobs his head, confirming this was indeed the information he knew. But he is still testing, somehow. I understand distrust in his eyes, a mission to solidify loyalty. They cannot veer off course, even a tad.

"There is a need for troops at the border of the Fae," he speaks instead. "A breach in security has caused widespread devastation. The King requires as many soldiers as can be spared until further accommodations can be made."

Kasismis is agreeable, bowing deep and low.

"Of course," he promises. "I will send one of my men on horseback to Praesidia at once to gather further troops. After the recapture of my wife, I will take our remaining men to guard the borders until relief arrives."

My mouth drops open, lips trembling. I wet them with my dry, painful tongue.

"Y...you can't do that!" I shout. "You can't take away their only way to treat their sick and injured. How will they survive?"

Kasismis peers to Silas. "Does...she know what elimination means?"

"Quiet." Silas' voice is sharp and forceful, to both of us.

"No!" I shriek at him. "It's not fair. How can your race claim to care for children, say that children are the most important piece of your civilization, and then take away their only way to care for the ones that aren't feeling well?! It's beyond barbaric."

I picture my sister at this time, her cherubic face. What if she is out there? In Limbo? What if she dies because her medical care is ripped out from under her feet? No one would take her in time...

Panic rises in my throat, suffocating me, tears streaming down my face faster than I can wipe them clean. Silas lurches forward, hand coming at the square of my jaw, but I jerk away.

"Don't touch me!" I scream without thinking, and then I stop.

Not because I want to. But because I can't help it. Because I am overwhelmed with...nothingness.

Emptiness. Solitude.

I am writhing beneath the feeling, his ability to dampen how I feel and control it in the most literal sense. But I just...can't think.

"You are going to stress the baby." He pulls me in close, and my body grows limp in response, eyelids drooping. "This is not appropriate conversation in the presence of a woman."

"N...nnnn..." I can't find the word.

Everything is cloudy in my thoughts. I want to cry, but the tears are lost behind my eyeballs. I am small and weak against Silas, slumping over as conversation begins to prattle on in my growing absence.

The last thing that touches my ears is a single phrase.

*A true nightmare will rain down upon them.*

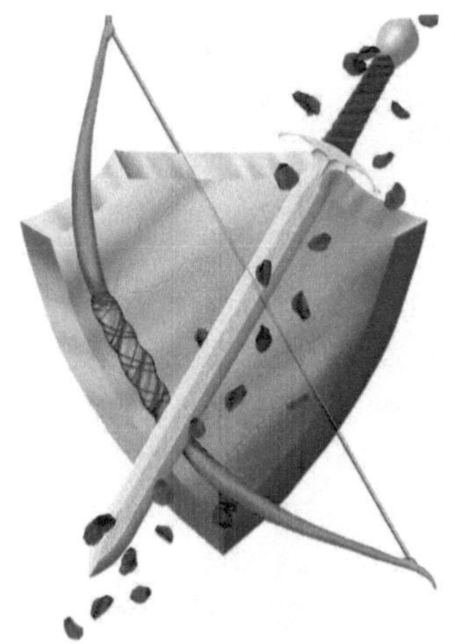

# CHAPTER TWENTY-EIGHT
## AIDAN

I T ISN'T SAFE TO BE AROUND HER. OR SANE.

Not Addie.

It is too...risky.

The lines and boundaries I have drawn up to keep myself invulnerable are beginning to blur into the unsketched patterns designed by my runaway thoughts until I am not sure where I am standing in the jaded mess it creates. Keeping everyone at arm's length becomes the new tragic game I play, because it is functional. Because I have to, for more than myself.

Everything has its place in this new world, and like the knick-knacks collecting dust on the shelf of a senile, childless old woman, these items must stay right where they're at. I can't leave anything to chance, or move across the board to meet others halfway, or get stupid. People die when they get stupid, and it happens all the time, everywhere I look.

I can't let Addie die.

We've come too far for it to come down to this. To admit that there is even an inkling of troublesome care bubbling inside willing to march us both to our deaths, when the risks others believe she already carries are so severe.

It is coming up on a week since Simone hit the ground, and I am stranded as Addie refuses to show her face for a single minute on the teams. The members grow increasingly critical in her absence, agitated and aggressive following delivery of the paperwork she minds, not that they weren't any of these things to start. She would have never won them over anyway, simply for being a woman on their turf, but more so for being a strong woman. She isn't nearly as intimidated as she puts off when she is in her element, especially when nudged the wrong way, and it is harder and harder for them to get up under her skin.

I feel more like one of them, a heaping piece of garbage the longer I don't spend the slightest effort to check in on her. As her partner. We have done everything else together up to this point, and she has always looked in on me without hesitation. It is the least I could do to just say hi, even if I can't.

Celestyn grows more bitter about my lack of hostility with Addie by the day, letting each hour roll on in less than pleasant arguments about my bad choices. There is always a new excuse attached to her side of the story. She claims that she has ideas on what is "wrong" with Addie, that she is a true monster and can't be trusted. We are all in inconceivable danger around her, at an increased risk for death and destruction. But she refuses to elaborate as to why, the theater of it growing old on my ears, like a record played on loop in hell. There isn't faith in a concept that I can't put proof behind.

If anything else, my life has become one spiteful, infernal cycle waiting on things to go back to the way they were. Never relenting, it always adds on one problem following another like a train collecting cars on its way to the next station in a thunderstorm without rain.

*No.*

The rain has let up for the hour. But it is coming.

This morning, I meet with Melody for the subject of late payments, also taking the time to fill out a formal request to meet with Master Amadeus for the answers I crave in absence of Ace to convey my messages. I realize it could mean the end of my stay in Limbo if it is approved, heart thumping and fingers sweating at the flick of the feather signing my name in faded ink, but the cycle of Limbo will end one day—some way or another. It is my choice how I let it happen for myself.

Melody tilts her head, rolling the scroll of paper and setting it at the rear of the counter to turn in at the end of the day. She is bent with her face resting in the palms of her hands, elbows grinding into the counter as if she were too exhausted to stand straight. It is almost easier to talk to her this way, though it has never stopped us from speaking in the past when she is sprite and about.

I've never seen a girl as tall as Melody when she is upright, closing in on seven feet high though still at least half a foot shorter than Ace. I could swear they are carved from two halves of the same stone, down to the oversized matching beanies they never take off that cover their foreheads to the square of their jaws, and their soft black hair. It is a wonder to me they've never hooked up, considering Melody is the only real person Ace lets close.

"How are you holding up?" I ask her, hands digging into my pocket.

Her eyes pop open, blinking slow, as if trying to comprehend what I just asked of her while she remains low to the countertop.

"I...I'm okay." She lets out a whistle of air. "I'm great. How are you, Aidan? Not dead yet?"

The stress is getting to her. It is getting to me too.

"Check back tomorrow." I knock on the wood of her counterspace.

She chuckles, and I spin away, ready to go meet with the teams out on Headquarters' lawn, but her high-pitched voice reins me in.

"How is Miss Green?" There is an unsteady twitch in her pitch. "Is...is she any better? Or is she still by that little girl's side?"

There is a ringing of coin at my backside, and I turn to see her snaking out from behind the desk, delicate and graceful. She has never much cared for Addie before, outside of seeing her on occasion to get cash, and the question throws me sideways.

I answer with caution. "Simone is still sick. Addie is very attentive."

Melody bites her bottom lip, bobbing her head in acknowledgement and pushing the extra sack of coins into my hands.

"Ace left this behind for her." I can see the faintest grin playing at the slick corners of her lips. "He really worries about her. It's super sweet if you think about it."

These words make my stomach churn, flipping upside down in my gut. My face scalds red until all I can see is bright white and fire, my breathing slowing to a trickle of air leaving my nose.

*I* worry about Addie, and Ace can step the fuck down.

But I force the hateful stream of thoughts to a close, shoulders relaxing as much as I can make them. Feeling this way doesn't make me any better than Celestyn, and no one deserves that. I have more control over myself than that, and I'm being dumb. If I was really worried, I would have come knocking at The Center door by now.

"I'll get the money to her," I promise, trying to devise a plan in my mind to get the task done without having to see her.

Melody walks me to the door in a weary shuffle, waving me out for the day. Outside in the lawn, the teams are waiting to converse and split, though I'm not much in the mood for talking. There haven't really been any vicious attacks over the past week to walk through in the report, and in turn that leaves little to find to bring to market.

All week I've been sending my men out on water grabs and limited hunts to feed the underpaid as monotonous tasks to keep them occupied. Not that we couldn't use any of these things, but the peace is alarming for me. It puts me more on edge than the constant attacks ever have. People are relaxing, letting their guards fall while the storm catches wind. Friends sit on their makeshift porches at night to see the stars like they've never been able, and children play in the streets long enough to see the moon shine bright overhead.

Last night, I fell for the fancy of it too, playing my guitar for a group of brats who giggled around a small fire while the adults roasted vegetables for dinner.

*People can actually eat dinner at nighttime instead of late evening.*

It is like a dream, except it is a living nightmare.

I am not asleep. I can't sleep.

It feels wrong. *Something* is wrong. I can't shake it.

"It was another clear night," I comment, strolling up to greet the lot of persons I am responsible for.

They look less happy to see me than they did upon finding out Ethan was forced to take my place. I wish Ethan would come back. Having him gone was never my intention.

"What are we even doing anymore?" Ben sighs, throwing his hands out in dramatic exasperation. "I don't want to hunt, *again.* I used to be vegan!"

I pity the luxury of getting to be eighteen and reminiscing about lost choices. Instead, I'm going on twenty-five and burdened with making snap neck decisions that only sometimes pan out how I want them to.

*Fucking hell.*

I shrug. "My bad. Fine, don't. You and Lukas can fetch water today for the livestock from the riverside."

"Oh, fuck you!" Lukas groans, flipping his stub of a middle finger high enough for me to see. "Let 'em be thirsty! See if I care that we don't have milk for cheese."

Being First-in-Command somehow makes these misgivings easier to ignore than when I was Second-in-Command and being harassed by the whole group. I simply don't care. I don't have the time to care what they think. They can quit and go hungry if they don't appreciate the orders.

"Complacency means we are safe right now." I reply. "Be grateful we aren't picking up corpses and do your job."

Dennis erupts with sarcastic fits of laughter, fitted with a wooden leg wobbling in the dirt to help him balance as a new amputee, and rolling his eyes, puffing on a cigarette.

"Sure, sure," he chuckles, slapping his bad leg. "But I've got myself so much time, I'll prob'ly go on by The Center, and give Celestyn a good ole dickin."

*Oh, shit!*

Everyone else breaks off into the riotous laughter of jackals, yelling and clapping and howling at one another. Dennis takes it as the encouragement to carry on, to take it one step further.

"Ya know what, boy? While I'm rootin' around for pussy on over there, I could scooch on to our good ole Second-inCommand's room, and give 'er some of the good shit too. I bet the freak's a real freak, don't ya think? I might be a bit much for her though. Split 'er in two, if ya know what I mean."

Everything goes dark.

I feel my eyes twitch, my arms tense. But I don't feel myself act. I don't recall my brain commanding my body to move. I am blinded by searing, scalding light aproning over my field of vision... and when it lifts, I find myself holding Dennis by the front of his shirt, hammering into his face with my balled up fist while streams of blood spurt from his crooked nose and cracked lips. The whites of his left eye have ruptured into crimson flowers the harder I hit, and he shrieks, scratching at my tender hip injury when the cracks at my jaw don't pan out.

The team around us has fallen dead silent, uncomfortable, and Melody breathing heavy in the doorway once more at the commotion. I fling Dennis onto the ground, flexing my bruising fingers and knuckles. It was a rash decision that I shouldn't have made.

But it felt *damn good.*

*So damn good.*

"Hey!" Dennis shouts, sputtering through the facet of blood he leaks. I face him at the pitiful noise, shaking my hand at my side. "What the fucking hell, boy? What the fuck was that fer?"

I don't answer, vocally, thinking it all over.

*What the fuck was that for?*

Ben and Paul rush to Dennis' aid. I can hear his wooden leg find footing, crunching dirt beneath his feet, approaching me fast as he yells.

"Yer gonna regret that fucking shit!" He sputters through swelling lips. "Ya lookin to get fucked up over the tiny bitch? Now I'll actually have to fuck 'er to prove a—"

Another twitch.

I clock him straight in his already broken nose, watching him crumple to the ground like a wet paper plane, and kicking him in the ribs so hard, he loses his breath.

"Talk," my voice is hoarse with rage, but loud enough everyone can hear, "and I'll fucking do it again. I'm done hearing about it."

He grunts, wheezing. The blood gushing from his nose like an expensive fountain catches at the rear of his throat, and he chokes, trying to find his voice.

"She might as well be dead," he tests through the pain, and I follow through on my promise, catching him in the gut. Dennis groans, whimpers, and still manages to mouth curled in the fetal position. "She never...shows up."

The rest of the team has chosen to separate themselves from Dennis, looking any other direction as if he weren't here at all. I want to cave the man's skull in, take my dagger and ram it into the base of his throat and out the other side. But I pull my gentler side into focus. Taking a deep breath, I run my hands through my messy brown hair.

"She isn't dead." I remain firm. "And she is *your* superior. So show a little respect for women in general. Go to The Center. Get cleaned up. Fuck Celestyn, if she'll let your trash fire of a face near her. But after that, get the hell out to the fucking forest, and do your goddamn job before I finish what I've started here."

It is the first time no one answers back, thinking they're being funny. Dennis' newest partner shoulders his brand-new bundle of shame up off the ground, and everyone splits to do their jobs as I have commanded. The power is almost a sickening rush, blowing over me and giving me chills from the tip of my spine and down my legs.

There is *no boy.*

*No bitch.*

Just, compliance.

I break from the scene, hand sore but having quenched its blood thirst for the late morning. I wander away from the forest where I would have taken Addie if she was present, opting for the place where the old village stood instead.

There isn't much use for me today, and if I were a less angry person, I would have sent everyone home. But scamming them out of a day's pay also felt cruel when all should be stockpiling for the future. It is important to prepare for the difficult when things are easy, because the worst is yet to come.

The worst is always just ahead. I'm not so easily fooled.

Out in the weeds, I wade through thorn thickets and tough rocks in places where fields had been planted years and years ago, vines still climbing carved wooden posts bearing small green tomatoes no one would be brave enough to eat. Sticks snap beneath my shoes, textured leaves grasping at my cheeks when I brush them by as I cut a good path with my dagger to my destination and leave a way for me to return.

I don't know a whole hell of a lot about the older village, if I am being truthful to myself. I am aware that it stood here at one time, and was centered around Master Amadeus' pre-built tower rather than the unused Center. Outside of rumors, it isn't understood why they moved, but when they did, they picked up and fled further uphill like it made all the difference.

The tower stayed, however. Amadeus stayed, as if he has no fear at all of what comes for him in the night. And maybe he doesn't. Perhaps the rumors are true.

He could be a "good" Ravager, if there is such a creature, that intends to protect humanity from his own kind. I'll believe it when I see it, but I can't exclude the possibility.

The one clear fact from the remnants of our fallen brethren is that the people preceding us were much better builders. Their homes are constructed sturdier, with superior material to keep people out that weren't invited in. Stone and metal were their go-to choice for housing means, and most people in Limbo now are too fearful to come this far out to take what they need of it. But I take as much as my hands can carry, snatching every opportunity I have to reinforce my home. My door definitely requires a touch up, among other things, so I get to work on the initial house I approach.

I remember it being harder the first time I stooped this low in comparison to now. I would come upon an old house, and I would look inside for items I could keep, allowing the guilt to swell up inside me as I did.

Parts of me would wonder, would question the necessity and anything else it could conjure in the brew of insanity.

*Who lived in this house*, it would antagonize.

*Were these people nice?*

*Friends? More than friends?*

*Did they get stupid?*

I climb on to a window ledge, gripping the metal overhang and hoisting myself up on top of the roof. As I army crawl my way up, my foot swings, shattering the glass, and snagging my jeans as I tenderly maneuver my way free, wedging myself high atop the home. From my pocket, I pull a makeshift hammer I had the single blacksmith craft me during my first two months in Limbo. I work to pull free any nails used to bind the sheets of metal together, counting them after I remove the first cluster. There are six sheets in total, half my size and just heavy enough for me to carry on my own.

But the inside of the home glares at me through the tangled web of support beams still holding me up.

It is a bit more sophisticated than our caveman huts, set with polished wood countertops and cabinets molded from the ashy white wood surrounding us that has stood the test of time thanks to a roof that keeps the rain out most days. The floors match the two other assemblies, dull but fit together without rivets or indentations. There is even a quaint table off to the side with three chairs, and homemade bowls set out.

A soft smile tugs are the corners of my mouth, wishing I were able to snag these too, and turning to scoot off the roof to the ground right as something else catches my eyes on the floor. A tiny, pale object resting below the table.

A self-made, burlap doll in a red dress cut from an old shirt smiles at me with a black, inky u-shaped mouth. It is coated in a layer of dust, pleading with beady black eyes to be found and rescued from its abandon. I slide the metal sheets I've disassembled to the grass and shimmy after it, veering around the side to the entrance and opening the door to the ghosts of our past.

It is a haunting, soulless place. My feet are heavy, thundering echoes inside, and I lean forward to pick up the doll right as an abrupt screech sends me skittering to the back wall, a small, iridescent dragon with the wings of a dragonfly prowling at the end of the hall. Growling and hissing.

This is a light area of The Dome, but it isn't the lightest. There shouldn't be magical creatures this close to home so early in the day, and I glance around. The reptilian asshole snorts, primal snarls deeper than that of a dog rattling at the base of its throat. I pocket the doll, racing for the exit as the gallop of its charge catches up behind me. I slam the heavy door shut in its face, listening to the resounding thud and a resulting shriek, wings flapping up to the broken window but unable to reach the ledge.

It is a fledgling, which means it hasn't mastered flight yet. So how did it get inside here at all?

I don't stick around to find out, hauling up the metal sheets and lumbering under their weight to the main village where I am safer. As I enter town, I am stopped by a familiar face staring off into the distant tower of Master Amadeus, studying its silhouette against the horizon.

"Hey, Zoey," I say from underneath my hard-won prizes. "What's up?"

She starts, a jolt rippling through her body as if I had tied live wires around her extremities and let them rip. It doesn't take the frown from her face upon seeing me, only raising her guard higher than I can climb.

It is understandable.

The woman is overdue. Scary overdue, and miserable, and enormous despite being so skinny. I don't know how she is sustaining a baby being that hungry for so long. She looks so...so fragile. Like a stick with an oversized cocoon suctioned to its midsection.

"Fucking nothing," she replies, crossing her arms over her belly. "What the fuck is up with you?"

I glance at the metal through wisps of my own shaggy hair, managing a weak smile.

"Reinforcement. No time like now to make sure I'm ready for the next attack, you know?"

"I get that." She laughs a bit. "All too fucking well considering I had to put our door back up."

I chuckle a bit too, apologetic, but finding the real humor is lost on me. The hurricane of disaster will hit us at full force at some point, and anyone who denies it is a liar.

Zoey would never deny it.

"Are you hungry?" I ask, shuffling next to her. "I need to drop this crap off, but I would be happy to buy you some lunch. If you'll let me, of course."

There is a reluctance hidden here. She doesn't want to say yes and appear like she needs anything from anyone else. I get it. But there is an undeniable fact that since Addie left house, she is struggling to make ends meet and chow the way she needs. Especially when she is in and out of the hospital.

"Yeah, okay, I guess."

A smile breaks just a tiny bit across her face, and we walk together to my home where I lay the metal up against my fortress to handle later.

I change my clothes while she waits outside, cleaning up with spare water collected in a bucket I keep out in the back room. Time has flown by in all my running about, inching closer to early evening by the time I am able to bring her into the markets for lunch or dinner, whichever she preferred it to be called.

I have always tried my best to be a gentleman around women, the way I was raised to be. When I was a boy who could barely see over the table's edge without a booster seat, I would have a lot of dinner dates with my mom where she would pretend to let me pay for the meal when we were through, and help clean up after. I'd like to think it rubbed off well.

I've strived every day of these recollections to be the kind of man she raised me to be in spite of everything willing me not to, and I don't think Zoey has ever been subject to that kind of person. Not since being awake, but maybe it goes deeper than that, too.

I could never see her in a romantic way by any means, but it is an honest belief of mine that every girl should understand what it's like to be treated with dignity and respect more than once in their lives where so many other men lack.

Zoey walks excessively close to me as we go through the markets, fearful and anxious of the villagers, and more so of what they might do or say. But for the first time since the night after our incident, I don't care. Let them do what they do, or say what they please, and they can see what happens next.

I wave as we pass people by, drawing attention to our duo, but letting her set the pace for conversation so she isn't too far outside her comfort zone. She doesn't speak at all until we hit the local butchery, and even then, it is granted only to me.

"It's been...real fucking quiet lately," she tries while I pick out some cuts. "I'm scared, I guess."

I don't want to lie to her, but I don't want to tell the entire truth either—a bad habit of mine.

"Everyone needs a break sometimes. Even the Ravagers. They'll be back."

"I don't fucking want them to be," she replies faster than I can finish. "I just...I don't know..."

I take the meat I've ordered from the butcher, exchanging him cash and moving on down the road, feeling the dry skin of her arm brush against mine. She's more than afraid—she's terrified, and I am not sure how to delegate appropriate comfort to a woman that has been assaulted.

"I understand," I tell her in lieu of physical contact. "You are not alone."

"I just wish there was a fucking way out," Zoey says. "I can't shake the feeling that we aren't supposed to fucking be here."

*You and me both.*

I change the subject, attempting to direct her somewhere happier for the time being. In place of furthering our conversation, I ask her to pick out some healthy-looking potatoes for me, and carrots to go with our dinner. In light of our time spent together, I let her pick out some strawberries for dessert as well. On our way home, I make one more stop to buy some fresh milk as a treat to drink instead of water.

Zoey is fidgety the entire way to my place, letting me lead the way and inching at my heels. I try to lighten the mood with more positive conversation. Things that inspire hope.

"I'm looking forward to playing music again...well, more often, when we figure out the mystery to this place. What about you?"

She sighs, racing to the area in front of my home as soon as it comes into view and spreading out while I unload our meal into the tiny fire pit I have made to cook over.

"It's fucking different for me," she tells me, watching me pull out the materials to kick start a fire. "I'm not the fucking minor I was when I first got here. I was really young when I got knocked up. Now I'm...nineteen? Maybe even twenty? I don't even fucking know anymore because I've been too scared to pay attention. But I know we haven't gotten any damn closer to the answer you're talking about in all of that time, Aidan. The mystery is just bullshit."

I don't bother arguing with her. I let her simmer instead. I want her to relax from all the things that keep her up at night and impossible choices she has had to make, not agitate them further by demanding she tell me her life plans. That is up to her.

I make a game plan for how long to cook the food, filling up a pot with enough water to cover the meat and potatoes and wishing I had a bit of salt to throw over it. If I were smart, I would stew the strawberries in a different pot so they get done around the same time, but Zoey has already dug into them. There is no way I am going to deny a pregnant woman a *damn* thing. Being pregnant in a forest full of violent murders and suffering the indignities she has, Zoey has deserved all the good for so long. She never earned an ounce of the neglect she received.

The sun rises and then sets low in the horizon. We eat and laugh, letting the time waste by. Zoey tells me things I never knew about her, personal things I wish I had, but never asked. She explains that her mom died when she was a little girl, and her dad spiraled into steep depression and alcoholism. Her friends in the pictures at home are actually a year older than her, like sisters. They supported her when there was no food in the house and helped raise money so that she could start college. She tells me that she never had a boyfriend in her life, but she lost her virginity at fifteen during a house party on a dare.

*A damn stupid dare*, she makes sure to add.

It makes sense more than ever when she says she never really had the chance to live life the way it should be lived, and that she feels like she will never be able to live it how she wants.

I let her ramble on for some time before I put out our fire in the growing dark and start walking her home, bringing my guitar to play and my bow...just in case. We pass Celestyn on our way through town, and she ducks her head in an angry shame that leaves me wondering whether or not she actually fucked Dennis, or if she thought I beat him on her behalf. She does not say a word to me, nonetheless.

When we get to Zoey's home close to the edge of space between The Center and the village, I give her the leftovers from our day of fun. She needs them more, and I've had my fill. It is strange to see her smile this way, but refreshing.

"No one has ever spent the day with me like this." She grins, sitting at the opening of her home and staring at the stars beginning to peek out from the dark blue sky.

"Addie has spent a lot of time with you," I point out, taking a seat and playing away on my instrument while I can.

The song is stuck in my head, the one I have been playing since the day we met. I can't seem to get rid of it no matter how hard I try. It's just so...solemn. I don't want to be solemn. I don't want to be like the tattoo hidden on my upper arm of a Gothic ballerina playing the piano with lines of notes erupting from the top of the instrument down my forearm.

But I can't stop.

I have to see it to completion. And every time I play, all I can see is her face instead.

Addie's.

The night I played it for her she smiled, as though it were the best piece she had ever heard. I watched her body relax to the melody of it, mismatched eyes drooping, pale lips releasing a gentle sigh.

I push this image from my mind.

"It was never fucking like that," Zoey finally answers, her voice laced with disappointment. "She is a good...protector? But she never tried to fucking know me. We are both projects to each other."

"You never gave her the chance to know you," I retort. "You've been burned so many times in this shit stain of a village, you don't know how to give people a chance anymore. It only works against you in cases like Addie. She's loyal."

Zoey claps unexpectedly, smirking. "Sounds like you have the fucking hots for her."

I stop for a moment, and then repeat the same sounds I have been playing.

"It's not like that."

"O-kay," she drawls. "But I'm not deaf. I fucking hear the

stories Celestyn tells the others in the halls. You don't sound like you fucking hate the bitch all that much."

"I...don't hate her."

Quiet.

"Neither do I."

"Then why did you kick her out?" I ask, regretting the question as soon as it comes out.

Zoey goes rigid, and I feel terrible.

"I was fucking afraid," she admits. "But...I told her I was sorry. I asked her to fucking live with me again. She said yes as long as I showed her the silver marks on my back."

I nod, remembering the commotion about those brands, and repeating the chorus of the song I've played, staring into the distance. Into the trees, all around us, and the lightning bugs flickering, yellow like traffic lights. Warning.

*Slow down. Trouble ahead.*

"Just...don't ask her to come back because you need her for some sort of financial gain."

"Fucking what now?"

Another bad idea.

"She commits to the downtrodden, Zoey." I try to put it more eloquently. "She would die for you if it meant she did her job."

There is a look of hurt written across her expression, but a small, willful smile finds its way back to her lips.

"I would fucking die for her, too," she whispers.

It is pained, but it is genuine.

I can appreciate that.

We sit in the mellow swell of my music a bit longer as other people buzz with chatter out the front of their houses, enjoying the fresh night air. But I notice it.

It seems like nothing at first—a figment of my imagination, red and blue flickers of light sparking vibrant flashes like fireworks at the top of The Center.

Just twinkles. Zaps.

But it can't be.

Vibrations rock the ground as an explosion of sound lights up dark figures on what remains of the glass ceiling—shattering it into a burst of crystalline fragments like glittering dust in the air, and bending the iron bars that held it inward into stunted, melted lines.

At the tree line I can see humanoid figures are on the move, sweeping through in organized lines and units. They bypass homes entirely on their march. Zoey freezes in panic. I shove my guitar into her open arms, cramming her behind the door. I look at her from behind my glasses.

"Push everything against your door," I tell her. "And hide under the hatch."

I slam the entry closed before she can protest, turning around and heaving in a deep breath.

I have to be fast.

I have to be...brave.

*Fuck. Fuck. Fuck.*

# CHAPTER TWENTY-NINE
## ADABELLE

I SKIP AHEAD A FEW PAGES IN THIS BOOK, SKIMMING SOME articles, and ignoring others altogether. I promise myself I'll go back and read through it where I can, when I can, but I can't handle any more information about the imprinting right now, as it happens to be a subject that covers a large section of the dark elven culture having to do with their family bonds.

Their families appear to be everything to them, and it is clear to me that they almost always stay close in housing or go as far as to live in the same home as parents or siblings. It is as easy as adding on to the structure they already inhabit.

I had to stop reading it out loud to Simone a long time ago, choosing to chirp up to her here and there instead to remind her I haven't left. Rape isn't an appropriate conversation topic for anyone, but she wouldn't understand why it is so terrible—if she could hear me.

I don't want her to have to understand. Ever.

Although, if I want to be technical, I suppose to the dark elves this is not rape. It is their own right, in their delusions. Their partners are considered a part of their own soul, a personal connection that they adore. Consummations are an act of this love unto them, the most dedicated, flamboyant display of it to be exact, and aggressively passionate. It binds the two spirits for the eternity to come, and solidifies a marriage preceding a public ceremony.

Not that any of that excludes it from what it really is. From what humanity knows it is. Because it doesn't require their partner's consent to pursue, and therefore, it is criminal.

Interestingly enough, however, the men also cannot survive without their fated partners after the completed process of imprinting, according to this author. Grace. It is a very literal life bond to them. If lady love happens to perish, the corresponding male will just shut off. And society allows him to.

He is considered unsustainable following the death of his spouse, and he will wither in an elongated depression spiral that ends in fatality. For this reason, most men of the race agree it is easier to die by sword in battle, or by torture, than it is to endure the death of a spouse. Taking a spouse is an uncalculated risk, an accumulation of extreme vulnerabilities, making the creatures overprotective and hostile to strangers.

It is the one part I can salvage of them. And it gives me several ideas on how to eliminate them entirely if granted the opportunity. It would bring on more casualties than I'd care for. Innocent casualties, if I took the easy way out. But I refuse to believe other women haven't thought of this, if what is happening to them according to the text is true.

I *want* to help the victims involved in this tragedy without becoming one. There just isn't a cut and dry answer that I can visualize yet that doesn't involve punishing the recipients of the problem.

I move on to the second half of the book. The one written by Ceridwen Rose. Her handwriting is a bit of a mess compared to Grace's, the scrawl of unfamiliar figures is sloppy and smashed together, small. But it is translated in the same handwriting, titled *The Fae*.

*I wither in this place where I had once lived—where all the Fae had once lived. I should have turned when I saw him there. If I had chosen to run with Ronin, I might have made it out. We might have made it out.*

*Ronin would still be alive.*

*And now, all I have left are the journal entries of another woman that sat on this bed before me—though she had done it on her own accord.*

*I am a prisoner here. My wrists are shackled to the posters so I can rest my arms but never leave, and I have been stripped of all my dignities. Unable to walk. Unable to fly.*

*It is due to circumstance that I think it is more important than ever to bring to light the third, and final, Master Race created by Our Great Mother and her enemy, The Nameless King. In case these bystanders of spite do not survive The Nameless King and his heirs.*

*I want the future generations to know that the Fae existed. That we were alive, and sentient, and kind.*

*Readers should know that we were slaughtered like lambs, torn from our mothers and fathers as wee children. There were unspeakable experimentations performed upon our bodies while awake, feeling ourselves being ripped apart just so we can be tossed aside to be processed later when we are dead. When we are eaten.*

*I could be the last of the pure Fae to ever survive at this point, for I do not know if Kai has made it out of this castle alive. If he has, it is my only hope that we will stand the test of time yet.*

*I am sorry to report, first, that Grace's story is one that ends in tragedy. She has been long dead at this time, and thus able to give life to my own tragedy that began both before, and as soon as The Nameless King laid eyes on me for the first time.*

*Grace of the Crows was a miserable being, ostracized from her own people for what she was, and begging death from the King and Our Great Mother. But the Nameless King had loved her in a kind way, never imprinting, but allowing her to live in close proximity.*

*They ultimately conceived a child together in their flings at attempting a true bond from what I understand, something that upset Our Great Mother quite dearly.*

*Our Great Mother murdered the poor girl in rage, cutting the baby from her womb and leaving it on this very bed, taking the corpse with her. Like a butcher, she chopped Grace into segments, making the ultimate sacrifice as a creator of love to bring forth the original members of the Fae from the individual body parts—her ultimate creation a rare, extraordinary Fae. Our King, Kai. A moon faery.*

*The Fae would be known as the most magically efficient creatures, you see. We are humanoid creatures smaller than the dark elves, only perhaps six and a half feet at our tallest, but usually measuring a bit smaller. Daintier.*

*Though we put on muscle mass better than our dark elven counterparts, we are not as quick. Not as observant. Our ears are somewhat less keen, and the point shorter to our head. Our pupils are not in a permanent state of vertical slits and may appear round at most hours. We are friendlier at first sight, and are greater magical entities known to this world.*

*Because of all of this, we no longer require the primitive urge to fornicate for reproductive purposes. It is all an endeavor of love, and magical strain, and nature...and a LOT of protein to sustain ourselves for the grueling process. Nonetheless, there is not a child born to our kind by accident.*

*Until now.*

*Well, soon.*

*I suppose this is only a tragedy to the Fae though, in a way it was not for the sprites that came prior. I'm not guaranteed to survive through a non-magically induced childbirth, as Fae never have completed a physical pregnancy without death following. The only piece I can take away from this is at least if I should perish, The Nameless King will inevitably fall as well so that we will rot together.*

*His death should be my gift to the world, if it happens.*

I close the journal yet again, promising myself that next time I will do it sooner. I can't handle the tragedy alongside my own. It is too much.

Was this person real? Is she a joke?

Was she part of the history here? Or fantasy?

Grace claimed the dark elves were kind, happy creatures. Celebratory and generous. She went as far as to become purposely intimate with their unbonded king who never imprinted but loved her anyway.

He must have been devastated to find her how he had. Or to not find her at all.

Ceridwen paints these creatures differently, claiming them as cruel, vicious monsters. But her own "Great Mother" was the person who dismembered Grace to give this glorious race life. To give their king, Kai, life.

Grace was a sacrifice. But was it a sacrifice she chose, if at one point she had wanted to die anyway?

The Nameless King changed following the death of Grace, and much of the text between what I can figure out seems to indicate Ceridwen was raped in the same way Zoey had been. Skimming through later pages for context confirms she lives through her labor, but it wasn't necessarily a happy ending. And she never kills the King. Which leads to the better question of if The Nameless King is still king.

Is he in charge of the atrocities being put upon us?

I huff a sigh, eyes growing tired from reading in dim candlelight, and tattooed hands still squeezing to Simone's cold, limp ones.

I've hardly let her go all day.

Her condition has been deteriorating at a much faster pace, and Celestyn has become frightened to push more fluids or honey or medicines in her wake periods than what we can get away with. She could choke, she says, due to the bewilderment of her conscious stages.

But Simone's seizures have increased without it, to the point we might be looking at brain damage. There was an instance this afternoon when she opened her eyes to see me and cycled without delay into seizure. The girl is all but skin and bones now, and I can't leave her like this. I can't make myself leave her like this. She needs a person here, more than anyone else in this whole godforsaken village.

So here I am. Waiting.

I rub my thumb across the protruding knuckles of her tiny fingers, using my free hand to push the disgusting journal into the top of my backpack. Our candles are close to going dark in this empty chasm where souls fly free after hard fought battles, and the water vase is bone dry. Simone could use a few wet rags as a subtle sponge bath, and some potential fluids if there was a miracle that allowed her to open her eyes. I wonder if she could ever forgive me if I got up to stretch my legs and retrieve a few necessities.

Could I, if I missed anything?

Usually, patients and late visitors are forbidden from roaming these halls at night for our own safety. But the evenings and stays have been so mild lately, no longer laden with danger. I hear quite a few people stretching their legs throughout the dark hours, talking and groaning. Tonight is a bit more quiet than those prior, but it hardly seems anyone could give less of a damn. What can it hurt?

I give Simone one more really good squeeze, and a smile.

"I'll be right down the hall, okay?" I whisper at the edge of her ear. "I'm just going to grab a few things for your belly...and maybe a little for mine, too."

It is hard to leave her, but I open the door, slipping out into the brighter, candlelit hallway. I take a deep breath right away, gulping down the fresher scent of better, more consistent ventilation while my legs thank me for allowing them this brief stretch.

I thank me for it too.

I could sure use it, going from intense cardio on the daily to absolutely nothing in an instant. If I can find my way home again soon, to my *real* home, the first thing I am going to do is order food from the closest place that delivers and sleep on the couch with the television blasting for the next week and a half.

I stumble, left foot just a touch numb and tingly from sitting on it for several hours, arms flailing out to the side to catch myself on the wall. There is a light moaning coming from several open doors across the hallway, smears of dried blood painting the path inside two of them in wavy finger lengths. Looking in each direction, I can't find the exact origin, droplets splattering across the floor and sprinkling over each inch of flooring.

*Maybe someone got a little clumsy. Fell or something. With a knife?*

At the caved desk, I duck underneath to dig out the supplies in the ample boxes packed in the residual space. Since the attack that snapped it down the middle like a twig in winter, Celestyn has had to opt to store most of the content in an empty patient room to be secure, but she keeps a couple day's supply out in direct reach at all times. I turn my head to the left, locking on to a bucket of fresh water hauled in from the well, or the river, that I can use to presoak the rags in, dipping the water vase in for a hearty take away. Behind it, there is a touch more honey hiding with the medicine that Celestyn has been giving Simone, and I grab both, piling it on my small tower of supplies. With folded rags, towels, and two spare pillows, it is difficult to remain steady, but I don't want to make an extra trip or keep Simone waiting any longer.

Holding air in my cheeks, I use my legs like springs, popping upright and teetering behind the mass of crap that I've accumulated in the last ten minutes with a satisfied huff. I am aching to turn back down the hall when a bleak shadow catches my attention, haunting the space where the doors have been erected into their original place once more. Except the doors are completely open, letting in the fresh air I had inhaled earlier like it were my last breath, moonlight streaming silver beams heavy with dust inside making me wonder how I never noticed it were open to begin.

I choke at the sight of it coming into view, in its subtle opening, fingers clutching to the wooden edges, one of *them.*

The Ravagers.

Dark elves.

Killers.

Rapists.

He is taller than the original I had witnessed—head half-shaved and dark brown hair braided over his right shoulder dawning pale, white rings that rattle in a dull clunk, quite dissimilar to regular jewelry. His clothes match this eerie presentation, neat and militant, but...old timey. Lightweight black armor steels in intricate designs over his chest and underlying tunic, spreading to protect much of his extremities, and ending in armored boots that glint in the torchlight at the other side of the lobby.

I swallow, meeting his sharp green eyes and shaking. Quivering.

His foot takes less than a step forward at my acknowledgment of his presence, and I let everything crash to the floor, the vase smashing into a million pieces as I crunch over them, racing to reach Simone. The Ravager is just as quick on me, weight careening against the desk as he jumps over it in an effort to reach me like a cat swiping at his prey.

The whole building quakes as if in response, but it is more than that. It is a thunderous roar, rocking me off my feet, and rolling me along the floor as The Center ignites in a bright, red fury. The Ravager is not far behind, perfectly balanced, maneuvering about crumbling stone and flashing a dark blue light at the small of his palm, burning like the flames of a gas fire. He throttles the flame my direction in a larger blast that grows the further away it becomes, and I bob away, legs scraping across the rough floor while I acquire my balance and rush for Simone's room.

I can't leave her to this for my sake. I have to get us both out, somehow.

A few more typhoons of fire are swung my direction, a deep crimson hose of it grazing my fingers as I slip into the room with an agonizing screech. The skin bubbles around my nail beds, swelling and sizzling and sparking as if I were disgusting and greasy enough to actually catch fire.

I want to throw up from the pain, crying out through my teeth to drown out the noise that is overcome by the bloodcurdling screams of everyone else. I wrap the injury in one of Simone's semi-damp rags, pulling on my backpack and cradling Simone's limp body against my own. I gather a bed sheet to tie her to me, fast, like a papoose. But there is barely time.

The Ravager stands in the doorway, guarding our exit as smoke fills the room and hallways in toxic waves of black. It won't be breathable soon. It almost isn't now, though he seems to have no problem with it.

I scurry to the closest corner of the room, breathing shallow and fast, Simone groaning softly in my collar bone as I cradle her tiny, fragile figure. I don't know what else to do, panicking and holding my hands out in defense.

"P...please..." I cough. "She's just a girl. Don't hurt us."

He rocks onward, slow and methodical. Like a snake, he weaves around stone that drops from the ceiling, jouncing ever closer, drawing his sword from its sheath in a decisive swish. It is pointing close to my neck, just above where I have Simone's face buried.

"I don't..." The Ravager presses to the skin of my throat to silence me. I am terrified to so much as inhale the wrong way, stilling my whole body in response. "No..."

He speaks in our tongue, cold and unfeeling.

"This will be a mercy for your kind."

And he swings back.

I scuttle backward as far as I can, shimmying up on my tiptoes, and spinning toward him so that his weapon cannot catch wind against the force of my brick like backpack. I am not as fast as I should be with Simone in my arms, grunting at the impact that rips the fabric and contents within. I use my dry hands to grasp the searing door, charging forward and slamming it shut on him with one arm before he has time to react. I don't have the key ring, so it won't slow him down much, but it should hurt like a bitch to open.

At every inch of The Center I can see beyond the smoke, red

and blue flames rage without mercy. Bodies pile and catch fire, enemies all over ripping doors off their hinges and tossing them aside like paper to be consumed by the greedy, extraordinarily hot monster they have made.

I duck my head at the sound of the elf beating on the other side of the door. He yells loud enough for his men to hear him, and there is a deafening roar as the door flies off its hinges, battering into the opposing wall.

The smoke is growing thicker, providing me better cover, but also leaving me to run blind on broken glass, crumbled stone, and something firm, but peculiar, that gives just a little when my shoes push on it.

I cough, hoarse and hard. So hard I nearly vomit, gasping but receiving nothing. I feel about with my shoulder, guessing where I am in the hallway, and slamming into something immovable. Hard. Exceptionally hot.

I jerk away, shrieking. Panting. From my hand, I remove the damp rag and lay it over Simone's mouth, hoping it would screen the worst of the poisonous clouds of air until we could make it out of here. I no longer know how the Ravagers are thriving inside the building all things considering, unless I account for magic.

But how?

I skirt about what can only be a door, trudging forward as another inhuman moan sends a piece of ceiling spiraling to the ground around me, catapulting fiery debris skyward in a steamy spray. I race from it as fast as I can, dodging a piece of support beam lumbering to the ground but unable to miss the rock it throttles to the side, smashing and melting into my ankle, bringing me to the ground with it.

As I look up, I can see the night sky being swallowed by a plume of black death, shadows perched atop the melting bars that caged in the glass topping the lobby. I cough, again, wobbling upright and freezing solid as a long blade narrowly misses the tip of my ear.

The scream of the Ravager I had locked away is one of fury

and agitation, rearing to swing once more as adrenaline pumps me forward. In a moment of clarity, I can see the moonlight beaming from the doors ahead of me like a guiding light, glinting. Winking. Beckoning. I race for it, almost blindly, another swing caressing my arm as a rumble overhead brings down another piece of the ceiling.

I yell in panic, lurching ahead faster and unable to tell whether he is still on my trail or not. But I am stopped at the doors, ramming into something both soft and hard, my dry lips cloaked in fabric. I screech, skittering backward as hands catch me around the shoulders and pull me in so that the night air clears a touch of the smoke around us.

"Addie, Addie," Aidan's voice rings at the same time. "It's me, okay? I've got you. I've got you. I won't let anyone hurt you, and I'm here to help. I just need you to be quiet."

I am sobbing, clutching to him like a small child with my free hand not touching Simone, and gasping for fresh air under the dense smoke. Aidan walks with mine and Simone's weight dragging on him like a pack mule, but more careful. Silent. We make it to the free air where dozens upon dozens of soldiers similar to the one that chased me down have gathered about women and children kidnapped from the hospital—a daunting realization overcoming us that we cannot escape to the village this way.

Aidan whips us toward the trees, pursing his lips and rushing fast. We make it to the midnight border of the forest before we notice a lone guard standing at the tree line, nearly running straight into him in our hurry. He is watching the building burn in sick satisfaction, spinning at us with only enough time to say *"He—"* as it is cut short by Aidan ripping his dagger free of its restraints and plummeting it straight through the beast's throat. We are both showered in blood, lips caked in a rich ooze as we jolt over the body, fleeing into the forest as far as our legs can carry.

In total exhaustion, spending what feels like an eternity on my crippling, agonizing injuries, we crash into a heap of dead weight within bushes ripe with berries falling to the ground. I take this moment to untie Simone, removing the cloth from her mouth and heaving in gasps of oxygen, terrified to so much as glance at my ankle.

I lean backward against Aidan instead, tilting my head up to meet his gaze. His hand comes fast at the side of my face to render it motionless, brushing the rawness of my cheek with his thumb as I struggle to find the words I need to say. My chest hitches, lips parting to speak, but his forehead comes down on mine, squeezing me closer, unwilling to relinquish this moment.

So I shut my eyes.

And we sleep.

# CHAPTER THIRTY
## AIDAN

I know what burning flesh smells like.

The odor is cruel and unpleasant, a chasm full of pungent pain that smells of ash and despair. Like something you can reach out and touch, taste in the back of the throat against every will in the body not to.

Because it tastes like memories.

Like gasoline.

I open my eyes to my chest struggling to rise and fall, a weight smelting through it and keeping it heavy. My lungs give way to a series of drool worthy hacks, abdomen trembling and bouncing as I look down to see Addie turned into the fetal position, limp head rolling off my sternum and face blanched. Simone is laid close, half across my lower lap and sunken cheeks buried against my belly and shoulder in Addie's stomach.

Neither of them are moving.

"No," I mumble. "No, no. Addie? Hey, Addie?"

My hand is soft at her shoulders, nudging her dead weight from my almost corpse, a frown deepening at her lack of response, my heart racing. I shake her harder this time, yanking so she is forced to sit upright, slumping into her own chest—or lack thereof. It is here I notice the shallow motions of her continued breathing moving her chin up and down in uneven beats. She rasps at the next, sudden shake, failing to breathe in deep but alive. Her mismatched eyes blink open, finding me with a slight, gentle smile and leaning forward.

I cringe at the hoarse sound of her coughing, retching as her gut slips under her rib cage, gagging so she vomits right beside me. My hand flies to the small of her back at the sound of her whimpering. I offer her some water from my canteen, allowing her to quench her aching throat while she wakes.

"We need to get home, Addie," I tell her after a minute, trying to get her glassy gaze to focus. "It will be safer there...maybe."

The Dome is almost gone. But I can't tell her that yet.

"Where are we?" she mumbles, mouth full of water that runs down her neck in cool, glistening streams. "How'd we get here?"

I almost laugh as she tries to speak through gulps of fluid, tired and weak, but the reality is a stark one that keeps me somber. Addie is confused. Confused on top of being confused, she doesn't understand what is happening.

She keeps muttering while she drinks, choking on the water that I provided her until I remove it from her needy hands that are far too weak to maintain their grip. Her voice is a bray, a rough whine, leaving me not quite certain what it is she is trying to say, and pretending to understand all the same. It will probably take some time for her to feel completely normal again. She's going to hurt quite a bit, for sure. The real question will be if she can walk well enough to get back.

Last night, it was a limp.

I give her a few more moments to sober up. Wake up. I'm not very awake either, and I am more than stunned we lasted the night after our unexpected murder to get out here. Their point of exit must have been the same way they came in, with little time to spare to hunt the fugitives who took the life of their ill-suspecting comrade.

But their plans went deeper than that. Just to where, though, I am unsure. It sends chills crawling along the curve of my spine to reflect upon.

Addie sways into my chest following a loss of balance, wheezing and quivering. I stay this way for a selfish second, arm coming up around her, touching her small, sagging shoulders. The scars bringing texture over them are smooth, though they don't look smooth. They just...

"Hey," I whisper into her sooty hair. It smells like death. "Hey, we have to go."

"Where?" She rocks her head, hitting my chin.

But her eyes don't open. I barely hear her.

"Home."

I want to be patient.

"I want to go home," she cries, and I cradle her, a tiny bit. "I want my mom. Can I have my mom?"

I shush her, reeling us back and forth in gentle motions as Simone rolls along my knees. We need to check her too, soon, but I can't let Addie alone like this yet. She's not in her right mind. She doesn't even know what she's telling me, or why.

"Can you walk?" I ask her, recalling last night.

I haven't tried to look at her feet or her ankle thus far, but I know it is coming. Now that the adrenaline has worn off, this could go one of two very grave ways, and I can't afford any scenario that doesn't end with all three of us making it home to Limbo.

Addie nods her head, however, but I'm not sure she remembers what she is moving her head to. It is absent, in a way, empty and the movements of a person that is only a shell. She is still crying, too, hands feeling up her own arms and touching the smooth, malformed scars where she reaches her shoulder, brushing my fingers. I pull away in a sharp intake, shifting upright and stiff.

"I was in a fire once," she mumbles, releasing her own

shoulder and gripping her calf. Squeezing it. Palpating it.

"Addie, listen to me..." I start. She isn't saying things that make sense. She is damaged, and puzzled, and I am growing unsure as to how I am going to get us back into Limbo like this. I might need help. "I can carry Simone, Addie, but I need to know you can walk."

She retracts a leg toward her body, whimpering as she tries to pull the shoe off to no avail. Beneath her black leggings, it is difficult to tell much of anything, but I slide Simone onto the grass with care so I can help, covering her tiny body with my plaid overshirt when I am sure she is breathing. Together, Addie and I tug the shoe off, and I use Addie's dagger in her backpack to sheer up the side of her leggings so we are granted clearance to the lower half of her leg.

She does not look me in the face for this, trembling and skin flushing dark red. I am unable to tell if it hurts simply to that extreme, or if she is embarrassed. The skin on her feet and around the region of her ankles and lower leg are much more distorted than that on her arms. Still scarred, but worse, they are divoted and lacking muscle tissue in spots. Her feet are gnarled and broken from years of dancing to top it off, toenails black and painful looking.

I only cut the fabric to the point where her skin has room to breathe for this reason, the swelling more than obvious even if it weren't for the imprint the hems of her clothing made in her skin. It is atrocious. She won't be able to bend it even if she can stand up. How we didn't have to cut her shoe off is beyond me, not to mention I am now noticing the deep, blackened blisters over her fingers.

Addie swallows, peeking down to it.

"I can walk," she wheezes.

"We..." I hesitate, trying not to linger. "We have to get back to Celestyn so she can take care of this. It is serious, Addie. What if it is broken? Not to mention Simone...I mean...Christ..."

Her bottom lip pushes out in a crippling pout, and I stop, helping her upright, letting her lean against a tree for balance while I pick up Simone. The kid weighs more than she looks, but still...

light as a feather. A bag of bones, and nothing more. I let her keep the shirt for warmth, stumbling in pace with my partner toward town in a daze, Addie occasionally reaching out for me as a balance and growing more and more conscious as she does. Limbo isn't the home she wants to return to when she speaks of it, but there are no other choices left.

When we enter through the trees, two figures catch our sight at the front of the ruins where The Center used to stand. Celestyn turns at the sounds of brush shifting and parting, Zoey spinning quick after her. They shuffle to us without delay, yelling words that are incoherent to my mind as Celestyn's hands reach for the sides of my face, cupping it gently. Frantic.

"I'm so happy you're okay," she whispers against my mouth, our lips almost touching as she stands on the points of her toes. "I was so worried. You had me so worried. I can't even explain..."

I can't help but feel Zoey's shadow looming over our interaction, judging. Her sharp, down-to-earth eyes say it all. That she doesn't approve. But she doesn't motion toward either of us, as if she expects someone else to comfort Addie.

Celestyn jerks away from me when I don't reassure her. Or speak. At all. Immediately, this turns her attentions to Addie, rearing back and slapping her so hard that the Ravagers can hear the crack miles away by this point.

"This is your fault!" She yells.

Addie stumbles drunkenly, holding her raw and blistering crimson cheek, all the more dazed. Her backpack weighs her down, and I move in behind her, using myself as a crutch to keep her on her feet.

"Uncalled for!" I snap as Zoey lurches forward, fists clenched and rearing back herself.

"It is not!" Celestyn argues, wiping her own face free of tears. "Don't you all see? She's an animal. She drew you in to come save her. An entirely reckless, criminal beast! You could have died, and you have nearly died on multiple occasions just being around her."

"I didn't ask for help," Addie fires back in her most coherent voice, keeping me from spitting out the very same words. "Celestyn, you're so smart, but you're being a moron right now."

She rubs her face where it blooms in specks of blood, blistered apart from where Celestyn struck her atop the places the fire had burned her raw just for being too close.

"I've been with Simone. Nonstop," Addie continues. "For days now, I have barely had a bite to eat tending to the needs of another person. I didn't have time to come crying for Aidan to save me—who I haven't seen in just as long. And why would I? I didn't know what was going on until I was being chased leisurely down the hall by a psychopath."

Celestyn's mouth drops open to shoot steam at Addie in response. I can feel my own voice rise to fight what I know is coming, but Zoey gets there first. Sharp.

"I have to fucking agree." She shrugs. "I was with Aidan when the attacks started. He's his own damn man, Celestyn. He acted on his own before I even fucking knew what was going on."

*Man.*

I've wanted to hear that for so long. To feel like I've earned it. I'm only twenty-four, but I have been living a life unlike so many ever have.

Haven't I earned it?

There is still a pity for Celestyn on a particular level of my breaking spirit. She is worried about me, and I've known her for a while in ways no one ever will. These feelings are hard to convey for her, and she acts out in place of them. Not to mention how jealous she has become, seething in this bitter stew that she cooked herself.

To be fair, it was a stupid move to run in after Addie like I had. It went against everything I have taught her to do in these situations, and it was painstaking to creep in around a condensed Center flooded with enemy men. But when I saw what I inevitably knew was going to happen, it was knee-jerk.

Instant.

I couldn't stop myself, and if I could, I didn't want to. All I knew in the singular moment I made the choice was that I didn't want Addie to die.

At least...not alone.

"You're all blind!" Celestyn shrieks. "Stop being stupid. You don't know what she is."

"What am I, Celestyn?" Addie shouts in return. "Since you know so well, spit it the fuck out. I'm all fucking ears, girl."

"A monster!" Celestyn screams. "An animal."

"It's just so *vague,*" Addie snarls. "You can do a little better than that, can't you, genius?"

"You're a fucking—"

"Stop it!" I shout over them both. "That is *enough.*"

Celestyn shakes her head in a stupor, throwing her hands up. Addie's eyes are void, staring off into nowhere but temper fading off. She can hear me, but I'm not sure she is listening. She is still shaking, even without the weight of Simone twitching in my arms.

"You don't know—" Celestyn starts up.

"I don't know what everyone's problem with Addie is, no," I interrupt, watching her whole face break. "What I do know, is that this was definitely the first attack the Ravagers have made against the village as a *whole.* They robbed us of our place for sick and injured people by burning it to the ground, killing plenty of people on their way out. Do you think that is going to get any better?"

Zoey inches closer, touching Simone's face with careful fingers.

"Absolutely fucking not." She quakes.

"We need to stay together." I nod. "All of us. As close as we can, if we want to survive the attacks to come."

"There is danger in numbers," Celestyn huffs.

I shrug. "That's what we have been told. Over and over. It is fed to us like lunch in prison. But people die alone too, and these things arrive in organized numbers. Like military operations. What good is one of us versus six of them? If we want to survive collectively, it's important to stay together."

Celestyn paces, skinny legs marching through the rubble that remains of her workplace.

"No," she states without hearing the rest of what I am to say.

"Yes." I am firm. "It is *my* home that *you* are choosing to live in, in spite of your protections. And it is better fortified than almost any other home around, inside and out. We could all live there together. Maybe we can work to build a trap door like the one in Zoey's place if we spend the day digging together. But either way, we should be protecting one another."

My arms are growing tired of holding Simone, and I need to get somewhere good to set her down. Home would be an excellent start to that, and even better if they could all call it home too. This can be manageable.

"*No*," Celestyn repeats. "I can deal with the pregnant bitch. I could even overlook the child. But allowing that *thing* into our home will be the death of everyone you see right now. And she has been granted one too many mercies."

Addie frowns, staring into the finger pointed straight at her.

# CHAPTER THIRTY-ONE
## ADABELLE

AIDAN IS FIRM, AND CELESTYN CAN'T MAKE HIM CHANGE his mind.

Whatever she knows about me, she isn't willing to spill on, so the evidence of my apparent monstrosity to bar me from living with the group is nonexistent. As per usual, the story of my life.

She ceases fighting an awful lot following this call out, however, and as a newfound family, we begin to follow Aidan home. Smoke still fills the air from the ruins of The Center, many of the homes on the outer edge of the structure crisped black with soot—mine and Zoey's functional piece of shit included.

There are throngs of people out the front of their residences, holding doors open and rummaging through the insides, grabbing what they can in heaps. Here, escapees or those too close to the incident nurse burn wounds and wrap horrific scars in dirty shirts. Others are fried to the ground, ashy and toneless shapes pleading mercy in silent cries that will never be heard.

I edge closer to Aidan, sensing the hardened stares of present villagers as we go. Something tells me there weren't a lot of survivors from The Center's onslaught, my night being a hard-won success unwelcome in this place of tragedy. Still, I find myself pitying them.

They're scared. We all are.

I can smell it and feel it, and hear it in the scant sobbing filling the air as I hobble along.

*I just want to live*, they cry.

*I want my sister.*

*I want to go home.*

I wish I could promise that I can make this possible. That there is a way to end this devastation that we have been all too complacent to as we try to find methods to simply survive. But it is so easy to die here, modern-aged civilizations unequipped for the environment we've been thrown into.

We need bullets and guns. Tasers and armor.

Cell phones.

An army.

I stumble, swollen foot dragging over a pile of bricks laid out on the ground, leaving me gasping in pain. Zoey waddles to my aid, bending at her backside against her better, pregnant judgment, and offering a hand to help me up. But I don't want to burden her already encumbered body with my own trash fire.

I smile, faintly, chewing my bottom lip while I climb to my feet, trying to find balance on my single good foot. We walk just a bit further when I gain my bearings, toward Aidan's home as things noticeably condense, a crowd generating in a single place close to the barn where the field we meet usually is.

Aidan glances about, a bit more anxious than he was prior. He bypasses the row of shacks and huts where his stands not far off, lurching forward to the crowd of survivors instead. Amidst them, I can see Melody, her long, soft black hair braided over her shoulder and covered up by her oversized red beanie.

She is taller than nearly everyone else in the crowd, and at least definitely all the women. Thin as a rail and shapeless, she smiles upon catching Aidan's attention, waving almost theatrically, and gesturing onward. Our band of misfits follow him in a line, robotic and stiff and exhausted, squeezing in between sweaty, hot figures until we reach her at the front of it all. Around us must be close to one hundred people, maybe a little less. The number doesn't include the nearly two dozen children remaining in Limbo, roaming the streets or clinging to their assigned guardians, if they were lucky enough to have one.

"What's going on?" Aidan glances to Melody who offers him the rickety chair she had brought out for her own comfort, allowing him to rest with Simone's tiny body cradled against him.

She pats him on the shoulder, stepping aside when Celestyn nudges her way forward, gripping onto him like an emotional leech. Our local witch doctor is possessive, and Melody could care less, not minding much of anyone outside of her brief acquaintances and friendships.

She is unattached. Not romanticized by survival or the desire to live.

It is an admirable mental endeavor.

"I've decided to host a town meeting," Melody replies to us as a unit. "Ace isn't here, so I'm not sure what to do. But I feel like this is what he would do, considering the attacks, and the damage it has cost us."

"What is it going to accomplish?" Aidan mutters in return, voice bitter and sullen as the night truly catches up with him.

I watch his eyes scan over the growing audience we acquire, the body count building—though not by much. The buzz of chatter reflects this, each person talking at the same time as the next. Whispering. Crying.

Would anyone be willing to listen for very long?

This holds chance to make our situation as outsiders a lot worse.

Out of the corner of my eye, I see Melody studying me, though I do not think she expects me to catch her. She starts, falling firm and a hint of a smile gracing her mouth.

"Don't let them get to you." She leans in close to me, so close that only I am privy to her words. "It is in their nature to fear us, just a little."

A wink.

I glance up.

"What?"

But my words are lost as Melody's voice rises above the others in a yell that silences the twittering birds in the trees, breaking a grin across her face as if she were softer than she led on.

*Shut the fuck up!*

And then the smile when all do as she commands.

I hobble away from her, closer to Celestyn and Zoey, cowering behind Aidan so that no one can see me. Mock me. Hurt me. I am tired of being knocked around more than anything.

"Last night was…hard," Melody starts, taking a deep breath to cleanse. "Real hard. We lost a majority of the town in this tragedy, and I don't think it's going to stop here. We need to make a plan. I know I'm not Ace, but if we want to survive long enough for him to return, I mean…"

She shrugs her delicate shoulders. It is apparent she isn't comfortable with leadership or the concept of pulling the reins in panic. But she would be damn good at it given a better oppor-tunity.

"You have no expertise beyond being Ace's fucking secretary," a woman shouts at the back. "We have no reason to follow a glorified ATM. The best you can do is teach us how to sit and die."

"Melody is more than a secretary," Celestyn fights without hesitation. "She helps Ace with everything he does down to coordinating the tactical plans for the Suicide Missions. Give a woman credit."

I am secretly impressed Celestyn can do more than think of herself, and all of the amazing things she is capable of doing. The capacity of her brain is making the dedicated venture of traveling beyond medicine, thoughts occurring to make a difference in someone else's life that isn't negative.

But it puzzles me.

Why does she feel less threatened by Melody than myself?

"It doesn't matter," Melody sighs. "None of it matters when we are boned. None of us know what to expect from here on out, or if this is our last night at all before they come back to finish what they started. We don't know, and in the big picture, we can't afford to be petty. You want a leader? A male leader? Go fucking find one. But what I want is a plan. A functional plan. Who has one of those?"

There is a sobering silence. Someone holding the hand of a near four-year-old girl speaks up.

"I say we go home, and pick up what we can carry," he declares, squeezing her little fingers with fear. "We need to get as far away from this godforsaken, almost absent Dome, as we can get in one or two nights, and not turn back. It seems to me that it is their primary target, and we are obviously upsetting these creatures by being here."

Melody shakes her head.

"Women and children are the primary target," she affirms, slow.

Her voice is full of resentment. I can relate.

"I agree," Aidan speaks up. "On top of that, Addie and I found these Ravagers in the third layer of our Dome on one of our outings. We didn't know they were even there until it was practically too late. If we walk out as a unit without a bigger plan in mind, they could be waiting for us. They know the area better than we ever could. They've lived in it much longer."

I shuffle closer. My good leg wants to give out, and I am out of air. Weak. My injuries are quick healing, but there is still a time frame, and it is lagging out.

Celestyn moves so I am unable to get too close to Aidan. Melody notices this out the corner of her eye, and shifts over, wrapping her arm around me so that I have no other options but to steady upon her. I mouth a quick thanks as a murmuring from the crowd burns in the morning light as panicked waves. A couple more people have joined us now, singed and scarred and confused.

"We can't just stay here!" A younger girl shouts. "They'll kill us!"

The voice is too young. Maybe thirteen, maybe younger. She shouldn't have this fear.

No one this age, especially, should have to sit with the anarchy of adults and wonder who in the hell they are, or what will happen to them next.

"They won't kill *you*," a boy about the same age taunts.

"It might as fucking well be the same thing," Zoey snaps, the crowd roaring into chaos.

"You shouldn't even be here!" someone screams back.

Her temper in full swing, she points at them, yelling a series of expletives. But everyone is entirely too loud. I can't hear what they're saying, and I am not sure I want to.

Melody's face pales, looking unstable amidst this circus she called to order now spiraling out of control. Celestyn bends closer to Aidan, combing over Simone's bald scalp in a nervous fidget that I allow against my better judgment.

"That's it!" Aidan shouts at the highest pitch he can summon, letting this rolling boil simmer while he regathers. "We aren't getting anything done like this. We *can't* get anything done like this."

Quiet.

Celestyn hesitates, patting him on the shoulder.

"What do you have in mind?" she mumbles.

He looks at her for only a second, frigid and uninterested.

"We go to the old village. Everyone, together. I've been there many times myself, and it is not cursed. Nothing has hurt me yet. But there are supplies there that we can use to reinforce our homes, weapons that are still good. There are some old clothes and medical supplies too, still sitting inside the homes. We need to reinforce what we have, while we have it. Not abandon the fortress we have started."

I release Melody, almost dropping to the ground and tripping forward. I yank Celestyn's shoulders for help, limping around into view as people look on. Disgusted.

"T-there's a shed." I pant. "I-I-it's out back behind The... Center? In the forest."

"The one you fucking found me in, and Aidan found us both in?" Zoey perks up.

"Yeah," I nod. "It had tons of supplies in it! Gauze and medicine. All kinds of crap. We could go get some."

I can't miss the way Melody's eyes grow to the size of dinner plates. She follows me to the front of our band, peering to see my face, searching, and finding nothing.

"We should raid it for any supplies left in there...but I've never heard of it. It isn't ours. So, we will have to be *careful.*"

"I'll go," I speak faster than I can hold the words in. "I mean, I can go. I guess. To get the supplies. But it will take me a couple trips. I would need a donkey and a wagon."

"Granted," Melody bobs her head.

A man in the front of our local mob rubs his head, an older gentleman in his mid to late forties. He is a bit on the heavier side and clean shaven, surrounded by three smaller children. I wondered if he had used a knife to get that close a shave. I need the advice.

"That doesn't give us any real answers, however." He grimaces. "We need a higher authority here. Someone that can give us wisdom. I don't know if I can go through with this otherwise. It seems safer to run while we can."

"You haven't been out there—" Aidan starts, but I interrupt.

"It's fine," I admonish, putting my hands out in peace. "I...I have a summons from Master Amadeus. A couple, actually. I'll go see him, and we will talk. I will find us some answers. I will keep us safe. Remember that."

A slight buzz.

I peek over, meeting Aidan's slack-jawed stare overflowing with concern.

It screams no. All but begs it.

But it pleads something else as well. I just can't place the emotion.

As I am turning away, a quiet whine catches my ears like

music, and I whip back. Simone's sunken, dark eyes flutter a few times, pained by the harsh, direct sunlight as Celestyn begins yelling for everyone to stand down. But I hobble toward them, dropping to my knees at Aidan's lap so I am face to face with her, touching her frail cheeks blistered with hot streams of tears.

"W-w-where's daddy?" she chokes.

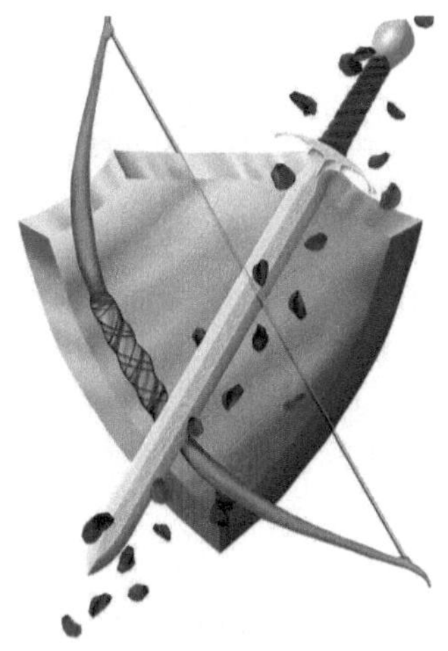

# CHAPTER THIRTY-TWO
## AIDAN

NO ONE *JUST* RECEIVES A SUMMON FROM MASTER Amadeus.

Most of the time, he ignores requests to meet at all with the common people of Limbo and reserves the right to banish those who he permits to see him in the flesh.

It comes with a serious risk to be called upon by him, and few people have been to his residence on the regular without consequence. On my fingers, I can count Ace, Melody, and Celestyn. But they are all people of extraordinary talent, skill, or use to the outcome of the village. They have something to offer this grim world that the rest of us cannot.

The only thing Addie has offered is death. In her very wake, she offers bloodshed and violence without ever meaning to, and it clings to her like an infant would its mother. So, I can't make sense of it.

What does this mean? And why?

I can see a smirk at the crooks of Celestyn's lips beginning to form, but I can't concentrate on the act. I can hardly think as the people surrounding us buzz louder and louder, like hornets knocked free of their nest. My fingers twitch, Addie pulling Simone free of my aching arms that sigh with ice cold relief when the pressure is lifted. She squeezes the little girl tight as Celestyn yells at her on the ground for a better look. Melody ushers people away at the commotion, Zoey sidestepping to be at her best friend's aid.

But I am dumbstruck.

Stupid.

How could I not know?

Addie never said a word, and I made...assumptions, about why Ace would come to see her. Why he cared about her.

I have been jealous.

Celestyn slides Simone out of Addie's lap against the child's own will to remain in place, safe from examination—far too weak to fight the action. I scramble out of the chair on my knees with Addie, taking her by the shoulders while her ward is occupied, and giving her a firm shake.

"What the hell are you thinking?" I lower my voice, attempting to engage the reasonable part of her. "I can't allow this, okay? The probability of you coming home at all from this little venture to Master Amadeus is slim to none. Don't throw your life away. I know you try like hell, but you are more than a sacrificial lamb."

Addie pulls away, soft and patient, head shaking.

"I am nothing," she replies, still hoarse but improvement noticeable in the speed her body restores. "No one. I will be nothing, and I will be no one when this all ends, as well. Don't you see? I am not made to be here in the same way as others, and if I can help just one person on my way home, wherever that ends up being, it will be worth my time."

I open my mouth, slack-jawed and frantic, but she wobbles upright with a pained smile, limping toward the barn to retrieve her donkey. It is a brief stop she makes to provide Simone a tight squeeze and a snuggle, promising to come home in a few hours, murmuring something incoherent to Celestyn, and disappearing beyond the wooden gates.

I hope she gets the same animal we had all that time ago, for her own sake. She deserves at least a touch of happiness before it all evaporates into the same gas we breathe. It isn't fair of the village to let her make such a reckless decision on their behalf, when she doesn't realize what she is getting herself into, and I almost wish Ace was here to talk her out of it like he has so many others preceding.

Except, he is in on this.

He must be.

Who else has delivered the letters requesting her presence?

And god knows what he has said about them.

It has always been him, the brute force weighing down Limbo like a brick in water.

I get up off the ground. Celestyn has finished her exam, speaking to Zoey and Melody of the child's prognosis to update Addie in her absence. Other villagers have already started to break for the old village as suggested, in the meantime, to build on the plan we have made while we wait for Addie's godforsaken court date.

I stumble toward the rest of my small social circle, hands feeling strangely empty since the warmth of her skin departed them. So unarmed, and upset, I clench and unclench them to fill the void, awaiting the feeling of nothing at all to greet me again. Melody holds out her normal, slender fingers to Simone with a fake smile, not so great with children, but trying her best to comfort.

Though weepy, Simone allows herself to be scooped up, wrapping still somewhat limp arms around Melody's neck, and eying Zoey with disdain. I approach them all with a more genuine grin, taking Simone's little fingers in mine like I would a princess, and rubbing them with the pad of my thumb.

"A-Aidan?" she mumbles, dark eyes glassy and peeking out from behind thick lashes.

"Yeah, Simone," I coo. "It's me. Are you ready to go home?"

"I want daddy," she frets, tears glistening over her gaunt

cheekbones and dribbling to her chin. "Where's daddy?"

I grimace, but I don't allow it to stay. Not now.

"Well, we haven't found him yet. But you know what? Why don't I have Zoey and Melody take you back to my place while you wait on Addie? They can give you some yummy food, and you can look at Celestyn's books with all the pictures. Maybe take a nap? And when I get home, I'll have something special for you. A present."

"Present?"

Her face lights up enough to look alive. I nod, feeling a weird delight in her resulting smile.

"What present?" she mumbles, leaning closer, and holding a single arm out.

I inch toward her too, nose touching her cheek as she giggles.

"It's a surprise," I whisper.

"Promise?" Simone is shaking, body shivering in the heat of day, droopy and tired.

She won't remain awake long.

"Pinky promise," I swear. "Those are the best promises, after all."

She watches me, filled with suspicion, and breaks, laughing, holding her forehead as she does.

"You're silly," she mumbles.

"What? Me? No."

Melody cradles the girl closer to heart with a bit of an eyeroll.

"Alright, alright." She tries to hide her own, reluctantly touched smile. "Let's get this kid back to the house so we can get her settled, and start pitching in. Zoey can watch her until Adabelle gets back, right?"

"Fucking gotcha," Zoey replies, a bit uncomfortable, but waving her over.

Simone wiggles her fingers while they leave, waving so I see to wave back, waiting till they are out of sight before I whip around to Celestyn who is packing up her minimal supply bag. I march for her as she glances up, smiling as if she can possibly be more naïve than Addie herself.

But we both know better.

We know so much better.

I grab her by the upper arm, close to the shoulder, and pull her upright. She yelps, complaining words I refuse to comprehend as I tug her toward the barn, clawing at my fingers with nails she has chewed to the beds.

*Hey! That hurts. What the fuck, Aidan?*

But I move her against the fence, pinning her with my leg and arms so that she has no choice but to look me in the face. There is no escape from this.

"What do you know about Addie?" I growl low, pressing my hand beside her hips on the wood posts to bar her in.

"Nothing!" She lies, trying to slip out from under my trap, but I steel my brace, locking her in place.

"WHAT DO YOU KNOW?" I roar, and she looks away.

Jittery.

"I don't..."

"Don't bullshit me, Celestyn," I interrupt. "Why is Master Amadeus summoning Addie?"

Her face grows somber and overcast, gaze falling.

"I. Don't. Know." She grits her teeth.

"You don't know, or you won't say?"

Her mouth is a hard line, sucked in, forehead stressed indentions, and eyebrows knit together. She doesn't speak a word, but it is obvious what she will say.

I sigh, arms dropping and hope melting while I mull this over.

"What is she, Celestyn?" I run my hands through my hair, sweeping it free of the tangles in front of my glasses.

Celestyn fixes her hair from being pushed to the fence, touching it lightly after tugging it every which way. And then she stops, and gives in.

"It isn't my place, Aidan," she replies at last.

"Are we in immediate danger with Addie present in our lives?"

I am hesitant to ask. I know what she will say.

Quiet. Almost everyone has left us, and we are almost alone—save the farm animals. The birds call from the trees, singing a hurried tale of warning and tragedy.

*Hurry up*, they call. *Time is almost up.*

The idea sends shivers down my spine.

"If she does not kill you," Celestyn counsels, choosing her words with care, "she will be the reason you die, Aidan."

My fist tightens, covered in sweat though it is barely noon.

"She heals," I think aloud, "at abnormal rates. Even her foot...I don't know how long she will continue to limp, but it won't be for more than a couple days. I've watched major cuts heal in less time, and not all of it can be accounted for by your medical concoctions."

Celestyn nods, as though she has known all along.

I mean, she has. She has *always* known.

She *does* know.

There is something wrong with Addie.

"If you care for me at all, or us at all, just let her go." She lays a hand on my shoulder.

Part of me misses it, her touch. Being touched. Feeling human, and not like a worthless sack of shit. At one point, I would have killed for just a second more of her hands on my skin. Caressing. Feeling. I want her voice, and her mind—the tangibility of what it is to have a conversation with her late in the afternoon, and to watch her laugh at the stupid things I do. I would be jealous of other men, warding them clear while she smirks, knowing they'd come back when I left her.

I'd overlook it because she was *mine*.

Mine.

Mine?

She was never mine.

And no matter how much I miss it, I never had it in the first place. Not a connection. Not a person or a romance.

Celestyn was never mine, and she was never any other man's. She never will be.

Because she is hers. Because we cannot own a person.

Still, I let her linger before I shrug her away, at least for a moment before the feelings of resentment flood back inside and overtake rationality.

"What do you know?" I am seething in my own pool of selfloathing. "You've always hated Addie, because you're no different than me. Jealous. Petty. Bitter."

She guffaws. Snorts.

"Jealous?" She rolls her eyes. "Of her? Boy, have you seen her? The girl has the complexion of curdled milk, and the scarring doesn't help."

"Then why care? Huh?"

This time, she winces, eyes growing to the size of dinner plates.

"Because I am afraid," she admits. "And I can't afford to be. Not when there are people that need my help."

I hold my face, rubbing my temples.

"Then why even save Addie?" I ask. "Why did you even bother saving her when Ebony could have killed her when the others were making that call. You said no. And now you decide that she should be treated like piss when she has done nothing but try and help?"

It is routine for her to fall silent, refusing to speak when I back her in a corner. I know she won't respond to her own hypocrisy. She isn't ready, if she still won't tell me what the problem with Addie is in the first place. But I want her to stew on the concept so that she is unable to escape the knowledge that she has treated someone beyond their own control like less than a living being.

"We will all be living together. That includes Addie," I repeat, picking up her bag for her and setting the supplies inside. I am angry, but I don't have to be a jerk. "That's the end of this argument. If you don't like it, you can either shut up and deal, or go live with Amadeus. But I am done with you being horrible to her for the sake of being cruel."

Celestyn rips her bag from my arms before I am done retrieving all her things, jars and tools rattling about inside.

"What are you not getting about this?" she yells. "What do you have to prove to *her*? She is only your responsibility in the search teams. Not in life."

I glance up to her, fuming, but her lip quivers, and the rest of her trembles with rage. She is just as, if not more, upset.

"Stop," I demand.

"No!" She shouts. "It is her, or it is me. But it can't be both of us."

I take in a big gulp of air. She won't like the answer if I make it.

"I don't owe you anything." I laugh. "We aren't exclusive."

And I turn my back on her, leaving across the fields in a hurry towards Headquarters.

I have some reading to do.

# CHAPTER THIRTY-THREE
## ADABELLE

OUT OF SIGHT FROM THOSE WHO HAVE TO BELIEVE I AM stronger than what I am, I can't stop coughing. I am wheezing, trudging toward my destination out behind the haunting ruins of our hospital, though I feel a bit better than I had upon waking this morning. The donkey provided to me brays in response to each hack while the cart it is hitched to squeaks over uneven earth, like it is a secret conversation we are having in the meantime, just me and him. Or her.

Her?

I don't know.

I'm too embarrassed to look, even now, twisting where we can fit through the once peculiar trees that I have since adjusted to, awaiting the next onslaught of violence that bears the promise to do me in for good. I wonder here, do animals value privacy at all? I still haven't been around them enough to find out, let alone seen any until waking up in Limbo, so it is hard to say.

I mean, they pee out in the wide-open glory of nature, but so do most men. So when I really think about it—

More coughing.

It grows harder to maneuver a jackass and wooden wheels through the forest, hitting patches of brush with underlying dragon nesting, creatures rife with discontent and chasing me clear so as not to crush their eggs. I don't know why I offered this route when there are no carved-out paths to trek, forcing me to wing it where I can. I guide the donkey where it needs to be, and I weasel it through areas it can't fit—or won't. But my limping shuffle slows us immeasurably, and there is a small voice singing concern at the back of my head that Aidan is right about the ceiling breaking my ankle when it fell. The injury wasn't a pretty sight to behold when we pulled the shoe off and snipped the leggings up to see, burned anew and attempting to scab without success. Encircling the open wound was a meaty, mottled bruising mounded with unmatched swelling that leaves me barefoot on one side and naked to infection.

If I am telling myself the truth, it hasn't stopped hurting for a second, and I want sympathy. I want someone to care for me, and feed me, and let me relax it off in the comfort of a bed that isn't a solid wood floor. I want to watch a bad holiday movie where I know exactly how it ends while I drink a full bottle of red wine to chase away the bad dreams that caused my painful, inescapable insomnia. I want to wake up, and teach my classes to the sounds of gentle and melodic piano euphonies and high-pitched giggles.

I want to go home.

But I can't. There is work to be done, and the only thing broken is my drama bone. I have too many people counting on me to fixate on it.

Still, I wouldn't mind a break from this chaos if I can manage it prior to meeting the Master. I hold a quiet daydream I can still make it home, maybe even go on a vacation.

Are there any vacation spots left? I am blurry on the details.

Surely I can rent a hotel, though. Flirt with a stranger. Drink at a bar, and sleep without fear. Without interference. Without *anyone* at all in the room.

It goes to say that leaving Simone was the hardest thing I have ever done in my time here. I wasn't ready for it, or for her to wake up as duty called. I won't be ready for it again when I meet Master Amadeus, and I won't be ready a third time when I go home, returning her to rightful guardianship or parents.

I'm not ready to be without *her*, but I want the universe to right itself.

Simone has family that isn't me, somewhere.

I have tried to substitute it the best I can with the help of Aidan. And Celestyn. And now, Zoey. But it will never be the same, and these people are a temporary adjustment at best. Nothing is permanent, and everything must change if we want to survive. Down to me, down to Celestyn, down to Zoey.

Fear and pain cannot be an excuse to hurt other people, or turn on them like wild dogs.

The shed is just up ahead, and I tie the donkey outside a short distance to one of the trees with roots blocking the path of our cart. I feed the coarse, fuzzy bastard half of an apple I kept in my pocket from the barn treat barrels, rubbing down the space between its ears and under its chin.

"You're such a good baby," I squeak through smoke damage, planting a kiss between the greedy eyes narrowing in on my shirt in search of more treats.

"I don't have any more." I laugh, stepping away in worry I will get bit as the donkey huffs. "Buu-t I will give you a little something when I get you home later. I promise, yes I do."

I spin away as the animal snorts, approaching the door and twisting the handle absently. I stop upon the realization that it is locked. My mouth goes dry, my head tilting toward either window that sports intricate panes of colored glass reflecting rainbows of light inside where it hadn't last time I was here.

I swallow, spit raking trenches down my gullet, tapping my finger pads over the clean, delicate panes that plink in response. There is no movement inside to indicate the acknowledgment of my presence, and I try again, louder this time with my knuckles, rapping so the glass vibrates.

Silence, other than the sound of my heart thrumming against the inside of my ears.

I turn away, searching the grass until I find a rock bigger than my fist at the side of the shed. Pursing my lips, I smash it into the window so that the colors spiral into hundreds of sharp fragments that twinkle to the floor in a shriek, as if it hurt to fall apart. I reach through the opening I have made, fingers feeling for a lock on the other side of the door but not finding it, realizing I will probably need a key rather than a simple twist of a deadbolt.

I stumble backwards, lurching forward and ramming the door as hard as I can on one good leg.

Again. And again.

It groans but remains steady. Tight, and well-constructed on hinges that aren't rusted.

Fine.

I scramble over to the window, minding my ankle and reaching into my bag, folding my old skirt down over the frame in case there is any glass leftover, hoisting myself upright with strong, but quivering arms. I sweep my injured leg over first, using the good one as balance, and sucking in air as I touch it to the inside wall. Pacing, I crunch the good side over, lowering myself to the floor in a hollow echo that rings through the tiny hallway.

I am overcome with hopelessness.

It is empty, mostly.

In every nook, every cranny where there had been heavy trunks layered ceiling to floor, clustered and stacked so tight I could hardly wedge down the hall, there is dry, barren space. In the right corner, settled below the window, a few trunks are sprung open, littered with dried, bloodied bandages and trailed ridges of crusty, reddish-brown needles glinting dull to the side.

I can't breathe, holding myself up onto the wall, and sliding to the hallway, shifting in a series of obnoxious thumps courtesy of my bad luck. I glance into each side room while I move, stopping at a closet space spread wide open, three trunks remaining inside and spilling defective objects haphazardly to the floor.

I shake my head, seeing red. I feel the color like it were an object, a warm, cancerous mass rising from my chest to the top of my throat, filling my cheeks and my ears. *Swooshing* with crimson, I can hear the sound red makes, exhaling it through my nose.

I cover my eyes, burning in a lava bath of vivid sanguine, pulling at my lids to relieve the sensation.

I want to smother myself in frustration. I want to scream this color into existence.

I *do* scream, loudly—straight into my aching, tingling palms. I shriek, hitting my fist into the wall above my meager find. I throw the mostly empty trunks into the hallway, hoping to dent the opposite wall.

"No...no, no, no, no. NO!" I shriek.

I reach into the pile of less than gorgeous materials, pulling out a dented blade and flinging it after the trunks like a ninja star.

What am I going to do?

I can't return to Limbo with *this*. With so little to offer. They'll crucify me. I promised big things, asking for an entire donkey to bring in the haul. At this rate, the biggest thing coming home will be my crybaby ass.

I fall over on my rear, scooping what I can find that will be useful into the trunks I tossed so that at least we have something. There are a couple usable rolls of bandaging, though it is a bit stained in comparison to the standard I had found before it. One of the trunks appears to be nothing but bandaging, and silver clips used to pin it—misshapen and older, but still much nicer and cleaner than any of what we have in the village.

I use some of the product to wrap my ankle to protect it on the way home, putting the rest away and almost unable to close the smallest trunk of the group.

The largest one that is flipped upside down thanks to my fit contains a series of imperfect little blades that are dented and rusted, looking as if they were made in haste and some even lacking a handle to grip. Most of the weapons are not perfectly straight or steadily thin, unpolished or chipped on the sharp edges as if they have been used, none matching the caliber of those I collected earlier. Nonetheless, I pack them away, scooting the separate pile from the last chest into a heap of small quilts, clean white rags, and minor dinner provisions. Potatoes being the most thriving item among what's left of the perishables I never knew of, but I am able to find some carrots as well. Dried meat. Dried fruit.

Whoever cleared this place out did it not that long ago. They must have kept everything in here fresh, too. Produce doesn't stay palatable forever, or so I have found. I get an eerie feeling about it the longer I stay.

I finish packing what I'm able, dropping each trunk out the window I came in through, checking on my donkey that flicks its head to the flies buzzing about it. I think we make eye contact, and I wave to the animal as though it actually cares, ducking inside with a tiny grin at how silly it seems.

It grows hotter the more I move around, but I check other crevices and closets in the front rooms to make sure I am not missing anything, dropping six more trunks out the window in a lopsided stack that will hopefully support my weight when I climb out after it. I find a few more articles of infant clothing checking around here and there, a broken arrow hiding under another bloodied roll of bandaging, and an ax. Onions. Some high-quality suturing material, and two needles on a windowsill in the first room.

I press my palms along the base of the window, scooting close and hoisting myself upward when it gets too cluttered, ready to move each trunk to the cart when a low, deep rumbling calls out from the last room I had not touched. The noise builds in intensity, inhuman and brazen. Sharp, like the prehistoric call of a bird.

There is a switch inside of me that flips off, a change blossoming lethal curiosity in an instant that leaves me stumbling from the windowsill back inside, though every stoplight in my conscious thought flashes red.

I know I should run.

I should fling myself out the window and drag myself to safety.

But I thump to the floor, pulling one of the better daggers I had stolen all that while ago from my backpack, and limping to the sound. I falter behind the door where Zoey and I had sat in, sifting through the strange baby clothes. My lips purse, heart pumping harder than it has since I was out in the woods with Aidan.

Broken glass on the other side of my small barrier crackles, screams with the rake of something sharp grinding over the top of it, and then grinding into the wood of the floor. I glance to my own foot, trying to decide if I am in any shape to take a look.

Is it wise?

But the idea clicks off as soon as it comes, and I toe into the room, working my way into the potential mess ahead.

I am surprised to find, as the other side comes into view, this area is bigger than I remembered without as many items to fill it, though there are still more trunks than any other room had. Not as many as there had been. But more than others had now.

More is more.

I won't complain.

Or maybe I will.

A sleek shadow glides across the room, gleaming and writhing like a snake. But it's not. It's different.

I edge further from sanity, casually picking up a small chest with one arm, and slipping around a small stack for a better view. By the broken window at the other side of the room is a metal trunk ripped asunder, like shreds of newspaper by a mischievous cat. Its lock is popped free in deep rakes, mixed contents of infant clothing and weapons thrown about like confetti.

The creature in charge is long, with feet like a chicken's—black clawed and feather crested around the neck, its haunches and abdomen are made up of dark blue scales that glisten like ocean water, rolling in different lighting like the beast were actually filled with it.

I am relieved it does not initially notice me, taking a peek and studying its form, no longer than an average-sized dog with scant, webbed wings folded over its back making me feel better about my chances of escape should it try to pursue me. Chances are in my favor that it is flightless with minuscule appendages hardly big enough for gliding, let alone flying for a creature of its size.

I crouch a bit lower, watching the front feet pick up knives as it chitters about like a child, sharp teeth gnashing dents into the blade and hissing at the taste, yet picking up another more polished one in delight.

I turn my head, questioning whether dragons are like small children with attention problems. The *ooh, shiny object* kind that are smart, but unable to retain conversation. Not that there aren't adults like that as well.

I hold my weapon close, keeping the blade out of sight and shifting to my next destination, the items in my backpack jangling against each other as I do so I freeze in place. The creature stiffens, bobbing its slender neck, and pivoting an angular, horned face to and fro, finding me with burning, yellow eyes.

I stay still, gulping down fear at the shredded metal still hanging in silver ribbons from its reptilian jaws, and waiting. It snorts at my concern, bending to its danger toys and tearing into another chest. Huffing. Yanking.

Is it safe?

Testing my boundaries, I creak on dusty floors a few steps. The dragon turns again, feathers rising, and fluffing out as it releases a hiss that reminds me of a house cat's, snapping vicious jaws at my feet. I pop away, groaning as my ankle catches a portion of the resulting weight, and crumpling into the floor, holding my hands out for protection.

The beast hisses a warning once more, returning in a swift whisk to its business of stealing treasures it can't leave with.

My brow furrows, and I push myself up on my feet, hobbling around the creature with confidence and assertion. It eyes me, watching me retrieve some of the clothing it hasn't torn apart, and other cloth material. I work at an even pace it can feel comfortable with, reaching for what I can, as close as I can without disturbing boundaries.

Another growl rumbles from the spiteful little prick when I pick up a blade, sending the beast lunging at my shins. I panic right away, tossing the object handle first at his head between the eyes, dumbfounding him as I push my own blade out in self-defense. Shaking, I scamper against the wall closest to the broken window.

The dragon grumbles at my threat, pacing the room while I move for my exit, holding out defense and picking up what I'm able as I go, using the knee on my bad leg to scoot a smaller stack of trunks. It makes him cranky to share, nostrils flaring and steaming curls of smoke.

The window is shut hard, the break not large enough for me to throw trunks through and squeeze out in one go. I keep my eye on the enemy, refusing to turn away and wedging my blade underneath to pry open my way to a small victory. It groans apart, agitating my newest friend—Human Barbecue Grill on Legs—its serpentine body coiling and uncoiling.

I bend fast, tossing trunks outside when I have the window open, much to the animal's rage. He flips from the door on the other side of the room, charging at me with what seems like a thousand teeth glinting in the sunlight. I squeak, dagger not enough to concern him any longer and adrenaline pulsing as I throttle myself out the open window backwards, crashing over the rounded trunks below.

There is a screeching that follows this, another lazy warning to keep out of a dragon's treasure through the open window. A proper, frightening display of power, to add.

I am not welcome here, either.

That's okay.

I move the trunks one by one to the cart with the donkey, sitting at the rear of the wooden wheels when I am done for a momentary drink break. I am afraid to sit on the actual wood where corpses had been hauled to their cliffside mass grave, their ghosts haunting me to do the right thing even while I have my doubts.

I hold my face one more time, screaming where no one can

hear me so I can get it all out of my system. I wriggle out of my backpack, swinging it to my front and hugging it to my gut like it were a person, trying to breathe through my anxiety. Trying to think clearly.

Why can't I stop myself from throwing my life away?

It never stops, the way my brain responds to life around me rolling at dangerous speeds ever forward, no matter if I'm on board or not.

I can't keep up, even when I try to plow ahead.

I am going to die here because I can't think. It is an unstoppable force becoming part of my reality.

I gasp in, and out. Fast. Hard. Coughing until I gag. But still trying.

After what feels like forever, my face growing numb and tingly and warm, I stop. I do what I have needed to do this whole time, reaching into my backpack, and pulling free the last unread letter from Master Amadeus I received, ripping it open.

*Miss Adabelle Shay Green,*

*The living monster.*

*A hero, in her own right. Reject of Limbo.*

*Why is it you avoid me?*

*I am inevitable, sweet girl.*

*Your fate is written in the sky as black as midnight, in the stars as bright as moonlight.*

*There is no escape from destiny. This was never a choice. This LIFE was never a choice.*

*We WILL meet.*

*Regrettably, my schedule is full for the next day or two. Dare say we try again at the next full moon?*

*It would truly be my pleasure.*

*Your Master,*

AMADEUS

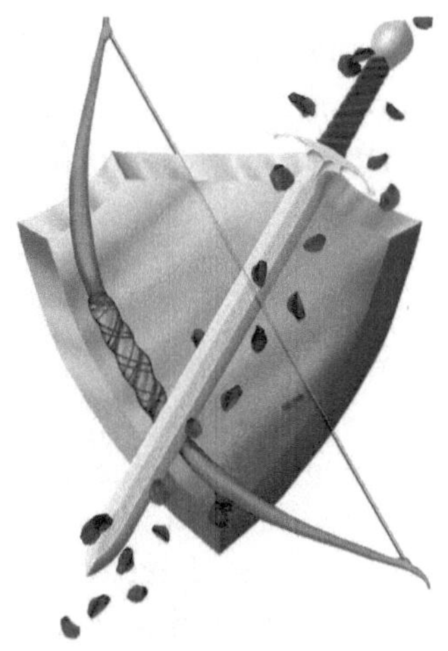

# CHAPTER THIRTY-FOUR
## AIDAN

I CAN'T STOP LOOKING OUT THE SMALL HOLE IN MY covered window.

Like a game of peek-a-boo, I pop up and down while part of my new household sleeps, pacing with journals from Ace's library in hand, and monitoring Simone curled tight with the doll I rescued from the home in the old village under her bony arm.

It was already dark when I came home to give it to her, having spent most of my long work hours attempting to do the research each resident should have always been duty-bound to do, with no such luck on what task I should perform next to avoid absolute extermination—my dyslexia making the information hard to sort.

But, to my delight, at least Simone favored the gift I snagged, mumbling weak gratitudes while Zoey attempted to shovel food down her gullet during our uncertain wakeful state.

Though maybe she really just loved receiving a gift. All women do. All people do.

I don't care. It is enough to see her happy before the real part of the night begins. Someone should be happy.

The rest of us are terrified, and I try to stay awake without playing my guitar, knowing if noise was risky prior to this stage of the game being played, it is lethal now. Unacceptable, at any cost, and those costs staking a high price as we focus on keeping Addie alive to the next full moon. To tomorrow night.

An admirable, arduous task, though no one seems to mind doing it.

It is a sudden, disgusting coincidence that people believe she is important following the acceptance of Master Amadeus' invitation to meet. They welcomed her return to the village when she came this evening, one and all, despite the absence of most of the supplies she promised. I cringed from a distance, overseeing the praise they showered her with that meant nothing when the behavior leading up to it was everything short of abhorrent.

The villagers believe she is a hero now. Because she *is* a hero. Their hero. She always has been, and these greedy bastards failed to realize it until she reconciled to either die or vanish for good—just like they wanted. It makes it a greater shame she fights for them anyway, even when they don't see it.

Addie is the only person here that deserves to be free of this hell. She's never wanted to leave anybody behind, and there isn't a person she wouldn't save based off any reason she could foresee. Though I suppose I can *maybe* categorize Celestyn in this imaginary save column too, considering how many people she rescues from death's cold embrace on the daily. It would be unfair to separate her person from the good she has done over the woes of our personal relationship.

But tonight, I am feeling small, and small people create hateful illusions when they're wounded. They see the ugly, gritty bad of a soul, and forget the light that brought them closer to that darkness.

Small people are bitter without cause.

She is also bitter. Celestyn.

She came home late as a consequence to our argument.

I know what she was out doing, just the same as any other time she has gone out of her way to upset me, but it always rakes across my chest like it were the first time. I can't help it. It is still an open wound while I am unable to surmount the past she helps me repress when we are together, leaving me not quite over the high of our sick, twisted beginnings. No matter how bad I want to be.

Nonetheless, I ignored her coming through the door an hour ago, her greeting met by low-key panicked, love starved Addie and no one else, the rest of us well aware of her ulterior motives down to the half-dead child. It isn't like she makes her extracurricular activities subtle when I've upset her. In my experience, most women understand the art of inflicting pain upon a person without ever opening their mouths like it was ground into their DNA at birth. Skilled masters of agony, the average female mental warrior can lift a man up when it's right and drop him like a corpse in the sea when he's too heavy.

I have a lot of baggage. It isn't Celestyn's job to carry me through it. But if she were my friend at all during the hurricane force of it, she would make it easier to let her go too, without going to every length to get me to notice what she's done. Without the added slap in the face of dark red hickeys peppering her slender jawline to her shoulders. Without the snapped ponytail holder swinging between her fingers like a blue ribbon she won for best sex on the block. Without unnecessarily carrying home her shoes, and the belt to her shorts, when she could have put them back on before leaving her adventure.

It isn't like I don't see that she has baggage of her own to deal with in the ways she sees fit. I'm not that blind.

There are parts of her life not in Limbo that she needs more help than I can give to understand, a stronger, metaphorical hand to pull her off the ground when the world spins too fast. I simply fear that neither of us have understood in this time that there can't be strings attached to the ways in which we help other people. And I have grown hyperaware over the last month that I cannot carry us both if I want to survive too.

I can protect us.

But that has to be the extent of *us.*

There can be no us.

Across the room from where I stand, I accidentally catch Celestyn glaring at me from behind one of her translated medical journals. Laying in her nest of blankets and pillows, she is more comfortable than the rest of us despite sharing the bedding with Simone, who hogs quite a bit of it.

Given her challenge for the day is over, Zoey rests in the backroom with all the medical supplies Addie brought in from the shed. It was collectively decided Celestyn should be the keeper of these items, seeing as she is the best fit to use them, and therefore our injured person's best chance at survival. This decision, to my disdain, opens my home during the day to strangers seeking medical attention like a functional fraction of The Center.

I can't make myself grow keen on the choice. I have enough people in my home already without having to worry about others coming in at all hours of the night. Four girls at risk for disaster, one of which is a child, and none of which get along very well. Addie and Zoey are the closest to being friendly as it gets concerning the adult women, but there is a trust broken there that isn't repaired yet. Simone has taken a bit of a shine to Addie, but it isn't a bond. Celestyn has too much of a god complex to particularly care for anyone outside of herself, not that I haven't spent some time around her to understand it.

I know many things other people do not about Celestyn. Dark, terrible things that make her hate herself more than anyone understands, in a way that no one else sees.

But the knowledge doesn't make for easier living. Especially when Addie is her target.

I can't bring myself to talk to Addie just the same. Not after our last conversation.

She said three words I never wanted to hear from anyone. Words I can't push from my mind, or clear from my conscience in the form of her voice berating them into my skull.

*I am nothing.*

As if it were true.

How do I come back from that?

With life crumbling all around us at an alarming rate, there are several veils being lifted from this reality I coexist within at her side. It is undeniable in these marriages of conclusions that I have a soft spot on my heart for Addie. That I can't draw myself away from her or stop myself from returning to her even when the consequence is a risk to my existence.

Addie is my comrade. She's a proper teammate.

She's the guilt I didn't think I had.

She makes me a better person. A person I feel like I could actually get to know, maybe even like.

I could like who I am...with her.

I just can't seem to trust her completely. A strange fact considering my life has been in her hands, and hers in mine. I don't know why I can't relinquish this fear of her, or her peculiar mannerisms. But I'm not ready.

I glance out the window again, and Celestyn aggressively flicks a page so it echoes from the back wall to the door where Addie sits, her nose buried in the book Ace gave her before leaving as if she cannot feel the tension, though perplexed anyway. Saddened. There is a gut feeling I have that she does not appreciate what she reads, as if it hurts her not-so-fragile soul to burn through. She licks her lips, folding the corner of a page, and setting the leatherbound monstrosity on her knee to look at the wall for a moment, glassy-eyed and quiet. Celestyn shatters this discomfort, voice low and calm.

"Did anyone find new villagers today?"

She reads at the same time. How?

"I've had a busy day, so I wouldn't know."

There isn't an immediate reply.

No one reported back to me today, the whole morning through sundown a blur of busy bodies whirring from one place to the next. At least two-thirds of the existing team didn't show up at all when I arrived at our meeting space, and I didn't try to question it.

I open my mouth, but nothing comes out. I don't know, at all.

"No," Addie answers in my stead. "There was no one. We actually, erm...we lost some of our search team members, I think. I saw a couple guys burying Dennis out by The Center on my way home."

There is an indifference to Celestyn's demeanor about this, a slump of her shoulders that throws me off kilter considering she fucked him.

Did she kill him herself? Or is she really that ruthless?

She flicks through another few pages, scribbling a few words onto page.

"Interesting," she mumbles.

"Not entirely," Addie replies, peering back down to the book she was reading in disgust of both person and literature.

Celestyn smirks.

"He was a jerk. We have plenty of those."

"You're a jerk," Addie hisses. "We still keep you around."

"Hey, hey, he-y." I wave my hands, trying to maintain peace so that neither sleeping volcano erupts.

Both women glance to me, and then return to their respective literatures, though Addie still hasn't picked hers up off her knees. Instead, she stares bullets through the front, rereading the cover over and over.

What is she thinking? What the hell did Ace give her?

As Celestyn turns another page, I notice her free hand moving to the floor, touching Simone's bald head, and stroking it in silence. It is melting, to a degree, to see she has a sweet spot for the kid. It is almost endearing, knowing she cares so little for everything else.

I want to say something out loud, but I refuse to ruin the moment knowing inside that no matter what, there is an indescribable goodness ready to protect Simone at all costs.

"Our numbers are diminished." Celestyn scribbles. "No one

has been found since just a bit after Simone, and a lot of people are dying. At this rate, humanity will cease to exist by the end of the month."

"Unless they conceive children." Addie doesn't look like she is breathing, unable to bring herself to touch the book in her lap. Frozen. Angry.

Celestyn tilts her head, peeking up from her work and eying the one Addie has, enticed. She puts a finger up in thought.

"With the dark elves, I assume?" she ponders. "Weird thought, but it doesn't work like that."

*The what?*

"What do you mean it doesn't work like that?" Addie growls. "There is every implication that these dark elves are raping women to conceive children. Those children would be half human, so humanity could carry on. Just not in the way we want."

Celestyn shuts her book, stilled by Addie's statement. I cross my arms, gaze darting between the two of them, both informed on something I am not, and making me feel a touch...dense.

"I don't know what Ace gave you," she speaks cautiously, "because he is the only one that could have given you what you are reading. But it doesn't work like that."

"Fill me in." I inch between them, sitting in the space they've set and ready to mediate, but realizing I might not need to.

Celestyn looks...relieved, that someone else has information like this. It is more like a weight has been lifted off her shoulders.

Is this what she's been researching alone this whole time? With no help? Has Celestyn been burdened with the responsibility of figuring out what to do next under Amadeus' nose with a trusted secret until action could be taken? So no one would panic?

It must be amazing to just...talk.

Celestyn's shoulders bounce.

"Their king doesn't allot for the survival of half-breeds," she states matter-of-factly. "I've read a couple entries in several medical studies he has done from Master Amadeus' library. He doesn't like them."

"T-that's impossible." Addie laughs. "The King—he married a

Fae. She had babies. It's—"

"What the hell are Fae?" I ask, pulling at my eyes and trying to catch up.

Celestyn stops. Smiles. This is an invigorating conversation for her, intellectually stimulating and a release.

"A faery," she replies. "A creature of magic and nature, founded from an act of violence, but peaceful in nature. They are much smaller than the dark elves, and closer to our size in comparison."

"And the dark elven king—"

"The whole damn world king," Celestyn corrects. "He runs the whole shit show here."

"Okay," I carry on. "But he married one of these...Fae?"

Celestyn shakes her head.

"The current dark elven king never imprinted. His father, however, did marry a Fae against her will in a time of war."

"That still makes my point." Addie crosses her arms. "He *is* a half-breed. He can't hate something that he actively is."

We both jump as Celestyn cackles, waving her hand with a genuine grin that is both unsettling and well meaning.

"A lot of people hate themselves, Adabelle." She rubs her forehead. "But his reasoning goes beyond that. Half-breeds are either incredibly powerful, or painfully useless without grey area. The problem with an incredibly powerful being is that all of their brains appear to be a bit...meh? On impulse control. They all pretty much act on whim. They're irrational, and hard to control without training. He mentions something about faulty connections in the medical journals. Of course, he has had millions of years to hone his problem, and his people practically worship him. But there are direct orders to kill half-breeds on sight to avoid any of the risks involved with their existences."

Addie frowns. I hate it when she frowns.

"He wants...something he can control?" She is bothered.

"That is politics, Adabelle." Celestyn sighs. "If he can't control his population, what is the point of his title?"

Still, Addie thinks this over, muttering something under her breath that I can't quite catch. I give her the privacy of it, focusing on Celestyn. She has an anticipatory look on her face, as if she is waiting for the roundabout question we haven't quite asked yet so that she can achieve her point.

I attempt to conjure this into existence.

"Zoey is pregnant," I point out. "By an elf."

"A-nd this is where I tell you that Adabelle has skipped pages in whatever she has been reading." Any chance to take a jab at Addie, clapping her hands together so loud Simone flinches in her sleep. "If she were thorough, she would know that the humans were also created through the blood of The Nameless King and Mother Nature combined, elves being a direct likeness and descendant of The Nameless Creator. Sooo—"

"Our...our genes just...blend in?" Addie is crushed. Defeated. "You're saying that we are just...weaker, dumber versions of them?"

"We are the defective prototype, but we are essentially the same." Celestyn nods. "The trial run that kept living. We can't hear as well or see as well. Our eyes can't change color on a magical whim and we can't run faster than a car. But we carry children better, and more often, usually more successfully considering nearly all of the baby girl gestations of their race don't survive."

I can't inhale, or exhale. My head is spinning, face burning, arms tingling.

"Are you telling me that you have known this whole time that they have been kidnapping women to use as breeding stock? Or gene replacement therapy? Or—"

"It's not like that." Celestyn's face softens. "I don't know for sure, and I don't want to say anything until I do. Zoey's case felt like a heavy confirmation of that knowledge, but stealing Amadeus' books and translating them properly based off of what he has taught me takes time I don't often have. They have three different ways to say love, Aidan, depending on who they are saying it to. It's not easy."

"They think they're in love." Addie bites her lips. "That's why it isn't as easy."

"Addie, what?" I wince. "No, that's—"

"They don't think," Celestyn interrupts. "They know. That is what imprinting is—a grand realization."

I cover my eyes, huffing into my elbows.

Kill me.

What the hell am I going to do to protect three full grown women from creatures who believe I am keeping the love of their life from them?

"I wish you two could have decided this morning to get along, and start talking," I groan. "We would have left like everyone else suggested. We are just dumb potatoes in this house, waiting to be harvested."

Addie places her ear against the cool metal of the door, careful but unafraid.

"We still have a chance to leave, depending on how my meeting with Master Amadeus goes," she insists.

The bitter part of me bites hard, like a dog unwilling to let go.

"Why can't you talk to him, Celestyn?" I grumble. "You've talked to him in the past."

"Through a curtain," she points out. "A-and if you knew what it was like, you wouldn't want to go there either. I left that tower in a hurry, Aidan, because I couldn't continue my research and live there at the same time. I STOLE from him on my way out. He's not just someone you piss off for shits and giggles. Adabelle should be afraid that he requested to see her at all."

I grimace, though Addie appears unaffected.

"What do you know about him, Celestyn?"

She meets my gaze.

"Just one thing for sure." She picks up her book. "He's not one of us."

# CHAPTER THIRTY-FIVE
## ADABELLE

THERE IS A LOT CELESTYN WON'T TELL US ABOUT Master Amadeus, perhaps out of fear I will change my mind last minute. There is information missing from my own set of facts that she knows, that Aidan knows.

The Master is elusive by all accounts according to Zoey, who is more honest with me than anyone has ever been. Clever, and powerful, he has gifted positions and protections to the rare elite by a wave of the hand. He has made other lesser members disappear off the face of the map all together with the same hand, but stories conflict as far as to where this goes next.

He is a person.

He is an entity.

He is a ghost.

He is a Ravager.

Celestyn claims that one time, she overheard him playing a harp, though it could have been someone else. Sometimes, there was more than one person at the opposite side of the curtain she spoke to him through, staring to her with glowering crimson eyes that seemed as if they were glowing in the dim lighting.

It brings me to wonder if Master Amadeus is more a collection of people than one in particular, and the strength of his identity lies in the incredible numbers. The strength in numbers should have occurred to us sooner, and we should have been building an army this whole time to combat our threat.

If we had ever acted as an organized unit instead of letting fear play every man and woman against the other, we might have drawn the same conclusion as the potential creature watching over us.

Though now it is too late.

I am meeting the Master tonight, for answers. Not just for the village, but for myself too.

I need these answers for myself, to know who I am and why I am here. The thirst of the undying questions plaguing our existences, crying out to know where we are and how we got here, can be quenched if I just rock the boat. It should only take a little motion to understand the brute force of our reality, and to reconcile whether or not there is any "going home". The one cost is my life, a small price to pay for whoever will take it.

Besides, Celestyn isn't all unhelpful when she *wants* to be cooperative. The research we have both done is a weak point in her hatred for me—sort of. She allowed me access to some of her translated books throughout the night to learn about the dark elven medicines, and a bite-sized chunk of their lore. It covers some basics already listed in the text belonging to Grace and Ceridwen, plus some off-hand comments written in by The King that make me smirk over his apathy.

But it does get me to think when I am through that the comments must mean at some point Master Amadeus has had access to The King. The idea gives me a glimmer of hope that I can put an end to all of this tonight—last night the moon was not quite full enough, making this one my big bang. And I have to be ready, even if I am not.

Everyone is counting on me.

It was peaceful again overnight, like it was before the attack on The Center. There hasn't been a single attack since that one, putting every villager more on edge than if they were occurring each night as per usual.

Following our conversations, hypothesizing, and deep readings, I found myself huddled up with Celestyn and Simone, laying between the two and covering my foster child in an attempt to conceal her if our small fortress was destroyed. But it wasn't, and I was permitted some additional human contact by our resident witch doctor in the process.

Ace still hasn't returned from the Suicide Missions come morning, which Aidan tells me brings more tension through Melody who panics, rumoring perhaps he was finally found out and done in this time. If Ace died, the whole team will have gone with him without question. It was bound to happen eventually without a better plan, these dark elves being primitive super creatures and us being advanced lackluster bags of trash.

But no one knows for sure, and when Aidan steps out to set up a meeting with our leftover search teams, I hold out hope.

In his absence, I sit in the pile of blankets Celestyn nests in, surrounded by her unending supply of books. She has already left for the day to do home visits at the appeasement and insistence of Aidan, carrying a Santa Claus-sized sack of our only medical supplies from the back room as she goes. I should be out too for my final meet up with the search teams, but after studying my ankle I am unsure if I am going to make it out of the house unless I have some serious help.

Most injuries I've incurred living in Limbo have healed at expedited rates. I don't have the initial thigh wound I was found with except for a ridged, nasty scar that can barely be seen against the porcelain plane of my skin. However, my ankle seems to have missed the memo for these few talents I possess. My functions are returning to an average healing mode as though my body is officially tapped out and exhausted, outside of my lungs feeling a bit lighter.

Which is great—except that I really need my foot right now, and my ankle is still busy looking like a raw and meaty, black and green beach ball. I still can't fit my shoe back on, and I've been afraid to wash the clothes on my body, seeing as how they might not fit going on again. I can revert to using an extra long stick from outside to help me walk if I need it, because god knows I will—and who foresaw me becoming a twenty-one-year-old cripple? But first, I have to actually get up.

*Fucking yay, me.*

I reach over the little area Simone slept to where Celestyn left some of her advanced, foreign elf creams, rubbing it over the tender area I am wounded and wrapping the area with new bandaging left behind to avoid infection. Simone and Zoey are both prepared to leave house by the time I am finished, dressed and having eaten breakfast while I was still trying to breathe life into this dead body.

I put on my single shoe, peering up to Zoey whose cheeks are puffed out and reddened, hands cradling her stomach like she could crush it back up inside her abdomen to mend the agitation it causes. If only.

She has been working with Simone in the barn lately for extra cash, a situation that is ideal for me so I can know right away if anything goes wrong. Especially when Simone isn't in peak condition and requires a lot of help throughout the day as it stands.

It's not like Zoey is in peak condition either—way overdue and cripplingly exhausted. So they get to keep track of each other, making my job easier, kind of. Maybe more convenient is a better term. I smile at her through her pain, through the purple pillows swelling beneath her eyes.

"Rough night?" I hobble to my knees, sucking in a gasp of agony, and squeezing Simone into a deep hug.

There is so much weight needed to be put back on to this kid, and we don't have any idea why she went down in the first place, or if she will do it again. But she smells good. Like honey soap. I bet Zoey helped give her a bath early this morning so I could take my time getting ready.

"I haven't been sleeping fucking well, at all." Zoey rubs her eyes so that she doesn't cry, pressing the tears up behind her eyelids. "My contractions are getting heavier, and fucking consistent. It feels like this baby is just going to fall out of my damn vagina, Adabelle."

I don't think I can possibly cringe harder.

"I'm...sorry to hear that?"

"What's vagina?" Simone pulls from our hug to look me in the face.

"It's where this damn baby's head is going to bust through like a scene straight out of a wicked sci-fi movie," Zoey groans, answering so I don't have to.

Simone thinks about this, and her little brow furrows, teeth clenched in a confused smile.

"Oh. Eww."

I snort, just a little.

*Damn right, girly girl.*

"It's the woes of womankind." I kiss her forehead. "Well, some of us, anyway."

There is no amusement for any of us when I say these words. It is a simple truth. It is Zoey's nightmare, and though she appears to love her baby, her baby is here for all the wrong reasons.

"Kasismis is going to fucking come back for me." Zoey fidgets with her long, Viking-esque braid. "It's going to be fucking soon, before this place goes to shit. I mean it. My contractions are almost unbearable. I don't have a lot of time left...and I don't fucking think he's going to let me and this baby stay here unless he's dead."

I shrug.

"He might be dead. Who knows? It doesn't matter. I promised you that I won't let anything happen to you, or the baby. I'm serious."

Zoey attempts to chuckle, but it is littered with anxiety.

"What? Your crippled ass? Are you going to scare the big bad guys away with your beastly rumors?"

I use the wall to help me stand up, clutching Simone's hand in mine.

"Believe and achieve." I grin, swinging my backpack on and hopping them out the door where I search for a makeshift cane so I can take them to the barn where we will part ways.

It is a beautiful morning, glittering white with sunlight and clouds to provide shade as a haven to the heat. The birds are singing, and the breeze is blowing hard enough to disturb my loose bun. The cows are grazing in the open space between the markets and the barn, donkeys groaning jealous brays inside the confines of the pen.

I don't want to ruin it too much by speaking aloud all the plans I have to make for the day so that it stays beautiful. I also don't want to mention to either of them that I haven't quite figured out how to uphold all my promises to them and meet Amadeus in the same instance. I just push it all aside for the sake of one proper morning.

Simone smothers me in a hug that sucks the air straight out of me, and I make sure to comment on how strong she is. It swells the little girl with immeasurable pride, and I leave her with it to meet Aidan and our teams not far from the structure in the field next to the tree line. When Aidan sees me, he breaks away from the group, meeting me halfway. He stops close enough that I can feel the weight of his body hovering over me, looking toward the ground to find me, face red.

I manage a small smile.

"Today is the day." I try to move around him, but he moves with me. So I stop.

"Are you...okay?" He pries.

"I'm nervous," I reply. "But I will be fine."

My backpack is heavier when I am slightly hunched, walking like an old man with a bad spine. I am going to end up with a wicked back disease before I get the hell out of here.

"You shouldn't go." Aidan looks me in the face. He makes a point to, and he means it. "I just...you could die. And I don't want that to happen."

My chest hitches. Hurts. But I force a crooked grin anyway.

"Why would I die?" I jest. "If anything, I'll vanish into thin air. Why would I die? Dying is for the birds."

Aidan pauses, sucking in a stream of air, and shaking his head. "It's fine. Just, never mind. If you don't know, you don't need to know, because you wouldn't listen anyway. It's not important."

This rubs me the wrong way. I feel my entire tiny form heat up in sick rage, hands clenched in taut fists at my side.

"Stop it!" I shout, startling him. "You don't trust me. Just like everyone else, and I'm so sick of it. We can't continue a partnership where you don't trust me. We can't make a reliable team if we don't trust each other."

Aidan crosses his arms, rolling his eyes. "Every time I have ever left you alone, it has been nothing but trouble. When we are together, it is nothing but trouble. Our existences together have brought nothing but pain, and I've put in all the effort to get close to you. Where is your try, huh?"

He has me, but I react without thought.

"I can't afford to be close to people," I huff. "But I haven't KILLED you yet, so grant me that. I haven't killed anyone yet, but you HAVE. Plus, I seem to recall saving your ass at least once. And despite your every 'better judgment', you have come to get me at every. Single. Turn. So if you don't trust me, then why bother?"

This is unexpected, and he tenses up in defense.

"I-I don't know," he admits. "It's like...a calling. I saved Zoey against my better judgment too without even knowing her an eighth as well as I know you."

I purse my lips, and he turns away to head over to our team. He keeps just a slow enough pace to make sure I maintain an impaired, but functional trail at his backside, the group having dwindled down to maybe six people, not including ourselves. Over half these faces are new, but I can still spot two old ones.

Part of me is relieved not to see Glue Man anymore, but the other tiny sliver of me feels guilty for this. Glue Man was dumb... and hateful...and cruel...but he didn't deserve to die. He helped save people, and he had the potential to turn his life around one day.

I don't know if stupidity should equate to a death sentence.

"Is this everyone?" Aidan looks over the men, a bit disap-pointed.

The tiny of group of heads bob nervously, peeking around to make sure everyone has their own dagger. This wasn't the first job most of them had acquired. I think nearly all of them had others prior to this.

One man I remember as Quinn from the markets, who looked about seventeen or so, started out as a baker in Limbo two years ago. He was recruited this morning when it was made known our numbers have dwindled next to none. Judging by his face, he knows what we do...and he doesn't want any part in it. Not that there is a choice.

I feel a bit sorry for him.

Aidan lets out a slow, decisive sigh.

"Okay," he heaves. "Here's what we will do today. We are going to section off into groups of two. When you get in the groups of two, Addie is going to give you one of the following assignments. She will tell you that you will either be collecting water rations, collecting edible plant matter from the forest, or hunting to build our meat stores within the village."

I turn to him. "What about looking for new people?"

He is firm. More so than I have ever seen him.

"If we come across anyone who needs our help, we will help. But at this point, we can't waste any more time on finding more mouths to feed."

My jaw drops. I can feel my eye twitching in distress, corners of my mouth falling.

"That's disgusting." I prep for a fight.

"Survival is disgusting, Addie. Lose your sympathy for a minute, and find the fighter in your sacrificial body."

"But what about THEIR survival?"

"Their survival doesn't particularly matter to me right now."

Aidan's rubber band patience is about to find its snapping

point with me. I can see it, and I want to stop testing its margins. But I can't find it in me, that ruthlessness he has. That he wants me to have.

"Fuck. You," I bark.

It doesn't affect him. "My skills on this team are currently superior to yours. It would do you well to listen just one time in your life. But if you can't, I suggest you leave and find a job more suited to your needs in this time of crisis."

Everyone is uncomfortably silent for a moment. I am huffing air like a bull, squeezing my fists tight, and wondering if I am tall enough to deck him straight in his four fucking eyes. I will have to aim up, but I think I can fucking do it.

Except I don't. I don't actually want to.

I bite my lip and look away.

"Fine."

I do as I am told, awaiting the group to pair off into teams, and begrudgingly giving them each an assignment based on the overview of what I know about them. I can't breathe, watching them leave and knowing no one will come back if they aren't being looked for. But Aidan bobs his head in a motion to follow him after they're gone, assuring that I do.

We walk in dead quiet through Limbo, resentment building while we approach the remains of the old village, wading through the weeds not trampled on as we do, and weaving our way closer to Master Amadeus' tower.

It isn't time, yet, but we bring a large sheet to fold up any material we might find in the area, holding it like a sack. The hours tick by this way, looking through crappy little houses, and scoping the area for useful products. It isn't a surprise we make a few interesting finds in the process.

Bowls. Spoons. A necklace, and another, empty backpack. Clothes. Daggers. Arrows Aidan can use for his bow. And then, an unusual beauty, as a distinct crunch shrieks below my good foot.

I nearly leap out of my skin at the rattle of ribs and bones, scurrying into Aidan's hardened form at the sight of the sunbaked remains of a long-passed corpse. I can feel the wrap of his arm around my shoulders, delivering a firm, grounding squeeze and following closer.

I bend fast, shimmying my way to the ground and pulling from the milky bone fingers a long, heavy sword. It is well built, I realize, a leather handle worn from the elements, but the grip still exceptional, the pommel embedded with rubies and sapphires. Nothing like what blacksmiths in Limbo have ever made.

Aidan inspects it for himself too, the silvery blade unrusted and almost untouched—as if it had never seen battle. There is not even a hazy smear of blood to cloud its immaculate design.

"This is a great find." He nods, placing the weapon in my arms, almost too heavy to hold, and searching the surrounding weeds for a sheath not attached to the body. "I can't believe someone didn't find this sooner."

"You can have it," I blurt out. Aidan stops searching, freezing in place, and I blush. "It's just, I've never used one. I don't think I could wield it with the confidence I would need to do it well."

He frowns.

"You could learn, you know," he offers.

"Who would teach me?" I scoff. "Besides, I don't think I have it in me to hurt anyone. At least, not in the way this thing could hurt."

It's true, if you don't count the mermaid, and he can't deny it. I've gone to every length to avoid serious damage to the very people who hate me the most, and beyond. Even at cost to myself. I can't see myself causing unnecessary pain if I can avoid it.

Aidan pinches his lips together, retrieving the sword from me and dragging it while we carry on with our search. We don't stop our scavenging until the sky is rich with the beginning twinkles of starlight. A bit too long to be out, but we both need the solidarity of it—the time to think.

We haul our glorious finds back into the village where many townspeople are shutting themselves inside for the night. There is a chill in the night air that feels good, prickling my skin under clothes drenched in perspiration, and making it easier to hobble on. We decide to meet with the teams in the morning to distribute our goods later in the day—if I am still around to see it through. Aidan will be the only one of us going home tonight, after all.

On the way to the house, footsteps crunch at our backsides, and a sickening groan makes me spin, reaching for my dagger and Aidan for his brand-new sword. But we are only faced with Zoey and Simone, both looking a bit shaken but unharmed.

"What are you doing out?" I balance on my stick.

But I already know. I see it now.

The blood.

There is so much of it, slipping down Zoey's legs in glistening waterfalls and creating a swirling trail where she has walked, trying to find us. In outside torchlight, I can see she is crying, quivering in pain while she slows her own breathing in an attempt to compensate.

*Why is there so much blood? Is this normal?*

"Adabelle," Zoey grits her teeth. "I think I'm...I can't...agh..."

She takes a deep, gasping breath.

Simone whimpers, racing for me and catching me on the bad side so I tumble over, catching myself on Aidan.

I wish I could pick them both up to take them home, my mind rolling a million miles a minute.

This is a bad time to go into labor. A really bad time. Can't this wait? Can babies wait?

"It's okay," I reassure, setting my crap down. I wrap an arm around Simone's shoulders, shuffling toward my friend in need. "It's okay. You'll be okay. Okay? I promise. I've got this."

"Where is Celestyn?" Aidan whirls in circles as if she would jump out from behind any of the corners like a fucking genie from a magic medical lamp.

Zoey cries out, hunching over and holding her rock solid belly.

"I don't fucking—" she wails, squeezing her eyes shut. "I looked for her at home, and...I can't..."

Crap.

"She has all the supplies with her, Aidan." I frown. "We're fucking screwed without at least some of that shit. We need to go to The Center and see if we can't find any that wasn't destroyed."

Aidan shuts this idea down, not missing a beat.

"Are you stupid?" he whispers. "Absolutely not. We need to get Zoey home, and deal with what we have."

"What if she needs something we don't have?"

"We make do."

"You're unbelievable, you know that?"

I start limping for The Center's ruins. It isn't far off, and we can make it on foot before it gets too late, I think. Aidan stands in place for a second, growling in frustration and whisking Simone off her tiny, precious feet. He drops our supplies in place, slinging her around to his back so he can follow close on my heels in defeat.

When we reach the remains, Zoey lays on the grass to reduce the flow of gravity on her lady bits, huffing slow and cursing the infant under her breath. I make a silent prayer we have enough time, or at least just a little, to look. To make everything safe, and bearable.

I step around walls that are still standing, sifting through layers of brick and crushed stone, fingers grasping at anything they can get a grip on while Aidan spins in a nervous frenzy. Unwilling to help. It feels like forever passes before he is willing to speak up around the wall.

"Addie, we have to go," he calls. "It is getting really late."

I have found a few dirty towels half-eaten by fire, and an empty, smashed jar of evaporated medicine. Everything else is far too buried, destroyed, or sullied with ash. I find the further I dig, the more I am acting unreasonably.

Do I even know what I am doing?

I just want a needle and thread. Celestyn took all that I had in my backpack this morning, and I just need something to hold her over if something goes wrong.

I can't lose Zoey.

"Soon," I promise, digging.

Zoey screams through gritted teeth, almost howling and sobbing. *Make it stop! I don't want to do this.*

I shovel stone aside faster, finger pads bleeding and nail beds breaking. I want to make it stop. More than anything, I want to help.

*"Now,"* Aidan commands quietly, but the tone feels the same as if he had shouted it.

It is harsh, and unrelenting.

"You can't tell me what to do in the real world, outside of work." I sniff, refusing to give in.

"No, no I can't. But I can advise you to do the right thing, and right now, you're being a moron. We need to get Zoey somewhere safe. Warm. Away from the elements where she can have her baby."

That's true.

I hold my face for a minute with filthy, blackened hands, raking them up my forehead and through my bangs. Still purple. And green. And blue. Sort of like a bruise, but faded now. Growing softer in shade as my hair starts to grow with me here. The realization grounds me, letting me think in my whirlwind of thoughts.

"Give me five more minutes," I request. "Just five, to find some needles and thread. This is still a medical event, and she is a first-time mother. We don't know how big that baby is, and it could tear her in half on the way out. It isn't like we have formula if she bleeds out."

Quiet. Other than the sound of Zoey's breathing, it is quiet.

"Listen," Aidan replies. "Listen to me, Addie. What you are looking for is probably gone by now. That fire burned real hot, for a real long time."

"Things can survive a fire, Aidan!"

There is hurt in this, but I don't mean for there to be. Still, it is visible across every fiber of my being. Like a stamp over my ugly face. Aidan tries to be gentle with his rebuttal. Reasonable.

"You made a promise to meet Amadeus, Addie. *To everyone.* You can't be present for the baby, and you don't have time for this. There are other obligations to fulfill that include our long-term survival."

"Adabelle!" Zoey's voice raises an octave with every bloodcurdling letter, and I jump.

I poke my head around the wall. There seems to be even more blood on her legs than earlier, and my thoughts muddy again. I whip inside, tossing rubble around like a twister to try and locate boxes below where the desk should have been. They have to still be there.

"I can find them faster if you help," I yell to Aidan.

But he is silent. Unmoving in the shadow he creates outside.

I hear him bend, setting Simone in the grass, and straightening in the dirt and grass. I stop, racing outside and holding to the charred, melted rock. I know what he is doing, where he is going, but my heart doesn't register.

"W...where are you going? What are you doing?"

He is upset, stressed and quaking with the last of his patience.

"Home. There is a bad feeling in the air tonight, and I'm not staying here so you can lead me to my death."

My voice lowers, uncertain and abashed.

"You're not...going to help me? What about Zoey?"

His response is a stab to an already open wound.

"No, I'm not, Addie. You're on your own. I'm going home, and hopefully on the way there, I can find Celestyn. That way, I can save at least one person worth saving if things go downhill. Zoey is a lost cause. She'll be carted off anyway if she screams even once, which she can't stop doing as we speak."

My eyes burn, and there is a heavy, suffocating thickness added to the air floating between us as he turns away, allowing the aura to swallow me whole. My bottom lip quivers, chest writhing in unmatched pain, arms losing the energy they had sustained earlier. At the doorway, I sit, digging at a lazy pace, finding two slim needles, and feeling validated—though questioning the worth of it.

I understand why he left. I don't blame him, despite the ways it hurts. But it also brings to light another feeling that I have always known inside, afraid to acknowledge the truth of it, which is that we were never a team. Never partners. It has always been nothing but business, and our business has concluded.

In the visible distance, I see the weeds and brush shift, Zoey sitting up as she notices as well. She winces, biting her tongue and groaning.

"I think I'm going to throw up," she sobs.

Simone starts to cry a little too, and I pat her on the shoulder at the same time.

But my heart stops. Restarts. Races.

"Me too," I choke.

Four figures emerge from the distant tree line, many more on their heels.

We have to go.

# CHAPTER THIRTY-SIX
## SAHANNA

I TELL MYSELF IT GETS EASIER, THE CLOUD OF TERROR EVER accumulating droplets of misery that is my life as I know it. I feed myself little lies similar to this one like decadent chocolates, flagrant attempts at making it easier on me, rather than facing the promises I have been fed.

At least I have control over my own fibs.

I was told early on that I would adjust to my new home given time exposed to the primitive lifestyle. I would grow to accept the strange husband I was forced to wed following a few mere hours of knowing his presence existed, and the agonizing stretch of him pressing his way into my body would become, if not pleasurable, bearable.

I was commanded to submit my entire person to his purposes, and my body to the gestation of his future children. It was a part of the public vows, and I spoke them into existence, making them a reality that blossoms the vibrant guilt of blame—as if the end result could possibly be my fault when I never wanted part in this.

It is an adjustment, I tell myself, to endure and understand the repeated pain of my uterus expelling small and unfinished life into the world so I can cling to the only power that remains within my grasp to this day. However, in my experience, "adjustment" is simply a cop-out. Because I can't stop feeling how it hurts, even if it somehow hurts less. I almost don't want to acclimate.

I should feel something, after all, right?

The moon looms like a silver, waxy ball in the midnight sky tonight, stings of pale white beaming down through the treetops like alien spotlights here to uncover my secrets at my most vulnerable moments. I wince away from it, trying to relax my legs from hours of walking, shuddering at the violent prodding of sharp wire stolen from the loose end of a trapper's cage pressing into what I assume is my cervix, digging in my best attempt to shred it apart within the time I have been allotted to urinate while Silas scopes the area.

It is much harder tonight, for some reason, and I hold my free hand flat against my lips, biting hard on my fingers to keep from gasping at the burning, unmatched turmoil that bleeds through my insides.

There will be no other time to get this done, I remind myself when my threshold pleads me to stop.

I need to be strong.

There is no other way, and it has to be done.

I need to maintain the illusion of control. To maintain what freedom remains of my shallow, endless life.

This nasty little brat has already survived too long in the first place, creating a filthy nest in my quarters, and swelling up my insides like a balloon that I would present to the universe at birth. In turn, these people would coo as if it were the sweetest creature blessed upon us, instead of the nightmare I live with every single day. Could live with, every single day, if this doesn't work.

Soon, the baby beast would be much too large, perhaps even salvageable.

Small bugs chant solemn music around me, filling the night's crisp air with the symphony of betrayal that is taking place. The breeze moves it along, whispering to the leaves of the next plant nearby in a forest that hisses with condemnation. A swish in the tall grasses a couple feet to the left freezes me in place before I edge the instrument in deeper, achieving the ultimate pain I've sought this whole time.

It is a sweet, victorious cramping that gurgles from within a warm, sick wetness reaching unspeakable peaks of affliction, and tapering so it leaves spasms of hurt in my wake. I try not to groan, gripping the ashy tree next to me until the bark crumbles beneath the power of my bony fingers. I decide I will wait to break the untimely news to Silas if it proves to be done, to draw away suspicion and avoid any violent reprimanding.

I pull the rusted wire from my inside with a surgeon's precision, relieved it doesn't catch or stick, tossing it into the noisy set of tall weeds. This will be the second hardest "miscarriage" I have ever been part of. There will be a real birth this time, probably on a bed sheltered at an inn if we can reach one in time after The King's dragon comes for us. It won't be like the others, where I can pretend like Aunt Flow was gifting me an extra heavy crimson river of Satan's piss.

There will be a body involved.

I will have to look at it, this parasite I am eradicating, and pretend I am sad.

I sniff, dusting my skirts, and arranging them so that the blood will not dampen through right away. I need to find a way to disguise the smell as well, but we are so close to the chaos it shouldn't matter.

I waddle back to where I was instructed to wait for my husband's return, blood bubbling, gushing from under my dress down each of my thighs, similar to if I had wet myself, but much more sinful. In my head, I am rehearsing what I will do this time when I can no longer conceal the distinct smell of personal death over those he is not familiar with.

What will I say when the black shadows roll in thick plumes to his nose like smoke he can breathe in? How will I release it to him, and the world, as unrelenting grief and failure?

I am very experienced in both concepts, very adept at understanding the shape of these feelings. I can bring them to life while I feel nothing at all.

I am empty, a lonely girl from the start.

So, I decide I will begin with the classic stunned silence, something uncertain and nervous when I see his nostrils flare at the scent of red. There will be a moment when I excuse myself from his presence to "check" my undergarments.

I'll tell him I feel a little soiled. It might only be discharge, which is sickly common in what appears to be all stages of pregnancy. I will reassure him, despite his reluctant knowledge. Maybe I peed a little. It happens too, much more than I care to admit.

I will disappear into the vast tree line, or washroom of the inn, to still my beating heart so I am able to deliver the news, so that I can try to mean what I say without producing a clever smirk because I have won yet another round. I will return in a silent, but hysterical sobbing, tears misting my face so that it leaves a rounded outline on his shirt. I will ask why, and plead with him to do something, anything to save our baby.

Of course, it will already be too late, and this will spare my womb a good few months of healing, as well as his heavy heart. Dark elves are particularly attached to their children, family being an important model in their structured society.

I fidget at the folds of my dress again, trying to perfect its design before his return so that I will seem normal upon arrival. Unnatural swathes of wind yank the silk against my legs in spite of it, as if protesting all that I can do to defend myself, mussing my hair so that I can taste the knotted braids and beads woven inside them.

I close my eyes, bringing a trembling arm up over my face as the dirt swirls, sticks and rotting debris grazing my palms and then settling where it belongs once more. It would little phase me, if it weren't for the pain.

There is nothing that can make me fear for this life I lead. Especially not when the primary reason for the rigid distaste that eats away at every inch of my being is, perhaps, not that far away. Not that this path is dangerous to start. The way home least laden with terror is the one that brings us so close to the village my own species dwells inside called Limbo. It is a path Silas always takes when we travel without his brother. It is longer, but with less confrontation, the dragon knowing to meet us four more miles out.

I brush the flyaway hairs from my face, raking fingers through to remove anything I might have picked up from the forest floor. It has been a long time since I have been this close to the village during the raids, and I have never been part of them in person.

Silas attempted to shelter me from this operation. He assumed I knew nothing of it, and ignorance might have helped me feel a little less deplorable inside for not doing as much to save them when I am in a position to do so. But I had questions the first time we passed through. There aren't a lot of easy answers when a girl can hear men dying, and women being shorn away from homes like ripe fruit from a vine.

"What is it you are doing alone, so close to the borders?" A deep, rough voice calls to me.

My feet skip and scramble at the acute realization it is not my husband speaking to me, but someone else I am not familiar with. My eyes travel the length of an elf who stops in his superhuman, dirt blowing speed, six feet in front of me.

I attempt to smile with pleasant grace, as is expected of a woman in my position, flashing my white teeth and batting my eyes. The green dress I wear happens to be sleeveless, held with a delicate tie about my neck that billows in sharp ribbons down my back, most importantly showcasing my husband's tattoo on my naked upper arm, snaking along my collar bone.

If I were an honest woman, I would call it a brand, a mark that tells other men of the race that I am his property and is universally understood as such. It keeps most other men of the species from seeing potential in my body, and sometimes, I am recognized as the wife of The King's closest advisor, giving me just a little more influence than the average woman. I caress the design with the tips of my fingers, tracing the visible imprint, and giving the man before me a look of sudden abash.

This man is tall like the others, and for awhile when I was adjusting to my new life, it felt good to be smaller than almost all men and women alike. I am rather statuesque myself as a human woman, and in my foremost memories of this place as well as the one that came before it, it wasn't all that commonplace to feel so small. Here, I look up to him, meeting his piercing, glowing green eyes that attempt to decipher the meaning of each symbol upon my arm.

"Only waiting on my husband." I speak in my most sugary tone. "He's not too far gone, I'm sure. I can call for him if you prefer."

A bloodcurdling scream pierces our conversation through the heart like a double-edged sword. It scrapes each limb, bush, and creature between ourselves and the darkest layer of the defensive shield protecting Limbo, prickling my skin into rounded gooseflesh that feels as if I have a needle slipped into every pore. It sounds again not even a minute later, but quieter, the anthem of defeat reverberating in a high-pitched whine that continues to echo long after the noise stops. My head turns toward the sound with little control, my neck just a scrawny stand for the rotating orb of my skull, memories of my own capture reeling inside my thoughts.

It's only...this sound is unusual. There are no resounding words, no pleas, though surely it is a woman.

I don't catch the swell of sobbing or calls for help. No desperate bargains.

Just pain, and only pain.

I wet my lips, sliding my tongue across their small surfaces while my heart races, drawn to the noise.

"Your imprints," the elf pulls me to our conversation, "they belong to a member of the royal family?"

"Yes," I affirm, mumbling.

Those who pay attention can tell. Everything belonging to the royal family is...different.

"Care to give them my regards?" The creature hesitates. "My

sister would have never survived the winter had it not been for the magics of your family. I am entirely indebted to our King, and his kin. Please, tell them?"

He bows deeply out of respect, as is tradition, bending his skinny body in a near perfect angle. I give him motion to rise in turn, dipping in a curtsy, though my eyes continue to stray in the direction of the village. Law dictates that I do not have to give him these sort of court manners. In fact, we can both end up in a lot of trouble if it were seen I paid him similar respects as I do my husband by the right snitch who knew who I was. But it is pleasant to hear of my new family doing good in this vile place, and it is better to feel complacent.

A new scream follows my movements, staggered by a decisive snap. I shake myself free of this notion I can be an equal commoner.

"Of course," I promise, absent. "What is your name? I will let The King know whence next I see him."

It is an uncomfortable silence now, a hefty void that the operations in the village do not fill with all of its vocalized suffering thickening the atmosphere. I understand why, wishing I had said nothing at all, but unable to take it back all the same. It isn't simple to feel pity for the awful creatures that make up this universe, but The King is rather...intimidating, to those subjects who have never been close to him. Hell, he is intimidating to me, and I find there is little to fear at all when death is at the center of my own yearning.

"Valemon," he says. "My name is Valemon." Another pause, and a quick look to the sky, as if it is watching over his slack in the raid. "Please, tell him that if ever he is in need of service, my family resides in the village closest to The Magholm Forest and The Pass."

"In the one past Praesidia?" I bite my lip. "I mean, yes, of course. Please, go on your way now. I am certain there is a night's work ahead of you. Happy huntings."

He nods, hand brushing the hilt of his sword sheathed in an elaborate leather scabbard at his waist. In my younger days, I might have cried a little. In the life before this one, that is, thinking about how many people will be murdered tonight, and how many women will be poached for the cause of The King.

It is a helpless thing, to know and to listen. To cradle my ears with invisible hands, and know that because I am a woman, I can do nothing here other than what I have.

But today, I only heave a sigh. I hope that his huntings are less than fruitful, and that innocent people are spared. I pray, I can keep what little piece of my conscience remains.

Silas emerges from underneath an overgrown root of white barked trees. I hold small doubt he had watched the whole conversation play out, collecting intel for his twin brother if there were any to be had, and awaiting one wrong move that would have the poor fellow killed.

They were savage beasts, in total, animals by nature considering they were the first perfected, major creation in existence. And I am *his* mate for life because he has chosen me for the job.

Silas takes my face in both his enormous hands, stroking my cheeks with his thumbs as he plants a kiss on my lips. I try my best not to pull away. Blood is now filling my shoes below my skirts, my thick socks absorbing what they're able and my feet coating in the rest. My fingers cross that the smell from the village dilutes this for a little longer so I have time to enact my own plan accordingly. We stand frozen in this thought of mine while chaos fires about us, a distant sobbing causing me to grimace.

It has been longer than I care to remember since I blinked away candlelight in a quarantine room on a sweltering summer day, but I find myself convinced that more time has passed than what is true without anyone to miss me, or relate to the pain I experience that soars to greater heights every day. I had a second or two of human contact before I left their makeshift hospital in a panicked hurry, leaving me in wonder at what would have become of me had I just stuck around to listen.

Not that there is much use in sulking. Exactly here is where my decisions have gotten me, and exactly here is where countless women lost their abilities to make important decisions again.

We walk in the path my husband directs, mostly along the darkest glow of the shield where the least amount of foliage stands in our way. If I were braver, I could leap through the purple hue and make a dive for the one freedom that exists in this world for my gender. But at this time of night, Silas could follow me with little issue. A reprimanding for such deeds is not a price worth paying. Still, I run my hands longingly through it, humming a gentle tune that I can hardly recall.

I used to have dreams of going home to these sounds. To waking up to the four walls of a dim lit hospital late at night, and blinking to the rhythmic chirping of machines that keep me on life support while this nightmare becomes a distant nightmare. My mom would start to blubber over me, tears of joy being the only wetness on my clothes ever again. My little sister would wrap her thin, deft arms around my shoulders, and my baby brother would climb up into my lap.

I would finally be *home...*

All at once, I find myself missing them all with a fierce intensity that cannot be confined to the privacy of my thoughts. My eyeballs burn, and I lean my face into my chest so that my long, dirty blond curls shade the sorrow that steams out my sockets against my will.

*Mom. I need my mom, so badly.*

I have no family here.

Just Silas. Just a stranger.

What would mom say if she could see me? If my baby brother were here, would he try to protect me?

I hate them for not protecting me.

"Are you okay?"

I sniff at the sound of Silas' concern. Mom would not be happy about how I dealt with the unborn problem, for sure. Old fashioned hag...God, why can't she be here?

"Oh, yeah...definitely." I sniff again, wiping away hot trails of tears with an emaciated wrist. "You know, I'm just thinking about my mom again. It's hard."

He stops, pulling me into him so that I can hear the beating of his heart, calm and slow. If he weren't a horrible jackass, this would be comforting.

"She lives a proper life," he assures, as if it possibly changes anything for me.

Fuck her, and her "proper life".

I nod anyway, as if it makes a difference, or soothes the eternal ache that plagues me. The cramping is beginning to intensify, but it is still enough to ignore as we move on.

The trees and weeds stir next to us a fourth-mile into our two-person caravan. Silas pauses, watching as from it bursts Kasismis, holding tight to a tall, mousy girl with a belly larger than my own. She is sobbing, as they often do, hysteria unparalleled by anything I have seen prior. The girl, younger than myself, beats him with tiny, ineffective fists.

*You killed her,* she screams through staggered, familiar groans and shaky breaths.

I sink behind Silas, peeking around his arm so I can eavesdrop enough to understand. It is unheard of under The Mass Extinction Plan to kill women, and I haven't caught wind of a rule change as of yet.

I tremble, legs quaking and eyes trying to find Silas'. Is he going to act?

He is paying attention.

"Adabelle..." The girl screams, pulling this way and that as she is moved deeper into the forest. "You fucking killed her...she was... and laid there with..."

Silas lets them leave, mulling the facts over and deciding he doesn't care.

The sound of this girl's voice is beginning to fade, and I catch my husband at least out of a peripheral glance, questions infesting my thoughts.

He touches my bicep, reassuring, but evil.

"Let's go."

# CHAPTER THIRTY-SEVEN
## ADABELLE

I SHUFFLE FORWARD USING THE STICK I'VE KEPT AS A balance to maintain steady footing in my newfound panic. My swollen ankle is angrier than ever at my continued missteps, putting pressure on the leg without thinking twice, feeling a distinct, loud pop at the final movement that nearly sends me to the ground. Simone paces in miniature circles the further I get from them for a better look, Zoey's head whipping to meet the figures emerging with violent grace and unison from the tree line in greater and greater numbers.

I can see the tears before I hear them, the squeal of pain that acknowledges defeat.

"Fu-ck," she sobs, and then loses an agitated groan. "They're fucking here, aren't they? Did you find what you need?"

I bob my head.

"Yes."

This is my fault, our exposure. I can't control my thoughts, and I can't undo this blame that overtakes me.

Zoey fights against my truth as a grim reminder of my shortcomings, repeating *no* like a chant that can make the enemy numbers dissolve into thin air. I wish I could have lied to her to make it easier. I want to make our dire situation as easy as a lie I would tell a child in the case of an intruder.

I want to be effortless.

Cover her head. Close her eyes. Tell her we are fine when we are not.

Why can't things be as easy as a tall tale?

Zoey is a sweet, innocent girl behind the tough mask she wears, and Simone is a child. Neither of them deserves this anarchy. Not ever. Not at this age. Not at this time. Not at this point in their lives, when everything else is so hard.

They should be doing tasks that are productive to their futures. Zoey and Simone should be in school, or in bed, being tucked away to a night of sleep, thinking about what they are going to have for breakfast tomorrow.

These girls should have friends. Romances. Recesses. Professional work lives.

Anything, but illness. Anything, but waiting to be split in half by another, smaller person.

I hold the air in my lungs, punishing myself with suffocation, and then letting it out slowly as another groan slips from my first friend in this whole world. I come to the conclusion we can't stay here, and I don't think Aidan wants us. We have more than likely already been spotted from such a distance by our eagle-eyed opponents, and it makes our escape all the more narrow.

Our best bet at this time is to run. Fast. And hide.

My ankle protests to this, however, panging with the haunting fact that I will slow my wards to a crawl, even with the benefit of adrenaline spikes.

I'm useless.

"We die?" Simone tugs at the hem of my shirt, peering back and forth between me, and the soldiers invading our village.

My throat clenches tight. I hook my arms up under Zoey's, dragging her to her feet as she wars with my action, crying to be set down. She's heavier than I anticipated, heavier than me, and it is a struggle I am ill prepared for. My ankle grinds like rocks underfoot, and I bite my tongue in an agonized moan, tears springing to the corners of my eyes. Zoey stiffens on the balls of her feet at the sound, hunched over like an elderly woman and finding my gaze. Simone repeats the phrase she spoke at our feet, over and over like a scratched disc.

I find my voice, small as it is, to respond to her. "No. Not today, sweetie."

My ankle cracks on the inside, and I am afraid to look at the outside.

"We no die?" Simone tears up despite my best efforts at comfort. "I want daddy! I want daddy! Right. Now."

Her voice raises in pitch with each word, rivers carving a path over either side of her face. I release Zoey, pulling Simone into my good leg to smother the sound of her furious cries, backing us into the only standing wall at the ruins of The Center.

Zoey trails us like a beat dog, tail between her legs. She is losing a lot of blood, and her complexion is blanching, face sinking. Her whole body is convulsing with unrelenting shivers of cold and pain, breathing growing fast but shallow. I move the stray hair from her face, her skin ice cold and clammy. Soft.

Will she survive a run?

I don't know if she will survive the childbirth. I don't know anything about childbirth other than where the baby is supposed to exit, and the little fucker isn't coming out. It's just...causing intense pain, and bleeding.

Fuck. *Fuck*. FUCK.

*Just breathe*, I try to tell myself. *I've got this. I can think on my own. I just need to stop panicking.*

"We need a fucking plan, Adabelle!" Zoey cries softer, leaning on the wall as if I am not trying, Simone attempting to literally bury herself in my body for respite.

I can hear someone scream in the distance, and I wince at the sound I have made myself forget in the times of peace. The panic I feel returns full force, demanding I find a more competent adult in the area.

I can't handle this.

I need a person with more experience willing to guide me to a solution that is functional and saves every person here.

Except, when I think about it, Zoey and Simone must feel the same. I am the oldest person between the three of us, and they believe that I will be the person to fix this mess I have created. And I will be the person to blame if it goes wrong...because no matter how badly I wanted to, I couldn't will myself to listen to Aidan.

*I'm so stupid.*

Zoey and Simone are practically children, waiting for my command. It isn't fair to them that I am the leader they are stuck with, and my decision rests our uncertain fates. I can lead us to safety, or I can lead us to a future unknown.

In any event, we can't stay here much longer trying to conjure the perfect idea. It isn't safe, and it offers us nothing in the way of protection. We are exposed, and covered in soot, which can't be sanitary if Zoey's labor gets any worse—which labors all eventually do.

I peer around the corner of the wall where it lines against the weeds that lead into the old village. Outside of a clear plan where there is nothing but grass and trees, blackened homes line up just out of our view. Our old one is there somewhere, touched by the heat of the fire that destroyed our hospital, but standing, intact as the rest of them are. They can make it if they get a head start on me. I owe them at least that, and Zoey could birth her baby below ground. It might disguise the scent of her copious amounts of blood, and muffle some of her shrill screams.

"We can't keep fucking standing here," Zoey pants, weeping and eyes rolling into her head for a minute. She's already exhausted without the task I am about to embark upon her. "Adabelle, pl... pl-ple-ease."

I try to keep my voice steady for this next part. Calm, like water on a windless day. Water is still, see-through and transparent when unspoiled. It does not stir unless it is touched, and I am untouchable. I am a beast. I am a monster.

I can be this *thing* they need me to be. I have to be.

"I need you both to listen to me, okay?" I bob my head, waiting for their attention.

"Please..." Zoey mumbles to me.

I take her by the shoulders, pulling her to Simone, and locking their hands together.

"You will have to run." I am vacant of emotion. A blank canvas for blood art. "Our old home is your safest bet. It is unlikely the Ravagers will go looking there considering how much it is damaged on the outside, but you still need to run. I can't rule anything out, and you need to avoid drawing attention to yourselves, if you can."

Zoey's gaze is dull and glassy, losing its sense of panic but finding mine, squeezing out hisses of air between clenched teeth.

"Hey?" she whimpers, leaning in to take my hand in hers.

I resist the urge to pull away from her subtle intimacy, giving her limp hand a brief, firm grip.

"I will be right behind you both," I lie. "But no matter what, I need you to promise me that you won't turn around."

Simone clings to my shirt with her free hand in a vice I'm not sure I can undo. But I have to.

Zoey blubbers, dehydrating herself in a salty ocean of despair, quivering harder, but keeping her grasp on Simone.

"Y-you'll be...right there?" she weeps. "Behind us?"

"Don't turn back," I reiterate. "Run—run harder than you have in your entire life. Don't stop for the contractions. Don't stop if you hear a noise. Just start, and don't stop. Knees to chest sprints, girl."

Zoey bobs her head, using both arms to wrench Simone free of me as I reach for my dagger in the side of my backpack. Old, faithful piece of shit. I toss her to the ground, retiring her for one of the better designs I had stolen from the chest, preparing for the inevitable confrontations ahead.

When I turn my head, the girls are gone, kicking up clouds of dirt and grass. I tremble in their absence with indecisive fear, a glint of yellow in the tree line beside the wall propelling me in a dead limp sprint after them. It doesn't take long before they are far enough at my front that I lose sight of them in my hobble to catch up. I knew it would be this way, that the chance I stand tonight is next to none. I will be forced to confront the enemy at their rear if they happen to trek through, and it is a more isolating despair than any I have experienced thus far.

But I hope that I have time, and that hope keeps me moving.

The night is cloudless, albeit windy, and the moon is full. It feels...strong, if a big rock up in space could feel as such. It does to me. Powerful, as if the light gives me the energy personally to persevere when my bones are paper thin.

Nearby, I hear a yell, but it doesn't sound like Zoey. Or Simone. I stonewall the sound out, hardening myself to the noise of it, and knowing there is not a second to spare for rescue. No matter how many times I hear a call for help, I have to power through.

I stumble over a small rock hidden in the grass, gasping for a sharp inhale, and cursing under my breath. I grip the better dagger harder in my fist, pushing it off the dirt with me and rolling onward. Faster now. I don't have time to be slow, but I am not getting anywhere as quick as I'd like in this condition. I need to use the foot, the bad one. I just—

I bite the bullet so passionately my teeth could go through my tongue. I am racing like I asked of Zoey and Simone, throttling through open space and housing and sheets of metal torn away from the old village for reinforcement.

I have to reach my friend and my ward at all costs, powering through the horror seething from my toes up my knee and thigh bone. As I reach the denser portion of the housing not skirting the clearing between The Center and village, I split through the first row for cover, slowing and peeking about every corner before carrying on to the next.

On the black, sooty side of one home is a foul red blob clumped in goo that is still fresh, dripping with no corpse in sight. I scamper from it, swinging around another home, and into the open, slipping across loose dirt into the sight of two armed men speaking to one another in in a foreign language.

Their heads tilt to see me, ears long and thin past the back of their skulls, hair past their mid-backs laced in pale white clips. They're taller than anything I have been witness to alive, even more so than professional basketball players. But...that is their average height. Right?

I break into tears, pointing my infantile weapon at them while I scoot on my bottom. They appear confused, glancing wordlessly at one another while gripping the hilts of their swords. They could catch me if they wanted to, this small woman frozen in fear with a blistering foot, sinking closer into the nearest home and awaiting impending doom. They seem to consider the idea, grinning back and forth. Muttering in their curious, unique language, eying me with enthusiasm.

But they stop. Instead, they turn toward where I came from, stepping over my legs so light they don't make prints with their boots, disappearing behind another row of homes. The last one hesitates as they leave, taking one final look over his shoulder and vanishing to do his dirty work.

I stagger to my feet, panting and forcing myself home. The finish line is so close, I can almost taste it in the way I can every conversation or sleepless night I've spent there. It feels like it takes forever, heart racing, ears helpless to receiving the terror going on around me.

The attack is serious this time. These creatures mean business.

And yet, somehow, when I am faced with them, most of them don't mean it at all.

They are...amused. Humored by my attendance.

I grit my teeth, pushing my injured foot to the ground and speeding to my destination in sight. If a woman in labor can do this, so can I. But when I reach our hut, the door is still open.

Wide open.

I inch for it, stumbling up closer, and touching the familiar door. Inside, I can swear I hear something. Shuffling. No...it is too human.

My hands go numb, hoisting me along the floor as I drop to my knees in pain, crawling inside. There is crying at the rear of the room, but not from a baby. Or Simone. The floor is wet, and I touch my cheek, crimson pulling from my skin to my fingers. More blood, but not my own.

"I can't..." Zoey's voice fills my ears.

My head spins, light and dark seeping into my field of vision in delicate curtains of color. I can see the stars in space. A television with no signal. Static.

I roll to my side, dragging my knees against the floor as the world comes into focus with a blur. Like seeing through wet goggles on a summer afternoon swimming in a pool.

"Please, not yet," Zoey says.

*Not yet?*

I prop myself up on the wall, swimming in the glittering distraction of static while surfacing for air. Zoey's voice erupts into a sob during this, the first time I've heard her shed genuine, aggressive, raw pain unrelated to her pregnancy.

I creep through the entry, searching for her in the kitchen, finding two figures that are standing close together. Both too tall to be Simone.

Where is Simone?

I don't hear her. Or see her.

My gut rolls, jumping to so many conclusions I am dizzy.

I move a little to get a better look. Atop the cold, dry floor balled up on the carpet that hides the trap door, I get a better visualization of Zoey, rocking against her pain on the trap door, holding to her stomach in unavoidable fear.

From this distance, it is easier to understand the depth of her malnourishment. It isn't as easy to notice when her belly steals so much of the show, but in the moonlight, it is all there. Her eyes are sunken and dull and purple underneath, spider webbed with red cheeks hollowed out around her jaw. Lips raw. Busted and chewed.

The unhappy figure standing over her disaster of a body is who I can only assume is Kasismis. He is long and lithe, rigid with a gold tunic and white undershirt. Chestnut brown hair falls over a quiver of arrows held to him by a black leather strap, and a sword is holstered to his side by a strong belt—a weapon that must be two-thirds my own size.

But when he looks about the room in curious whiffs to her life, his eyes are softer than I imagine—for Zoey. Bothered. As if he means her no harm, though he had caused so much of it a long time ago.

It is now in his very real presence I know I have failed to do anything I have promised my friend I would. The defeat is taunting, flashing neon lights on the inside of my eyes, burning to my core with shame. The hair on my arms and legs rise in painful gooseflesh, biting at the surface of my skin.

*Do something.*

It chants this like a song in my forethought, guilt building towers of pressure until it is spilling out to the tip of my tongue, the words not quite reaching the air.

*Do something.*

I drove everyone I ever cared about into the arms of the enemy. I can't deal with the remnants of this lethal mistake. How can I? This can't be happening. It shouldn't. I won't let it.

For a split second, Zoey's eyes meet mine. She mouths something to me, lips forming each word slow and careful, fingers tapping the small rug she sits upon.

My eyes never leave her, creeping along the wall, and raising my dagger to my side on my feet for the last time. I want her to look away. To not have to see what is about to happen. This is what I have to do, the only thing I can do to make this right.

Kasismis has not taken notice of me, focused on Zoey and his unborn baby. He quietly beckons her to her feet if she is able so they can leave, offering a hand to help her up that she refuses, tears flooding her eyes.

*Please, look away. I'm not tall enough to reach his neck.*

My hand is sweaty on the dagger. Slick. Like butter. Like blood.

I grip tighter.

*Don't watch this.*

I use the wall for leverage until I am straight and level. I am a coward for less than a second longer, and then I am lunging forward in a dead sprint.

My legs pump faster than every dance I have performed in my life, burning and exhaling at the same time. Zoey mouths another series of words that I pay little mind to, but mouthing something back in turn I can't quite understand from my own lips at this time, pushing myself off the floor in a small jump as I use my entire body's weight to plunge my dagger into Kasismis' mid-backside. It sends him screeching, reeling while he regains his bearings, though the stab wound not as deep as I had hoped. Or in the proper place.

The scream could have been more shock than pain, reality whirling fast as no blood pours from the wound. The only certain part is that the injury does not dampen his murderous spirits or slow him in the least. His recovery time is nil.

My bottom lip trembles, watching Kasismis rise from the floor and start toward me, touching the dagger in his flesh with care. Removing it with less care. The silence of the action is deafening, loud and quiet all at once, a steady rage that brews across his face at the realization of my sheer audacity to do as I had unto him.

Everything else happens slowly, and yet, so fast.

Zoey screams.

I remember the sound ringing like a bell in my skull like a dial tone.

Monotone.

Or maybe that is me, screaming.

It fades into the background all the same.

I step to the door, hands up and crossed to protect my neck. My face. My brain.

The only weapon I thought to arm myself with is gone. Defense is my option. I can't outrun him.

I try.

And it is followed by the screaming of what feels like a thousand voices singing the bitter music of my demise.

Kasismis snatches my wrist in a bone shattering twist from my body. My initial reaction to pull away is subverted by the pain of the bones in my arm grinding together in his hand, breaking this trance in time. Popping. Snapping.

Is that me? Is this the sound I make when I break?

I cry out, but it is short-lived. He uses my own limb to swing me back against the wall, the whack of my head on the wood leaving me dizzy and incoherent. Breathless.

I gasp, and take in nothing but panic. My feet are sliding out from beneath me, his less than delicate grip holding me by a wad of my own hair, my fingers seeking to hold the warmth oozing from it in vibrant color as Zoey screams. Begs.

*Please, don't beg. I'm okay. This is fine.*

*Don't give him that control. The control is exactly why I am doing this.*

The pull of his strong hands jerks me upright as my body slips further to the floor, shaking me firm on my feet so I have no choice but to stand and fight. I ball my fists in front of my face, trying to keep my head straight and my eyes open. But I am seeing spots, clouds of darkness floating in place, prickling against my lashes. I am swaying side to side as this occurs, or maybe that is the world doing it for me, rocking me, like a mother would her infant to keep me calm when I should be terrified.

A comfortable pressure builds within the confines of my skull, meanwhile, at first like the worst headache of my life, and then a release, more like ice melting across the plane of agony racing through my horizons.

The screaming around us is more frantic now. Words reach my ears but make little sense. I can't comprehend them, like a new form of gibberish.

My head drops to my collarbone, neck unwilling to support its enormity, but my body remaining in place. Weak. Numb—but pained.

I can't feel his hands, but one of them has to be there. Somewhere. I can't stand on my own. I can't even see. I am blind to this thing happening to me, paralyzed by it, and silenced. Conscious, if but barely. Everything is blending into the same light, the movement of his arm a breeze carving a subtle path backward that I can trace with my other senses.

I brace myself for it, knotting with fear.

But of what? I can only guess, until the pain ensues.

*One.*

My tensed muscles give like butter. No, like water. It parts, as though it were not really flesh at all, but something malleable. Like putty. Or gelatin.

That is it.

I am not a person at all. Not here, where my body accepts this foreign object of cold steel through its outer walls like it were made to be the sheath just below my sternum.

I am an object.

I hear myself scream in this first assault, but I do not register the sound as my own. It is an alien noise, inhuman and threatened. Out of body. It is a burn at the back of my throat as fluid warm and wet rushes to aid the dry field it sears into my vocal cords.

*Two.*

I don't expect this one, another attack on my person.

But I can hear it, the strange sound of my own flesh splitting apart, sort of like a zipper peeling open. My body opens to reveal fleshy bits that keep me running like clockwork, leaving me cold where I should be hot. Safe. Seen, in these vulnerable spaces, turning and ticking. It is apparent now, how they work, and how they throb in panic.

My fingers tremble at the new openings in my gut, my chest. I think.

There is a thick gurgle the start of my chest, bubbling like lava to the neck of this volcano of pain. Throbbing with urgency.

Suffocating me, as I choke on the coppery taste. Because I can't spit it out, and I can't swallow it either.

*Three.*

Like a muffled tea kettle, I am only able to produce a high-pitched whine, almost inaudible to my own ears.

I like tea.

Did my mom ever make me tea?

Someone did.

I find sanctity where it is warm, and sweet. A pool of light brown dissolving scoops of sugar.

*Mm...*

"Kasismis!"

*Is that Zoey? She sounds...so far away.*

Where am I again? What am I doing here?

"Please," Zoey sobs. "Just...leave her alone. Please."

The blade slips from my body as easily as it crept inside. No pull. I am allowed to crumple to the floor like a wet bag, trembling fingers searching the places in which I was struck, hot and soaked. Something slick pulsates in my palm, bulging.

I want to gasp, but I don't know that I can.

Am I breathing right now?

Between my fingers, his blade slips through in a shallow wound one final time for my reckless defiance to continue living, and I shudder. A sack of meat. Nothing at all.

*No!* Zoey shrieks. I can't catch every word. *You...she...oh god...*

She is crying.

Don't cry. Please. Don't.

I'm right here. And this is fine.

I am fine.

I'm not crying. I'm not afraid.

Fear is obsolete in this state.

I am just cold. And warm.

Numb.

Numb is a feeling, right? Or the absence of it?

How good it feels, to feel nothing at all.

A high-pitched wail pierces my far away thoughts, kissing the shores of my subconscious and waving from the other side some tantalizing. Familiar. Loving.

It pulls me forward like the tide, carrying me out to sea, down into the abyss of noise and further from the absence of feeling. My fingers can flex here, touching the walls of my mind to guide me without my sight.

I am still blind.

A wave of heat swaddles me, like the blasts of hot air from the space heater my mamma used to keep in her room when I would first turn it on in the morning, giving me goosebumps as the temperature change sets in. This only draws me deeper into a much more comfortable darkness I can hide within, like a small child. Where the walls of this anarchy cease to exist, and the freedom to live in solitude washes over me in waves of black water, caressing my feet.

Is this what it feels like to die?

"Addie?" A voice calls from all around.

*Aidan? He's not supposed to be here.*

"No, Addie. C'mon. Addie? Look at me!"

*I can't, don't you see? Everything about me is but time and space. You are not here.*

"Addie, hey." I can feel the heat of his breath at my ear. His voice is loud. Almost migraine inducing.

"ADDIE! Look. At. Me. C'mon. C'MON! I'm so sorry, Addie. *Please*. C'mon. Hey! HEY!"

The way he screams is painful. Ineffable.

I've never heard these sounds before in this way. It seems impossible to make them up.

The black tides are rising higher around me, to my knees, and then my waist. They eat away at who I am outside of this realm. The waves thrash to push me down into the emptiness below, to drag me to a place where he does not exist, and I can rest. It speaks to me the nickname he branded upon me when we first met.

*Addie.* Splash. *Addie.*

*Mm...*

I can feel my face twitch. Or pinch. Did he pinch me?

"Somebody help!" He screams over the waves. "Help!"

The waves smart against my cheek.

And then everything stills.

Just like that, the water absolves into silence, and the endless black horizons rot to ash. I groan in the thick abyss that has immobilized me, eyes lolling into my head, and body giving into the demands of the forces beyond my control.

Though I do not sink in this water at all.

Death...just feels so kind.

*Addie...*

Splash.

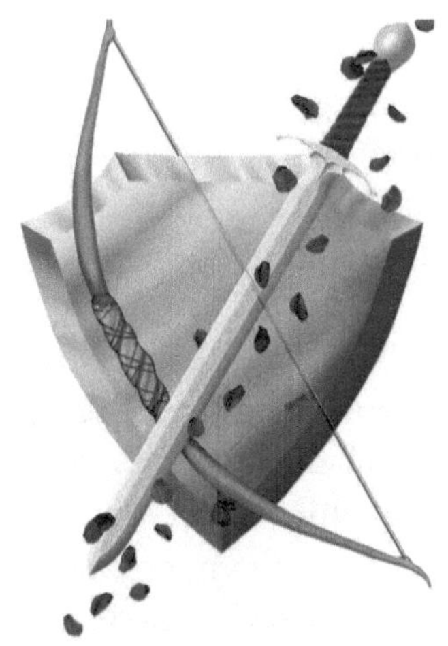

# CHAPTER THIRTY-EIGHT
## AIDAN

I DIDN'T GET FAR INTO MY DEPARTURE, AND I NEVER should have left her.

I know that now. I knew that then.

Addie is so...impulsive, and temperamental. It is just who she is, and who she has always been since she rediscovered herself in Limbo. She doesn't think with any kind of clarity, and this is something I have grown to understand to help her stay alive.

But in the moment I left her, I was thinking about my life. My very unfinished life.

I couldn't stay, let alone get her to come with me unless I threw her over my shoulder kicking and screaming.

I left her. And Zoey. And Simone.

Like the coward I know I am, I abandoned the vast majority of people I vowed to protect. The people I opened my home to, and promised to give them my world if we all could give a little to hold the next person's back.

Why couldn't I uphold my end?

I am stupid, but in spite of every red flag, I could swear we had another few days before the next attack tore our little village limb from limb. In my mind, the Ravagers would wait just a bit longer, at least long enough for us to get home. Surely, nothing could go wrong. Not to my household. Not to Addie.

She is an invincible force, I told myself, walking away. Unstoppable. Resourceful in the face of danger. She can get home, deliver a baby, and then she will go see Amadeus. It can work out and life can go on a little while longer.

But I knew better, deep down, and at this moment I see the shadows of our opponent weaving between the homes to end it all. Armed, and calm. Voiceless. Noiseless.

I am not so close to home yet that I can't turn around, and I have to anyway. Something inside screams the inevitable, roars that I should go find Addie—as it always does. Because a part of me is eternally with her, even when I'm not.

It doesn't take a lot of looking to find the chaos she is linked to. I see her slide into the dirt on her bad foot, rolling in front of two Ravagers like a rag doll as I arm myself, ready to lunge to her defense should she need it. She shakes in fear, as if she does, similar to a small girl rather than the grown, powerful woman she presents as of late. The beasts laugh, though, for one reason or the next, paying her little mind and passing her over in an event I have never witnessed in my life. As if she were a ghost. A phantom. A bug.

I try to catch up with her in the minutes following, but it is difficult. She can run unencumbered by the enemy, ducking through bodies I am not sure she sees in her blind charge. But I have to stay out of sight, out of mind from all the creatures filling the streets, lining the occupied housing in groups, while simultaneously praying I can keep her trail. In certain dark, niche places she seems to vanish altogether, rushing out the other side in vibrant torch light, and losing me once more. At the end of it, I can't find her again. Until I hear the scream.

It is the worst sound imaginable. It is blood in my ears,

swooshing at the fragile, protective drum in decisive beats. It is a heavy, earth-shattering weight on my chest that I cannot lift.

I am a moron, or I would have darted straight for Zoey and Addie's original residence at the start of their search. When I arrive, following the sound of familiar screams, it is just in time to see Kasismis carrying Zoey out of the home, drenched in blood up to the elbow. He does not see me when they pass, perhaps too focused on Zoey's labor to care, and needing to get her somewhere safe. But I can recognize him from anywhere, from any distance. I know who he is, right here in this place, making apologetic eye contact behind the safety of the side wall with the one woman I saved and mouthing my condolences.

I give it a second to make sure they're gone, and then I speed into the home. My eyes work faster than what my brain can comprehend, and at first, I see nothing out of the ordinary. There are no disturbances, other than the rug over the trap door being pushed aside, and I dart for my glimmer of hope. I rip the wooden square open, listening to the staggered groan of hinges not oiled, finding Simone at the bottom, her bulging little eyes flashing back to me in abandon.

I put my finger to my lips, knowing we are still not safe, and straightening upright. I turn my head all about the room, heart pounding against my sternum. A small dent in the wall next to the counterspace leads my eyes to a crumpled, wet heap in the corner where it meets the wall.

The whole world stops.

I drop to the floor, shuffling forward on my knees to see the misshapen lump of person. To see what is left of *her*.

Addie.

I can't seem to stop saying her name, touching her face.

I can't swallow or breathe or hear.

It is panic consuming me, and I have become the notion of this emotional disease.

Afflicted. Affected.

I can't stop trying to wake her up, pleading with her to open her eyes so we can get her help from Celestyn. Begging her to heal herself like she always has, just this once when it counts.

How can I let her go? How can I continue watching the little puffs of her chest rising and falling, knowing she is turning from a living, breathing creature to a corpse, and struggling to stay while I sit idly by—useless?

I can't let this happen. Not this way. Not yet.

She can't go.

I won't let her.

I pat her face, rolling her limp head back and forth. I speak her name into existence as if I am breathing life into her body. I try to breathe life into her body, knowing CPR is only so effective when someone is crashing, and trying anyway.

My own face hurts.

It tingles with boils of pain, resting against hers, murmuring simple comforts to the pain frozen on her shut-eyed face.

At some point in all of this, I use my dagger to tear my plaid shirt into strips that I tie around her wounds, hoping it will keep her from bleeding out further while her body's uncanny abilities work a magic all their own. I am terrified to move her, to hold her, but she needs medical attention I can't give her. Soon.

Simone clambers out the trap door as I am positioning myself to scoop Addie into a loving cradle. It is a motion that feels... ethereal. I can't focus. I am sniffling. Panting. Her dead weight is so much heavier than I anticipated—more especially on my conscience than physicality.

Somewhere in the background of this mess, Simone whines tearful questions to my ears that I can't quite hear in my stupor. I can't quite answer as my psyche is torn apart at the drips of blood that follow my partner's body from the floor. I am in stunned silence, turning out the door into the remaining anarchy with this little girl clutching to the back of my white T-shirt.

I am aware of the tired weight of this child, clinging to me as I walk without feeling through the village. Numb and clumsy, I realize certain areas have already been vacated, most of the enemy absent in the innermost housing as I glance in all directions, my focus down every avenue.

Where is Celestyn?

Addie is nearly a corpse now, taking in air as shallow rasps that flop her chest in uneven tilts. Rattling. Growing sweaty and cold.

In the streets, we step over so many bodies, a river of blood and guts that connect one home to the next like a channel of water we could row in on. There are rake marks in the dirt where some of these people fought for their lives, splintered doors where they lost, and wasted weapons that will never be used.

It is a cemetery where we walk. A graveyard for the lost and confused. A path of harrowing despondence leads the way home where I shimmy the door open to see exactly who I needed wide awake in a mound of blankets. She peeks out of her rabbit hole when she is certain I am not danger. But then she freezes.

Celestyn's mouth drops open at the sight she is witnessing, rolling out of her soft burrito to meet me halfway through the main room. My voice comes out as a quiver. A terrible, painful sound.

"W-where were you?" I choke. "We...w...looked everywhere. WE LOOKED!"

She eyes Addie, guiding Simone to the bedding, handing her some food off the counter, and lighting as few candles she can spare. Thorough, she makes sure the door is shut, speaking in whispers as she goes.

"I was late," she responds, shaken, "home—I was late getting home. But I was here, this whole time. They almost got inside."

When she rounds in front of me, I charge her with Addie's body, pushing it closer so she can have a better look. But still gripping tight.

I can't let her go.

I want to—but I can't.

Celestyn's eyes grow wider than ever. She puts her hands up in the air like I had pointed a gun at her instead, treading toward the backroom.

"Aidan." There is pity in her words. "Honey, she's...not okay."

"You can fix her." I nod. "Yeah, you can. If you try. You have to try. Look, she's already done half the work for you. She's barely bleeding anymore."

Celestyn purses her lips, gaze a bit softer. Her hand comes out in a hesitant contact, pity her form of condolence. Though I don't want either one.

I want her help.

"I'm not a genie that can just grant your wishes," she explains. "I am a person, with limited capabilities and medical studies. I'm really sorry, Aidan, but she's dying. She deserves to be let go instead of used as a pin cushion in what will only be a poor attempt at salvaging her life."

I collapse onto the floor with Addie, pulling one of Celestyn's cleaner blankets over, and spreading it thin with my free hand to lay her down. I rub my face and eyes as I do, burning dark like the flames of hell.

My face hurts so damn much. It stings and pulls like molten rock. Like fire.

I am on fire.

I need someone to make it stop hurting.

"It's my fault." I snap in two, tossing my glasses to the floor and holding my searing eyeballs. "I left her all alone, and I knew better. I fucking knew it."

"It isn't—"

"It is. Okay?"

"Adabelle was an—"

"Celestyn," I mumble, "please. Please, help. You can't let it be my fault. I don't want to be the reason she dies. I don't want to outlive her like I have everyone else. Please."

This hits a nerve, but it is the right one. It is the one that withholds her feelings.

My pain saturates her, the understanding of it eating her alive like her own so often does me. She reaches for the bag of supplies she carried today, pulling out a few books for Simone, and asking her to look away. I hear her promise the sniffling girl that everything would be okay, though refusing to give me the same swear.

I am swollen with guilt, pacing the small hut I made. Like I can explode at any second with remorse.

I hate me. So. Much.

Celestyn works through the night on Addie, maintaining an ever-faint heartbeat come morning after a night of repeated stitching inside and outside, and CPR coupled with Addie's own little self trying to heal up before our very eyes. I don't sleep through any of this, forever awake. Focused. I am afraid if I shut my eyes, Addie will stop taking in air, though Celestyn insists the village will be safer and better off with her dead.

But I can't accept this.

I won't.

At sunrise, Celestyn is taken aback. Addie's heartbeat is stronger. Stabilizing. Her breathing has deepened a bit more, though we aren't out of the woods.

It should be impossible with the amount of blood loss she suffered in the attack, the injuries she sustained rupturing vital organs that could still grow infected. Normal people don't just live through an attack like this and begin healing on their own within hours of it happening.

It is alarming, but Addie stands a chance. Enough of one that I am comfortable stepping outside when I receive the news for a breath of fresh air.

There are other people outside too when I open the door, gathering where they know Celestyn lives for immediate medical attention, though I wish I could shoo them all home. Addie needs round the clock care. Still I see at least ten adult men, twenty adult women, six children Simone's age or just a touch older, several teenagers, and one person I had not expected to see ever again.

Ace.

He stands with Ethan, dried blood at his temple, and shellshocked at the remains of our industrious village. I have never seen him wear such an expression before, catching my gaze and striding around a bruised, albeit okay First-in-Command. I don't stop Ace from pushing his way inside, following his lead and casually inspecting the gash on his head as we walk.

He needs medical attention. Badly.

And to be updated on the status of Limbo.

Maybe he can speak with Amadeus.

"What happened?" Ace inquires, sitting against the boarded window, and catching sight of Simone still fast asleep.

Celestyn hurries, emerging from the backroom with the necessary, but minimal supplies she can offer. She sits on her knees next to him, angling his face toward a mixture of candlelight and sunlight streaming in through the cracked door. I am quiet, for a moment, a lack of sleep getting the better of me.

"Maybe I should be asking you the same question," I reply, tired and bitter.

This attack rolls straight off him. He doesn't care that I dislike him for any reason or another. His answers are matter of fact.

"Suicide missions aren't easy. Ethan and I made it here alive by the skin of our teeth. A few of our men were picked off by mermaids early on, but the rest...they were massacred in the middle of the night while collecting supplies. We weren't able to bring home much, and I was forced to scrap the whole affair."

I watch Celestyn wash the wound at his temple with soap and water, humming along as she goes. She has always had a pretty voice.

"We were also attacked," Celestyn speaks in my stead. "A couple times. We are all but diminished here."

Ace jerks, passing a look between us.

"Melody?" He poses a not all too serious sounding question. "Is Melody okay?"

I bite my lip.

"I...haven't seen her outside this morning. But I saw her just a day or so ago. She seemed fine then. Just a bit shaken."

Simone yawns, grumbling and rolling. She is still weak and unstable—so quiet at times I forget about her when things get a bit more active. Ace's eyes roll from her to Addie, laying in the entryway to the backroom, bandaged tight and crowded with pillows. Her chest has a more even rise and fall today, eyes shut in a peaceful way so that she looks tired rather than comatose. Everything about her looks to be an improvement upon last night, but Ace...his face contorts in a sick pain.

He jerks from Celestyn's cleaning, rising and stumbling toward her. Bending down, he reaches for Addie's hair in a motion that makes me livid. Just a touch, fingers grazing through it in a tender manner that makes me like him even less. Immediately, even less.

But Addie gasps, inhales loudly as if in response to it, melting the features on his blank, monotone face. There is a pain, retracting from her when her breathing levels out to an even better measure than before. But he releases her all the same.

"I have to go," he murmurs.

Celestyn scoffs. "I haven't fixed you up."

"It doesn't matter." Ace shrugs her off.

I am on my feet, moving for the door so I am in his way.

"Where are you going?" I roar.

Ace is malicious in this second, and the energy makes me hesitate, standing firm but not as much as I'd like to be.

"It is none of your concern," he insists, elbowing me in the ribs so hard I double over out of his way, careening into the floor.

"What the fuck?" I groan.

But he is gone, and more patients flood into my home to be seen.

It doesn't take an official meeting this morning to understand the search teams have been either depleted or disbanded. Ethan wants no part in leaving his home since the missions, scarred beyond simple repair, and I see no point in leaving Addie's side if no one else plans to commit to the betterment of our survival.

I have money saved. I can dedicate round the clock time to Simone and Addie.

No one has been found since a bit after Simone anyway, and

survival has become a key focus.

Day by day runs us by in a blur since the attack that almost killed Addie, talk in the town all the way up to Ace and Melody discussing the idea of picking up the village to leave. To find a new settlement somewhere safer.

On the sixth day post-attack, a mob arranges outside our door, demanding Celestyn begin rationing the medical supplies for more minor scrapes, or immediately life-threatening injuries that can be managed. They implore we stop sustaining Addie, who needs daily bandage changings. Washings. Ointments. Care. Dedication.

I chase them away with arrows. With my new sword Addie gifted me. I throw a dagger at one man when he refuses to leave, flinging it right in his shoulder. Celestyn is furious at the extra work I create for her some days, fixing them up as they come.

*What the fuck is wrong with you?* she screams.

But my mind is made.

I will eliminate survival for anyone who attempts to take Addie's life, when she tried so desperately to save theirs. Every. Day.

Celestyn grows increasingly upset at these declarations. I am sure she hates me for them. She hates Addie for them. Addie would probably hate herself for them.

But I can't help myself. I can't stop. I'm through denying it.

It isn't until we hit the week-and-a-half mark that Celestyn confronts me again. I have never been more furious at the words she speaks, though Addie still isn't awake to hear them. Though there is truth in them.

"The chances that she will wake up and pull through are next to none, Aidan," Celestyn tells me. "Let her die with dignity."

# CHAPTER THIRTY-NINE
## SAHANNA

I T ISN'T EASY.

I don't expect it to be. I just didn't expect it to be quite so hard, either.

The labor is excruciating. I think I have ruptured my own insides with the wire, Silas spending hours to heal me afterward without drawing any conclusions as to why I could be so hurt. It is an unusual experience, when taking into account he prefers to let most bodily injuries heal on their own.

Our baby is born in the grass a few miles outside of the nearest village, traveling by dragon to our home from our next rendezvous point, but not quite making it there. Because she couldn't wait, and she was alive for a few seconds at most. Long enough to take measly gasps for air in her father's arms as he tries his best to deliver every lifesaving magic he was taught from his father and older brother.

It is a desperation I have never quite seen, knowing the baby was born alive, and being helpless to her death. He attempts regular CPR when all else fails, their race almost never having to resort to this. But he does, anyway. Frantically. Pleadingly. The poor creature struggles to survive in his arms, until her little heart gives out. Until he has no choice but to admit it is over.

Silas clutches his pointy-eared daughter to his body as if his grief could breathe the life back into her, quivering in angst, and realizing all at once that I still need medical attention. He presses the little girl into the crook of my arms, pulling aside his medical pouch he carries on hand to begin work.

Perhaps one of the worst parts.

All of the men in this race are trained early on in female anatomy. They have to be. They are generally the acting midwives for the birth of their children later in life, so they are taught young to hone the knowledge and skill of what they will be working with.

Mid-husbands? Man-wives?

It is ritualistic in any event that they help bring their very own into this world, symbolic of their responsibility toward a life they helped create out of love for another.

Out of force, in my case.

Not that it stops him from feeling the same.

The whole dark elven race cherishes children. The death of one is life-altering.

And we have lost many.

Just never this far along.

I am afraid to look at my baby in this moment, focusing my attention on the trees. The night. The metallic smell of blood. Anything.

But my face is wet, and when I bend my neck to wipe my eyes on the upper breast of my dress, I see her exactly as she is.

Sleeping.

Anemic, and pale—lips faded blue and skin like wax paper.

*Under done.*

Her hair is barely there at all, wispy and white like his. Like I imagined it would be.

My daughter is a wisp of a creature. Fully formed. Whole.

I am swollen with an indescribable feeling, but I bury it deep down, feeling my jaw tremble in grief. I continue to tell myself I made the right choice. That this world is no place for a little girl. I have done right by her. She doesn't deserve to suffer here with me. I'm not ready to be a mother.

I wish it wasn't this way. I wish she didn't have to go, struggling against the shadow of death in his arms.

She could have passed against me. Against the sound of my familiar heart. Anything that didn't make every painful attempt to preserve her, outside of a loving whisper that sets her free.

A part of Silas still yearns to save her, unable to take his eyes off her in my arms, and cringing at the reality that crashes over him. His brother would have been able to save her without question. Sustain her, without hurting her.

Silas is a failure in this moment, in his mind. He feels it, unable to shake the guilt gnawing away at him inside and out.

I want him to feel it too. I want him to hurt. Worse than me. I want him to feel like he has done something wrong, because he has.

I want to feel unstoppable. Ruthless, and cruel.

Hateful, like him, so that it feels like I have been victorious, even when I haven't been.

No one has won today.

The King is the entire reason why I had to do it now, when we are finally free of him for such a short time, and within this game of chess I play against him, I have finally found a balance. A steep price to pay for it, but I have.

Still, physically, I feel toasted.

Sick. Exhausted.

Silas' hands leave me for a second, shuffling, and then fluttering. At my front, his soft, fur cloak blankets over my arms and the baby's tiny figure, tucking neat under her neck so that her head remains exposed. Quiet.

Pure hair stains in crimson where his bloody hands have touched. My eyes move from her to him, unable to keep contact for long as he returns to his work. To everything he knows is sure, and sound. To me.

"She is cold," he tells me.

The breeze would have a bite to it for no one with body fat—but she is a corpse.

Do corpses get cold?

I feel like that is the definition of what they do.

I don't understand why it matters to him if she does as well.

But it does.

He never takes the cloak back.

The rest of the way home is spent almost entirely on dragon flight with him. We stop to rest with Bastian in the city of Praesidia, who hires skilled laborers overnight to build the deceased child a casket that will last until we can get her back in the mountains to bury out behind the castle in the gardens.

Time passes in a strange way through these days, one blurring into the next, leaving me winded and unsure as to where we are at, or when we are leaving. Yet, sometime later, we are home.

Well, we are at our second home. Most of our home life is spent within the walls of The King's castle. It is certainly big enough to house us, fully staffed and isolated from civilization.

A girl could really sleep out here—if that girl wasn't me.

More days pass inside the castle walls, and I am plagued with the images of her running through my thoughts. How little she was, and...complete. Scrawny. Fragile. Helpless. Sinful.

A month more is all it would have taken. Silas probably could have saved her. He could have washed the blood off of her, filled her tiny lungs with air so gentle they wouldn't risk bursting. I would have fed her at my breast, currently aching with an overflow of milk meant for her belly.

Preemies are so different here than they are on Earth.

Elven men aren't skilled medics like women, excluding their King. But a couple months early can be helped with extraneous measures. It would have been draining on him until his twin returned to assist, but our daughter could have been someone with little fingers. Small feet. And a heartbeat, if I weren't so hasty.

I keep thinking of the way she didn't move in his arms, like a doll, his cheek brushing over hers. Pining. Grieving. A sensation that makes me loathe myself without having earned it.

This is his fault.

Why is it that my hands still shake? Why does my heart hurt this way?

Neither of us have slept much since our return, Silas refusing to speak to the staff unless required of him. He has shut off entirely, something that is a glimmer of light in a pit of despair, as he spends less time about me. Less time showering me with his affections and time.

He spends most of it out where he buried the baby, close to the water. I forget exactly where. Part of me wants to make sure I don't remember. I want to lose this image of her like she was never there at all. Flexing. Grasping.

I feel sick.

Dee and Blythe are in the kitchens this morning to avoid disturbing our dining. One of the ladies provides me with tea to calm my nerves, the sound of rain blasting the enormous windows lining the dining hall with a warm, welcome static while I drink. It is a safe place in a not-so-safe space, even with Silas sitting across from me, dead-eyed and staring out the glass frames, far beyond the trees. Perhaps to where she is.

It isn't as if he didn't take the others hard as well. But they never stood a chance. So much smaller, sometimes not visible as I was only two or three months in. None of them had ever taken a breath outside the womb—until this daughter.

It must feel very unfair.

"We were very close," Silas tells me as I sniff the tea, inhaling the steam and sweet aroma.

It smells...fruity. I wonder if Dee told Blythe to stew some peaches with the leaves this time.

I peek up to him over the rim of my glass. He still isn't looking at me, and I am relieved. It is easier to lie to him this way.

"She is resting," I whisper. "It is no one's fault."

A faint smile tugs at the rear of my thoughts. Cruel.

It is *his* fault.

My hands tremble in rage, glass cup rattling against its plate.

"If my brother had chosen to follow us home as I had implored him to do, she would have survived." Silas' voice does not raise, though I can detect his resentment in the words alone. It is often difficult without knowing him personally to understand when he is angry. Or upset.

But I know.

Monotone is a sound he performs well, but the words bite the same. He is furious with the oh-so-magnificent King for not heeding every red light.

*Poor thing.*

"It is not his fault," I mumble into the warm brown fluid, taking a quiet sip and scalding my tongue. "It is his job to assure the security of all regions, including the Fae. No, especially, the Fae. And you have to be here, for the security of the home. The staff."

Silas is quiet. Painfully so.

I take another, smaller sip of my tea. When I glance back up to him, he is standing, moving toward the windows, golden eyes searching over the treetops from so high above the world. It is beautiful out there, a proper resting place for our nameless girl.

I enjoy his misery in my own silence, swallowing his pain, though shaken by what it cost me.

Still, I can't let myself forget I have a role to play as his wife. Out of fear, I play it well, and I scoot from my chair. Weak and sore, I have lost all the weight from this past pregnancy in a form of self-starvation while he has been distracted, and it has pulled me deep into a pit of exhaustion. Of ache.

I set my cup on the table and shuffle up behind him, reaching to touch the back of his arm, a gesture he stiffens to. I wait, letting him relax all the same.

"I am sorry," I offer, remaining for a second longer. "I will be in our room if you require my presence."

I turn, but his hand wraps about my bicep, yanking me into him so that both arms sweep around me in a death grip. Like I am all that is left in his life. Like he is ready to hoard me if possible, keep me locked away in a tighter box than he's already fit me into.

"Not yet," he tells me, planting soft kisses against my head. "I need you right now. For a moment, at least. Stay."

I am none to refuse him. It is never a good idea in the first place, and I am weak to the pain I am in. Childbirth is a series of agonies for me that I am fragile to, feeling as though I can't every time I have been meant to push, and doing it anyway.

Last time, I asked Silas to knock me out cold for the event, and to wake me up when it was through. But he claimed it "didn't work that way". That I wouldn't want to miss it, anyway.

Such an advanced, primitive race. I would think with all their magic they could have something similar to an epidural around here. Or pain medicines that I could get strung out on.

My heart races for a second, a sensation he can feel despite everything I try to hide it. Before I have time to resist, he slides us to the floor so his head can rest on mine, arms locked in a prison around me. My emotions fade into a clean slate, pulse slowing until everything is...tranquil. Calm, on the outside, as though I am floating on a fully-stocked cruise ship in the middle of an uncharted sea while I try to fight this sensation of emotional abandon. This ability of his isn't always a mastered technique, and a storm brews below the surface of my subconscious—one I can't quite reach to feel.

"I will do better," he promises at the cusp of my ear. "Next time."

Next time?

Please, don't let there be a next time.

Hard, heavy footsteps enter the room, and Silas' firm body grows rigid, head tilting up to acknowledge the presence in the room. I assume it is The King. He should be home any day with the advantage of dragon flight on his side. I peek from the safety of my husband's arms to greet the person invading our space—to my surprise finding another brother from this enormous family I'm part of.

Finn. A strict man, like his eldest brother who raised him, and all business. He has to be. He dwells within and guards the most dangerous borders in all this world. Not that it is a long travel here, but to leave his post is a big deal for that very reason.

"It is a bad time," Finn muses aloud. "I see. It cannot wait, however. I must have audience with our brother, The King."

Silas draws me in closer. Debating. I can almost hear the gears turning in his mind as they always do.

"He is not present," he replies. "I am standing head of house in his stead."

It is...sort of true? I suppose?

Silas is entrusted to protect the home from our current threats while his brother is away. All of it, down to the staff. He is charged with the responsibilities his brother bears to keep a smooth operation.

But head of house?

Finality on important decisions wait upon The King, don't they?

Finn also appears suspicious of this, despite Silas' role in raising him. It is a strange story of many children having three dads better told for another time.

"Where is our brother in this time?"

"Hard to say," Silas responds, collected. "We were sent ahead of him from the Fae at my own insistences. You are welcome to wait here for the next month or so if it is not urgent. But you do know how he roams."

It is true.

The King is always on his own personal watch. Time and space run on his agenda here. Just for him.

He did create this whole universe, after all, following the death of their father. So why shouldn't it?

It isn't like he will let us be for long, though. He and Silas have too much history for him to trust us like that, and there is a reason Kai protested Silas as an advisor.

Finn grimaces at this thought.

"Very well," he submits. "I am due home as it stands. Fighting our brother's battles leaves my wife quite lonely."

It is easier for Finn's wife. He imprinted upon an elven woman. A woman who was raised accustomed to this lifestyle. A woman who understands it. She welcomed him into bed with her. They have a son. The whole family spent an entire month in the city to celebrate when she gave birth just over two years ago.

Finn hands Silas the letter, which my husband tears open with simple grace, keeping his arms wrapped firm around me. It only takes him a couple seconds to read the contents before folding it away into his tunic.

"Where is it you acquired this?" His voice is strict. Not as desperate or wanting as it had been just a moment earlier.

"The original contents were sealed away by Amadeus," Finn says. "I only thought it proper to relay the message."

Silas bobs his head, hand falling from me to his lap.

I am returning to reality in shutters of depressing, bright light.

"I will let our brother know that all is going according to plan." Silas pats my leg, helping me return from the emotional stupor he caused.

"Is it?" Finn's smile is crooked.

Silas manages a coy smile in return for the first time since our baby's death.

"Sahanna?" His voice is empty of the amusement playing upon his face.

I attempt to remain polite.

"Yes?" My tone is as soft as I intend.

His large hand comes down to my skull, stroking my hair. Gentle. "Take your tea. Go lay down for awhile."

My cheeks burn, but I can't refuse him. So I appease instead.

*It will not always be this way,* I tell myself, doing as I am told like the dog I have become.

> Things will change eventually.
> One day.
> When I am brave.

# CHAPTER FORTY
## CELESTYN

S TABILITY. THAT IS OUR WORD OF THE DAY.

Adabelle has stability, and the hope of it giving new life to Aidan's dreams that she might wake up makes me sick, watching day in and day out how he hovers over her practical corpse, attached to it by some invisible tether he cannot seem to cut at any benefit to himself. There is not a single one of my gentle insistences that can persuade him otherwise, not a grim threat from other villagers that can make him afraid as he launches a deluge of arrows upon their, often violent, defiance. Because without her, he appears to feel as if he has lost his own stability—or sanity.

I move her body to the backroom in hopes that the absence of the fumes from her festering wounds will clear his head space and give room to reason. But if anything, it provides him a quieter place to dwell on her unconscious state, waiting for a miracle while Simone follows him come nightfall like a puppy in need of guidance—as if he doesn't have enough time to do that already.

He doesn't work anymore following the disbanding of the search teams, able to sit by her side where he wouldn't have prior, and refusing to move, let alone function. Most days, I am certain he does not eat either, terrified to sleep as he waits for her to wake up, or stop breathing. The exhaustion noticeably eats away at him, same as the guilt, his moral compass for anything outside duty growing thin and absent.

It is easy to feel bitter and sad seeing him this way, knowing that my whole life as I remember it has never had anything close to what he gives her in these days that pass like years. In my youth, or what I called youth, my life revolved around chasing people who could never fully commit to me—love me. My parents held powerful positions, careers that called them all over the world while I stayed home with a nanny that never spoke a word unless she had to. In school, I couldn't find a connection with my peers, advancing grades faster than any other student, and graduating college with my degree at the top of my class. In a hospital setting, I sat by while more people left me than ever before, in death or in health.

Even now, no one stays.

I am alone.

I can't stop hurting people to prevent them from hurting me first. Aidan took a genuine interest in me from the very first day we met, and immediately I wanted to keep him at arm's length. A relationship with another person has never turned out well for me. The only stable foundation I have ever built was a financial one, and whoever said money could buy happiness has never sat in a sea of bodies so thick that the air conditioning can't halt the perspiration, and yet simultaneously feel like a lone soul in a haunted house.

I seek commitment I can't give, just to get a piece of what I've lost. I need someone to need me more than I do them, someone to love me more than I can myself. I need to fill this void that Aidan is leaving in my life for a dying freak with something bearable, anything that makes me feel good for a fraction of time, and helps me forget that I am alone. This morning, I try harder than I ever have to feel complete on my way to drop Simone off at her work in the barn, stopping for a house visit along the way and making her sit outside in the living area.

It doesn't take long. I promised her it wouldn't.

It can't.

I'm nauseated, sick to my stomach and ready to blow chunks. Tired and weak. Sad.

I don't know if I am going to make an entire day of house calls a possibility, but this one is special. This one is for me. It is a quick spin in the sheets on top of a wood floor with two people I'd been active with a couple years ago. Nothing long or drawn out. Quick and to the point. Fun, but not see you tomorrow good. It isn't until I am putting my clothes back on that I lose all control of my composure, weeping in front of my sexual acquaintances and trying to pull myself together at the same time.

"What is wrong?" I hear at the brink of my ear, feeling sets of arms wrap around me as I pull free, slipping on my shoes and trying not to stay in this pity party I have made. But I can't *not* say it out loud. I need to say it.

"He's left me for her," I cry. "Aidan left me for Adabelle."

But we were never together. I told him that.

How can I feel this way if we were never together?

I don't bother letting them console me, wiping my eyes clear and rushing Simone out of the house. We walk to the barn for drop off, and I listen to her talk along the way, babbling the way children her age do about what she sees, who she knows, and what she likes.

Her daddy is tall, she tells me.

Her daddy gives the best hugs, she insists.

Her daddy has big ears, she laughs, holding my hand.

I like it...holding her hand. It is warm. And real. More real than anything else in this world.

I leave her at the barn with Farmer Ray and the promise to come get her at sundown, finding a place to throw up when she is out of sight, and deciding to go home rather than chance house calls and vomit waterfalls. Inside, I nibble on a few overcooked potatoes, and settle into bed to sleep a couple hours away. Something that turns into more than half a day wasted resting and eating, just to throw the mess straight back up.

Aidan doesn't pay me much mind, having pulled Adabelle into the living area again, and watching her breathe. I fall asleep to the mediocrity of it, like counting sheep, waking up only to a rough shaking and Aidan's panicked voice, claiming his poor pitiful monster has stopped breathing.

I am groggy, caught in the moment and unaware of the time, crawling to Adabelle and placing my hand on her chest to start compressions, only to realize she is still breathing after all, but not well. And something else.

Jesus.

The girl is on fire, all color that filled her skin lost, if it were possible.

Aidan frowns as I put my hands to my side, refusing compressions and turning to get my canteen so I can wash out the acrid taste of vomit residue on my tongue.

"W-what are you doing?" He stammers. "S-she needs help. Aren't you going to help her?"

I take a couple swallows. "What am I going to do, Aidan? She's breathing. She's just...not doing well."

"Your creams, the ones that promote healing." He runs his fingers through his hair. "You need to try those. I can go get them. Which jar is it?"

"I'm not doing it." I am firm, watching her struggle. "Aidan, this is wrong."

"Not helping her is wrong."

He is starting to yell. The sound of it makes me want to yell too, an uncontrollable urge to fight building in my vocal cords and coming out as a brutally honest scream.

"She has a CRAZY fever, Aidan! It is a death spiral right now. Don't you see?"

"I see she is still fucking breathing," Aidan snaps. "It means something."

"It means that we are literally torturing the poor girl into stabilization." I pull my hair in frustration. "Do you think these creams feel good, Aidan? That because they work so well, they don't hurt? She's in pain, if she can feel it, and that is a pretty big if."

"She's alive."

"She's as good as fucking deceased. She has one foot six feet under, and the only thing that is keeping her head above water is your ties to me. Good people could use the care I'm giving to her."

"She. Needs. It. More."

I scoff. "What? To ease your conscience? Because you left a grown woman all alone? Grow up, Aidan. She made her choices, and I don't think she regrets it. Let her die."

The floorboards creak, and we both stop. Dusky sunlight turning to moonlight beams inside around the body of Farmer Ray holding Simone in his arms.

I'm late. Fuck.

"I-I'm so sorry." Aidan steps over Adabelle as Simone is set on the floor, whisking her over to sit next to the woman who is supposed to be taking care of her while I try to find my words.

But I can't, watching the child curl up next to the extra warm body and placing her nose against Adabelle's neck. When the room clears, and Aidan has given his extra apologies for being late, shuffling to pull together a dinner for the child, I can hear her mumbling into the sanctity of someone who can't respond to her. Sniffling, the last word catching me at my worst, pulling at the only good parts left of me.

"I like you," she whispers.

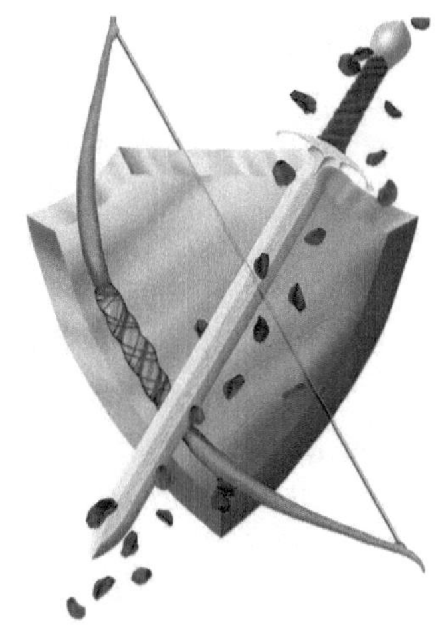

# CHAPTER FORTY-ONE
## AIDAN

I T HAS BEEN TWO WEEKS SINCE ADDIE WAS STABBED AND any progress she has made has started to evaporate into thin air.

I was told she was running a fever as of this morning, the wounds festering a rancid, glossy red no matter what Celestyn put on her to make them better.

It shouldn't have surprised me, though it did.

She has lost a lot of weight due to not being able to feed or hydrate effectively, lowering her body's ability to fight these infections, her cheeks sunken below her eyes and making her once porcelain skin an ashy, skeletal grey against my olive hands. We don't know what is sustaining her any longer other than an inhuman drive to survive.

Celestyn tells me Addie's heart is racing, as of this evening. Fluttering. Trying its best.

*Just keep trying*, I want to tell her.

But it doesn't matter when she can't hear me.

The attacks from the Ravagers have ebbed off again, and I no longer understand the aim outside of the fact it never seems to be a good sign when there is a long intermission. The whole village is preparing for the worst while they can in the very same mindset, most of them wanting to pick up and move by the end of the week at the latest.

Celestyn has propositioned me with a different idea, however. She has grown keen on the concept that she can crawl back to Master Amadeus on her hands and knees to beg for his divine mercy, taking with her myself and Simone on the condition that I leave Addie behind to die.

After all this effort to help.

After all this effort to bring her this far.

We would leave her to die, because she is taking a turn for the worse.

Celestyn is still yelling as I help Simone out of her strangely wet clothes into a dry set. Addie tied long shirts into individual dresses for the girl, and it always did the trick okay, more so when she puts a pound on here and there.

When I am done with this, I set her down for dinner and a book. I only catch the end of what Celestyn is saying as I turn around to get Simone some water from Addie's unused bottle, debating on whether four years of age is too young to start teaching a child to read.

"I will not let you die for her." Celestyn is almost shouting now. "There is an attack coming. You know it. I know it. And Adabelle isn't stable. We can't move her, and we can't protect a corpse."

I hand Simone the water bottle, rubbing her hand and taking a moment to appreciate her studying a picture of speckled, plum-hued flowers with wonder.

She's adorable, I have to admit.

I never imagined Addie would ever consider herself competent enough to take on a charge in Limbo, but Simone is the perfect one. Quiet and docile, the child doesn't make much of a fuss unless she's hungry, and adjusts to circumstances with very little question. Down to the tightly curled black fuzz growing on her scalp in small patches, and the way she cuddles up underneath my jaw at night, I've come to see why this kid can't be turned away under any circumstance.

I look to Celestyn, grabbing the corners of the blanket Addie lays on, and dragging her to the window out of the way with Simone so that they can still be together, but also out of the argument zone.

"We have to protect her, Celestyn," I say, returning to the center of the room. "I have to."

Celestyn touches her forehead, taking a deep breath as if she has a headache. Outside, I can hear a rumble of thunder in the distance, clouds rolling in to take the bite off the heat from the air blowing in through the door and cracks in the window.

"She's covered for your ass once. ONCE. I've covered for you hundreds of times. Neither are a lifelong obligation. You hated her not that long ago. You made it pretty clear."

Her honest points rip to my core in savage, jagged streaks. I clench my fists.

No one understands.

The person who made that point, and who I am now, are not the same people. Addie could see that.

Why can't anyone else?

"Only a coward of a provider chooses not to help someone simply because they hate them," I reply. "It isn't your job to decide who to save. You job is to do your best to save those who can be helped. Addie can still be helped."

"The rules are different here," Celestyn hisses.

"Only if you make them different."

Raw, stiff quiet.

Simone chews and slurps away at her food and water.

It occurs to me I should have put another blanket on Addie to assure that no crumbs get on her body. The stab wounds are really infected—swollen and oozing despite the rapid, inhuman healing that salvaged her insides. Even without the cream, Celestyn was adamant she had never seen anything like it. Almost all the internal bleeding was stunted before I got her home, though scar damage was freshly evident when we cleaned her up.

The condition of her body beneath layers and layers of clothes brings up another series of questions—but not then. Not now.

Everything is falling apart too fast for questions. Everyone is getting ready to leave, and I am the only person debating on staying. To protect Addie.

There is widespread devastation and panic. I saw three children left behind by their guardians yesterday morning who probably vanished to find better cover in the forest despite the risks.

The chaos is mind boggling and hard to get a grip on at times.

People are going hungry.

One of the cows was stabbed to death and gutted in the field when the farmer took a break, though no one knows how the assailant survived the feat.

There is a sharp knock at the door, and I grab my dagger to defend the home. When I spin to march forward, Celestyn has already opened it wide to reveal Ace standing in the frame, grim as ever with Melody at his side.

It isn't often I see them this close. Side by side, Melody is a tad smaller than Ace, but only by a head or so, and still impossibly tall for a woman. She steps inside ahead of him though not formally invited, her long, black ponytail swishing in her wake. Ace eyes Addie for a second, averting his gaze to Celestyn and I almost immediately.

He doesn't want to see her, I suppose.

"Our Master has written for Miss Green," he tells me, holding out a small, handwritten letter stamped with red wax. "Again."

There is something inside of me that snaps.

I can hear it, the way it breaks inside my skull like glass plates under soccer cleats. Shatters, as my eyes grow large and nostrils flare, snatching the invitation from Ace. In my own hands, I rip it to shreds, throwing the pieces like confetti into the air that float to the floor like shapely snowflakes.

"She isn't even awake!" I scream. "Tell him to fuck off."

There is a deep sadness to Ace at this statement that I can't quite write off.

It encompasses him. Gnaws away at his exterior.

I think he has lost weight alongside Addie, though it would make sense, considering there isn't much to offer in the food category anymore.

He does not react specifically to the letter, however, looking toward the door with a sigh.

"I will be abandoning my post with a group of villagers in three days after we gather our things. There is hope that this will be our better survival outcome," he speaks low, in a whisper. "You each may accompany us."

Simone calls for us across the room, but I can't think. No one can, buzzing to one another, pinging ideas off the next voice that blends into the first about paths we could take or where we would go. I look to Celestyn who is with Melody on the other side of the room, sifting through creams and salves in amazement.

Through it, I am...empty.

I can't leave. Not with them. And not without her.

"Aidan!" Simone calls once more. "Hey! Hey! HEY!"

"This is extraordinary." Melody gawks at a jar of blue salve Celestyn has been using as a disinfectant. "You are a woman of many talents, I see. We can really use someone like you when we leave, you know."

Celestyn grimaces.

Her vice is me. And I don't want to go without *my* vice.

"I know," she replies to the first half of Melody's statement, confident though pained with decision. "I...still need some things though, before I think about going anywhere."

Melody tugs Celestyn upright, toward the door as excitement spreads across her face.

"I could help you!" she exclaims. "If you sit on the porch with me for a minute, we can make a list of things, and I can help you retrieve them if you agree to come with us."

Ace minds this with some annoyance. It is better lit inside and sitting on the porch appears to have purpose outside of Melody's outward agenda. He leans forward with them, as if to assure that outside is still calm. Motionless and black. Thundering.

He has always been perceptive. Cold and calculating. But knowledgeable.

I've never not trusted his best judgment on the inside.

It is quiet, other than Simone whimpering in the forethought of my mind, and Melody and Celestyn murmuring with a scrap of paper they snatched off her books on the way outside. I don't like the feeling.

"The child and yourself are welcome to accompany our journey as well," Ace tells me after some time spent dwelling on our uncomfortable situation.

He studies everything in the room. My guitar case, and the blanket crumpled in a heap next to it. My bow. Food. Water. The dried blood on the floor that I can't seem to completely scrub clean, leading to the door frame and Addie's backpack that is sliced and disheveled, leaning into it all.

I haven't gone through it...as much as I would like to.

To pry.

To understand Addie, or the rumors surrounding her.

Maybe it is all true, after all.

She heals so fast.

A lot of the medicinal fighting she's done in this time has been on her own terms. Like something in her body preserves itself, powering through the internal damage and keeping her from bursting at the seams.

Regular people don't do that.

So she could be a monster. If monsters were just based on something that is different than what we know.

I have no further doubts she belongs to this world, at least.

But she dresses like the rest of us. Talks like the rest of us. She has a job, and faint memories of the place where we came from.

It makes what I know...uncertain.

"I could maybe foresee sending Simone with you," I comment, tucking my hand into my pocket, thumbing my very last guitar pick. "It might be safer. Addie would want her to be safe. But I can't leave here. Not until she wakes, or until she doesn't."

"Ignorant," Ace snaps. "I never once took you for a fool. A coward, perhaps, but I never judged your insolent hiding when I came for the Suicide Missions. This, however, is beyond basic stupidity."

I shrug. "Take it as me making up for all the hiding and cowardice this far. It has been a long time coming."

"You will die with her." His voice is ice.

"I'll take that chance."

"It is not a chance. It is a choice. An idiot could see this. Wouldn't you rather live in love than die in vain?"

I don't answer right away, and his gaze narrows.

Dangerous. Squinting.

I don't like it.

A jealousy? A hatred?

"I see," he speaks when I don't. "It will be the other way around then. Have you told Celestyn?"

I glance out to her and Melody. The night is peaceful when we aren't being attacked. Chillier with the storm coming in, with a symphony of bugs calling out all around. It would have been nice to enjoy it more before this.

"She knows I intend to stay if Addie doesn't wake."

Ace grimaces, shaking his head with a sigh.

"We could use people like you," he insists. "Bowmen. Fighters."

I laugh.

"No." I half-smile. "We could use people like Addie. And right now, that's a loss."

Thunder booms, and sprinkles of rain splatter the ground. Melody and Celestyn are saturated in it, placing the paper back inside on the floor, but still speaking with one another.

It is silent, except for the static of life happening around us, and all at once, I can hear Simone yelling my name again, as if the chaos has vanished with the sound of rain, bringing in another noise I hadn't heard yet.

An uneven gasp for air.

A groan.

I spin, but Ace has already made strides ahead of me, mouth open.

At the other end of the room, with shaky elbows slowly propping her upright, Addie sits staring wide-eyed at her gut, gingerly cupping the wounds bleeding through their wrap.

# CHAPTER FORTY-TWO
## ADABELLE

M Y DREAMS ARE VAST IN THIS STATE.

Endless.

There are swirls of color unlike which I have ever seen, pooling in a lake of black and white.

I am here.

I am gone.

Time does not pass, nor is there such an existence that limits what can be done in a single motion. It could take a year to raise an arm from this tar that bursts in pale fireworks around me, fringing out in beautiful flamboyance.

But it is okay.

I am in no hurry here, my mismatched eyes dead of feeling, but my mind still very much alive. Screaming for me to wake up.

This isn't where I belong—in waiting.

I don't want to be here.

So why am I here?

What happened?

The violent, purple sky rips open with lightning in fantastic divides through the clouds up overhead, but no thunder erupts. It is silent in the water, for not even an echo calls back to my hollow voice when it rings into the void.

I sniff, face lingering above the surface of the water, and hair fanning out around me.

There are many things that I can see from this place now that I have adjusted to the darkness of death. The faces of the people I once knew flash in picturesque flip books when the sky is about to break with light, like home videos of the mind playing stories of my life featuring the people I know. And some that I don't.

I used to laugh—a lot.

Aidan's voice, frantic and toiled, sometimes whimpers over this. It lurks in my innermost thoughts like a roach, climbing up inside of me, and picking at the edges of my brain like rotten food on an unclean counterspace. Yelling. Celestyn occasionally responds to this in ways that remind me of glass breaking, tears that fall in her cries like raindrops pounding the shores of this steady lake, only settling when her voice is alone to me.

*I'm not sorry. But...*

Their words fade in and out to me, breathing air into my lungs that possess little yearning to either expand or deflate, but rather remain in some permanent hitch so that I may reside in the warm company of death's embrace that sinks me deeper and deeper by the hour.

But something changes in this time. Shifts.

Distinct, brutalized screams berate the sanctity I have found in this little world I've hid inside, bringing forth vibrating ripples that lap this thick, tasteless darkness over my face like fingernails carving paths into my flesh. Excruciating.

I can hardly stand to listen to it, the way it buries itself within my pores, and seeks pity somewhere inside. Begs mercy of me.

*Girl!* A familiar voice of my past bellows.

The scream that follows penetrates all time and space.

And I blink this time, at the sound. Cringe.

For I am cold.

A single tear rolls down the course of my pale cheek, and my fingers long to trace it, flexing as begrudging, minute movements in a macrocosm of nothingness. My chin tickles in response to the face water, itching and cooling to the frigid temperature of my skin.

Another wave of misery rises to wash it all clean, slapping my corpse with a sting, and this time leaving me to cough, retching out the contents. The lock in my joints dissipates all at once, allowing me to thrash in panic before I drown.

All around me as I sink, I can hear voices. Like a psychopath, they are on the inside of my head. Etching into the grooves of my skull.

They argue. Bicker back and forth like children.

Their words are like vipers, snaking about my ankles, and pulling me below.

And for the first time since I found myself here, I can't quite reach the surface.

Instead—

I jerk awake.

It is a flutter of my eyes.

A gasp of soured spring air in a humid downpour that beats the windows, and slips through the gaps in the ceiling is all I can take in as the pain sends me rigid. Or limp.

It could be both.

I'm not sure which feels better.

I groan, tremulous hands holding the bandaged peaks in my skin at horrid remembrance of what I had reckoned with. I can hear Simone's voice at my ear as I power through small puffs of air, extending an aching arm just far enough to pull her closer.

My eyes burst with waterworks.

"Thank goodness," I croak into the curly fuzz sprouting from her happy little head.

A clamor of footsteps approaches us, stopping short of our moment as I already feel the panic set in. But when I look up, it is only people I know.

Aidan. Celestyn. Melody. Ace.

They stare at me in genuine astonishment, though something in Aidan is so boldly broken. Softened.

"A-Addie…" He drops to his knees, shuffling closer. "Oh my god, I just can't believe…I mean, wow. It's just…you're bleeding. Oh, fuck. Let me he—"

The only warmth left of me is that of a slick trickle from my belly button to the waistline of black, loose fitting shorts Celestyn must have changed me into after she wrapped the wounds earlier. I frown, the material barely enough to cover the worst scarring on my legs, let alone my ass. The hem drinks the crimson liquid as well it can, overflowing much too quickly and spilling onto my legs for everyone to see. For all attention to draw to the brutal, wrinkled scarring. The divots.

I am practically bare, I realize, my face boiling.

There is too much blowing through my mind in this moment, Aidan's calloused hand reaching out open-palmed to help. His fingers lace into the baggy grey shirt I am wearing, doused in blood, and I writhe away in terror. My heart beats out of my chest, legs rocketing faster than my brain can think to stop.

It is a blinding white haze of motion that sends me reeling against the wall. I can no longer contain my pain even in fear, howling and unfurling as everyone looks on, Melody's voice floating above the rest in an attempt to calm me down.

A confused torment spreads over Aidan's face as his hand drops in understanding. He won't dare touch my bandages without an okay, but he is hurt, fingers coiled to a loose fist and eyes losing mine in a sudden abashment. The burning red flushes over his face in dreaded silence, trying to pace his elation at my waking better.

Celestyn whips away to grab her bag of dwindling supplies, and Ace darts to a different end of the room for a canteen of any kind. My eyes dart over each of them, arms wrapped tight around Simone as I attempt to take in the situation that has encumbered my welcome back to hell.

Simone smothers herself into the dip of my neck, inhaling what is a very much alive me as Ace returns.

"You need water, Adabelle," he all but commands. "You have been down for quite some time now. Hydration is important if you want to start using those muscles any further."

I shouldn't be able to use them at all.

"Set it down," I reply, voice soft and still coming back to me. My gaze flickers around the room. I can't stop the fear. "On the floor. Please."

"Unreasonable." He does not comply, holding the canteen within arm's reach.

I am in no condition to fight him, but I am petrified.

He is tall and lean in comparison to my short and waning mass since I became unconscious. The weakness of fat stores being devoured by my body for fuel can be sensed in every plod of every limb upon my being.

It must have been quite some time they have pulled together to keep me alive.

But...

"I was hurt," I say, avoiding the scenic memory of touching my own guts.

"Yes," Celestyn returns with gauze, needles, and jars. "Very badly, I am afraid. Do you remember much of it?"

She almost sounds sympathetic. It is eerie.

"No," I reply, lying and edging further into the wall. I want nothing sharp near me. At all. "Not...a lot, anyway. Erm...where is Zoey? I need to talk to her."

I swallow.

There is a deafening silence, and Ace thrusts the canteen at me. "Water first."

My head cracks against the window as I hurdle backward from him.

Ace has never hurt me aside from when he smashed my hand at Headquarters for touching files. I know this. But fear burns through me like lightning.

I am afraid. And embarrassed. And exposed.

Ace rolls his eyes, relenting to setting the canteen on the floor in front of me, murmuring something about the hope of all humanity and returning to Aidan's side.

*Aidan.*

He still sits, glasses crooked on his face which appears forlorn at best.

"Zoey," I repeat, uncapping the water and taking a few, decisive sips.

It feels good. Not so much like drowning. I am alive now.

"You were attacked, Addie," Aidan tells me. "We will talk about Zoey later."

Both Ace and Celestyn nod in agreement, but my heart beats harder, blood rushing to my head in a heat wave I can't sweat through. Another large drink of water, and I toss the canteen down, letting the resource spill across the floor like an agitated child. Steam blows through my bloodless ears, body rocking with such impetuousness the words almost don't pass through my clenched teeth.

"I promised her," my voice cracks. "I told her that I would not let anything happen to her. Don't you understand? Have any of you made such a promise to anyone other than yourselves?"

They are frozen. Celestyn drops a spool of thread that rolls against my bare feet.

It is hard to say how long I have been beneath the surface of reality, in a haven that is not quite life and unparalleled to death. I want to be back in there all at once, to relish what was an unburdened soul and to carry none of this with me.

None of this hell.

"I did," Ace speaks. "But we will not speak of that. Rest first, Adabelle."

"Zoey, first," I growl. "Did. She. Have. Her. Baby."

Aidan's eyes flicker from the floor, catching mine in dull

candlelight. "We. Don't. Know." His lips are pressed, his brow knit. "I saved you, not her. There wasn't time, Addie."

My bottom lip quivers, curling to keep my jaw shut with little success. Hot tears burn my dry eyes, dripping to my chest as I cannot deny them their way. Celestyn scolds Aidan under her breath with large eyes that remind him I am not at an optimal strength for bad news. But we both know, no—all know I would have ventured for the truth in spite of their well-placed lies.

Because something inside of me knew.

I can remember the way she sobbed when I was throttled into the wall like a heap of garbage. The way she begged, and I yelled into my own hands, trying with fail to keep the sword from blistering through my flesh. It is troubling to keep track of the events after that, the resonating of her shrieking punching holes of pitch into my vision until I can see nothing. Hear nothing—but Aidan.

Aidan never left.

Not me, anyway.

"Did you..." My grip on Simone falls to my lap and I struggle to find my words. "Did you at least look for her?"

Celestyn nudges Simone at the side, muttering at her ear to scoot over so that she can work without the disturbance of a small girl. I feel split, holding to the edge of my shirt in outward defiance to her help. I don't want it, though I have little reason to refuse it if I do not wish to die.

But maybe I do.

Perhaps I don't deserve to live.

My legs twist closer to my gut as Ace steps closer. The look on his face is more unfriendly than I've ever seen him, and his hands are braced to steady me so Celestyn may work without the magic of anesthetic at her will. The fear of being held still is a jab through bone that keeps unwinding, my tongue wetting bruised and split lips. All I can see are restraints, all I can hear is myself with a sword through my midsection, sloppy innards spilling between my fingers.

"The search teams disbanded after the last attack," Aidan calls against every other person in the room telling him not to. "We have a population of less than fifty and those numbers have dwindled since last count. We will have to move soon."

"Must you do more harm than this misery you have subjected upon her, boy? It is a magnificent fortune she has lived at all." Ace's voice is a hiss, head over his shoulder long enough for me to bolt around him in a guttural squelching.

I can see that they are afraid to follow, terrified to disturb me in the notion I might run further. Cause more damage.

My gut grows sleek, rushing little streams of blood to my legs as an adrenaline surge springs me through the front door, and out into the cold of rain so heavy it comes at me sideways. I cry out when it stings my cheeks, slowing in puddles that cling to my toes as I pry them free.

Lightning smashes in brilliant spikes at the treeline, threatening to crash and burn all at its feet if it must, the thunder granting voice to such deafening power.

At my back, I can hear Ace above the others. The rain is a mist that drowns away his image, but the voice that comes from him is one that cannot be denied—except by me.

I shake my head to it with little understanding to the garble, knowing that at all costs I must not be caught as a bystander in Limbo if I wish to complete my final mission in this nightmare, to save my only friend.

Because I promised her.

I did, and it means everything in a world that means nothing.

Cold fingers wrap around my arm, and I screech from the onslaught, spinning just enough to clamp down with what pressure I can force behind my teeth in a final crunch to his skin, the release granting me the ability to pick up my heels once more, leaving nothing but a ribboning of crimson in my wake.

I almost cannot hear the yell that results from my attack, but I know I will be forgiven if I return to meet them alive.

One of us will surely perish before I come home, but grace given, it will not be them.

I just need this.

Zoey needs this.

She needs *me*.

They will understand.

They have to.

Or else this is all for nothing.

The trees break raw along my arms, my nose giving in to a light crunch against the bark, spiraling me into a mess of bramble that tugs at the loose skin stitched together inside my shirt. I audibly inhale, nothing left in me to cry out as blood spills over my pained lips, staining my teeth a deep crimson. It bubbles in my slack jaw, flowing in gluey blobs at the neck of my shirt and bra until I am on my stiffening toes. Spitting what I can into the dirt and trekking onward.

It is not long until the voices of the people I have come to know on personal levels fade and mesh into the wilderness of steep hillsides and rushing river water.

I do not know where I am as I rip aside plants that blow recklessly in the wind, wishing I had the time to pull on my shoes before departing in such a hurry. This brain allows for little rational consult and even less since waking back to this terror.

With all my being, I wish to be free of what binds me indefinitely here.

I want to go home. To know all the same people, but not at this cost.

"Zoey!" I scream into the storm, topping a hill that leads to a thinner part of the river. The Dome is nowhere to be seen. "Zoey!"

There is an inaccessible whimper carried just on the breeze downhill and I slide down the muddy banks into the rocks that have only started to overfill with loose sediment and river water. I call again, bangs drenched against my forehead and hair gradually picked loose from my bun with the help of stray, low lying branches to untie the good work Celestyn must have put down in my sleep as part of patient care.

I pull it down anyway, letting it sop on to my drenched shoulders while the adrenaline pulls back from my limbs starting at the extremities furthest from my heart.

I have to make a choice.

"Zoey!" I holler to the other side of the rushing waves of water carrying leaves and fish helpless to its current downstream.

No answer, but I feel the consequence in my pelvis, this time turning my innards to slush. I pant, removing my hand from the afflicted region to see the crimson residue wash into the soil. Another whimper beckons to my anguish, however, and my head bobs above the pain to take in the opposing side of the river.

It is a wall of trees with black and white trunks, like silver carved into the night sky and willow branches that drop to the grassy ledge with permanent leaves of rich, ripe red death blowing like loose whips that tangle with each gust of air. I feel along its borders like a blind woman, gasping as the wind picks up and I am slapped in the face by a labyrinth of branches.

As I am about to give in though, my hands fall through open space and my feet race to catch up. I stumble into briers that seem to suck me inside, racing as far in as I can go as pain riots through my body.

And then...moonlight.

Clean air blisters against my fresh scrapes as adrenaline pumps to fill the void. I am barely breathing, huffing in small bursts so that I don't have to move my chest too much.

It is a beautiful clearing here. A field of tall grass and flowers, trees behind me built like a wall against my backside. In every corner around as far as the eye can see, branches sway and blow red petals into the sky.

My mouth drops, and I hold as much of my gut as I can. Panting and groaning.

The rain has slowed in this spot, much of the skyline blotted out by the treetops, but what I can see...peaceful.

Black clouds have parted like magic to reveal the sliver of moon out tonight. Its beams feel good against my skin. Like love. Like power. I feel almost primal here. Breaking, and yet putting myself together.

The small whimper I heard before recaptures my attention, and I turn my head around in the tall grass. I see nothing, but it is nearly as tall as I am in some places, much shorter in others. Like a maze. I creep forward, calling out again.

"Zoey? Are you here?"

A voice answers back. "N-no. B-b-b-but I am."

I am floored.

Making my way through tall weeds I see the very thing I had hoped not to have to see again.

A Ravager.

But this one is different. He is a child.

Tears fall off my face, and I squeeze the river from my shirt, stomping bruised, bare feet into the grass at the sight of the tiny boy left alone. His blond locks are smeared with mud down his fat cheeks, his blue snake eyes welled with immeasurable fear of the only creature to have located his pitiful pleas in this hidden part of the world.

My heart pounds against my chest, thundering inside the wall of trees lapsed around us like a bowl of rich blood against flesh, where the moon shines while outside it rains with hurricane force winds still billowing through the unseen entrance to make ghostly wails.

Because what else can it be?

I can see nothing else living here but plant life, a guarded section of even further forgotten time that neither of us should be within.

But here we are.

Both sobbing. Disappointed. Knowing better.

We shouldn't be here.

I shouldn't be here.

I am so stupid.

"Miss," the boy calls.

I scurry back. My heart thuds and my gnarled dancer's feet tangle with terror, knocking me to my backside where I am gasping.

"I'm lost. Please."

There is an innocence to crime lying beneath waves of tears, his little shirt untucked and tiny knife on the ground. In his inhale a stuttered whine draws forth, jaw quivering and nose crimson to the tip. He steps in my direction, unsure that I am friend but seeing no enemy in my presence either.

Though I am, his enemy per se. I think.

My belly pangs with every movement, my legs stretching to propel me further away though I can't motivate my body beyond the gut-clenching agony any longer. I turn my head to my shoulder, propped on trembling elbows. Coughing, I spray blood down the side of my biceps, watching it roll in fat drops to the grass while I can no longer afford to catch my breath, but instead collapse into nothing more than an outline in the earth.

*I am a monster,* my thoughts conclude, *for if he comes any closer to me, I will surely kill him. I can't stop. I'm afraid.*

"My father can help you," the boy says, "if you help me. You're hurt."

"Leave me," I gurgle.

It is a warning, and also a plea. Like a viper that has been nearly ripped in two, I hiss something dead to the ears of an unforeseen passerby, that I will defend myself until I am no longer sucking in air beneath my ribs, so helpless and far from home.

I do not want their help.

*Your father is not here, and I don't want to be alive when he finds us.*

I think of Zoey, and the way her face contorted upon seeing me drop inside through the doorway. Her muddied eyes watered with one of two ways we knew the scenario would play out, depending on how I was going to proceed. How she knew I would proceed when I saw Kasismis attempting to whisk her from me like luggage to be lost.

It was on her lips before I had even acted. Those words, the ones that lulled me into painless comfort, that opened the sky back into this nightmare.

Just Zoey, mouthing words through streams of tears.

*Adabelle, no.*

And I said...what did I say? I mouthed something.

*I can't live without you, Zoey.*

I said it, right?

I can't. I can't live without her. Or that baby.

My only friends in this whole world.

She was the first person to ever treat me like I wasn't an abomination. I could have been satisfied with such an end I had met, guilt nonexistent in the colorless void of black water that I rested in. Where instead I am now filled with this indescribable anguish that races over the surface of my body against every will to fight it. Remorse that I am not better. Or stronger.

More powerful.

And less ordinary.

If only I could have been cleverer. A tactician of some kind. White hot tears are all the heat left in my body, clouding what is left of such a hazy world as I shriek in semi silent sobs, sniffling and rolling my laden, aching neck so I can see the sunny sky. Only it is shut away by the wet face of the blue-eyed boy, kneeling over me like a trained vulture to pick away the remnants left in my wake.

I screech, though the boy tries to speak. Something to the effect of *Miss, are you okay,* but interrupted by my elbow cracking into his sternum from the ground, winding him with abrupt force so he is flattened on to his backside. And then, I am over him, reaching for the blade he had left on the ground, sharp edge slim against the thin of his neck while he makes little attempt to fight me. It might win him a bloody smile to move, or it might kill him anyway.

His pulse throbs against my bloodied fingers, smearing my own gore in messy fingerprints to the lobes of his ears as I hum against the red stain of my teeth, blood bubbling through my lips and filling my collarbone with rich butterflies.

My own heartbeat is in my head, playing a violent drum that resounds in my soul.

One. Clean. Cut.

It roars to me, and I groan over it, shutting out the pain

flowing through every inch of my body.

The little boy's screams drown this out, wailing at last, and begging aloud to me.

Please after please.

Just like Zoey had.

Just as every man, woman, and child who could be heard through the walls every single night that I have been alive here had. Wondering if they will be next. If they will die trying to avoid being next.

The inherent wants that can never be attained for the sake of one greedy, Ravager—

*Boy.*

Again, I shuffle back. The boy flies up on to his bottom right away, and our eyes lock.

It is a sheer terror. Ashamed, I am deep pink with abashment, hot from my ears to my toes. For he may grow to be an adult who preys on women and small children one day, that hunts me relentlessly until my mark on humanity is missing forever and I am but dust on the porch come morning light. He could be a beautiful horror to behold, killing with lack of mercy, jesting alongside many comrades in a language I do not understand as though it were just another day's work while bodies pile about them, and fluids flowed in recognizable stenches through the streets, leaving us to hold what family we have known and bury what is left.

But today he is a boy. With little ears, and eyes that quiver in the presence of a stranger. Small hands. Feet clad in boots that have dampened with urine flowing down his legs, making him cry even harder, vision straying to the tree line I block. He wobbles upright and makes a beeline, the air that comes off his stride blowing my hair completely free of my shirt, still wet as ever.

"I'm. So. Sorry," I whisper, though he is gone. Though she is gone. "There was nothing I could do, and I'm sorry."

My voice cracks, and my palms come to my eyes, smearing yet more red across my cheeks as I rise to my feet. I need to go home, if

I can make the journey back.

I can die with dignity if I am able. Let the time pass and warmth consume me until there is nothing left but the bones of what I have become.

I need to *feel* home one more time. Relish it, instead of fighting it.

I need warmth. And love. Family. People.

A flood of tears drops from my cheeks, even when I feel as if I have nothing left inside. My whole body trembles, begging me to stop as the adrenaline fades as fast as it came, like another trick pulled out of the magician's hat.

I turn around, suffocating on myself, and throwing my arms out for balance, still gripping tight to his little dagger.

But when I look up, I am frozen again.

*Fuck.*

He isn't so far away, but he blocks my only exit. A grown Ravager. A dark elf. The tallest I have seen yet, and scrawny, despite being well built. Toned enough to stretch a bowstring tight, so that the arrow is locked straight between my eyes from the distance he set.

I swallow what I can, studying his pale skin that is a bit more ashen than my own, his eyes flickering from dark yellow to orange as though he is a mood ring unable to decide what he is feeling today.

*Froggy, perhaps?*

The mood bounces between unadulterated disgust and... nothing at all.

Who said it?

I remember—Celestyn? She said they can change certain features such as eye color like camouflage. It is why they blend into nature so well, and why we can't always see them in the dark.

Is he distressed?

Why wouldn't he be?

I attacked what is undoubtedly his son. I nearly killed the boy. Out of fear, and out of hate.

I *hate* what they are, and what they do.

I'm angry.

I can't stop being angry, even when I am scared. But my tears dry up at this standstill.

My belly throbs, hands saturated as I drop the knife like it were a loaded gun, raising my arms in compliance.

I can be submissive for my life.

I can say I'm sorry. I think.

I'm no soldier.

I just want to go home.

And he hasn't shot me yet. He's undecided.

"Y-you..." Blood spills from the corners of my mouth, and I whimper, bursting at the literal seams. "I'm...ssss-so sorry. I didn't mean to hurt your boy."

I choke, coughing.

The Ravager turns to the side, losing his aim if for but just a second and straightening back up. Perhaps an involuntary twitch of curiosity. Disbelief? Maybe he wants to torture me for what I've done.

I shuffle forward, hoping in some way I can weasel around him, and make a timely exit. It would be slow a dance, but just maybe...

The arrow follows me, like the animal I am. I stop for a moment, shaking wildly. Like a little girl.

I hold my breath, trying my hardest to stay calm. For a second, it seems to work. His arm relaxes for a singular fraction in time, and his eyes move to me instead. Studying. Listening.

I look like a mess in comparison to himself. I am wearing a bloodied shirt reaching halfway down my thighs. Even bloodier shorts he probably can't see that are drenched, rivers of crimson roaring down my knees, and staining the spaces between my toes. My hair is undone, soaked and hanging in my face like a gremlin, many of the scars I have tried to keep secret for so long on display like a walking zoo.

Meanwhile, he looks *very* well kept.

He wears a clean black cloak and red tunic, trousers, and boots that glisten with familiar, black scales I can't place—though armored well. His shoulder-length black hair is a bit disheveled, hanging over a single eye.

No braids. But well kept.

Covered. Groomed.

*I look like the ravager right now.*

I take a deep breath, and another mighty step, stopping again directly after, trying not to cry. When I look up at him, he is no longer looking at me at all, but instead at the sky, almost as though he is growing bored of this pitiful game we play.

I try to talk to him, to appeal to his inner good, if it is there.

"I...I was attacked not long ago," I whisper so that I don't strain myself. His eyes flick downward in my direction, attention piqued. "By one of your kind. I...I'm really sorry. I was jj-just so..."

*Afraid. Say it.*

I squeak, holding my abdomen. When I glance up to him this time, he is making eye contact, bow lowered but string still stretched tight. The gears are turning in the back of his mind, as if he were a cat watching his local mouse bleed out on his doorstep.

But much more majestic than a cat.

He is...sleeker.

Stronger.

A regular house cat wouldn't challenge him to a fight.

I sure as hell wouldn't.

"I was trying to protect a friend," I offer information. "She was pregnant, and I promised her I would—" I am coughing up blood again. "I promised, okay? I swore, and I failed. But it wasn't my fault."

He stands straighter, allowing his full height to come into view at my next step, lowering his bow just a bit more. His long, pointed ears move just barely, zeroing in on what I have to say, as well as other noises in the night. Perhaps his son, somewhere just out of sight.

I decide to watch the inflections of my voice if I can—the

proper way to manipulate. Every movement has to be made with the utmost caution and respect while he is becoming increasingly less threatening.

I bite my lip and shuffle.

"It probably sounds strange to you, or maybe not," I force a bit of a laugh, "But we are terrified of you guys where I live. Have you been there? We are so small...and weak."

I'm a bit closer than before. A couple arm's lengths away. He seems to allow it okay, eying me closely.

This near, he is admittedly handsome in a more rugged way. They all are, to a degree, in a way that humans aren't. But he is especially so in my mind. I enjoy his features, even his pity to a degree, if that is what this is.

I want to even mistake it for sympathy.

But I know what he is. What his race is. And it erases much of the good that my hormones beg to see.

"A lot of us have died r-recently," I gurgle. "I w...w...was stabbed. Pretty bad. I almost died...and...I'm scared. I don't think I'm...going...to make it home."

The tears start falling against my will.

He watches this entire show, raising his bow again for a moment as I straggle, bowing my head in preparation for the end. Wondering if it hurt to be shot with an arrow. If I would die instantly or if it would take some time.

Would anyone look for me?

I wipe the tears from my face as more come.

My legs feel as though they are on fire, carrying the weight of a thousand elephants while I inch closer on my very own death march. Sobbing.

I can't carry on too much longer. I am going to die just as alone and afraid as I always feared. Just within his reach. Shaking.

"I'm so *stupid*," I say out loud for the first time where no one else can hear me. "I can't believe I am so stupid."

I don't look at him for this part, keeping my head bowed.

"I've tried so hard just to fit in here. Just to belong somewhere at all. And I scare everyone away in spite of myself. I can't control myself. I think things into existence...all the time. I...I..."

More crying.

I wonder if this is uncomfortable for him. I wish I could stop.

Red petals blow off the willow branches, whispering my secrets through the open air. The breeze sends chills down my spine, making every hair on my body stand on edge as I try to pull myself together.

I sniff, peeking to him as he glances away again.

I am suddenly very certain he was looking at my legs. The horrendous divots and burn scars.

I look away too, blushing as fear courses through me.

"Why do your people hurt mine?" I ask, waiting for an answer that doesn't come. That I know won't come. "What did we do? How do we make it stop?"

Cold metal presses into my temple, and I suck in a gasp for air. Waiting.

His bow bounces to the ground. I can hear him grind his teeth, his large hand grabbing my wrist for leverage to blow whichever weapon he now held clean through my skull. I try to imagine the sound it will make. If it will crunch, or shriek like a vase smashing into the floor. But all at once, this rage seems to dissipate, and he releases me. In his hand a sword is slipped back into its sheath.

"I'm sorry," I whisper, pathetic.

No answer.

But I can't carry on any longer. I will die here, whether he kills me or not. My feet slip from the ground, the trees rolling into sky for a moment as I brace to hit the grass and rocks below. Head pounding. Heart racing.

But the ground never comes.

Long arms slip around me, holding me upright as tears and blood stain his rough clothing. It is an effortless motion, attempting to balance me as I slump forward against him, my breathing shallow and stiff.

I am panicking, but all at once, I feel safe as well. Secure. Tired.

I can stay here...for a moment.

"I think I'm dying," I weep into him. "C...could you....help me? Just don't let it h-hurt too bad. M'kay?"

My eyes flutter. I am growing tired. The Ravager shifts, just a bit, cradling me against him and looking around us for a moment.

I am fully supported by him, feeling his fingers glide against the hem of my blouse. My shorts. And then slides with care beneath the drenched fabric, something that makes me choke on my own spit in abashment.

My desperate, frightened hands fly to his, cupping his fingers gently. I am awkward—panting and reeling. Embarrassed as his sharp nails rip away at the gauze.

Disemboweled doesn't sound like a painless death.

"I...please..." I force a small smile as he searches for the wounds below my clothes in need of care. "At least buy me dinner before you round second."

Why can't I shut up?

It is an awkward joke. He makes a strange face, but I can swear it is almost a smirk. A suppressed chuckle.

*Gotcha. You have feelings.*

They have feelings.

His fingers splay between my hips and across my belly, flexing. Burning. I tense up, and he pushes down at the same instant, so I grunt in pain. A garbled scream escapes my raw, torn throat. The sound of his long, sharp nails across my open wounds is a strange noise from this action, like a zipper. A prickling of the skin. But the longer his hand remains, the better I feel.

I try not to look down, the smell of burning flesh reaching my nose, and making me shake. I clutch to him for dear life.

It makes him hesitate. My hands grabbing at him and pulling me closer as sharp pangs ring through my stab wounds, like he is holding back.

Resistance not to kill me instead, perhaps.

I am a strange, needy human girl who attacks children. Pitiful little lady asking for help dying. I don't even get to be a cute dying lady.

Still, instead of giving me a quick death, I am feeling a bit better. Slowly.

It is hard not to squirm in agony. I both want to feel better, and want to run with what I've been given.

He works in one area at a time, the rupture at my pelvis being the worst and saturated, but moving up as everything starts to feel more and more like a really bad bruise than a gaping wound.

There is a hesitation at the wound just below my sternum, fingers twitching. I can see now that each of his long fingers from the nail to the knuckle is slick with blood. Glistening and black at this time of night.

He glances down to me, noticing my attention on it in a barely, but quietly self-admitted fascination. Another small grin. Just enough to break the stern features of his face.

It is fast. I am almost not sure it happened. But these things can't be hidden forever.

I just...don't know why he is doing me this favor. His kind has committed serious grievances against mine.

Is this where I will disappear? Is he a soldier on his way to ravage the village? Why would he bring his young son to such an event?

I had never seen children in the attacks before.

The small clouds above have almost completely vanished now, letting the moon blast cold light down upon us. It is when I notice that the bloodied tips of his fingers have lit afire, a pale yellow flame that burns without melting away his flesh. The first extent of their powers we don't know.

Magic.

He moves it close to the last injury and I scurry to turn away, blowing at the flames before he grips tighter so I am still, so I have little choice.

My heart gallops, the heat from the fire quite real, lapping away at the skin as I bite my lip in pain that lessens as he works.

I don't know how long it takes.

When I stop tensing, and I relax, I stop keeping track.

A few minutes. A few hours.

He's thorough. And the night is...beautiful, when I'm not always running from it.

A few bats flutter overhead, squeaking before a slightly bigger dragon swoops through, snagging one from the sky. The screeching makes me stop looking at the sky. Another shake from him reminding me of another suppressed chuckle.

I frown.

"Things are so violent here," I tell him as he presses each finger sparingly along the parts of the wound that hasn't sealed shut in a nasty red line. "I...I want to go home."

Hesitation.

His hand drops over the wound, sweeping across it one more time in a bright gold flame and then he pulls my bloody shirt back over it.

We stay still for a second like this. I wonder if his son is still close by or not. Protected.

I feel horrible. They are protective over their children, and I could have really hurt his.

"I was more of a person before this," I say, and he listens, sitting with me laid across his lap still. "I would have never attacked a child before this. Or anyone. I just...freaked out. My friend was pregnant, and I tried to save her. And the...what are you guys..."

I snap my fingers.

He stares in silence.

I look like a moron. We both know it.

"Dark elf!" I find the words. "There was one and he tried to take my friend. When I tried to save her, he...stabbed...me. I think, maybe, he had *imprinted* on her. I read something about it. It makes the men especially aggressive...but I don't know. I-I almost died."

I stop the tears before they start again, choking on each word as I say them.

"There are so many things I haven't done yet, you know?" I whisper. "I'm still young."

He doesn't appear overly sympathetic.

I don't expect him to be. I'm rather accusatory toward his kind. Whatever they are doing, they seem to think they are justified for it.

But he listens, and right now, I need someone to listen to what I'm saying. Get this off my chest without opposing aggression. Or laughter.

"I'm twenty-one," I admit, sitting up slowly. "I...I'm twenty-one, and I barely remember anything about my life. It's like I'm just starting over clean. And it hurts for some reason. I miss who I was, and I don't know her."

His hand comes at my back to help me sit upright. I'm still very sore despite his healing efforts. Like my whole abdomen is a giant bruise and the rest of me has turned to gelatin. It is going to be a tough trip home, if I start right now. Which I'm not sure I can.

"I don't remember a lot." I sigh, holding my upright position.

The elf moves, rising to his feet and offering help to get me upright as well. I attempt the venture on my own, scrambling and wobbling. Groaning as I attempt to straighten out on my own two legs. The trees blow hard with another wind, and I wonder if the storm is moving back in.

"I was a dancer," I vent, peering at my exit. "I taught children to dance, and when they left, I sat on my couch in my underwear and ate ice cream until I fell asleep. It wasn't much of a life. At least not what I can remember of it. I didn't go running to bars. I never kissed a stranger because I was afraid to be turned down or had sex with a man I took home from the clubs because...I'm terrified that it will hurt...and that's lame, but I'm not keen on pain. The freakiest I got was this damn hair dye and these tattoos. And look at me. I'm a mess. The enemy had to use his extraordinary fire magic to make sure I didn't die, and I'm probably going to end up dead at some point anyway because I just can't stop being stupid."

*Am I rambling?*

*What am I saying?*

The way I came is maybe half a mile behind him. I don't think he will stop me from passing at this point, but it is a matter of if I can get there without fainting.

I'm still in pain. I still want to hunch over and scream. But not scream. Because that would hurt too.

I shuffle forward, stumbling.

His hands catch me at the arms. Again, *effortless*.

I feel warm at this. On fire. Frozen, but like every part of me has been delightfully blasted with delicious heat.

I...I like effortless.

That anything can be effortless with me.

My lip quivers, and for the first time, I don't look at him, not because I'm embarrassed, but because I think I am blushing.

This is part of their charm, is it not?

It doesn't feel like charm.

It feels like me.

I suck in a breath, staring at the ground as another gust of wind blows through the trees. More soft red petals free themselves from the willow branches, falling all around. I shake some out of my hair, pulling two off the sleeve of his tunic and rolling them between my fingers. After a moment, I straighten out, looking up to him. Still bright red.

I clear my throat and grab his hand, rolling the petals into his palm and closing his fingers over them with a brief smile.

"I-I don't have anything to give you." I nod. "For helping me. I have another chance to find a way home because of you, and I don't think I can ever repay you for that. Just...take these as a form of truce? I'll do better to learn more about your race...and you can...just remember me? We aren't all bad. Just scared...and confused."

There is a strange motion with his eyes, the way they dilate for a minute, and watch me. My every move.

I can't tell what it is. If they're pained. Or concerned. Frustrated or annoyed. Confident?

I am still burning, and his free hand comes at the side of my face, holding for just a minute. Cold. But warm. Calloused.

Effortless.

I gulp down another breath, unable to speak. His hand trails softly down my neck. Shoulder. Bicep. Wrist. His fingers curl around my wrist. Firm. I step into it, closer to him. I'm so small in comparison. Ridiculously so.

He steps away, something in him reluctant about letting my arm go, but allowing himself to do so, bending in a bow. To which I return, holding myself as I do, feeling like I am going to fall apart —something which appears to both confuse and amuse him.

It amuses me too, this custom.

I can't seem to unbend completely though, in agony. I have half a mind to ask him to walk me back, having a bet that no one would attack a girl already in the company of a dark elf.

But I don't know if it works like that. If he has to go.

I don't want to be a burden after already pushing the boundaries.

Plus...it is hard enough to ask regular people for help...I can't ask him.

"I...have to go." I try to smile. "I..."

My legs give out, weak and shaking still. Recovering.

*Of course I am still recovering. I can't act like I am completely well when the only reason I am able to be here at all is because of him.*

The elf keeps me from hitting the ground, this time leaning slowly back until we are both on the grass.

It is at this moment I look up to him. I can't control what I do next. I try, but I can't. I pull myself up as best I can, pressing my lips against his. Locked, and trembling. Love starved.

I'm shaking, pulling away, but he yanks me forward so that our lips touch again. His tongue is begging entrance to my mouth, which I hastily allow, this time moving further up into his lap before I am stopped by the agony of what is left of my injuries.

And so I slide down, weaker. Gelatinous.

I am goo.

I am woman.

I have kissed a stranger. And he didn't run.

The moon glows brightly, and I curl into myself, head against his chest, trying not to breathe too deeply. I am growing too tired to stay awake, despite my need to get home.

But I feel safe here.

I am safe here.

I shut my eyes, feeling his arm brush against me, holding me in place as a barrier against the world.

It is strange this way, but I like it. Relish it.

It's just as I drift away that I notice something else. It might be nothing at all. His clothes are quite thick so it is harder to tell for sure but...

I don't think he has a heartbeat.

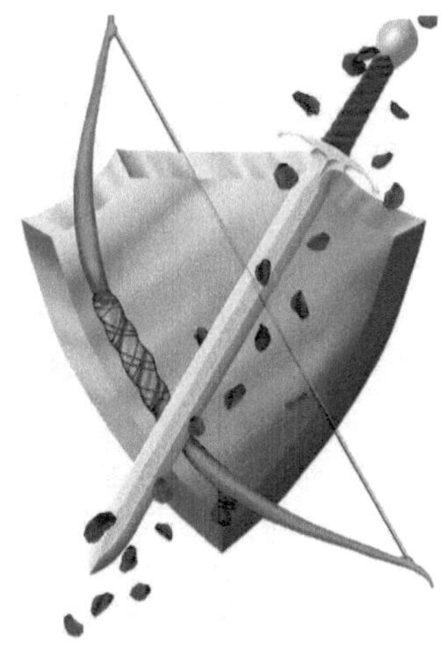

# CHAPTER FORTY-THREE
## AIDAN

ACE CAN'T KEEP HOLD OF HER, NOR CAN HE CATCH HER in time once she is lost.

Addie is too slick.

And fast.

And mean.

*God,* is she mean.

When Ace lumbers back inside, he is defeated, shaking small showers of rain off his clothes and from his slicked wet, jet black hair from his face. His head hangs, puffed cheeks letting free a slow, steady exhale of exasperation, eyes void of anything that can be classified as regular human emotion.

I throw my hands out at him as no words come to explain the loss, or to make a game plan on how to get her back home. I can't allow myself to give in quite as easily, my pathetic voice a stuttered whine of incoherent syllables and legs racing me out the door with Melody on my trail while Celestyn pleads for me to stop.

Outside, heading for the trees in the direction she ran, I scream for Addie until my throat is hoarse with pain. Melody screeches just as loud for me to stop, stumbling over her own heels in the thick mud created by the rain.

I can get killed acting like this.

It won't do anyone a favor to off myself in pursuit of my friend.

It is what she says, but I can't make sense of it in the moment. I'm running, faster and faster. The water is bleeding down from the sky in blinding strings, stinging my face and eyes, but slowing down as Melody catches up, laying a hand on my shoulder while I huff for more air. Stopping short of the trees, lungs feeling as though they have shredded themselves from the inside.

The distress of loss hits me all at the same time here, bending me into impossible angles of grief as I attempt to hold the pieces of myself together.

I didn't guard Addie's unconscious body against all odds this long just for her to run off like a scared dog on a sensory overload so she could die somewhere else.

It isn't right.

Melody's grip on me tightens, hard enough to hurt, like she is angry with me for leaving. Her squeeze feels like she could snap my shoulder to bits in the twitch of her palm, and I believe it, placing my hand on hers in a subtle bargain for release.

"We will look tomorrow," she tells me, slow but loud to assure I hear her over the rain.

I turn to see her, watching her gaze swivel around us. Nervous.

She has every right to be at nighttime as a woman. Or as a person living in Limbo, period.

She shouldn't be out here with me. This is something I should have done alone.

Why did she follow?

"She'll be dead tomorrow," I counter.

Melody bites her lip to this, scanning the trees to our left, and then to our right.

I'm not used to girls being taller than me, dominating the area I stand by a good head or more above. Quite a few of my male comrades would take it as the perfect opportunity to stare straight into her nipples, peaked through her shirt without a bra as gooseflesh rises on the surface of her skin against the elements. But other than a vague notice as I study her, I veer clear of intimacies with her the same as she does me.

We are more like...good friends. Very good friends.

And despite trying to break my shoulder, she is trying to help me.

"Adabelle takes care of herself, wherever she goes." Melody blinks away rainwater. "We can't risk looking for her right now, though. It would leave the village with even less people than what it has and compromise our remaining population. We need everyone we can get for when we leave tomorrow."

It is reluctant, but I know she is right. I agree to go home with her, vowing to return to the area tomorrow for a better look through if Addie doesn't come home.

The walk home is bitter, excruciating and long. Ace and Melody share a look upon entering the home again. A story reads between them that is unspoken, but knowing. Severe. Perhaps neither of them believes Addie will make it out there all alone.

Why even create such a façade if they know better?

Celestyn shrugs. She holds a sobbing Simone, rubbing her frail shoulders in an honest attempt to comfort her.

"I say let her go," she tells the room. "She is an animal, and she belongs in the great outdoors with the way she acts."

"Uncalled for," Ace snaps. "Miss Green had just awoken from a very traumatic experience. There was too much information offered as to the conclusion of her event, and emotionally, that can put a person in a friable state of mind."

Melody leans to the door frame, eyes roaming about the room, taking it all in as if it were the last time she will ever do so.

"It does call to mind that woman who escaped from the quarantine units two years ago following a psychotic break." The storm roars around us, though the rain is a soft solace of static.

"She never came home...although, I guess, you probably don't want to think about that. Lost to the forest, I imagine, if not worse."

Celestyn touches the very subtle, often overlooked twist of her nose, moving to the scar covered by her thick hair above her temple.

"I remember that," she comments, as if she wouldn't. She should remember better than anyone else, considering the damage she received from the crazy bitch. "I can't remember her name for the life of me."

"Sahanna," Ace replies. "Sahanna Leanna Gillens."

There is a quiet that only the rain can fill, tapping against the rooftop, and dropping inside where it isn't as foolproof.

I don't want to think about Sahanna, or what happened to her. Not now.

Melody is right.

"Has it ever occurred to any of you that it would have made a world of difference to be kind to the girl despite her differences to this world?" Ace snaps as another gust of wind sends rain sprinkling inside through the gaps in the window and open door.

"Excuse me?" Celestyn raises her voice. "You hit her!"

Ace is firm. "She touched my things."

"You're touching *my* things!" I shout.

The room is quiet—again.

I lean toward my guitar, touching the strings, but not quite playing the instrument. Ace and Melody let themselves out as the rain lets up after a few hours of awaiting Addie's return.

I leave the door cracked all night, just in case she comes home —or wants to. But the night is more silent than ever, and I don't wake up until close to noon the next day, glancing around the room in a frantic mania to find Addie is still not here.

She never came home.

Celestyn is sitting up with Simone in the corner, chowing on a meager breakfast of berries and bread, reading medical studies to her, and assisting her in the sounding out of simple words as I yank my shoes on that I took off to dry before sleeping last night. I grab the sword Addie gifted me from under the blanket, as well as my bow and quiver with few arrows. On my other arm, I swing Addie's backpack up by a single strap.

It is heavy. So heavy, the woman must have the traps of a goddess to haul this bullshit around all day. But she still has extra gear in there that will come in handy if I can find her, so I can't bring myself to leave it.

"Where you going?" Simone calls from the corner.

I stop, peeking over my shoulder with the quiver that blocks less of her image so we can make eye contact.

"I need to find Addie." I don't bother lying to the child. The explanation goes for Celestyn too. "She's alive, and if I can find her, she probably needs help. If I can find her and help her, she will be able to leave with us when we get out of the village."

A better word for *village* is *hellhole*, but I attempt to be careful in regards to preserving what remains of this child's innocence.

"This is stupid." Celestyn's voice is begging, soft tone not matching the hate it spreads like butter over toast. It gives me pause, though I don't know why. I don't want to. "No one wants Adabelle here, except you. Let her go. It will be safer. We never had this kind of trouble before she came along. I don't know what hints you aren't picking up!"

"Just stay home then," I reply sharply.

I step out the door. Outside, what is left of the villagers gather what they can. Several children are crying, and voices shout back and forth. To my own shock, The Purple Dome that protects us has faded so much more, barely there at all, the blue sky winking to me in full color, uninhibited by the lavender film.

In my mind, it doesn't seem coincidental that as Addie left, The Dome did as well. But she also wasn't here when the structure was first erected, so the assumption doesn't make a lot of sense.

Nothing makes a lot of sense.

My mind rewinds to what Melody said last night, about the girl that had the psychotic break. Was she implying Addie, too, had a mental breakdown? That she couldn't handle any more of this place, and that is why she left?

It doesn't seem right.

It doesn't *sound* like Addie.

Addie is stronger than that other woman. Physically. Emo-tionally.

She's unlike anything I have seen. She doesn't have meltdowns or breakdowns or psychotic episodes.

Whatever happened had to be part of her weird hero complex. Her irrational need to save everyone alive. To make sure no one has been left behind.

Closer to the tree line, I start to ask people if they have seen Addie today. The rain will have washed away most of the blood trails she might have left. Other sets of feet are bound to shroud her own, making them hard to track. But if she came back, someone is bound to have seen her. It is a small village now more than ever, and everyone knows who she is.

Still, the realization I am out of luck comes at no shock. No one has caught wind of her since before the attack that put her in the miniature coma, and most people had not even known she woke up last night. Which means if I continue beyond this point, I will really be searching blindly in the trees in the directions I think she *might* have gone, without The Dome's second layer of protection.

A voice calls at my backside.

*Hey! Wait.*

I turn around. A couple houses down, Celestyn is holding Simone's tiny hand, rushing toward me. Together, they stare at the enormous trees that begin the true forest, like the legs of wooden giants rising to the leafy sky. Celestyn is not usually quite this close and personal with nature as she, of all people, knows what is out there.

"A...are you leaving?" Celestyn asks me, trying not to appear as if she cares too much.

"I'm going to look for Addie. Dead or alive, but I believe she is alive."

Tension clings to the air like a toddler to his blanket, soaking in what is left of the good while preparing for the worst. Celestyn's medicine bag clinks at her waist, shuffling closer to my side so that I can feel the heat coming off her body. She is especially warm today, I notice. And fuller, in the hips. I can't be sure, but I think she has gained a little weight.

Is it possible for her to gain weight?

"You can feel it, can't you?" she asks me in a low whisper. "The tension in the air? Last night was our last good night."

"Perhaps, only good for some of us," I respond, stepping into the woods, though her free hand catches mine, squeezing it as tight as she can.

"Her injuries were critical," she implores. "The depth of the infection spreading, and tissue that was growing necrotic...I tried to keep it from you, so you wouldn't hurt as much, but Aidan, I don't know how she woke up. There is no way she is alive right now. Any animal could have found her, preyed on her weak state. We don't know."

I rip my arm from her, heaving the backpack higher up on my shoulder so that it clamors against my quiver.

"I guess I better hurry then."

I can feel her tense up. She is getting angry. I expect her to hit me. Like she had done in the past. Waiting until I turn my back to punch me in the arm. The first time she did it, I just sat there. Like a moron. I couldn't believe it, and I shoved it off like a bad joke.

She was all I knew at the time, the only person I was comfortable around. It was easy to share my dark, haunting secrets with her, and I was in love with her.

*All girls get a little slap happy when they're upset,* I told myself. *No big deal. I am here to be her punching bag.*

But the more it happened, the more I could feel my insides boil.

She would hit me in the arms, the back of the head, the hip, the legs, the neck...

To this day, I am rotting against her, seething in bitter discontent.

I bite my lips, awaiting her worst, but it never comes.

Celestyn does not hit me, the contents of her medical bag shifting, a few jars sounding as though they are broken as she knocks me aside with the point of her elbow. There is a dagger in her hand, swinging through some of the bramble in crazy waves of her hand into the forest ahead of me while Simone toes at her legs. A woman scorned, a child learning.

I hold my hand out to Simone upon catching up, which the child cautiously takes. We set out as a group to find our friend, looking for signs that anyone has been in the area, though I am having a hard time deciding whether Celestyn's intention is to help find Addie, or kill her.

It takes some time, heads moving in all angles, watching the ground and examining rocks that look as if they might have blood on them. We come across several trees in the miles up ahead that appear to have the remnants of bloodied handprints smeared on their ashy trunks, ridges of mud splattered in a stumble for the unknown. We follow this trail for hours, slowly, starting to talk the more discouraged we become, the signs of her potential existence all but evaporating.

"Why do you go to all this effort for her?" Celestyn asks me, lifting leaves and touching trees.

I release Simone's hand, examining the ground, and crouching to find anything that looks like shoeprints in the area.

"She's my partner." I tick left over right.

This answer isn't good enough. We both know it isn't.

"Your last partner died, Aidan. You didn't make near the effort to recover his corpse. In fact, you didn't make any effort."

The river isn't far off. I can hear it. Addie would be stupid to go near the water, including a smaller branch of it, covered in blood. But it is Addie, so...

"What are you getting at?" I sigh, trudging through weeds and trees.

I can feel Simone at my heels, picking up cool rocks and watching bugs crawl.

"Do you...like her?" Celestyn veers closer.

It is something I have been waiting for her to ask. She has

passive-aggressively hinted at the question long enough, and it is not like I have ever done anything to abate these fears, or reassure her. She had never reassured me either when I had similar concerns.

But something about her sounds vulnerable in this minute. I can't refuse it.

"She is a reliable friend," I admit. "She is...she is a good person."

"Is that it?"

"Is what it?"

"You don't...I mean, you aren't in love with her or anything?"

I frown.

The memory of Addie sleeping on me after the fire crawls into my mind, picking apart my brain with sharp, spindly legs. Dangerous. Painful, and warm.

"Why do you care?" My inner defenses wall in the sensation, afraid to give it up.

She waves me over, a bare footprint still encased in mud. Simone thrashes through weeds to catch up, clutching to the hem of my shirt, and then letting go when she is sure I won't run.

"We have history," Celestyn tells me while I scan the direction it is pointed for more. "I care about you. I have since the first day."

I half-smile. "I hated those quarantine units so much. I was so damn happy to see another human being that day, and you were... gorgeous."

"I was elbow deep in blood from another patient." She laughs, moving parts of a bush to check inside where the prints lighten up.

I laugh too. It is genuine, and it surprises me as it comes.

"What can I say? You made death look hot."

She slows to a stop. "You asked me out for the first time before the first ten minutes of your examination were up."

I wish I could say I knew what I wanted. That I wanted her, more than anything. But the truth is, then, I had latched on to anyone that appeared like safe company. I didn't know anything about myself, or where I was. It was terrifying, and she was a beacon of light that I could walk into.

"You deserved better than that." My voice is solemn.

"It was funny," she reassures. "Cute, when I think on it."

I adjust my glasses, the roar of river water closer than ever.

"I shouldn't have pursued you for as long as I have," I say. "Or try to convince anyone we were something we weren't. The truth is, I knew it would never last. You would come over, and I would have sex with the hottest woman alive, but there were never any attachments to be had between us. No matter how hard I tried to create some bond. It was just never there."

She is quiet. Listening. So I carry on in my ramble.

"There has been a void inside of me since I woke up here that I have been trying to fill with anything I can get my hands on. It is like part of who I am has been ripped out, and tossed into this empty space of who I once was. I've always tried to make that darkness fill up with you, so that I don't have to confront it. But it isn't fair to either of us."

Celestyn purses her thick lips. It is almost like she isn't breathing at all, but she nods. Willful, but rejected.

"I agree." She clears her throat. "W...we should definitely end this. And be friends? Can we be friends?"

I turn to her, without missing a beat, pulling me into me with a tight embrace. Her hands are trembling, desperate as she holds me in turn, tears trickling off her cheeks.

"Absolutely." I stroke her rough, curled hair.

I mean it.

She will always be an important part of my existence here, but the worst of our dynamic has to end. When I release her, both of our hearts stop in unison. Everything stops. Looking in circles, neither of us see Simone anywhere. We race in opposite directions to cover more ground in the same area, looking in overgrown brush or behind trees that could shield her little body from view. The worst idea of all hits me when I think about where she could have gone.

*The river.*

I yell for her, over and over, throttling over legions of rocks and dirt.

"Simone!" I scream, Celestyn's own echoing mine as we subconsciously compete to arrive at the riverside.

*We should have split up, my mind nags. What if she's not here?*

"Simone!" I scream louder, zigzagging for the bank.

At the top of the steep, rocky banks of a shallow, small branch of overflown water, we both stop.

The whole universe feels dead, and Celestyn pants, skidding deep trenches at the soft incline where we stand, eyes widening so large they practically bug out of her face.

Simone stands where the water laps at her feet, right on the river's edge where current is fast enough that it pushes her sideways, but not crazy deep enough to drown her. The opposing side of this snaking section of water is littered by a wall of red petaled trees, willow-like vines arching into the shallows where schools of smaller fish wiggle without fear.

Under this veil of branches is *her*.

Addie.

She stares back at us with a soft, weak smile, T-shirt crusted in blood and soiled in dried mud. A small dragon coils around her once injured ankle that she now stands on without issue, chittering with great need up to her as she shuffles toward her side of the bank, as if not injured at all.

The beast does not appear to enjoy this, crying out to keep her, but not biting as they usually do, watching her step into the water and mourning the loss of the very creatures it lives to terrorize. It shuffles its way to shore, watching her slosh her way toward us, and squeaking for all to hear like a child that lost its mother.

I see the terror spread over Celestyn's face while this occurs, fingers trembling between her medicine bag and dagger.

But my chest drops in relief, sliding to meet her in the water.

I won't let anything else happen to her from this point on.

It is my one, silent promise.

# CHAPTER FORTY-FOUR
## ADABELLE

I WAKE UP ALONE.

Like a phantom, the elf who granted me life has vanished from existence altogether, leaving me to find my way home in the hopes I have enough time to set my life straight. Not that I mind. I am grateful for the help he provided, even more so that our abrupt meeting could turn into a one-time event that does not brand everlasting scars into my future. I have been given the opportunity to do more in this life, and today, while I am empty-handed, I am going home with the family I have made in Limbo. A second chance. With a new perspective, and a lot to think about.

It takes me some time to find my way out of the boxed in, weather changing clearing, unable to locate the way I entered through as I thought I could. When I am out, I stroll the riverbank for where I believe I came in at during my frantic idiocy, searching for the part of this branch of water I know is shallow enough for me to cross.

It is where I find Simone. It is where I find home.

Through the water, on the other side of hell, Simone is the very first person to reach me, wrapping her lanky arms around my legs that are not quite as weak as they once were, and crying for the whole woods to hear. She begs me to never leave her alone again, shrieking sobs reaching me where I could not have been touched less than a day ago. I wish I could make her these promises right this minute, to console her in every which way she demands so that the tears can dry, and we can live like we had. Poor, yet happy.

But I still have one more duty left in this world before I can attain the freedom of decision. I have one more promise I can't escape. I have to speak with Master Amadeus. I have to set things straight and get to the bottom of this madness. For everyone. For Zoey, because I haven't given up on her, no matter how far away she might be from me.

Aidan trembles from the incline overlooking the riverbank as I squeeze to Simone, softly so as not to disturb my new bruising and fresh healed injuries. He rushes our direction immediately, Celestyn wobbling after him with her medicine bag. I allow her to examine my shirt and injuries without lifting too far in the presence of everyone I care about.

"Are you okay?" she asks, suspicion a rigid guard protecting the sanity of her outer walls.

"I am...okay." I nod, stepping around her, and reaching for my backpack from Aidan, who drops its weight into my eager arms. "I am enlightened."

I am not entirely certain I am ready to carry the weight of it yet, but I am going to try my best. I have to, so that they can trust I am in charge of the situation here.

"Enlightened?" Celestyn scoffs from behind me. "Is that why you're so sprite, when earlier before you left you were sucking death's dick?"

I don't want to talk about my condition, and the experience that brought it full circle out in the forest. None of them are ready to hear that sort of thing. It is my dirty secret, my moment of vulnerability, and my safe place where for a fraction of time, I was heard and understood when all else was chaos.

I can't expect them to be ready for that kind of truth, and if I were to speak it aloud, it would exacerbate other issues that can't afford to be pressed any further. So I shrug my shoulders in a light bounce.

"What can I say?" I reply. "I've always been a fast healer. A freak. Whatever you want to call me, that's the correct term."

Celestyn's jaw comes unhinged as Aidan chuckles.

"You're home, with us. That is all that matters. And just in time, too!"

I swing my arms into my backpack straps, taking Simone's soft hand in mine. She clings to me like a baby koala, squeezing around my forearm, and pressing her cheek into the bare skin of my scarred legs. It takes no time to comprehend how clammy she is, and I debate carrying her. I hold doubt many people have since my trouble began, and she is such a cuddly girl.

Aidan and Celestyn walk at either side of me as we move, waiting for me to stumble in the dirt, and allowing me to speak any part of my piece that I'm willing to give—an afterthought of Aidan's sentiments occurring to me.

"You said I am just in time...just in time for what?"

Aidan is hasty, but happier than I have seen him in all the time we have met. "We are picking up the village and leaving tonight. Ace and Melody are going to be leading people out, and we are going to travel the paths these beasts usually don't enter on...there is barely anyone left, Addie. It is catastrophic."

"And you both are going too?" My brow furrows.

"And you," Aidan assures. "Now that you're awake. I...never gave up on you."

I stop, my stomach fluttering up to my chest. Up to my throat. I can't help but smile, nudging him in the sternum with my shoulder.

"C'mon, now," I try to laugh. "That was your free pass to get rid of me, and you didn't ride that bitch to freedom?"

"I could have," Aidan grins. "Damn it. Why don't I think these things through?"

I can see Celestyn glower at my other side, watching her feet kick the dirt and sticks where we walk. I try to make do in the department of forcing amends though, moving a bit closer to her and leaning in.

"Thank you," I say. "For helping me when I needed it most. I know it was you, and you didn't have to. But you did."

Celestyn grows sour, and rigid. Sad. Her whole figure droops and recoils, sucking into itself.

"I did it for Aidan," she replies, glancing up at him. "He—I mean, he acted like a big pussy and shit carrying you back. It was the least I could do to keep his blubbering ass quiet."

I look to Aidan, my lips twisted and ornery.

"You cried?"

He doesn't answer this question right away, so Celestyn does for him.

"Like a bitch!" She starts digging in her bag, pulling out a handful of berries to eat. She takes bite after bite, talking again after a couple swallows. "Sorry you missed it though!"

Aidan is more silent than death himself, looking every way but mine, face glowing dark red. I pat him on the shoulder though, awkward as I am. I'm not good at this, but I want to be—for him.

"You...carried me all the way back?" I try. "That's incredible. I'm so heavy, and it must have taken a lot of effort. You saved me."

This seems to ease his tension a little bit, and I'm glad. I need them to calm down and stop fighting like they usually do.

When we reach the village, all eyes are on our little group. Melody and Ace, who are instructing a group of men and women with whatever livestock we have remaining, drop everything and rush over to greet us.

They stop short of our small, numbered presence, inching a respectful, clinical distance from me. Like I'm toxic.

Not like friends any longer, but more like acquaintances I don't know.

Ace eyes me up and down, jaw clenching shut so his teeth

grind together, Melody touching his shoulder with slender fingers. Gripping it.

*The scars are unsightly...I get it. I'll be back in my normal clothes soon.*

"You found her." She smiles, but it seems fake. It *is* fake.

"Yes." Celestyn is tart, but victorious. "And she's...healed, somehow. Mostly."

"Somehow," Ace repeats darkly.

I don't like it. I edge closer to Aidan who looks to the ground at the shadow who follows, swinging Simone off of her tired little legs. Melody tries to keep from frowning, locking arms with Ace so enthusiastically, I expect them to break out in square dance— her teeth flashing a bleak, solemn feel rather than a pleasant welcome home.

"Well, why don't you get her dressed in something not so... bloody, and then she can help get things ready to go?" she recommends.

Ace's demeanor changes at this thought, and he nods. Straightening.

"You could come with us," he says, as if remembering that I am still a person with two working legs.

I shake my head. I need them to slow their roll.

"I want to," I insist. "But...I have to talk to Master Amadeus first."

"Why?" Ace and Aidan exclaim at the same time.

"There is no point," Ace growls. "We are leaving. He has nothing to offer us when he is already failing us."

I grimace.

"I want answers," I say. "Answers that maybe he can give me. I want to set things straight so that maybe we can figure out what happened here. Why we're here. I want to know how we can live in peace with these creatures while we try to figure out how to get home."

The whole group is following me to the house, each one talking out of turn. Arguing their side as if it will sway me like a bad bridge ready to collapse.

"We can't live in peace with them." Ace is adamant. "It is impossible."

"I think she should go," Celestyn says with a mouth full of more food. "Why not? What are we going to lose?"

"Her!" Melody scoffs.

"This is stupid, at best," Ace growls.

I shrug, stepping inside the house. There is medical supplies and books littered everywhere. Not quite how I remember it, but it still looks like home. Feels like home. Like everything I have missed.

"It's my last line of defense," I state at last. "Take it or leave it, but that's what it is. I think there is more to this situation than meets the eye, and I'm going to figure it out. Get back to minding your own business if you don't like it."

The yelling only gets louder until Aidan's voice breaks the sound barrier of disagreement.

"I want to go with you." He surprises the mob. "To meet Amadeus."

I walk to the back room with a change of clothes, slipping into my green, knee length skirt and white shirt I was wearing when I first arrived, along with black leggings. And shoes.

*Fuck, yes. Shoes.*

"That is madness!" Celestyn protests, choking down her stress meal. "Why?"

"I want answers too." Aidan frowns. "I don't see why not."

The arguing continues for a couple hours longer than we can afford, through lunch, and a little while in the afternoon prior to Ace and Melody being officially through with work.

Aidan helps me gather everything into my bag that I will need. Just in case. He scours the house for medical supplies, books, and documents. He arms himself with his bow, bringing along the sword I gifted him as a safeguard.

It is nearly nightfall by the time we are ready to see Master Amadeus. The sun is setting behind the skyline and the musical chittering of birds turns into the unharmonized screaming of insects. I touch the soft, textured white line where I had been split as we walk into uncertainty. Pelvis to collar bone, the father of Zoey's baby didn't miss an inch. But neither did the elf out in the clearing.

My face burns, remembering his large hand at the bottom of my hip bones, a gesture I feel too guilty to speak to Aidan about. Not that I am entirely sure why. It doesn't matter. Yet something about the affair makes me feel treasonous to the entire village, despite the fact I felt, for the first time, that I was exactly where I needed to be.

I might have left with him if there wasn't so much to return to here. My senses had been altered entirely when we were together, and I don't think there is a shout on this planet that could reach me over the gravitational pull of my own hormones.

The overhead branches that shroud some of the older homes in the ancient settlement surrounding Master Amadeus' tower into darkness bounce with impending demise—a death rattle of quivering foliage. I can feel different sets of eyes on me, whispers sending gentle messages through the breeze that pass me by as the first Ravager hits the dirt a good ten feet ahead of us without so much as a thud.

Just an earthy silence.

Aidan's eyes roam around the tall creature, giving him little thought for the first time since we met, instead hand falling to his quiver while his neck raises with the height of the incredible black tower ahead us, as if it were also his first time seeing it this close.

I shuffle backward, the glowing blue eyes of the Ravager shimmering back into mine. The trust isn't there, the trauma of my previous situation crawling out through my pores like spiders from an egg sack. Aidan steps in front of me, bow readied and locked, preparing to loose on my command or any sudden motion.

The Ravager only glances us over, casually peering back to the overhead branches. He blinks, nods, and dips into a genuine bow. It is similar to the elf in the clearing, only much less personal, and I still have no idea what it means.

I nudge Aidan's bow arm aside, bowing in turn as I had before.

Again with the peculiar look?

He looks troubled, back to the forest, as if to make sure no one had seen him, and then proceeds to walk the length of the trees, probably into the village, without another word or gesture.

"What the hell was that?" Aidan asks, lowering his weapon.

I can't answer. It means speaking secrets I cannot reveal yet. Sacred things.

His eyes are trying to find mine, but I avoid the warmth of their search for kindred inquiry. I slump my shoulders, crossing my arms over my chest. It is enough to make him give in as we approach the tower together. At the base, we stand so close there is not even air to breathe between us.

It is gargantuan in person, made of weathered and damp smelling black stone with a single metal door at the bottom for entrance. I can see, only barely, a sturdy balcony at the highest floor of the tower that sits level with the stronger branches of the tall, overpowering trees, golden drapes billowing over the edges like glittering waterfalls every time the wind gushes.

There are no other openings in the tower outside of the evenly spaced windows. Just the two exits and a pointed roof that appears stronger than any other structure in Limbo for there is not even a bulging piece of the roof where rain is causing it to cave.

Thunder rolls in the distance as clouds I cannot see, challenging the strength of the tower for another fight.

It strikes me then. That every night Celestyn made this journey by herself through the old fields of skeletal remains where the village once stood, past the weeds taller than her own self and through the deafening silence of at least an hours' worth of walking just to be somewhere safe for the night.

In my head, I can see it with absolute clarity. The way she probably watches her back on the late nights, wondering if she will make it to the safety of the tower in time before hands reach from the darkness all around her to take her away to the misery beyond.

And how safe is she really? If Master Amadeus was at least any of what the Ravagers were? What motivation does he really have to protect any of us?

I feel the weight of his last letter in my bag, the words of what felt like urgency after the first meeting I neglected to attend ringing in my ears. It feels like trouble, like something terrible that has yet to happen. But will. If it can go one of two ways, I am bound to get the latter.

I am not like Celestyn. There is no use for me that is worth special rights and privileges. I have never wielded proper weapons like Aidan to know if I have any skill in that area, and I haven't had the time to learn. I'm no born leader like Ace or Melody.

But I also don't recall villagers ever being removed for being useless.

*It never said anything about removal*, I remind myself. *You're just scaring yourself. This has more than one possibility, and therefore more than one outcome.*

"I'm here," Aidan says, attempting a shy smile, and hiding his free, fidgeting hand in his pocket.

I nod, looking to the clouds that have begun to steal away the distant stars. A passing thought wonders if Celestyn is caring well for Simone at home. If she can help rescue her during the invasion about to occur.

In the time I have known her, I have not even seen her approach a child other than Simone. Will she continue to care for her if something happened to me?

The door is cold against my hands, numbing my fingers so that I don't have to feel myself open it. It doesn't seem as difficult as I had imagined it would be from a distance. A pull of the handle, and the slightest nudge. I am left dumbfounded on how none of the Ravagers never once decided to just pull open the door and scoop Celestyn out from inside like ice cream. But maybe, the power of this Master is as much a legend out there as it is in Limbo.

The squeal of metal against cool stone floors reverberates to the core of my spine. I clench my teeth and hunch over, holding my ears until the door settles in place. Aidan steps into the room ahead of me without flinching at what could lie in wait for us. My head ticks in either direction, leaning forward to attempt a better view of the room, and all of its potential traps to keep intruders out. A Master of any city in constant anarchy would want to protect himself, wouldn't he?

A hot burst of dull orange brings a small circle of visualization to the room. Aidan waves a metal torch back and forth with his stupid grin I've grown to love.

"Celestyn said this would be here," he says. "I'm pretty sure this is the area of the tower that she slept in."

"You don't know?" I ask, legs quivering with adrenaline. My footsteps echo off the tall walls that reach to a ceiling so far up I cannot see it just by craning my head. Aidan waves the torch again, finding another to light just a few feet to his left, and leaving me alone in the open doorway.

"I've never been here," he affirms. "Celestyn always visited me when we had our...dates."

"Dates," I repeat with finger quotes, a smile playing on my lips. "You mean, those things she only shows up to when it is convenient for her?"

"The exact same." There is small comfort in the fact he no longer denies what is happening between the two of them.

The room seems to grow with each torch Aidan sets fire to, the dull light eating away the dour blackness that had consumed it prior, revealing the true splendor of the tower before us. I rub my arms, little bumps prickling from each inch of skin and mouth dropping at the glory of the practical extravagance Celestyn had lived in for all these years. It almost feels unfair, seeing how much space she was given, that the Master should only protect one person out of hundreds in need.

It is undoubtedly the area where Celestyn lived at first glance, the bottom of the tower being so grand in size that one could ride a horse straight across without worrying about needing more room to turn around. A blue rug with intricate silver etchings and dragons stretches from the door to the other side of the room, splitting the living quarters and the side with the stairwell straight down the middle like the uncomfortable residence of a feuding married couple.

On Celestyn's side, I can spot one of her long white shirts draped over a mahogany chair upholstered in red velvet cushioning. There is a long, similarly designed slender couch, and a feathered pillow at the farthest end alongside it that seems to serve as her bed. Or at least, did, at one point. A patchwork quilt is bunched at the floor in front of a heavy wooden table to confirm my theory—a great wonder it hasn't been cleaned up.

I saunter closer for a better look, running my fingers over the spines of what must be hundreds, if not thousands of books clustered on massive shelves built into the walls, each piece of literature having its own distinct title—some in English, and others in letters that do not appear human at all. I look closely at the pages, the thickness, wondering how there can be so many books in an era where there are no computers to have written them on.

It must take ages to get just one finished.

On the long, sturdy table in front of the seating and bedding area, is five other medical studies Celestyn had pulled from the shelves, sprawled haphazardly on top of one another. Some are open, others having a couple pages torn from them with only the first three letters of each sentence hanging on to the leather spine to tell their story. I squint, trying to read the words still left in failure.

"I think we need to climb the stairwell," Aidan calls from the other side of the room, torch still in hand. "The balcony is at the top, and the doors are labeled, from what I was told. None of the doors down here appear to be our great Master's office."

"Sure," I consent, closing the book on top of the stack, and parting with the goodies, following my closest comrade up the first flight of stairs that lets off on a platform that branches off into two separate corridors with doors placed on each end.

I poke my head down the right corridor, quiet calling me to nose through every room lining either side of the short, straight path. Distraction is easily my Achilles heel, followed close by curiosity, everything having a story it wishes to tell me if only I dig a little deeper.

Aidan pokes me in the ribs with his elbow, passing around to the next set of stairs to keep me on track and further our ascent. I tip forward, feet stumbling to keep balance on slick, grey stone steps with no railing, hands flailing to find anything to hold on to, and catching his shirt. My fingers grasp the soft cotton, firm, so that I steady myself and avoid pulling him down with me.

It is fortunate that we are only yet high enough that if we did fall, so long as we didn't land on our heads, there might be a few broken bones and nothing more. We would not die. Though I have to admit that compared to the rest of the home, these stairs were made in a hurry, with poor design.

Who makes stone stairs with no railing to hold a person inside? There is nothing to keep one from plummeting to their death if they happen to look at the floor on their way up, and while I can gain some vertex in a grand jeté, there is an innate fear of heights and falling from high places instilled inside me.

I wonder if Master Amadeus would mind leaving his office at the highest part of the tower to meet me on the lowest floor. How much can it really inconvenience an all-powerful being who remains untouched by anarchy, anyway? He has all the time in the world. It is the actual inhabitants who are limited, waiting on us to finish this last step.

I clutch Aidan's shirt tighter the higher we climb, pacing my breathing and trying not to watch my feet too much, though a voice in the back of my head taunts that my shoes are probably untied.

At the top of the staircase, the wind whistles from the space between the bottom of a thick wooden door with a round silver handle and the thin, crumbling platform we stand on. I can feel my chest spasming in fear that if I do not lock my knees into stiff boards and squeeze my legs and ankles shut, I will overflow from the platform and fall, taking my best friend with me.

Aidan rocks forward, and I try not to whimper, shutting my eyes instead of looking down, making us rock even more. He finds the handle in time to get a good grip with the tips of his fingers on his free hand before we tumble, breathing suddenly as heavy as mine.

"Addie," he chokes, body quivering. "Addie, I need you to either let me go, or open your eyes. I don't think I can hold us both."

It pains me, but I concede to opening my eyes, shuffling on his heels so that we both fit on the top of the staircase. Letters on a silver plaque across the uppermost half of the door below the peephole spells out **Offices of Amadeus Grunwald**. I stretch an arm around Aidan to knock on the door, unsure of if we are naturally permitted inside simply because the Master had requested an audience with me.

People are often never seen after meeting the Master.

What will happen here? And will Aidan be protected from the outcome? If we weren't crammed on to the same staircase, I might have made him leave just for his own sake.

There is no response to our knocking, and I can feel Aidan's weight shift at the sweaty discomfort between us. I swallow, and knock again. When another silence follows, I do one more beating on the wood to be safe. Just in case the office is as large as the bottom of the tower, and perhaps, he had not heard us. The minutes that come after the final tap to the door are spent in dead silence. Not even the wind blows. It is just us, and a crippling anxiety of failing before reaching our ultimate goal.

How many people have met their fate here alone?

"For fuck's sake..." Aidan grumbles after a heavy sigh.

With a groan and a tug, he yanks our body weight forward, swinging open the door to reveal a dark and narrow hallway. He steps in first, flinging his torch ahead of his body so that it doesn't catch my hair when I barrel inside behind him, ducking under his arm and jogging blindly down the hall to be as far away from the height of the staircase as I can be.

It is no wonder the Master didn't answer his office door. He has a maze for a home.

The hallway twists on in what seems like a puzzle for at least a couple minutes, but for what is really much shorter. I stretch my arms to either side, touching the walls to reaffirm to myself that I know where I am going, and that I am not going to dip down into a bottomless hell where Aidan's torch won't be bright enough to see.

A light can finally be seen at the end of this chaos, however, and I race for it, stopping short at a small set of stone steps that lead into a peaceful, well-lit room.

It is smaller than the bottom of the tower, cozier even, with an unlit fireplace off to the right of us encircled by several red cushioned chairs that are decorated with enough pillows to make a really great fort. An animal skin of some kind lays at the feet of this furniture, and a few pokers rest in a blue vase on top of a wooden table.

Closer to the window is a desk larger than the one at The Healing Center. It is an aesthetic smoky color that stretches in all directions so that it overwhelms its home in the room with an empty leather chair behind it. Mounds of dusty, yellow paperwork crowd either side of the surface of the desk, and an open leatherbound book sits on its front with a pot of ink and a quill next to it. The same as the bottom of the tower, the walls were carved in beautiful, elaborate bookshelves that shelter hundreds of aged, withering texts.

I swallow, stepping away from Aidan to confront the desk alone, though the Master is nowhere to be seen, the silk curtains moving with the grace of liquid at the rear of the desk, fluttering with each caress of the wind. Beckoning.

I brush the surface of the desk with my fingertips, letting the polished wood squeak beneath the dryness of my fingers, peeking into the contents of the open book.

It doesn't appear to be anything incredibly important at first glance. A touch of history. Small handwritten words that pop out in the faint cat scratch of someone with poor penmanship.

*Did Lady Ceridwen plead for her life?* The first paragraph of the page starts in the boldest ink. *Why, of course she had. But her life had become all it could be, and there was little respite to come, for her future had been sealed in the minute his eyes had set on her. She would come to...*

I hesitate. I remember that name.

"It is true what they say about you, Miss Adabelle," a small voice rings from wall to wall.

I turn my head to Aidan who is rolling his own eyes around the room in a fruitless endeavor to find the source of the voice. He creeps closer to me, torch in one hand and sword in the other. It has to be a trick of some kind, something to make us let our guard down, for the voice isn't that of a grown man. It belongs to a child. Prepubescent. Maybe someone Simone's age...or younger.

Still, the speech is more...sophisticated than that.

"What would that be?" I entertain the phantom child, ambling around the desk with Aidan close, checking every nook or cranny along the way.

A cynical laugh. "You do enjoy putting your nose where it doesn't belong, don't you?"

I listen.

"I would like to think I am just trying to piece together a puzzle no one else has quite put together yet." It is not too often I have heard any of the Ravagers so much as utter a full sentence. The father of Zoey's baby had such a powerful presence, he did not need to speak. One single, horribly violent aura that made me wish I had thought twice about stabbing him, leaving me petrified when I so much as relived it in my memories.

But this voice does not frighten me at all. It sounds almost as casual as Aidan's. Not so threatening as it is challenging.

I glance to the area in front of the fireplace, and then stride toward the open window and balcony. I can feel Aidan attempting to keep a healthy distance, protecting my backside on the off chance our enemy has been behind us the whole time.

"You are bold though, aren't you?" the child asks.

"Hello?" I call into the night that consumes the balcony.

There is no answer this time. I take another survey of the room, and with willful legs, I take baby steps onto the balcony. The force of the fresh, pre-storm air whips my hair into my eyes, and my hands clamor to move it so that I can see clearly. Aidan sets the torch on the wet stone, padding on ahead of me before I realize why. I touch my own dagger with uneasy anticipation, barely breathing and shaking all but stilled.

The balcony extends out into the forest, like a stone road with no end into the darkness amidst the treetops. Dozens of glowing eyes glower at us from the higher branches, shadowy figures ebbing fluidly through the thick treetops to get a better look. Blue. Green. Yellow. Orange. They all glimmer with hunger and curiosity, silent judges of our fates. Jackals.

I back away from the painted white railing, afraid to veer so close to the creatures that I had at one point been safest with. Aidan's fingers curl around my forearm with a gentle fierceness, his breathing quickened. These are impossible odds. One of us will die if we tread any closer.

There is a flutter as the curtains collapse into a golden veil behind us, closing our easy exit if we don't want to trip on our way out.

"A pleasure to meet you, Miss Green," the little boy's voice sings. "Truly. I have waited quite some time."

We both spin from the curtains with such speed that it is a wonder Aidan has not broken my arm. There, only a few feet from the trees, stands a Ravager child just a tad younger than Simone.

His long, pointed ears stretch past the back of his head, looking unfit for his body by even Ravager standards. Little eyes glow red like hot coals with tiny black slits for pupils focused on our faces and spelling murder in their tone. His messy black hair is in disarray around his pale, round face and robes of crimson and gold trail to the stone in puddles of silk about his short, skinny body. He looked small for the voice that had been granted to him. I try not to sigh too loudly.

"Oh my..." I breathe, and I can hear the tension draw from Aidan's chest as well. "Oh no. You...you startled me, kid. Whoa." The boy's head ticks to the side, facial expression unchanging. "Where is your dad?"

His lips hardly part, jaw not so much as twitching.

"I'm afraid it would be inappropriate to bring a lady to a place for the dead. Women are not permitted entry to The Shadowlands." There is no stutter, no illusion of humor to his voice. "Though...I haven't yet decided if you are a true lady. I suppose it is debatable."

I retract in slight toward Aidan. The eyes in the branches above never remove themselves from the situation, though I can hear distant wailing that says their brethren were already in the village.

"This...this is a joke, right?" Aidan replies, hand squeezing the pommel of his sword. "This whole tower is a joke, right?" The boy is silent. "No one answers doors. We go through a maze to get here. I almost *died* on the staircase. Where is your dad, kid? I am done with the games."

The small child blinks, as if attempting to find an appropriate response to Aidan's inquiries, and then deciding there isn't one with a boyish smirk.

"What proof need you that I am the person you seek?"

Again, his lips part in calm, hushed motions as he speaks. Yet the adept figures in the trees appear to hear the sentences that come from him.

Aidan slips his sword in and out of its makeshift wrap, unable to feel threatened in the presence of a child, but uncomfortable all the same.

There isn't a possibility in the universe that such a small, impish boy could be an all-powerful master, but rather an ornery Ravager with no parent to keep him in line. Surely, he has snuck inside from the tree line, or at best he could be the Master's son.

"What proof could you possibly provide?" I turn to the curtains, readying myself for another eventful journey back down the stairs. I try not to laugh, but the sheer exhaustion of this situation escapes me in a frustrated huff that leaves me tickled in a not-so-delighted way. "Get your father. Or your brother. Or your uncle, for all I care! But I will be damned if I get three letters from this Master Amadeus only to be stood up when I finally arrive to his urgency."

The boy's eyes narrow, and he tilts his head high to the trees. Several eyes hone back on him, a couple seeming to speak words that only he understands, though he does not respond. There has to be some realism to this skepticism. The Ravagers were known for their superior magical qualities. It can't be out of the realm of possibility for a small boy to play a trick.

"I'm disappointed, I suppose," he says at last, knees bending beneath the heavy clothing and feet launching him high enough to settle on the railing with the finesse of a cat. "With such talk, I expected much more out of Miss Adabelle than what I see."

My arms fly outward in instinct to catch him should he fall. He teeters, feet snagging on his clothing.

"What talk?" I am breathless, Aidan motionless, his eyes frozen in the same fear that this boy might plummet to his death.

The boy walks in spite of me, and I follow, all eyes on us. He grins.

"The trees talk, don't you know?"

"I don't." I stumble to snatch him from the railing, and he runs the remaining length to the curtains in little less than a second, clutching the fabric and swinging to the stone in a single stride. "Tell me about these trees that speak."

He glances to the figures in the trees, boyish grin becoming clownish and giggling. "Miss Adabelle is very disappointing indeed. Not very clever either. Not even a little."

I threw my hands on to my head, fingers raking through my hair.

"I might hate children," I whisper to Aidan.

The little boy grimaces at this, as if it were a personal assault.

"That's a shame," he says, and his voice is sincere for the first time.

Our spectators remain as stone now, like each of them had been molded to the trees for years. The wind tussles the boy's hair, leaving it messier than it had been and in need of combing. I frown, releasing a sigh and shaking my head.

"I suppose I deserve this," I say. "I had no excuse not to show for the first letter. I just didn't want to. The rumors were awful." I walk closer to the end of the balcony, or at least the end that I can see. The obvious end is not always the factual end, after all. "I was going to show up after the second letter, but I—"

"You were split down the middle," the little boy finishes.

I meet his evil red gaze, bobbing my head.

We both jump when Aidan makes an awful, loud buzzer noise, turning his thumb down in disagreement of the truthful statement.

"Try again, kid," he said, tone stern. "Everyone in the village knew about Addie and what happened. I'm sure it isn't a stretch to say the Ravagers talk too. Your card tricks don't convince me."

I feel a small amount of gratitude that Aidan insisted on accompanying me today. He is far more well-versed in speaking to other people than I am, and quick on his feet when I am knocked flat.

The small boy rolls his eyes though, and gives in to a troubled sigh.

"I see," he hums. "So protective. Do I make you jealous for her affections?"

Aidan's powerful voice is stifled.

"In my father race, it is common for men to be very possessive of their partner's affections," the boy continues. "It is their lifeline, Mr. Powell."

Aidan purses his lips, still unsure of whether or not he is going to shiv a kid.

"She is my friend," he replies.

"A friend?" The boy's little head ticks again.

"Can we go?" Aidan immediately shoots back to me.

The boy speaks even faster than I can answer.

"Have you told him yet, Miss Adabelle?" He speaks as my mouth opens. "About your time in the forest? What you found there?"

I swallow, shaking my head as Aidan's voice rings at the hollow of my subconscious. Repeating my name. My throat feels dry, and I clench my teeth. There should be no way anyone knows that.

"Master Amadeus," I interrupt Aidan. "That is who you are? A literal incarnation of a man-child? Or are the children of your race just smarter?"

He is triumphant, brushing against my skirt and walking back toward the curtains. We follow, Aidan holding up the rear and glancing back nervously as slender legs climb down onto the balcony. Just shapes.

At his desk, Amadeus sits, leaning down to grab several books and pulling them forth. Aidan is reluctant to sit across from him, following the lead of a child seemingly far from his realm of possibilities, though I am somewhat more convinced, descending to my chair slow, as though it were built with knives.

Aidan stands still, leaning over from behind me to keep an intimidating presence, frustration growing.

"Why did you call her here?" He demands answers right away. "We are wasting time we could be spending getting the fuck out of here."

Master Amadeus smiles, a bit of a devilish charm attached to him.

"Why, that is the entire reason I have called Miss Adabelle here," he replies. "To, get the fuck out."

My mouth drops. Heart stops. I can't breathe. Am I having a panic attack?

Fuck, fuck, fuck.

"I...don't understand." I attempt a smile. "You have been trying to make me leave? This whole time?"

Master Amadeus loses his smile for a second, opening a book and flipping the pages.

"Don't take it too personally," he muses. "I don't like any of you that much. I just have a soft spot for humans, hence the barrier."

He gestures outside to the fading barrier.

"I'm a human," I reply quietly.

"The barrier is fading," Aidan speaks at the same time. "It's almost gone."

Amadeus looks between us, trying to decide which is more deserving of a response and pausing at the page he is on. The text is in a different language, untranslated. Old and faded.

"My magic is fading," he tells us. "I can't support the weight of the controlled area and the magics fighting it when my own magic reservoirs can never expand past youth without causing my heart to literally shred into bits."

I look around in frustration, biting my nails and speaking up again. Did he hear me?

"I...I'm human. I'm human," I say over and over.

It does not seem like either of them hear me this time.

"Magic reservoirs?" Aidan raises an eyebrow.

The boy rolls up his sleeves, exposing his milky arms for us to see. With a pointed nail, he pricks the skin apart so a near black fluid draws down over his forearm, running over on to his desk like blood...but it doesn't look like blood. It is more like...dark brown ink.

In turn, glowing black markings race up along that arm as far as the sleeve is raised, crawling up his neck and face, and fading as he closes the wound in a five-minute-long trace of his finger as Aidan and I watch in silent amazement.

"Every one of us are born with a certain amount that builds as we age. The weaker bloodlines of both elf and fae are born with none and get very little as they grow, while the stronger are born with many that strengthen and multiply as they get older. These inner workings control what kind of magic we have and how it functions. They can be directly sensed by other magical beings... sort of like what you guys would call...an aura?"

I shake my head, opening my mouth to say it. To make it true.

*I am human.*

But he smiles, revealing sharp canines like that of a wolf glimmering back at me.

"Are you?" He taunts.

I close my lips, and he flips another page. Aidan does not fight this attack on my character, as if he has already been sold on the concept.

"You are weak, Miss Green," Amadeus continues. "Un-expectedly so, but it happens in some half-breeds. In your case, it is fortunate."

I shake my head, glancing to Aidan. Waiting for him to speak up. He doesn't.

"I-I'm sorry." I breathe. "I...I was told your King doesn't allow half-breeds. So I think you're mistaken. I would be..."

"Dead?" Amadeus interrupts. "Wouldn't that be the dream? I'm sure he had every intention to kill you, but that's tricky. Especially when there are laws protecting the Fae. It could start a war to kill you, and we would win by sheer number, of course. But that wouldn't make him a very good King, disrupting progress he's made. It wouldn't make him a very liked King either."

Aidan pushes Amadeus' books aside, sitting down.

"Prove it," he replies. "I want to see her magic reservoirs. If she is part Fae, she will have them."

He gestures to my arm, and I hold it out. But Amadeus only laughs.

"As I said before," he replies, "she is weak. The ones she possesses are in her heart where the primary ones are always held. We could not see those if we tried. There are other signs that could be easily overlooked with her oh-so-human exterior."

Aidan leans back. Waiting. He seems impatient, as if all the answers should come at once. But...we aren't on our schedule. Master Amadeus does not seem to mind this a bit. He plays it like a game. Enjoying the passes involved.

"So restless," he croons. "Rude, too. Do you come into everyone's home with such hostility?"

I shake my head, putting my hands out.

"No. No. He...it's just been a long time. The village is about to be ruins, and there has been so much...stigma surrounding me, and this world and all of it. We just want answers." I say, wondering how to appease a literal man-child as I talk.

He's smart for a little boy. His speech is eloquent. Uncomfortably so.

Amadeus appears to find this satisfactory.

"Half-breeds are strange creatures," he comments. "There haven't been many to conduct research with. The royal family bloodlines have the best examples for proper observation. Through them, The King collected a list of items that all half-breeds seem to possess for those that cannot smell the filth on them. The most obvious sign being the inability—or close to—to control basic impulses. These creatures have a lot of misfire, and it takes hundreds of years to learn how to properly resist acting out on basic wants."

My mouth drops, and Aidan stiffens.

"What if it is a risk to their own lives?" He fires.

"There is no difference to their brains," Amadeus explains. "They understand danger, but they don't always understand how to react to it. Say that their closest companion as at risk of drowning, but they don't know how to swim. There is no point A to point B reasoning. They skip point B entirely. Hence why almost all half-breeds die early and are not a problem prior to discovery."

Aidan grips my upper arm, pushing me back just a bit. I can feel every hair stand at attention. My whole body feels numb, trembling. I feel weak all at once, like when I was hurt. As if all the healing that had been done could be plucked apart.

"I...should have been here the whole time?" I pose it as a question. I want it to be denied.

*Say no.*

It's the only fact I can take from this. That even though I am here, that I don't remember my beginnings the same as everyone else, I belong here. With this...evil.

"Don't despair too much." Amadeus waves his hand. "Your mother is very much human. She was the whole reason you got to live what your kind considers a normal life."

I interrupt before he can continue.

"Was? Is she...?"

"Dead?" He smiles, and stops. "I am not permitted to say. But don't misconstrue her intentions. She bypassed The King's law to get you there. There is an entire story there that has yet to be spoken."

He eyes the scars on my arms. Aidan brings me back to reality.

"Adabelle's mother was here at some point? Twenty-one years ago, there were still people?"

Amadeus shrugs.

"I don't see why not. The King has allowed the passage of souls from deceased and comatose individuals to relive a second chance here for at least a century."

Aidan slams his hand on the desk.

"Then it's not our fault we are here," he growls. "Why are we being attacked if this is something The King did? We don't deserve to be eternally punished for what he did without asking. We don't even remember who we are, and people are dying."

"We are dead." I laugh at the same time. I can't focus. "We aren't even real, and they're killing us?"

Amadeus laughs. "I'm not at liberty to speak much, but your soul is the realest form of yourselves. You are very much alive right now in this forgotten place, and could even be so much as brought back to your world in The King's power under certain circumstance. Think of it as sort of a...parallel. Of course, your little village is being decimated as we speak. Most of you would never make the journey anyway. Humans alone are not strong enough."

"How long?" I whimper, hitting my fist on the desk following Aidan's.

The boy is nonchalant, tracing the movement from my arm to my shoulder. He does not startle, as though he knows that he can take me in a fight.

*Go ahead.* His face contorts in the quiet. *You can try.*

But something feels wrong about hitting a child as I shake. Contemplating.

"Look at you," Amadeus teases. "You're trying so hard. It is impressive how well-behaved you are."

"She's not a dog," Aidan snaps.

I can't breathe.

"How long?" I repeat, emphasizing each word. "I can't...I want...I need...answers. Please."

My teeth are grit. The boy grins in delight at this, my struggle. Our struggle. My comprehension.

"It doesn't matter now, does it?" He replies. "You're home now, Miss Adabelle. Welcome to your homeland. To Draedalys. To, *immortality*."

He continues to smile, eyes a void as I speak in panic, Aidan gripping to my arm. His voice at my ear.

*Addie. Addie.*

He shakes me.

"N-no. No." I shake my head. "I promised everyone answers. I didn't come here for this. I need to know how to fight this. How to fight *them*. What do we do—*you* do? Why are they hurting everyone? What's Draedalys? How do we...we..."

I choke on my own words. Aidan's arms come around my shoulders holding me still. The boy tenses just a bit at my mania. There is something hiding in his gaze that is soft. Sympathetic, masked behind this cruel amusement. There is a reason he has protected us this long. Why is he so avoidant?

"Your answers are as follows," the small master replies. "The humans here serve purpose to The King and his subjects—a purpose to which each person here belongs, whether by choice or not. Those that do not serve this are eliminated. My protections are through as of yesterday, and I will also be making my exit as of this night. You, Miss Adabelle, will not play a part in the rebuilding of Limbo, if it were to happen. You must separate yourself from regular civilization as per my request, since you are of magical descent."

I shake my head.

"That's not fair." I breathe. "I've been nothing but good for society, and you're magical. And you're still here."

My skin is boiling as he speaks again.

"Don't you think I also serve The King's divine purpose here?" He whispers. The little master grins, each corner of his lips curled devilishly to his ever-pointed ears, and his messy hair tousled to his face, "Miss Adabelle Green still does not understand. But she will. Because if she wants to live this life in which she desires, she cannot play by her laws any longer, but instead by mine which belong inherently to our King. Her King. And if you have a problem with this, attempting the journey to meet him is the only path to take. He is, after all, the only one who can grant passage between our world and yours."

"Fuck his divine purpose!" I scream, ripping from Aidan's grip, and sweeping every last paper off Amadeus' desk, gripping the book he had laid open and swinging it hard into his face so he spins from the chair.

The child shrieks, blood spilling from his split lip as I climb on to his desk and Aidan hurries from his seat, arms wrapping around my waist and tugging me backward. The boy flings his hands out, constructing a translucent red shield about himself like another, smaller dome, nursing his small wound as I attempt to kick Aidan in the shins.

"You're a dreadful bitch," The Master growls as his mouth swells. "I've lived millions of years, and not once have I met a woman I have disliked more than you. And you deserve everything that will happen to you."

His shield vanishes as Aidan drags me toward the door. I still hold the book that I swung in my hand, but with the other, I reach for his bookcase, taking a heavy metal bookend that I hurl at him so that the crunch of it against his shoulder brings me both relative satisfaction, and guilt.

A child that has lived for millions of years? But never aged into an adult? Is he a defect?

Aidan rushes us outside, and I give in to the urgency of his pulls as we reach the staircase, head hung as I can already hear the screaming of the night ensue. We look at each other in this moment, unsure of what to do next. Whether to run or stay.

Should we go home? Wait out the storm with Celestyn and Simone and hope it misses us? Die on our feet?

I cover my face. Laughing, almost.

"I'm a half-breed? *A monster*," I scoff into my palms. "Just like everyone said."

Aidan shakes his head, reaching out, but not quite touching

me. Hesitant.

"No," he says. *"No.* You were never a monster, Addie. You have always been a hero. You've made me a better person since the second you arrived, and you haven't stopped trying to do the right thing without being able to help yourself at all...we're the monsters. Not you. It was a witch hunt."

"I'm sorry," I murmur, but before I can finish the final word, he collects me into his arms again, squeezing me against him until I stop shaking. Until I relax in this darkness that consumes the night around us.

Until I can't hear anything but the sound of his labored breathing against my hair, his voice at my ear in a tickle.

"I'm sorry too, Addie."

# CHAPTER FORTY-FIVE
## ADABELLE

I FEEL NO RISK ON MY END, BEING OUT IN THE OPEN WHERE I am seen, and vulnerable, and empty.

I am one of *them,* even if I am not.

It is what I tell myself like a ritualistic incantation that could make me invisible as Aidan and I break apart from our embrace, forced to face one decision among many to come. Our bashful, skittish ogling drops to the grass we tread on in knowledge of where we must go next as we venture among legions of dark elves that have the village surrounded, boxed in where The Dome is no longer erected. There are even, square uniforms of men in coordinated stance allowing little to no escape unless accompanied by those already marching through the village in lines. Aidan claims we should be careful, slipping through their ranks like mice among a pride of lions. But there isn't much to take care at this time for myself, hoping that it means he will be safe as well if by my side.

*I belong among them, see?*

I don't. Please, tell me I don't.

But I have to believe that those who intend me harm will do so as they see fit whether or not I mesh inside their leagues like a corner piece to their puzzle, and those that pay me no mind, won't. I will be in as little, or as much danger as I put myself in, Aidan's presence overlooked by my "weak" magical aura, if I just believe it to be true. If I just take the dive, which I do. I have no choice. Our friends are in the eye of this storm and we have to get them out.

My plan works to some extent, many eyes assuring that we do not go unnoticed falling upon us in the statuesque divides in their ranks, but none necessarily following our path home to stop us. The sets of looks that do are careful not to get in the way too much, heads tipping down to see, but mindful of our presence, even a bit confused on our direction.

Everyone in this lifetime has been confused on my direction, why I am here. I should never have existed at all, but more especially, I should have never been in Limbo. It is why I was found on the borders of the third Dome layer. I materialized here to be home after injury or death, to be separated from this tragedy occurring now, despite humanity holding half my heritage.

I suppose I should thank my mother for that bullshit, for fucking some celibate Fae man sideways until I popped out. Maybe I still can, one day, when I leave Limbo—if I leave Limbo. I have an end goal, after all, if I want to return to what I had instead of living my unnatural life out here with none my own. I have to find The King. I have to convince him to set me free, to wake me up. Perhaps to do all of humanity that he has entrapped here such favors.

Aidan jogs to keep up with me, hunkered over himself like a frightened pup at my haunches, glancing over his shoulders and quivering while we pass elf after elf. It is usually harder to see at night until our eyes adjust better, but many of the men carry long, spear-like torches that they are using to set fire to abandoned housing, moving in toward the ones with people still inside, giving the village a sweltering yellow glow as flakes of ash drift in the stormy air. I can hear a bloodcurdling scream in a home we pass by out in the village streets, the sound alone singeing the hair on my arms, making my eardrums wither to the curdled shape of chewed gum.

*Men.* All of the pained, agonized noises are that of grown men or teenage boys, crying for help as the flames consume them alive.

For the first time, I shut it out, because I have to. I need to carry on if I want to save anyone that has a chance to get out of here. I am making plans as I go, intending to leave with Simone and Aidan. I will get my things from the house if it isn't already a crispy husk, and I will plead with Celestyn for jars of her miracle speed-healing salves and creams. Together, we can gather what food can be carried in bags if we have the time. I'm not much of a hunter, so when I part from them to go my own way, I'll have to learn to make the rest of the journey as a vegan.

From behind, Aidan grabs me by the elbow, jerking me backward before I run straight into a group of five soldiers who all glance to us as I skid in the dirt. I flutter against Aidan who smiles briefly and takes a sharp turn to the right while one of them begins to unsheathe his weapon. I whip after him, shorter legs scrambling to carry me out of sight. But a strong hand catches my forearm, twisting it painfully around so I feel the start of a crunch, making me stop. Gasping. Aidan halts at the sound.

I am shaking, memories returning in a sanguine flood of Kasismis plucking me from this world. My bottom lip quivers, jaw unhinging, soundlessly wanting to beg for my safety in a riotous panic. At his side, Aidan's fingers brush the hilt of the sword I had given him in contemplation. We both know he should use the bow instead. He has more experience with it. The long range is better in this scenario. What is he thinking?

The soldier who took hold of me steps closer at my rear, jerking my arm further back and up for inspection. I squeak, biting my tongue to avoid giving him the satisfaction of my half-bred agony.

"Interesting," he holds my limb for the others to see, "yes?"

Aidan and I are both frozen, afraid to make a move for certain.

The wrong one could end us both here and now. We have to tread lightly, no matter the cost.

*He should run,* my thoughts yell over the hope he doesn't.

"What is it she is thinking?" Another of the five soldiers approaches, laugh dark. His largest finger runs from the tips of my own to my elbow, up my shoulder and neck. "Awful brazen girl, isn't she?"

One more shakes his head, walking so my view of Aidan is partly blocked, and I feel my arm twist to its breaking point. I take in a quick, audible inhale.

"No. What is it *he* is thinking?" the newer one croons. "So much for intelligence. What a waste."

They aren't speaking their own language. They want me to hear this. To scare me.

The one with my arm yanks me tight to his body, sword pulling free of its sheath in a clean, glinting movement, and rising to my throat. Aidan draws an arrow to his bow, ready to fire and aim locked on the elf blocking his full view of me. The ears of the soldier standing at the side of the one holding me twitches to the inaudible sound of it, turning his head to see, and sending the soldiers into a fit of laughter. My attempted murderer waves his weapon to Aidan in a sweeping gesture, calling to him in a challenge.

"Have at it! If you want to. If you're as brave as the bitch. The end will come just the same. But, we could make it fun for the second it takes to kill you as well."

When it comes back, the blade presses harder into my throat. I choke, scuttling as far backward into the armor of the elf as I can. I am squirming, like a rat, looking for a place to lay my teeth in a hearty bite, yet unable to find an angle that won't be met with steel. Aidan purses his lips, bouncing forward at the cacophony of shrieks reverberating throughout the village, and glancing around himself, paranoia growing. He doesn't feel safe to fire when the danger is all around. Where will he run?

The soldier in front sneers, knocking the one with my arm in the shoulder so his grip falters.

"Go on, do it quick," he jeers. "If you don't, bigger problems will come. You know how it goes."

I tremble. Shake.

I don't want to die yet.

Swallowing, the thin canvas of skin protecting my windpipe connects with the blade, just barely, and I use my free hand to travel low, careful, finding exactly what I want to. I grab his groin fast, squeezing as tight as I can like a stress ball, twisting and using as much of my remnant nails as I can through the fabric of his trousers.

Their fault for not wearing armor lower than their waists.

He screeches, grip instinctively removed as the others draw their weapons to halt my escape. That is when Aidan fires his arrows, loosing them in careful repetition while the men attempt to gain their wits about them. The dark elf at my front collapses, the dull shine of our ill-constructed arrows jutting out through his eye in a nauseating squelch as I dart over his corpse where there is space. The next assailant on my heels is shot through the Adam's apple, piling on top of his comrade in my dash for escape.

I flail out to Aidan as he lowers his bow impending my arrival, hands stretching for him in the split second it takes to be whacked in the back of the skull by the broad side of a sword, leaving me spinning into the dirt with a staggered scream. Aidan unsheathes his own sword at this range, swinging just in time to catch what would have been a fatal blow to my neck before he is repelled by the sheer strength of these creatures.

I watch, dizzy as our only hope and protection clatters into the dust, Aidan throttled so hard next to me that I hear something crack. He gasps simultaneously, a wheezing intake of air, clutching at his own chest.

I climb to my hands and knees, met at the nose by another sword, and freezing solid. My hands twitch for rocks that I can't bring myself to pick up as the taunts rage over our heads, Aidan rolling to his sword in a groan that lets me know he is still alive.

"Look at you." The soldier tilts my face with a flick of his blade so I am forced to follow. "Look at these *scars*. This...naiveté. Killing you is almost too easy, no? In this manner? But it would send a message, wouldn't it?"

The two comrades that survived cackle in response. I hear Aidan shriek as a soldier smashes his fingers with a quick boot to the hand right as he reaches our blade and one chance at survival. I shuffle away from the sword pointed at me in the silence that follows, rearing toward Aidan who now has a soldier's sword hovering over his crumpled body. From the side pocket of my backpack, I pull free one of the many weapons we packed, a stolen dagger out of the shed in the woods, swinging it toward our assailant. I am unable to connect, kicked swift in the arm so hard I flop over Aidan's legs. The attacking soldier takes a stab after this, and I jerk, skimmed in the bicep and Aidan in the calf.

"I'm sorry," I tell my friend, holding the wound on his leg as blood slips through the spaces in my fingers. Aidan's free hand touches mine, the one that isn't smashed, shaking in silence over my delicate tattoos, and intertwining. The soldier in charge of the onslaught laughs, making a mockery of it while I watch Aidan cover his face, struggling to breathe.

"Is it love?" the monster jests. "Should it be they die in each other's arms?"

Another stab, and I use all the strength I have to push myself and Aidan forward, closer to one of the many burning homes, just to be stopped short, kicked in the head while trying to stay low to the ground by another soldier at our front. Somewhere close by, another home sets alight, burning with fierce intensity as Aidan and I are forced closer and closer to it for each swing taken at us.

I lick my bloody lips, tasting the familiar flavor sliding back and forth over my teeth. Like oil.

The soldier in charge steps forward when we have nowhere else to go, raising his sword into the air for the killing swing, only to be halted by a deafening crunch. A gurgling.

There is a hot, sticky spray that coats our huddled bodies, and the tall form flops to the ground like a sack of potatoes. The other two soldiers turn their attentions to the new attacker, but they are caught in the wave of quick assaults, slicing through them like onions until they fall one by one around us in a series of yells.

As the last one drops, Aidan's head lolls upright, and he reaches for one of the dropped swords from the dirt, protecting our shivering forms from the next inevitable hit as it becomes clear our savior is also not our friend. He stumbles to his feet, as do I, the next clatter of sword on sword knocking the new weapon from hand. It is then I get a look at the creature in question, heaving large breaths in and out. Wounded like us, but worse, an entire ear cut away from his body and leaving a still healing stump.

This beast is closer to our size than the dark elves, maybe about Aidan's height or a bit taller, ear still attached similar to our own but with a smaller, but defined point. His skin is thin, like paper, and sheet white with an orange hue that matches his strangely structured hair pointed in stiff spikes...like peaks of fire. His eyes are like two pools of mercury, without pupils and shimmering with disgust and hatred. It is his armor though that is most intriguing of all, blue and silver plates covering his vital places raked with deep trenches along the gut, the shoulder plates adorned in long, lethal spikes that close in around his head as if for protection.

The next strike the creature makes is weak but fast, aimed at myself. Aidan throws his hands up, catching the blade without hesitation by his own palms at the sharpest edge in a high-pitched exhale.

Rich crimson ribbons from Aidan's hands, billowing in satin plumes around his elbows and dripping into the dirt. The sword makes a squelch when the blood is produced, his sneakers crunching into the dirt as he slides against the force of his opponent and his screams pierce the pitch abandon of the forest, overwhelming the outside world around us.

Or is that the sound of me?

No air appears to fill my lungs, stunted in a semi-permanent exhale of terror, mouth agape. I rush to my friend's side, uncertain as to how I should assist, hands extending up to the blade, and back down as the enthusiastic spray coats my touch while Aidan attempts to pace his breathing. He wants to remain calm, biceps quivering but adrenaline sharp. He mouths something to me I don't make out in my panic, repeating it when my eyes bore right through him to focus on the agony at hand.

*I have been in worse fear,* I remind myself, but I still cannot seem to find my voice.

My hands reach toward the blade, tracing its flat side just above the canyon it carves in my friend's hands. It is a strange weapon, though familiar to this world, attached to an even stranger man whose deep grey eyes bore straight into us as if we are his one true enemy without any kind of knowledge as to who we are. Or what we are.

He is not like us, after all.

Our gazes finally, truly meet, I think. He has no pupils in these pits of silver, glistening misguided aggressions, so it is hard to tell. I attempt to smile at him, even in fear.

"We didn't mean to startle you." My words are shaken, feet traipsing closer without releasing his blade.

I don't want him to turn on me, to swing it from the curl of Aidan's fingers thick with rich, cherry shadows, and knock my head from my shoulders. The sheer image of it floats around the hollow of my skull, bouncing from side to side in vivid detail, leaving nothing but a clean, bloodied stump and a meaty, mangled corpse to abandon while my friend could do nothing more than watch, his hands a soured mess.

"I am not startled," the creature growls, breathing deepened with the fear he denies sinking claws below the sheet of skin that covers his insides. "You are not startling, child."

I nod with reassurance, a swallow and a genuine upturn of the lips, releasing his weapon and letting the weight fall into Aidan's fresh wound. Everything in this oddity's gait begs to differ from his words, arms quivering with violence, as if he is seizing with a direct consciousness of his environment. He cannot even maintain this gaze he has met with me, wandering about from shack to shack while the terrible screams of so many people rain down from every viable inch of this earth. Something about it is unsettling to someone who has yet to experience it often enough to make it routine, and I try to recall my first few weeks adjusting to the noise, the way it began to wash over me. Through me. Like music being played until I could fall asleep with a fraction of the fear I used to possess, drifting in and out when the choir of bedlam drew too close.

"It is horrible, isn't it?" I tilt my head, trying to find him again. "Terrifying, I think. To live this way."

There is a wretch, something twisted in agony, a falter in Aidan's legs, dropping him to one knee, arms still extended enough to keep the weapon from splitting his skull like a nut. But I can hear him vomit just the same, smell it, acrid fumes running down the front of his bloodied shirt, the food he had consumed hours ago revolting under the torture of staying alive.

If I could work faster, I would. But if I make the wrong move, we could both end up at the mercy of this creature. Something I can't allow. I chew my lip, skipping sideways as a dark elf strolls past me, looking out of the corner of his eye at first and then a double take, stumbling as if he cannot decide the appropriate action.

The creature in front of me looses something similar to a crackled hiss at the dark elf, orange strands of hair folding closer to his scalp as though it is live, pulsating wildly. Aidan cries out at this, the sword baring deeper with tension, and weeping crimson to the dirt, the dark elf little reacting, eyeballing myself and back to the forest as though more confused than myself as to why I stand in this village of nonmagical things when I belong to the universe itself.

His voice drifts to me in a language I do not understand, a question of concern as the pitch raises at the end and head tilting back to the forest. Aidan wretches once more as the question repeats itself, breathing audible and whisper pleading. The dark elf glances to him, hand pulling to the hilt of his weapon as I step back, shaking my head, attempting to retrieve every ounce of information I had absorbed since the elf in the clearing.

What did I do? And say? So that I was not attacked. He could understand me, though he never spoke a word. I know they can mock the human tongue in any language with little effort, understand it, even if they preferred their own. Their intelligence is incredible, beyond our comprehension.

"Addie," Aidan's voice whimpers.

I turn to see him for a moment, afraid to take my eyes off either threat presented. The question comes louder when I turn, firmer, head motioning toward the trees this time. I shake my own head in defiance.

"I don't understand," I say at last, and the dark elf's eyes pop in realization, gears turning, reveling in some sort of knowledge. He finds words, long lost, in a way I understand them.

"Is *he* close?"

I don't comprehend the context of his words, though I play along for my own sake, listening to the frantic chitters our frenzied enemy makes.

"Absolutely, yes," I lie. "Very."

There is an uncertainty to his stance that glimmers with doubt, but he nods, moving along. The creature at hand's attention turns to me and Aidan in a confused delight, as if we had repelled the dark elf with a phenomenal, invisible force of nature rather than appeasing words.

"We have to leave." The beast huffs, coming to the chaos unfolding around him as though he had not noticed it until this second. "It is not safe here."

"I...I agree." I nod. "But my friend needs help first. Y-you injured him, you see? We need to take him to our healer."

The creature follows the length of his own sword to Aidan, pulling the weapon from the flesh of my partner who nearly drops in agony. With care, and a bit of guilt-tripped coaxing, we motivate this newfound species to follow us through town as our very own personal killing machine, should we need it. In every way, he is stronger than us, single-handedly slaughtering lines of those who stand in our way too long until most are forced to clear the area, allowing our worn passage home. But my heart drops when we get there.

Blazing in a blinding red and orange, the little space we called ours for a short time has been ablaze for more than a couple minutes. I look around the place we stand in a dizzying haze, the smoke coming out the top and through the windows a melting, black cloud growing thicker and thicker as I hear our names being called.

Ace and Melody stand at the rear of a burning shack aside ours, Celestyn and Simone at their backs. We trudge forward, our new companion immediately alarmed by our old ones. Particularly Ace. The creature moves his sword, ready to swing and snarling as Ace lifts his hands for mercy, shuffling in retreat.

"Who—the fuck is this?" he yells over the snap of flames and cries for help.

I look to our enemy savior with a shrug. "Hey! What is your name?"

Everything in his aloof stature suggests he does not want to tell us, but he answers with relative caution.

"Titan."

Ace nods with a faux sympathy. "Ah, I see. Well, strange...thing... we need to leave. Now. I think there is a chance we can get out if we can scale the wall next to Headquarters. But we have to hurry."

Titan shakes his head, still ready to cut Ace down, but putting a hand out to stop him.

"I wouldn't," he tells us. "You're not safe anywhere you go. Not with *him* lurking about this world."

Celestyn pushes out from behind Ace and Melody, rushing to Aidan and looking over his injuries. She takes a quick survey of the area before she digs in her medical bag of glorious goodies.

"Him?" I ask, heart breaking as I watch Aidan suffer in his best form of silence while Celestyn performs temporary mends. As I turn, Ace is reaching toward me, slowly, carefully. I can see his hand in the light from the darkness, how it longs to grab my arm, pull me from this creature called Titan.

But he isn't sure.

I step closer to Titan, the only instincts I have telling me to steer clear of his grasp.

"Their king," Titan answers, armor ringing as he shifts to face Ace. "Disgusting, vile creature."

I stop.

"You've met him?"

"Once. Never again. I am finding where it is I came into this world from, and I am going home."

I stumble, Ace just missing my hand yet again in his reach, and Melody grabbing him by the shoulders, pulling him into her. She doesn't appear to feel safe around Titan either.

"I-I need to see the King. I...he is our only way home."

Titan looks us over with suspicion, planting his sword in the dirt, and free hand reaching forward to touch my ears, my round cheeks, my hair.

"You are...human. You are all..." He looks every one of us over. "Almost all, human. You should not be here."

"The King can get us out." I nod. "I just need help reaching him."

Celestyn's mouth drops as she finishes the wrap on Aidan's hands, and she pauses before putting her things back into the bag. At her side, I notice she saved Aidan's guitar, a relief for me in an unspoken way as he needs it, in an emotional sense.

"The King won't do a thing that doesn't benefit himself," Titan spits. "Save your time, child. Find another way."

I move closer, in front of him so he cannot leave.

"Save *me* time," I insist. "Take me there. I promise, I wouldn't go if I didn't have to. There is no other way."

There is a loud crash, and fire billows from above. Ace and Melody step away, though Ace holds his hand out to me, calling through a division of sparks and flame.

"Come with us," he yells. "You don't have to travel with a stranger. Travel with friends."

There is a reluctance in Titan's eyes. A back and forth between us, the screaming, and them. Something sets in stone in these moments.

"We have to leave, child." He sheathes his sword, taking me by the arm as Celestyn gathers Simone.

"Wait, wait." Aidan looks around, unsure of which side to take.

I can hear yelling from every person I know. The whole lot of them moves with us, and I jerk at the tug of Titan's insistence, dragging me like a rag doll toward the tree line where he will have to cut through more bodies to get us through. He stops the closer Ace comes, pulling free his sword again and aiming it for the chest. Ace leaps backward, gaze catching mine.

"Don't..." he pleads. "Please, Adabelle. Don't go where you think you want to go. It won't end well. You have to believe me."

I grimace, listening to the fire crackle, feeling a tug of my heart at this place, the one home I have to recall, and the people inside of it.

It's not enough.

"I have to."

Aidan's bloody hand waves past Titan's weapon, catching me around the shoulders and pulling me into him, Celestyn and Simone on his heels, leaning into him for safety.

"Don't leave us," he tells me. "We...we can go too. Together. You don't have to face The King alone."

I choke on air, sniffling, finding my grip around him, and feeling an unusual grip upon my fingers. Celestyn's.

"I...I don't?"

"You could still, you know, travel with friends. If you want."

"We have to go." Titan is impatient.

It is true. Limbo is crumbling around us, falling apart and eaten alive by destruction and chaos. I take Aidan's wrist, feeling Celestyn hold his shoulder tight in a silent plea to follow as I am quick to relent, allowing them at my side.

I lead the group into the radius Titan protects, awaiting his worst as my mind has been made. Under his breath, I hear Titan mention something about compensation, shoulders squaring and readying for attack. Thunder rolls overhead, louder than ever, lightning ripping the sky apart to allow a cleansing rain to fall as we march for either freedom, or certain demise. The white veil in my mind that has stood between myself and all I know flutters at the core of my subconscious, allowing me a glimpse of my own truth as we attempt to leave Limbo, a city of ash and smoke.

712

my mind that has stood between myself and all I know flutters at the core of my subconscious, allowing me a glimpse of my own truth as we attempt to leave Limbo, a city of ash and smoke.

# ACKNOWLEDGMENTS

I don't know where to start when it comes to this small honorary section of my book. This book has been over ten years in the making, starting as a small project I conjured up as a teenager and morphing day by day into what is now written on page. I would never have dreamed of pursuing this idea further than doodles and scribbled notes on a page if it weren't for the encouragements of my husband, who was the first person to really believe in me, pushing me up a steep slope of self-doubt to conquer my fears.

He is my hero. My anchor.

Other acknowledgements go out to the people who took time out of their lives to read this book in its infantile stages, to give input that would help it grow into something more than just words on a page. There is a special dedication as well to my closest friend and her cat, who helped me read through this book before I sent it to an editor, staying up countless hours after each chapter to nitpick and laugh ourselves to sleep.

Without any of you, this book means nothing. I am forever grateful.

# ABOUT THE AUTHOR

Wake Me Up is the debut novel from dark fantasy author, Obsidian Corvus. Growing up, Obsidian had always possessed a deep love for books, reading just about anything she could get her hands on and falling in love with epic fantasies and fictitious worlds she could get lost in. She learned to write her own the more her love for literature expanded, weaving intricate stories and building magical worlds. She has spent countless hours curled up on her couch with her bird, Falcor, burning daylight with a book in hand. Her favorite reads are often twisted and dark, with a touch of magic.

www.ingramcontent.com/pod-product-compliance
Lightning Source LLC
Chambersburg PA
CBHW031042110726
47900CB00003B/778